JOHN COLVILLE

The author was born in 1915. Educated at Harrow and Trinity College, Cambridge, where he won a Senior Scholarship and first class Honours in history, he passed the Diplomatic Service exam at an unusually early age. He was a close friend and associate of Churchill, whose trustee and executor he became. He served as a fighter pilot in the RAF and took part in the D-Day operation. As Private Secretary to the Queen when she was Princess Elizabeth, he married one of her ladies-in-waiting, Lady Margaret Egerton, and has two sons and a daughter.

He is at present chairman of two companies, including the Ottoman Bank, President of the New Victoria Hospital in Kingston and an honorary fellow of Churchill College, Cambridge, where his diaries are lodged.

Sir John Colville is the author of seven previous books including FOOTSTEPS IN TIME and THE CHURCHILLIANS.

VOLUME TWO: OCTOBER 1941–1955 will be published in 1987.

John Colville

THE FRINGES OF POWER
Downing Street Diaries 1939–1955
Volume One: September 1939–September 1941

First published in Great Britain in 1985 by Hodder and Stoughton Ltd

Sceptre edition 1986
Sceptre is an imprint of Hodder and Stoughton Paperbacks, a division of Hodder and Stoughton Ltd

British Library C.I.P.

Colville, John
   The fringes of power: Downing Street diaries 1939–1955.
   1. Colville, John *1915*–
   2. Private secretaries –
   Great Britain – Biography
   3. Diplomats – Great Britain
   – Biography
   I. Title
   941.082'92'4   DA585.C64

   ISBN 0-340-40269-5

Printed and bound in Great Britain for Hodder and Stoughton Paperbacks, a division of Hodder and Stoughton Ltd., Mill Road, Dunton Green, Sevenoaks, Kent (Editorial Office: 47 Bedford Square, London, WC1 3DP) by Richard Clay (The Chaucer Press) Ltd., Bungay, Suffolk. Photoset by Rowland Phototypesetting Ltd., Bury St Edmunds, Suffolk.

Dedicated to Mary Soames with affection and with penitence for some of the less complimentary references to her in the early part of this diary.

CONTENTS

ACKNOWLEDGMENTS

I am indebted to Messrs David Higham Associates, who act for the owners of the copyright of Miss Dorothy Sayers' books and papers, for permission to reproduce the hitherto unpublished poem, "The Burden of Ireland", which she sent to Winston Churchill at the beginning of January 1941.

I also thank the Society of Authors, on behalf of the Estate of Bernard Shaw, for permission to publish his letter to Winston Churchill on p. 200 and Sir John Peck for allowing me to include his "spoof" minute written on October 31, 1940.

Miss Sheila Legat kindly typed the many thousand words of my manuscript diaries twenty-five years ago and I am grateful to her, as I am to Miss Joyce Macleod who with unfaltering accuracy retyped them for publication together with the narrative and the notes included in this volume. I am also much indebted to Mr Hilary Rubinstein of A. P. Watt & Co., to Mr Thomas C. Wallace of W. W. Norton & Co. and by no means least to Mr Ion Trewin of Hodder and Stoughton whom I have discovered to be the eighth Pillar of Wisdom.

PREFACE

In the England of my youth primogeniture held sway, as indeed it still does in families with real estate to maintain and bequeath. My father and mother both came from well-known and by no means indigent families, but they were younger children and therefore, thanks to primogeniture, comparatively poor. I say comparatively, for in the twenty years between the two world wars we wanted for none of life's essentials, always had six or seven domestic servants, owned a fleet of small boats in the Isle of Wight and had a house in one of London's less fashionable squares. We had no motor-car (for my parents, both born long before the motoring era, equated a car with a carriage, complete with coachman and groom), we had no country house and we had no fine possessions. We always travelled about London by bus or underground; we never fed in restaurants, only went to a theatre on the last night of the school holidays and were constantly admonished to turn out the electric light. I remember going to the Opera at Covent Garden in full evening dress, my mother wearing her tiara and a large diamond brooch; and we travelled there and back in a Number 11 bus, covering the first and last few hundred yards on foot.

However, the money saved by my parents' carefulness (which never verged on meanness) went on providing their three sons with the best and most expensive education available; and though they were far from being cadgers, they had enough devoted friends and relations to provide their children with pheasants to shoot, horses to ride, yachts in which to race and pleasant country houses in which to stay.

Thus in 1936, when I came down from Trinity College, Cambridge, at the age of twenty-one, I had not been stinted of pleasures and had even, in the days when travel was still an adventure, been to the Soviet Union, steamed down the Danube in a barge, crossed Asia Minor in a third-class railway carriage, spent ten days as a guest in the monasteries of Mount Athos and learned to speak both French and German with fluency. I had also won two scholarships. However, I was well aware that I must soon earn my living with greater urgency than some of my university friends. This provided an incentive for hard work.

My two elder brothers had gone in to the City of London, one as a banker, the other as a stockbroker. To me, fascinated by political history and current affairs, the Foreign Office beckoned, though in those days the honour of belonging to the Diplomatic Service was thought to outweigh the need for reasonable remuneration and my father doubted if I could afford such a career.

The first problem was to get in: the entrance exam consisted of eighteen three-hour papers and four interviews. The competition was formidable. I was remarkably lucky: contrary to all expectations I succeeded at the age of twenty-two and at the first attempt.

In September 1937, after a memorable tour of Italy with my American friend Henry B. Hyde who, stimulated by a visit we made to the famous sage, Bernard Berenson, introduced me to the greatest of the Florentine and Venetian paintings (showing a sensitivity I shall never forget), I presented myself at the Foreign Office in Whitehall and was allotted to the Eastern Department.

The important problems confronting that department related to Palestine, where a plan to partition the territory between Arabs and Jews had succeeded in infuriating both parties, where the Mufti of Jerusalem was believed to be in the pay of the Germans and where the British Government was viciously attacked by Zionists who wanted more entry permits granted to Jews, and by Arabs who wanted all immigration stopped.

It is strange, on looking back, to remember that in the other territories over which we kept a watchful eye, peace reigned in Iraq under the firm rule of King Feisal's trusted old adviser, Nuri Pasha, not a ripple of commercial interest stirred the sandy wastes of Saudi Arabia and the Gulf States, and the few apparently insoluble problems related to an Iraqi claim to some date-gardens belonging to the Sheikh of Kuwait and to that of some distant heirs of Sultan Abdul Hamid to the Mosul oil fields.

My parish, with of course a senior First Secretary in charge, was Turkey and Persia. Persia was just a little tiresome, as the Shah, Reza Pahlevi, was a temperamental despot. We had to be particularly polite to him because of the enormous interests of the Anglo-Persian Oil Company (now British Petroleum) in the country, and there was an administrative complication in that the seven or eight British consular posts in the country reported (for some obscure nineteenth-century reason) to the Viceroy of India, though the Foreign Office were sent copies of their despatches.

Turkey was more exciting. Standing at the cross-roads joining Russia to the Mediterranean and Europe to the Middle East, and by no means remote from the route to India, the country was of political importance to both Britain and Germany. It was ruled dictatorially by Kemal Ataturk, the Grey Wolf, whose early inclination to the Germans had been sapped by the diligence of the British Ambassador, Sir Percy Loraine, able to stay up night after night gambling and drinking with Ataturk and becoming, in the process, an intimate friend and counsellor. The Germans tried to counter Loraine's influence by sending as their Ambassador the notorious Franz von Papen, more slippery than any eel; but they were too late, Loraine had landed the Turkish fish.

I was living with my parents at 66 Eccleston Square, immersed in all this oriental intrigue, and especially in coaxing unwilling supply departments to provide arms for Turkey and Persia in competition with German and Italian offers, when the world almost went to war over Czechoslovakia. It was September 1938, exactly a year after I joined the Foreign Office, that Britain and France stepped back from the brink of the precipice and signed the Munich Agreement with Hitler. Neither Britain nor

France was ready for war. The French had a vast army; the British had the world's largest navy; but the Germans already had a powerful air force whereas by then the Royal Air Force had only received two or three operational Spitfires: not even two or three squadrons. The French Air Force was in a lamentable state.

In those last days of September 1938, trenches were dug in Hyde Park, plans were made to evacuate school children, gas-masks were prepared for distribution and every young man I knew, not already a soldier or sailor, joined a "Supplementary Reserve". However, after the signing of the Munich Agreement Neville Chamberlain assured us that there would be peace in our time; and he really believed it. So I returned to my middle-oriental ploys, to be rudely shaken when on March 15th, 1939, Hitler, contrary to the solemn promises he had given at Munich, sent his troops to seize Prague and, shortly afterwards, Danzig. On Good Friday Mussolini invaded Albania and Hitler began to make menacing threats to Poland.

On August 22nd, 1939, came the signature of the Molotov – Ribbentrop non-aggression pact between the Soviet Union and Germany, secretly partitioning Poland and agreeing to hand over the prosperous little Baltic States to Russia. It meant that short of a miracle war was certain.

On August 23rd I had been due to sail to New York on my first visit to the U.S.A. for a month's holiday in Wyoming where some close Anglo-American friends had rented a ranch. I looked forward with excitement to seeing America; and I had a strong emotional incentive, which had been growing throughout the summer. Hitler put a stop to all that, for all leave was cancelled just before my ship was due to sail, so at the beginning of September 1939 I was waiting at my desk in Whitehall for war to be declared, twenty-four years old, a Third Secretary in the Diplomatic Service of two years' standing and tempted to resign before, on my twenty-fifth birthday, my employment should become a reserved occupation from which there would be no escape while the war lasted. Unsure of what was going to happen next, I decided to keep a diary.

I have used extracts from it in several books I have written, and I lent a large part of it to Martin Gilbert for background information and quotation in the concluding volumes of his official life of Winston Churchill. Now, a long time after it was written, I present it in consecutive form, having eliminated a high proportion of the trivial entries which are of no general interest, but leaving in a few which may perhaps help to recapture the "atmosphere" of the time.

Since there are many for whom memories of those distant years are blurred, and at least two generations who had no first-hand experience of them, I thought it might be helpful to insert from time to time brief explanations and comments on people and events which, if familiar to my contemporaries, are scarcely so now.

In order to reduce the number of footnotes, which some may find informative but others distracting, I have compiled a series of biographical notes, inserted at the end of the book, and have marked the names in the text with an asterisk*.

PART ONE

SEPTEMBER 1939–
SEPTEMBER 1941

ONE

THE WAR BEGINS

The British and French Governments, rapidly followed by all four of Britain's self-governing Dominions, declared war on Germany on September 3rd, 1939, as soon as Hitler's forces invaded Poland. He had already recovered the Rhineland, seized Austria and Czechoslovakia and proclaimed that "Today Germany is ours; tomorrow the whole world".

It was a warm and bright Sunday morning, on which the early services in all the churches were packed with worshippers, many of whom had not been seen in church for a long time. When, after following their example, I arrived at the Foreign Office I was informed that I had been assigned to the Ministry of Economic Warfare which was in the course of being established in the vacant lecture rooms of the London School of Economics. It was to be a primary instrument in imposing an economic blockade on Germany, a policy which, combined with our control of the seas, many deluded optimists believed would bring Germany rapidly to her knees.

On reporting to this new and bewildering organisation I was given an empty desk and nothing whatever to do. I sat contemplating the green leather desk-tops until somebody switched on a wireless set (the word "radio" was not then much in use) and we listened to Neville Chamberlain announcing we were at war. We knew it was coming, but all the same Chamberlain's broadcast, made with slow, solemn dignity, induced a numbness from which we were rudely revived by the sirens moaning out the war's first air-raid warning.

I say we, for there were others sitting equally unemployed in the London School of Economics. It was widely believed that London would be reduced to rubble within minutes of war being declared, as recently depicted to an alarmed populace in the film of H. G. Wells' book called *Things to Come*; and it seemed that this was indeed about to happen. So we scuttled, preserving what semblance of nonchalance we could, to the air-raid shelter. There I played bridge with David Eccles,[1] Rufus Smith[2] and another new conscript to the Ministry. After the first rubber the all-clear sounded, for the sirens had been set off on account of a single unidentified aircraft spotted miles to the east of the Thames estuary.

We returned to our empty desks and at lunch-time, being assured that I should have nothing to do or even to read that day, I went home reflecting that we seemed remarkably ill-prepared for Armageddon. It was a lovely afternoon and so my brother Philip,* awaiting his call-up to the Grenadiers, motored me to Trent Park,[3] formerly the home of Sir Philip Sassoon and now owned by his close friend and cousin, Mrs Gubbay. It had an excellent private twelve-hole golf course on which my brother and I peacefully spent the first afternoon of war. A few days afterwards I went to the Foreign Office and pleaded, successfully, to be restored to my familiar and reasonably busy occupation in its Eastern Department.

On September 10th I began my diary. I wrote copiously in the first, undramatic months of the war; but I have drastically curtailed the extracts from the early pages and have excised many of the references to my private life and social activities. I have not, however, tampered with the text of the Diaries themselves even when they contain views on people and events which now seem to me dubious.

---

[1] Subsequently 1st Viscount Eccles. Holder of several ministerial offices and eventually Chairman of the Trustees of the British Museum.

[2] Later 2nd Lord Bicester and Chairman of Morgan Grenfell Ltd.

[3] Near Cockfosters. A splendid Queen Anne House.

Sunday, September 10th
From the point of view of the civilian this war has hardly begun in earnest, and only the black-out at night, and the barrage balloons by day, remind one that Europe has finally toppled over the brink of the precipice upon which it has been balancing precariously for the last twelve months. Doubtless there is much in store for us that will dispel our cherished illusions of peace; but for the moment the war seems very unreal.

Ever since war was declared the sun has shone with unremitting splendour, and there is nothing about the gaily dressed, smiling crowds in the streets to remind us of this great catastrophe – except perhaps for the gas-masks slung across their backs and the number of men in uniform.

Monday, September 11th
Getting up at 7.30 I read the colourless newspapers in the sun on the balcony outside the back drawing-room, and walked to Coutts' after breakfast. Many of the bank clerks were wearing special constables' uniforms instead of their usual sober frock-coats.

I arrived at the F.O. just before 11.00 and spent a busy day there. The most interesting work I had was to assess the claims of Persia to receive support in armaments and flying instruction as compared with other countries. Persia has every intention of remaining neutral, but her goodwill is essential to us both on account of imperial communications and because of the Anglo-Iranian Oil Company, on which the navy to a large extent depend for their oil supplies. It is therefore important to please the Shah[1] by supplying him with aeroplanes and instructors, even if our effort in so doing will be wasted on incorrigibly neutral soil.

In general the impression to be gained at the F.O. is not as encouraging as that which the newspapers give. It seems likely that Mussolini's neutrality is very much of a put-up job and that

[1] Reza Pahlevi. Brigade commander who overthrew the effete Qajar dynasty and was proclaimed Shah in 1925. In 1941 he was deposed by the British and Russians, acting jointly, on account of his pro-German sympathies.

he is still on the best and most intimate terms with Hitler. Italian neutrality is, however, clearly the wisest policy for the Axis powers: as far as Hitler is concerned it ensures Turkish neutrality and thus makes it less easy for the Allies to help Poland from the East, as well as introducing complications about the passage of warships, etc., through the Straits; from Mussolini's point of view it is eminently desirable, because the Italian people are at present violently opposed to war and Mussolini is bound to increase his prestige by keeping them out of it.

Russia remains the most uncertain factor. From reports that I have seen in telegrams, I have formed a shrewd suspicion that she is preparing to seize the eastern districts of Poland if and when Germany subdues that country.

Stalin's latest double-cross has been at the expense of the Poles. He promised them arms a short time ago, and now he says that the entry of Great Britain and France into the war has altered the situation and he can no longer supply any armaments at all. I begin to think he is more villainous than Hitler, and even Marshal Voroshilov[1] and M. Molotov[2] are said to be ashamed of this continuous duplicity.

Tuesday, September 12th
For the first time there was a feeling of autumn in the air, and it was unpleasantly chilly as I sat on the balcony in my dressing-gown reading in the papers that the British Expeditionary Force had landed in France. It is as if one of those war films was being acted again in real life, only one misses the secure feeling of sitting in a comfortable armchair at the Curzon Cinema.

I had an interesting day at the F.O. trying to arrange for railway material to be shipped to Persia so that the Shah's susceptibilities may not be ruffled. I spent a good deal of thought on the subject, and was rewarded by being told that the action I proposed, and the drafts I submitted, were admirable. I shall probably be abashed before long by being told quite the opposite.

---

[1] Marshal K. E. Voroshilov. Red Army leader in the Civil War. Eventually head of the Russian state.
[2] V. M. Molotov.* Soviet Foreign Minister.

Mother[1] came up from Badminton for the day with Queen Mary.* She is furious at being marooned in the country and talks as though she were Ovid eating her heart out at Tomi. She was extremely funny about the effect of the air-raid alarms on the Queen. Apparently they so upset the old lady that she had acute and urgent stomach trouble, with disastrous and undignified results on the motor-drive from Sandringham to Badminton. They were forced to stop at a lonely inn, where the inn-keeper was most helpful. The Queen sent him a small silver knife as a thank-offering, and he replied by sending her a beautiful little carved silver chain (which, as Philip remarked, was a most suitable souvenir!). When they reached Badminton the Queen, who had spent three sleepless nights owing to air-raid warnings and thunderstorms, looked forward to a welcome rest, but was aroused the next morning at 6.00 a.m. because the kitchen-maid turned on the private air-raid warning in mistake for the electric light.

Wednesday, September 13th
At the F.O. I wound up the affairs of Turkey and Persia before transferring my attention to Palestine and Arabia. Of war news there was little, except for the fact that Poland has exhausted nearly all her resources of aerial defence, and that our comparative inactivity on the Western Front is causing general uneasiness. Why not bomb military objectives instead of scattering pamphlets is the question everybody is asking about the R.A.F. (Incidentally that body has not begun too well: it has violated Dutch neutrality, bombed a Danish town, and fought some Belgian planes over Belgian territory. Moreover, in the air-raid warning on September 5th the only casualty was one of our own planes falling to one of our A.A. guns.)

Encouraged by the postponement of petrol rationing for a week, so that enough coupons could be printed, I went for twenty-four hours to stay with my father's sister at Kenswick near the village of Broadheath in Worcestershire.

[1] Lady Cynthia Colville.*

Sunday, September 17th

I went to the early service at Broadheath. After breakfast, when the others went to church, I walked through the fields for about an hour, and returned to the house in time to hear, on the 12.00 p.m. wireless bulletin, the harrowing news of Russia's invasion of Poland. The announcement by which the Soviet Government attempted to justify their act of unequalled greed and immorality is without doubt the most revolting document that modern history has produced. For the first time since the war began I felt really depressed, and frantic at the impossibility of our taking any effective action to prevent this crime. And yet I remember thinking, less than a year ago, that the Poles deserved the darkest fate in view of the way they treated the Czechs and that nobody could feel sorry for them if their turn came next.

After lunch and a game of billiards I motored Philip to Middleton via Stratford and Banbury. The house is occupied by a horde of Roman Catholic children, in the charge of a dozen nuns, and the family are living in the cottages. Old Lady Jersey (ninety years old now), Ronnie and Cynthia Slessor,[1] Ann Elliot,[2] David[3] and Joan,[4] and Grandie[5] and Virginia[6] were there, all with their respective children.

It was a glorious September evening and we sat about in the garden trying to concentrate on the peaceful sound of church bells and to forget Russia and Poland and the rest of Europe's infected plague spots. Virginia returned from America yesterday in the *Manhattan* and was so frightened by the thought that she and her fellow passengers might be the incident to bring America into the war that she developed a temperature, as a result of which she walked about the sunlit garden looking like a ghost.

---

[1] Daughter of the 4th Earl of Kilmorey. Married first the 8th Earl of Jersey and then Rodney, formerly her children's tutor and brother of Marshal of the R.A.F. Sir John Slessor.

[2] Younger daughter of the 8th Earl of Jersey, married to Alexander Elliot.

[3] My eldest brother.*

[4] Elder daughter of the 8th Earl of Jersey, married to my brother David.

[5] 9th Earl of Jersey, owner of Middleton Park near Bicester and of Osterley.

[6] Lord Jersey's second wife. Formerly Virginia Cherrill; played the part of the blind girl in Charlie Chaplin's *City Lights*.

Monday, September 18th

The Foreign Office was less depressed by the Russian monstrosity than I had expected. Turkey seems to be standing firm, at the cost of our promising financial support on a scale vaster than we had ever contemplated. With such momentous news on everybody's lips, I find it difficult to concentrate on minor Palestinian or Arabian problems.

I lunched at the Travellers, which has fortunately reopened, and learned that the *Courageous* [large aircraft-carrier] had been sunk – our first naval disaster.

On leaving the office I called on Mary Roxburghe,[1] and found Middy Gascoigne[2] already there. We discussed the situation heatedly, and condemned the Government's inactivity severely (though one can but hope they are in reality doing more than they seem. But if they are, the Ministry of Information should give some indication of the fact, or the public will begin to lose confidence). Middy was looking lovely; Mary rather ill (she is to have an operation tomorrow).

Tuesday, September 19th

I rode through Wimbledon Common to Richmond Park on a horse incongruously called "Peaceful". Riding is an agreeable sedative and I find it easy to dream placidly and forget the slings and arrows of outrageous fortune.

The Poles are still gallantly resisting, though their government has fled; but the Russian invasion has been decisive and the Polish campaign is now over. The German people are unfortunately elated by their series of rapid successes, and Hitler evidently hopes that he can now conclude a generous peace settlement. He made a speech at Danzig this afternoon in which he threatened that if we carried on the blockade, the Germans had a terrible weapon in store, which could not be used against them, but which they had no wish to employ. This is probably meant to intimidate, but it does give one a slight feeling of

[1] Youngest daughter of Lord Crewe. My mother's half-sister. Married to 9th Duke of Roxburghe.
[2] Hon. Mrs Gascoigne. Daughter of Lady Annabel Dodds, my mother's eldest sister, and mother of Bamber Gascoigne.

uneasiness, because even Hitler and his satellites usually have something on which to base statements of this kind. For instance Ribbentrop[1] said last May or June that he was preparing the greatest diplomatic defeat that England had ever known, and though we laughed scornfully at the time we are now obliged to admit that the Russo-German pact does deserve that definition.

The war looks like being an immobile affair on the Western Front, with neither side bombing the other's civilian populations for some time to come, and the real test being whether Germany's economic resources and the morale of her people can defeat the navy's blockade and the morale of the Allies. This will be dangerous because it will be boring; and in wartime boredom is certain to breed discontent at home. However I do not think the Germans will begin their proverbial "frightfulness" until they feel they are losing or winning, so that London can probably sleep in peace for a good many weeks, or even months, to come.

Friday, September 22nd

At the Foreign Office I had very little to do except compose a few dreary letters to the Colonial Office about Palestine. In the morning, however, I attended a meeting of the Middle Eastern Sub-Committee of the Committee of Imperial Defence, to discuss means of gratifying the Sultan of Muscat. Except as a means of studying the psychology of elderly civil servants, such meetings are invariably tedious.

The most interesting telegram of the day was an explanation of why the Government has been doing so little lately, and is intended for the use of H.M. Representatives abroad who are met with the complaint that we have not lifted a finger to save Poland. The gist of the Government's argument is that "strategy is the art of concentrating decisive force at the decisive moment". The Poles knew we could give them no effective help and realised that we could only save them in the long run – when Germany has been defeated. "To have devoted hundreds of British planes to bombing raids in Germany would have meant

---

[1] Hitler's Foreign Minister, Joachim von Ribbentrop.*

spectacular successes, but the inevitable loss of machines which will be used more effectively on the Western Front." There may be something to be said for this policy, although its effect is exasperating to public opinion. Dr Brüning[1] told somebody I know – Eric Duncannon[2] I think – that the best way to treat Hitler is to keep him guessing, and perhaps our inactivity, if he thinks it hides some sinister purpose, may have that effect; but there is always the danger that he will take it for irresolution and degeneracy. In some circles it is thought that his first active move in the West will be a massed air-attack on the British navy and its bases.

In France there is calm but fixed determination: *"il faut en finir"*. The Consul at Rouen reports, however, that the French are showing some uneasiness about our declared intention to wage this war against Hitler and Nazism, and not against the German people. The French believe in the original sin of the German race and point out that in every major war from 1860 to the present day Germany has been the wanton aggressor and the disturber of European peace. The French consider that the leader and his ruling clique are of real insignificance: the character of the German people is such that they will always produce bellicose leaders with an ideology of force, and it does not matter if one calls the leader Frederick, Wilhelm or Hitler, or if his satellites are Junkers or Nazis. The German mentality is dangerous and incorrigible.

I do not believe this is true. If it were, there could be no alternative but to exterminate the whole German people, and such an act – even if it were possible – would be against the laws of God and man, besides being repugnant to the conscience of a world which claims to be civilised. If we win this war I am convinced that the only hope of a lasting peace, based on principles of justice and goodwill among men, will be to treat the Germans with the utmost generosity and to make a clean sweep of the past – whatever may be the feelings of bereaved wives and mothers. There must be no "guilt clause", no repara-

[1] Dr Heinrich Brüning, German Chancellor 1930–32.
[2] Viscount Duncannon, subsequently 10th Earl of Bessborough.

tions and no public humiliation of Germany. Instead Germany must be placed on her feet economically, as far as it may be possible for us, in a devastated world, to do so. She must be disarmed; but so must the Allies. None of her rightful territories must be snatched from her, nor must she be partitioned; but she must be given free access to foreign and colonial markets. As far as possible the German people must be made to feel that they are not "pariahs", that they own and have produced much that is universally admired, and that their former enemies are willing to trust them, even to the extent of giving them colonies or mandates to govern. If this can be done, I believe they will respond and will appreciate such generosity; if they do not, then indeed the time will have come *pour en finir*. But it is going to be a task of unequalled difficulty to persuade the English and French peoples, hardened by years of war and suffering (and vitally affected in their pocket!) that this is the only wise and Christian course to pursue, and that it is the only chance of sparing future generations the curse of perpetually recurring wars. He who can convince the victorious side that such is the truth will deserve to be considered humanity's greatest benefactor; but he will need more than human powers to enable him to succeed.

Saturday, September 23rd

After lunch I went by train to Stansted[1] to spend the week-end with the Bessboroughs. They were just *en famille*, Lord and Lady Bessborough[2] and Moyra,[3] Eric [Duncannon] having joined his regiment. There were also sixty or more orphans, who played cricket happily on the lawn in front of the house but were carefully excluded from the main part of the house itself, which remains as cheerful and comfortable as ever.

[1] Stansted Park, Rowland's Castle, standing in a park laid out by Le Notre, some fifteen miles from Portsmouth.
[2] Vere, 9th Earl of Bessborough. Governor General of Canada, 1931–35. Married to Roberte de Neuflize.
[3] Lady Moyra Ponsonby. Afterwards married to the distinguished surgeon, Sir Denis Browne, and herself Superintendent in Chief of St John's Ambulance Brigade.

We had an excellent dinner (nowhere is the food better than at Stansted) and afterwards Moyra and I alternately played backgammon and played with an unusually elaborate wireless set, from which we heard a German announcer broadcasting rather ineffectively, in English, about the wickedness of the English blockade measures. To be legal, he said, a blockade must be effective: let us hope that it may be, in every sense.

Sunday, September 24th

I woke up, in a very attractive bedroom, to see a powder-blue sky and the sun shining brilliantly on the lawns and borders. As I get older I very seldom have a feeling of present happiness: it is rather anticipation or reminiscence, and chiefly the former, which makes my heart swell with happiness. But this morning, as I lay in bed turning the pages at random of a sentimental novel, and contemplating the charm of my surroundings, I felt blissfully contented.

Wednesday, September 27th

Warsaw has surrendered after a heroic defence against overwhelming odds. Hitler is therefore free to turn his attention westwards, but it remains to be seen whether he will have the courage and stupidity to strike the first serious blow. For the moment the position can best be summed up in the words of the Italian Ambassador in Paris to Sir Eric Phipps:[1] "I have seen several wars waged without being declared; but this is the first I have seen declared without being waged."

I lunched with Charles Ritchie,[2] from Canada House, at La Coquille. He was in quite good spirits, and said what really got him down was the attempt to resurrect all the songs, scenes and emotions of 1914. It was like sitting in the dentist's waiting-room and turning over the pages of some twenty-five-year-old magazines.

It is, I think, essential that no gratuitous humiliations be

---

[1] British Ambassador in Berlin, 1933–37 and in Paris, 1937–39.
[2] Second Secretary at Canada House. Canadian High Commissioner in London, 1967–71.

heaped on the German people and that no reparations be taken. Moreover, purely German areas, like Danzig and the Sudetenland, should be included in the confederation. Of course the trouble will be that while many will agree that Germany should be treated with magnanimity, others, and especially the French, will be in favour of the harshest peace terms. I suppose the result will be a compromise, like Versailles, and in consequence discontent and resentment in Germany on which another Hitler will be able to build his diabolical system.

Thursday, September 28th
After breakfast I perused, with melancholy, the report of last night's budget – 7/6d income tax! [A fifty per cent increase.] Father[1] is sunk in depression; personally I find it impossible to be really horrified by anything impersonal these days.

I am afraid the budget may have a chilling effect on public opinion which, unable to appreciate the essential merits of a waiting policy (waiting until we and the French are in a position to assert our mastery of the air), is already showing signs of impatience and is asking what we are fighting for. In some quarters this war has already been named "The Bore War". But it is clearly right to let Hitler take the initiative, both from a material and a psychological point of view: he will have to do so very soon (unless Russia takes some drastic and unexpected step) or else we and the French shall have won the mastery of the air and the blockade will have begun to take effect. But I am inclined to think Hitler's first move will be a gigantic air onslaught on the navy – and not on London.

On leaving the office I spent an hour talking to Mary Roxburghe, who is full of worries about the apathy being shown by the public (and also, not surprisingly, about the budget). We agreed that it would probably be a good thing if Chamberlain resigned soon and left the conduct of the war to some younger and forceful successor. Unfortunately I can see no Lloyd George on the horizon at present: Winston is a national figure, but is rather too old; and the younger politicians do not seem to include any outstanding personality. Halifax* would be respected, but

[1] The Hon. George Colville.*

he has not the drive necessary to keep the country united and enthusiastic.

Aunt Nancy[1] came to stay, and Brian O'Neill[2] dined with us. We talked incessantly of the war, and Brian, though he was in one of his silent and semi-sulky moods to begin with, was quite interesting when he discussed our war policy from the army point of view. Apparently the army think very highly of Ironside.

London, illuminated by the pale light of the harvest moon, looks more beautiful than ever before.

Friday, September 29th
So the Germans and Russians have consecrated their Unholy Alliance by a formal partition of Poland, a Gilbertian statement about responsibility for continuing the war, and an impressive but (hopefully) empty declaration about supplying Germany with raw materials.

Sunday, October 1st
We dined with Dorothy Cambridge[3] and heard Winston Churchill's inspiring speech on the wireless. He certainly gives one confidence and will, I suspect, be Prime Minister before this war is over. Nevertheless, judging from his record of untrustworthiness and instability, he may, in that case, lead us into the most dangerous paths. But he is the only man in the country who commands anything like universal respect, and perhaps with age he has become less inclined to undertake rash adventures.

Monday, October 2nd
Mallet,[4] one of the Private Secretaries, sent for me and asked me whether I should like to be one of the Assistant Private

---

[1] Lady Annabel Dodds,* eldest daughter of the Marquess of Crewe.
[2] Hon. Brian O'Neill, adjutant, the Irish Guards, second son of Lady Annabel Dodds by her first husband, the Hon. Arthur O'Neill, M.P.
[3] Dorothy Hastings. Married George, 2nd Marquess of Cambridge, a nephew of Queen Mary.
[4] Sir Ivo Mallet. Second Private Secretary to the Foreign Secretary. Subsequently Ambassador in Belgrade and Madrid.

Secretaries to the Prime Minister. He said it was an interesting job, which would mean "being in the know" the whole time, but that it would entail a good deal of drudgery. I said I would, because I knew that to have such an appointment is likely to be an excellent stepping-stone in the Diplomatic Service.

Consequently after lunching rather dully with John Cairncross[1] (a very intelligent, though sometimes incoherent, bore) at the Travellers, I went to the Treasury to interview a man called Douglas and Rucker,* the Prime Minister's chief Private Secretary. The latter impressed upon me that my new job would imply very long hours and a good deal that was utterly boring, but it would also mean a certain amount of attendance at the House of Commons and the control of appointments to bishoprics! There are several other candidates in the field, so I shall not know for certain whether I have been accepted at any rate until tomorrow.

After dinner we listened to a speech on the wireless by the Archbishop of York,[2] which contained some wise words about the peace to follow the war and even suggested European Federation. What a glorious dream, but how difficult in practice when one takes into consideration differences in language and prejudices based on national pride or history.

Tuesday, October 3rd
I have been selected for the post at No. 10, which is most exciting, and am to begin next week.

---

[1] What I did not know about John Cairncross, so clever that in 1936 he passed first into the Foreign Office a hundred marks ahead of a brilliant Fellow of All Souls, Con O'Neill, was that he had been busy making notes about the opinions of his Foreign Office and Civil Service contemporaries for the benefit of the Communist Party. When Guy Burgess fled to Russia with Donald Maclean in 1951, these notes were found in a trunk he had left behind. Cairncross had ill-advisedly dated each note and so, in 1953, by referring to my old 1939 engagement book, I was able to tell the security authorities, at a loss to identify the hand-writing, with whom I had been lunching on the day a note about me had been written. I asked them what Cairncross was then doing. They replied that he was working in the Atomic Energy Division of the Ministry of Supply. They said he had renounced his Soviet sympathies, but all the same I almost fell off my office chair in astonishment.

[2] William Temple.

Wednesday, October 4th

Rode at Richmond before breakfast. It was cold and bright and windy, and very exhilarating. There is little war news, but every effort is being made by the Germans for their great peace offensive, which is almost certain to be launched this week. Meanwhile Russia is systematically compelling the miserable Baltic states to accept her suzerainty and, having got her booty, seems not indisposed to take part in the peace moves. But Stalin's real intentions remain completely obscure: personally I suspect the worst and rather agree with Mother who says she feels Russia is a great "force of evil", which, long stationary, has now been set in motion by Ribbentrop's blind stupidity and is rolling gradually westwards. Mother has admirable faith and relies on the assistance of St Michael and All Angels against this disguised Beelzebub!

Thursday, October 5th

I spent most of the day wrestling with such problems as Ibn Saud's[1] desire to buy armaments from Germany, the Mufti's[2] not entirely disinterested wish to make a declaration to the Arabs in favour of the Allies, and the legal technicalities involved in deporting Foreign Legion deserters from Palestine to Syria (where, being Germans, their fate would probably be certain death).

There is little military activity: Hitler's peace proposals are expected tomorrow, and he seems to be having trouble with Italy. There is a sinister calm before the storm bursts and the war begins in fearful earnest. Herr Weizsäcker (of the German F.O.) is reported to have said that Germany will probably last till the New Year and then go Communist. Propaganda is said to be rife in the factories and to be likely to infect the army (who must be furious about the suspected murder of von Fritsch).[3]

[1] King Abdul Aziz of Saudi Arabia.
[2] The Mufti of Jerusalem. Pro-German and an incorrigible plotter.
[3] Werner, Baron von Fritsch. German Commander in Chief, 1934–38. He was opposed to Hitler's policies and was probably murdered by the Gestapo.

Friday, October 6th

Went over to No. 10 for half an hour in the morning and was shown by Miss Watson[1] how some of my new duties are to be executed. She seems to be a kind, efficient, unassuming and rather wizened old thing (she tells me the Treasury are furious at my appointment – as being too young). I also met Captain Dugdale,[2] but could not see the Prime Minister or Sir Horace Wilson* as the Cabinet was meeting.

I was rather busy at the F.O. with the Mufti and other Palestinian questions. In the outside world the event of major importance was Hitler's long, overwhelming and slightly hysterical speech. Rather surprisingly he did not threaten us with destruction in its most appalling form; but the terms he offered are, as was to be expected, unacceptable to all except a few intellectuals suffering from senility, like Bernard Shaw (whose article in this week's *New Statesman* is typical of a man whose particular form of exhibitionism is a constant wish to espouse lost causes in such a way as to irritate the majority of his fellow citizens. In this case his attitude will probably be genuinely harmful and be misrepresented abroad).

I dined with Diana Quilter[3] at Quaglino's. It was interesting, if macabre, to see all the khaki-clad dancers, but the place was miserably full, very smoky, and, of course, outrageously expensive. However Diana was, as ever, very agreeable and original, and it was pleasant to have a glimpse of "night life" in the new world.

Saturday, October 7th

I am indulging in an orgy of spending, in the belief that materials will grow worse in quality and more expensive. This morning I tried on a new suit and an overcoat at my tailor's, and two ruinous pairs of shoes at Peal's.[4]

---

[1] Formerly typist, promoted to be a private secretary with responsibility for parliamentary Questions.

[2] Captain Thomas Dugdale, M.P. Created Lord Crathorne* in 1959.

[3] An agreeable and intelligent childhood friend. Later married Archibald Tennant.

[4] The "ruinous" shoes, hand-made and fitted on a last, cost £2.10.0. a pair.

After saying goodbye to Aunt Nancy, who is off to Nice, I caught the 1.50 to Stansted.

Sunday, October 8th
I looked from my bedroom window at the vistas which stretch away from Stansted, and saw the leaves of the trees, now turning yellow and red, perfectly still in the cold, windless and brilliantly sunny morning. I could not have enjoyed *Byron*[1] more (but I *am* being slow with it!) which shows how important it is to read in agreeable surroundings. Usually when I settle down to read the sun is shining too brightly, the fire is too hot, or somebody is being disturbing.

Hal Goodhart Rendel,[2] who never knows when to stop talking but certainly talks well, was loud in his denunciation of the German people as opposed to Hitler. He said that the Germans could never understand others (i.e. us) acting from principle instead of from interest. But are we? Surely it is at least convenient that for us the two coincide.

Lord Bessborough thinks we should have a War Cabinet, as in the last war, with members freed from departmental duties. He points out that Lloyd George left the leadership of the House to Bonar Law, and only appeared there himself on rare and important occasions.

Monday, October 9th
Travelled up to London with Zara,[3] and discussed our late hosts very favourably. She looked very pretty, in black with an astrakhan hat, and has great vivacity.

At the F.O. I cleared up all the work I had left, and then took a rather sad leave of Lacy Baggallay (who was certainly the perfect Head of a Department) and the other members of my department. It is just over two years since I entered the F.O.,

[1] André Maurois' biography of Byron.
[2] Gifted and affluent architect, artistically erudite and a talented pianist. His face alternated between green and yellow in colour and was much commented on (behind his back).
[3] Younger daughter of Sir Harry and Lady Mainwaring. Married first Ronald Strutt (later Lord Belper) and secondly Peter Cazalet.

and it seems an age. But it has been a pleasant "age", because I have had delightful people to work with, and plenty of free time with which to enjoy the vanished pomps of yesterday. Yet I think I have learned a lot. Miss Glasse, one of the typists, observed, when in saying goodbye I remarked that I should probably have a lot of work to do, "well that will be a change"!

TWO

THE WHITEHALL SCENE

Even when I moved to 10 Downing Street, there was at first a monotony only sometimes varied by events or discussions worthy of record by one who saw all important papers and heard much political and military gossip, but was too junior to play any part in decision making. Nor, except in relation to Scandinavia, were a great number of notable decisions made in those dreary, depressing months of what was generally called the Phoney War. Only the war at sea was waged in earnest.

Once it was realised that the Germans had no immediate intention of bombing London or Paris, and that the expected offensive on the Rhine was delayed, there were lingering hopes in some breasts that the full impact of war might even yet be avoided for all but the unhappy Poles, whose spectacularly gallant but tragically ill-equipped army had been smashed, and whose country was being systematically devastated by Germans and Russians alike.

These hopes were expressed in the Cabinet by Lord Halifax and found a strong echo in the staff at 10 Downing Street, as indeed with many who had had personal experience of the First World War massacres. Neville Chamberlain was not anti-German, nor indeed was Winston Churchill; but Chamberlain, to whom the very thought of war was abhorrent, would have gone further than Churchill in making concessions to a new German Government, even if it had contained some of the Nazi leaders. On one point, however, he was adamant: nothing would ever induce him to deal with Hitler, whose supersession would be an essential prerequisite of any settlement. Mussolini might perhaps be tolerated, and might even be helpful in arranging a settlement: Hitler was beyond any conceivable pale.

This was because Chamberlain realised that Hitler's brutality was matched by his unreliability; but I think there was also an element of damaged vanity. At Munich, in September 1938, he had trusted Hitler in the face of strong remonstrances from the Foreign Office, but with encouragement from our gullible Ambassador in Berlin, Sir Nevile Henderson. Hitler had betrayed that trust and made a dupe of Chamberlain. One evening when I was returning with him from the House of Commons, he spoke angrily of some Opposition member who had been attacking Government policy. "I believe," said I, "that he is sincere in his views." "What of that?" replied the Prime Minister sharply. "I am sure Hitler was sincere at Munich, but he changed his mind a few days later." I thought that remark explained quite a lot about Chamberlain's ingenuous faith in the Munich agreement – and perhaps something about Chamberlain himself.

He was courteous to his staff, as were those close to him, like Sir Horace Wilson and the invariably delightful Parliamentary Private Secretary, Lord Dunglass.[1] The two senior Private Secretaries, Arthur Rucker and Cecil Syers,* were not only helpful to me and encouraging, but also men with a well-developed wit and sense of humour, so that the sound of laughter seldom failed to resound in the Private Secretaries' rooms and did much to relieve the gloom of those grey winter days.

The Prime Minister was encouraging to the young and inexperienced. The first time I was asked to prepare a memorandum, on a fairly complicated matter, for inclusion in the nightly Prime Ministerial box, it came back the following morning with a most complimentary red-ink note in Chamberlain's handwriting – far more complimentary than it deserved.

This was in marked contrast to the Chancellor of the Exchequer, Sir John Simon.* He also had a young, new Private

---

[1] Alexander Douglas-Home, subsequently 14th Earl of Home, Sir Alec Douglas-Home and Lord Home of the Hirsel,* Prime Minister, 1963–64.

Secretary, Burke Trend, who became many years later Secretary to the Cabinet. Trend was entrusted, at about the same time as I was, with the task of writing his first memorandum for the Chancellor. Since he is a man of exceptional ability, I have no doubt it was an admirable document; but on the following morning it was returned neatly torn into four pieces and without comment. To those who did not work under him, such as myself, Simon was friendly, forthcoming and often agreeably witty. I was one of a sadly restricted company who actually liked him.

Chamberlain was austere, and he seldom said to me anything not strictly related to business. At week-ends he retired to Chequers, where there was only one telephone (and that in the pantry). He disliked being disturbed, telephonically or otherwise, at weekends or after dinner at 10 Downing Street. He never took a Private Secretary with him to Chequers; nor did he ever invite the members of his staff to lunch or dine with Mrs Chamberlain and himself. That was in marked contrast to Winston Churchill, who treated his Private Secretaries as part of the family, and indeed to Clement Attlee. Yet this austere man had such integrity, such devotion to duty and such high ideals and standards, that if it was at first difficult to feel affection for him it was impossible not to feel esteem.

The men of power in the Cabinet were Sir John Simon, Sir Samuel Hoare,[1] Lord Privy Seal (who invariably replied "m, yes, m, yes, m, yes" when one ventured to address him), and Lord Halifax, formerly Viceroy of India and now Foreign Secretary. Halifax was a sincerely religious, intelligent and by no means ingenuous man, who because of his political acumen and his deep love of both the Church and the hunting field was generally known as "the Holy Fox". To these was added on September 3rd, 1939, Winston Churchill, First Lord of the Admiralty and a stronger, more colourful personality than any of them. Many of his colleagues, and most senior civil servants, regarded him with suspicion, an attitude reflected by the staff at 10 Downing Street and one to which I was daily subjected.

There were also men of power behind the parliamentary

[1] Subsequently Viscount Templewood.*

screen. Of these Sir Horace Wilson* was the foremost, for Neville Chamberlain did little without his advice. It was not Wilson's fault that he was frequently required to advise on matters, such as foreign affairs and defence, of which he had scanty knowledge; for he had been brought to Downing Street from the Ministry of Labour by Chamberlain's predecessor, Stanley Baldwin, and he had been made indispensable. He was not ambitious: he was kind, high-principled and frequently wise; but being the Prime Minister's *alter ego*, he had come to believe himself as infallible as Chamberlain considered him to be. There were others – Sir Edward Bridges,* Secretary to the Cabinet, General Ismay,* Military Secretary to the Committee of Imperial Defence, Sir Alexander Cadogan,* Permanent Under-Secretary at the Foreign Office, to mention but a few – who were men of the highest character and calibre; and there was the attractive, extrovert Chief Whip, Captain David Margesson,* who saw the Prime Minister every morning at eleven o'clock and shared with Sir Horace Wilson a commanding influence on political appointments.

The leaders of the Labour Opposition were Clement Attlee and Arthur Greenwood; and the leader of the Liberal Party, Sir Archibald Sinclair,[1] had been Winston Churchill's second in command in the trenches during the First World War. All three were good and honourable men, Attlee being by far the most outstanding. Greenwood's value was impaired by his addiction to the bottle; and Sinclair, high-minded and patriotic, could seldom, when the time eventually came, stand up to the stronger personalities with whom it was his fate to contend.

While in the first months of the war Ministers and civil servants were striving to keep the administration on its competent, if unimaginative, track, the British Expeditionary Force, first two divisions, then four and after a few months ten (with an eventual target of fifty-five), disembarked in France. It contained the best professional soldiers in the British army and all the equipment which, after a shamefully late start, the country had been able to provide. It was led by a gallant hero of the First World War,

---

[1] Subsequently Viscount Thurso.*

Viscount Gort, V.C., D.S.O. and two bars, M.C.*, who had as his two Corps Commanders Sir Alan Brooke* and Sir John Dill.* Dill returned to London, to be Vice Chief of the General Staff, shortly before the Dunkirk campaign began.

The B.E.F. was subordinated to the French General Georges and, above him, to the Commander in Chief, General Gamelin,* who was mistakenly rated a military genius. The French, with some eighty divisions but a totally inadequate air force, had built what they believed to be an impregnable defence, the Maginot Line, stretching from Switzerland to the Belgian frontier. Behind this they were confident of their ability to resist any German onslaught, especially as leading military experts, such as Basil Liddell-Hart,* had declared that in modern war a defensive strategy must prevail. The main French objective, leading them to be enthusiastic exponents of Scandinavian adventures, and by contrast resolute opponents of bombing the Ruhr or mining the Rhine, was to keep the war off French soil. They felt they had suffered enough from previous Teutonic incursions.

Unfortunately, despite what had happened in 1914, the French Government had seen no need to extend the Maginot Line along the Franco-Belgian frontier which was only defended by an unimpressive ditch. This sector was allotted to Lord Gort and his B.E.F. who therefore had to spend the unusually icy winter of 1939/40 building pill-boxes and constructing a somewhat more defensible line. It could never, in the time available, have been strong enough to resist a determined German attack by armoured divisions, of which the British themselves had only one and that not as yet ready to take its place in the line. Such was the position on December 31st, 1939.

Meanwhile I had moved my diary physically to a drawer in my writing-table at 10 Downing Street where succeeding volumes were kept locked and where I made daily entries or, when I was away for a day or two, hastened to record my activities as soon as I returned.

The following are extracts from what I wrote between October 10th and December 31st, 1939.

Tuesday, October 10th
My first day at No. 10. It began at 9.30 a.m. and finished at
6.30. In the course of it I met the Prime Minister, who was shy
but welcoming, Mrs Chamberlain (who looks utterly vague), Sir
Horace Wilson and Captain David Margesson. The latter said,
"You know my daughters, I believe", with a rather penetrating
stare!

> *The penetrating stare was due to his knowledge that I was deeply*
> *in love with his younger daughter, who was beautiful, gay and*
> *intelligent. Another of her suitors was Nicko Henderson, later*
> *Ambassador in Bonn, Paris and Washington. He told me that*
> *if she did not finally say yes, he would never marry anybody*
> *else. I said the same applied to me. We both did marry somebody*
> *else and lived happily ever after. As for the delectable young*
> *lady, she married a third equally ardent suitor and also lived*
> *happily ever after.*

I sit in the same room as Miss Watson and Lord Dunglass.
Miss Watson showed me how to deal with some of the enormous
post which arrives every day now, and I also began looking into
the question of the Ecclesiastical patronage with which I am to
deal, and about which my predecessor, Jasper Rootham, came
to talk to me in the morning.

I read with interest the various drafts, by the Prime Minister,
Churchill, Cadogan, Vansittart[1] and Corbin,[2] suggested for
the reply to Hitler's peace proposals. When the proposals are
rejected it is thought likely that Hitler will launch a tremendous
onslaught. For the moment calm reigns on land, sea and air.

Wednesday, October 11th
My appointment announced in *The Times*.

At No. 10 I made an effort to grasp the intricacies of the
Ecclesiastical Patronage of the Crown, read the Cabinet
minutes, etc., appointed one man to a Crown living, and

---

[1] Chief Diplomatic Adviser to the Government. See p. 189.
[2] French Ambassador in London.

answered a lot of irritating letters. One of the Prime Minister's correspondents said: "You may put this letter in the waste-paper basket; but remember you and I will meet face to face before the bar of judgment, and then it may be taken out of the waste-paper basket." A solemn thought if one is to spend one's time in purgatory dealing with neglected correspondence!

I left at about 6.00 p.m. and went to have a drink with the Stirlings (Margaret,[1] Bill[2] and Peter[3]). Peter leaves for Cairo tomorrow. Pam Berry[4] was there, obviously determined to lead a gay social life, war or no war. There was also a pretty girl, Prim Rollo,[5] and another not unattractive one, Lavinia Shaw-Stewart.

Dined with Lord and Lady Cambridge to meet the Duke of Beaufort. On the way there I fell headlong down an area, mistaking it for a porch in the black-out!

Thursday, October 12th

At No. 10 by 9.30, which is the disgustingly early hour we start work. Everybody was humming with excitement about the Prime Minister's statement in reply to Hitler, which is to be made this afternoon.

Mother and I dined with Grandfather[6] and Peggy[7] at Argyll House. We had a delightful, intimate evening, and it is clear that Grandfather, although he suddenly looks rather old, is still very alert mentally. When Mother and Peggy had left the dining-room, I sat a long time with him, sipping old brandy, and hearing him talk of his active political days. He told me that when at the India Office and Colonial Office he had known every member of the staff and had always considered it important that a Secretary of

[1] Afterwards Countess of Dalhousie.
[2] William Stirling of Keir, eldest of the family, leading figure in the Commandos and subsequently chairman of Keir and Cawdor.
[3] Entered the Foreign Office the same year as I did. A keen steeplechaser and one of the best shots in the kingdom.
[4] Daughter of Lord Kemsley. Later married the Marquess of Huntly. Not to be confused with Lord Birkenhead's daughter, Lady Pamela Berry.
[5] Later married David Niven and was killed by a fall downstairs.
[6] The Marquess of Crewe.*
[7] His second wife, born Lady Margaret Primrose.

State should be able to judge the individual capacities of those beneath him. He spoke of the difficulty of forming a war cabinet of non-departmental heads, because the Foreign Secretary must be included, and if you retain Lord Chatfield,[1] but dispense with the Service Department heads, then what becomes of Winston? It might, he thought, be possible to have a cabinet consisting only of soldiers and sailors, but that would amount to martial law and should only be resorted to if the prosecution of the war really required it. He thought it most important that Winston should not become Prime Minister, and considered that Chamberlain ought to continue in office since he has both the necessary drive and the confidence of the public. He agreed with me that there was no younger man of outstanding ability on the political horizon.

After dinner I talked to Peggy (who has genius for using anti-climax) and then Grandfather discoursed amusingly about family history. He also said that as a small child he had been taken to tea with a Lady Blakistone, aged 101 (born in 1759, the *Annus Mirabilis*) who remarked how sorry she was that "her eldest boy was not there to play with him". Her eldest boy turned out to be eighty-one!

Friday, October 13th
The Germans are furious with Chamberlain's speech, but show no signs of an immediate offensive. One cannot help wondering whether Hitler really does want to start the war in earnest, or whether all that has happened has been part of a gigantic bluff. It is probably wishful thinking; but while there is life there is hope, and I should not be surprised if Hitler now put forward further peace proposals. However, short of a revolution in Germany, I do not see what can stop it. The important thing is that every day's delay is so much gain to us as far as war production is concerned.

Arther Rucker says he thinks Communism is now the great danger, greater even than Nazi Germany. All the independent

---

[1] Admiral of the Fleet and former First Sea Lord. Appointed by Chamberlain Minister for Coordination of Defence with a seat in the War Cabinet.

states of Europe are anti-Russian, but Communism is a plague that does not stop at national boundaries, and with the advance of the Soviet into Poland the states of Eastern Europe will find their powers of resistance to Communism very much weakened. It is thus vital that we should play our hand very carefully with Russia, and not destroy the possibility of uniting, if necessary, with a new German Government against the common danger. What is needed is a moderate conservative reaction in Germany: the overthrow of the present régime by the army chiefs.

George Steward,[1] the Government press chief, tells me that Dugdale is much the ablest man in the junior ranks of the Government. The Whips are much the weakest spot in the present Government, and David Margesson's appointments (e.g. Sir J. Gilmour[2] today as Minister of Shipping) are usually deplorable.

Three German submarines sunk. As the B.B.C. announcer said, Friday the 13th has been a bad day for the Germans.

It was said in Whitehall that Sir John Gilmour's appointment was the worst since Caligula made his horse a Consul. This witticism has been repeated ad nauseam *since the war about numerous people; but it was the first time I had heard it.*

I repeated it to my Father who smiled and said that when he was a young man he had heard it said of one of Disraeli's cabinet choices. Thinking it funny, and believing it to be original, he told his father (who was Derby's and Disraeli's Chief Whip in the House of Lords). His father replied: "When I was a young man, Lord Melbourne made an appointment . . ." Where and when this now hackneyed joke originated I do not know – doubtless centuries ago.

Saturday, October 14th
It is a pity the B.B.C. were so boastful. This morning comes the news of the loss of the *Royal Oak*, at Scapa Flow and surrounded by the Fleet.

---

[1] Press Officer at 10 Downing Street.
[2] Home Secretary, 1932–35. Not to be confused with the other Sir John (Jock) Gilmour, a much-respected stockbroker and father of Sir Ian Gilmour.

I was alone with Arthur Rucker all day at No. 10. He thinks it all-important that the war-mentality should not be aroused (he blames Winston with his submarine-hunts "not without relish") because he still hopes real war may be avoided.

In the afternoon, while I was alone in the room, Winston came in, carrying a large red box which he said was to be opened by the Prime Minister in person. He looked rather distraught, but said, as he went away, "Tell the Prime Minister we have got another submarine: that makes four yesterday." I had the red box before me for over half an hour, but managed to resist the temptation of opening it.

It has been a long day – 9.30 a.m. to 8.00 p.m. – and very tiring. What a drab world this is; especially when it rains all day.

Sunday, October 15th
Went to No. 10 for a few hours, to relieve Cecil Syers, about tea-time. Apparently a big offensive on the Western Front is thought imminent. Talked to Sir Walter Monckton about the Ministry of Information, of which he is a part: he says all the best men are threatening to resign because of the chaos. Lord Macmillan[1] must go and we need some Northcliffe-like propagandist to put life into the place.

Monday, October 16th
Lunched with Milo Talbot,[2] who is at the Ministry of Economic Warfare. I like Milo provided I only see him once in six months.

Dined with the Kemsleys.[3] The party included the Aly Khans,[4] Sir Godfrey[5] and Lady Thomas, Beverley Baxter[6] and

---

[1] A distinguished judge, but far from distinguished Minister of Information.
[2] Lord Talbot de Malahide. A contemporary at Cambridge and in the Diplomatic Service.
[3] Lord Kemsley was owner of the *Sunday Times* and *Daily Sketch*. Brother of Lord Camrose (owner of *Daily Telegraph*). His second wife was Edith du Plessis.
[4] Son of the Aga Khan, married to the Hon. Joan Yarde-Buller.
[5] Seconded from the Foreign Office to be Secretary to the Prince of Wales (Edward VIII) and thereafter to Prince Henry, Duke of Gloucester.
[6] A Canadian who became a Conservative M.P. in 1935 and was editor of the *Daily Express*.

Lord Davidson.[1] We none of us dressed (to show it was war-time) but in every other respect it might have been a party of pre-war days; all the rooms were open, there was a galaxy of footmen, the dinner was vast and excellent, and wine flowed like water. Vulgar, perhaps, in these days; but certainly a pleasant relapse into the gilded past.

At dinner I sat between Sir Godfrey Thomas, whom I found most agreeable, and Pam Berry. Afterwards I talked to Lord Davidson who was interesting on the subject of Ribbentrop, whom he had known well and whose blindness about this country he had done his utmost to cure. He also spoke of the bad appointments recently made by the Government (e.g. Sir J. Gilmour to be Minister of Shipping) and said that Sir S. Hoare was largely to blame. He also thought David Margesson's advice bad. At the end of dinner Lord Kemsley read out a telegram he had received to the effect that the expected German offensive near Saarbrücken had begun.

Afterwards I played bridge with Beverley Baxter against Lord Kemsley and Prince Aly Khan. It was amusing and at the same time quite good bridge. My partner is a talented bounder, and good company. I succeeded in winning £2.

Tuesday, October 17th
In the afternoon I went down to the House, heard Mr Hore-Belisha[2] having a rough time over Questions, and left after the P.M. had answered his (it was my duty to check what he said). Arriving back at No. 10 I found Lady Astor[3] on the doorstep having some raucous back-chat with the police about their wives. Interviewed the Bishop of Willesden.

Friday, October 20th
Not a very busy day. Received a delightful letter from Gay,[4] who still seems uncertain about coming back from America. Her

[1] Viscount Davidson. Private Secretary to a series of Prime Ministers and later Chairman of the Conservative Party.
[2] Secretary of State for War.*
[3] Viscountess Astor. An American by birth and the first woman to take her seat in Parliament.
[4] Captain David Margesson's younger daughter.

father tells me he consulted Winston about the safety of returning on an American ship: "Perfectly safe," said Winston, "but of course there is a risk of their being torpedoed or mined!"

Caught the 5.30 train to Winchester, where I found Eddy Rothschild[1] and Peter Trehearne[2] awaiting me and looking very martial in their heavy military overcoats. We motored to Exbury[3] and arrived in time for dinner.

Saturday, October 21st

It was a day like summer, and although the leaves were by no means off the trees we could scarcely have had a better shoot. Pheasants were plentiful, the shooting was good, and we killed well over 250.

At lunch I sat next to an American girl called Gracia Nevill, who gave me a description of an hour's conversation she had had with Hitler at Berchtesgaden and described the complete difference in him when he was talking of politics and when he was talking of other matters. In the former case he was a fanatic, in the latter a quiet and very impressive conversationalist.

Sunday, October 22nd

I walked round the garden, which was a sight of unparalleled beauty with its blaze of autumn red and gold, and talked to Lionel de Rothschild,[4] who was at his most agreeable. He suggested that our war aim should be to give Germany to the Jews, and divide up the Germans among the races of the world: in other words to make the two races change their position. But then, I said, the Jews in Germany will complain that the Germans control world finance!

---

[1] A close friend of mine at Harrow and Trinity. Later Senior Partner of N. M. Rothschild and Son.

[2] Another school and University friend, notable for his height, courage and good nature.

[3] Exbury, in the New Forest and on the Beaulieu River, has hundreds of acres of gardens devoted to rhododendrons, azaleas and the rarest of shrubs and trees.

[4] One of the two partners in Rothschilds. Creator of the magnificent gardens at Exbury.

Tuesday, October 24th

Went to the House in the afternoon. After Questions the P.M. saw Attlee and Greenwood, and afterwards Sir A. Sinclair, to harangue them about the disloyalty of the Opposition who, oblivious of the fact that we are at war, are seeking every opportunity to criticise the Government and increase their difficulties. Evidently the P.M.'s words were effective, because Attlee and Greenwood came out looking very chastened. Sir S. Hoare, with whom I had a short conversation, told me that in the last war the Opposition never made themselves unpleasant in this way: criticism of Haldane, etc., was always from outside the House. Probably the explanation is that the war seems scarcely to have begun, and nothing sufficiently drastic has happened to break the long-established traditions of party intrigue.

Wednesday, October 25th

In the morning I walked to Lambeth Palace to discuss Ecclesiastical matters with the Archbishop of Canterbury.[1] He was very charming and patriarchal, spoke charmingly of Mother ("one of the most excellent and distinguished members of the Church Assembly"), and every now and then introduced a sly sense of humour into his conversation which was most disarming. "That," he said, pointing to a barrage-balloon in the garden, "they call the Arch-blimp!"

Helped Arthur Rucker a little with the statement which the P.M. is to make in the House tomorrow, and which contains a forceful but dignified reply to Ribbentrop's fantastic speech at Danzig last night. It was said of Sir Stafford Cripps* that every time he opened his mouth he lost 100,000 votes for the Labour Party, and I begin to hope the same may be true of Ribbentrop and the Nazis. But then it is probably easy to persuade the Germans that their cause is just, because they are so inherently stupid; and they will certainly fight, because they are so incon-

---

[1] Cosmo Lang. Close friend of King George V. Widely, and in the main unjustly, criticised for his broadcast condemning Edward VIII's motives for abdicating.

testably brave. When you get a cross between a Lion and an Owl, the result is a very curious phenomenon; but that is as close as I can get, biologically, to accounting for the German mentality.

Sunday, October 29th

The most interesting papers concerned a possible basis for peace. Two Englishmen, called Christie and Conwell-Evans, have been talking to high-placed Germans, of whom one is Prince Max von Hohenlohe, in Switzerland about the possibility of getting rid of Hitler and coming to terms with an anti-Nazi Government under Goering* on the basis of restoring independence to Poland and Bohemia, disarming all round, and agreeing to leave inviolate the unity and boundaries of Germany proper. It seems that the upper classes and high military authorities in Germany are anxious to avoid the outbreak of a real war, since they believe that Bolshevism in Germany would be the final and inevitable outcome. Prince Max produced nine points as a possible basis of negotiations. Lord Halifax proposed a rather cautious reply, to the effect that our war aims had already been clearly announced in the P.M.'s speeches (that we should declare our aims was considered by Prince Max indispensable, in order that the German people should abandon their conviction that we intend to partition and humiliate Germany) and that we could do nothing without consulting our French allies.

I am afraid the F.O. are rather defeatist about the possibility of procuring peace. The P.M., on the other hand, is in favour of a much more encouraging reply, and is prepared to accept eight out of the nine points, only stipulating that Hitler himself shall play no part in the proposed new order. In return for a change of régime (or at least a modification), restoration of frontiers and disarmament, the P.M. would be prepared to agree to economic assistance for Germany, to no demand for reparations, and to Colonial discussions. He wishes, however, to insert some safeguards for the Jews and the Austrians.

Monday, October 30th
On returning to the office after luncheon I found Lord Portal[1] waiting to see the P.M. He is anxious that business should return to London because of the disastrous effect decentralisation is having on our economic life. He feels, as I do, that our greatest danger through the coming winter will be growing apathy, and he is seriously concerned at the poverty of our propaganda as a weapon to combat this.

Tuesday, October 31st
Sir Eric Phipps, in his last despatch, makes out the French case against Germany and supports that country's opposition to our theory that we are fighting against Hitlerism instead of against Germany. Much of what he says seems plausible, and no doubt his views represent very accurately those of the French; but in the interests of world peace I trust he is wrong, because there now seems just a chance of separating the German people from their leaders if we can convince the former of the purity of our intentions towards them. One can sympathise with the feelings of the French; but it was, after all, their intransigence which bred the bitterness and despair upon which Hitler rose to power.

The Government White Paper on German Concentration Camps is a sordid document calculated to appeal to people's lowest instincts, and reminiscent of the "Corpse Factory" propaganda in the last war. It does shed a lurid glow on the bestial sadism of the Germans at their worst; but after all most of the evidence is produced from prejudiced sources, and it is in any case undesirable to arouse passions before the war has begun in earnest. Lord Halifax, of all people, is said to have pressed for its publication, but I understand that the fanatically anti-German Kirkpatrick* is the man behind it all. Alec Dunglass, Cecil, Arthur and I all agreed in condemning its publication.

Thursday, November 2nd
I saw further papers about the Hohenlohe proposals. H. wants to come over to England, but this request has been refused and

[1] Viscount Portal of Laverstoke.*

I gather Christie is going out to see him in Holland. Poor wretch, if Hitler should hear of his machinations! Van[1] and Halifax refuse to entertain seriously the idea of negotiating with Goering, but there seems reason to think that Hohenlohe and his friends, goaded by their fear that Hitler may turn Bolshevist, are only using Goering as a "stalking horse". One of Hohenlohe's more curious recommendations was that we should hastily start bombing military objectives in order to prove how serious are our intentions: pamphlets are not sufficiently impressive.

Saturday, November 4th

The Cabinet seem rather excited about the Russo-Finnish dispute. Personally I think that if the Finns stand firm the Russians, who are more hyaenas than bears, will not attack them.

David Margesson says he is in despair about the Cabinet. He would like to recommend the P.M. to get rid of Sam Hoare and Simon, who are egotistic intriguers; but the difficulty would be to find someone else to put in their place. Arthur Rucker thinks Sir Kingsley Wood[2] * would do as Chancellor of the Exchequer, but he is such an appalling speaker. Some people consider Reginald McKenna,[3] of whom David had thought, dishonest. The trouble is that there are no promising young men on the horizon and it is necessary to fall back on such unattractive bureaucrats as Sir John Anderson.[4] David M. is even thinking of him as a possible Chancellor, but the appointment would be almost as unpopular as that of Gilmour as Minister of Shipping.

There is a first-class row in progress between Hore-Belisha [Secretary of State for War] and Kingsley Wood [Secretary of State for Air] about the provision of aircraft for the army; Belisha

---

[1] Sir Robert Vansittart (see p. 189).

[2] Beachcomber, the consistently funny columnist in the *Daily Express*, wrote at about this time:
Democracy gives us the men that we want,
And those that we chiefly adore
Are colourful, vital Kingsley Wood
And glamorous Samuel Hoare.

[3] Chancellor of the Exchequer in Mr Asquith's Liberal Government and subsequently Chairman of the Midland Bank.

[4] Later Viscount Waverley. *

wants 250 bombers to be handed over to the exclusive control of the C. in C.; Kingsley Wood thinks that this would be disastrous in principle and in practice. It would mean the removal of nearly half our striking force of bombers from the R.A.F.

One feels some sympathy with David Margesson's anxiety to get rid of all the service ministers; but, as he says, it would be necessary to leave Winston in the Cabinet without portfolio, and heaven knows what that would presage.

The P.M. and Halifax are busy thinking out what reply can be sent to a communication from Daladier [French Prime Minister]* about war aims. The trouble is that any suggestion that Germany would be partitioned would unite everybody in Germany behind the Nazis, whereas a sensible moderate statement would dishearten the French. It will probably be necessary to confine any statement to the vaguest of generalisations, merely including something specific to the effect that the autonomy of the Poles, Czechs and Slovaks will not be disregarded. Halifax and Chamberlain both think that one of the chief mistakes at Versailles was the establishment of small autonomous states which had not the strength to withstand the onslaught of ravening wolves. When Germany has been defeated it will be vital, Halifax thinks, to establish some form of federation in Central and South-Eastern Europe, at least in the financial and economic sphere. We ought to start working for that now. I am afraid, however, that the French tend to think these areas ought to be left to their hegemony.

Sunday, November 5th

The general situation now seems to be as follows. On the credit side, Germany has not yet attacked despite her armed superiority, and it seems incredible that if she really means to wage war in earnest she should have allowed these valuable months to slip by. The Empire, except perhaps for India, is solidly behind us, and the material support which Canada, for instance, can lend is as great as is her determination to do so. Neutral opinion is convinced of the justice of the Allies' cause and is disposed to be helpful when it safely can, e.g. the courageous decision of the Norwegian Government yesterday to intern the *City of Flint*'s German prize crew. Finally the U.S.A., as much no doubt for reasons of commercial profit as any other, has at last passed the new Neutrality Act, and the Germans are thoroughly disgruntled thereby.

On the debit side, I am alarmed to read in Cabinet papers how long it will be before our production of armaments, and particularly aeroplanes, is satisfactory. I am not impressed by our efficiency or ability to "get a move on". With the exception of the P.M., Halifax, Churchill and Kingsley Wood the Cabinet are not a striking collection, and the junior ministers do not seem to include any outstanding personalities. Our Intelligence Service seems very weak, despite the number of sympathisers we must have in Germany: we never seem to have accurate or certain information about German fleet and troop movements, whereas the Germans know all our movements within a few hours of their taking place – probably by means of very low-wave wireless transmitters in this country which it is difficult to detect. At home the public is inclined to boredom and apt to forget that a war calls for sacrifices. The press and the Opposition maintain an endless campaign of criticism and grumbling, which embarrasses the Government and provides the enemy with propaganda. The power of our propaganda in the U.S. and elsewhere does not seem very formidable. Finally trouble is brewing in India where Congress is attempting to blackmail us into constitutional concessions, as the price of its support, and is now threatening a campaign of non-cooperation.

Tuesday, November 7th

Went to the House for Questions. Hore-Belisha, as usual, was having a rather difficult time with questions about dependants' allowances, etc. The P.M. had arranged for a private notice question to be put down about the *News Chronicle*'s allegation that an "Inner Cabinet" existed which excluded the Service Ministers. He rebutted this false statement amidst universal applause.

After Questions Sinclair and Attlee came to see the P.M. and, after them, Sir P. Loraine.[1] Attlee said he was getting an

---

[1] Successful Ambassador to Turkey before the war, winning Kemal Ataturk's friendship, and then Ambassador to Italy. A keen racehorse owner.

enormous number of telegrams demanding the imposition of rationing: as Alec Dunglass remarked, it is astonishing that people grumble when one is doing one's best to let them live normally and to save them inconvenience.

Loraine, whom I had last seen in Istanbul in 1934, was full of conversation. He told me that he found Ciano[1] likeable, though conceited, and very quick. He also genuinely believed that C. was now disgusted with the Axis, largely because of the abominable way he was treated by Hitler and Ribbentrop at Salzburg. Loraine further said that it was a mistake to forget that Italy was fascist, and that being such she did not like democracies. On the other hand the King was determined not to fight against France, and throughout modern history Italy, when in danger, has always turned to the House of Savoy. The Crown Prince, he said, was anti-fascist, but he had not got the King's intelligence.

Wednesday, November 8th
Went down to the House for Questions. I waited to hear Winston Churchill make a statement about the loss of the *Royal Oak* and the naval situation. The best point he made was when, referring to the Nazi claims of destruction of our ships, he said that the British navy would be prepared to fight the whole German navy merely with those ships which the Germans claimed to have sunk.

The latest German claim is to have sunk H.M.S. *Kestrel*, which turns out to be a naval sea-plane base some miles inland.

Thursday, November 9th
An attempt on Hitler's life unfortunately failed. It was probably genuine, but I should not be surprised if Hitler made use of the occasion for a great internal purge. He may even use it as a pretext for beginning the war in earnest. Let us hope it will not increase his popularity at home, as did the Rye House Plot that of Charles II.[2]

[1] Mussolini's son-in-law and Foreign Minister.
[2] Unsuccessful plot by disgruntled Whigs to kill Charles II on his way back to London from Newmarket. Its failure restored the King's waning popularity.

The P.M. has gout, rather badly. This may give a useful handle to those who think he is too old for the job and ought to retire. But there is really nobody to take his place: Halifax has not the forcefulness and Winston is too unstable.

The morning was spent in hectic preparations for the Mansion House speech, which Simon will now make in the P.M.'s place. Simon proved obstinate, unbelievably unhelpful, and ended by leaving half of the speech behind. Arthur Rucker pursued him with it to the Mansion House in a taxi.

The Cabinet and Chiefs of Staff think that an attack on Holland really is imminent, and the Dutch and the Belgians are in a state of terror. I rather doubt it: even Hitler would find this hard to justify, and there does not seem to have been any attempt to "prepare" German opinion. However, there is always a chance that Hitler may do something on November 11th – to wipe out the slur of twenty-one years ago – and it is conceivable he may choose the Low Countries for his gesture.

In any case, as Halifax said to the Cabinet, Hitler will find it difficult to remain inactive after the threatening speech he made in the Bierkeller at Munich yesterday. He said he would attack England and, in the words of the *Evening Standard*, one cannot count on his *always* telling lies!

Sunday, November 12th

Our secret reports claim that it would be a mistake to expect any collapse of German morale until serious military reverses have been suffered.

We listened to Winston Churchill's wireless speech, very boastful, over-confident and indiscreet (especially about Italy and the U.S.A.), but certainly most amusing.

Monday, November 13th

Winston's speech has made a very bad effect at No. 10 but the F.O. and the City take a favourable view (War-Loan rose a point!). The Italian and Dutch Representatives protested at the F.O., and Rab Butler* tells me he thought it beyond words vulgar. The Cabinet were evidently embarrassed; but Hankey* (who, I am told, always "sucks up") expressed great approval to Winston.

Tuesday, November 14th
The Belgo-Dutch crisis seems to be passing over. Alec Dunglass thinks that Hitler will take no drastic measures because the Germans think they can win a long war. I suspect he is right: there can surely be no other explanation for the waste of these precious ten weeks – unless Hitler really has got a "secret weapon", to which he can resort at any moment and with which he can make resistance impossible.[1] But that seems unlikely.

Cabinet meeting at the House at 6.00, which the P.M. did not attend (though he was carried down to this morning's meeting). I went down for the meeting, and sat there with Alec, helping him with parts of the speech which the P.M. is to make to the 1922 Committee.

Thursday, November 16th
The Cabinet are considering, very secretly, the possibility of bombing the Ruhr, which is the centre of German industrial life, if Belgium is attacked. They do not wish to do so because:
  (a) It would entail bombing the civilian population.
  (b) It would invite drastic retaliation.
  (c) We should lose a great many planes, which we can ill afford to lose.
Moreover the French are not anxious to take such a step before the spring, and do not think it would pay. The important question is whether an invasion of Belgium would be a decisive phase of the war. Our Chiefs of Staff think it would, and Gamelin* is prepared to use all his forces to stop a German advance on the Scheldt or on the line Antwerp–Namur. However he doubts whether an invasion of Belgium *would* be decisive. The British view is coloured by the fact that we do not want the Germans to be allowed tamely to occupy the Dutch and Belgian ports

---

[1] Hitler's secret weapon was the magnetic mine, which caused much damage to Allied shipping until it was neutralised by what was called "degaussing", a method devised in a comparatively short time by British scientists.

from which they could launch intensive attacks on England. The matter is to be discussed at a meeting of the Supreme War Council in London tomorrow.

Friday, November 17th
A hectic day. The Supreme War Council met in London to discuss the question of bombing the Ruhr, and I went to Victoria Station with Oliver Harvey[1] to welcome Daladier and Gamelin on the P.M.'s behalf. They both look very undistinguished. The Council met at No. 10, owing to the P.M.'s inability to move, and there was a great deal of flurry in the morning with French A.D.C.s and camp followers. The Council decided not to bomb the Ruhr if Belgium was invaded, but only if French and English civilian or paramilitary objectives were attacked. In case of invasion the Allied armies will try to hold the Antwerp–Namur Line.

After lunch I saw the party off at Victoria and had a talk with Oliver Harvey. He considers that Eden[2] has a first-rate brain (contrary to No. 10 opinion) and is not merely a "glamour boy" with a facility for speaking, but may easily be a future P.M. He thinks that if anything happens to Chamberlain, Halifax would be his successor if things remain quiet, but Churchill in the event of serious military reverses (God forbid!).

Saturday, November 18th
I went to Chandos House[3] and was driven down to Farnham[3] by Pam Berry and Ian Fleming.[4] Lord and Lady Kemsley were there, and he was full of conversation. He thinks that Sam Hoare will slip into the premiership if anything happens to N.C., but doubts his holding it for long.

---

[1] Principal Private Secretary to Lord Halifax. Ambassador in Paris after the war. Created Lord Harvey of Tasburgh.
[2] Secretary of State for the Dominions till May 1940. Later Lord Avon, 1961.*
[3] The Kemsleys' London house in Queen Anne Street and country house at Farnham Royal.
[4] An officer in Naval Intelligence. Author of the James Bond stories.

Sunday, November 19th

Lord Kemsley and Baxter are carrying on a journalistic war against the *Sunday Pictorial* which has lately contained scurrilous attacks on the P.M. (and which George Steward thinks is run by Winston's supporters).

Tuesday, November 21st

Went down to the House where the P.M.'s statement about seizing German exports was well received. He saw Kingsley Wood and Lord Macmillan, and afterwards I drove back with him to No. 10. He was quite conversational for once, but his favourite topic is the weather.

Wednesday, November 22nd

The mine warfare continues with a vengeance and about a dozen ships, including Italian and Japanese, have been sunk in the last few days. German aircraft have been dropping mines by parachute, and none of the waters on the south-east and east coasts can now be considered safe. The neutrals do not like our retaliatory measures, but the U.S. seem satisfied.

We are now dropping pamphlets over Germany in the form of a small newspaper called *Wolkiger Beobachter*,[1] of which I saw a copy this morning. It is extremely well done, with cartoons (one *very* obscene), verses, and short facts about the war.

It has been decided to lay a mine barrage right across the North Sea, to prevent the egress of submarines and raiders, but this will cost much and will take a long time to put into effect.

Winston is agitating for an alleviation of the black-out and makes the silly proposal that street-lighting should be restored and switched off on receipt of the Yellow warning. As the P.M. Points out, this would make the Yellow into a Red warning.

Saturday, November 25th

Simon looked in and said that his speech on the wireless, urging people to save, had been much criticised as damaging to trade

---

[1] Wolkiger meant coming from the clouds. A play on the title of the German newspaper *Völkischer Beobachter*.

and he hoped the P.M. would not mention the matter in his broadcast on Sunday. He wished, he said, that he had told people to go on shopping, but nevertheless to save all they could. "A Chancellor of the Exchequer expects to be cursed; but we must encourage National Savings in order to raise the money we require. Nobody realises yet what privations we have got to face."

Monday, November 27th
When I got home I found Lady Snowden[1] with Mother. She thinks a defeatist spirit is growing in the country (Alec Dunglass told me the other day he had the same impression and was afraid it might spread to the House).

Tuesday, November 28th
Lunched with Mariora Swinton[2] to meet Captain Troubridge,[3] lately Naval Attaché in Berlin. He says there is little anti-English feeling in the south and that Goering is undoubtedly anxious for peace. Goering did not expect war: he had even ordered 600 young pheasants for delivery in October. He thinks the military leaders will soon get rid of Hitler and offer peace on their own terms – terms which we shall find it difficult to refuse in the face of popular opinion here. He also thinks it is silly to talk about making a martyr out of Hitler: he will in any case be a martyr to the Germans who will always revere him as the greatest figure in their history. Speaking of Hore-Belisha, Troubridge said women liked him because women always like Jews: they are both oppressed races!

I cannot help feeling that there is something very wrong with

[1] Ethel Snowden. Passionate teetotaller and social reformer. Wife of Philip Snowden, formerly Labour Chancellor of the Exchequer.
[2] Attractive wife of Lt-Col. Alan Swinton, Scots Guards, our next-door neighbour in Eccleston Square.
[3] Bluff and entertaining officer, subsequently a Vice-Admiral, who came of a family famous in naval history and had been naval attaché in Berlin. His father commanded the Mediterranean Cruiser Squadron in 1914; his grandson was the first husband of Princess Michael of Kent.

a code of honour which, as in the case of the *Rawalpindi*,[1] prescribes that a ship must go down with all hands fighting to the last when cornered by a bigger vessel and unable to escape. Why should not the crew scuttle their ship and take to the boats? The effect would be the same except that hundreds of lives might be saved from a fate of flames and impotent horror. Codes of honour are often relics of a barbarous age, and it is tragic that modern opinion should remain so obscurantist on these matters. But it is undeniably true that if the *Rawalpindi*'s crew had scuttled their ship and saved themselves, their action would have been represented as disgraceful at home and abroad.

Wednesday, November 29th
Dined with Dorothy Cambridge to meet the Duke of Beaufort,[2] who had been told (by the King, I think) that Mr Kennedy,* the American Ambassador, is talking about our inability to win the war. To the P.M. and the F.O. he poses as the greatest champion of our cause in the U.S.

Thursday, November 30th
Evidently the Russian threats were not bluff. Using the same technique as Hitler, a technique which does not gain in dignity for being second-hand, they invaded Finland this morning.

Arthur Rucker thinks this may ultimately be a good thing: it incontestably brands Russia, Germany and Japan as the wolves in the sheepfold and destroys any remaining illusions about the Soviet's altruistic intentions. He laments that after the last war the statesmen of Europe did not see Russia was the great menace and did not make friends with Germany on that basis. There might then have been no Hitler; but now we are hopelessly divided in the face of a common foe and, as the Hungarian Regent said to our Minister in Budapest, it is on the fields of Europe ploughed up by German and Allied gunfire that the seed of Bolshevism will take root.

[1] The *Rawalpindi* was an armed merchant cruiser found and sunk by the German pocket-cruiser *Deutschland* against which she had no chance at all.
[2] Famous Master of the Beaufort Hounds. Master of the Horse. His wife, Mary, was a sister of Lord Cambridge and a niece of Queen Mary.

The Pope [Pius XII] put it all admirably in his recent encyclical, when he spoke of this "age of technical and civic progress tormented by spiritual emptiness and poverty". There lies the fundamental tragedy and the *fons et origo malorum*. Mankind has deposed God and deified the state, while substituting a kind of sentimental philanthropy (which stops at the barrier of self-interest) for a code of morality based on religious principle.

Went down to the House where the P.M. answered a Private Notice question about Finland, the references to the Russian invasion being greeted with cries of "shame". However, the P.M. privately thinks the invasion may not be a very serious matter.

The P.M. elaborated to Arthur his ideas for the future, after the war is over. He thinks there will have to be a World League, but its jurisdiction will only extend to economic and social questions. Within or beside that there would be a European League, the members of which would agree to bring their differences to a council table and would attempt to bring about disarmament by slow stages. He does not think an International Police Force is practical politics.

Sunday, December 3rd

At Cambridge I looked in for a short time at King's Chapel to hear the exquisite singing and generally to enjoy the unique beauty of the place. Afterwards I went to Newnham to see Janet Margesson,[1] with whom I walked along the sunlit "backs", ending up with sherry and a fervid political discussion in Alan Hodgkin's[2] rooms. Jan is an intelligent and agreeable companion, but is at present passing through the earnest undergraduate stage of finding nothing right with the world. Alan Hodgkin is a brilliant scientist and an unusually attractive personality – very unassuming.

Wednesday, December 6th

Returned to the House with the P.M. at 7.15 for the division on the socialist amendment to the loyal address. I listened to

[1] Elder daughter of the Chief Whip, Captain David Margesson.
[2] Eminent physiologist. Master of Trinity College, Cambridge, 1978–84.

part of Herbert Morrison's* speech, fluent and moderate and rather impressive. He spoke of the World Revolution which had taken place in this century: a technical revolution which began in the West and moved Eastwards. In the East it gained much; for instance the Russian experiment proved that collectivisation could work; but it also broke down disastrously in the East because it was accompanied by a doctrine which denied the Rights of Man (Liberal cheers). Eden replied for the Government, speaking easily and sometimes amusingly, but never descending from generalities to deal with the concrete facts for which the Opposition asked. As Alec Dunglass said, it was difficult to realise one was listening to a speech by a man who had been Foreign Secretary.

Thursday, December 7th

Awoken at 2 a.m. to deal with a letter to the P.M. from Winston, who has decided on the spur of the moment to proceed northwards to investigate the situation caused by the temporary disablement of the *Nelson* and the *Rodney*. The *Nelson* has struck a magnetic mine and will not be repaired for two months. This is not being divulged.

Lunched with Chips Channon* at his highly ornate house in Belgrave Square. Sat between Lady Cunard,[1] who is certainly most amusing, and Alice von Hoffmanstahl.[2] Lady Cunard spent her time trying to persuade me (as if I could help) that Archie Sinclair ought to be in the Government and that, despite the war, the Government ought to subvention music, possibly by diverting money from the Churches! Covent Garden, she tells me, is shut probably for good.

Friday, December 8th

Sir W. Seeds,[3] our Ambassador in Moscow, thinks Germany and Russia are now hand-in-glove and that there is little hope of

---

[1] American by birth. Scintillating conversationalist, indefatigable hostess and intimate friend of the celebrated orchestral conductor, Sir Thomas Beecham. Ardent supporter of King Edward VIII and Mrs Simpson.

[2] Alice Astor by birth. Married Raimond von Hoffmanstahl.

[3] Former Ambassador to Brazil, but only lasted a year in Moscow.

a rift between them. He suspects that the Soviet intends to control all Scandinavia, and he thinks that the reasons against our declaring war on Russia are now less strong. Moreover he believes all the neutral states consider Russia more dangerous than Germany, and would welcome our changing our present state of undeclared war against Moscow into a real one. There are signs that when the League meets next week there will be strong support for Russia's expulsion from the League and for sanctions against her. Meanwhile Italy, Sweden, Great Britain and even Hungary are sending armed support to Finland, and Italy may be prepared to favour a Balkan bloc against Soviet aggression in that direction.

Lunched with Michael Grant[1] at the Travellers. He is working in Military Intelligence at the War Office, and is as good company, as brilliant and as egotistic as ever.

Wednesday, December 13th

Horace Wilson told me of the naval action being fought against the *Graf von Spee*. He and Edward Bridges were seeing the P.M. about a first-class row in progress between Hore-Belisha and Ironside [Chief of the Imperial General Staff]* on one side and Lord Gort on the other. The first two are, as usual, behaving disgracefully.

Thursday, December 14th

Tommy Dugdale tells me that Sinclair's speech last night was the best he had ever made. He showed, though not directly, that he knew a great many details about production, the number of divisions we propose to send to France, etc., which he could only have obtained from official sources. His speech must have been prepared either by Winston (who is quite capable of such a thing), or by Hore-Belisha via Sir Walter Layton.[2]

---

[1] A friend of mine at Harrow and Cambridge. Brilliant Classicist, successful author and expert from his early youth on Roman coins.

[2] Chairman of the *News Chronicle* and Editor of the *Economist*. A leading member of the Liberal Party. Made a peer in 1947.

Friday, December 15th

The P.M., accompanied by Arthur, General Ismay and Alec Dunglass (in uniform, but looking very unmilitary) left by aeroplane for France, to inspect the troops and G.H.Q.

Consequently we had a quiet day at No. 10, with nothing but a large number of letters from boring members of the public to keep us busy. The only interesting paper that I saw was an account of a conversation between Alec Cadogan and the Duke of Würtemberg, who hopes for a military uprising in Germany soon (under two anti-Nazi Generals and with the support of three tank divisions) and thinks (optimistically, I fear) that the country will divide itself up into its former little states (though the Hohenzollerns would be excluded). He expects the new capital to be Munich, or possibly Stuttgart, and not Berlin. But he declares that the essential preliminary is that the generals shall be convinced the Allies will not make use of the occasion to crush Germany.

Saturday, December 16th

Main papers of interest were:

(1) A memorandum by Winston on German iron ore supplies. He considers it essential to use drastic, and even illegal, methods to prevent ore being shipped from Norwegian ports, and he wants Cabinet authority to lay minefields in Norwegian territorial waters (with the justification that German U-boats are sinking ships in those waters) in order to drive ships carrying iron ore out of territorial waters into the hands of our contraband control.

(2) A Foreign Office appreciation of the situation in Scandinavia, weighing the possibilities of German intervention in the south if the Russians attack in the north. Sweden may very likely intervene on the side of Finland, but Norway and Denmark are determined on neutrality. Probably Germany will try to dissuade Russia from seizing Northern Norway and Sweden because in that case the iron ore, upon which Germany so much depends, would fall into Russian hands.

I have a feeling that Scandinavia may well end by being the chief theatre of war and that we may have to send troops there.

(3) A report on the Balkan situation, which has been changed by the Russian threat. Roumania is the weak spot, in danger of attack from three sides, from Russia, Bulgaria and Hungary, and susceptible to German pressure. Roumania (i.e. King Carol) would probably choose German domination rather than subjection to Russia.

Bulgaria is threatened by Bolshevisation, of which the King and ruling classes live in mortal fear. Her relations with Turkey are improving.

Yugoslavia is very cautious but, except for her Foreign Minister, very pro-Allies.

Turkey will not fight Russia if Bessarabia is seized, but would probably consider her vital interests threatened if the Russians tried to cross the Danube.

Hungary is increasingly anti-Nazi, terrified of Russia and looks to Italy as her mainstay. If the Bulgarians and Russians take their pound of flesh from Roumania, no Hungarian Government could prevent their people from going for Transylvania.

Greece, though pro-Allies, is becoming very anti-war as a result of commercial difficulties and a fall in the standard of living.

(4) A statement by the Chancellor on the financial situation. If the war begins in earnest, our military expenditure will amount to half the national income. We must face the fact that there will be a great fall in the standard of living, that we shall not be able to obtain luxuries and even supplies to which we are used, that wages will not be able to rise in proportion to prices (without causing inflation), and that the burden will have to be borne equally by all classes. Even the confiscation of the incomes of all surtax payers would not solve the financial problem. A grim outlook, but I suppose these hardships will only make themselves felt gradually. The question is whether the morale on the home front is good enough to bear them. Judging from the raucous criticism of hitherto minor inconveniences, I am inclined to doubt this, unless the public's enthusiasm and determination is increased by sensational events in the war – which from a

wider point of view is just what we want to avoid. From this angle Germany, and any totalitarian Government, is in a better position to wage war than we are.

Moreover I have no confidence in our propaganda.

Tuesday, December 26th [On Christmas leave at Helperby in Yorkshire]
Anthony, [1] Philip and I hunted with the York and Ainsty (North) near Ripon, hiring horses as it was too far to hack. The country was lovely, much prettier than at Helperby, and the going good. After a somewhat ineffective morning, during which every time the fox tried to sally out into the open he was thwarted by zealous holiday-makers, we had two first-class runs in the afternoon. The first was short but with a lot of jumping, the second lasted over an hour and was finally ended by the death of the fox (everybody being in at the death, except the Master, the Whips and Anthony who got lost). At one stage I followed the wily Arthur Collins[2] and had a magnificent hunt alone with him, the hounds, the Master and the Whips.

Wednesday, December 27th
At Downing Street by 9.30 where I found Cecil Syers very disconsolate, having spent a depressing Christmas alone with Miss Watson at No. 10.

A dull day, the only excitement being the question whether or not we should take drastic steps to prevent Scandinavian iron ore reaching Germany. If we do, it may shorten the war, but it may mean our having to send an expeditionary force to Sweden. Winston, of course, is in favour of immediate action; but the Cabinet and the Chiefs of Staff are less enthusiastic.

Thursday, December 28th
The P.M. has another attack of gout, and is worried at the prospect of not being able to carry on if these attacks increase

[1] Anthony Coates, younger son of my mother's twin sister Lady Celia Coates. Immensely popular, sincerely religious and possessor of a sparkling sense of humour. Joined the Coldstream Guards and was killed in Normandy in 1944.
[2] Later senior partner of Withers, the well-known solicitors.

in number and violence. Meanwhile very secret soundings are being taken regarding the possibility of an enabling bill to allow a peer to speak, but not vote, in the Commons, so that Lord Stamp[1] can succeed Simon as Chancellor of the Exchequer.

The story of these negotiations was committed to paper by Lord Stamp. When his house was bombed, in 1941, and he killed, an envelope containing the account was blown into the street and found by an A. R. P. Warden who brought it to No. 10 Annexe. As I was on duty, it came to me. On reflection I did not show the paper to the Prime Minister, who had known nothing of the plot, but forwarded it directly to Sir Horace Wilson, then Secretary to the Treasury and, with the Governor of the Bank of England, Montagu Norman, one of the originators of the scheme.

Friday, December 29th

There are signs of a renewed peace move. The Vatican and Mussolini are putting their heads together and may enlist the support of Roosevelt, to whom the R.C. vote is important.

Our (or rather Van's) conversations with German army leaders and Hohenlohe, through Conwell-Evans, are continuing and all hope of engineering an internal coup d'état does not seem to be abandoned. It is said that Hitler and his generals are at loggerheads over an invasion of Holland, which Hitler still favours (and which Ciano thinks probable).

A dull, but quite busy day. From conversations between Arthur and C. J. Harris[2] and Arthur and Horace Wilson, I gather Cabinet changes are under consideration, with a view to being rid of Hore-Belisha from the War Office. Kingsley Wood and others want him to go to the Ministry of Information, but Halifax opposes this (presumably because his brand of propaganda would be too vulgar) and it seems that the influence of Horace will also be wielded against this proposal.

---

[1] Celebrated statistician, economist and expert on taxation. He had been ennobled in 1938.

[2] Secretary to successive Chief Whips at 12 Downing Street and a welcome habitué of No. 10.

Sunday, December 31st

Here at home, at the end of 1939, people seem to be resigned to the war without fully realising the hardships which it must, and the physical terror which it may, imply. Everybody is talking gaily about a changing world, a new social order, a complete revolution of national and international ideals; but do they realise what effect all this, if it comes to pass, will have upon them personally? It is easy to sit in the warmth, beautifully dressed, after an enormous meal, and talk academically about the inevitability of change and the charm of doing one's own housework; but it may be less easy to accommodate oneself to the grimness of reality.

At sea the war is going better for us. The *Graf Spee* affair, and the damaging of German warships by two of our submarines at about the same time, have greatly enhanced our prestige abroad and have given much-needed encouragement at home. The mine menace, the possibility of violent air onslaughts against our harbours or the Fleet at sea, and the slowing down of trade due to the convoy system are the major dangers and inconveniences with which we are now faced.

In Europe interest is, for the time being, centred on Finland, where the Russians are apparently meeting with unexpected and overwhelming setbacks. Germany may well be alarmed at the effect which the action of her new ally is likely to have on opinion both at home and abroad. The Italians are openly disgusted and frightened ("this monstrous aggression": shades of Abyssinia and Albania!), and it is increasingly clear that Ciano is now in the Allied camp. He even gives Loraine information which is obviously to the detriment of Germany, and he is a restraining influence on his father-in-law who hates democracies and cannot forgive or forget sanctions.[1] The newly cemented friendship of the Vatican and the Quirinal will probably strengthen the hands of both parties, who feel, I think, that the war should be stopped soon and that the belligerents should unite against Bolshevism.

As always throughout history, the situation in the Balkans is

---

[1] The sanctions imposed by the League of Nations in 1935 when Italy invaded Abyssinia.

obscure, explosive and liable to change. The two most likely causes of trouble would be a Russian invasion of Bessarabia or a decision by the Germans that they must secure a firmer grasp on Roumania's oil supplies. The latter is not improbable as Germany's own consumption, even during the present period of inactivity, far exceeds what she can import and what she can safely draw from her stocks.

The U.S. is aloof, and critical of what everybody in Europe is doing and thinking, without showing the least inclination to step in to redress the balance of the Old World.

In general, we seem to be floating on a sea of stagnant waters and in ships not built of the soundest timbers. Whether the much-advertised spring offensive will come off remains to be seen, but it is very doubtful whether we can reach next winter without something drastic happening, and I think the odds are fifty-fifty on peace or the real outbreak of war. The conditions in which the former could be made are at present unforeseeable; but at least each side is aware of its own shortages and weakness and both are afraid to begin the carnage. The consequences of the latter are only too easy to predict.

THREE

INDECISION
JANUARY–MARCH 1940

Monday, January 1st

The breakfast supplied by Mrs Chamberlain is really hardly edible, and so after sleeping at No. 10 I went across to the Travellers to feed well and in comfort. It is the Prime Ministerial coffee which is at fault: it tastes of strong burnt chicory and is, curiously enough, a source of pride to the Chamberlains and their staff who believe it to be unique in its excellence.

The Cabinet, instigated by Winston, are considering a daring offensive scheme in Northern Scandinavia, which they think might bring Germany to her knees but which also, to my mind, is dangerously reminiscent of the Gallipoli plan. Briefly, they have decided that if Germany could be denied her Scandinavian supplies of iron ore she would have to give up the struggle. They contemplate either (a) blockading Narvik, in Northern Norway, by means of destroyers and minefields, or (b) more boldly, landing a force in Northern Norway to take possession of the ore deposits and thus prevent shipments to Germany from the port of Lulea in Sweden. They hope to be able to force Norway and Sweden into the war on our side in order to put the major scheme into operation; if, as seems likely, this is not feasible then they might resort to the first and minor scheme, despite Scandinavian opposition. The effects are likely to be (i) a German invasion of Southern Scandinavia, (ii) a violent air-attack on this country by way of reprisal. The essential requisite is speed, and if the plan is adopted in either of its forms it will probably be put into execution before the spring. The Cabinet will debate the matter tomorrow.

Extensive Cabinet reconstruction is proposed: Macmillan to leave the Ministry of Information and become, eventually, a Lord of Appeal; Hore-Belisha to become Minister of Information (to the satisfaction of everybody connected with him in his present job); Oliver Stanley* to become Secretary of State for War; Lord Stamp to be made a Commoner by Act of Parliament (an unprecedented step) and be Chancellor of the Exchequer instead of Simon, who will be Lord President and do much of the Treasury work in the Commons. Arthur Rucker is doubtful about Stamp whom he considers the Sir James Jeans[1] of the economic world; David Margesson would secretly like Bob Brand[2] to be Chancellor, and hopes to have him in any case appointed to the Treasury in an advisory capacity. I suspect that the fact that he is a neighbour of the Margessons at Boddington, and a friend of David's, accounts for this whim of the Chief Whip.

Dined at the Travellers with Con O'Neill[3] and John Cairncross. The former says that the thing that he most dreads is a breach in the Russo-German alliance. If Germany turned against the Bolsheviks she would do so with the sympathy, and probably the active assistance, of all the neutrals, and her own crimes would be forgotten in an anti-Russian crusade. We and the French should be faced with the choice of coming to terms with Hitler, on a basis which left him in power in Germany, morally strengthened, or of attacking him when he himself was fighting against an enemy whom half our own people consider more venomous than the Nazis themselves. A great man, and perhaps Hitler is a great man, could use an opportunity such as this to re-establish himself in the eyes of his own people and of the

---

[1] Author of *The Mysterious Universe*. Considered to be a popular scientist rather than a profound one.
[2] Hon. Robert Brand, son of the 2nd Viscount Hampden and married to a sister of Lady Astor. Fellow of All Souls and eminent in the City of London. Treasury representative in Washington at the end of the war.
[3] Son of Sir Hugh O'Neill, M.P., later Lord Rathcaven. A Fellow of All Souls. Joined the Diplomatic Service in 1936 and resigned several times. Finally Ambassador to Finland and to the E.E.C.

world. And at the end of it all we should be faced with the same situation as we were in six months ago: a Germany armed to the teeth, loyal to its Government, and ruled by an unscrupulous clique whose word was not trustworthy and whose aggressive instincts were patent to the whole world.

Con, who is secretary to Grigg[1] at the Ministry of Information, has been invited to return to the F.O.; but Horace Wilson has apparently imposed his veto, inspired, of course thinks Con, by the memory of Con's resignation as a protest against the Munich policy. It seems an unlikely hypothesis: I cannot believe Horace would bother his head about a twenty-five-year-old Third Secretary.

Tuesday, January 2nd

The most hectic morning I have had since being at No. 10. The Cabinet discussed the Scandinavian project and more or less agreed to adopt the proposal to stop the Narvik iron-ore trade, Winston hoping that this may lead to a German invasion of Norway and the consequent facilitation of our undertaking the major project of seizing the iron-ore fields with an armed force. The Cabinet decision will depend on the Chiefs of Staffs' consideration of the position if the Germans occupy the south Norwegian air-bases (from which aerial attacks on this country would be a grave menace).

The P.M. saw Stamp who was reluctant to become Chancellor. The curious constitutional suggestion of making him a Commoner has therefore been dropped and Sir J. Simon will maintain his position, blissfully unconscious of the schemes which have been evolved for his removal.

Wednesday, January 3rd

Miss Watson returned from her holiday which, nice as she is, rather disturbed the quiet and efficiency of No. 10.

Miss Watson, who had been a typist at No. 10 since the days

---

[1] Sir Edward Grigg, M.P., formerly Secretary to Lloyd George and later Governor of Kenya. Parliamentary Secretary at the Ministry of Information, 1939–40. Created Lord Altrincham.

of Lloyd George and Bonar Law, was promoted to the rank of Private Secretary and dealt conscientiously and well with the preparation of replies to Parliamentary Questions. She had an admirable character, loyal and affectionate, but she was not over-endowed with brain-power and her incurable tendency to make a fuss could be exasperating. She did not, however, lack acumen and one afternoon she assured me that the man at No. 10 with the greatest political sensitivity was Lord Dunglass. He was the only man round the Prime Minister who understood the House of Commons.

"He will be Prime Minister one day, Mr Colville."

"But, Miss Watson, he will be a peer before he reaches that seniority, and you couldn't have a Prime Minister in the House of Lords nowadays."

"That's as may be, Mr Colville. I shan't live to see it, but the day Lord Dunglass becomes Prime Minister, you just remember what Miss Watson said." I did.

There is now some doubt about the proposal to appoint Hore-Belisha Minister of Information, as the fact that he is a Jew would make him a target for the Nazis, who would represent all British propaganda as an inspiration of Judaism. This argument has impressed Horace Wilson and the P.M.

The Bishop of Lichfield (Woods)[1] came to see me to discuss Ecclesiastical appointments, with especial reference to the vacant see of Leicester. He wants Neville Talbot appointed, and also suggested the names of Canon Raven and Canon Barry, who are in his view two of the finest intellects in the C. of E., as men who should be given Bishoprics. Lord Halifax, last night, put forward the name of the Bishop of Willesden for Leicester.

The Cabinet seem disposed to go ahead with the Scandinavian plan, partly because they believe that the extension of the war would add to Germany's commitments and be definitely to her disadvantage. We are to prepare expeditions of a thousand men or so to seize Bergen, Trondhjem and Stavanger if, when we stop the Narvik traffic, the Germans invade Southern Norway.

[1] Right Rev E. S. Woods. Two of his sons became bishops.

We cannot prevent them from taking Oslo and Christiansand, but the air menace to this country from German bases there will be incomparably less than Stavanger, etc. The chief dissentient in the Cabinet to the whole scheme is Hore-Belisha who, aptly I think, recalled that throughout history small military expeditions, like those contemplated at Bergen, Trondhjem and Stavanger, had been useless and had led to wider and more expensive undertakings, e.g. Walcheren in the Napoleonic Wars.

Thursday, January 4th

The Cabinet reshuffle is causing a lot of heartburning and proving very difficult. Halifax has come down so strongly against making Hore-Belisha Minister of Information that the idea has been dropped. Originally it had been decided that Malcolm MacDonald[1] should be President of the Board of Trade, "Shakes" Morrison[2] Secretary of State for the Colonies, Rob Hudson[3] Minister of Food. Now Hore-Belisha is to go to the Board of Trade and Sir John Reith,* to the Ministry of Information. As Lady Oxford[4] writes regularly to her "Darling P.M." recommending Sir John Reith, she will probably think herself responsible for the appointment. But it may not be well received by the outside world who look upon Reith as the man who failed first at the B.B.C. and then at Imperial Airways.

After lunch Hore-Belisha came to see the P.M. and looked nervous and "on edge" (he had, I think, no idea that his resignation was to be demanded). As he went out I was alone in the room: he looked very worried, clapped his hands together gauchely and talked about the weather. Afterwards I heard that the interview had gone badly and Belisha had taken it all amiss.

[1] Son of Ramsay MacDonald. Secretary of State for the Colonies, 1935 and 1938–40. After the war served with great distinction overseas, in India as High Commissioner (1955–60) and in Kenya as Governor and later High Commissioner (1936–65).

[2] Held many ministerial posts but never reached the dizzy heights foretold for him. Chosen Speaker of the House of Commons in 1951.

[3] Former diplomat who became an M.P. in 1924 and was Minister for Agriculture for most of the war. Much disliked by most civil servants.

[4] Margot, second wife of the Prime Minister Herbert Asquith. Born Margot Tennant.

One cannot help sympathising with him: as President of the Board of Trade he will not even be in the War Cabinet, and after all he has in some ways done extremely well at the War Office and shown particular energy. But he has a way of antagonising people, very often just when he is trying to be at his best and most efficient. In him one sees very clearly those characteristics which inevitably, but inexplicably, make Jews unpopular.

Cecil Syers returned from leave, Miss Watson came to sit in the same room as me, and the peace of the last ten days vanished.

Friday, January 5th

After some hesitation Hore-Belisha has declined the Board of Trade and so will be out of the Government altogether. A businessman, said to be of considerable capacity, called Sir Andrew Duncan[1] is to have the Board of Trade. Rob Hudson will go to the Post Office and Tryon[2] will be given a peerage.

Lord Bledisloe[3] has written to ask the P.M. for the Governor-Generalship of Canada. It is extraordinary how shameless people can be.

The Cabinet have decided to give considerable assistance to the Finns (whose successes against the Russians continue to be astonishing) and it has been suggested that we should apply those "principles of non-intervention" so successfully followed by Germany and Italy in Spain.

Mother, who has taken frantically to knitting since war broke out, took me to buy some navy-blue wool for a pullover. It takes a war to domesticate some people!

Sunday, January 7th

Arrived at Downing Street at 6.00. Charles Peake,[4] who was there, thinks that the newspaper violence over Hore-Belisha's

---

[1] Chairman of the Iron and Steel Federation and of the Electricity Board.

[2] A gallant soldier. M.P. for Brighton from 1910. Minister of Pensions and later Postmaster General. Made a peer in 1940 and given the Office of Works, but died a few months later.

[3] Former Governor General of New Zealand. Nicknamed Lord Bloody-Slow by King George V.

[4] Witty member of the Diplomatic Service who was a friend and adviser of Lord Halifax. Ended his career as Ambassador in Athens.

removal is a good thing, as there is now nothing left to say and the agitation must die down for lack of material.

Sir Walter Monckton and Sir Kenneth Lee of the Ministry of Information also came in and gossiped. The latter told me that within a quarter of an hour of its being known that Lord Macmillan had resigned, the following notice was produced in the Ministry:

DEMISE OF LORD MACMILLAN

NO REITHS BY REQUEST.

Read a number of Cabinet and other papers. There are concentrations of troops at North German ports who are undergoing intensive training in embarking and disembarking, from which it seems possible that an attack on Southern Scandinavia may be imminent. On the other hand whenever a dramatic German move appears to be contemplated, and suitable precautions are taken, nothing seems to come of it: either Hitler and his advisers are continually changing their minds or, as Germans would be likely to do, they are making preparations for every conceivable move – an attack on Holland, an expedition to Scandinavia (to seize the aerodromes), an invasion of England or a move south-eastwards – so that there may be a large and carefully prepared choice of action available. It is also significant that the Germans are pressing on with the erection of fortifications in the east so that they may be ready for every contingency and may have an *Ostwall* as a bulwark against their present Russian allies.

Monday, January 8th
The Belisha excitement continues in the press, the *Daily Express* and other irresponsible pamphlets taking the line that Oliver Stanley's appointment is due to intrigues in "High Society". Hore-Belisha himself is obviously making mischief by having photographs published of himself at home, with little dog, etc. Moreover Paramount Films have produced a pro-Belisha film, with an inflammatory commentary, which was shown in the cinemas last night and loudly applauded. All this may, as Charles

Peake thinks, be a nine-days' wonder; but H.-B. is certainly experienced in the art of publicity and can probably be trusted to make all the capital he can out of the situation. It appears that the P.M. handled the affair rather badly and lost his temper when arguing with H.-B. (this is a report of Miss Watson, subsequently denied by Arthur Rucker).

Lunched with Michael Grant at Simpson's. He tells me the War Office is almost unanimous in favour of H.-B.'s resignation.

Tuesday, January 9th
Dullish day at No. 10. The Belisha storm seems to be settling and despite the prayers and supplications of David Margesson, the P.M. listened to Arthur Rucker and made no mention of the matter in his speech at the Mansion House.

Thursday, January 11th
The Finns are performing miracles against the Russians in their frozen forests, and attack after attack is being turned into a rout. The Soviets have succeeded in alienating the sympathies of the whole world and even if, by sheer weight of numbers, they finally succeed in overcoming Finnish resistance, it seems likely that the Finnish fiasco may have as unsteadying effect inside Russia as did Napoleon III's Mexican adventure in France. (What a poor historical analogy!)

The Cabinet now think of compromising about the Scandinavian plan, by using the threat of action at Narvik to induce the Norwegians and Swedes to give us what we want. The reaction of both countries to the notification of our intentions which we gave them was unexpectedly severe, and although Norway might not matter the P.M. feels we cannot afford to estrange Sweden. On the other hand both the Cabinet and the army feel that to extend the war to Scandinavia would be greatly to our advantage, and it seems that the most likely way of achieving this would be to incite and support Sweden in her assistance to Finland. The whole situation is very delicate: would the Germans dare attack Scandinavia, thereby risking the total loss of their iron-ore supplies if the attack failed or were too slow; on the other hand could they allow the Russians, when the snow melts in the spring, to smash their way through Finland and threaten Northern Scandinavia or even occupy the iron mines? Personally I am against our interference: (i) it would be dangerous and might involve disaster or withdrawal and the consequent blow to our prestige: (ii) the idea of wilfully extending the war to Scandinavia, and involving the Northern countries against their wishes, is a callous contradiction of those very principles for which we are fighting.

Met the famous Tom Jones,[1] who was a discovery of Lloyd George and has since devoted his life to "helping the under-dog". He has extraordinary natural charm and a Celtic quickness of mind. He told me of his meetings with Hitler, who he said was before all else an artist and whose *Weltanschauung* had in 1936 "paralysed him with terror". Ribbentrop he knew well, and said that the F.O. and particularly Eden had made a tremendous mistake in snubbing him so consistently. They had taken the line that R. was a stupid man with no humour and that that was the end of it; what they should have been considering was the way to deal with a stupid man who had the ear of Hitler. Snubs and laughter were unprofitable tactics.

Saturday, January 13th

Arthur and I alone at Downing Street. Fairly hectic morning. In view of the violent Swedish reactions, the Cabinet have more or less decided to drop the Narvik project (despite Winston's fulminations), but to prepare an expedition to Scandinavia in case the Swedes require help against the Russians or Germans in the spring. In the latter case we should be able to attempt our plan against the Gallivare iron-ore field with Norwegian and Swedish assistance.

The Cabinet has received information that an attack may be launched by the Germans against Holland and Belgium during the next few days while Europe is still frozen up.

Monday, January 15th

The Belgian crisis has intensified over the week-end and the Cabinet has decided to move troops into Belgium if the Belgians

---

[1] Valued adviser to Lloyd George. A wise Welshman, dedicated to social reform, at one time Deputy Secretary to the Cabinet.

invite them, in order to seize the Wavre–Namur Line and forestall the Germans. Yesterday it seemed probable the Germans would advance at dawn on a line covering Holland, Belgium and Luxembourg; but today the situation is better and it looks as if an attack will at any rate be delayed. The German plans were divulged by some papers found in a German aeroplane which made a forced landing in Belgium, but the landing itself, the ostentatiously ineffective efforts of the pilot to burn the papers, and subsequently to commit suicide, are suspiciously like a "put-up job", and it seems that the whole thing may have been arranged on purpose either: (a) in order to induce the Belgians to invite the Allies to enter the country, so that the Germans themselves may have good reason to attack, or (b) to forewarn the Allies, so that the plan of invasion may be abortive (i.e. a *coup de théâtre* on the part of the army who are thought to look unfavourably on Hitler's invasion project).

Tuesday, January 16th

The House met, and after Questions Hore-Belisha rose to make his resignation speech. The House was packed, even Lloyd George being in his place, and it was in a combative mood. Hore-Belisha spoke smoothly and well, with many soft phrases, and the feeling which his speech left on one was "Well, if he and the Generals, the Cabinet and the P.M. saw eye to eye on every question of policy, why was he forced to resign?" The P.M. rose to answer and did it, to my mind, very poorly. He categorically denied the rumours of why H.-B. had resigned and led everybody to believe that he was going to state the facts of the case; but he ended, amid a storm of questions and interruptions from the Opposition, by saying that there was no reason for him to give the House any explanation why he had taken such action. H.-B., in order to curry favour with the Opposition, had spoken much about the "democratisation" of the army, and I think his speech took the honours and made the P.M.'s seem lame. As Arthur Rucker said to me in the box, the trouble is that Belisha, while apparently playing the game and refusing to make mischief, is in fact intriguing behind the scenes.

After this affair the P.M. made a statement on the general

situation which was too long and which seemed to bore the House with its dreary details about the help coming from the Dominions and Colonies. For some reason no subject is more boring to the average Englishman than the British Empire.

Wednesday, January 17th
Spent a good deal of the morning talking scandal with Alec Dunglass and the Chief Whip, who is certainly an unusually agreeable man. Talked also to the invariably and perhaps excessively cheerful George Townshend,[1] who is Ironside's A.D.C.

Went down to the House late in the afternoon and heard Cross,[2] the Minister of Economic Warfare, giving a review of his Department's not inconsiderable achievements. Dalton* replied for the Labour Party with a smooth but disobliging speech, which considerably annoyed the P.M. who confided to me afterwards how disgusted he was with the eternal carping and intrigue of the Opposition. He said that they only paid lip-service to the universally accepted doctrine that everything must be subordinated to the efficient prosecution of the war, and that in reality they were always searching for an opportunity to score off the Government and were saturated with the pettiness of party politics. I suggested that when air-raids or real fighting on land began in earnest (which one can still hope they may not), this attitude would change, and Mr Chamberlain agreed but said that even the blessings of peace at home could not make him wish for such a violent remedy.

He further told me that the Labour Party were angry with Attlee who yesterday made a speech on the Belisha issue which was sensible and sincere: his supporters argued that he should not have wasted such a splendid opportunity for attacking the P.M. Obviously the poor old man, who is doing his very best and is personally very sensitive in spite of his external coldness, feels these attacks deeply and, not without justice, considers

---

[1] 7th Marquess Townshend. A Harrow contemporary. Later Chairman of Anglia Television.
[2] Sir Ronald Cross. Later Minister of Shipping and High Commissioner in Australia, whither Churchill despatched him as he wanted his portfolio for Lord Leathers.

them to show an incomprehensible lack of patriotism and common-sense in the face of an enemy who is the common enemy of all parties alike.

Thursday, January 18th
Had breakfast at the Travellers, where I read a good article on war aims in *The Contemporary Review* by Grandfather, called "Looking Ahead". He writes extremely well and has an attractive way of expressing himself but, like his grandson, is sometimes inclined to ramble.

I went down to the House for Questions and spent most of the time talking to Alec, Chips Channon* and the Chief Whip. The P.M. is deciding against the publication of the Blue Book on our negotiations with Russia last summer, partly because the course of those negotiations would evoke criticism (of which there is too much at this time), and partly because there is no point in provoking the Russians before we actually go to war with them (if we do). Our present relations with the Soviet Government are just about as bad as they could be.

Sweden is behaving badly about the despatch of volunteers to Finland across Swedish territory. I am glad to see we are going to send the Finns 100 aeroplanes and some volunteers.

Sunday, January 21st
Went to church with Father at St Peter's [Eaton Square]. Bitterly cold: it has been freezing now for a good many days, the temperature is as low as I can remember it, and it looks as if we may be in for a "cold spell" as acute as that of 1929 (when we skated at Harrow for six weeks on end).

After lunch Philip and I went down to Trent, now a camp for German prisoners. The house is surrounded by barbed wire and guarded by sentries, but we managed to force our way into the park and skated, unmolested by the military, for an hour on the large and deserted lake. It was snowing a little and all the surrounding country was white. The air was bitterly cold and we felt most exhilarated.

After tea went to Downing Street, where I found Cecil Syers

who tells me that he has been appointed to a post in the Treasury and is leaving No. 10 shortly.

Monday, January 22nd

Miss Watson being ill, I had an agreeably busy day, most of which was taken up with Parliamentary Questions (her special preserve).

Another flotilla leader, the *Exmouth*, has been lost: the second in two days.

Lunched at home with Mother, who had come up from Badminton for the day and brought me a box of chocolates as a present from Queen Mary. The old lady is extraordinarily thoughtful and methodical, and is always fond of doing small things which give pleasure. She still continues to send me large packets of monograms, the envelopes addressed by herself – a practice she began when I was ten.

Wednesday, January 24th

An utterly hectic day, largely due to the continued absence of Miss W. It began with a scene. There has been a good deal of trouble over the proposed Blue Book on the Anglo-Soviet negotiations last summer. The French do not want it published; the Cabinet had decided to bow to the French demands. However the Opposition demand that it shall be published in spite of the French objections, and the P.M. could not persuade Attlee to the contrary. In a minute on a Parliamentary Question Frank Roberts[1] expressed himself rather tactlessly, said the P.M. "had failed" to do this and had "not succeeded" in doing that. When he saw this minute the P.M. was furious, called Frank Roberts insolent and impertinent, "damned his eyes", etc., etc. I could see that he resented it particularly as coming from the F.O., and I think he is unable to forget the opposition in that department to the Eden resignation in 1938, the Munich policy, and the whole influence of No. 10 as represented by himself and Horace Wilson. I was surprised at the violence of his fury which I could never have expected in such a cold man.

[1] One of the ablest and most dynamic members of the Diplomatic Service. Ambassador in Moscow, 1960–62 and in Bonn, 1963–68.

After lunching at No. 10 I went down to the House with the P.M. who had to answer nearly twenty Questions on behalf of the F.O. and himself. Some of these were embarrassing, including one about Unity Mitford's return from Germany, to which I had drafted the reply. Herbert Morrison alleged class distinction, etc., and was, as the P.M. said to me afterwards, "as poisonous as usual".

On the way back in the car we discussed a rumour, which Alec Dunglass has heard, that French morale is deteriorating, that an increasing section of French public opinion is for peace at any price, and that a number of politicians, including Bonnet[1] and Laval,* are intriguing for Daladier's downfall. The P.M. told me he considered Laval the most unscrupulous and unreliable of all French politicians – which is saying a lot!

Thursday, January 25th
The P.M. was again a bit acrimonious over Questions, but this time I was partly to blame because I had not insisted on the F.O. providing a really adequate reply to one of his marginal comments on a paper.

Friday, January 26th
So busy that by the end of the day I was almost blind with overwork. I was largely busy in compiling a complicated memorandum on the depressed state of the motor trade, and the efforts of the Government to remedy the matter, from evidence supplied by nine different departments. The main point seems to be that nothing can make up the loss suffered by garages, etc., owing to the withdrawal of so many private cars from the roads; and the necessary extra petrol allowance to attract these cars back cannot be supplied owing to shipping and foreign exchange difficulties. The question will be included in the debate on economic coordination next Thursday.

Mine is a curious job: sometimes, as today, I am dealing with

---

[1] Georges Bonnet held at one time or another almost every Government portfolio in France and was Daladier's Foreign Minister at the time of Munich.

matters of the greatest significance; at other times I have not enough to keep me occupied and am acting as little more than an office-boy. There are really too many of us for normal day-to-day work, and the difficulty is aggravated by Arthur (who otherwise has most of the known virtues) being so conscientious that he likes to keep everything in his own hands. Thus the remainder of us are often in the position of being mere spectators of events which are themselves of world-wide importance.

Saturday, January 27th
Another exhausting day, perfecting the memorandum, etc., and I had to go back to Downing Street in the afternoon.

Winston made a first-rate "fighting" speech at Manchester, which was broadcast. He is indeed an orator – perhaps the only one in the country today – and he does not read his speeches tamely like Halifax and the rest of them. Nevertheless he is a dangerous person unless kept well in control, as his Narvik-Lulea scheme shows.

Lady Maggy Bulkeley[1] died. She was a remarkable figure, rouged up to the eyes, short-sighted, witty and absurdly over-dressed; and she certainly succeeded in remaining young in mind and in spirit long after she had, for all her paint and dyed hair, become very decrepit physically. She loomed so large in my childhood, presiding in state in the Squadron Garden, that her death symbolises a very definite break with the past. Of course Cowes, with its Edwardian tradition and atmosphere, was already merely a survival; but in many ways it was an historically interesting one, to which the personalities of Lady Maggy and her contemporaries contributed greatly. Father, who had known her for nearly seventy years, and I composed an obituary notice at the request of the *Sunday Times*.

Sunday, January 28th
Reached the mature age of twenty-five in a world covered with the deepest snow.

---

[1] Daughter of 5th Earl of Hardwicke and wife of Sir Richard Williams-Bulkeley, Commodore of the Royal Yacht Squadron. Grandmother of Zara Mainwaring.

I spent the day at Tadworth, near Epsom Downs, with Pamela Foster[1] who has evacuated her children there. The snow was so deep that the railways were all out of working order and the journeys there and back were long, cold and tedious.

The return journey took three and a half hours instead of forty minutes, but it was enlivened by a brilliant fireworks display (caused by the ice on the electric cable) and by the entertaining and original conversation of two Austrian refugees, called Wassermann (he a Jewish chemist, she an Aryan doctor) who had been staying with Pamela's aunt. The husband tells me he expects a crack in Germany about next August – before a second winter sets in.

Monday, January 29th
Waded to No. 10 through drifts of snow and slush.

Cecil Syers goes to the Treasury today and an apparently delightful and estimable man in his forties, called Anthony Bevir* has arrived from the Cabinet offices to take his place.

The French are becoming excited about Finland and Scandinavia. They claim to have alarming evidence of energetic Russo-German collusion to force the issue in Finland. Consequently General Gamelin and Admiral Darlan* want to *prendre les devants* and to send a naval expedition to Petsamo,[2] followed by Chasseurs Alpins who can seize the iron-ore fields. They think this will mean war with Russia and thus an opportunity to bomb the Baku oilwells from Syria, to the discomfiture of all our enemies. The Supreme War Council will meet in Paris next week to discuss the question, although the French, impressed by the urgency of the matter, want the meeting to take place immediately.

A number of people seem to be thinking that Hitler will not take the offensive, but may even be in a position to win a long war of inactivity – or at least to ruin us economically and so, like Samson, to bring down the roof on himself and his enemies

[1] Pamela Wilberforce, married to Anthony Foster, a childhood friend of my family. Her brother, Richard, became a distinguished Judge and Lord of Appeal.
[2] In the extreme north of Finland, close to the Russian frontier.

together. There is thus, for the first time, a feeling that we may have to start the fighting, and Winston even gave a hint to that effect in his speech on Saturday.

Dined with David and Joan, forcing my way miserably through slush and piled-up snow which formed itself into innumerable snares and pitfalls in the black-out. Father was there and Philip, who arrived just in time for dinner after an eight-hour journey by train from Kenswick. We drank champagne in honour of my [twenty-fifth] birthday, and I departed reluctantly from a cheerful atmosphere to grope my snow-bound way back to bed at Downing Street.

Tuesday, January 30th
The newspapers point out that the year '40 has always been a bad year for Germany, or at least for the Hohenzollerns who represented it. Margraves, Electors and Kings, they died regularly in 1440, 1640, 1740 and 1840. Now Hitler has taken their place let us hope history will not let us down.

The Italians are already making good use of their neutrality and it looks as if we shall have to spend millions on unwanted imports, such as "horticultural produce" in order to get them to provide us with the few ships and guns we want and to buy coal from us instead of from Germany.

Wednesday, January 31st
The report of the West Indies Royal Commission shows such a deplorable state of affairs, with regard to health, housing and standard of living, that the Cabinet have decided not to publish it because of the outcry it would cause. However they propose to set about providing a remedy.

War with Russia seems now to be seriously contemplated, and we are examining methods of helping Finland which would include a naval expedition to Petsamo and the crushing of Russian resistance. If we do go to war, Germany and Italy are almost bound to become formally allied and Italy will then find it impossible even to use the threat of joining Germany as a bargaining counter.

M. Prytz, the Swedish Minister, wants us to go ahead with

our Scandinavian project, whatever the apparent reactions of the Norwegian and Swedish Governments. Halifax says that Prytz's views are clearly far in advance of his Government's; it is a curious example of a diplomat working independently of and contrary to his orders. The present intention is that we shall stop the Narvik traffic and operate from a Norwegian fjord; however I think we have wasted too much time to make this worth while (unless we *want* to provoke a German invasion of Southern Scandinavia), because in a month or two Lulea will be free from ice.

Went to the House where the P.M. had rather a rough time from the Opposition, especially Shinwell,[1] about a Private Notice Question on shipping. Afterwards I had a long talk with the Chancellor of the Exchequer (Sir John Simon), who explained that while the Government are now spending £50 million a year to stabilise prices, they will abandon this policy if the Opposition refuse to take the hint and the Trade Unions demand wage rises. Wages will rise to some extent, he says, but the workers must realise that we have got to export cheaply in order to meet foreign competition and that if wages rise inordinately this cannot be done. It is worth spending large sums to avoid "the vicious spiral of rising wages and prices", but if the Trade Unions refuse to co-operate (despite the fact that the Government have not tried to use their present policy as a bargaining factor) then the Chancellor will let prices rip and will try to reserve the money, now being spent on stabilisation, to meet the inflation which will inevitably follow.

Sir J. Simon said that we are going to make a tremendous effort to export, and so to earn foreign exchange by maintaining our normal exports (e.g. cloth) that we shall be able to afford to import steel, etc., from America and thus avoid diverting our present factories to war-manufactures for which they are unsuited and inexperienced. Moreover if we can keep our industry on a peace footing it will be less difficult to return to normal

[1] Emanuel Shinwell. First elected as a Labour M.P. in 1922. Served in Attlee's Government successively as Minister of Fuel and Power (1945–47), War (1947–50) and Defence (1950–51). Created Life Peer 1970. Died in May 1986, aged 101.

conditions after the war, and we shall have retained or even expanded our pre-war markets. One of our troubles, said Sir John, is due to the fact that in the last war countries such as Italy and Yugoslavia, which are now competing with us very strongly in the export market, were themselves belligerents and unable to compete. Moreover the American industrial machine was not then so developed and all-embracing as it is today.

George Steward pointed out that after 1931 our exchange position had been greatly eased by the fact that other currencies followed England off the Gold Standard and formed a sterling bloc. "Yes," said the Chancellor, "whereas today the sterling bloc consists of England, Scotland, Wales and doubtfully Ireland!"

Thursday, February 1st
Extremely bleary-eyed and depressed by the thaw.

Lunched at the Travellers with John Cairncross and subsequently talked to Sammy Hood,[1] who says that Reith is a fountain of energy at the Ministry of Information.

Debate on economic co-ordination and on the demand for an overriding Economic Minister, responsible for all the departments concerned and representing them in the War Cabinet. The P.M. will turn down the proposal because he, and his advisers H. J.W. [Horace Wilson] and Lord Stamp, feel that the creation of such a minister would involve divided authority over departments and would not in the least add to the efficiency of our war effort. (The present agitation is partly aimed at the Chancellor, who resents it and is hurt. Great emphasis is laid on the fact that he has to represent both finance *and* economics in the Cabinet.)

The Cabinet have received a report to the effect that all Soviet ships have been ordered to return home, or to be in neutral ports, by a certain date. This looks ominous. Meanwhile M.

---

[1] 6th Viscount Hood. Joined the India Office on leaving Cambridge and was Private Secretary to Lord Zetland. Private Secretary to successive Ministers of Information in the early part of the war and then transferred to the Foreign Office where his wisdom and quiet efficiency were much esteemed.

Maisky [Soviet Ambassador] has had the impertinence to suggest that we should apply to Finland the same doctrine of strict non-intervention to which we adhered in Spain – which, when one thinks of Soviet policy in Spain, is an almost incredible proposal.

Friday, February 2nd
The Chancellor apparently made the speech of his life last night and I wish I had not felt too tired to go down to the House to hear him. Also Herbert Morrison was much less poisonous than usual, but the P.M. failed to respond or to pick up the olive branch. This is rather hard on Arthur Rucker who has been working behind the scenes to get Morrison to moderate his tone, but, as Arthur points out, the P.M. is incapable of being gracious at the right moment. He is a curious mixture of qualities and defects: I have nothing but admiration for his forcefulness, precision and capacity for hard work; and yet at the same time he is obstinate and vain. Vanity is a failing common to Prime Ministers – Ramsay MacDonald for instance (I remember his talking about himself to Mother and me for a solid hour and a half, before breakfast at Cowes one morning, at the time of the Schneider Cup); and I suppose it is natural in view of the adulation they receive but to which they are not, like Kings, accustomed. In N.C.'s case this vanity takes the form of resenting any kind of criticism or mockery. He feels it acutely when he is attacked personally in the press or in Parliament; his wrath against Frank Roberts the other day was due to a suspected lack of respect in the minute which offended him; and there is no surer way of gratifying him than to make some allusion to the exceptional importance of his position. In other words, he likes to be set on a pedestal and adored, with suitable humility, by unquestioning admirers.

General Ismay came in during the morning and gave an account of the Chiefs of Staff meeting in Paris, about Finland and Scandinavia, which is to be followed by a meeting of the Supreme War Council early next week. The French plan is for a landing at Petsamo, the consequent cutting-off of the Russian forces at Murmansk, and the movement of Finnish troops northwards against them, assisted by four divisions of Allied soldiers. Apparently the Petsamo expedition will involve our using a Norwegian fjord as a base, and the British view is that if we are going to violate Norwegian neutrality anyhow we may as well be hanged for a man as for a sheep and put the whole Narvik-Lulea project into effect. Our objections to the French plan include the points (i) that the Petsamo landing will necessitate the diversion from this country and the Western Front of anti-aircraft guns and aircraft which we can ill afford; (ii) that the four divisions which are to assist the Finns have got to be (a) raised and (b) equipped. The French talk vaguely about foreign subjects, living in France, who could be used. Both sides agree that if anything is to be done it must be done quickly, before the ice in the Gulf of Bothnia melts, the Germans can reach Lulea and the Russians can overwhelm Finland. Complete secrecy is also essential, but with the French "in the know" is it possible?

General Ismay thinks this French plan is political, sponsored by Daladier, etc., because of the ill effect of this continued inactivity on French morale. He says the French General Staff, and even Gamelin, are not really in favour of it, although Gamelin has now for the first time admitted the possibility of the Germans not attacking on the Western Front and says he thinks it is desirable to extend the war. Personally Ismay can see no point in all these risky proposals and thinks we should do better to stick to our original thesis that we can win a long-drawn-out siege by outstaying Germany. I agree with him except in so far as we may wreck our economy and ruin our prosperity in the process. Perhaps even that would be preferable to a real *guerre acharnée*.

Most of the morning was taken up listening to a long conversation between David Margesson, Arthur and Alec about the ineffectiveness of "Shakes" Morrison as Minister of Food and the possibility of removing him. Like Walter Elliot he is one of those exploded "future Prime Ministers".

Sunday, February 4th
Monty Sherman [Claims Adviser in the Foreign Office] died suddenly. Although not a brilliant person, he was certainly a

remarkable one, as is proved by the affection felt for him by all sorts and conditions of men and by his friendship with such varying personalities as D. H. Lawrence and T. E. Lawrence. Bon viveur, dilettante, collector of pictures and books, he was a wonderful host and a most sympathetic companion. He brought the secluded and academic charms of the university into the practical and hard-headed world of London and the Foreign Office. His boundless hospitality, made possible by a handsome fortune, was inspired by motives of genuine kindness and philanthropy. He will leave a gap in a lot of people's lives, and in particular in those of many members of the Foreign Office – where he held a position involving little work and enabling him to win the well-deserved affection of a great many people.

Monday, February 5th
The P.M. has gone to France for a meeting of the Supreme War Council about Scandinavia. Certain information about our project has inevitably leaked out owing to the necessity of enlisting volunteers from the army. Brian O'Neill told me yesterday that he would be going and he knew that Norway would be his destination. Others, less well-informed, imagine we are contemplating armed intervention on behalf of the Finns (because persons with ski-ing experience have been asked to volunteer).

There is trouble about two I.R.A. terrorists who are to be executed. Their death will make them martyrs in Ireland (where martyrdom is very coveted and very effective in its results) and will sway Irish opinion in the U.S.A. against this country. The Cabinet have discussed the matter, but seem disposed not to give way, despite the warning of Lord Lothian[1] and a personal letter from De Valera to the P.M. They are keeping no records of their long discussion on the subject, because a reprieve is not really a matter for them, but for the King's Prerogative, exercised through the Home Secretary.

---

[1] Philip Kerr, 11th Marquess of Lothian. One of "Milner's young men" in South Africa, Editor of *The Round Table*, Secretary to Lloyd George and Ambassador in Washington, 1939–40.

Tuesday, February 6th

The I.R.A. executions continue to occupy everybody's mind. Cabinet Ministers are heavily guarded and the policeman outside No. 10 replaced his ordinary helmet by a tin one. De Valera is making a desperate effort to have the men reprieved as he feels that their deaths and martyrdom will strengthen the I.R.A. in Ireland and weaken his own position. Bomb outrages occurred in London, Birmingham and elsewhere.

The P.M., Halifax, Winston, etc., returned from Paris where they have been for a meeting of the Supreme War Council. According to Arthur the discussions went very well and I presume our Scandinavian plans are finally determined.

I lunched with Jim Bowker[1] at the Wyndham,[2] but was called away very soon as the P.M. had scarcely set foot in London before he went down to the House to take Questions. His energy is remarkable; but he also hates to feel that anyone else is usurping his place as Prime Minister.

President Roosevelt is proposing to send Sumner Welles[3] over to Europe to visit the various capitals concerned and to examine the prospects of peace. This has been expected, because Hitler well knows how to play on neutral fears of an extension of the war and on the world-wide terror of Bolshevism. The P.M. thinks this move comes, very indirectly of course, from Germany, where Goering and others have long been posing as moderates and have been putting out peace feelers. The danger is that Welles' visit will give an opportunity to the peace-at-any-price minority here to raise their voices, while the controlled public opinion of Germany will present a united front. Moreover such an initiative, which could never really achieve anything since the destruction of the Nazi régime is, from our point of view, an essential prerequisite of peace, would open up endless possibilities of which the German propaganda machine would know only too well how to make use.

---

[1] Diplomat of singular charm and cultivation. My immediate senior (and instructor) when I joined the Foreign Office in 1937. Subsequently Ambassador in Ankara and Vienna.

[2] The Wyndham Club, 4 St James's Square.

[3] Under Secretary in the State Department.

Wednesday, February 7th
Read the minutes of the Supreme War Council. It is now decided that we shall carry out our iron-ore plan on the pretext of sending help to Finland through Norway. The Finns will publicly appeal to the Norwegians and Swedes to allow foreign volunteers through their country, and we shall then demand permission to land our "volunteers" (in the approved "non-intervention" manner) at Narvik and Trondhjem, at the same time offering further troops to defend Norway and Sweden against any German invasion from the south. In the event – which Mr C. thinks *most* unlikely – of the Norwegians offering armed resistance to the Allies, and cutting the Narvik railway, we should probably be obliged to revert to the plan for a naval expedition to Petsamo in order to save our prestige and the Finns. Chamberlain and Daladier agree that the defeat of Finland would be a defeat for the Allied cause. Our expedition to Narvik will be ready by March 20th – orders to begin preparations were telephoned from Paris immediately the Supreme War Council had reached its decision – and it will consist of three British divisions (who were to have left for France today), some French Chasseurs Alpins, etc., and some Polish battalions. It will be under British command, and of course its primary objective will be, on its march to Finland, to seize the Gallivare iron-ore fields and occupy or incapacitate them.

Despite the serious foreign exchange position, the Supreme War Council also decided to order 3,000 aeroplane engines in the U.S.A., M. Daladier proclaiming that he would rather sell the art treasures of France than risk Germany maintaining preponderance in the air.

Friday, February 9th
Spent most of the day preparing for the P.M. a summary of the findings of the tribunal which investigated the *Thetis*[1] disaster. The Duke of Buccleuch[2] called and spent the morning trying to

[1] The submarine H.M.S. *Thetis* sank in the Irish Channel in the summer of 1939 with great loss of life.
[2] Walter, 8th Duke of Buccleuch. As Lord Dalkeith an M.P. for twelve years. Entirely patriotic but an admirer of Hitler and strongly opposed to war.

persuade Alec that peace was essential: in a year's time the same people would be in power in Germany and we should eventually have to make peace with them. Why not do so now, when comparatively little damage has been done and when there is still time to avert economic ruin?

Thursday, February 15th
The French cannot keep a secret: rumours of the Supreme War Council's decision have already permeated to Stockholm from Paris.

Went to the House for Questions. Had a long talk with Sir W. Citrine[1] (who is just back from Finland) about the economic interpretation of history and of other things. Citrine said that the Russians had even discovered an economic interpretation of Sex. We also discussed, with reference to Hitler, whether the man produces the hour or the hour the man, and agreed that neither was the case. Hitler could not have come into power without the peculiar circumstances that, in post-war Germany, gave him his opportunity; but it was the personal characteristics of the man who so came into power that made events take the course they have.

Citrine then talked for an hour to the P.M. about his impressions of Finland, while Alec and I discussed Munich and the attitude of the F.O. to the P.M. and Horace Wilson. Alec told me that our lack of armaments in September 1938 weighed very heavily with the P.M. during the Munich crisis, but that also it was only fair to admit that he and Horace believed that by the sacrifice of Czechoslovakia they could achieve permanent peace and that Hitler would be satisfied. The F.O. were equally mistaken in thinking Hitler was bluffing about war, and if the truth be told the only justification of Munich was *salus populi suprema lex*: war would have been disastrous to us and we had to sacrifice principle to security. This fact will probably be the salient one when future historians come to judge, but it should not be forgotten that the P.M. and Horace were prepared to use questions of principle as bargaining counters in the diplomatic

---

[1] General Secretary of the T.U.C., 1925–46. Made a peer in 1946.

game and looked on Munich as a permanent settlement, not as the postponement of an inevitable war. "Peace with Honour" was a blunder, but Mrs Chamberlain made him say that.

On the way back in the car the P.M. said that Citrine, like all the Labour Party, was very discursive and kept on going off the point (this is agony to the P.M.). Nevertheless he was very interesting about the deplorable morale of the Russians, who were shot and bullied from behind (he had talked to Russian prisoners), and the heroic resistance of the Finns. The P.M. thinks that once our Hurricane aircraft, and other foreign aircraft, are in action on the Finnish side "there won't be a Russian left in Finland". I am afraid he may be over-confident.

Saturday, February 17th
There was great excitement at No. 10 over the *Altmark*[1] affair, news of which reached us early in the morning. It is a perfect conclusion to the victory over the *Graf von Spee*.

I was going to Terling[2] for the week-end to stay with the Rayleighs and to see Sidney Cuthbert,[3] who has just returned from India. But at lunch-time I felt so unlike the journey, and so little inclined to the prospect of shooting pigeon in the deep snow, that I took my temperature and, finding it was nearly 103°, retired hurriedly to bed.

Sunday, February 18th – Monday, March 4th
Languished in bed with jaundice. Kind people came to see me and relieved the tedium.

For a few days it was pleasant to lie in bed with a cheerful fire, eating grapes and oblivious of all the world's cares, but it

[1] The *Altmark*, a German merchant ship, was returning to Germany crammed with British prisoners taken from the ships the *Graf von Spee* had sunk. She took refuge in a Norwegian fjord, but H.M.S. *Cossack*, commanded by Captain Vian, entered the fjord, boarded the *Altmark* and freed the prisoners.
[2] Home of Lord and Lady Rayleigh in Essex.
[3] A great friend of mine and fellow traveller in the Balkans when we were both at Cambridge. Killed in action in Normandy in 1944 as a Major in the Scots Guards. He had had meetings with Gandhi by whom he was impressed and influenced – though not in the direction of pacifism.

became exceedingly wearisome, and I was very glad when, after more than a fortnight, I was able to get up.

Friday, March 8th – Sunday, March 17th
Stayed at Uppark with Meg Fetherstonhaugh.[1]

It is the perfect country house, ideally situated in the loveliest country of the Sussex Downs and preserving much of the eighteenth century within its beautiful walls. There is nothing ugly inside or out, and at the same time it is very comfortable and pleasant to live in.

Uppark, near Petersfield, originally belonged to the Fetherston-haugh family. Sir Matthew, last of the line and a notorious Regency rake, married a milkmaid at the end of his days. The house was left to the milkmaid's sister, who in accordance with Sir Matthew's will, took the name of Fetherstonhaugh. Many neighbours looked askance at this upstart; but the Commander-in-Chief at Portsmouth, Admiral of the Fleet the Earl of Clanwilliam, was kind to Miss Fetherstonhaugh. So, after a life tenancy for Lord Winterton's brother, who had also been kind to her, she bequeathed the estate to Lord Clanwilliam's second son with a proviso that the name Fetherstonhaugh be retained.

While still a Cambridge undergraduate I was invited for a week-end. The Meades had only just moved in. Little had changed in a hundred and fifty years: wallpapers, curtains, furniture were all much as Sir Matthew had left them.

A fellow guest was H. G. Wells whose mother had been old Miss Fetherstonhaugh's housekeeper. He had spent his childhood at Uppark, kept firmly in the housekeeper's apartment, well out of sight of Miss Fetherstonhaugh who, a milkmaid's younger sister though she might be, held firm views about keeping her own servants in their proper place.

He had not been back since he was a boy. At luncheon he told us that in the afternoons, when Miss Fetherstonhaugh went

---

[1] Attractive wife of Admiral Sir Herbert Meade-Fetherstonhaugh, known to his friends as Jimmy.

*out driving in her carriage, he used to creep up to the library
and read a book, his ears cocked for the sound of returning
carriage wheels which necessitated a hasty departure. At the end
of one shelf there had been a copy of Plato's* Republic, *which he
read and re-read and which had a profound influence on his
thought, then and in later years.*

*We left the dining-room and walked through the library.
There, at the end of a shelf, untouched since he had hastily
replaced it at the age of twelve, was the dusty and much-thumbed
edition of Plato.*

Meg was there, in excellent form, full of laughter and always
charming so long as she can be prevented from talking on serious
subjects, when she becomes fatuous. Jean Meade[1] was also
there and I was very much struck by her cheerfulness, kindness,
energy and competence. Nobody could be simpler or more
anxious to help others or more ready to put herself out.

In order to keep Uppark going – which with its silver plate,
its large rooms and its periodical repairs is no light task – they
have taken some paying guests for the duration. This was all
the more necessary as Jimmy Meade* has thrown up his job at
the House of Lords and gone off to sea in command of a convoy,
thus sacrificing a considerable amount of income. It is tragic that
such courage and self-sacrifice should be wasted on something
as futile as war: it ought to be possible to produce such qualities
in peacetime and utilise them for a constructive purpose.

The P.G.s included Lady Mary Glyn,[2] a rather trenchant and
occasionally quite interesting relic of another age, who knew
Ruskin and remembers Garibaldi. There was also "A" Cecil,[3]
nephew of the Prime Minister Salisbury, who is a little old-
maidish but a very good talker and a man with great literary
knowledge and experience. He was interesting as having known

---

[1] Sir Herbert and Lady Meade-Fetherstonhaugh's younger daughter. Married
Michael Babington-Smith after the war.
[2] Meg Meade-Fetherstonhaugh's mother. Daughter of the 8th Duke of Argyll
and widow of the Bishop of Peterborough.
[3] Algernon Cecil, a barrister and former President of the Oxford Union.
Brother-in-law of Oliver Lyttelton.

A. J. Balfour well and as being one of the "Souls". After dinner he read aloud to us, quite beautifully, short stories and fantasies by Oscar Wilde. By way of contrast to this bearded blue-stocking there was Mr Charles Mead, whose interests centred on hunting and shooting. Lastly there was Audrey Paget,[1] aged seventeen, very attractive and refreshing with her enthusiasm for life and her passion for enjoyment. She has plenty of conversation and though strikingly "ingénue" is evidently not stupid.

I spent much of the time walking with Audrey or Jean on the lovely downs. Otherwise I read or played picquet. In the evenings, when "A" Cecil did not read to us, we played round games and laughed a great deal. Meg also showed me some interesting and amusing manuscripts, including letters from Lady Hamilton to Sir H. Fetherstonhaugh and eighteenth-century accounts of the estate.

Monday, March 18th
Returned to Downing Street. While I was away the Finnish resistance to Russia collapsed, despite the fact that we had been prepared up till the last to send the assistance we had promised. But Norway and Sweden proved recalcitrant and the Finns were exhausted. Probably it is all to the good: we have certainly lost prestige but we have reserved our strength to face Germany instead of dissipating it in the forests of Finland (and in all probability the Caucasus and Batum as well).

Tuesday, March 19th
Busy day. Big debate on Finland in the evening, during which the P.M. won great personal success. His birthday yesterday has caused us to be inundated with a flood of letters and telegrams.

Wednesday, March 20th
Daladier resigned.

News of our gigantic air-raid on Sylt, as a reprisal for a raid on Scapa Flow the other day, very well received by the public,

[1] Seductively pretty daughter of Lord Queenborough by his second marriage.

which is otherwise rather depressed by the defeat of Finland. It looks as if this may be the beginning of a more active phase of the war, since the Germans will now probably undertake another raid by way of reprisal and so things will go on until somebody goes so far as to bomb civilians. Lord Hankey thinks that an intensive German attack on shipping is now to be expected, but doubts whether it will be extended to the ports as that would mean an attack on civilians and, as the Germans well know, immediate counter-attacks by us against the Ruhr, etc. The Pope has also hinted that considerable air and naval activity is to be expected and thinks that in another month the Germans may begin land operations. However, he alludes darkly to the likelihood of certain unexpected events occurring in the meanwhile and has admitted to the French Ambassador that these would include the elimination of Hitler.

Thursday, March 21st

Lord Hankey has produced a strategical survey in which he emphasises the value to us of the present "static warfare" until such time as our war production has approached more nearly to its maximum. He doubts the Germans attacking Holland (which is of value to them economically) but believes they will concentrate on destroying our blockade (i) by heavy attacks on shipping, (ii) by attempting to establish their sway in the Balkans, if possible by peaceful methods. This second plan is probably the motive of the recent Brenner Pass conversations between Hitler and Mussolini. Italy is anxious to be friendly with the Allies, but Mussolini is personally hostile and he will certainly go as far as public opinion, the King and Ciano will let him in pursuing the old Axis pro-German policy. Loraine thinks that M. alone is responsible for this attitude and that he alone caused the recent breakdown of Anglo-Italian trade conversations. He cannot forget sanctions and he hates democracies.

Saw our Ambassador in Paris, Sir R. Campbell,[1] who told me that the political horizon in France was as bare as in this country.

---

[1] Succeeded Sir Eric Phipps as Ambassador in Paris, 1939. On the fall of France he became Ambassador in Lisbon.

There is no sign of a new Clemenceau, with the possible exception of M. Dautry.

Friday, March 22nd
It is to be hoped that Hitler can resist the temptation to commit some nefarious act on Good Friday.

We, for our part, are debating the possibility of seizing Dr Schacht (Governor of the German Central Bank) at Gibraltar on his way to America in the *Conte di Savoia*. The F.O. are strongly opposed to this breach of international law, the advantages of which would be small. Winston, who is always for "action" in any form and at all costs, is pressing for Schacht's arrest.

Saw a paper by Boothby,* who has been travelling on the Continent. He paints a clever and lurid picture of young Germany, solid behind Hitler, confident in its role of an enthusiastic and virile civilisation fighting against the decadent democracies of the West. He speaks of the new German moral code, according to which it is no disgrace to be dishonourable or brutal: the only unforgivable sin is to be weak (what a lesson for Good Friday!).

From all sides come disgusting accounts of the German terror in Poland: young men shot in hundreds, girls sterilised and conscripted for the soldiers' brothels, old people sent to hard labour in concentration camps or driven from their houses to die of exposure. At the same time the Germans continue their attacks on neutral ships, firing torpedos without warning and leaving the crews to their fate. I suppose there is a natural strain of brutality in the German character and as great an insensitivity to human suffering as there is a sensitivity to beauty. Certainly the Nazi doctrine has sublimated all that is most despicable in human nature, and it is difficult to see how this pernicious philosophy can be eradicated from the minds of the rising generation in Germany. However I still refuse to believe they are wholly abominable, and I think we ought sometimes to try and see ourselves reflected in their eyes: pharisaical, oblivious of the acts of aggression in our own history, rich and anxious to keep those riches for ourselves. Undoubtedly we are, as a nation, irritatingly self-righteous.

Motored Jean Meade down to Camfield Place [near Hertford] to stay with Lord Queenborough[1] for Easter. It is a comfortable modern house, part of the exterior covered with wood like a German or Swiss chalet, and it stands very well, looking across a valley to a distant horizon. Besides Lord Q. there was Audrey Paget, brimming over with life and good spirits and looking very attractive; Ann Paget (daughter of Peggy's friend Bridget Paget) who promises to be good looking but is at present shy, downtrodden and speechless; Mrs Stuart-Wortley, mother of Lady Loraine, who is pedantic and has a passion for high politics, about which she knows nothing, but is not disagreeable for all her self-assuredness; and finally a man called Kreck, effeminate, very talkative, intelligent and possessed of infuriating opinions about astrology, fortune-telling and Confucius which almost drove me to distraction. However he seemed to have a nice side to him.

Monday, March 25th
Sufficiently sunny and warm for us to sprawl in a heap in the middle of a field, on Audrey's coat, and laugh helplessly for the best part of an hour.

An interesting talk with William Teeling[2] who takes a gloomy view of post-war conditions in this country (owing to the fact that the middle classes are being ruined) and thinks that Conservatives, Liberals and Labour may have to combine against the extreme Left in order to fight revolution. We seem far from such a possibility today, but of course wars upset all calculations.

He agrees with me that our objective as far as Germany is concerned should be to smash her politically and militarily as a prelude to treating her with the utmost generosity.

Kreck told me that someone had once said: "Germany hates England with the love of a jealous woman."

[1] Almeric Paget. Conservative M.P., 1910–17. Married the rich Miss Pauline Whitney, by whom he had two handsomely endowed daughters (Olive Bailey and Dorothy Paget), and then another American, Edith Miller, by whom he had three exceptionally pretty daughters. He took little interest in them as he resented having no male heir.
[2] Elected M.P. for Brighton in 1944.

Tuesday, March 26th

Politically there are two topics of importance: (i) a mooted change in the War Cabinet involving the removal of Chatfield, Hankey and Oliver Stanley from the Cabinet, the appointment of Winston as Minister for Co-ordination of Defence as well as First Lord, and, probably, the retention of Kingsley Wood in the Cabinet in some other capacity (because the P.M. and David Margesson put great trust in him), (ii) the approaching meeting of the Supreme War Council to debate the French thesis that the war should be prosecuted with greater vigour and that (a) Norwegian territorial waters should be violated, to stop the iron-ore traffic, and if possible Norwegian ports seized so as to make Germany retaliate and thus extend the war to Scandinavia, (b) Russia should be attacked and her oil sources at Batum destroyed by aerial attack from the Near East. With regard to (ii) the point is that Daladier fell because of criticism that the war was being prosecuted without energy or resolution, and M. Paul Reynaud,* D.'s successor, has therefore got to take, or try to take, some active measures. This, of course, suits the book of Winston whose policy is one of "action for action's sake"; personally I feel it would be very wrong to sacrifice lives merely in order to defend oneself from the accusation of irresolution unless there was some worthy objective for which those lives should be sacrificed. There is all the difference between being resolute, capable of seeing one's opportunities and able to use them, and taking some spectacular but valueless action merely in order to impress public opinion. To attack and to fail would be very serious in a war which is, at present, more psychological than military in character.

Wednesday, March 27th

While I was still in bed the Assistant Air Attaché in Paris rang up to ask about arrangements for the meeting of the Supreme War Council – oblivious of the fact that the cross-Channel telephone is almost sure to be tapped. When I suggested that he should ask the Embassy he implied that he had not thought of that!

The Cabinet undertook a thorough review of our strategy in

view of the meeting of the Supreme War Council tomorrow and in particular of the new French Cabinet's wild proposals for drastic action. The Chiefs of Staff pointed out that we were not really in a position to take the offensive: our aircraft production was being built up on the basis of a three-year war and in consequence our immediate output was smaller than if we were budgeting for a *Blitzkrieg*; the Germans need only concentrate their defences on a short line from Luxembourg to Switzerland, whereas the Allies must be ready for an attack anywhere from the Channel to the Mediterranean; on the other hand if Germany were enabled to maintain her present inactivity she would, in six months' time, have remedied her present weak position in respect of oil by imports from Russia and Roumania.

So it seems that we shall have to be careful not to launch a major offensive and yet active in preventing the Germans from profiting by our waiting policy. A German attack on our ports and shipping by the new aerial torpedo, which they are thought to have devised, would mean the diversion of our trade to west coast ports and would seriously complicate our daily life. We can do the same to Germany by tightening the blockade (preventing the Germans using Norwegian territorial waters and "rationing" Italy more strictly for oil) and by putting into operation the mysterious ROYAL MARINE project about which there has lately been much talk, but which the French are frightened of our putting into effect. (It is a new river mine device.)[1]

The question of bombing Baku and of attacking Soviet oil ships in the Black Sea by means of submarines must depend on the attitude of Turkey. At present our Ambassador in Angora does not think the Turks would consent, although they might be ready to do so later in the summer. We could bomb Baku by flying over Turkish or Persian territory, but there is danger of retaliation on the Anglo-Iranian Oil Company's refineries. There is also the question of public opinion in this country to be considered: the extension of the war to Russia without a *very* good cause would

[1] It was a plan to drop mines from the French-held left bank of the Rhine so that they would float down and destroy German shipping in the river. It was finally implemented, far too late, after the German offensive on the Western front had begun.

arouse much criticism. Personally I feel that if we were going to take these steps we ought to have done so before, while the Soviet Government had their hands full in Finland. But dilatoriness is inseparable from democracy, it appears.

The P.M. is anxious to do something spectacular – on the lines of the Sylt raid – which will help to keep public morale and interest high. The ROYAL MARINE operation would serve that purpose and it *might* make the Germans attack on the Western Front, which would be all to the good.

A report from the Vatican says that German conditions and morale have deteriorated in the last few weeks. In that case Hitler will be forced to show his hand.

The objects of the recent Brenner Meeting between Hitler and Mussolini remain obscure, but they probably related to the Balkans, especially Hungary (in which both the dictators have a lively interest) and Roumania.

The possibility of Cabinet changes is still in the air, and I think Lord Chatfield will almost certainly be dropped. David Margesson also wants to drop "Shakes" Morrison, who is a manifest failure, and appoint Rob Hudson Minister of Food. But apparently the latter is quite incapable of working with Civil Servants.

Talked to Sir John Reith who told me that he had given up smoking, because he regarded it as a "dirty, pernicious and childish habit", and had put on two stone as a result. He gives the impression of being a forceful personality.

Dined with Arthur Rucker at the Travellers and listened to an interesting exposition by him of the Fourth Dimension and the meaning of Time. My brain reels beneath such problems.

After dinner Charles Peake, who was in the Club, showed us an alarming communiqué to the effect that the French had "leaked" about the project of laying a minefield in Norwegian waters and stopping the iron-ore trade. Subsequently I saw a Secret Service report of a telephone conversation between M. Reynaud (who arrived in London this evening) and Paris. M. Reynaud was genuinely horrified, but it is clear that in France the most extraordinary things can be done, for internal political reasons, behind the back of the Government.

Thursday, March 28th

The Supreme War Council met at No. 10.

The Norwegian waters and ROYAL MARINE projects were agreed upon and are to take effect next week.

The Baku bombing scheme is to be carefully examined by the two staffs. If the Low Countries are invaded the Allies will march into Belgium without awaiting an invitation to do so.

Means of tightening the blockade are to be examined.

Cabinet reconstruction has now reached its final stage. Chatfield is to be dropped and to go to New Zealand as Governor General (if he will accept it). Sam Hoare is to go to the Air Ministry and Kingsley Wood to be Lord Privy Seal. Kingsley Wood is tired and is also a little out of his depth in the Air Ministry; Hoare is very much disliked by the H. of C., and David Margesson, Arthur (and I think Horace Wilson) would like to be rid of him altogether; but the P.M. refuses and so he is destined for the Air Ministry, where at least he will have to face open criticism and will be less easily able to intrigue. Rob Hudson is to go to the Ministry of Food, the discredited Morrison to the Board of Education and Lord De La Warr* to the Post Office. Hoare's appointment will be ill received.

FOUR

SCANDINAVIAN ADVENTURE
APRIL 1940

Monday, April 1st
The French are making difficulties about the ROYAL MARINE operation and wish to postpone it, possibly because Daladier, who is now Minister for War, does not want Reynaud to get the credit, or possibly because the French fear instant retaliation which they are not in a position to withstand.

Tuesday, April 2nd
Whole Ministerial scheme changed again: Sam Hoare to Air, Kingsley Wood Lord Privy Seal, Morrison Post Office, Ramsbotham[1] (who is an educationist) Board of Education, Woolton* Food, Hudson Shipping, De La Warr Office of Works, Geoffrey Shakespeare[2] Department of Overseas Trade.

Thursday, April 4th
The Cabinet changes have met with a mixed reception in the country, being considered insufficiently drastic in some quarters. Sam Hoare is very much "in with" Beaverbrook* and so his appointment was hailed with delight in the cheap press, but *The Times* was very disagreeable.

The chief centre of interest is the attempt to make the French

---

[1] Created Lord Soulbury in 1941 and made a Viscount in 1954, after being the first Governor General of independent Ceylon.
[2] National Liberal M.P. Later Parliamentary Under-Secretary, Dominions Office.

revoke their refusal to let the R.M. operation take effect. The P.M. has written personally to Daladier and Winston is going over to Paris to do a little personal persuasion. We are trying to blackmail the French by maintaining that we may not undertake the Norwegian territorial waters project unless we can combine it with the other.

Dined at the Travellers where I found Charles Ritchie, who was very good company and most amusing about Canadians. He says that all those who come to the top are sons of the Manse – from Mackenzie King to Beaverbrook. Perhaps that is why Lord Tweedsmuir[1] felt so much at home in Canada. Charles Ritchie is Private Secretary to the Canadian High Commissioner and is greatly exercised because he has to write a speech to the Youth of the Empire, and Lord Halifax, in his recent speech at Oxford, has stolen all the thunder.

On returning to No. 10 I had a talk with the Chancellor of the Exchequer, who is disgusted because the Ministry of Information have been trying to popularise themselves and persuaded Lord Stamp (who, says Simon, is not competent to talk about financial policy) to give a talk to journalists. As a result the Government have been declared by the press to be in favour of the Keynes Plan (which suggests forced loans, not bearing interest, and a capital levy at the end of the war to repay them). Simon was furious and became eloquent on the subject of Sir John Reith whom he described as "a self-advertising ass" who should never have been made Minister of Information. He told me he thought Lord Woolton a good choice as Minister of Food and that Lennox-Boyd[2] would do the Ministry of Food work well in the Commons as he knew the subject really well. He thought Sam Hoare would be good at the Air Ministry, as he is

---

[1] John Buchan (1875–1940), author of *The Thirty-Nine Steps*. Governor General of Canada, 1935–40.

[2] After a gallant war record in the navy, held many responsible ministerial offices, ending as Secretary of State for the Colonies under Churchill, Eden and Macmillan. Loved and respected inside and outside Parliament, he was created Viscount Boyd of Merton in 1960. He was run over and killed in the Fulham Road in 1983.

an excellent administrator, but the appointment had not been well received in the Conservative Party.

Friday, April 5th
Winston went over to Paris to try and convert Daladier to the ROYAL MARINE operation and then telephoned in the middle of the Cabinet to say that he had been converted by Daladier! This much amused the P.M. who said it was like the story of the pious parrot which was bought to teach good language to the parrot which swore, but ended by itself learning to swear. So now we shall proceed to lay a minefield in Norwegian waters but shall postpone the R.M. operation until the French have had time to remove their vulnerable aeroplane factories, etc., from places where they would be in danger from German retaliation.

Lunched with Arthur Rucker at the Athenaeum. Arthur says, with justice, that it is to the P.M. we owe our excellent case in the present war: if it had not been for Munich and the policy of appeasement our case would have lost half its strength, our desperate anxiety to maintain peace might have been questioned and, of course, we should in 1938 have been in a hopeless position of inferiority as regards armaments.

A young man called Anthony Gibbs (son of the writer Sir Philip Gibbs) came to see me and tell me of his discussions in Holland with the German General Wenninger about possible peace terms. The General said that the Nazi Party felt themselves hemmed in and would welcome a face-saving peace. He suggested terms including the reconstitution of Poland with the 1914 boundary (i.e. minus the corridor but with rights at Gdynia) and Czechoslovakia as at Munich. I took these terms to the Foreign Office where there have been other similar schemes put forward by people of this sort – all of whom claim that Goering is a moderate and would favour such proposals. The F.O. rightly regarded Goering with the deepest suspicion.

Saturday, April 6th
The laying of the minefield in Norwegian waters is timed for dawn on Monday. It may arouse some criticism, particularly as

it will not now be accompanied by the spectacular ROYAL MARINE operation. A sharply worded note was sent yesterday, as a prelude, to the Norwegian and Swedish Governments, intended to justify the technically illegal action which we now propose to take. The Swedes have reacted violently, have asked what reason we have for the accusations we make against them, have talked about our previously friendly relations and have even said that we have brought the two countries near to war.

Rab Butler told me the F.O. were not very much in favour of this action and were definitely opposed to any project against Lulea (by laying mines from the air) on the ground that we had recently signed an agreement with Sweden allowing her to export a certain quantity of ore to Germany: we cannot thus violate a treaty we have signed. Rab said that this Norwegian project had gone through because the "Winston" policy of H.M.G. had gained a triumph over the "Halifax" policy. Halifax had only agreed to next Monday's move because of his loyalty to the P.M.

The P.M. for his part is not over-enthusiastic, but feels that after the expectations aroused by the meeting of the Supreme War Council the other day some effective action must be taken. He does not believe (like some people) in "action for action's sake", but he recognises the importance of the psychological factor in the present war and the necessity of throwing occasional sops to public opinion. The question is will it be only a sop? May not the Germans be stung to retaliate forcibly? Rab thinks not, on the ground that the German mind works like clockwork: they are now preparing to destroy our air force and shipping by concentrated attacks, and this activity on our part may, by destroying the clockwork precision of their plans, throw them into some confusion.

As regards Sweden, Rab thinks the key to their attitude is a determination to avoid fire and the sword at all costs. They would rather sell their souls and their country to the Nazis (provided the sale were effected without bloodshed) than stand up boldly for their beliefs and their independence. They would invite Germany to occupy their country peaceably rather than risk an armed invasion.

From Denmark comes a rumour that the Germans are proposing to invade Norway on Monday and to land troops at Narvik. It is also reported that German naval forces are moving northwards.

From the U.S. come reports of a conversation between Lothian, Roosevelt and Sumner Welles. Roosevelt is in favour of an Allied declaration to the heads of neutral states announcing that it is not the Allies' policy to partition Germany or destroy her sovereignty. Lothian thinks the difficulty would be that such a declaration would be taken as heralding a peace plan and might encourage the Germans to put up their terms (if they have any) by way of bargaining.

Lunched at the Travellers with Robert Cecil,[1] who gave me very secret figures intended to show that the Ministry of Supply is being mismanaged and our ammunition output utterly neglected.

Monday, April 8th
Arthur has 'flu, and so Tony Bevir and I are alone, in the very centre of the vortex.

At dawn British destroyers laid minefields in Norwegian waters. On the way back one of them, the *Glow-worm*, stopped to pick up a man who had fallen overboard and was intercepted by the Germans. At the time of writing no more signals are being received from her and she is thought to have gone down. Throughout the morning came rumours of an impending naval action and our ships were searching for a German force containing the *Gneisenau*. Then after lunch the Chancellor looked in and (with his liking for the sensational) told Tony and me that the Germans were "going into" South Sweden. We immediately set the wires buzzing, but the Chancellor's statement soon resolved itself into a Norwegian report that German ships were steaming across the Belt in the direction of Sweden. As a matter of fact such a possibility is not unexpected and we have an

---

[1] Intelligent and well-informed member of the Diplomatic Service, expert on German affairs. Director General of British Information Services, New York, 1959–61.

expedition to Narvik waiting to embark immediately information of a German move is received. Hence the tension.

Tuesday, April 9th

Woken early by a message to say that the Cabinet was meeting at 8.30. Got up in a hurry and rushed round to Downing Street to hear that Norway and Denmark had been invaded by the Germans. Meanwhile most of our fleet is busy chasing German ships towards the North Pole.

The morning was hectic (Tony and I were alone). Messages came to and from the Cabinet, which met again at 12.00, giving reports about the latest German moves or sending instructions for appropriate action on our part. The room was full of people, Sir John Reith, the Chief Whip, Alec Cadogan and various officials, and the question everyone was asking was why did our fleet allow the Germans to establish themselves at Bergen and Trondhjem. It seems that our ships were drawn off northwards by a well-executed feint, but certainly the result is unpleasant and I am not clear where the troops we are now despatching will be expected to land (unconfirmed reports say the Germans have taken Narvik too). However it is cheerful to remember that the last episode in which the British navy was drawn off by a feint ended in Trafalgar!

During the Cabinet "Pug" Ismay came out and said that as far as he could see the Cabinet were proposing to do the only thing that could lose us the war: namely *not* to take vigorous action. The measures at present envisaged are the sending of small naval units to clean up Bergen and other ports while the main fleet is chasing the *Scharnhorst* and *Gneisenau* northwards; the despatch of soldiers to occupy or recapture Narvik, Trondhjem, Bergen and, most important of all, Stavanger, which is the best Norwegian air-base; to take up once again with the French the R.M. operation and try to persuade them to agree to it; and to make fresh approaches to Holland and Belgium. Meanwhile it is not forgotten that this whole affair *may* be meant to occupy our attention while an attack is made on this country.

Lunch-time was spent drafting, with Rab Butler, Horace

Wilson, Gladwyn Jebb[1] and Collier[2] (from the F.O.) the statement on the situation which the P.M. is to make in the House
this afternoon. Generally speaking there seems to be a great deal
of uncertainty as to what is happening, and my own impression is
that the Germans have got a long start of us both in time (which
is hard to explain as we knew that some violent reaction to our
mining operations must be expected) and in decision. From our
point of view the whole thing seems, as the Chief Whip said, to
be "rather a fog". But, of course, if we can secure a naval victory
the balance will be redressed in our favour. Bad visibility and a
heavy sea have made things very difficult.

After the P.M. had made a statement in the House the
Supreme War Council met, at 4.15, Reynaud, Daladier and
Admiral Darlan having flown over from Paris. They decided to
approach the Belgian Government with a view to the allied
armies entering Belgium in order to man their lines: an attack
on Holland and/or Belgium is expected in the course of the next
few days and the French are anxious to forestall the Germans
for once.

The situation is becoming clearer. The Germans have scored
a considerable success by seizing the Norwegian ports despite
our command of the sea, and we, who started the whole
business, seem to have lost the initiative. Nevertheless the
German hold on the northern ports must be precarious, we may
be able to dislodge them without much difficulty and the operation
may give us a chance of putting into action the original project
for denying the Gallivare iron-ore fields to Germany. The First
Lord (who at last sees a chance of action) is jubilant and maintains
that our failure to destroy the German fleet up to the present
is only due to the bad visibility and very rough weather in the

[1] Private Secretary to Sir Alexander Cadogan and then adviser to Dr Dalton
at the Ministry of Economic Warfare. Worked under Sir William Strang on
plans for post-war Europe. Later British representative at the United
Nations and Ambassador to France, 1954–60. Created Lord Gladwyn in
1960.

[2] Sir Laurence Collier. Head of the Foreign Office Northern Department.
Subsequently Ambassador to Norway. Son of the Royal Academician John
Collier.

North Sea, while if the German ships fly for home they will leave their garrisons exposed to our expeditionary forces. Horace Wilson is rather perturbed because he feels that now the Germans have got Denmark (and incidentally incarcerated our Legation), they will find it no difficult task to establish an overland line of communication with Bergen and Trondhjem. Arthur Rucker is convinced that if this affair goes seriously wrong the Government will fall or be re-formed.

I dined with David. We listened to the news which was derived almost entirely from German sources: scarcely a word from our own. This is, I think, shocking and I know from his remarks this morning that Sir John Reith feels bitterly on the subject – but nobody will supply him with the necessary material.

When I got back to No. 10 the Chancellor confirmed the rumours I had heard from David that the Germans seized Narvik by a Trojan Horse manoeuvre: they congregated a lot of iron-ore ships in the harbour with soldiers disguised as seamen and hidden in the holds. "Very clever," said the Chancellor, "and we were ninnies, we were ninnies!"

About 10.00 news came through that our Wellingtons had returned safely from Bergen where they had scored a substantial hit on one German cruiser. I told the P.M. who seemed considerably cheered and said, "That is better than some of the news we have heard lately."

Wednesday, April 10th
Talked to the P.M. just before he set out on his morning walk.[1]
He seemed rather depressed by the situation and admitted that the Germans had reason to be elated by their success. "The lesson to be drawn from it all is," he said, "not that the Allies are cowardly and slow-witted, but that it is impossible to help neutrals who will not help themselves. If the Norwegians and Swedes had agreed to our plans to help the Finns, we should now have been in possession of the Norwegian ports."

[1] He and Mrs Chamberlain used to walk round the lake in St James's Park every morning acknowledging the greetings of passers-by as they went. Nobody was worried about security.

David Margesson says that the P.M. never expected the war to flare up as it now has.

News from the Air Ministry is not encouraging and the Admiralty are not cheered by the reports which have so far reached them. However the German air-attack on the fleet failed, though the *Rodney* was hit; and one of our submarines torpedoed a German cruiser last night. So far our naval expedition outside Narvik has failed to achieve anything. Apparently "things" are still happening in the North Sea.

The Supreme War Council conclusions show that we are to concentrate on occupying Narvik once the seas have been cleared. The ROYAL MARINE operation will be put into effect if the Germans attack on the Western Front or if Belgium is invaded.

After lunch reassuring news came about our expedition to Narvik: far from failing to achieve anything we succeeded in doing a great deal of material damage, though we lost two destroyers in the process. The P.M. decided to make a statement to this effect in the House, and I went over to the Admiralty to get the details. I waited in the Private Secretaries' squalid little room while the First Lord toyed with a draft, and was shown a number of interesting telegrams from the fleet. Apparently there are still two large German squadrons at sea. Tonight aircraft from the *Furious* will make another attack, with aerial torpedos, on Bergen. I finally rushed the material for the statement back to No. 10, whence it was transmitted to the House with about two minutes to spare and read by the P.M. to an elated House.

Thursday, April 11th
Warm and summery weather at last.

A French mission arrived early at Downing Street to see the P.M. and Halifax. It is on its way to Stockholm to try to persuade the Swedes to come into the war, and is headed by M. Coulondre.

The press are full of extravagant and untrue stories about the recapture of Bergen and Trondhjem.

The Cabinet have indications that an attack on the Western Front is now imminent. It seems likely, therefore, that the

Norwegian affair is really a diversion, especially as the generals commanding the German armies are insignificant men and the armies themselves are small. It is difficult to see why Hitler should be prepared to sacrifice his fleet for the sake of a diversion, because he certainly does seem to be sacrificing a large part of it. Possibly he thinks it is worth losing the navy in order to seize places, such as Stavanger, from which intensive aerial attacks can be made on this country. Meanwhile we are concentrating all our available troops for the seizure of Narvik and, if possible, the subsequent denial of the Gallivare ore mines to Germany.

In the afternoon I heard Winston make a speech in the House about the naval situation. He was witty, but less polished than usual. He caused much amusement by saying that Denmark had had most to fear from Germany of all the neutrals, because she had been the most recent to negotiate a non-aggression pact with her. He wisely damped down the absurd over-optimism of this morning's newspapers, but made a good case for the navy's achievements during the last three days.

The general atmosphere is one of nervous expectation. Where will the blow fall? Will it be Holland and Belgium, or the Maginot Line, or a great air attack on this country – or all together? The Belgians have rejected the Anglo-French approach for an immediate entry into Belgium, but they may think better of it if we agree to move straight up to the Albert Canal–Meuse Line instead of merely halfway across the country to the Antwerp–Namur Line.

Mother and I dined with Grandfather and Peggy at Argyll House.[1] Grandfather is getting to look rapidly older but retains a great deal of his unrivalled charm. Peggy, with whom I gossiped for hours on a sofa, is at her best and most natural in conditions such as this. She often shows herself impractical, but is invariably witty in her conversation and shrewd in her judgments. It is amusing to hear both Grandfather and Peggy, who have always lived sumptuously and in state, expressing the most liberal and

---

[1] In the King's Road. The Crewes had moved there shortly before the war after selling Crewe House in Curzon Street to Messrs Thomas Tilling.

democratic theories. Peggy is sometimes quite revolutionary in
her sentiments – but very aristocratic in her tastes.

Friday, April 12th
P. J. Grigg,* the Permanent Secretary to the War Office, came
in and told us that many people in the War Office are pressing
for us to concentrate on retaking Trondhjem instead of Narvik
(the Norwegian Government is also asking us to do this). Grigg
says that Ironside ("Tiny") and Stanley are not adopting a
sensible attitude and he remarked to Arthur: "We must get the
P.M. to take a hand in this before Winston and Tiny go and
bugger up the whole war."

Then the Chancellor arrived and stayed most of the night. He
wanted to talk to the P.M. about the Budget and the particular
difficulties connected with the proposed Register of Wealth
which is to help the Government assess war profits for subsequent taxation. The Governor of the Bank thinks that such a
measure will cause general uneasiness: it will be thought to be
the precursor to a Capital Levy – at any rate under a politically
more advanced Government – and will discourage people from
contributing to Government Loans. The Chancellor said his
Budget was perfectly horrifying and he could only trust that the
attack on the Western Front would coincide with Budget Day!

Then the Chancellor saw Tony's Homer, picked it up and
insisted on reading to Arthur and me long passages from the
Iliad about Priam begging Achilles for Hector's body. He went
on interminably about the beauty of the passage, but I could not
help being impressed by his erudition (which, of course, was
what he intended). He is always quoting learnedly from the
Classics.

P. J. Grigg came back and the conversation turned to India.
Simon was quite amusing in describing what he called "the
masculine and simple view" adopted by Winston in the Cabinet.
Winston rejoiced in the quarrel which had broken out afresh
between Hindus and Moslems, said he hoped it would remain
bitter and bloody and was glad that we had made the suggestion
of Dominion status which was acting as a cat among the pigeons.
Both Simon and Grigg agreed that this was not the moment to

give anything away in India: we must remain firm as a rock, because British rule was today essential to India.

Monday, April 15th

Although I was busy all day with Ecclesiastical and other matters, there was very little happening. We are all waiting for a number of prospective operations in Norway, which go by such deceptive names as MAURICE, HENRY, PRIMROSE and ALPHONSE, to mature, and the centre of interest has shifted from Narvik to Trondhjem which, in order to keep up the spirits of the Norwegians, we are to make a rapid and determined effort to recapture. The destruction of half the German fleet has greatly improved the morale and recaptured the interest of the general public and, it appears, has had a correspondingly depressing effect in Germany. It is therefore to be presumed that another German coup is expected, and the general uneasiness about Italy, and in particular her designs on Dalmatia and Corfu, make it seem possible that some Italo-German coup is hatching in the Balkans. Mussolini's prestige is so great that he could probably carry an unwilling people into war or some perilous adventure if he so chose, though it would undoubtedly be his destruction in the end. Holland still languishes under the threat of invasion and sinister movements on the German side of the frontier.

Tuesday, April 16th

Little news of our fortunes in Norway, but there is still some reason for disquiet at Mussolini's sudden hatred for the Allies and all their works. He seems to be doing his best to work on Italian feeling and there is a fluttering in the Balkan dovecots.

In the evening the Chancellor came in, seized me by the shoulders and said: "Since we are quite alone I want to discuss a Classical matter with you: Aeneas was not the son of Priam but of Anchises." This was because the other night when he read to Arthur and me about Priam's plea for the body of Hector, the last of his numerous children, I, wishing to show an intelligent interest, interjected, "What about Aeneas?" "Oh," said the Chancellor, "Priam was being effective, which is not necessarily the same as telling the truth." That he should remember and correct himself and me on such a small point shows what an amazing grasp of detail his remarkable brain possesses.

Hardly had I gone to sleep at No. 10 when I was informed that the P.M. wanted to see me. He was rather taken aback at seeing me in my dressing-gown, but told me that as a result of a conversation with the First Lord he wanted a meeting of the Military Co-ordination Committee summoned at 10 a.m. in the morning. I gather that our forces at Narvik, under Lord Cork,[1] are rather loth to make an attack because of the snow, but Winston feels that a long delay would be disastrous both for military and psychological reasons. There are signs that the Norwegians will lose heart if they are not quickly assured of substantial support.

Wednesday, April 17th
Plans for an attack by the Guards, Chasseurs Alpins, etc., on Trondhjem are being matured (Operation MAURICE). They will land after the enemy guns have been silenced by battleships and will be supported by a move southwards from Namsos by General Carton de Wiart[2] (Force HENRY). Lord Hankey hinted to me that he was a little worried by Winston's determination to direct the war: he remembers, he says, the operations at the Dardanelles all too clearly. He is going to warn the P.M. Ronald Harris,[3] who is Secretary to Sir E. Bridges, says that Winston has been presiding over innumerable committees, talking a lot and getting nothing done, but that now the P.M. has begun to preside over the Military Co-ordination Committee things are beginning to move, more practical plans are being made and there is a definite sign that the difficulties and opportunities of the situation are being handled in a realistic manner.

---

[1] Admiral of the Fleet the Earl of Cork and Orrery. Commanded H.M.S. *Repulse* in the First World War and the Home Fleet in the 1930s. Appointed to command the Norwegian expedition in 1940. Known in the navy as "Ginger Pop" on account of his red hair and occasionally explosive reactions; but highly esteemed by all ranks.

[2] Legendary hero of several wars who helped the Poles defeat the Red Army in 1920 and survived many severe wounds.

[3] Later held high rank in the Treasury and was eventually First Church Estates Commissioner.

Went to the House for questions and met Major Astor,[1] who was waiting to be harangued by the P.M. about the unhelpful carping attitude which *The Times* has been adopting recently.

Thursday, April 18th

Went to the House where I met Sir J. Wardlaw Milne[2] who says that the public are beginning to believe, through constant repetition, the extravagant German communiqués which claim that the Germans have sunk half our fleet. He felt some authoritative dementi was required, but the P.M., to whom I mentioned this on the way back, disagreed on the grounds that there will always be people anxious to believe the worst but who do not represent the real feeling of the country.

Dined with Gordon Etherington-Smith[3] who, after varied and exciting adventures, has just returned from the Legation at Copenhagen. He described how the staff burned the last confidential paper as the Germans arrived at the Legation, how the Germans told him that he was a filthy Englishman and that if he wasn't careful he would be shot, and how, finally, after being paraded through the streets in drays, the staff were released by the Germans and treated very courteously.

Monday, April 22nd

The P.M. left for France to attend a meeting of the Supreme War Council. We have landed two forces successfully in Norway, one north of Trondhjem and one south, but partly owing to dangerously truthful prognostications in the press we have abandoned the difficult project of a landing from the sea under the guns of the navy and have adopted a pincer scheme instead. Strong forces will attack Trondhjem from Namsos in the north (if General Carton de Wiart can overcome transport and other

---

[1] Afterwards 1st Lord Astor of Hever. Bought *The Times* in 1922 from the estate of Lord Northcliffe, but refrained from interfering with editorial control. M.P. for Dover, 1922–45. Not on good terms with his sister-in-law, Nancy Astor, nor by any means always with Winston Churchill.

[2] Senior backbench Conservative M.P. who later ran an unsuccessful campaign against Churchill's handling of the war.

[3] A former colleague in the Eastern Department of the Foreign Office.

difficulties which are increased by heavy German bombing) and from Aandalsnes in the south, where the railway is to be seized. Simultaneously a feint landing will be made and H.M. ships will bombard the town, which will thus be invested and not spectacularly stormed.

Dined with Herschel Johnson[1] (Minister at the American Embassy) at White's. He told me of his admiration for Lord Halifax whose mind, he felt, was always open to conviction and who would never be afraid of yielding a point, if he believed he had been wrong, except on a question of basic principle. Afterwards we talked of Anglo-American relations and deplored the ignorance and misunderstanding on both sides and especially the increasing bitterness in England against America's attitude of critical and ineffective sympathy in the present war. He emphasised the real anxiety of the administration to be helpful.

Herschel Johnson spoke of the feeling in America that England was decadent and its ruling class effete. He himself realised that, whatever their external appearance, there was no tougher race than the English.

Tuesday, April 23rd
Represented the P.M. at a Memorial Service for H. A. L. Fisher (who was run over by a bus) at St Margaret's, Westminster. The Bishop of Winchester (Garbett)[2] gave a moving address and the Archbishop of Canterbury read, in his musical voice, the beautiful lesson from the Book of Wisdom. Immediately behind me sat Lloyd George: he paid little attention to the service, but when we reached the last hymn his Welsh blood got the better of his indifference and he shouted "For All the Saints who from their Labours Rest" in a high-pitched tenor which reached above the voices of the congregation.

[1] A friendly, hard-working and Anglophile member of the American Foreign Service who tried unavailingly to keep Joseph Kennedy on the right track, but was highly esteemed by Kennedy's successor, Gil Winant. American Ambassador in Stockholm at the end of the war.

[2] A deeply spiritual cleric who was Bishop of Winchester for ten years and from 1942 Archbishop of York. Brendan Bracken thought him a saint and tried hard to persuade Churchill to promote him to Canterbury when Archbishop Temple died.

Went to the luncheon of the St George's Society at Grosvenor House to celebrate St George's Day. Sat next to Audrey Paget and an attractive girl called Elspeth Ogylvie. Duff Cooper* spoke, in the place of Winston, and his eloquence was remarkable. He praised the absent First Lord (unduly, I thought – but then Winston is trying to get him back into the Government) and spoke of Germany with blood-curdling hatred. He castigated those who blamed the Nazis and whitewashed the Germans, maintaining that the German people as a whole were responsible for their repeated crimes. I thought of Burke's wiser statement: "I know no means of indicting a whole nation." After Duff Cooper the Canadian and Australian High Commissioners spoke.

Budget Day: it was less fearful than the Chancellor had led me to believe.

The P.M. returned from France and they all seemed rather elated. Here, on the other hand, gloom reigns (H.J.W.[1] and the Chancellor) because of the difficulties which General Phillips' brigade are meeting at Namsos. It appears that the snow is deep, that the men are obliged to keep to the roads and have no snow-shoes, that enemy aircraft attacks are bad and can be met with no adequate defence, that the Chasseurs Alpins (who are equipped for this sort of fighting) are remaining at the base and doing nothing.

Dined with Sidney Cuthbert at the Travellers. He is anxious to go to Norway because he says he would prefer to die, if die he must, in beautiful scenery!

Returned to No. 10 to sleep. The Military Co-ordination Committee met and discussed the situation. Edward Bridges said afterwards that Winston was being maddening, declaring that we had failed at Namsos, and making the most unreasonable proposals. As for Oliver Stanley, Bridges said that he hadn't an "ounce of guts".

The P.M. is depressed – more by Winston's rampages than by the inherent strategical difficulties with which we are confronted in Norway.

I gather that the Supreme War Council have decided to go all

---

[1] Sir Horace Wilson.

out for Trondhjem and Narvik (bearing in mind that stoppage of
the iron-ore supplies is the main objective), to enter Belgium
without an invitation if Holland is invaded (and incidentally to
bomb the Ruhr), to pursue investigations about the bombing
of Baku, and to take measures (such as naval movements in
the Mediterranean, when ships can be spared, and military
moves in North Africa) to prevent Mussolini doing anything
rash and bellicose – a possibility which is now decreasing in
likelihood.

Wednesday, April 24th
A large map of Scandinavia, studded with coloured pins, now
stands in our room and groups of people cluster round it all the
morning discussing the prospects of our adventure. General
Ismay points out that we have only a small stake near Trondhjem
and that it does not much matter if we lose it – a cold-blooded
military way of looking at things. Actually I think the psychological cost would be considerable. Rob Hudson, Minister of Shipping, is chiefly interested in not losing the person of King
Haakon, because while he is secured to us we can make use of
3,000,000 tons of Norwegian shipping.

I have an uneasy feeling that all is not being as competently
handled as it might be. The failure to send snow-shoes for our
men at Namsos (while the Germans have them) is unpleasantly
reminiscent of the Crimean War. Moreover I do not put great
faith in the judgment of the Chiefs of Staff or of our military
pundits. There is not that appearance of thought-out, clockwork
efficiency which I should like to see; but it may just be that
the English way of doing things is superficially slipshod and
unimpressive. Of one thing I am convinced: we make up our
minds lamentably slowly and we do not insure against every
eventuality like the Germans do. Time and again we have
"missed the boat" (e.g. Finland, Norway) owing to excessive
deliberation and fear of unnecessary extravagance.

Went back to Downing Street in time to greet the First Lord
and take him into the P.M. The latter has been much less
forbidding of late and has even taken to calling me Jock. His
incredible capacity for hard work, and his apparent immunity

from fatigue continue and seem even to increase as the problems become more difficult and the days heavier with work. His seventy-one years lie very easily upon his shoulders. I gather that his talk with Winston did not go too well: he is proving a difficult colleague.

Italy is moving still further from war. Mussolini is reported to have said, "Germany is trying to drag me into the war by the hair, but luckily I am bald." If Italy did come in, the Allies would probably send an expeditionary force to Salonica, provided Greece were complaisant.

Thursday, April 25th
The trouble about Winston, which has been brewing for the last few days, arises from his demand to be appointed Chairman of the Chiefs of Staff Committee. This would not only annoy the other service ministers but would also probably cause chaos among the Chiefs of Staff and planning experts because, as was shown when Winston presided over the Military Co-ordination Committee, his verbosity and restlessness make a great deal of unnecessary work, prevent any real practical planning from being done and generally cause friction. But if the P.M. refuses to acquiesce, Winston threatens to go down to the House and say he can take no responsibility for what is happening. To let this happen in wartime would be unthinkable: there would then be a first-class political crisis, because the country believes that Winston is the man of action who is winning the war and little realise how ineffective, and indeed harmful, much of his energy is proving itself to be. On the other hand if the P.M. gives in, Winston will have won his point by blackmail and he is likely to pursue the same tactics in order to get his way in future. Winston, for his part, professes absolute loyalty to the P.M. (and indeed they get on admirably), but complains that the Chiefs of Staff and the "Joint Planners" are making a hopeless muddle. A possible solution is to make Winston Minister for Co-ordination of Defence and make somebody else (Alec suggests David Margesson) First Lord; but unfortunately Lord Chatfield was asked to resign only the other day on the grounds that the office is now superfluous.

Drove down to the House with the P.M. who is in an agreeable frame of mind, but obviously depressed and at a loss how to solve the Winston impasse. Stanley Baldwin lunched with him and he probably drew on his experience in dealing with such awkward problems.

At this point I should perhaps say something of Winston Churchill's views on Stanley Baldwin. At a later stage of the war, he showed him considerable magnanimity. However, he certainly believed that Baldwin, more than Chamberlain, was culpable of a neglect and an idleness which contributed much to the outbreak of the "most unnecessary war in history". I think, too, that there was a certain personal animosity based on the curious fact that Stanley Baldwin had once out-manoeuvred Churchill without the latter realising it until after the event. Few people ever did get the better of Winston Churchill and the case which I describe now is the only one which I ever heard him admit. It appears that after the famous Westminster Election, which Churchill just failed to win in 1923, Baldwin saw in him a menace to his own leadership and to the serene unanimity of the Conservative Party. He therefore skilfully offered him, in his 1924 Government, the great prize of the Chancellorship of the Exchequer. Churchill afterwards believed that Baldwin did this for two reasons: first because he knew that he would serve the Government loyally and that, being in one of its highest posts, there would be no likelihood of his giving trouble; and secondly because he did not think Winston would be a success at the Treasury and his political future would therefore be jeopardised. I do not know whether these were in fact Baldwin's motives, but Churchill believed them to have been so. It appears that during his Chancellorship of the Exchequer, lasting four years, he was only once asked inside 10 Downing Street other than on an official occasion, and he thought, probably rightly, that Baldwin had a personal antipathy to him.

In the evening I took down the record of a meeting of Ministers over which the P.M. presided. Nearly all the Ministers not in the War Cabinet were present and the P.M. gave them an account of the events of the previous week. He described the meeting of the Supreme War Council which had been entirely cordial, despite his anticipation of a quarrel with the French. The French Government had given way over the question of the control of French troops in Norway and had agreed to let us bomb the Ruhr and German military objectives in the event of an invasion of the Low Countries. The latter concession was unexpected in view of the French fears of retaliation on their aircraft factories, a consideration which had led them to veto the ROYAL MARINE operation.

The P.M. said that he had liked M. Reynaud on this occasion: he was a man who definitely improved on acquaintance. Turning to Norway, the P.M. painted a very black picture and said that we might well have to evacuate all our forces in the Trondhjem area. He told how the French anti-aircraft cruiser, which had been sent to cover the landing of the Chasseurs Alpins at Namsos, had been inexplicably withdrawn and the Germans had thus been enabled to bomb the French successfully and destroy their supplies. (This action of the French Admiral was not brought up at the Supreme War Council, a restraint which the French much appreciated.)

As faces round the table grew longer and longer (because even Ministers have been partially misled by the extravagant optimism of the press), the P.M. described the landing of German troops *by sea* at Trondhjem and the cutting off of Carton de Wiart's men. He told of the difficulties which snow and ice presented to Lord Cork at Narvik, of the exhaustion and the unhelpful attitude of the Norwegians (who could not even blow up a railway line) and the appalling problems caused by lack of air-bases and aircraft. The P.M. discounted the probability of Italy coming into the war, on the grounds that the army and air force were not ready, the people and the Pope wanted peace, and the country's resources were inadequate. He believed that at the Brenner meeting Mussolini had agreed to create a diversion while Hitler undertook his rapid and bloodless conquest of Scandinavia. Finally Mr C. spoke of the transports for German troops which were reported to be concentrated at German Baltic ports: he did not believe this portended an attack on Sweden (at any rate until the ice round Lulea melted) but thought the Germans might intend to seize the Aaland Islands.

The P.M. took the meeting admirably. He sat back in his chair, spoke slowly and rather colloquially, showed a certain sense of humour (which I had always doubted his possessing) and obviously commanded the undivided attention of all present. For my part I wrote more hectically than I had ever done since the days of lectures at Cambridge.

Friday, April 26th

The Military Co-ordination Committee (presided over by the P.M. and attended by the Service Ministers and Chiefs of Staff) decided to evacuate our troops from Southern Norway, on the grounds that even if we captured Trondhjem we could not expect to hold it. We shall concentrate on Narvik, in order to be near the Swedish frontier and the iron-ore fields in the event of a German attack on Sweden. The Cabinet agreed, and the withdrawal will be effected slowly and be combined with a concentrated attack on Narvik. I fear the psychological effect will be deplorable: inside Germany Hitler will gain a much-needed triumph; and the effect on Italy may be dangerous. P. J. Grigg goes so far as to say it is a wrong decision and hints that it is a political manoeuvre of Winston, who sees that the P.M. will be discredited and his own position strengthened. Could he be quite so black?

One consideration which influenced the decision was the fact that our operations in Central Norway would involve a greater strain on our own resources than on those of the enemy, whose communications are so much easier.

The Winston problem is still much to the fore. The proposed solution, if W. accepts it, is that he should have a secretariat of his own, headed by General Ismay, who will be a member of the Chiefs of Staff Committee and there represent Winston's views. W. will become a kind of Deputy Prime Minister in matters connected with defence. The P.M. is wisely humouring Winston, whose position in the country is, quite unjustifiably, unassailable.

The French have heard of our proposed withdrawal from

Norway and have gone up in smoke. The C.I.G.S. (Ironside, whom P. J. Grigg thinks the worst and most incompetent of men) was to have gone over to Paris today to explain matters, but the French seem to have obtained previous information and Gamelin has arrived this evening to harangue the P.M., Halifax and Winston. Meanwhile the Norwegian Minister in Brussels gloomily prophesies a second Gallipoli in Norway.

There must be something wrong with me: it is all so depressing and the Whitehall world is crowded with dark looks and knitted brows, but I just *cannot* take it tragically or feel nearly as depressed as I ought or, indeed, as I write.

Dined with Cynthia Keppel[1] at Luigi's where the food is delicious but the prices scandalous. We went to a propaganda film called *For England*, which was too long, and then proceeded to the Bierkeller in Leicester Square where, for the first time in the West End, I saw a group of bespectacled intellectuals remain firmly seated while God Save the King was played. Everybody looked but nobody did anything, which shows that the war has not yet made us lose our sense of proportion or become noisily jingoistic.

Saturday, April 27th
A talk with Rab Butler who agrees that the Chiefs of Staff have an appalling lack of foresight (at least so it appears), that nobody can make a clear-cut decision, that everybody is unnecessarily rattled about Italy and that, in general, the Government and its advisers are not conducting themselves as creditably as could be wished.

The French are reported to have decided that if we withdraw our troops from Norway they will nevertheless keep theirs there. So it was decided to hold a meeting of the Supreme War Council and at 11.30 Ivo Mallet, from the F.O., and I motored down to Heston to meet Reynaud, Daladier, etc. Unfortunately the aeroplane arrived early and we missed them. I drove back

---

[1] My second cousin, daughter of Lord Albemarle. In 1944 she married the distinguished historian, Professor Postan, whose first wife had been another well-known historian, Eileen Power.

with a French staff officer who told me that the French thought, like us, that Narvik and the iron ore was all-important but that for psychological reasons, and especially in order to stiffen the Swedes, we should at least maintain ourselves in Central Norway. The plain truth of the matter is that we have unadvisedly landed an insufficient number of troops without adequate equipment or support from the air, and we have met or are meeting with a serious reverse. Its political importance is greater than its military importance, for unless we can make some counter-stroke at Narvik or elsewhere the effect on public opinion at home and abroad will be serious. From what I can see the Chiefs of Staff are much to blame, also Winston who fusses but does nothing and Oliver Stanley who from all accounts is hopeless. Horace, David and Arthur seem to have got their knife into him, as they had it into Hore-Belisha before, and I suspect therefore that his days at the War Office are numbered. If Norway goes seriously wrong, then I suppose the popular outcry may force a reconstitution of the Government and Winston, to whom as much blame should attach as any other single individual, will ride triumphantly forward on the wave of undeserving national popularity.

One of Hitler's cleverest moves has been to make Winston Public Enemy Number One, because this fact has helped to make him Public Hero Number One at home and in the U.S.A.

The Supreme War Council met in the afternoon just after "that swine Rib", as Halifax calls him, had made a speech condoning German aggression in Norway on the grounds that the Allies were contemplating such action with Norwegian connivance. It was tragic to hear the conversation of the Polish Ambassador and Norwegian Minister, who waited in our room to be summoned in at the end of the meeting. What, they asked each other, was it all about? Had some interesting news been received from Norway? Obviously they sensed that something was amiss and felt alarmed.

The Supreme War Council apparently reached agreement and decided to evacuate the Trondhjem area by degrees.

Monday, April 29th

At No. 10 gloom still prevails. We have lost most of General Morgan's brigade, Aandalsnes has been bombed to pieces and it is clear that nothing but a miracle can save us from evacuating the country south of Trondhjem. We may be able to hang on at Namsos until we can retire northwards to fortified positions and can reduce the German garrison in Narvik.

Among the P.M.'s visitors during the afternoon was Grandfather, as one of the leaders of the Liberal Opposition. I went and sat on the sofa with him in the hall and talked to him while he waited.

Arthur thinks we ought seriously to consider the possibility of a German invasion of the British Isles, first by air and then by sea, as in Norway: once German air-bases are established in Norway such an apparently fantastic scheme would be more feasible. Hankey has produced a book, written by a German military expert, according to which the Shetlands should be the next step after Norway: meanwhile we are hoping to adapt those unfortunate islands to aerial use.

Slept at No. 10, but was aroused in the early hours by General Dill[1] in connection with a telegram which showed that the Norwegians thought of capitulating unless they could be certain of more substantial help. I refused to awake the P.M. and Dill sent off a reply on his own account.

Tuesday, April 30th

Apart from adverse weather conditions and the lack of aerodromes from which British fighters can be operated, the two main sources of our troubles in Norway seem to be the following:
 (i) Cowardice, ineffectiveness and even treachery of the Norwegians. They fight half-heartedly (shades of the Finns last winter!) and they even refuse to allow their bridges, etc., to be blown up when our demolition squads arrive.
 (ii) The lack of training of our troops, most of whom, in the Trondhjem sector at any rate, are inexperienced territorials

---

[1] Just back from commanding a Corps in France under Lord Gort to become Vice Chief of the Imperial General Staff.

or reservists called up on the outbreak of war. The French
are averse to our removing regular divisions from France,
but the Norwegian situation certainly calls for them – and
for adequate supplies of equipment and A.A. Protection.

Went with Betty Montagu[1] in the lunch-hour to hear one of
the daily concerts at the National Gallery, where the admission
is one shilling and various artists give their services free, in
aid of charity. There was a large audience and we heard a
performance of Mozart's Sonatas in E Flat, C Major and A
Major by Eileen Ralph and Thomas Matthews. It was very
enjoyable and a good relaxation. There was a buffet in an
adjoining room where one could procure excellent sandwiches
and coffee.

[1] Lady Elizabeth Montagu, daughter of the 9th Earl of Sandwich. She and her
family were kind and hospitable friends with whom I frequently stayed at
Hinchingbrooke, near Huntingdon. She was generally known as "Betts".

FIVE

CHANGE OF GOVERNMENT AND DUNKIRK

MAY 1940

Wednesday, May 1st

Sir Roger Keyes* has written to Winston a letter condemning the pusillanimity of the Naval Staff, and has sent a copy to the P.M. He says that the navy have let down the army, that Trondhjem fjord could and should have been forced and the German positions bombarded by naval guns. He blames Pound* and maintains that the prestige of the Royal Navy is at stake (Charbonnière of the French Embassy tells me the same is true as far as French public opinion is concerned). Keyes ends by asking to be re-employed himself.

I feel it is most important to be rid of Ironside as C.I.G.S. and replace him by Dill. I have less and less confidence in the Chiefs of Staff, especially as far as the War Office is concerned, and Winston's unco-ordinated energy is not reassuring. "If I were the first of May, I should be ashamed of myself," Winston said this evening as he gazed at a sudden blight which had descended on the face of the earth. Personally I think he ought to be ashamed of himself in any case.

Friday, May 3rd

Our troops were safely evacuated from Namsos last night. This morning the press is full of the withdrawal from central Norway which is admitted to be a reverse, and there is a certain amount of criticism, though less than might have been expected. Sir

John Reith says that "the situation is in hand, but not entirely restored". Berlin and Rome are jubilant and Sweden, that most lily-livered and defeatist of nations, has the cheek to be extremely critical of our action.

General Dill said this afternoon that militarily the situation was by no means precarious and that he did not think the German army was in really good fighting shape. Their soldiers were young and enthusiastic, but not steady. The only dangers to his mind were (i) the effect on Italy and the neutrals, (ii) the effect on the home-front and the intrigues to put in a more "active" Prime Minister, (iii) the effect on our Allies. He is a man who gives one confidence and who will, I hope, soon succeed Ironside as C.I.G.S.

Lord Portal, who also called at No. 10 this afternoon, told me that his information went to show that Winston himself was being loyal to the P.M., but his satellites (e.g. Duff Cooper, Amery,* etc.) were doing all in their power to create mischief and ill-feeling.

Sir A. Sinclair wrote a letter to the P.M. in the most unmeasured terms protesting against having the wires tapped during his telephone calls. Everything goes to show that he is a most untrustworthy person who is quite capable of passing on to the press what the P.M. tells him in confidence as an Opposition Leader.[1] In addition he is blinded by prejudiced hatred of the P.M., and gives frequent proof that his feelings are more powerful than his brains. To what depths of futility and even banefulness the Liberal Party has fallen, and what a dearth of brain-power there now is in a party which, in 1906, produced the most intellectually brilliant Cabinet in history.

Sir Victor Mallet, our Minister in Stockholm, has sent home an appalling description of our ineffectiveness and lack of defensive weapons in the Namsos area, which was provided by a man called Binney, of the British Steel Federation. Binney described a conversation with French officers who said, "The British have planned this campaign on the lines of a punitive expedition against

---

[1] Totally unjust to Sinclair who was wholly honest and patriotic even if he did detest Neville Chamberlain.

the Zulus, but unhappily we and the British are in the position of the Zulus, armed with bows and arrows against the onslaught of scientific warfare." Both Binney and Mallet sum up their criticisms in the complaint that "we have allowed the situation to develop instead of developing the situation".

There was also a somewhat alarming report from the Conservative Central Office giving the observations of their agents in the provinces on the internal situation. It seems that the war is not popular among the lowest sections of the community, that there is a suspicion it is being fought in the interests of the rich, and that there is much discontent about the rising cost of living. This is but a slight foretaste of what we shall have to face after the war.

Monday, May 6th

At Downing Street all interest centres on tomorrow's debate on Norway. The P.M. is very depressed about the press attacks on him: he needs a tonic, says David Margesson; but in fact I think he suffers from a curious vanity and self-esteem which were born at Munich and have flourished, in spite of a good many wounds, ever since. David, Alec and Rab Butler think the position is good politically, even though strategically and diplomatically it may be precarious. Obviously the Government will win through tomorrow, but there will be many awkward points raised about Norway, and I am afraid that the confidence of the country may be somewhat shaken. But if we are to win this war we have got to be able to stand reverses and take them philosophically.

Tuesday, May 7th

Rode at Richmond before breakfast under cloudless skies and among trees in full bloom.

After lunch I went to the House for the keenly-awaited debate on the Norwegian contretemps. The P.M. spoke well, though he began unimpressively, and he put his arguments cogently, declining to be rattled by the constant interruptions from the Opposition benches. When he had finished speaking, it was generally agreed that the Government was going "to get away with it". Attlee made a savage attack on the ineptitude of the Government and declared that the confidence of the country would remain unshaken only provided the people were sure of good leadership.

Sinclair, for the Liberals, made an eloquent and venomous speech (though he was badly tripped up by the P.M. and by Winston on two occasions) in which he showed, as usual, a remarkable store of inside information, e.g. he knew all about the failure to send snow-shoes with our troops. He is a good debater, but his arguments, though often original (unlike Attlee's, which are commonplace) suffer from the petty-mindedness which is inherent in him. I was disappointed that L.G. did not rise to his feet. Sinclair made one telling point (at least it told with the Opposition) when he compared the policy of the Government to that of Lord Galway[1] at Almanza in 1707, as described by Macaulay: "He thought it more honourable to fail, according to rules, than to succeed by innovation."

Lord Hankey, who has got to open a similar debate in the Lords, complained to me that he would be addressing most of the members of the Fifth Column!

George Lansbury[2] died.

Reports received of a projected attack on the Western Front tomorrow.

Wednesday, May 8th

The debate took an unexpectedly unfavourable turn last night and as a result the Government is rocking. Sir Roger Keyes came down in full uniform and made a dramatic, if vulgar, oration about Trondhjem (based on Winston's justifiable refusal to re-employ him), Amery* made a slashing attack on the Government, and Oliver Stanley, winding up, was weak and ineffective. He impresses nobody and has obviously got to go.

---

[1] Henri de Massue de Ruvigny, 1st Earl of Galway (1648–1720), was a French soldier who settled in England, became a general in the British army, commanded the British forces in Portugal during the War of the Spanish Succession, won a number of battles, but was defeated by the French at Almanza in 1707.

[2] Devoutly religious Leader of the Labour Party after 1931. A dedicated pacifist.

So this morning everybody is at the nadir of gloom, lower than I have yet seen them. Alec, Rab Butler, David and Arthur are all talking about reconstituting the Government and seriously discussing schemes such as a bargain (to be put by Halifax to Morrison) whereby the Labour Party should be asked to come into the Government in return for the dropping of Sam Hoare, Kingsley Wood, Simon, etc., but on the condition that the P.M. retains the leadership. If, at their Whitsun conference next week, the Labour Party burn their boats and refuse co-operation, then the P.M. might have to resort to a Government of national figures (L.G., etc.).

What disgusts me is that everybody is concentrating their energies on an internal political crisis (*à la française*) instead of taking thought for the morrow about Hitler's next move. We must not be caught napping again; but I have the impression that an invasion of the Low Countries is the only German coup for which we are thoroughly prepared and to counter which we could take vigorous action.

Very soon after the beginning of the debate in the House, it became apparent that the fate of the Government hung in the balance, not that there can be any doubt they will win the division (which the Socialists today decided to force), but because all the attacks on the Government were personal attacks against the P.M. and it is clear that his position in the House is shaken. There were a series of venomous speeches by Herbert Morrison, Stafford Cripps, Lloyd George and Duff Cooper. In reply the Government could produce nobody of any power except Winston, who will wind up tonight. Sam Hoare was ineffective and, indeed, Conservative backbenchers are more or less demanding his resignation as the price of their allegiance.

Lloyd George made probably the most forceful speech he has made for years: I could see that he held the House spellbound as he flung his arms about and denounced the incapacity of the P.M. and the Government. He said that our promissory notes to Czechoslovakia, Poland, Finland and Norway were so much waste paper and he expressed the hope that Winston would not allow himself to be used as an air-raid shelter beneath whom the Government could hide their blunders. The Opposition shouted themselves hoarse as L.G. became more and more vehement and less and less reasonable. Horace Wilson, who sat with me in the official gallery, said that the hatred written on their faces astonished him: it was the pent-up bitterness and personal animosity of years. Duff Cooper was vitriolic, but his oratory is certainly impressive.

Arthur, Kingsley Wood, George Steward and Alec Dunglass all seemed to think the P.M. would have to resign unless he could get a majority of a hundred votes; so much depends on whether the Conservative waverers can be induced by Amery, Duff Cooper, Spears,* Gunston,[1] Lady Astor, etc., to summon up the courage to go into the Opposition lobby to vote. Personally I feel that if the P.M. is firm he can win through: the pendulum is bound to swing back the other way, and all depends on how much his tough but sensitive personality is wounded by this terrific onslaught and manifest detestation of his enemies.

Horace said that what caused him the greatest anxiety was the encouragement this debate, with all its indiscretions, would give to the enemy and the opportunity they would have for launching a great attack (as is hourly possible in Holland) now that the whole vigour of the country is bent towards internal political strife.

A hurried dinner at Luigi's with Middy[2] (whose backbench friends think that the majority of Conservative waverers wish to give the Government a severe shock but not to overthrow it), Terence[3] and Jean Meade.

I went back to the House to hear Winston, but unfortunately the gallery was full and, despite Rab Butler's effort to smuggle me into a forbidden place, I failed to hear the speech. The Government got a majority of 81 – they had hoped for 100 – and were fairly satisfied. It had been a hard day, with the whole weight of opinion against the Government, and they will now be both obliged to reconstruct the Cabinet and to prosecute the

---

[1] Long-serving Conservative M.P. who had been Parliamentary Private Secretary before the war to Neville Chamberlain and to Sir Kingsley Wood.

[2] Mary Gascoigne, formerly O'Neill.

[3] My first cousin, Terence O'Neill, later Lord O'Neill of the Maine.

war with greater vigour; so perhaps the shock they have received may be a healthy one. Slept at No. 10.

Thursday, May 9th

At 2 a.m. Mr Kennedy, the American Ambassador, rang me up to say that President Roosevelt had just telephoned to say that Germany had presented an ultimatum to Holland the previous afternoon. I rang up Sir E. Bridges, the F.O., etc., and caused a great deal of excitement but the report, as is so often the case in those from America, proved to be quite unfounded.

The Cabinet met at the House, which assembled in the morning. The air was full of rumours of impending resignation, etc., and in fact the P.M. spent the whole day discussing the future with Halifax, Winston, etc., and the Leaders of the Opposition. But I have not managed to glean much yet, except that the formation of a Coalition is not out of the question. But will Labour serve under the P.M.? The fundamental difficulty is that no alternative Prime Minister seems to be available, though it is possible that Mr C. might serve as Minister without Portfolio and right-hand man in a Government headed by Winston or Halifax. It is clear that if the freedom of the press is to be curbed, as is temporarily most desirable, and conscription of labour to be introduced, as may in the long run be inevitable, only a truly national Government could perform the task.

Dined with Mrs Henley[1] and went on afterwards to dance at the Savoy. Sat between Mrs H. and Mary Churchill (Winston's youngest progeny) and the others at dinner were Juliet Henley, Juliet Peel, Judy Montagu,[2] Mark Howard,[3] Julian Berry[4] and

[1] Daughter of the 4th Lord Stanley of Alderley, sister of Venetia Montagu and cousin of Clementine Churchill. A member of the Asquithian Liberal set. One daughter, Juliet, was a Principal in the Treasury during the war; another, Rosalind Pitt-Rivers, a brilliant scientist, was one of the first women to be a Fellow of the Royal Society.

[2] Daughter of Venetia Montagu.

[3] Eldest son of Hon. Geoffrey Howard of Castle Howard, former Liberal M.P. Killed in action in 1944 as was his youngest brother, Christopher. The second son, George, became Chairman of the B.B.C. and died in 1984.

[4] Youngest son of the 1st Viscount Camrose. Later Lieutenant Colonel commanding the Royal Horse Guards.

two Grenadiers whose names I missed. I thought the Churchill girl rather supercilious: she has Sarah's emphatic way of talking, and is better looking, but she seemed to me to have a much less sympathetic personality.[1] The Savoy was stuffy and I felt jaded, devitalised and utterly uninteresting.

Friday, May 10th
Rode at Richmond in summer heat. As I dismounted the groom told me that Holland and Belgium had been invaded.

At No. 10 the fog of war was too thick for me to gather very much of what was happening, but the Cabinet had met at 8.00 and things are obviously moving fast. The Government crisis will have to be postponed. Last night Attlee and Greenwood made it clear that they thought it unlikely their executive would agree to their serving under the P.M. In that case the P.M. may have to go to the Treasury and a Coalition be formed under Winston. The 1922 Committee have shown great animosity against Horace Wilson and he will probably have to retire upstairs in any case.

This morning Archie Sinclair apologised to the P.M. for any insolence or rudeness he had shown him; presumably he wants office.

Halifax is said to have declined to form a Government; so if the P.M. does go I am afraid it *must* be Winston. But the Belgian move has slowed matters up for the time being as the present moment would be a bad one for a change in departments.

Rab Butler tells me that the Secret Service told him yesterday that there was no chance of an invasion of the Netherlands: it was a feint. An attack on Hungary, on the other hand, was imminent. So much for our renowned foreign agents.

Since the above was written I have discovered that last night the P.M. told Winston and Halifax he would gladly serve under either of them. Halifax categorically refused to lead a Government; Winston licked his lips. This afternoon we all, Arthur,

---

[1] Mary Churchill, to whom I soon became and remain devoted, was not, at that particular time, feeling well disposed to Mr Chamberlain's Private Secretary and was also, quite understandably, much keener on her other neighbour at dinner, the attractive and intelligent Mark Howard.

Alec, David and the whole gang of hangers-on, sat discussing the future form of the Government and weighing the unlikely chance of the King, who (remembering perhaps the Abdication) is understood not to wish to send for Winston, being able to persuade Halifax to recant his determination not to be P.M. We awaited the decision of the Labour Party, who, it was feared, might refuse to serve in any Government of which the P.M. was even a member. At about 4.45 Attlee rang up to say that they would agree to join a Government provided Neville Chamberlain was not P.M.; so now David's idea is that he should lead the House, as Lord President, like Bonar Law in the last war, while Winston is the new Lloyd George. Provided the P.M. and Halifax remain in the War Cabinet there will at least be some restraint on our new War Lord. He may, of course, be the man of drive and energy the country believes him to be and he may be able to speed up our creaking military and industrial machinery; but it is a terrible risk, it involves the danger of rash and spectacular exploits, and I cannot help fearing that this country may be manoeuvred into the most dangerous position it has ever been in. One thing, however, is certain: if Winston thought the P.M. were trying to hold on to the reins of power he would create such mischief in the House of Commons that a really serious crisis would arise. Nothing can stop him having his way – because of his powers of blackmail – unless the King makes full use of his prerogative and sends for another man; unfortunately there is only one other, the unpersuadable Halifax.

Everybody here is in despair at the prospect. Personally I shall be sorry too, because I feel a greater loyalty towards the P.M. than I had supposed. And I shudder to think of Brendan Bracken* sitting in this room instead of the charming, inoffensive and extremely sensible Alec.

7.05 p.m.: The P.M. has come back from the Palace. Ministers not in the Cabinet have been sent for and told they will have to resign. The King has sent for Winston (fortunately, because Halifax, true to form, had gone off to the dentist!).

7.15.: Alec and I went over to the F.O. to explain the position to Rab, and there, with Chips, we drank in champagne the health of the "King over the Water" (not King Leopold, but Mr

Chamberlain). Rab said he thought that the good clean tradition of English politics, that of Pitt as opposed to Fox, had been sold to the greatest adventurer of modern political history. He had tried earnestly and long to persuade Halifax to accept the Premiership, but he had failed. He believed this sudden coup of Winston and his rabble was a serious disaster and an unnecessary one: the "pass had been sold" by Mr C., Lord Halifax and Oliver Stanley. They had weakly surrendered to a half-breed American whose main support was that of inefficient but talkative people of a similar type, American dissidents like Lady Astor and Ronnie Tree.*

I went home to a solitary dinner and read *War and Peace*. At 9.00 I listened to the late P.M.'s broadcast which was well worded, although he is least effective when he raises his voice and tries to indulge in rhetoric.

On many subsequent occasions I heard Winston give an account of his talk with Mr Chamberlain and Lord Halifax, of which indeed he gives an account in his own history of the Second World War. He always believed, I think, that Mr Chamberlain would have liked Lord Halifax to be Prime Minister. Indeed, from the extracts already quoted from this diary it is clear that all at No. 10 Downing Street and many others, such as R.A. Butler, trusted that some miracle could achieve this. The King, although he gave Winston all the support in his power once the choice was made, certainly disliked the change and would have preferred Lord Halifax; and the feeling in Conservative, or at any rate old-fashioned, circles, was represented by a letter which Queen Mary wrote to my mother saying how much she hoped I would remain with Mr Chamberlain and not go on with the new Prime Minister.

At any rate Winston told me several times that when Chamberlain had summoned Lord Halifax and himself to the Cabinet Room he looked at him sharply and said, "Can you see any reason, Winston, why in these days a Peer should not be Prime Minister?" Winston saw a trap in this question. It would be difficult to say yes without saying frankly that he thought he himself should be the choice. If he said no, or hedged, he felt sure that Mr Chamberlain would turn to Lord Halifax and say, "Well, since Winston agrees I am sure that if the King asks me I should suggest his sending for you." Therefore Winston turned his back and gazed out on the Horse Guards Parade without giving any reply. There was an awkward pause, after which Halifax himself volunteered the suggestion that if the King were to ask Mr Chamberlain's opinion about his successor, he should propose Mr Churchill.

Saturday, May 11th
Rode early at Richmond. The balloons are all up again and London is looking as it did last September.

At No. 10 there is a prevailing air of uncertainty. Who will go and who will stay? "We are hanging," said Arthur, "suspended between Heaven and Hell." At about 10.30 N.C. received a letter from the new P.M. offering him the Lord Presidency of the Council, which he has accepted. It was pointed out that as Chancellor of the Exchequer, a post for which he is admirably equipped, he would have to bear the full brunt of socialist criticism on Treasury questions and the factor of personal animosity would assuredly be dragged in.

Lunched at the Travellers and talked to John Dashwood[1] and Nigel Ronald.[2] The latter, who represents one very definite section of opinion in the F.O., told me he thought Rab Butler a public danger, flabby in person and morally and mentally as well; a young man whose whole influence was that of an old one, whose inclination was to put a break on all initiative. He knew Kingsley Wood to be dangerous too: he had always advised the P.M. wrongly about the state of public opinion in the country, because he represented a small nonconformist world. At No. 10 both Rab and Kingsley are considered supermen, and so it is always refreshing to hear the other side of the case.

[1] Owner of West Wycombe Park in Buckinghamshire and formerly a member of the Diplomatic Service. Married to an agreeable Canadian, Helen Eaton, who was a generous but discriminating hostess.

[2] Foreign Office Wykehamist, all but mortally wounded in the First World War. Close to infallible in all matters relating to art, literature and gardening. I served on his staff when he was Ambassador to Portugal after the war. The only Ambassador Dr Salazar saw regularly.

I cannot bear this indecision and idleness any longer and so have proposed myself to Hinchingbrooke for the night.

Sunday, May 12th, Whitsunday
Back in London I looked in at No. 10 and found Arthur looking very depressed. He is to go with Mr Chamberlain. Tony and I are to remain with Seal and Peck[1] from the Admiralty; Horace has been told bluntly that his services at No. 10 are no longer required; and Miss Watson is to be relegated to a back room to deal with "the post".

*   *   *

At this point in history one of the greatest administrations which has ever governed the United Kingdom was in the process of formation. It is therefore appropriate to attempt a character sketch of the man who led it, not in the light of what I knew or felt on May 12th, 1940, but of what I learned by personal experience in the subsequent twenty-five years. It is a formidable task because few public figures in all history have assumed so many mantles, displayed such an unlikely mixture of talents, experienced over so wide a span of years such a variety of triumphs and disasters, and been successively so suspected and so trusted, so disliked and so admired by his fellow countrymen.

I hope that in the pages of this diary some aspects of his character will by degrees unfold themselves. For the moment I will merely list those which, in retrospect, seem most striking to me. In his judgment, no less than in his activities, he was entirely unpredictable. A Private Secretary who works intimately with his master over a long period can usually say with little risk of error what the reaction to a given proposition is likely to be. With Winston this was impossible, as even his wife found and admitted. I was often asked what the Prime Minister would feel about something and there were occasions on which I thought I knew the answer for a certainty. Sometimes I was right, but just as often I was wrong. There were none of his

[1] See p. 149.

associates who would have claimed to do better. This was due to some strange intuitive power which he held and which might induce him to take a line contrary, as it appeared, to logic and contrary to the normal mental workings of everybody else.

Perhaps examples of this will appear in these pages and it is certainly true that his unaccountable attitude to apparently reasonable proposals was a frequent source of irritation as well as of astonishment to his Cabinet colleagues and to the Chiefs of Staff.

He always retained unswerving independence of thought. He approached a problem as he himself saw it and of all the men I have ever known he was the least liable to be swayed by the views of even his most intimate counsellors. Many people made the mistake of thinking that somebody – it might be General Ismay or Professor Lindemann – for whom the Prime Minister had the utmost respect and affection, would be able to "get something through". Unless the Prime Minister was himself impressed by the argument, pressure by others seldom had any effect. If a subject bored him he would pass it, however important, to somebody else for a decision and would scarcely pause to consider the grounds on which that decision had been reached. But once his personal attention was engaged he had to be convinced that his initial reaction was wrong before he would agree to change his line. He was open to persuasion, although it often needed courage to press the point, but he was never persuaded by the fact that those who argued a certain course were people whom he liked and respected. There were indeed a number of occasions when he showed a quite inexplicable facility for reaching the right decision on faulty logic and against all the best advice.

He had an unusual capacity for affection and an intense loyalty to those whom he had known long or who had served him well. Sometimes this loyalty went too far, as in the case of Sir Roger Keyes, and sometimes his affection for his children and his friends led him to take actions which gave rise to mutterings of nepotism. He had great compassion which he combined with personal generosity and his sympathy for those in misfortune was particularly marked in the case of humble people whose unhappiness was somehow drawn to his attention. Although he had a few enduring dislikes, his magnanimity was a far more remarkable characteristic and he hated vindictiveness above all things. When the bloodhounds were on the scent of Robert Boothby about charges relating to some Czech gold, he said to me that he could not endure "a man hunt".

His anger was like lightning and sometimes terrifying to see, but it lasted a short time. He could be violently offensive to those who worked for him and although he would never say he was sorry, he would equally never let the sun go down without in some way making amends or showing that he had not meant to be unkind. His sarcasm could be biting, but it was often accompanied by an engaging smile which seemed to say that no harm was really intended. He had a great liking for young people, of either sex, and he treated his Secretariat as if they were his children.

He was not easy to work for, particularly during the anxious days of the war. Patience is a virtue with which he was totally unfamiliar. As soon as he had ordered something to be done he expected that it had been completed. Many was the time when he told me to do something and before I had had time to get back to my telephone he had rung the bell to enquire the result. He would ask for a draft, either from his Private Office or from one of the departments, and would expect it to be ready long before it was humanly possible. His own rapidity of thought and expression was partly responsible for this, together with the fact that having been in a position to give orders all his life, and seldom obliged to execute them, he had no conception of the practical difficulties of communication and of administrative arrangements.

He also possessed, to an unusual degree, the ability to assimilate quickly the main points in a complicated story. He would read a long Cabinet Paper and pick out one or two aspects of the case, frequently those which did not seem the most important. He would pursue them with the utmost vigour. It was strange how often they turned out in the end to be the principal points at issue.

Lovable though he was, and indeed an object of affection to

everybody who came in close contact with him, he was at the same time curiously inconsiderate. In the war years, when feeding was difficult, he thought nothing of keeping the Cabinet in their seats until, for them, all hope of getting any food had passed, because he himself had only to walk upstairs to lunch or dinner. Equally, it never occurred to him to suppose that anybody might be tired or over-worked. He thought nothing of sending for one in the temporary sanctuary of one's bath about some trivial point which could well have waited until one was dressed. During meals at Chequers I used often to be sent to the telephone half a dozen times and even when I knew him well enough to suggest that a call might wait until after dinner, or that indeed the answer was already available, no excuse was accepted. Yet what would have been resented from any other man was accepted with almost complete equanimity from him; and this went not merely for his Private Secretaries, but also for the typists who might be kept up until three or four in the morning even when there was no work to do, and for the servants who might have to wait till after midnight before they could clear the dining-room table.

He often made impetuous remarks, both about people and events, and I have doubtless recorded some of these without realising, till I knew him much better, that a statement made with fiery vehemence, which few would dare contradict on the spot, was often modified on reflection. His reputation was for impetuosity, but that was, at least by the time he became Prime Minister, partly due to the forcefulness with which he expressed himself. He usually thought deeply about the matter afterwards and seldom acted without careful consideration. This applied, most strikingly, to his relationship with General de Gaulle.

He digested the more important of his decisions slowly. Sometimes it took him weeks of cogitation before he reached an answer which satisfied him. He would talk half aloud, half under his breath, about some matter which was occupying his mind. He might address apparently inconsequential remarks to his family or his staff, or even to the yellow cat, while under his breath you could hear him preparing some Minute to the Chiefs of Staff Committee or speech to the House of Commons. He would repeat again and again some phrase or quotation which would appear, most appositely, in a speech a few weeks later.

His interests were predominantly defence, foreign affairs and party politics. He cared less for domestic problems or the home front except when he was aroused for sentimental reasons, but he would wax furious, and send fiery minutes to his Ministers, over some apparent miscarriage of justice reported in the newspapers.

To matters of defence he gave the deepest thought, based on years of study and experience, and nothing influenced him more in a man's favour than an act of gallantry on the field of battle. It was at least partly to this that Lord De L'Isle, V.C., owed the Secretaryship of State for Air in 1951 and that Lord Louis Mountbatten* owed his promotion to be Director of Combined Operations in 1941, though he subsequently lost favour because Churchill doubted his judgment and disliked his overt support of the Labour Party.

As far as foreign affairs went, he was more interested in events than in trends and he was in the main oblivious to the growth of nationalism as a force in British imperial affairs. For him India, Egypt and Africa were and should remain as they had been at the time of Omdurman. He mistrusted the Foreign Office whose members he regarded as defeatist and prone to socialism. It was, however, a source of regret to him that he had held every great office except that of Foreign Secretary and during Anthony Eden's absences he usually contrived to be the acting Secretary of State, much to the chagrin of Eden who would have preferred a more compliant *locum tenens*. There were even occasions on which he said to me that he would take over the Foreign Office and run it from 10 Downing Street. No word of this ever reached the corridors across the way, but I think that he seriously considered it.

Finally, in politics and indeed all his life, he was as strange a mixture of radical and traditionalist as could anywhere be found. He was certainly not conservative by temperament, nor indeed by conviction a supporter of the Conservative Party. On the other hand he was, as Lady Churchill once said to me, the only surviving believer in the divine right of Kings and his respect for the monarchy amounted almost to idolatry. He disliked the abolition of anything which had colour or tradition behind it. As regards religion he was an agnostic who, as the years went by, and I think more particularly as a result of the Battle of Britain, slowly began to conceive that there was some overriding power which had a conscious influence on our destinies. He seldom went to church and, curiously enough, only enjoyed christenings; but he unquestionably developed in his later years a conviction that this life was not the end. Once, driving back from Aldermaston, where he had been awed by the apocalyptic forecast of nuclear devastation, he told me that he thought he would soon die. He went on to say he could not help wondering whether the government above might not be a constitutional monarchy, in which case there was always a possibility that the Almighty might have occasion to "send for him".

*   *   *

Monday, May 13th
Winston is still in his lair at the Admiralty, but will begin to work at No. 10 this afternoon. He looks like keeping a double establishment until the Chamberlains move out of No. 11 as they will do in about a month's time. Neville Chamberlain sent for me to say goodbye and told me he would watch my career with interest.

Winston Churchill brought with him from the Admiralty his principal private secretary, Eric Seal, and also John Peck. Seal, who was a man of intelligence and integrity, was not fully on Churchill's "wavelength", though he understood him well. He remained at No. 10 for a little less than a year before leaving to take up an important defence assignment in the U.S.A.

John Peck, brilliant, a master of light verse and parody and invariably a pleasant companion, was at No. 10 until the end of the Coalition Government in 1945 and stayed on for a time with Mr Attlee before transferring to the Foreign Service. He was Ambassador in Dublin when a mob burned his embassy to the ground.

Went down to the House with Seal to hear the new P.M. ask for a vote of confidence in his Government. He made a brilliant little speech. Maxton[1] denounced the Coalition with wit and vehemence: he is a great idealist and not ashamed of being so. He sees no way of putting his ideals into practice at present and is not ashamed of admitting the fact. Lloyd George also spoke and was afterwards invited into the P.M.'s room and offered the Ministry of Agriculture (for which the cheap press has always tipped him). He refused it because he thinks the country is in a hopeless position and he is generally despondent.

I spent the day in a bright blue new suit from the Fifty-Shilling Tailors, cheap and sensational looking, which I felt was appropriate to the new Government. But of course it must be admitted that Winston's administration, with all its faults, has drive; and men like Duff Cooper, Eden, Lord Lloyd* and Herbert Morrison should be able to get things done. Moreover the Government has the complete confidence of the country.

Seal and Peck arrived at No. 10. From what they tell me of the First Lord's ways I am going to be much harder worked than of late.

Another crisis is brewing in the Mediterranean, and it begins to look as if Italy really may come in against us. Winston apparently thinks so, but I feel sure that much will depend on events in the Low Countries.

Tuesday, May 14th
Rode at 7.30 in glorious weather.

There is still a certain air of "malaise" about No. 10, which is largely due to the contrast between the fixity of the late P.M.'s habits and the inconsequential nature of Winston's. I suppose we shall get used to it; but the prospect of constant late nights – 2.00 a.m. or later – is depressing.

Went with Mother, David and Joan to see Philip off to the front. He looked very happy and extremely well, and I feel sure

---

[1] James Maxton. Eloquent Leader of the Independent Labour Party. M.P. for the Bridgeton district of Glasgow. His honesty, sense of humour and independence of judgment won the admiration of his opponents and of few more than Winston Churchill.

he will be an admirable soldier. Father could not face the scene at Waterloo and did not come.

Some of Winston's correspondence today was entertaining. The Duke of Windsor wrote to congratulate him and spoke of his "great measure of practical and sympathetic support in the past"; Randolph Churchill* spoke of the caucus which had kept him out of office for nine years and hoped it was not now too late; Oliver Stanley refused an offer of the Dominions' Office in view of the contemptuous way it had been offered and referred to Winston's blunt accusation that he lacked drive – why then had he been offered the post?

In the evening the military news was disturbing. Holland is to all intents and purposes lost, the French are being pressed on the Meuse, the Germans look like breaking through at Sedan, and we are besought to send more fighter squadrons to France if the enemy advance is to be checked. The French speak ominously of the lack of defences between Sedan and Paris.

The ROYAL MARINE Operation has now been put into force and mines have been placed in the Rhine and Moselle; but the Cabinet have decided not to bomb the Ruhr yet, until the position is clearer, because it may be necessary to conserve our long-range bombers for use in the land battle or against Italy if, as becomes increasingly likely, she comes in.

After dinner I went to Admiralty House, where Winston proposes to work at night. He has fitted up the ground floor for this purpose: the dining-room in which the private secretary and one of Winston's specially trained night-women-typists sit; the lovely drawing-room with its curious ugly dolphin furniture, which is used as a kind of promenade; and an inner room in which the Great Man himself sits. At the side of his desk stands a table laden with bottles of whisky, etc. On the desk itself are all manner of things: toothpicks, gold medals (which he uses as paper-weights), special cuffs to save his coatsleeves from becoming dirty, and innumerable pills and powders.

Peck and I arrived at about 9.15 and waited till 10.30 before anything happened. In the meanwhile I read some of W.'s correspondence which we had ready for him. There was a letter from the King, two or three days old, urging that Lord

Beaverbrook* should *not* be made Minister of Aircraft Production in view of the effect likely to be produced in Canada. Also a large number of letters suggesting various appointments. A note by Brendan Bracken* referred to a number of "our friends" disliked by "the parachutist", by whom he meant David Margesson (who, owing to the reconstruction, has landed in the enemy camp, I suppose).

At about 10.30 Winston came down, and then by degrees a motley gathering appeared. David Margesson, Sinclair, Eden, Beaverbrook, the American Ambassador (who told me the most disquieting evidence of Italy's intention to enter the war) and Pug Ismay. Strange bedfellows indeed! They walked about talking to each other while Winston popped in and out first through one door and then through the next, appointing Under Secretaries with David, talking about the German thrust at Sedan with Eden and listening to the alarmist and, I think, untrustworthy opinions of Mr Kennedy. Eventually Tony Bevir came in to relieve me, Peck having gone home early, and I walked home through the warm night at about 1 a.m.

Wednesday, May 15th

A day of great trivial activity for me: incessant appointments, telephone calls, etc. Most of the afternoon was spent offering Under Secretaryships to various politicians and it was my difficult job to explain on the telephone to Kenneth Lindsay, the Duke of Devonshire, Lord Denham and Captain McEwen that their services were no longer required.

Pug Ismay is not too happy about the military situation. He says the French are not fighting properly: they are, he points out, a volatile race and it may take them some time to get into a warlike mood. Pray Heaven not too long!

Dined at Bucks with Pat Hancock[1] who has just returned from H.M. Legation at The Hague, where he was in constant danger from snipers, parachutists and bombs. We had a most

---

[1] A contemporary at Trinity who passed the Diplomatic Service examination in the same year as I did. A first-class brain coupled with an engaging touch of eccentricity. Afterwards Ambassador in Oslo, Tel Aviv and Rome.

agreeable dinner (which did not begin till 9.00 as Winston was busy drafting a message, which was intended to be both strong and conciliatory, to the Duce) and both the food and drink were delicious. But I noticed a curiously worn and strained look about Pat which was no doubt partly due to physical weariness and partly to having had the meaning of war really brought home to him, an experience which is still in store for us.

Thursday, May 16th
Apparently the French are still not putting their best leg forward and a serious German incursion into French territory has taken place in the direction of Laon [north-west of Rheims]. I have always been a little afraid of the unbounded confidence placed in the quality of the French army, but now that the soil of France has been invaded they may show their traditional toughness. However for the moment things are serious, the air situation is bad (we have lost too many machines, although we have inflicted far more serious losses on the Germans), and our troops in Belgium may have to fall back in order to maintain a line with the French.

During the afternoon the operational news became increasingly alarming and it was evident that the German breakthrough was jeopardising not only Paris but the whole French army. Winston was away and so we could sit in the garden at No. 10 and enjoy the sun; but none of us felt like enjoying anything. Gossiped with the Chief Whip.

The Cabinet met at 11.00 p.m. to discuss a terrifying telegram Winston had sent from Paris and to decide whether seriously to weaken our defences by sending out fighters from this country. I will not describe the situation: it will be in every history book of the future; but evidently there has been lamentable staff work on the French side and Paris has been left undefended by reserves. We had hoped that only armoured divisions had penetrated the French defences, but it now seems that infantry divisions are pouring through the gap on a fifty-kilometre front.

Winston's telegram was decyphered in driblets and I rushed it into the Cabinet by instalments. W. wants us to mass all our air strength to stop the advance in order to save the collapsing

French morale. He speaks of "the mortal gravity of the hour" – which made Arthur Rucker say "He is still thinking of his books" and Seal talk of his "blasted rhetoric". Everybody is on edge, except the soldiers.

W. wants a reply from the Cabinet by midnight and Cornwall-Jones, of the Cabinet Offices, is to give it to Ismay, who is with Churchill, in Hindustani.[1]

The Cabinet's decision was to send the ten fighter squadrons for which the French asked. That means denuding this country of a quarter of its first-line fighter defence. The reply was telephoned by Cornwall-Jones and I could not help laughing when he referred to "Lord President Sahib" and "C. A. S. Sahib". But it is dangerous, this Hindustani trick. It has been done too often now and I suspect the Germans know what language we use. Slept at No. 10.

Friday, May 17th

Rose at 6.00 to go down to Hendon to meet the P.M. on his return from France. He looked quite cheerful, having slept and breakfasted well at the Embassy. However Dill, Ismay and the rest of the unfortunate staff had had a miserable time. Winston had told them to be ready by 5.45, and it then transpired that he did not wish to leave until 7.00 and he had gone on sleeping while they wandered about aimlessly and could get no breakfast. He is very inconsiderate with his staff.

I drove back from Hendon with Ismay and two other officers, who were all heavy with sleep and had eaten nothing but a rusk. Ismay was very pessimistic and said the French were not merely retreating but were routed. Their nerves were shattered by this armoured warfare and by the German air superiority, and the French Government were upended by this sudden shattering of their faith in the invincible French army. Another General in the car – his Christian name was Otto, but that was all I could discover – was more optimistic. He thought that if we and the

---

[1] In the First World War Lloyd George and Tom Jones used a similar deceptive device, but spoke in Welsh, which must have puzzled the Germans even more than Hindustani.

French could concentrate our air strength on the battle front so that the French can, as Winston puts it, fight "under a clean sky", the French troops might sit down, have a cigarette and turn round and fight. If they do, there is a good chance the present dark prospect may brighten into a major success.

The P.M. and Mrs Churchill lunched at the Japanese Embassy and I was asked too. It is a charming house in Grosvenor Square with attractive Japanese furniture and decoration. Corbin, Rob Hudson, Grigg[1] and Geoffrey Shakespeare were there. I sat next to the inscrutable First Secretary, who was polite but not sufficiently oriental to be attractive, and after lunch I talked to Geoffrey Shakespeare (the new Under-Secretary for the Dominions) who is longing for Italy to declare war on us.

Heard from the War Office that Brian O'Neill was among the soldiers killed on the troopship *Chobry* which was sunk off the Norwegian coast yesterday. This is the first casualty of this horrible war that has really brought the full meaning of it home to me. He had great charm and was, I believe, a most efficient soldier. He also had considerable brain-power of which he might one day have been able to make real use.

Winston is depressed. He says the French are crumpling up as completely as did the Poles (I hope and believe this to be an exaggeration) and that our forces in Belgium will inevitably have to withdraw in order to maintain contact with the French. There is, of course, a risk that the B.E.F. may be cut off if the French do not rally in time.

Saturday, May 18th
The position is still critical, and Admiral Phillips,[2] the best brain in the navy, observes to the P.M. that the Cabinet have now got to take a fundamental decision. They can either send most of the fighters from this country in the hope of turning the scale on the Western Front, in which case the war might be appreciably shortened; or they can maintain them here for

[1] Sir Edward Grigg, Parliamentary Secretary at the Ministry of Information.
[2] Vice Chief of the Naval Staff. Small in stature, but outstandingly clever and disarmingly simple in his tastes. Drowned in the *Prince of Wales* when she and the *Repulse* were sunk off the coast of Malaya in December 1941.

defensive purposes, on the assumption that even if France's resistance is overcome we shall still carry on the war from here. If we send the fighters and lose them, then this country will be left at the mercy of concentrated German air attack and can hardly avoid destruction. It would be a terrifying gamble, but I am afraid it is one we ought to take.

Back to work by 3.30 and, after dining at home, went to Admiralty House. Winston was in excellent humour. He first of all dragooned the Chiefs of Staff and Ismay in the War Room upstairs, and then came downstairs, turned me out of my room and started dictating. So I repaired to his room and discussed with Brendan Bracken and Professor Lindemann* why, if we had a large number of unused aircraft in this country, we could not increase the quantity of our fighter squadrons. Apparently the wastage, especially in training, is something appalling. Bracken is a cad, "slick" and amusing, and quite likeable in his way; but rather too talkative and apt to make the most ridiculous pronouncements. Lindemann is supremely unattractive but has an air of competence and efficiency.[1]

Winston, who is full of fight and thrives on crisis and adversity, dictated a few brief notes, containing questions on strategical points for the people concerned to answer, and then wrote a letter to General Georges[2] about the situation in France. Referring to the rapid advance of the German army he said, "The tortoise is thrusting his head very far beyond his carapace." In reality I think we are the tortoise, and Germany the hare. The tortoise will win in the end, but the hare is "making the going". I hope – but perhaps it is wishful thinking – that the present position is comparable to March 1918, with the Germans carrying all before them but with November 11th not very far ahead.

A. V. Alexander,* the new First Lord, came in and W. showed him the sharp and uncompromising reply Mussolini today sent to his firm but very polite telegram on becoming P.M. Alexander thought that as Italy's participation in the war was now virtually

[1] I soon became great friends with them both and admired their respective abilities. Professor Lindemann was created Lord Cherwell in 1941.

[2] In command of all the armies in north-east France, from the Channel to the Swiss frontier, 1939–40.

certain (which I do not believe) we should seize the initiative and occupy Crete. Winston answered that our hands were too full elsewhere to enable us to embark on adventures: such is the change that high office can work in a man's inherent love of rash and spectacular action.

Sunday, May 19th

Heavenly weather again. It has been cloudless for at least three weeks now and we can none of us really profit by it.

At No. 10 by 9.45 where I met and talked with Amery, the new Secretary of State for India. After the Cabinet I went to Admiralty House and found Mrs Churchill who said that the preacher at St Martin-in-the-Fields had preached such a pacifist sermon that morning that she got up and left. "You ought to have cried 'Shame'," said Winston, "desecrating the House of God with lies!" Then he came back and said to me, "Tell the Minister of Information with a view to having the man pilloried." It is refreshing to work with somebody who refuses to be depressed even by the most formidable danger that has ever threatened this country.

After lunch came the astounding and, if true, nerve-racking news that the French army south of the B.E.F. has melted away and left a vast gap on the British right. Winston was summoned back from Chartwell, where he had gone for a few hours' sunshine and to write his broadcast speech for tonight. At the moment Lord Gort's choice seems to be to retire to the sea, forming a bridgehead round Dunkirk or to fight his way south-eastwards, leaving the Belgians to their fate, in order to rejoin the French. Lord Gort has asked for a Cabinet decision on the action he is to take.

Our fortunes are at a low ebb, but I am still confident we shall win in the end and perhaps a shock to our self-esteem and feeling of security is not unwholesome. In any case, whatever Winston's shortcomings, he seems to be the man for the occasion. His spirit is indomitable and even if France and England should be lost, I feel he would carry on the crusade himself with a band of privateers. Perhaps my judgments of him have been harsh, but the situation was very different a few weeks ago.

The Cabinet met at 4.30 and decided that the B.E.F. must fight its way southwards towards Amiens to make contact with the French. Winston decided to fly to G.H.Q. to see Gort and to visit the front line, and I was to have gone with him. To my bitter disappointment the project was abandoned just as I had reached home to pick up some clothes. I stayed to have tea with Mother, Father and Peggy Crewe. The latter was delighted to hear that Weygand,* whom she knows well and respects greatly, is to succeed Gamelin.

The P.M. started writing his speech at 6.00 to broadcast at 9.00. I heard it from home, where I dined. It was good and it brought out the full seriousness of the hour, but it was not Winston at his best, nor quite the clarion-call I had expected.

At Admiralty House there was the usual "evening party", the Chiefs of Staff, Beaverbrook, Eden, etc. The P.M. sent a telegram to Roosevelt asking for fighter aircraft and implying that without them we should be in a parlous state, even though this country would never give up the struggle. Considering the soothing words he always uses to America, and in particular to the President, I was somewhat taken aback when he said to me, "Here's a telegram for those bloody Yankees. Send it off tonight." I duly sent it to Herschel Johnson at the American Embassy and was somewhat annoyed to be woken up at 2.30 a.m. and told that the P.M. wanted it back to review what he had said – particularly as he made no alteration after all. In telegraphing to the President he always calls himself "A former Naval Person".

Winston also dictated a telegram to Reynaud, expressing his distress at the plight of the French army and insinuating that we had been rather let down. I gather the French Government are in a deplorable state of pessimism and depression.

Monday, May 20th
Every morning now at No. 10 there is a time of feverish activity when the P.M.'s box returns. It contains all the work he has done overnight, in fact everything that it has not been possible to thrust under his nose during the previous days – telegrams, letters, Cabinet papers, C.O.S. reports, etc. Many of them

come back untouched and have to be placed in the next night's box; others have illegible instructions scrawled on them in red ink and have to be dealt with immediately.

The B.E.F.'s march to the Arras–Amiens Line begins today. I said to Seal: "It looks like the retreat from Mons beginning all over again. It is awful the way history repeats itself." He replied: "I wish history would repeat itself, but I am afraid it is not going to. There seems to be no proper liaison or co-operation between the French, British and Belgian Staffs and the whole thing is dropping to pieces through sheer ineptitude." We need another Charles Martel,[1] but let us hope the decisive battle will be fought and won before the invaders reach Poitiers.

David[2] came to dinner. He is proposing to join the R.N.V.R.

Tuesday, May 21st
The situation in France is extraordinary. Owing to the rapid advance of armoured troops, the Germans are in many places behind the Allied lines. Enemy columns have reached Amiens and are thought to be on the way to Abbeville; it is clear that the main thrust is north-westwards towards the Channel ports.

To the House with the P.M. for Questions. He intends to take them once a week.

News that German tanks are approaching Boulogne. Listened in, rather unscrupulously but with the approval of Tony and Peck, to a green-line telephone conversation between the P.M. and C.I.G.S. They expect to be able to hold Boulogne, but it is a shock that the Germans should have penetrated so far and obviously the B.E.F.'s communications are in danger. The German advance is now really dangerous, and it is staggering that France should have so far put up less resistance to invasion than did Poland, Norway or Holland. Preparations are being made for the evacuation of the B.E.F. in case of necessity.

Dined at Betty Montagu's flat with her and Zara Mainwaring. We cooked our own dinner consisting of an omelette (which

---

[1] King of the Franks who stemmed the tide of the Moorish invasion of Europe by his great victory at Poitiers in A.D. 732.
[2] David Colville, my eldest brother.*

I made), peas, asparagus and stewed raspberries, and tried unsuccessfully not to talk about the war. From what Betts and Zara said it is clear that the full horror of the situation is dawning on people, and perhaps they think it even worse than it is. But I think Betts was typical of the whole country when she said, "We shall not be beaten; even if Paris and London fall we shall win."

At Admiralty House there was chaos owing to the lack of information being received, because communications have broken down. I have not seen Winston so depressed, and while I stood by him, trying to get M. Reynaud on the telephone, he said: "In all the history of war, I have never seen such mismanagement." Against the advice of the Chiefs of Staff and all present, he decided to go to Paris early tomorrow morning to see Weygand* and Reynaud and to impress upon them that it is no use concentrating on the destruction of German motorised columns which have penetrated far into France, but that we must withstand the main German advance and ourselves attack. Sir C. Newall,[1] the Chief of Air Staff, told me he thought the B.E.F. was in grave danger; but at least they seem to be fighting well, unlike their French allies.

At about 1.30 a.m., just after the P.M. had gone upstairs, the Air Ministry rang up to say that General Billotte,[2] whose weakness and vacillation are thought to have contributed to much of our discomfiture, had been seriously injured in a motor smash. They thought the P.M. would be relieved. I found him in his bedroom, a comic sight clad in nothing but a vest. All he said was "Poor man, poor man" – but without much sign of grief in his tones!

Wednesday, May 22nd
Pouring rain for the first time for months. A quiet day owing to the P.M.'s absence in Paris.

About 7.00 p.m. the party returned. Pug Ismay said that at

[1] Later succeeded by Sir Charles Portal. Given a peerage and appointed Governor General of New Zealand.
[2] Commanded the first French group of armies. Lord Gort's immediate superior. Unhinged by the speed of the German advance.

least they now knew the French had a real man to command them. Weygand was magnificent, youthful despite his years and capable of realising what sort of war this is. We had asked him point-blank whether he could get the French army to fight and he had replied, "I will try"; but reports of their fighting spirit were bad. Pug said he was really worried. He was afraid the Germans would offer the French generous terms, the latter would then ask us for forty divisions and fifteen more fighter squadrons, and when we replied with a *non possumus* would say they were very sorry, they could not continue the struggle. So we have got to think of a first-rate C. in C. for our forces in this country and to prepare for the worst. I think Pug is unduly alarmist, because I cannot see the French shaming themselves quite to that extent.

Thursday, May 23rd
Yesterday the Government obtained permission from the House to take over fuller powers than any British Government has ever possessed. The purpose is largely that if we are invaded, or otherwise *in extremis*, the rights of individuals and institutions must not be allowed to stand in the way of the country's safety. Houses must be demolished to stop advancing tanks, labour must if necessary be coerced, industrial plant requisitioned. Now if ever *salus populi suprema lex*, and in a totalitarian war even a democracy must surrender its liberties. But what a precedent for future peacetime Governments; and will state control, once instituted, ever be abandoned?

The situation this morning is still blacker. The B.E.F.'s communications have been cut and their food supplies are in danger. Moreover enemy infantry columns have nearly reached Amiens, and strong armoured columns are very close to Dunkirk, Calais and Boulogne.

A dramatic afternoon, mostly spent in the Upper War Room at the Admiralty. It began with the news that the Germans were in Boulogne, that the B.E.F. could not break through southwards to join up with the French, and that they only had two days' food left. It seemed all but certain that our army would have to retire precipitously and try to embark, under Herculean difficulties, for England. Then the P.M. spoke on the telephone to Reynaud and Weygand. The latter claimed that the French had recaptured Amiens and Peronne. If true the news is stupendous, although the position of the B.E.F. still remains critical and they will have to fight their way southwards against heavy odds.

After dinner the Admiralty became normally hectic. Brendan Bracken insulted Philip Broad[1] on the telephone. Most immediate telegrams were despatched to most of the existing Generals, Prime Ministers and Presidents. Lord Beaverbrook was sent for and plied with whisky. Pug Ismay was dismal and depressing. And I got to bed, at No. 10, about 1.45.

Friday, May 24th
Went early to Admiralty House and met the P.M., dressed in the most brilliant of flowery dressing-gowns and puffing a long cigar as he ascended from the Upper War Room to his bedroom. He had one or two telephone conversations with the C.I.G.S. and Sir Roger Keyes (from Belgium), emerging from his bath in a towel in order to do so.

We have two new faces at No. 10, a private secretary called Martin* from the C.O. and a clerk from the Ministry of Pensions. We are thus ridiculously overstaffed, but at least we shall have somewhat shorter hours. At the moment we are not overworked, but overtired by the length of time we remain on duty.

Sunday, May 26th [*At Oxford*]
Gay[2] and I had a tremendous discussion on socialism, she just having become affiliated to the Party. I understand and sympathise with her point of view, which is founded on a sense of pity for the poor and disgust at their lack of opportunity. But I do not feel socialism is the proper remedy: private enterprise is valuable because it is efficient, while state control makes for petty tyranny by Government officials and for lack of drive or

[1] Resident Clerk in the Foreign Office.
[2] Gay Margesson, younger daughter of Captain David Margesson. Married the Hon. Martin Charteris, later Lord Charteris of Amisfield.

imagination. Local government is now in socialist hands and the result has been overspending of public money and the spread of corruption in local government. The Conservatives, on the other hand, have failed to take sufficiently strong measures: as was said of Erasmus, they have "sought to heal by incantations a wound which required the surgeon's knife". They and we may have to pay dearly for it in the social unrest which must inevitably follow this war.

Before dinner the sun came out and we were able to walk placidly in Christchurch Meadows. We dined once again at The Trout, but in glorious conditions this time: a blue sky, a setting sun and enough clouds to make the sun still more effective. We ate on a seat by the river, and then walked along the tow path, watching children at play and listening to plovers calling. There has never been a more beautiful setting in which to be happy and I have never felt greater serenity or contentment. Gay did too and said that she believed happiness could only be attained if one lived for the moment.

Monday, May 27th
At Downing Street I was distressed to find the situation much blacker than when I left on Friday. It appears that a grave deterioration has taken place in the last forty-eight hours: the B.E.F., unable to force their way southwards, have got to retreat to the coast as best they can and re-embark for England from whatever Channel ports remain open to them. The French seem to be demoralised and there is now a serious fear that they may collapse. The Cabinet are feverishly considering our ability to carry on the war alone in such circumstances, and there are signs that Halifax is being defeatist. He says that our aim can no longer be to crush Germany but rather to preserve our own integrity and independence.

Fortunately Ironside has gone and Dill, who inspires great confidence, has taken his place; but I do not envy him, confronted as he is with the problem of salving the wreckage of the B.E.F.

I still feel convinced that we shall win, even if the French collapse; but we have reached all but the last ditch and a timely miracle would be acceptable.

In the afternoon came a telegram from Lothian describing a conversation with Roosevelt, who seems to think that if we really are *in extremis* the U.S. will come in. R. suggests that with the resources of the Allied empires, and provided the navy remains intact, we could carry on the war from Canada; but he makes the curious suggestion that the seat of Government should be Bermuda and not Ottawa, as the American republics would dislike the idea of a monarchy functioning on the American Continent!

There was a Cabinet at 10.00 p.m. to discuss the situation caused by King Leopold's determination, despite the opposition of his Government on English soil, to ask for an armistice. This defection of the Belgians leaves the B.E.F. in an exposed and extremely dangerous position. Duff Cooper told me he was afraid "a lot of them will be scuppered".

After the Cabinet I went over to Admiralty House with the P.M. He said he did not think the French would give in and that at any rate they ought not to do so. At midnight, after reading a few papers and saying "Pour me out a whisky and soda, very weak, there's a good boy", he went to bed.

Tuesday, May 28th
Sir R. Keyes, who arrived from Belgium this morning, says that Lord Gort, whom he saw recently, does not rate the chances of saving the B.E.F. very high. Winston, in his statement to the House this afternoon, spoke of "hard and heavy tidings to come", and Duff Cooper made a sensible but intentionally depressing broadcast in the evening. We have lost the first great battle of the war, but it is by no means the last.

Sir R. Campbell, from Paris, says that Reynaud is firm, but Daladier cannot be counted on. The best of the French Ministers is Mandel,[1] at Home Security, who is both efficient and determined.

As it was my early night I got away at 6.00. We have arranged

---

[1] Clemenceau's *Chef de Cabinet* in the First World War. Churchill hoped to lure him to England to lead a Free French movement, but he declined to leave, though strongly opposed to surrender. He was murdered by the Vichy *milices*.

that John Peck and I shall take alternate late nights, so that every other day will be an easy one. I went to see Betts and Rosemary Hinchingbrooke,[1] the latter very relieved that Hinch. has returned safely from France. I then took Betts home to dinner with Father and Mother, both of whom were interesting about their reminiscences of London as it used to be. Father said he remembered how on the 1st of May men used to walk through the streets with Maypoles, surrounded by a throng of dancing people. He remembered Northumberland House and Princes' Cricket ground which was where Cadogan Square, etc., now stands.

I have decided that if the war continues I must make a determined effort to go and fight; but I gather there will be opposition from the Foreign Office authorities. However, in present circumstances what is reasonable has to take second place to what one's conscience dictates. I shall wait a month and then move heaven and earth to go.

Wednesday, May 29th
Ciano has told Loraine that Italy's entry into the war is now certain and will be a matter of days. The fault is Mussolini's alone and on him the entire blame must rest. He is presumably convinced that Germany is going to win and he considers the moment for a diversion to the southwards to be opportune. There are signs that the attack will be made through Switzerland.

Lunched with Tony Bevir at the Travellers. Sir Kenneth Clark,[2] who came and talked to us during lunch, is trying to arrange for the pictures in the National Gallery and Royal collections to be sent to Canada. He also spoke of the pacifism in Wales, which he says is largely due to the attitude of the clergy. Tony sensibly suggested calling in Tom Jones to assist. After lunch Tony and I talked about socialism, and I made the

[1] Rosemary Peto, married to Betty Montagu's brother, Viscount Hinchingbrooke, M.P.
[2] Director of the National Gallery, 1934–45; Chairman of the Arts Council, 1953–60; at one time Chairman of the Independent Television Authority and a widely praised demonstrator of the finest works of art on television. Made a peer in 1969.

point, which I believe to be justified, that socialists almost always create their Utopia in theory and then attempt to work backwards from it. It is wiser to struggle forwards, with a definite objective in view, but prepared to adapt that objective as obstacles on the way and the conditions prevailing at the end may necessitate. *Idées fixes* are always dangerous when they relate to the future, because it is past human ingenuity to guide the course of events. It is for this reason that cut-and-dried peace plans are so futile, since it is impossible to assess the conditions of peace. We may win outright or we may be obliged to compromise: that we shall lose I do not for a moment believe.

News received that we have taken Narvik. We sorely need some restorative just now.

Dined with Zara at Luigi's. She is so attractive and her vivacity is a tonic in these depressing days. We used to dislike each other so profoundly and now we get on admirably.

At Admiralty House after dinner. The evacuation of the B.E.F. is proceeding more satisfactorily than had been expected and 70,000 have been saved already. While the P.M. was in the Upper War Room with the Chiefs of Staff I heard that we had shot down seventy-seven German aeroplanes today for the loss of sixteen. When I told Sir Cyril Newall, the Chief of Air Staff, he refused to believe it possible. I saw a letter from Lloyd George to the P.M. refusing to accept office except on the most unqualified terms. L.G. said he was "genuinely anxious to help to extricate my country from the most terrible disaster into which it has ever been plunged by the ineptitude of its rulers. Several of the architects of this catastrophe are still leading members of your Government and two of them are in the Cabinet that directs the war" (i.e. Chamberlain and Halifax). The P.M. replied by saying that he would not abandon the loyalty he felt for Chamberlain, who had stood by him and was giving him all the support in his power.

Winston's ceaseless industry is impressive. He is always having ideas which he puts down on paper in the form of questions and despatches to Ismay or the C.I.G.S. for examination. Sometimes they relate to matters of major importance, such as the measures to be taken against invasion, or the provision of more aeroplanes, and sometimes they relate to quite trivial questions. This is the sort of thing: "General Ismay. Inquire into the number of German guns now trophies in this country and whether any can be reconditioned for blocking exits from beaches against tanks conceivably landed thereon." Another today asked whether wax could be supplied to troops to put in their ears in order to deaden the noise of warfare.

Thursday, May 30th

Back to No. 10 by four o'clock and heard that half the B.E.F. were now away but that Dunkirk, the port of embarkation, was scarcely usable any more.

Returned to No. 10 to sleep. I am glad to see the Cabinet are already thinking about building up a new expeditionary force, based on St Nazaire, and Winston has already telegraphed in this sense to Reynaud and Weygand.

Friday, May 31st

Everybody elated by the progress of the evacuation. One of the world's greatest defeats is being redeemed by an outstanding achievement of organisation and gallantry. The B.E.F. rear-guards, though decimated, are standing firm against fearful odds; the R.A.F. activity over Dunkirk is ceaseless; the navy has attempted and achieved the incredible. Two hundred and twenty-two men of war have been used in the evacuation and 665 other vessels. The sailors are so tired that they are working automatically, but they are apparently quite undaunted.

Meanwhile the Secret Service reports from Germany show that the difficulties there are increasing and that the Nazis are terrified of failing to win the war this summer. There is general apathy at home in Germany, the casualties have been heavy, the shortages of food and raw materials are making themselves felt, and the production of tanks and aircraft is falling off by forty per cent. If these reports are true, the war may well be over by Christmas, despite the German people's and army's famous staying power.

The P.M. flew to Paris this morning with Attlee and the C.I.G.S., but, alas, without taking a Private Secretary. As a result I had very little to do but gossip with Brendan Bracken, the Chief Whip, etc.

Indirect attempts are being made, through the Dominions' High Commissioners, etc., to bring the U.S. into the war by painting to members of the Administration the most sombre portrait of what we expect from Germany and by harping on the possibility of France giving up the struggle.

Although Italy is making every preparation for immediate war, I think there is still a chance it is all stupendous bluff. If Musso were serious he would scarcely be so blatant about it all.

Had a long talk with Eden from whom I gathered enough information to make me almost sure that Philip is south-west of the Somme and thus comparatively safe. Eden is amazed by the success of the evacuation. As Brendan Bracken put it "we should have sold out for 40,000 a few days ago", and now 170,000 are already home. Edward Bridges said cynically: "Evacuation is becoming our greatest national industry."

SIX

COLLAPSE OF FRANCE
JUNE 1940

Saturday, June 1st

Very busy all the morning, especially when the P.M. returned from Paris with a box full of straggling papers. His minute on the paper in which Tony had asked about sending the National Gallery pictures to Canada was: "No, bury them in caves and cellars. None must go. We are going to beat them."

Brendan Bracken is always complaining about "yes-men". It was therefore amusing to see somebody not behaving as a "yes-man" as far as he personally is concerned. The P.M. wants to make him a Privy Councillor. The King has caused Alec Hardinge[1] to write and expostulate. Winston, however, who is nothing if not loyal to his friends, has taken up the cudgels vigorously and, in his reply, complains that it is indeed hard if his most loyal supporter, who has stood alone with him in the wilderness prophesying the wrath to come, is to be refused this honour. I suppose Winston will get his way, but it is clear that the King has a mind of his own.

I had a somewhat stormy passage this afternoon with the P.M., because the Chiefs of Staff were not at Admiralty House when he wanted them. He rated me soundly, but I did not mind as my conscience was, in this case, clear and as he always

[1] Assistant Private Secretary to George V. Private Secretary to Edward VIII, with whom he got on badly, and to George VI. Succeeded his father, who had been Permanent Under Secretary at the Foreign Office, Ambassador in Paris and Viceroy of India, as Lord Hardinge of Penshurst.

pitches upon the first available person to display his wrath, irrespective of who is to blame. But he bears no grudge. Spoke to Lord Gort who returned from Dunkirk this morning.

Had tea with Mrs Churchill in the drawing-room of the flat on the top floor of Admiralty House. She was full of conversation and pleasurably excited at the prospect of going to Chequers for the first time. She and Winston went down there in the evening, but there was enough happening to prevent my going down to Cambridge to stay the night as I had intended.

Seal agreed that, as far as he was concerned, I could go and fight and he promised to arrange to get me a Commission in the R.N.V.R. But Mallet, of the F.O., whom I immediately went to see, said that there were many similar aspirants in the F.O., but that for the moment Alec Cadogan had refused to release anyone. I could not be released unless others were also. He said he thought there might be a change soon, if operations continued at this intense pressure, and he promised to let me know as soon as possible.

Sunday, June 2nd

Lunched with Grandfather and Peggy. Talking about Italy, Grandfather said that the Italians had a certain grievance against us. We made lavish promises in the secret Treaty of London of 1915 and we could not fulfil them. In the last war we had been prepared to do almost anything to win new Allies and the results had often been disastrous – viz. the Balfour Declaration.

After lunch I walked through Chelsea with Peggy who is much exercised about Fifth Columnists and the lack of deep air-raid shelters.

I returned to No. 10 just before the P.M. got back from Chequers. The Chiefs of Staff arrived and I gathered that the evacuation was proceeding smoothly. Now all attention centres on two matters: the expected drive against the French towards Paris and the provision of equipment for a new B.E.F. Reynaud has telegraphed for more fighters, more bombers and more troops in order to withstand the great attack expected shortly on the Somme and on the Aisne. This annoys Winston who considers the French grasping and whose main energies are now turned to consolidating our home defences, conserving our air strength, and building up a new army from the remnants of the old and from the troops now in India and Palestine. However, it is vital to sustain French morale and give no excuse for a collapse.

I went back to Admiralty House after dinner, but little happened and I was able to get home early. Eden made an admirable speech before the 9.00 news about the success of the evacuation from Dunkirk: a first rate performance.

Monday, June 3rd
Winston is tired of our always being on the defensive and is contemplating raids on the enemy's territory. "How wonderful it would be," he writes to Ismay, "if the Germans could be made to wonder where they were going to be struck next instead of forcing us to try to wall in the Island and roof it over. An effort must be made to shake off the mental and moral prostration to the will and initiative of the enemy from which we suffer."

Found Horace Wilson at lunch in the Travellers and sat down beside him. I thought he was a little depressed, as indeed the loss of his powers behind the throne is likely to make him, and especially as there is inevitably a great deal of criticism now aimed at those thought to be responsible for the deficiencies in our armament and aeroplane production. I broached the question of being allowed, as a civil servant, to go and fight, because he is still Head of the Civil Service and might be able to help me. He showed himself sympathetic and promised to see what could be done.

Tuesday, June 4th
Our evacuation of Narvik, which I am sure is a mistake, is being delayed to allow the discussion of a Swedish plan for a settlement with Germany which would leave the King of Norway the northern half of the country.

The problem of the day is the French Government's demand for fresh divisions and more fighters. Apparently our aircraft losses in the last fortnight have seriously weakened our air defences, and Newall says that unless we have a respite he cannot guarantee the safety of this country against concentrated air attack for more than forty-eight hours. So we cannot afford to send fighter reinforcements to the French. We are sending two more divisions but our ability to provide more is dependent upon the speed with which we can replace the equipment we have lost.

Went to the House to hear the P.M.'s statement on the evacuation from Dunkirk. It was a magnificent oration which obviously moved the House. Speaking of the awful possibilities in store for us, and the chances of invasion, he made the following impressive peroration:

> Even though large tracts of Europe have fallen into the grip of the Gestapo, and all the odious apparatus of Nazi rule, we shall not flag or fail. We shall go on to the end. We shall fight in France. We shall fight on the seas and oceans. We shall fight with growing confidence and growing strength in the air. We shall defend our Island, whatever the cost may be. We shall fight on the beaches. We shall fight on the landing grounds. We shall fight in the fields and streets. We shall fight in the hills. We shall never surrender. And even if, which I do not for a moment believe, this Island or a large part of it were subjugated and starving, then our Empire beyond the oceans, armed and guarded by the British fleet, will carry on the struggle until in God's good time the New World with all its power and might sets forth to the rescue and liberation of the old.

He did not finally mention in his speech (although he had originally intended to do so) that King Leopold, whom he castigated soundly, had given Lord Gort a pledge of continued resistance.

At Admiralty House after dinner Winston was a little on edge. He kept on ringing the bell and complaining that we were making too much noise. The last time he did so, he said, "What is all this bloody jaw? Who is it?" I said, "It's the First Lord, sir," and he smiled, saying, "Well, you've got me this time."

The First Lord, Alexander, was full of talk. He told me that he had tried three times to oppose the evacuation of Narvik, but it had been decided upon and he could do no more. He did not think much of the French navy. We talked about Maxton and I said I admired him for being an idealist and for having the courage to admit in Parliament that he did not see how his ideals could be put into effect. Alexander said Maxton was muddle-headed and that it was people like me, who listened to people like Maxton, that were responsible for the country being where it is today. Tony, who came in just then, hinted that this responsibility rested with the Labour Party as much as with anyone, and Alexander had the grace to agree. A. showed me an extraordinary telegram from Lord Cork at Narvik saying that the Norwegians were frightened of the Russians taking over the country, were therefore thinking of capitulating to the Germans, and would like us to leave our equipment behind so that the Germans could use it against the Russians!!

An encouraging report on aircraft production which shows that the number of new planes has exceeded those destroyed in the past few weeks. Lord Beaverbrook is producing the goods in an astonishing way.

Wednesday, June 5th
Winston is still full of offensive zeal and thinks that the Australians should be used for small forays on the coasts of occupied countries such as Denmark, Holland and Belgium. "Enterprises must be prepared," he minutes to Ismay, "with specially trained troops of the hunter class who can develop a reign of terror down these coasts, first of all on the 'butcher and bolt' policy, but later on, or perhaps as soon as we are organised, we should surprise Calais or Boulogne, kill and capture the Hun garrisons and hold the place until all the preparations to reduce it by siege or heavy storm have been made, and then away." Light armoured units must, he says, "crawl ashore, do a deep raid inland cutting a vital communication, and then back leaving a trail of German corpses behind them. It is probable that when the best troops go on to the attack on Paris, only the ordinary German troops of the line will be left. The lives of these must be made an intense torment."

Turning to more trivial subjects, the P.M. wrote this morning to Eden suggesting the restoration to officers of the leather shoulder-strap, abolished by "your foolish predecessor, Belisha".

Lunched with Cecil Syers at the Travellers. He agreed with me that history would probably judge King Leopold's action very differently from people today, and that he had proved a most useful scapegoat to the Allies.

The Germans have today begun another great offensive towards Paris, being anxious, no doubt, to allow our routed armies no respite. The French are demanding immense fighter support from us. Winston would like to send more than the air experts will agree. The latter say that we must have time for reorganisation and that we cannot leave this country exposed.

Thursday, June 6th

In the early hours I was disturbed by a Yellow warning, but fortunately the raid did not reach London.

Interesting censorship report on public opinion, as shown in letters. There is no frenzied fury against the Germans but much cold and reasoned hatred. The war has now for the first time become the question of paramount importance to the average Englishman. There is no sign of bad morale, and little wish for peace at any price, but it is noteworthy that discouraged and defeatist women outnumber men by two to one.

Lunched with Janet Margesson at Luigi's (incidentally the Home Secretary reports that the waiters at a lot of restaurants, including Quaglino's, the Café Royal and the Dorchester, are thought to be dangerous). Afterwards Jan and I sat in the shade in St James's Park and thought what a lovely town London was.

Dined with Lady Wolverton.[1] The Dutch Minister and his wife were there, also Sir George Clerk.[2] The latter said that in order to wage war Democracies had to convert themselves into

---

[1] Daughter of the famous beauty, Georgiana, Countess of Dudley. Lived in St James's Place till her house was destroyed by a bomb. She had a forceful personality and her contemporaries found her alarming, but she was kind to young people. She told me to marry Audrey Paget, but as far as I know did not consult Audrey. And I had a matrimonial obsession elsewhere.

[2] Ambassador in Paris in the 1930s.

Dictatorships. We had our Dictator; in France there was only one potential one, M. Mandel, and he, as a Jew, would find it difficult to establish himself, particularly when M. Blum[1] and the Front Populaire were still so vividly impressed on the minds of the French bourgeoisie.

The P.M. went to a cinema, to see the Dunkirk film, and returned to Admiralty House in rather a bad temper. He bade me light the fire, although it was the hottest of hot nights, and then proceeded to work till 1.30. He was cross with the French, who are being persistent in their demands for further air support. Pétain* and Weygand are saying that if we do not send fighters, the present battle will be lost and France will have to capitulate. Pétain told Reynaud that if he had not the courage to do so, he, Pétain, would undertake the task. I think the French are trying to frighten us, for bargaining purposes, but Winston is justifiably angry with Vuillemin[2] who referred to our tremendous air efforts in the first battle as "tardy, inadequate but nevertheless of value". Pug Ismay says the French are nothing short of outrageous: we have thrown no bricks at them despite the fact that they let down our Expeditionary Force; and they, without one word of gratitude for the help we gave them in evacuation and in air fighting, do nothing but sling mud at us. All this talk on their part of Allied solidarity is shown in effect to refer only to the necessity of preserving the sacred soil of France. We should be insane to send them all our fighters, because if they were lost this country would be beaten in two days, whereas even if France surrenders we shall still win the war – provided our air defences are intact.

The P.M. was in an impatient frame of mind. He was angry with the First Sea Lord, who is being excessively cautious about Winston's cherished OPERATION PAUL (which is to interrupt by mine-laying the Lulea iron-ore traffic), and with the Secretary of State for War (Anthony Eden) who is making difficulties about bringing battalions of trained troops back from Palestine. "We

[1] Leader of the *Front Populaire* and twice socialist Prime Minister of France in the 1930s. A patriot and idealist.
[2] Commander in Chief of the ill-equipped and largely ineffective French air force.

are indeed the victims of a feeble and weary departmentalism," he wrote; and after comparing the success of our efforts in providing divisions in the last war with our inability to do so in this, he wrote, "Our weakness, slowness, lack of grip and drive are very apparent on the background of what was done twenty-five years ago."

Friday, June 7th

As Winston went down to Chartwell at lunch-time there was very little to do and I sat in the shade most of the afternoon in the garden at No. 10, reading a book of war stories called *The Green Curve*.

After tea I motored down to Uppark for the night. Herbert Meade, who represents I suppose, a large section of opinion in the country, said he hoped that when we had won the war we should bomb German towns and show the German people it did not pay to make war. Perhaps there is much to be said for firmness, but I think sheer vindictiveness is neither a right nor a paying policy.

There is great excitement in Sussex over the organisation of the new Local Defence Volunteers.

Sunday, June 9th

At Stansted.

Lord Bessborough is wholly occupied with the Fifth Column, which he avows is very powerful in Sussex and will not be squashed until the Fascist party is declared illegal. I shall arrange for him to come to No. 10 and see Morton.* Meanwhile the most decisive battle in history is at its climax.

Monday, June 10th

Left Stansted at 7.30 and drove up to London, dropping Eric at Petersfield *en route*. The roads are now barricaded and guarded by soldiers.

In the afternoon there was chaos at Admiralty House. Winston made one of his lightning decisions to go to Paris, and just as he was about to leave for Hendon, a telegram was thrust into my hand to say that the French Government were going to leave

Paris. "What the Hell?" was all the P.M. said, but subsequently as there was no aerodrome available at which he could land he reluctantly concluded that "there was no perch on which he could alight" and gave up the plan. After much telephoning and shilly-shallying, Mary Churchill turned Winston out of "the flat", because she had Mark Howard coming to tea, and we all moved downstairs to the state rooms.

The news from France is distressing. The Germans have taken Rouen and the French are making more and more extravagant demands for air support. Winston thinks it good that the French Government is leaving Paris because it shows that they intend to go on fighting; but he is afraid that Flandin[1] and other "Quislings"[2] may stay behind and make terms with the invader.

Mussolini decided to come into the war, and we had to wake up Winston from his afternoon slumber and tell him of this added complication. At least it was not unexpected – though I personally thought it might not happen. There has never been such a flourish of trumpets to announce a grand entry; but the Italians have a sense of the melodramatic. In any case they have given us time to make our dispositions and move heavy bombers to the south of France. We are to make a grand attack by air tomorrow night.

At Admiralty House the possibility of the French giving in, or being defeated, was of greater interest to all present than the approaching entry of Italy into the war. All Winston said about the latter event was, "People who go to Italy to look at ruins won't have to go as far as Naples and Pompeii in future." He was in a very bad temper, snapped almost everybody's head off, wrote angry minutes to the First Sea Lord, and refused to pay any attention to messages given him orally. We all listened to Roosevelt's speech from America: it mentioned Italy's "stab

---

[1] Had been French Minister of Commerce, of Finance and of Foreign Affairs and, briefly, Prime Minister. Arrested by the Free French in Algiers in 1943, but acquitted of collaboration when brought to trial after the war. Abetted by Randolph, Churchill did his best to help him and his support possibly swayed the verdict.

[2] The word, taken from the name of a Norwegian traitor, was already coming into general use.

in the back" and was about as useful as it could have been in the circumstances.

Tuesday, June 11th
The P.M. went to France to bolster up the fainting French morale.

Wednesday, June 12th
The news today is darker than it has yet been. General Haining[1] says Paris will almost certainly fall within the next forty-eight hours. The French, although fighting with grim determination, are at the end of their tether, and although Reynaud wishes to fight to the end Pétain is willing to make peace. He is worse than Bazaine[2] in 1870. Meanwhile our 51st Division is cornered at St Valéry and has been ordered to surrender by the French. Its commander has refused, but as evacuation of the remaining men is now all but impossible submission may be inevitable. The French troops at St Valéry are already hanging out white flags. Pray God Philip is with those of our troops who are at Havre and whose embarkation at Cherbourg for home seems to be progressing favourably. Some of his luggage arrived today, labelled Havre, and so there is every hope; but the journey home by ship will be very dangerous.

Last night the French tried to prevent our bombers setting out to attack Italy. They even placed lorries on the aerodromes to prevent the Wellingtons taking off. Such is their spirit of co-operation. They are afraid of Italian retaliation; but, poor things, they are naturally in a state of desperation.

After dinner I read the account of Winston's conversations with the French yesterday (he returned at lunch-time today). Apparently the Generals have no reserves left. Their divisions are decimated and every man and weapon has been thrown into the line; but nothing can stop the German steamroller. Weygand and Georges talk about the impossibility of carrying on the

[1] Vice Chief of the Imperial General Staff, 1940–41.
[2] Marshal François Bazaine. In the Franco-Prussian War of 1870, having lost the battle of Gravelotte, he surrendered the fortress of Metz with 173,000 men and without putting up a fight.

struggle, at any rate on co-ordinated lines, but Reynaud is as indomitable as Pétain is defeatist. There is the usual cry for the use of our whole air force, and we are now going to send far more than we can afford. But we must save enough to carry on the war victoriously in the event of France surrendering. There is apparently a young French General called de Gaulle,* of whom Winston thinks a great deal, and perhaps he might organise further resistance in Brittany or on the Atlantic seaboard, to which our divisions could be sent. Soon we shall have another army, but as Weygand says it is no longer a matter of weeks or days, but of hours.

Winston has sent a graphic telegram to Roosevelt, describing the impending catastrophe, and he seems to hope that America will come in now, at any rate as a non-belligerent ally. But can American support, in materials, be made effective in time?

At Admiralty House there was great activity. Beaverbrook made a lot of noise, presumably hoping to cheer people up thereby, and all the Air Ministry heads were there concocting a telegram to France about the number of bombers and fighters we can send tomorrow. Unfortunately the effective range of our fighters will not enable them to go far up the Seine, but it would be suicidal to send them to aerodromes in France where they would be destroyed on the ground.

After midnight Reynaud rang up. Winston could not hear him, because the line was so bad and eventually de Margerie[1] and I had to carry on a conversation through the intermediary of telephone operators. Reynaud asked that Winston should go back to France tomorrow, arriving at the Prefecture at Tours by 2.45. This looks as if the French mean to give in, because Reynaud promised to consult Winston again before any fundamental decision was taken, and this sudden summons is ominous. Perhaps W. will be able to persuade them to carry on the war, west of Paris, on a guerilla basis. The Germans must be exhausted and their lines of communication are immense, so if

---

[1] Roland de Margerie, Minister at the French Embassy in London under Monsieur Corbin, was now *Chef de Cabinet* to Reynaud. His son was a popular and effective Ambassador in London in the 1980s and was then posted to Washington.

only the French could hold yet a few days the skies might clear.

Winston was furious because Reynaud would talk of the hour of arrival and destination over an open line: he thought it very dangerous and spent a long time considering how to deceive the Germans who had, he felt sure, listened to the conversation. Finally he decided to go very early in the morning with a strong escort of fighters; but at one moment he was ordering me to ring up de Margerie and say, untruthfully, that it was impossible for him to go. This would have caused chaos at the other end and, at the risk of having my head bitten off, I dissuaded him.

Speaking of the surrender of the 51st Division, W. said it was the most "brutal disaster" we had yet suffered.

Thursday, June 13th

Winston came back from France about dinner-time; but as it was my early night I gave Moore Crosthwaite[1] dinner at the Apéritif, in payment of an ill-advised bet that Chamberlain's Government would not fall. He tells me there is great rancour against Chamberlain and his colleagues because of the lack of equipment, and that much of the credit for the recent rapid improvement is being given to Morrison and Bevin as having called in the Trade Unions to redress the mistakes and omissions of the manufacturers and ruling classes. This is unfair, because although the Trade Unions have certainly co-operated handsomely, it is Winston and Beaverbrook who have really galvanised the country and the Government departments. I think that Moore is probably right in saying that the Prime Minister's personality has a great effect on the speed with which Government departments work and the energy they display. Chamberlain had drive, but he had not Winston's probing and restless mind: he expected his subordinates to work with the same tirelessness and efficiency that he showed himself, but never questioned their ability to do so. Winston, on the other hand, is always looking for shortcomings and inspires others to be as

---

[1] An intelligent Fabian intellectual, with an acerbic wit, who had been a colleague of mine in the Eastern Department and was in due course Ambassador to the Lebanon and to Sweden.

zealous ferrets as himself. But, of course, Chamberlain never had the "complete powers" or the universal support which events have given Winston.

When I got back to No. 10, to sleep, I found that Winston had returned from Tours and was recounting his experiences to the Cabinet. Apparently Weygand was suggesting an Armistice in order that he might still retain the vestige of an army to deal with disaffection. "They were very nearly gone," Winston said, and they asked to be released from their pledge not to make a separate peace. This W. refused on behalf of the British Government.

At an opportune moment came a message from Roosevelt to Reynaud, promising support. This raised in Winston's mind hopes of approaching American intervention as an active Ally, but I fear these hopes may be doomed to disappointment because it is for Congress and not for the President to decide. However the message cheered up the French, who are desperately anxious to see "some gleam of light at the far end of the tunnel". Winston therefore telegraphed to Roosevelt asking leave to publish the telegram to Reynaud: such action would revitalise the French and prevent Hitler from dictating peace in Paris. "All the far-reaching plans, strategic, economic, political and moral which your message expounds may be still-born if the French cut out now," Winston continued: "We fully realise that the moment Hitler finds he cannot dictate a Nazi peace in Paris he will turn his fury on us", and he explained that we much regretted our inability through force of circumstances, to take our full share of the present battle on land.

Friday, June 14th
Mr Kennedy rang up to refuse permission to publish Roosevelt's message to Reynaud. It seems that the P.M.'s expectations last night of immediate American help were exaggerated. Roosevelt has got to proceed cautiously, but the plain truth is that America has been caught napping, militarily and industrially. She may be really useful to us in a year; but we are living from hour to hour.

News that Paris has fallen. I am still reading *War and Peace*, which I never have had time to finish, and have reached the point where the French are entering Moscow. The position is in some respects analogous, except that the winter with its cold and ice is further off today than it was in September 1812. If the French will go on fighting, we must now fall back on the Atlantic, creating new lines of Torres Vedras[1] behind which British divisions and American supplies can be concentrated. Paris is not France, and provided defeatism in the French High Command can be thwarted there is no reason to suppose the Germans will be able to subdue the whole country. Guerilla warfare on long lines of communications should be most effective.

In the afternoon came a telegram from our Military Mission in France to Dill, who brought it over to show the P.M. It said that organised resistance in France was at an end, that the French army was disintegrating into disorganised groups, and that Weygand, Georges and Brooke were agreed as to the impossibility of holding Brittany. Obviously a French collapse can now only be averted by a miracle or by the heroism of France's leaders. The former seems the more probable of the two, although Reynaud, de Gaulle, etc., are full of zeal. America's attitude is of vital importance to French morale; but America is the slowest to act of all the democracies, and that is saying much.

The Churchills are moving into No. 10 today, but the P.M. thought it best to spend the night with Lord Beaverbrook. He came to No. 10 after dinner and had a long conference with David Margesson, Desmond Morton, Brendan Bracken and Duncan Sandys[2] (who shows no *gêne* about sitting here and drinking in all the most secret information) regarding the suggestion that 250,000 French troops should be brought here with their equipment in order to make this Island stiff with soldiers and lessen the likelihood of a successful invasion. It is now almost certain that the French will ask for an armistice as their powers of resistance are at an end and Reynaud can scarcely stand up alone to the pressure from his Cabinet and his Generals.

---

[1] The three concentric lines of defence, built by Wellington to cover Lisbon, which halted the advance of Marshal Masséna in 1810.
[2] Later Lord Duncan-Sandys.*

It is thus a question of salvage: the 120,000 British troops in France and as much French material and manpower as we can evacuate.

About 2.00 a.m. Herschel Johnson brought round from the American Embassy Roosevelt's reply to the "Former Naval Person's" last telegram. It promised all support possible, but was careful to define what that possibility was. Active and open support does not seem as near as the P.M. thought and encouraged Reynaud to believe. W. told Eden he thought France would crack internally in a day or two.

The general opinion now is that nothing can save France, whatever may be the fate of her Colonies and fleet, but that nevertheless if we can hold on until November we shall have won the war. The holding-on is going to be a grim business, a chance for the whale to prove his superiority to the elephant.

Saturday, June 15th
Had intended to go to West Wycombe for the night to stay with the Dashwoods, but it was decided that I should go to Chequers with the P.M.

After tea Winston dictated long telegrams to Roosevelt and to the Dominions (whose premiers had all sent the most touching and encouraging messages) pointing out that we had now got to face the most trying ordeal of heavy bombing and saying to all that he personally was convinced that the carnage and destruction in this country would bring the U.S. into the war. He said that the French condition for carrying on had been a promise of active U.S. support: the promise of redoubled supplies which had been received was not sufficient, and though France might fight on from her Colonies her resistance at home would now almost certainly come to an end. "If words counted, we should win this war," he said, as a comment on his own telegraphic efforts.

We arrived at Chequers in time to dine at 9.30. The party consisted of Winston, Duncan and Diana Sandys, Lindemann and myself. It was at once the most dramatic and the most fantastic evening I have ever spent. Before going into the dining-room Tony Bevir told me on the telephone that telegrams had been received from Bordeaux to the effect that the position was deteriorating fast and the request to be allowed to make a separate peace was being put in a more brutal form. I imparted this to Winston who was immediately very depressed. Dinner began lugubriously, W. eating fast and greedily, his face almost in his plate, and every now and then firing some technical question at Lindemann, who was quietly consuming his vegetarian diet. The Sandyses and I sat silent, because our spasmodic efforts at conversation were not well received. However champagne and brandy and cigars did their work and we soon became talkative, even garrulous. Winston, in order to cheer himself and us up, read aloud the messages he had received from the Dominions and the replies he had sent to them and to Roosevelt. "The war is bound to become a bloody one for us now," he said, "but I hope our people will stand up to bombing and the Huns aren't liking what we are giving them. But what a tragedy that our victory in the last war should have been snatched from us by a lot of softies."

Winston and Duncan Sandys paced up and down the rose garden in the moonlight while Diana, Lindemann and I walked on the other side of the house. It was light and deliciously warm, but the sentries, with tin helmets and fixed bayonets, who were placed all round the house, kept us fully alive to the horrors of reality. I spent most of the time telephoning, searching for Winston among the roses and listening to his comments on the war. I told him that fuller information had now been received about the French attitude, which appeared to be slipping. "Tell them," he said, "that if they let us have their fleet we shall never forget, but that if they surrender without consulting us we shall never forgive. We shall blacken their name for a thousand years!" Then, half afraid that I might take him seriously, he added: "Don't, of course, do that just yet." He was in high spirits, repeating poetry, dilating on the drama of the present situation, maintaining that he and Hitler only had one thing in common – a horror of whistling – offering everybody cigars, and spasmodically murmuring, "Bang, Bang, Bang, goes the farmer's gun, run rabbit, run rabbit, run, run, run."

Kennedy telephoned and Winston, becoming serious for a minute, poured into his ears a flood of eloquence about the part that America could and should play in saving civilisation. Referring to promises of industrial and financial support, he said such an offer "would be a laughing-stock on the stage of history", and he begged that "we should not let our friend's (President R.) efforts peter out in grimaces and futility".

About 1.00 a.m. Winston came in from the garden and we all stood in the central hall while the Great Man lay on the sofa, puffed his cigar, discoursed on the building up of our fighter strength, and told one or two dirty stories. Finally, saying "Goodnight, my children", he went to bed at 1.30.

Sunday, June 16th
Woken at 6.30 by the telephone and shortly afterwards by a despatch rider who brought the full facts about the French from London. When I heard that the P.M. was awake, about 7.30, I took them to his room and found him lying in bed, looking just like a rather nice pig, clad in a silk vest. He ruminated for some time and then decided to call the Cabinet in London at 10.15, abandoning his project of having the French General de Gaulle, together with Eden and the C.I.G.S., to lunch at Chequers. So I hurried back to my room, ate a hasty breakfast, and was ready to leave by 8.30. I had to wait till after 9.00 before we started, being called from time to time to W.'s bedroom, where he was wasting time with Duncan Sandys, to receive orders. Finally we drove back to London in pouring rain, disregarding traffic lights and speeding down the Mall, to arrive just as the Cabinet assembled.

On the way to London the P.M. dictated a number of minutes to Mrs Hill[1] and did enough work to keep us all busy during the morning. It is one of the great differences between Chamberlain and Churchill that whereas the former, in reading Cabinet papers, seldom made any comments and only on questions of the highest policy, Churchill scrutinises every document which

---

[1] Kathleen Hill, the senior of Churchill's personal secretaries, who looked after his personal and constituency affairs and took his dictation (often straight on to the typewriter). She was patient, long-suffering, good-natured and a skilled violinist. Churchill was devoted to her.

has anything to do with the war and does not disdain to enquire into the most trivial point.

The Cabinet met again at 3.00 and I ushered Corbin and de Gaulle into Desmond Morton's room to wait until they were summoned. Shortly afterwards I saw Morton who told me what the meeting was for and why the stern telegrams sent off this morning, refusing to release France from her "No separate peace" pledge, but in reality agreeing to an armistice, were being held up. Apparently there is a stupendous idea of declaring the political unity of England and France, and Reynaud has said that in these circumstances France would fight on, having seen "the ray of light at the end of the tunnel". I am not clear about the details of this epoch-making idea; but apparently Chamberlain is "in on it" with Salter,[1] Amery, Lloyd and Vansittart, and de Gaulle is one of its most ardent supporters. "De Gaulle is a magnificent crook," said Morton, "another Max Beaverbrook, just what we want!"

Bridges came out of the Cabinet and dictated the Declaration of Union to Mrs Hill in my room. It sounded inspiring, something which will revive the flagging energies of the French and invigorate our own people. It is a historic document and its effects will be more far-reaching than anything that has occurred this century – and more permanent?

Morton tells me that Horace Wilson has been working like a black on this proposal, that Van, one of its principal sponsors, has suddenly returned into the limelight, and that Monnet[2] is the man to whom the chief credit for the idea should be given. Apparently most of the day has been spent telephoning to Reynaud and Mandel, persuading them to hold fast and not give in to the defeatist pressure of their colleagues. De Gaulle has been strutting about in the Cabinet, with Corbin too; the Cabinet meeting turned into a sort of promenade, Winston beginning a speech in the Cabinet room and finishing it in Morton's room;

---

[1] Distinguished academic and expert on shipping. Fellow of All Souls. M.P. for Oxford University from 1937. Chairman of the World Bank Advisory Council after the war and Minister of Materials in Churchill's 1951 Government. Ennobled in 1953.

[2] A founding father of the Common Market.

and everybody has been slapping de Gaulle on the back and telling him he shall be Commander in Chief (Winston muttering "*je l'arrangerai*"). Is he to be a new Napoleon? From what I hear, it seems that a lot of people think so. He treats Reynaud (whom he called "*ce poisson gelé*") like dirt and discourses familiarly on what he will do in France; yet he is only a Major General just recently discovered.

Meanwhile the King does not know what is being done to his Empire. The Lord President is going to see him at 7.00 and will break the news. Who knows, we may yet see the "fleurs de lys" restored to the Royal Standard!

7.00 p.m. Since writing the above I have obtained a clearer idea of the events of this astonishing day. On Friday night one of the Whips put David Margesson in touch with a Frenchman, called Pleven, who produced this idea of union together with that of evacuating French troops to the U.K. David got in touch with Desmond Morton, who welcomed the idea which was similar to that on which Monnet had been working, and David went up to No. 11, where the Halifaxes were dining with the Chamberlains, to propound the scheme. He became eloquent (he says) but was not enthusiastically received. Finally, after discovering that Horace Wilson knew about the matter, David and Desmond persuaded Brendan Bracken to let them take Pleven to see Winston. W. was bored and critical, but eventually went upstairs to discuss the matter with Chamberlain. Nothing more occurred here and certainly, last night, the whole idea was far from Winston's mind and he was preoccupied with the necessity of saving the French fleet if France capitulated. At this morning's Cabinet a telegram was drafted and actually despatched to Reynaud which said, in effect, "ask for an armistice and let us have the fleet" (though it did not release the French from their pledge not to make a separate peace). Winston lunched at the Carlton Club with Corbin, de Gaulle, Eden, C.I. G.S., and presumably de Gaulle persuaded him to consider seriously this revolutionary project – on which, of course, Monnet, Amery, Salter, etc., had busily been working behind the scenes. The Cabinet met hurriedly at 3.00; the declaration was re-drafted several times; and it was agreed that Winston, Attlee,

Sinclair, Ismay and the Chiefs of Staff should tonight go to Brittany and meet Reynaud.

I went back to No. 10 at 9.00 and found that a telegram had been received from Bordeaux cancelling the meeting with Reynaud. Why?

Monday, June 17th

Reynaud has resigned, unable to withstand the pressure, despite the fact that the proposed Declaration was telegraphed to him yesterday afternoon. Pétain has formed a Government of Quislings, including Laval, and France will now certainly ask for an armistice in spite of her pledge to us. However a telegram from Baudouin, the new Minister of Foreign Affairs,[1] makes it appear that the surrender of the fleet will be refused. The Spanish are to be used as intermediaries and not the Americans as was expected. I gather that French demoralisation is complete and that Weygand is afraid that the troops may turn on their officers. In any case the internal explosion, which Winston prophesied the other day, is now quite probable. Perhaps the new Government will, in the end, accept the Declaration, if they consider Germany's terms cannot honourably be accepted, but it is all too likely now that yesterday's "cloud-capped towers, the gorgeous palaces . . . shall dissolve and . . . leave not a rack behind", and that the visions of a golden future which the Declaration held out are doomed to vanish. I feel like a deflated soufflé.

The Cabinet met at 11.00 and shortly afterwards we heard that Pétain had ordered the French army to lay down its arms. Lord Lloyd told me that he had seen Weygand a few days ago and that he was shrivelled up physically and mentally by the ordeal he had been through. If only the Declaration had been approved twenty-four hours earlier, Reynaud, supported by Mandel, de Gaulle – and, who knows, "by a whiff of grapeshot" – might have saved the situation, and the terms of the Declaration "against subjection to a system which reduces mankind to a life

---

[1] A banker by profession. Strongly supported Pétain, Laval and the "Peace Party" against Reynaud.

of robots and slaves" would have assuredly found response in France and the U.S. There would have been great difficulties to surmount, but we had before us the bridge to a new world, the first elements of European or even World Federation.

After the Cabinet the P.M. paced backwards and forwards in the garden, alone, his head bowed, his hands behind his back. He was doubtless considering how best the French fleet, the air force and the Colonies could be saved. He, I am sure, will remain undaunted.

4.00: Went over to the F.O. to see if I could discover any news. I met Van, who said that he thought the Declaration was by no means dead, that the German terms would very probably be such that the French could not accept them, and that he had just drafted a telegram in French from the P.M. to Pétain appealing to the latter's sense of honour, which was very real, talking about the *"vainqueur de Verdun"*, etc., and stressing the things we could do to help France. It was important to get at Pétain's feelings of honour before it was too late, and if telegrams were impossible the message must be taken by Lord Lloyd in an aeroplane immediately. General Spears was no good; he was too implicated with Reynaud. Van looked well and full of energy; he has come into his own, like so many black sheep and discarded statesmen.

Sir Robert Vansittart, made a peer by Churchill in 1941, was a man of striking intellectual ability, profound literary knowledge and poor judgment. He was Permanent Under Secretary when I joined the Foreign Office in 1937 and had established a high reputation at home and abroad. Indeed it was too high for his comfort, Anthony Eden much disliking the general belief that Van (as he was always called) was the power behind his throne and the real originator of all diplomatic initiatives. With the support of Chamberlain who, like most Prime Ministers, resented the Foreign Office, Eden arranged for Sir Alexander Cadogan to succeed Van. He was given the high-sounding but empty title of Chief Diplomatic Adviser to the Government, was left in the Permanent Under Secretary's corner office on the ground floor and was deprived of all active work in the department.

When Churchill came to power, Van doubtless hoped for renewed influence since he had constantly warned of the German danger in the years before the war. However, though Churchill felt the usual Prime Ministerial distaste for the Foreign Office, he did not seek to interfere in that department's internal arrangements. He was always ready to read the memoranda Van addressed to him, but he was well aware of his tendency to box the compass every twenty-four hours if some fresh intellectual concept obsessed him.

Lady Vansittart, whose sister was married to Sir Eric Phipps, Ambassador both in Paris and in Berlin, had beautiful green eyes and was an entrancing companion. Her son by her first marriage, Sir Colville Barclay, was an exact contemporary of mine in the Foreign Office, agreeable and serious minded, but keener to be a painter than a diplomat. He was, at this time, deeply enamoured of Winston Churchill's niece, the beautiful Clarissa; but his passion was unrequited and she soon had many other dedicated admirers, one of whom, Anthony Eden, she eventually married.

I have a feeling that today may have been rather wasted. We ought surely to have been spreading sedition among French Colonial Governors and instructing our agents to commit sabotage in France. Perhaps we have not been inactive, but the necessary orders do not seem to have come from the top.

The P.M. telegraphed to Pétain expressing his disbelief that "the illustrious Marshal Pétain and the famous General Weygand will injure their ally by delivering over to the enemy the fine French fleet. Such an act would scarify their names for a thousand years of history." Van's telegram in French does not seem to have been approved.

Tuesday, June 18th
The day of Waterloo – a poignant anniversary.

The French are apparently continuing to fight on the Loire and there are indications that Darlan does not intend to let the fleet fall into German hands. I spoke to Hartington[1] on the telephone and he told me that Philip was with the Beauman force, which seems to have borne the brunt of the fighting. The Central War Room informed me that the headquarters of this force were at Avranches, on the sea; so if Philip has survived he should be home at any moment now.

On a minute about the proposal to take away the King of Italy's Garter, the P.M. has scribbled: "I think there should be the utmost ignominy and publicity in the case of this miserable puppet." So much for the House of Savoy! Mother thinks that the Pope should have protested powerfully against Italy entering the war, and that in omitting to do so he has sacrificed great kudos which the R.C. Church might have won.

I see from the Cabinet conclusions that many of our Territorial officers have shown themselves inadequate and Storm Troopers are to be formed. In order to win this war we have to approximate closely and still more closely to the Nazis: complete governmental powers, internment camps and now Storm Troopers.

Mother rang up in the morning to say Philip was back – the last Guardsman to leave France. An indescribable relief.

This morning the Cabinet is discussing a declaration which de Gaulle wishes to make in French on the wireless in this country. Though not *apparently* disloyal to Pétain's Government, it is so in effect, and is intended to rally Frenchmen in this country and elsewhere to de Gaulle himself. He had better not go back to France just yet or else, as David suggested yesterday, all Gaul may be divided into three parts once again.

The Declaration of Union has been published in today's press not, Desmond Morton tells me, because it is a dead letter but in order that it may have its effect on U.S. opinion. It may still be practicable if Herriot[2] and a Government of die-hards succeed Pétain and fight on from outside France.

Went to the House and heard the P.M. speak on the collapse of France and the question of invasion and air bombardment

---

[1] The Marquess of Hartington, elder son of the Duke of Devonshire. Married Kathleen, daughter of Joseph P. Kennedy. Killed in action in 1944.

[2] French elder statesman. President of the Chamber of Deputies and at one time a Prime Minister and Foreign Minister of European renown.

here. He spoke less well than on the last occasion, and referred more often to his notes; but he ended magnificently. I was amused that he brought in Marvell's lines,

> *He nothing common did or mean,*
> *Upon that memorable scene,*

because he has been repeating it consistently and often for the last fortnight. Last Saturday he came out with it several times in the course of the evening and could not resist quoting it to the American Ambassador on the telephone while demanding assistance from the U.S.

After the speech I told him Attlee wanted to see him. He was performing his toilet (!) and said: "So does Amery; he is very tiresome, always wanting to air his views about how to win the war, on behalf of the Junior Ministers, instead of getting on with his work at the India Office."

General Spears came in, asking to see Winston. He said that the Cabinet had turned down de Gaulle's broadcast, because they were anxious not to offend the present French Government yet; now, however, he had evidence to show why it was essential that de Gaulle should speak. It was a question of saving in time a large number of aeroplanes at Bordeaux. Winston told Spears he would agree provided the rest of the War Cabinet concurred, and Spears, looking miserable and hot, set forth on his tour of conversion. Later in the afternoon Vansittart and Morton insisted on my going up to wake Winston, who had just taken to his bed: they wanted to urge on him a new scheme of Van's which entailed Lord Lloyd flying out to Bordeaux to put H.M.G.'s views fairly and squarely to the French Government. Van thought that this would be preferable to, and would exclude, de Gaulle broadcasting.

I went up to the P.M.'s bedroom. The blinds were drawn and Winston himself was right under the bedclothes. When he emerged he had a bandage over his eyes to keep out the light. Finally it was agreed that Van's project, which Halifax and Morton think a forlorn hope, should be put into effect *and* that de Gaulle should broadcast. Halifax thought that we should pull all strings at once: they might get crossed, e.g. Lord Lloyd might get a cool reception if de Gaulle spoke; but there was already such chaos in France that a little more would scarcely do any harm.

Just before dinner a telegram came in from Campbell,[1] saying that the French thought it would be dishonourable to negotiate an armistice unless their armed forces were still intact, but it seemed likely that the fleet would be denied to the Germans. I took this telegram up to the P.M., who was dressing. When he saw me coming with a telegram he said: "Another bloody country gone west, I'll bet."

As I went out to dinner I met Morton and Lindemann and together we gossiped, at the top of the steps leading down to the F.O., about the extraordinary de Gaulle intrigues, etc. Lindemann said cynically that the only thing in which production was going ahead really fast was theories.

Dined with Sylvia Henley. Her brother Oliver Stanley,[2] Juliet Henley and Judy Montagu[3] were there. At 9.00 the P.M. spoke on the wireless, almost word for word what he had said in the House. It was too long and he sounded tired. Juliet said it was like listening to a bishop. He smoked a cigar the whole time he was broadcasting.

Back at No. 10 after dinner. The usual evening party assembled, i.e. Beaverbrook, also Van, Morton and Cadogan. Beaverbrook told me that the Air Ministry was a rotten Ministry and Sinclair a thoroughly bad Minister who was hoodwinked by his subordinates. Pug Ismay says the Chiefs of Staff are too old and slow. There ought to be a chairman who could preside over them and enforce decisions. He thought the P.M. would end by being appointed C. in C. of all three forces.

Winston was furious because the morning papers, which he

[1] Sir Ronald Hugh Campbell, British Ambassador in Paris.
[2] Brother of Lord Stanley of Alderley, not to be confused with the well-known politician.
[3] Only child of Edwin Montagu, member of Mr Asquith's Government and author of the Montagu–Chelmsford constitutional reforms in India, and Venetia Stanley, for whom Mr Asquith, when Prime Minister, conceived an irrepressible passion.

likes to see before going to bed, had not arrived. In his emotion he upset his whisky and soda over all his papers. I asked him if he would see General Sikorski[1] tomorrow. "I will see him," he said, "at noon," and then went on to quote some entirely bogus quotation about that time of day, which he pretended was spoken by the nurse in *Romeo and Juliet*.

I had a long conversation with General Spears outside the door of No. 10. He told me: (i) That he had been with Reynaud when de Gaulle telephoned to him the text of the Declaration of Union. R. had been immensely impressed, but his colleagues had said that the British were trying to make France a Dominion. (ii) That the importance of de Gaulle's speech lay in the fact that Germany was bound to inundate France with propaganda and that it was, therefore, vital to be sure of a focus for Frenchmen on foreign soil, around which all the men and material that escaped could be grouped. Inside France itself a Government of Traitors would soon be established and it would be said that France had been uselessly sacrificed on England's behalf. (iii) That Weygand's strategy in the late battle had been unbelievably bad. The French troops could have no confidence in their High Command which had made mistakes that any intelligent boy-scout could have avoided.

Wednesday, June 19th
Full moon last night: the air-raids will now begin. They were bigger last night than hitherto, and Cambridge was hit, a row of houses being destroyed. David has been called up and will join his unit at Hove on Friday. Philip is to return to the Holding Battalion at Wellington Barracks.

A comparatively uneventful morning, though there are now signs that the French navy is not going to allow itself to be taken. The French Colonial Governors are wobbling but their military commanders are almost all threatening to arrest them if they give in. I told Morton that I did not think enough capital

---

[1] A hero of the Polish campaign against the Red Army in 1920. Prime Minister and Commander in Chief of the Poles in exile in Britain. Killed in an air crash at Gibraltar in 1942.

had been made out of the Declaration of Union, especially in the French Empire. He agreed, and the B.B.C. are, I hope, going to remedy the matter in their broadcast tonight.

President R. has turned down our demand for forty destroyers, but at Van's instigation the matter is not to be allowed to drop. We need them badly.

Saw a letter from Bob Boothby who claims that there is now a revolutionary spirit in the country which ought to be turned to advantage. He is for drastic measures: the conversion of the War Cabinet into a Committee of Public Safety, the adoption of really dictatorial powers, the proclamation of Martial Law. He says: "This is essentially a young man's war . . . It is this incredible conception of a movement (in Germany), young, virile, dynamic and violent, which is advancing irresistibly to overthrow a decaying old world, that we must continue to bear in mind; for it is the main source of the Nazi strength and power." Boothby claims that our leaders (as Pug Ismay said last night), are too old for this kind of war and that there is growing discontent with the fact among the younger officers. He thinks, however, that Lloyd George is an exception and should be brought back to office.

Boothby also claims to have information, gained in Switzerland, that the German invasion of this country will have three elements: by sea from ports stretching from Petsamo to Havre, and including amphibious tanks; by parachute landings in the West Country; by violent bombardment of the ports.

He is certainly a man with drive and, as Tony Bevir remarked, will probably obtain a seat in the most revolutionary post-war Government.

There is evidence to show that Spain is likely to enter the war against us at an early date, and that the military in Japan are bringing great weight to bear in favour of not letting the present opportunity slip.

Went with Mother and Aunt Nancy to see *The Tempest* at the Old Vic. Prospero is not the part for John Gielgud, but Marius Goring as Ariel and Jack Hawkins as Caliban were excellent, and Peggy Ashcroft made an enchanting Miranda, even though she is beginning to look rather too mature for these maidenly parts.

The stalls were practically empty, owing presumably to the general preoccupation with other things, but the gallery was full and enthusiastic.

Thursday, June 20th

Miriam Pease[1] came to breakfast. She is a factory inspector and told me that the conditions in armament factories are now appalling. Even boys of fourteen are working a seventy-hour week, and as it is impossible to work in shifts owing to the lack of skilled labour, efficiency is bound to suffer. Ventilation of factories is bad, she says. The Ministry of Labour cause confusion by setting up innumerable committees to deal with matters which had better be dealt with by experienced and trained experts in industrial conditions.

Heavy air-raids last night in which Southampton, Yorkshire and South Wales seem to have suffered. I suppose the real air armada will come soon, troop carriers and all. Spears thinks we are not by any means sure of being able to deal with it or with tank landings. Winston is goading the C. in C. Home Forces (Ironside), who seems to lack imagination, and he is busy forming special anti-tank forces of mobile troops. He is also taking the question of supply very seriously and has meetings almost every morning now. Lindemann is his right-hand man in this.

The real trouble about air-raids is that night-bombing is unexpectedly accurate and anti-aircraft fire extraordinarily ineffective. To intercept aircraft at night is apparently impossible so far, but we have a new very secret device called A.I. which is expected to help. So far there are only six sets with properly experienced handlers and these are in the Thames estuary.

Secret Session at the House on Home Defence. There was apparently some trouble when Hore-Belisha, replying to Bellenger,[2] implied that one of the reasons for his resignation in January was a difference with the Generals about fortifications from the Maginot Line to the sea. This was quite untrue and

---

[1] Daughter of Lord Gainford and an old friend of my mother. A professional factory inspector of long experience.

[2] Captain Frederick Bellenger. Subsequently a member of Attlee's 1945 Labour Government.

Chamberlain got up and rebutted the accusation. Winston spoke later, with great success I hear.

At about 11.30 p.m. Winston went back to No. 10 taking Alexander and Duff Cooper with him: "two dreadnoughts and a battleship", as he described the party on getting into the car. I had great difficulty in returning in my car owing to the formidable defences of Whitehall, and I found the Grenadiers on duty most unhelpful. Eventually I more or less forced my way through barriers on to the Horse Guards Parade and had quite an acrimonious *"passage d'armes"* with the officer in charge.

Lord Lloyd was at No. 10, just back from Bordeaux. He said things were much better and that continued resistance in North Africa, and the departure of the Government from France were now almost certain. Pétain was hopeless, as was Weygand; but Admiral Darlan was full of spirit.

Friday, June 21st
Winston sent the following note to the Foreign Secretary: "Do you think there is much use in promising to discuss the cession of Gibraltar to Spain after the war? The Spanish know that if we lose they will get it anyhow, and they would be great fools to believe that if we win we shall mark our admiration for their conduct by giving it to them. The news that we were willing to entertain the idea of giving up Gibraltar would do no end of harm."

We were all awaiting the German peace terms to France. I fear that they may be sufficiently generous to tempt the French Government, but the general opinion is that they will be crushing. The chief excitement of the day is the possibility of six cruisers intercepting the *Scharnhorst*, escorted by destroyers, off the Norwegian coast. She was torpedoed last night by one of our submarines, the *Clyde*. As I write, 8.30 p.m., the two forces ought just to have become engaged; but of course the *Scharnhorst* may turn into Stavanger fjord. Winston, with whom I drove back from the Upper War Room at the Admiralty, remarked that a few weeks ago we should have thought this news thrilling, but now it seems like a minor incident.

Saturday, June 22nd

The expected naval encounter has not come off, the enemy having fled into Stavanger where he is to be bombed today.

The news from France is not good, and there are signs that the determination of the French Government to continue their resistance is weakening. Laval is said to be busy with members of the Chamber and that is a bad sign.

During the Cabinet a telegram came in to say that the German armistice terms were being telegraphed from Bordeaux, and that the part concerning the fleet was following fast. I telephoned this down to Chequers, and everybody is waiting anxiously to know what the terms will be. Can the Germans be so foolish as to make them unacceptable and so drive the French Government overseas to continue the battle? I fear not, even though a day or two ago all preparations for the President and Government to go had been made.

Sunday, June 23rd [at Ardley – my sister-in-law, Joan Colville's house near Bicester]

In the afternoon we played a little bridge, and after dinner listened, between hands of "Slippery Jane", to the crushing terms which Marshal Pétain has thought it honourable to accept. De Gaulle broadcast at 10.00, preaching sedition – an action which I later heard was resented by many Frenchmen. H.M.G. published a message supporting de Gaulle, and this, I gather, was done by the F.O. on Lord Halifax's authority; but again the reactions from many French quarters were bad. Very tired.

Tuesday, June 25th

When I reached No. 10 I found that things had not been going well. Noguès,[1] in Algeria, is half-hearted; there is every reason to think that Darlan is behaving badly; the French fleet does not seem disposed to fight on under British orders, or even as an Ally, against the Germans and Italians; and, incredible though it may sound, the Bordeaux Government seem disposed to accept Hitler's assurances about the fleet and to trust his word. The

---

[1] Commander in Chief of the French troops there.

name of France will assuredly be blackened, as Winston said, for years to come. And, of course, they, the French, will maintain it is all our fault for not providing more support on land.

De Gaulle does not appear to have enough prestige to rally the more determined Frenchmen to himself, and it is a thousand pities that nothing is being done – so far as I can discover – to form a really strong Imperial French Government which could disavow Bordeaux and win the allegiance of military, naval and civil authorities in the French Empire. At present only Syria, the Cameroons, the French West Indies and Indo-China are steadfast.

Ismay has produced a first-rate note (which was, I understand, written by Colonel Jacob*) about the offensive action which we can take. When we have the equipment and the aeroplanes we must invade the continent, because Germany will not be defeated until her armies are defeated on the field of battle, a result for which the blockade will contribute much but will not alone suffice. We have got to plan this offensive now and discover an excellent young general to whom its preparation can be entrusted under the direction of the Chiefs of Staff and of Winston himself.

Dined with Seal at the Travellers wisely and well. He was interesting about Winston, explaining how much he had changed since becoming P.M. He had sobered down, become less violent, less wild, less impetuous. Seal thinks that W. believes in his mission, to extricate this country from its present troubles, and he will certainly kill himself, if necessary, in order to achieve his object. He is superstitious: Seal cited the case of the *Royal Oak*, which sank at the end of a day, Friday, November 13th, on which Winston had mistakenly put on a black tie instead of his usual spotted one – facts to which he attached great importance.

Everything now seems to point to my being released for active service soon. Seal says that the Treasury agree, and I have more or less persuaded the F.O. But I am afraid eyesight will bar me for the navy and I shall try the Guards.

Returning to Downing Street we had great trouble with the barricades, which infuriated the somewhat easily provoked Seal.

General Sikorski (Polish P.M.) came to see Winston. His

A.D.C. said that the way in which the French ran away was indescribable: they showed no fighting spirit. I hear from all sides that the Poles have been fighting magnificently in France: they seem to be our most formidable allies.

Slept at No. 10 on a bed which has been set up in the room in which I work – a rather sordid arrangement.

Wednesday, June 26th
Slept well in spite of the surroundings and various Yellow air-raid warnings, alarums and excursions. First thing in the morning Captain Pim[1] came round from the war room to report the news: 150 planes over England, eight brought down, practically no damage. The Germans seem to have no training in night bombing, and in this we have a great advantage.

Yesterday the P.M. received the following letter:

Dear Prime Minister

Why not declare war on France and capture her fleet (which would gladly strike its colors to us) before A.H. recovers his breath?

Surely that is the logic of the situation?

Tactically,

G. Bernard Shaw.

Belgrade and Bucharest, which are always prolific with their reports from Berlin, foreshadow a peace offensive or the summoning by Hitler of a European Economic Congress, excluding Great Britain and Turkey. From Berne comes a report that the plan of invasion has been postponed, if not abandoned, and that the Germans were surprised by the intelligent heroism of our troops in France. Personally I think a peace offensive is almost certain, unless it has dawned on Hitler that we shall not stop fighting until we have won. When his terms are rejected, very heavy bombing is, I suppose, inevitable.

Smuts has telegraphed to Winston saying that arms and

---

[1] In charge of the Prime Minister's private and personal map room. Afterwards head of the Royal Ulster Constabulary.

men should be poured into South Africa. The British Isles will withstand the threat of invasion, providing no vital mistakes are made, but the Near East, India and Africa are in deadly peril, and from them Hitler could obtain enough resources to maintain himself and his régime. In his reply Winston says that, as far as Germany is concerned, he does not think that winter's strain will prove decisive, but next year, or even this, he hopes that we shall take the offensive and begin "large-scale amphibious operations" on the continent. This will keep Hitler occupied because he "has vast hungry areas to defend and we have the command of the sea".

At tea George Steward told us of a conversation he had had during lunch with French journalists. These said that although de Gaulle was an honest straightforward man, he was not the person to establish a new French Government and they mistrusted the judgment of Spears, who had launched de Gaulle. (Actually it was never intended that de Gaulle should be any more than a rallying point for expatriated Frenchmen: it was the fault of the Ministry of Information that a false impression on this point has been given.) The new French Government must be established on French Colonial soil, in liaison with the British Government, and they thought Peyrouton[1] was the man to lead it. But much depended on the decision which Noguès finally adopted.

Orders have been given to our ships to capture the new French battleship *Richelieu* and, if she puts to sea from Casablanca, the *Jean Bart* as well. Unless things go much more satisfactorily in North Africa than we now expect, we shall end by seizing by force as much of the French fleet as we can intercept.

Thursday, June 27th

Went up to the P.M.'s bedroom at about 10.00. He was lying in bed, in a red dressing-gown, smoking a cigar and dictating to

[1] Marcel Peyrouton, Vichy Minister of the Interior. Rallied to the Western Allies in 1942 and was appointed, on American initiative, Governor General of Algeria. Removed by de Gaulle.

Mrs Hill, who sat with a typewriter at the foot of the bed. His box, half full of papers, stood open on his bed and by his side was a vast chromium-plated cuspidor. His black cat Nelson, which has quite replaced our old No. 10 black cat, sprawled at the foot of the bed and every now and then Winston would gaze at it affectionately and say "Cat, darling".

Among this morning's minutes was one he wrote to the Secretary of State for Air about the shortcomings of the Air Ministry and the flaws in its organisation (criticisms based on a memorandum sent from the F.O.). He described the Air Ministry as "a most cumbrous and ill-working administrative machine".

During the Cabinet news came out that both Noguès and Mittelhauser,[1] in Syria, had abandoned all idea of resistance and were going to be loyal to the Bordeaux Government. This is tragic news as it virtually delivers North Africa, with its vast supplies, into the hands of the enemy. In France itself the Germans will procure large stocks of petroleum, steel, fats and an immense sum in gold. Now, with North Africa gone, the position is more serious still and our lifeline in the Near East is threatened. It is doubtful whether the French, even those that are loyal to their Allies, will do much effective sabotage: the way in which they delayed handing over to us captured German pilots, when they might still have done so, until it was too late, is not encouraging.

It seems years since we had even a gleam of good news!

There is a good deal of Anglophobia in France and Algeria, partly on account of Winston's hard remarks about the Pétain Government and partly because it is said that we did not provide France with enough support. There is a good deal more Francophobia in England. Such is the fate of the Entente Cordiale.

America is disheartened, inclined to blame us for the defeat of France, and less ready than before to counter Japanese designs in the Far East.

---

[1] French General with a command in Syria.

Friday, June 28th

The Russian ultimatum to Roumania about Bessarabia may be good news. It is possible that the Soviet will impede the supply of oil from Roumania to Germany. They can scarcely be overjoyed by the prospect of German hegemony over Europe; but unfortunately events have shown that it is impossible to put much faith in Russia.

The P.M. is, as ever, actively interested in every small question relating to the war. This morning: "Home Secretary: Let me see a list of prominent persons you have arrested."

In a minute to the P.M. Amery examines the possibility of developing India's resources in men and armaments. We must, he says, visualise the possibility of being driven out of Egypt and Palestine during the next few months, back on to Iraq and Aden. "After that, if not next year then in 1942, a great Army of Liberation from the south-east, carrying forward with it the armies of Turkey and the Balkan States, may march into the heart of Europe to meet our Army of Liberation from the west."

Went to Chequers, driving down with Mrs Churchill in her car. We talked a good deal of politics, about which her views are as ill-judged as they are decisive. She spoke much of the time wasted in the last nine months and I tried to convince her laboriously that Chamberlain's Government could not achieve great results without full powers and that full powers could only be obtained by a National Government. Until the Norwegian affair this was impossible, because Labour and the Liberals refused all invitations to co-operate, maintaining that an Opposition and criticism were essential in war-time. "Then Chamberlain ought to have resigned," said Mrs C.; and I could not make the proper retort that there was nobody to take his place and that the country would never have accepted Winston.

Lindemann was at Chequers, also Mary Churchill, Judy Montagu and Ismay, who came to dine and sleep. We arrived just after 9.00 p.m., at the same time as the guests for dinner, Sir Robert and Lady Vansittart and M. Léger.[1] During dinner the

---

[1] For many years permanent head of the Quai d'Orsay (French Foreign Ministry). Much more involved with internal politics than his British equivalents, Vansittart and Cadogan.

P.M. said to Lady Van, who was on his right, while I was next to her: "He wants to go and fight, but I won't let him." I asked him if he would let me go eventually, and he promised he would if the country really needed me but said that at present my duty was to stay in the job for which I was trained.

When the ladies had left the dining-room, Winston, Léger and Van discussed the collapse of France. Winston told Léger he was speaking to a *"cercle sacré"* and must express himself frankly. He foresaw the possibility of France declaring war on us and he wanted to know how we could maintain the goodwill of the French people, for whose salvation we were the last hope, while we were obliged to starve them by blockade and destroy their towns by bombs. How could we convince them that we were being cruel in order to be kind? It was essential to keep the French well disposed to us, even if their Government went to war with Great Britain. Léger replied that it was important to maintain contact with the Bordeaux Government, to send a chargé d'affaires to France and not to leave this country unrepresented there.

Apart from that he saw three ways in which we might influence the French people:

(i) By clever use of the press and wireless. English broadcasting was more heard in France than was French broadcasting, and now it alone could be expected to provide news from untainted sources. Similarly English newspapers would find their way into France. They must be sympathetic and avoid recrimination.

(ii) By not doing anything unnecessarily provocative to French sentiment. It might be necessary to oppose the Government, e.g. by bombing French ports in occupied territory and by tightening the blockade, but French national sentiment must not be antagonised. As regards the fleet, which was, he agreed, the major problem of the moment, he suggested that the French might be asked to invite a third power to act as an intermediary in keeping it immobilised in French ports. This the Axis powers would refuse to allow, and then we should have a good pretext for seizing as much of the fleet as we could with the probable compliance of the French navy and approval of the people.

Winston was not impressed by this suggestion: he is contemplating violent action against French ships in African ports.

(iii) By doing all possible in the U.S. from the point of view of propaganda. The U.S. had always been sympathetic to France and they might easily be led to believe that France had only collapsed because we had given her inadequate support. If the British were blamed in America, the French would increase their own propaganda on these lines (which in their heart of hearts they must know to be untrue) and the effect of American opinion on France was immense.

Winston would have none of this (although Van backed Léger up): he has received such reports from Lothian, whom he and Van think little of; he has been pressed on all sides to pander to American opinion; and he maintains it is entirely a waste of time. "Propaganda is all very well," he said to Léger, "but it is events that move the world. If we smash the Huns here we shall need no propaganda in the United States." It was, he said, "the night before the battle. It may be long: now we must live; next year we shall be winning; the year after we shall triumph". But if we could hold the Germans in this coming critical month of July, and deny this country to them, then our position would be quite different from today and "a very different wind will be blowing on the world".

Léger said that Reynaud had been less devoted to the Allied cause than we had supposed. He was under the thumb of a mistress who was in the pocket of the pro-Axis party in France, and on the advice of "*cette femme*" Léger himself had been dismissed, de Gaulle had been sent off to the front, and Baudouin, etc., had gained Reynaud's ear. R. had long been thinking on the lines of a German–Italian–French entente and only the P.M.'s visits had served to keep him to the straight and narrow path. "I wish now that I had stayed there ten days," said Winston, "and had left Neville to carry on at home." I felt sure (and I think Winston did too) that Léger's remarks about Reynaud were coloured by the fact that it was from Reynaud he had received his dismissal.

The Vansittarts and Léger left about 1.00 a.m. and afterwards the P.M. discussed with Ismay the organisation of the War

Office and Air Ministry. The latter, in particular, disturbs him and it is the cause of serious differences between Sinclair and Beaverbrook. He told Ismay there was too much "top hamper" in both departments: they would have to be simplified and useless officials must be ruthlessly eliminated. Speaking of the Chiefs of Staff, W. said he thought a lot of Pound, although he was slow; Newall had many good points (but Beaverbrook says "he was an observer in the last war, and he has remained an observer ever since"); Dill had, unfortunately, aged a great deal in every way (c.f. Weygand's sudden senility in the course of a few weeks).

Saturday, June 29th
Prof. (Lindemann) says that the French collapse has helped Germany a lot economically, even though, as far as fats are concerned, the effect may not be visible until next spring. But I am afraid it is very likely to lengthen the war by saving Germany the necessity of tightening her belt still further. Winston is perturbed. He writes this morning: "It seems to me the blockade is largely ruined, in which case the sole decisive weapon in our hands would be overwhelming air attack upon Germany."

I awoke at 8.00 and made telephonic enquiries about the results of last night's air-raids and the naval situation. But the P.M. did not send for me till 9.30 and he lay in bed all the morning working. I was able to give him the news about H.M.S. *Dainty* which, in the Mediterranean, reported that she had sunk three Italian submarines and was pursuing six more. I also told him that Balbo had been killed flying and suggested that this had been engineered by Mussolini. He said he thought it very probable.

Beaverbrook and Brendan Bracken came down to lunch. The conversation began with a discussion on the evacuation of the Channel Islands and the food which had been left behind. Turning to me Winston said: "Tell the Ministry of Food to evaluate it, and the Admiralty to evacuate it." I carried out this peremptory order which, of course, led to much trouble – the cattle in Jersey had foot-and-mouth disease, etc., etc. Winston was obviously pleased with his epigram and did not look beyond. After lunch

Beaverbrook raised the question of whether we should continue to increase our aircraft production or should improve the engines and armaments. There is an important decision to make: should we aim at quantity or quality? B. says he can maintain our present level of output in any case and that should give a certain measure of safety.

I sat in the garden much of the afternoon with Mrs C., Mary (whom I find very much nicer on closer acquaintance) and Judy Montagu. The P.M. talked with Beaverbrook, and later with Alec Hardinge, who came after tea. They discussed the position of the Duke of Windsor who is in Madrid trying to impose conditions, financial and otherwise, about his return to this country. It is incredible to haggle in such a way at this time, and Winston proposes to send him a very stiff telegram pointing out that he is a soldier under orders and must obey. The King approves and says he will hear of no conditions, about the Duchess or otherwise.

We had tea in the morning-room upstairs and while we were there the Sandyses arrived. Shortly afterwards came Randolph Churchill and his wife.[1] I thought Randolph one of the most objectionable people I had ever met: noisy, self-assertive, whining and frankly unpleasant. He did not strike me as intelligent. At dinner he was anything but kind to Winston, who adores him, and he made a scene in front of General Paget about complacency in high places, inefficiency of the Generals, lack of equipment, etc., etc. Duncan Sandys appeared charming by contrast, although I daresay he is an opportunist. Diana Sandys I liked.

In reply to a request from the P.M., the Home Secretary sent a list of 150 "prominent people" whom he had arrested. Of the first three on the list two, Lady Mosley[2] and Geo Pitt-Rivers,[3] were cousins of the Churchills – a fact which piqued Winston and caused much merriment among his children!

[1] Pamela, daughter of Lord Digby. Later wife of Leland Hayward and, after his death, of Averell Harriman.*
[2] Diana Mitford, daughter of Lord Redesdale, wife of Sir Oswald Mosley.
[3] Mosley's second in command in the British Union of Fascists. Married at one time to Rosalind, Mrs Henley's scientist daughter.

General Paget,[1] who did so well in South Norway against tremendous odds, came to dine and sleep. When the ladies had gone, Winston got going and gave an interesting résumé of the French campaign as it appeared to him. He said that there had been a rot in France which had affected every class and stratum of the community: it was not merely the Generals and the politicians but the whole country. There had, said Winston, been "nothing like it, ever", and its feeble reaction was now apparent in the outbreak of Anglophobia. Winston described how Gamelin had said to him, after the breakthrough at Sedan, "They are superior in numbers, they are superior in armaments, they are superior in method." When W. asked him what he was going to do about it, G. just shrugged his shoulders, and Winston remarked to us bitterly: "Gamelin was occupied in saving not France but his own position." He still believed, however, that Georges had been a good commander.

Winston went on to expatiate on the incredible success of the German armoured divisions and the curious inability of the French to evolve any method of dealing with them. He said it was something new in warfare which he did not fully understand. It was astounding that 4,000 excellent troops in Calais should so easily have been driven out and he thought Gort had missed an opportunity in not making a lightning move to the relief of Calais with one of his divisions. Such action would almost certainly have been successful and would have given the B.E.F. a far larger area from which to evacuate.

After dinner I went for a short walk with Mary and Judy, and we were challenged in the most alarming way by ferocious sentries. I had thought the P.M. was walking with Paget, but unfortunately he had changed his mind and I had to run precipitately back, at the risk of my life, and screaming the password "Tofrek", in order to be ready for his commands. Later in the evening the Air Ministry, in giving me details of the raids then taking place said that enemy planes were passing south of Aylesbury. I told Winston who said, "I'll bet you a

---

[1] Chief of the Home Forces General Staff. Later Commander in Chief, Home Forces.

monkey to a mouse-trap they don't hit the house", and hurried excitedly out of the house to see if he could see anything, shouting at a sentry: "Friend – Tofrek – Prime Minister" (a formula which entirely nonplussed the unfortunate soldier). General Paget and I followed behind in a leisurely way, the former saying to me "what a wonderful tonic he is".

I see from intelligence reports that the German long-range bomber *Geschwäder*[1] will be refitted and ready by July 8th. Their fighters are already prepared for action, and it is considered that a major offensive is likely about July 8th and is possible any time after June 30th. The nightly raids we now endure are presumably just intended to test our defences.

Winston went to bed shortly after 1.00 a.m. and I resisted the now drunken Randolph's attempt to make me sit up with him and discuss the Fifth Column (which, incidentally, Winston thinks a much less serious menace than had been supposed). Randolph was in a horrible state, gross, coarse and aggressive. I felt ashamed of him for Winston's sake and yet W. said, when he asked to be allowed some more active part in the war, that if R. were killed he would not be able to carry on his work.

Sunday, June 30th
Winston asked for me at 7.30 a.m., which was inconsiderate, to find out if there was any news. As he lay in bed all the morning, dictating to Mrs Hill, I was at a loose end, but did not dare to go more than a few yards from the house in case Winston or the telephone should ring. So I sat in a chair in the sun outside the window of my sitting-room, reading descriptions of the Pavilion at Brighton and a small German Court before the war by Mary McCarthy. The ladies of the party (except Mrs Randolph) went to church.

It is a curious feeling to stay for the week-end in a country house, not as a guest and yet, for a number of reasons, on fairly close terms with the family. It was much like any week-end party except for the conversation which, of course, was brilliant. It is a pleasure to hear really well-informed talk, unpunctuated

---

[1] Approximate equivalent of an R.A.F. "Wing".

by foolish and ignorant remarks (except occasionally from Randolph), and it is a relief to be in the background with occasional commissions to execute, but few views to express, instead of being expected to be interesting because one is the P.M.'s Private Secretary.

Chequers itself, though not arranged with perfect taste, has an air of calm and happiness about it. The surrounding country is exquisite. Looking through the Visitors' Book I saw that Marshal Foch had written in it: *Les affaires de l'Angleterre iront encore mieux quand son premier ministre pourra se reposer à Chequers.* Let us hope he will not be as wrong about that as he was about Weygand. ("When France is in danger send for Weygand.")

Mr Amery and General Thorne[1] (commanding XIIth Corps, south of the Thames) came to lunch. Randolph said something unpleasant about the former Government and claimed that its leaders ought to be punished. "We don't want to punish anyone now – except the enemy," replied Winston. W. is, however, less cautious about his criticism of Baldwin, etc., even though he never countenances a word against Chamberlain, and when I told him that the Germans had bombed the works of "Guest, Keen and Baldwin", in South Wales, all he said was: "Very ungrateful of them."

I told Amery at lunch the dictum about the Harrow and Eton opening batsmen (Harrow: W.S.C. and Lord Gort; Eton: King Leopold and Captain Ramsay[2]) and was amused to hear Amery include his own name in the Harrovian list, and exclude Lord Gort, when he repeated the story to Winston.

After lunch Winston and Thorne examined the whole question of invasion and all the possibilities. Thorne thinks 80,000 men will be landed on the beaches between Thanet and Pevensey (which is Thorne's area); Winston is less pessimistic and thinks the navy will have much to say to this. W. is not sanguine about

---

[1] A gallant Grenadier with three D.S.Os. Had commanded a division in the Dunkirk campaign and now commanded a corps in the threatened invasion area.

[2] M.P. of genuine patriotism, however misguided, who made no effort to conceal his admiration for Hitler and fascism.

our ability to hold the whole expanse of beaches and points out that a river line has never proved a real obstacle to an enemy. He thinks it will not be difficult for the enemy to find soft patches into which he can probe. Thorne, who was Military Attaché in Berlin, is convinced that the Germans, acting according to their rule, will concentrate all their forces against one place, even if they make feints elsewhere.

Winston is inclined to think that Hitler's plans have had to be changed: H. cannot have foreseen the collapse of France and must have planned his strategy of invasion on the assumption that the French armies would be holding out on the Somme, or at least on the Seine, and that the B.E.F. would either be assisting them or else have been wiped out. The situation is now very different: on the one hand many more ways of invasion are open (although if the invading troops are to be escorted, it will still be difficult for the escorting ships to penetrate the Straits of Dover): on the other the whole of the B.E.F. is now back in this country to defend it. Thorne agreed, but said that the Divisions in his area were scarcely equipped at all and only partly trained. He thought the German left wing could be held in Ashdown Forest, but he did not see what could prevent the right wing advancing through Canterbury to London, especially if his only trained and equipped Division (the 3rd) was to be moved away to Northern Ireland. The P.M. Promised that this should not be done.

We left Chequers about 4.00 p.m., I driving up to London with Mr Amery and General Thorne (both of whose sons were with me at West Downs). [1] We had a very pleasant conversation on every kind of subject. Amery said he thought Winston ought to be Minister of Defence and P.M. only in name: I said that this was in fact the case – he spent most of the day with the Chiefs of Staff. General Thorne said that that was as it should be: it was most desirable that one of the greatest students of military history and of war should himself play the leading part in the direction of this war's strategy. Winston was more vital to this country than Hitler to Germany, because the former was

---

[1] A preparatory school near Winchester.

unique and irreplaceable and the latter had established a school of leaders. The obvious comment is that Hitler may be a self-educated corporal and Winston may be an experienced student of tactics; but unfortunately Germany is organised as a war machine and England has only just realised the meaning of modern warfare.

It was interesting to hear from Brendan Bracken, when I got back to No. 10, that Mr Alexander had told him he and the other Labour Ministers were beginning to realise what Chamberlain was and to admit that their condemnation of him had been to a great extent unjustified.

I have among my papers a note which I gave to the Prime Minister in June, 1940, which shows the bitterness of our feelings over the French collapse. For the first and only time in my life I became, for a brief period, a Francophobe; and I was certainly not alone in that. It is a quotation I found in Shakespeare's Henry VI, Part 3:

HASTINGS: *Why, knows not Montague that of itself*
              England is safe, if true within itself?
MONTAGUE: *But the safer when 'tis back'd with France.*
HASTINGS: *'Tis better using France than trusting France.*
              Let us be back'd with God, and with the seas,
              Which He hath giv'n for fence impregnable,
              And with their helps only defend ourselves.
              In them and in ourselves our safety lies.

SEVEN

ALONE
JULY 1940

Monday, July 1st

On a secret F.O. Paper Roger Makins[1] has written: "What happened at Bordeaux was a coup d'état engineered by the most corrupt elements in France making use of famous names." It is accepted here that the anti-Bolshevik feelings of Pétain, Weygand, etc., were exploited by Laval and Baudouin; and the general Anglophobia, spreading over the country, is a natural reaction to events. It has an element of justification, in that we did not provide many divisions, but it really springs from the unwillingness of the French to admit their own shame. It was thus that Leopold was the scapegoat for the incredible French blunder on the Meuse at Sedan (of which neither Winston nor Paget could find any explanation last Saturday at Chequers), and now inadequate British assistance is the thin excuse used to explain the total collapse of France.

The Prime Minister has instructed Ismay to investigate the question of "drenching" beaches with mustard gas if the Germans land. He considers that gas warfare would be justified in such an event. The other day he said to General Thorne: "I have no scruples, except not to do anything dishonourable," and I suppose he does not consider gassing Germans dishonourable.

[1] Later Lord Sherfield.*

Tuesday, July 2nd

Tomorrow at dawn we put into operation a plan called CATAPULT which entails the seizure of all French ships in British ports and, later in the day, an ultimatum to the big French capital ships at Oran.

The P.M. says that in the event of invasion London should be defended. To take it would cost the Germans many lives. Secret Service reports from Norway make it clear that invasion is being prepared from there as well as from other quarters. It is suggested that Iceland and the Shetlands may be among the first objectives, that a feint will be made against the East Coast, but that the real attack will be from the West.

Beaverbrook wants to resign because of his difficulties with the Air Ministry and, in particular, with the Air Marshals. Winston won't hear of any such thing at the present moment and, of course, it does rather look as if B. wanted to leave now, at the peak of success in aircraft production, before new difficulties arise. It is like trying to stop playing cards immediately after a run of luck.

Brendan Bracken is apparently to be allowed to supervise the appointment of bishops – which I find a little hard to stomach. Brendan is all very well – intelligent, forceful and often sensible – but he is not the man to deal with bishops.[1]

Winston returned about 10.45 p.m. from a tour of defences in the South and life became both hot and hectic.

Wednesday, July 3rd

At No. 10 chief interest centres on the Operation CATAPULT. First we heard of the operations at Portsmouth and Plymouth, then that the attack on Oran was to take place at 1.30. During the afternoon came news of various postponements in the hope that the French resolve to fight was weakening.

At about 7.00 p.m. signals began to come through that we were heavily engaged with the French. I was alone most of the time with Lord Lloyd and Sir John Dill. The former had been

---

[1] I did not appreciate Brendan's genuine and conscientious interest in things ecclesiastical, hidden behind a mask of agnosticism.

summoned to consider a project for making the Duke of Windsor Governor of the Bahamas. The latter, who had been sent for presumably to discuss some question of defence, told me that Winston confined himself to telling him the story of the situation and to walking up and down saying "Terrible, terrible". Dill said that he had never seen anything comparable: the two nations who were fighting for civilisation had turned and rent each other while the barbarians sat back and laughed. It is indeed the most tragic irony in history and an event that could not have been entertained as possible a fortnight ago.

There was the greatest excitement about the operations taking place and an 11.30 p.m. meeting of the Chiefs of Staff. Winston said to the First Lord that the French were now fighting with all their vigour for the first time since war broke out. He did not see how we could avoid being at war with France tomorrow.

Apparently Brendan Bracken had been indiscreet and given the whole situation away at a dinner party, so it will have to be published quickly. The shock to public opinion will be greater than any to date. War is said to be always full of surprises – but this is a fantasy.

While we were standing about outside the Cabinet Room Edward Bridges declaimed on the danger of "looking over our shoulder". We have got to withstand the new technique of war, an offensive against our morale, and nothing is more helpful to Hitler than to say we must start thinking about preparing skeleton Government departments in Canada, etc. Already incalculable harm is being done by attacks on the Civil Service, Mr Chamberlain, the Chiefs of Staff and the C. in C. Home Forces (Ironside). If enough people say that these people and institutions are rotten (which they are not), it will be believed and the Germans will have cause to rub their hands. We should burn our boats, stand firm and refuse to contemplate anything but victory. Being on the defensive brings many disadvantages and dangers.

Before going to bed the P.M. rang for me and asked me to take down a telegram to the Duke of Windsor, offering him the Governorship of the Bahamas. Before dictating a sentence he always muttered it wheezingly under his breath and he seemed to gain intellectual stimulus from pushing in with his stomach the chairs standing round the Cabinet table! "I think it is a very good suggestion of mine, Max," he said to Beaverbrook, who was there. "Do you think he will take it?" "Sure he will," said B., "and he'll find it a great relief." "Not half as much as his brother will," replied W. When I gave him the dictated telegram he said: "What a beautiful handwriting(!!), but, my dear boy, when I say stop you must write stop and not just put a blob." (He is always pedantic about small things.)

Thursday, July 4th
The action against the French fleet at Oran was very successful, although it was unfortunate the *Strasbourg* escaped. At Alexandria we heard, early in the morning, that trouble was brewing and it looked as if the French would scuttle their ships and block the harbour.

The P.M. made a statement in the House, to which I listened. He told the whole story of Oran and the House listened enthralled and amazed. Gasps of surprise were audible but it was clear that the action taken was unanimously approved. When the speech was over all the Members rose to their feet, waved their order papers and cheered loudly. Winston left the House visibly affected. I heard him say to Hore-Belisha: "This is heartbreaking for me."

Jarrett[1] (Alexander's Private Secretary) and I sat in my room at the House and received news from the Admiralty. Part was good and unexpected: a satisfactory agreement had been reached about the French ships at Alexandria. Part was bad: a serious air-raid had taken place at Portland and much damage was done. Twenty dive-bombers took part and were not intercepted – a bad look-out for the future if this can be done with impunity in broad daylight.

Dined with Grandfather and Peggy at Argyll House and felt very much better for his remarkable old brandy and her witty conversation.

---

[1] Sir Clifford Jarrett, Permanent Secretary to the Admiralty, 1962–64.

Friday, July 5th
The world's reactions to the Battle of Oran are favourable, it seems. As Mother says, there is a strange admiration for force everywhere today, even among those who suffer from it. It is a curious disease: even exiled German Jews have been known to speak with awe and respect of the Nazi power which is responsible for their distress. Thus it may be that even in France our action will be approved.

The P.M. has telegraphed again to Roosevelt explaining our dire need for an immediate supply of destroyers and motor-torpedo boats. With the whole French coast in enemy hands the importance of our naval strength is double as great, and America's responsibility will be heavy (or "grievous" as the P.M. puts it) if she fails us now.

[*He has not sent this off owing to objections from Halifax on certain points. (JRC – 13.7.40).*]

From German sources it is reported that the French Government has broken off diplomatic relations with us. But we have heard nothing!

Saturday, July 6th [*at Cambridge*]
In this halcyon summer the only rain we get invariably falls during my week-ends off. This is no exception.

After dinner I called upon the Vice Master of Trinity, Winstanley,[1] and drank beer with him as I used so often to do. He told me that the Master was failing and it might soon fall to my lot to consider the appointment of a new Master of Trinity. We discussed the matter and he said that Adrian[2] would be the appointment most congenial to the Fellows.

In speaking of the war I expressed the opinion that the two most disappointing and discredited men of recent months were King Victor Emmanuel and the Pope. The House of Savoy, though opposed to war, had not had the courage of its convictions; the Pope, who must realise that as never before this war

[1] Historian of Whig politics in the eighteenth century and of Cambridge University.
[2] World-famous physiologist, Nobel Prize winner and holder of the Order of Merit. Succeeded Professor George Trevelyan as Master of Trinity.

was one between right and wrong, Christianity and barbarism, should have boldly laid the Fascist Government under an Interdict. In so doing he would have martyrised the Italian Church and himself, but he would have raised the prestige and power of Catholicism to great heights throughout the world and the Church would ultimately have benefited. Winstanley, though agreeing about the House of Savoy, was less sure as regards the Pope. But I am convinced that a spiritual power should never compromise between justice and injustice and in standing aloof Pius XII has betrayed the memory of Hildebrand,[1] whose dying words were: *"Dilexi justitiam et odivi iniquitatem: ergo morior in exilio"* [I have loved justice and hated iniquity: therefore I die in exile].

Monday, July 8th
Today is supposed to be the day on which the German bomber force should be ready and refitted. I have the impression that Germany is collecting herself for a great spring; and it is an uncomfortable impression.

I went up to see the P.M. in bed and he gave me a note, for instant despatch to Lord Beaverbrook, of which the following is an extract:

> When I look round to see how we can win the war I see that there is only one sure path. We have no continental army which can defeat the German military power. The blockade is broken and Hitler has Asia and probably Africa to draw from. Should he be repulsed here or not try invasion he will recoil eastward and we have nothing to stop him. But there is one thing that will bring him back and bring him down, and that is an absolutely devastating, exterminating attack by very heavy bombers from this country upon the Nazi homeland. We must be able to overwhelm them by this means without which I do not see a way through.

[1] Hildebrand, Pope Gregory VII, died in exile at Salerno in 1085 after a long struggle with the Holy Roman Emperor, Henry IV, over the rival claims of the spiritual and temporal powers.

This is a curious war. Early today we think we inflicted serious damage on the *Richelieu* at Dakar. Now we are suggesting that our Consul General there might be able to discover how serious that damage in fact is! Meanwhile the French are becoming very ferocious and one of our submarines has inadvertently sunk a French cruiser at a time and place when it should not have done so. Result: an apology by H.M.G. to the French Government at the same time as we are tentatively suggesting the appointment of a Chargé d'Affaires in unoccupied France.

Tuesday, July 9th
The invasion and great attack is now said to be due on Thursday. Meanwhile Russia seems disposed to try bullying Turkey about the Straits.

Spent part of today reading Sir R. Campbell's account of the last days of France. From the time that the Somme could no longer be held the politicians and Generals apparently gave up hope: "a lamentable influence was General Weygand's mystic mood which led him to believe that France, having made mistakes, deserved to suffer." Campbell does not think the seed of France's decay lay in her constitution, even though the multiplicity of small parties made it impossible for a real leader to emerge. It was the inconceivable collapse of the army which destroyed all further will to resistance and made France "like a man who, stunned by an unexpected blow, was unable to rise to his feet before his opponent delivered the *coup de grâce*".

Lunched with Pat Hancock. He is private secretary to Dalton at the Ministry of Economic Warfare, and thinks him good. He says that there is a good deal of attempted jobbery by the Labour Party, which still thinks very much on party lines.

Winston went off to see some new aeroplanes, an improved Hurricane, a machine called the Tornado, etc., and I took the opportunity to go and have an hour's sleep at the Travellers. Just as I was leaving I heard from the Admiralty that the C. in C., Mediterranean, was engaging a superior Italian fleet, consisting of three battleships, thirteen cruisers and fifteen destroyers. Unfortunately the Italians quickly scuttled for home. But we are now proposing to take offensive action in the

Mediterranean, to raid the Channel Isles and (Operation SUSAN) to establish a force at Casablanca. On duty late. Spent most of the time trying to instil some semblance of order into the P.M.'s box and listening to Beaverbrook's philippics against the Air Ministry, Lord Halifax, the employment of old men, etc., etc.

Wednesday, July 10th

Winston is displeased with the War Office. In a letter to Eden[1] complaining of a number of things, he says: "I do not think we are having the help from General Dill which we hoped for at the time of his appointment, and he strikes me as being very tired, disheartened and over-impressed with the might of Germany." It is a pity, because no man has greater charm or was expected to give greater confidence.

There is some indication that Hitler will propose an economic conference of European powers (excluding this country) in order to air his grandiose views about the organisation of the future. Such a plan could be attractively worded and might win favour in a war-weary world, although of course it would imply German economic, and thus political, domination. Accordingly we are consulting with the U.S. about the best method of countering such a move in advance and an admirable telegram has been sent to Lothian. It is suggested that the principle to be followed is that "a plan much discussed and exposed beforehand can often be made to fall flat when it is launched". We might try to anticipate Hitler by public discussion of the likelihood of his dressing up German and Nazi–Fascist domination in the guise of an economic paradise. We could show that it is merely a device to harness all European wealth and production to the Nazi chariot wheels – an extended German "autarky" – for the military aggrandisement of the "superior" German race and for the suppression of freedom everywhere.

At the same time it is proposed that we ourselves should make some more positive suggestions defining "the advantages of the international economic structure which we and the U.S. wish to see emerge as part of the peace settlement". "Our two

---

[1] Secretary of State for War.

nations firmly believe that undue interference by the State frustrates the real economic aims and functions of mankind as well as involving the negation of liberty. We prefer to do things because reason tells us they are worth doing, not because we fear the sanctions attaching to failure to do them." (What do Messrs Attlee, Greenwood, etc., say to this?)

In general our aim is "to break down the artificial barriers to trade which impede any general rise in the standard of living"; but I personally think that our positive proposals, if they are to carry any weight, must descend from the Olympian height of principle and deal with practical details.

On the way home to lunch I met Horace Wilson in a bus. He said he was sorry Winston had thwarted my wish to join up, but that he always, in every question, took the short view rather than the long view. It was the latter that was really important in the end. Is this a fair criticism? I think it is; but the short view is forced on us at present and there is no greater master in dealing with that than W.

Thursday, July 11th
Went to see the Dean of Westminster about Brendan's suggestion that Bishop Hensley Henson[1] should be offered the vacant canonry of Westminster. The Dean seemed to jump at the idea.

Left at 2.30 to visit the defences of the South-East Coast with Winston. We travelled in a special – and very comfortable – train to Dover, the other members of the party being Ismay, Duncan Sandys, Colonel Jacob and Commander Thompson.[2] At Dover we were met by the Admiral in Command and General Thorne and proceeded to the castle, into which we penetrated

[1] A controversial and contentious cleric who had been Bishop of Durham.
[2] Commander C. R. Thompson, Flag Lieutenant at the Admiralty, brought to No. 10 by Churchill. He arranged the Prime Minister's journeys at home and abroad and was near to the foreground in most photographs. More esteemed by Churchill than by his staff. At the end of the war he unscrupulously purloined the official diary of the Prime Minister's activities which had been meticulously maintained by the private secretaries. 10 Downing Street, Chartwell and the Cabinet offices were vainly searched for them when Churchill required them for the writing of his History of the Second World War.

by subterranean passages through the chalk. We hoped for an air-raid (yesterday 150 machines were dog-fighting off Dover) but although we saw the A.A. gun men show sudden signs of activity, no enemy planes came. From the Admiral's room, in the face of the cliff, we looked across the sunlit Channel to France and could scarcely bring ourselves to realise it was enemy territory. From Dover we drove to inspect the emplacement for a 14-inch gun which, owing to a caprice of Winston's, is being prepared at considerable risk, and with immense labour, for the purpose of bombarding the coast of France. It will require three valuable and vulnerable cranes to put it in position and will only last for 100 rounds: the military authorities call it "a pure stunt".

We looked at defences, pill-boxes and troops the whole way along the coast, from Dover to Whitstable. The countryside was strangely deserted, most of the population having been evacuated, but it was encouraging to see the fields of waving corn and cultivated land – an unaccustomed sight in England. There were road blocks and guns and soldiers everywhere, and from Deal we looked at the masts of a large number of wrecks, sunk by mine or by collision since the outbreak of war. We also saw a German hospital plane beached quite intact after having been forced down the previous day. It was painted white with a Red Cross in front and a Swastika on the tail.

It was a glorious evening with excellent visibility, and we could see Cap Gris-Nez thirty miles away over an expanse of rolling Kentish downs. But it was too clear and cloudless for enemy planes and for an aerial spectacle we had to be content with patrols of Spitfires glinting in the sun 10,000 feet above us. Winston was disappointed; the whole object of his journey had really been to see an air-raid!

We boarded the train at Canterbury and dined on the way back to London. I sat at a table with Colonel Jacob and tried to listen to what he had to say when his words were not drowned by the adjacent Winston. Jacob is in a good position to see the events of the last few years in their proper perspective; he is a soldier, and thus practical in his outlook; and he has been working in the Committee of Imperial Defence and Cabinet Offices, where the best information is available. His view of Chamberlain was that he had a heavy load of responsibility for our present state of unpreparedness, although his work for peace could not be overestimated. As Chancellor of the Exchequer, and afterwards Prime Minister, he had starved the fighting forces and refused seriously to consider their expansion, because he believed in – and staked all on – the maintenance of peace. Had war never broken out, as it appeared to many good judges that it might not, Chamberlain would have rightly been thought a superman; but as events have turned out he cannot escape a large measure of blame for what we now call short-sightedness.

Jacob said he thought Winston was the only man who could hold the country united, but if he had a fault it was his inclination to go too much into detail. All these tours of defence areas, and his ceaseless output of minutes to Ministers and to Ismay, are the very antithesis of Chamberlain's practice; but they are not really the function of a Prime Minister. Jacob bewailed the fact that there were no politicians of outstanding merit. I ascribed this fact to three causes: (i) that the flower of a whole generation was destroyed between 1914–1918, (ii) that entrance into politics, as a Conservative, postulates considerable private means and, as a Labour member, influence with the Trade Unions, (iii) that modern education turns out mass-produced material which is essentially inferior to the "handwoven" product of a hundred years ago, when the syllabus was simple and unvarying but the inducement to think for oneself great.

We were back by 10.00 p.m. I suggested to Brendan Bracken that the remedy for inefficiency in the Civil Service is the grant of pensions at an earlier age than sixty, so that men who lack drive and imagination can, without undue cruelty, be shelved. The younger men would thus be given a chance to prove their worth. I suggested that now was the time for such a measure, when opinion in the country was influenced against the Civil Service. Brendan was taken with the idea and promised to put it to Winston.[1]

I see that we now have definite evidence that the Germans

---

[1] This proposal, which was subsequently adopted, had not, at least to my knowledge, been mooted in 1940.

are assembling a force in Norway which could be used for a descent on Scotland, the Orkneys, the Shetlands or the Faroes. The reports of our bombing in North and North-West Germany are extremely encouraging and come from too many different sources to be untrue. So I think we must expect retaliation soon.

Friday, July 12th

At 6.00 p.m. I left with the P.M., Ismay, Sandys, Seal and Elliot[1] (from the Cabinet Offices) for Kenley, to inspect the Hurricane squadron of which Winston is Honorary Air Commodore. Winston was arrayed in R.A.F. uniform which, curiously enough, suited him well. We inspected the men and machines in pouring rain, watched twelve Hurricanes take off for patrol and went to see the operations room from which the activities of all aircraft in the area are directed. Then we got into a large machine, called a Flamingo, and flew very low, some 400 feet off the ground, to Northolt. The visibility was too bad for us to fly nearer Chequers. Ismay and I drove on together and he discoursed to me about polo!

Mrs Churchill and Horatia Seymour[2] were at Chequers. Generals Paget and Auchinleck[3] (who are two of the best younger generals and very much finer soldiers than Dill, Haining, Ironside, etc.) came to dine and sleep, as did Ismay and Sandys.

At dinner I sat between Ismay and Paget. The latter is charming and particularly easy to talk to. Winston began describing yesterday's tour of the South-East area and said that he had enjoyed a real "Hun-hate" with one of the Generals there. "I never hated the Germans in the last war, but now I hate them like . . . well, like an earwig."

After the ladies had left the conversation became more serious and Paget and Auchinleck were put through their paces. They gave a good account of themselves. Winston then gave a brief

[1] Subsequently Air Chief Marshal Sir William Elliot.
[2] Beautiful and cultivated member of the pre-First World War Asquithian set. Lived in one of the Churchill cottages at Chartwell.
[3] Field Marshal Sir Claude Auchinleck,* Wavell's successor as C. in C. in North Africa.

account of what he thought might be the course of the war. He could not see much hope of a decision before 1942. For the next three months we must fight for the negative purpose of preventing invasion and defeating it if it comes. The winter will be terrible for Europe, but "Hitler will take the other children's candy" and W. does not think it will put an end to German resistance. Next year we shall be building up a great offensive army and we hope to have fifty-five divisions. We shall plan large-scale "butcher and bolt" raids on the continent and Hitler will find himself hard put to it to hold 2,000 miles of coast line. Moreover we shall be approaching numerical equality in the air. By 1942 we shall have achieved air superiority and shall be ready for great offensive operations on land against Germany. But, said Winston, it is impossible to be precise: in the last war we kept on saying "How are we going to win", and then while we were still unable to answer the question, we quite suddenly and unexpectedly found ourselves in a winning position.

The discussion turned to invasion. Winston does not think this is feasible in fishing boats from Norway, as is now said to be likely. Paget and Auchinleck thought that advance troops might arrive in this way in quite insignificant numbers. Simultaneously troop carriers, gliders and parachutists would be utilised to seize a port from which the main body could land. W. does not believe in dispersing our troops along the beaches, but in concentrating effective and mobile divisions behind so that they may quickly be moved to any area where a serious threat materialises. He emphasised that the great invasion scare (which we only ceased to deride six weeks ago) is serving a most useful purpose: it is well on the way to providing us with the finest offensive army we have ever possessed and it is keeping every man and woman tuned to a high pitch of readiness. He does not wish the scare to abate therefore, and although personally he doubts whether invasion is a serious menace he intends to give that impression, and to talk about long and dangerous vigils, etc., when he broadcasts on Sunday.

There followed an argument about encouraging the populace to fight. If they meet the invader with scythes and brickbats they will be massacred. Paget thinks they had better stay at home; Winston says they will not and Auchinleck says they ought not. W. is sufficiently ruthless to point out that in war quarter is given, not on grounds of compassion but in order to discourage the enemy from fighting to the bitter end. But here we want every citizen to fight desperately and they will do so the more if they know that the alternative is massacre. The L.D.V. (Local Defence Volunteers) must be armed and prepared (but not, insists Paget, at the expense of the regular army) and even women must, if they wish, be enrolled as combatants. Sandys here pointed out that in Spain the fact of women fighting made the men fight still more keenly. Today large quantities of arms and ammunition have arrived from the U.S. and are being distributed to the L.D.V. (or Home Guard as Winston wants to call them). The outlook is not gloomy.

After dinner Winston, Sandys and the three Generals retired with a number of maps to discuss the details of invasion and I thought it discreet to leave them to themselves. To bed by 1.30.

Saturday, July 13th
I was up by 8.30 procuring the latest news from the Admiralty and taking it to Winston in my dressing-gown. I told him that the French Cameroons had renounced their allegiance to the Pétain Government and were to continue fighting. Of course the French dependencies are more bellicose in proportion as they are further away from Europe, but possibly the defection of the Cameroons may start a very satisfactory Colonial rot.

At lunch I sat between Horatia Seymour and Duncan Sandys. I shocked Miss S. and Ismay deeply last night by saying that I couldn't help liking the Germans; however she seemed to have recovered and we got on admirably. Winston showed greater animation and exuberance than I have seen before. He began by maintaining the arguable thesis that "Human beings don't require rest; what they require is change or else they become bloody-minded". He then went on to praise brass bands, to curse Hore-Belisha for abolishing them, to say they should return to every regiment and to ask what that large instrument was that he liked so much. I tentatively suggested a saxophone, whereupon he beamed philanthropically and said: "You haven't been brought up in the army; you have been brought up in night-clubs", proceeding to tell the general company that I wanted to go and fight and desert him and he jolly well wasn't going to let me until the killing really began, etc., etc.

He reiterated his now familiar scheme of our future strategy and said it gave him confidence to be able to see clearly how this war could and should be won instead of groping forwards uncertainly. This week-end he felt more cheerful than at any time since he took office. He spoke of the "armoured panther springs" which our mechanised divisions would make on the continent next year and of the bombing supremacy we should attain. Even if "that man" (as he always calls Hitler) were at the Caspian – and there was nothing to stop him from going there – we should bring him back "to find a fire in his own backyard and we will make Germany a desert, yes a desert". Hitler could do anything he liked where there was no salt water to cross, but it would avail him nothing if he reached the Great Wall of China and this Island remained undefeated. He could not survive if we devastated his homeland and if our excursions on the continent, made whenever we chose to land, were continually taxing his strength outside Germany. Therefore in the end he must probably be driven to attempt invasion, even if he decided against it now and went eastwards; and he would not succeed. Thus our vigil might be long and trying, and we shall have to be on our guard against surprise attack at any time of year and in any conditions. We should be put to the greatest test.

After lunch Auchinleck departed and Ismay too. Paget had left after breakfast. I walked up to Beacon Hill, when Winston was safely asleep, and sprawled on the grass, gazing for miles and miles across country. The air is most invigorating, the Chilterns green and the woods sublime. As I lay on the hilltop, thinking that England was the most beautiful country in the world and I could never bear to leave it, Mrs Churchill and Miss Seymour appeared and I walked back with them, gossiping.

Sir Henry Strakosch* arrived at tea-time and during that meal we looked at the ring which was taken from Queen Elizabeth's dying finger and carried to James VI to prove to him that he was King of England. It is a lovely jewel with an E that opens and shows two tiny jewelled miniatures of Elizabeth herself and of Anne Boleyn.

Air Marshal Sir Hugh Dowding* (C. in C., Fighter Command) and another R.A.F. officer came to dinner. He began by telling the P.M. that the only thing that worried him in life was the ridiculous dreams he had every night: last night he dreamt that there was only one man in England who could use a Bofors gun and his name was William Shakespeare. It was, he said, most disturbing.

During dinner we talked of air matters. Winston said the last four days had been the most glorious in the history of the R.A.F. Those days had been the test: the enemy had come and had lost 5 to 1. We could now be confident of our superiority. The discussion turned to technical questions of the superiority of the Hurricane, the defects of the Defiant,[1] and the curious fact that the Germans had not yet put armour behind their engines. If they should do so, said Dowding, our tactics would become much more difficult. They also spoke of the new German beam, called Headache, which guides the enemy machines to their targets. The Germans do not know that we have discovered this, and Lindemann, who arrived this evening with all his albums of statistics, was horrified that Winston should mention it before Strakosch, who is a chatterbox.

We have reports, from Maisky amongst others, that the Germans will use gas if they invade us. So perhaps Winston is wise to contemplate "drenching" the beaches with mustard gas.

W. started dictating his speech at midnight and I got leave to go to bed.

Sunday, July 14th

One of the amenities of Chequers is being called with one's breakfast, and I confess it is a form of laziness I begin to appreciate, even though it makes me feel still more emphatically that I am not suffering my full share of hardship in this war.

There is an ominous calm. For the first time in a month there were no air-raids last night, all the German submarines except

[1] A newly-developed fighter aircraft intended primarily for night interception.

two have gone home, and it looks as if *der Tag* may be imminent. The P.M. thinks it highly probable and keeps on repeating that "Hitler must invade or fail. If he fails he is bound to go East, and fail he will."

I went to church with Miss Seymour, having obtained permission from the P.M. who said, "Go and pray for me: *ora pro nobis.*" It is a lovely church on a hill and there was an immense congregation. Returning from church I played backgammon with Mrs Churchill whose skill is slight, but who talks so much that she wins by *force majeure*. She said that she had been intended to marry Lord Bessborough and had been left with him in a maze all one afternoon.

The Jimmy Rothschilds[1] came to lunch and Winston walked about with him afterwards expatiating on the beauty of the pictures. There is, in particular, a little Rubens in the dining-room about which Winston went into ecstasies. I thought he was a little tactless to Dolly Rothschild in talking about the disgrace of France.

At about 4.00 we left Chequers and went to look at the R.A.F. establishment at Halton, by which the P.M. was obviously bored. I nearly got into hot water for leaving tonight's speech behind but, by undeserved good fortune, Mrs Hill had a spare copy and I was saved! It is fun driving in the P.M.'s cortège: no attention is paid to traffic lights or speed limits.

The P.M. has strong views on food rationing. He thinks it absurd to make it excessive when our supplies are as good as at present. In a letter to his Minister of Food, Lord Woolton, he says: "Almost all the food faddists I have ever known, nut eaters and the like, have died young after a long period of senile decay. The British soldier is far more likely to be right than the scientists. All he cares about is beef . . . The way to lose the war is to try to force the British public into a diet of milk, oatmeal, potatoes, etc., washed down on gala occasions with a little limejuice." The ideas are, I think, taken from Nat Gubbins

---

[1] Son of the French Baron Edmond de Rothschild. Liberal M.P. for the Isle of Ely and owner of Waddesdon in Buckinghamshire. His wife gave it with its superb contents to the National Trust. He married Dorothy (Dollie) Pinto, a knowledgeable and most agreeable lady.

in the *Sunday Express*, whom Winston and all his family read
with avidity.

Monday, July 15th
St Swithin's Day and pouring rain, a fact to cheer the farmers
in this year of drought.

Very little work apart from the normal drudgery of answering
letters sent by the well-meaning or self-seeking public. The
latter predominate.

Lunched with Tony Bevir and Seal at the United Universities
Club, which is the haunt of respectable Civil Servants. We
talked, deprecatingly, of a scurrilous unsigned attack on Horace
Wilson handed to the P.M. by Attlee. The influence of Ismay
will be used to smooth matters out. We also spoke of Winston
who, think Seal and Bevir, will one day bring about his downfall
by excessive loyalty to his friends and a natural disinclination to
hurt anybody's feelings. This vice – or virtue – has already cost
him much in leading him to support King Edward VIII: by so
doing he forfeited the confidence of the House of Commons and
of the country.

Tuesday, July 16th
Lunched with George Steward at the Travellers. He seems to
have conceived the strongest dislike for Kingsley Wood and he
says that Arthur Rucker is not advising Chamberlain well.
Neither Horace nor David Margesson nor Arthur were really
helpful to the old man because the first could never tell a
dishonest man and the other two had no judgment of men's
capacity. Beaverbrook he described as twenty-five per cent
thug, fifteen per cent crook and the remainder a combination of
genius and real goodness of heart.

On late duty. Nothing much happened except the usual nocturnal visits, which included Dr Dalton, whom I thought agreeable.
Speaking to Beaverbrook on the telephone the P.M. said: "I
feel better. The air boys have done it. We live on their wings."
I was, however, rather depressed to read a note by Dowding
on our inability to prevent indiscriminate night bombing (once
Hitler has got over his fear of retaliation) and on the increased

dangers as the nights grow longer. Apparently we are almost certain to evolve an effective technique for intercepting bombers by night ("the smeller", Winston calls our device), but we have no night fighter capable of making real use of this invention and even if we had the effect would be limited. Dowding thinks each side must sooner or later begin a race for the destruction of the other's aircraft industry, and this, of course, will imply bombing the civilian population. Then the real test will begin: have we or the Germans the sterner civilian morale?

Wednesday, July 17th

The P.M. went off with Seal at 8.45 to inspect defences at Portsmouth.

I see M. Corbin has written to the P.M. on leaving the Embassy: *"Je souhaite que malgré les évènements des dernières semaines nos deux nations ne perdent jamais de vue les intérêts permanents qui les unissent et que leur amitié renaisse un jour plus forte que par le passé."* Actually I can see little hope of the French forgiving us, especially if we win and restore their freedom. Halifax thinks that the plans of permanent Anglo-French co-operation, which reached their climax in the proposed union of the two countries, will have to be abandoned in favour of more intimate relations with the United States. I think this is logical and it is surely natural that the beginnings of world co-operation should come through closer co-operation between the two great English-speaking Empires. Spain and the Latin Americas might then follow suit.

Brendan tells me that the Germans have a 2-ton bomb – which would certainly create havoc. The big aerial onslaught is expected daily now, followed perhaps by a peace offensive rather than by an invasion. But since St Swithin's Day it has rained and blown ceaselessly, so we may expect a respite until the sun shines again.

There is a great deal of feeling in the country against Chamberlain and the "Men of Munich" and a demand for their removal from office. This W. would never countenance unless he considered them incompetent; and he does not.

Friday, July 19th

Apart from the fact that the Duke of Windsor is being cantankerous and maddening there is no news, only waiting.

Lunched with Lord and Lady Lloyd to meet Madame Tabouis.[1] Sir Harry and Lady Joan Verney[2] were there and also Sir John and Lady Shuckburgh (he is Permanent Under Secretary to Lord Lloyd at the Colonial Office). I sat next to Madame Tabouis who was a bit *effarée*, understandably as she has been proscribed by the Germans and has had to leave her family in France. I said that I had heard (from Sir Orme Sargent at the F.O.) that the Bordeaux Government were thinking of restoring the monarchy and that the Comte de Paris was in France. Madame T. said: "The Pétain Government will make every mistake except that one."

Monday, July 22nd

The Germans in Washington are telling our Embassy that they can produce the terms of peace which Germany would accept. Now, I think, is the psychological moment to define our own war aims and state our terms. They would be such that Hitler must refuse them, but in so doing he would lose credit in the eyes of the outside world and also in those of his own people. Mr Kurt Hahn,[3] former headmaster of Salem, has produced an interesting note on this subject which Tony Bevir has obtained and passed on to the P.M. But I fear the Government lacks the imagination to make such a move, even though I think they have been right to keep their war aims vague up till now (and in any case agreement with the French on the subject was unattainable).

Hore-Belisha has written to suggest that we should support the Duc de Guise,[4] in an effort to rally the royalist French fleet and the Colonies to our side. He thinks that such a move would

---

[1] A widely-read, left-of-Centre French journalist.

[2] Formerly Private Secretary to Queen Mary. Lady Joan was a lady-in-waiting.

[3] A liberal German educationalist who was a profound thinker. He left Germany, and came to Britain, when Hitler came to power, and founded Gordonstoun School near Elgin.

[4] Orleanist Pretender to the French throne. Father of the Comte de Paris.

attract both the Left (which wants to carry on the war) and the Right (which would like a monarchy) in France. He forgets the Centre which is numerically and politically the most important element in France.

Late at No. 10, where I slept. I talked to the Prof. about his secret weapons, the U.P., the P.F. (proximity fuse), G.L. and P.E. He thinks these may be really effective next year and if they are, there is a distinct possibility that aircraft will be ruled out as a weapon of war, because anti-aircraft fire will become not merely effective but deadly.

Professor Lindemann believed that since the enemy had military supremacy, the way to defeat them was by scientific ingenuity. The U.P. weapon was an aerial minefield which might have been a valuable deterrent to dive-bombers, but was not put to much effective use. The proximity fuse, which caused a shell to explode when close to a metal object such as an aeroplane, was eventually perfected and mass-produced in America, though it was a British invention. The G.L. was a radar-controlled searchlight and the photo-electric fuse (P.E.) was the parent of many successful later developments.

There were others, including the A.I., which would lead night fighters to enemy bombers, the Sticky Bomb for dealing with tanks, and the Blacker Bombard. The Prof. with the Prime Minister's support, was tireless in promoting these devices, but few of them were far enough advanced to play a significant part in the achievement of victory.

The Prof. was also, with Sir John Anderson, Churchill's liaison with the most important of all Anglo-American scientific activities, the development of the Atomic Bomb, given the code-name Tube Alloys. This ranked with the breaking of the ciphers of the German armed forces as the most jealously guarded secret of the war.

The P.M. was in a cantankerous frame of mind, demanding papers which were not available.

At about 1.00 a.m. Brendan, Prof., Tony and I had a discussion about Kurt Hahn's proposals, which are generally thought to be intelligent. It is important that the odium of saying "No" to peace terms should be laid on Hitler and not on ourselves. Hahn thinks that Hitler, who must realise that the aid to be expected from Quislings in this country is small, might hope to discover a Lansdowne, who would advocate a compromise peace.[1]

Wednesday, July 24th

The P.M.'s comment on a long telegram of July 22nd from the Viceroy (Linlithgow)[2] about the proposals for new Indian constitutional measures is "long-winded as ever and a piece of hypocrisy from beginning to end".

On a note from Vansittart about a possible answer to the speech Hitler made last Sunday, Winston has written: "I do not propose to say anything in reply to Herr Hitler's speech, not being on speaking terms with him."

Thursday, July 25th

David, having returned from Liverpool where he has been coping with French sailors, told me horrifying stories of the casual and tactless way in which they have been handled. The climax of idiocy was to repatriate these highly susceptible Latins on a mule ship from which the mules' manure had not been removed. I repeated the story to Desmond Morton who told it to Winston with a view to having this question of the French in England co-ordinated under Lord Hankey. Winston passed it to the Chiefs of Staff for a report.

The Archbishop of York[3] has written to the P.M. complaining (i) of the recent Burma Road Agreement[4] with the Japanese, whereby we have betrayed China, (ii) the wholesale internment

---

[1] In November 1917, Lord Lansdowne, a former Foreign Secretary, wrote a letter to the *Daily Telegraph* calling for peace terms. Despite the devastating losses on the Western Front and at Gallipoli, he was bitterly attacked as an unpatriotic defeatist.

[2] "Hopey", 2nd Marquess of Linlithgow, Viceroy of India, 1936–43, Chancellor of Edinburgh University and, after the war, Chairman of the Midland Bank.

[3] William Temple, whose influence on the Church of England was profound and who became Archbishop of Canterbury in 1942.

[4] The Burma Road was the main route by which China, having lost most of her sea ports, was supplied in her struggle against Japan.

of enemy aliens and the accompanying hardship to many well-disposed and technically useful Germans, Austrians, etc. Both of these questions are causing a stir in the public mind, and the Government are wisely temporising over the second. As regards the first, the argument is that when we are fighting for our life we cannot afford to risk Japanese hostility. But it is a moral defeat to sacrifice in one part of the world the principles we are defending in another, and I feel sure we shall in the long run suffer for yielding to Japanese pressure. The Archbishop says that at least we should boldly admit the reason for our action: "nothing 'saves face' so completely as the honesty which has no interest in face-saving".

Dined with Mrs Churchill and Mary and went with them to see Sarah[1] act in a play of Ivor Novello's, *Murder in Mayfair*, at the "Q" Theatre. Sarah has the reputation of being a thoroughly bad actress, and so I was agreeably surprised to find that she gave a good performance and looked much lovelier than she in fact is. Her mass of red hair was very effective on the stage. I sat beside Mary who was in raptures; she has a naive and rather charming adoration for everything connected with her family (except Randolph). After the play we went on, with the Sandyses, to have supper with Sarah and Vic [Oliver] in their extremely luxurious flat. The Churchills *en famille* were delightful and very amusing. They made a certain amount of fun of the Chamberlains and Mary described how Mrs Chamberlain had taken her for the wife of one of the officers on the *Exeter*. Sarah seems much older (she is only my age), but apparently thrives on the life of movement, instability and restlessness which she and Vic have chosen. Vic, munching a sandwich while the rest of us swilled champagne, talked of the broadcast to the U.S. which he was due to make in half an hour. I devoured

[1] She had long tresses of beautiful dark red hair and was perhaps Winston Churchill's favourite child. I had known her since we were both eighteen (and even took her twice to see the Grand National). She had an obsession with the stage, but in the war joined the W.A.A.F. and was a competent analyst of the R.A.F. photographic surveys. She wrote good poetry and had great depth of feeling. None of her three matrimonial experiments ended happily.

cherries, gossiped with Diana, and aroused Mary's indignation to a high pitch by telling her that when Chamberlain was P.M. I had refused to wake him up to see the papers which Winston sent over sporadically from the Admiralty at 2.00 a.m. "You dared to do that to Papa!" she said. Mrs Churchill told me of her disapproval of Sir John Anderson[1] (a feeling which is widely shared).

Friday, July 26th

There is some agitation for an authoritative reply to Hitler's speech, and I think Winston should make one, stating our terms and our aims subtly but clearly. However W. remains adamant and Vansittart encourages him to maintain "a forbidding silence".

Halifax's speech on the wireless, in which he spoke of God more than of Hitler, has aroused a certain amount of criticism in the *New Statesman*, etc.; but generally speaking it has been well received here and apparently appreciated in the country. Though his delivery is bad, Halifax's speeches are invariably beautiful to read.

Amery, whose policy with regard to India has been almost universally opposed in the Cabinet, came to see Winston after tea and from all appearances they had a "blood row". It looks as if Amery will resign. Later Winston produced a telegram which he wanted sent to the Viceroy without Amery or the India Office knowing; so I had to go over to the India Office, suborn one of the men in the telegram despatch room, and cypher the telegram with him. It was a sharp rebuke to Linlithgow for carrying on a secret correspondence with Amery behind the backs of the War Cabinet and demanded permission to show this correspondence to the Cabinet.

Back at No. 10 I talked to Arthur Rucker.[2] He defended Sir J. Anderson over the refugee question, saying that he had been averse to locking them up indiscriminately in the first place and had pleaded for a reasonable policy. He had given in, or rather

---

[1] Later Viscount Waverley.*

[2] He had remained Private Secretary to Neville Chamberlain, who was now Lord President of the Council and living at 11 Downing Street.

had been forced by the Government to give in, owing to popular clamour and fear of Fifth Columnists. Now Sir John was anxious to avoid swinging the balance too far the other way just because people were beginning to feel sorry for the refugees. Left to himself he would have preserved a sane policy of discrimination. Arthur also defended the Government's Burma Road policy on the ground that without this concession we should have had to fight Japan. He claimed that our great fault in recent years had been to let our diplomacy outrun our strength, to threaten what we could not fulfil. It was essential to return to a system of *realpolitik*.

Saturday, July 27th
Alone at No. 10 with John Martin who is a most agreeable companion. We had a reasonably quiet and undisturbed day, except that I had to go over to the India Office and decypher the Viceroy's humble reply to Winston, suborning another cypherer in the process.

The press have made fools of themselves by harping on our wonderful supply of destroyers – just when we are crying poverty to the U.S. in the hope of procuring fifty from them. Winston is now appealing eloquently to the President, both directly and through Lothian.

From Berne the Minister reports that Paravicini[1] – who cannot be suspected of anything but benevolence – has reliable information that the majority of the German General Staff, formerly opposed to an attack on this country, have swung round in favour of it. Dowding, C. in C. Fighter Command, estimates that one mass raid of 3,000 machines could be launched against us, but that over a period of days a maximum of 500 a day and 200 a night could be maintained. It is significant that yesterday and today German raiders turned away when they saw our fighters approaching. They have been "grievously mauled", as Winston would say, on their recent daylight visits.

[1] Swiss Minister in London for many years before the war and, with his wife, popular in social and political circles. Madame Paravicini was of invaluable assistance to British prisoners of war in Germany and to their families at home.

Sunday, July 28th

Spent the morning at No. 10, where I was in constant touch
with Chequers about India. The story, in brief, is that Amery
has been telegraphing to Linlithgow about a public declaration
which it is proposed the Viceroy should make concerning the
attitude of H.M.G. to India's status and Constitution after the
war. Amery has tried to push his ideas (which would give a blank
cheque to an Indian Constituent Assembly of the future) through
without really consulting the Cabinet, and his telegrams, which
Winston demanded to see on Friday and which may now be
circulated as a Cabinet paper, contain a number of ill-advised
references to Winston himself and complaints that he is driving
the Cabinet to adopt his own views about the form this declaration should take. The Viceroy has been placed in an embarrassing
position by Amery's impetuosity and now, as far as Amery is
concerned, the fat is in the fire. Winston, after consultation with
Lord Simon,[1] has redrafted the last paragraph of the declaration.

Went back to No. 10 at 6.30 to meet Winston on his return.
Talked to Edward Bridges about Sir John Anderson. He says
that the latter is really a very sound administrator, the best we
have. He supports Arthur Rucker's view of Anderson and the
refugee problem and says that he has been much maligned and
made a scapegoat for actions that were taken too quickly owing
to the caprices of public opinion which were reflected in the
Government.

After dinner I had a conversation with Attlee about Public
Schools and Universities. He was much more agreeable and
forthcoming than I had thought.

Chamberlain has been taken ill and may have to have an
abdominal operation, poor old man. Brendan tells me that Lord
Beaverbrook is to be brought into the Cabinet as Minister of
Production if Herbert Morrison (who may object to playing
second fiddle as Minister of Supply) can be squared. Brendan
also wants to bring in Lloyd George and thinks that with the
temporary disappearance of Chamberlain the opportunity has
come. I said I thought that with the examples of Hindenburg

[1] Lord Chancellor. Formerly Sir John Simon.*

and Pétain before us, we should be careful of enlisting the support of hoary survivors from the last war.

Brendan and I also talked about the Ecclesiastical patronage. Although an agnostic he feels very strongly the importance of good appointments being made and of deeply spiritual and saintly men being encouraged to enter the Church. We need Saints, he says, not good administrators, and the P.M. should rely on the advice of men in the Government, such as Halifax and Caldecote[1] (as representatives of the two extremes of churchmanship) who take their Ecclesiastical responsibilities seriously.

Monday, July 29th
It is being put about, Attlee has discovered, that Amery's liberal and statesmanlike proposals with regard to India are being sabotaged by Churchill. This is not true because Amery had merely wanted to make a woolly promise that H.M.G., after the war, would assent to whatever constitutional proposals a representative body in India should propose. It would be impossible to collect a really representative body and, secondly, such a wide and general promise would arouse expectations which might, and almost certainly would, be unfulfilled in the event. However, there is a real danger that if Amery goes, as I think he must, his resignation will be misinterpreted and the Government branded as reactionary.

My final visit to my masseuse.[2] She talks a lot of nonsense and insists on my living on tomatoes, but curiously enough I do feel much better and less sluggish for her ministrations.

Tuesday, July 30th
Rode at Richmond before breakfast, despite the tank traps. The P.M. and the First Lord are having a bit of a tiff, owing to the

[1] As Sir Thomas Inskip responsible for rearmament before the war. He approached this task with excessive caution. A devout low churchman in contrast to the high-church Halifax. Created Viscount Caldecote by Chamberlain. Briefly Lord Chancellor in 1939–40, he was appointed Lord Chief Justice in October 1940.
[2] As the antidote to long nights, insufficient exercise and a general feeling of unhealthiness I had placed myself in the hands of an energetic but ugly masseuse.

former's comments on the sinking of five ships and the damaging of six others in a raid on a Channel convoy last Friday. The P.M. complained that the Admiralty's precautions were "utterly ineffectual", and said: "I must consider this one of the most lamentable episodes of the naval war so far as it has yet developed." A. V. Alexander flared up and wrote asking that this minute might be withdrawn. In his reply, refusing to do so, Winston said: "I was naturally wounded to read of the massacre of all these poor little ships and I do not think I was wrong in describing the episode as 'lamentable'. The word lamentable expresses grief and not necessarily judgment."

Wednesday, July 31st
Rode again at Richmond, where a searchlight was attacked by machine-gun fire last night. The ford which I usually cross from Wimbledon has been blocked with pits and barriers and in the park itself, near Louis Greig's* house, a village of unsightly grey huts with blue windows has sprung up. Fortunately the sun and the early morning air are proof against warlike preparations.

Winston has gone off on one of his tours of inspection, this time to the North. Desmond Morton tells me that "C", the head of the Secret Service, has now received news of imminent invasion from over 260 sources. The main attack will be against the South, with diversions against Hull, Scotland and Ireland, which will be exploited if successful. Parachutists will be used only in the South. It is clear that all preparations have been made; whether they will be used depends on Hitler's caprice. It is significant that German troops are concentrating in the East and it is on the cards that Hitler has immediate designs against the Ukraine.

One of the items on the Chiefs of Staffs' agenda is the situation caused by the insistence of innumerable spectators on crowding the pier at Dover to watch the aerial battles. It is encouraging that the passion for sightseeing should still be greater than that for self-preservation.

Winston has finally sent an appeal to Roosevelt for destroyers, flying boats and motor-torpedo boats. He says: "We are hitting that man hard both in repelling attacks and in bombing Germany;

but we have lost a lot of destroyers lately and we cannot get a substantial reinforcement. The whole fate of the war may be decided by this minor and easily remediable factor . . . I am beginning to feel very hopeful about this war if we can get round the next three or four months."

After dinner I talked to Desmond Morton about the Foreign Office proposal that a number of American foodships should be allowed to sail, under safeguards, to ports in unoccupied France. Desmond, and the Ministry of Economic Warfare, feel violently that the Foreign Office is trying to "appease" the Vichy Government in the same way that, throughout the winter, they tried to prevent Italy coming into the war by relaxing the blockade in her favour. Halifax, Ronnie Campbell and Van maintain that to allow enough food into unoccupied France would not affect Germany's position but would suffice to keep the French people, as opposed to their Government, well-disposed to us, to counter German propaganda about our brutality in starving women and children, and to allay misplaced humanitarian feelings in America. I should feel more open to conviction by the Foreign Office arguments if they could produce one example of successful appeasement. I am afraid that as far as France is concerned we shall have to harden our hearts and block our ears.

Japan has arrested a number of British subjects on charges of espionage and feeling is running high. New Zealand and Australia are naturally anxious that we should avoid war.

The Italians are said to have bombed one of their own battle cruisers in mistake for the *Hood*.

EIGHT

BATTLE OF BRITAIN
AUGUST 1940

Thursday, August 1st

David's story of the treatment of French sailors at Aintree, repeated by Desmond Morton and sent by the P.M. to the Chiefs of Staff, has returned with the comments of the First Sea Lord and C.I.G.S. They deny most of the allegations and say that the trouble was largely due to the sulky and unco-operative attitude of the French themselves.

Priestley[1] has sent the P.M. an article he has written pleading for Government benevolence towards the people's recreation. We will give up our Bank Holidays, but let us have laughter and fun and untaxed books (the Chancellor in his much-criticised budget proposes to tax books and has aroused a justifiable storm of protest). Priestley declaims against the drift towards dreariness. What is far more dangerous, as Mother points out, is the film-fed public's insatiate longing for sensation. It has often been said that the Dictators could only survive if they took some dramatic action every six months, and now the British public, drugged by Hollywood and by the stirring events of recent months, seems to need incessant change and excitement. It is already being said in the provinces that Churchill is "played out" and must go. There is no such murmur in London, but London does not represent England any more than Paris does France.

[1] J. B. Priestley, the novelist.

At tea we talked of the Civil Service and I complained of the slow promotion in the F.O. "You'll never get beyond the rank of Second Secretary," said Seal. "Oh yes, he will," said Desmond Morton, "he has got such a capacity for intrigue!"

The Archbishop of Canterbury came to see the P.M. about the appointment of a new Bishop of St Edmundsbury and Ipswich, a matter which has been occupying me for some months. After a good deal of discussion I recommended Archdeacon Brook of Coventry, a safe but not spectacular appointment for this rural diocese. The P.M. and the Archbishop agreed to make the offer.

Friday, August 2nd
During the night the Germans dropped pamphlets in England, containing part of the text of Hitler's speech.

The German press is busy educating its readers not to expect an immediate success against England. It looks as if the military authorities are becoming doubtful of their ability to invade us rapidly and successfully. Meanwhile German dive-bombers have arrived in South Italy and I feel sure that the Axis powers contemplate forceful action in the Mediterranean.

Lothian has telegraphed the American reaction to Winston's demand for destroyers. The President would like to send them, but does not think he can obtain the consent of Congress unless one of two conditions is accepted: (i) that Canada is given a lien on some of our fast cruisers which could be used in the defence of North America if this country were defeated; (ii) we should agree, without transfer of sovereignty, to give the U.S.A. military facilities in Trinidad and the West Indies. Although the Americans are not showing signs of appreciating the full seriousness of the situation, and are themselves showing the lack of realism for which they so freely criticised us before the war, this is evidently not a time to haggle, and Lothian points out that there is much to be said for constructing an Anglo-American battle front in the West Indies and Western Atlantic.

In an interview with Lord Halifax, the Duke of Alba[1] asserted that the French have always laid the blame for their national

---

[1] Spanish Ambassador in London.

disasters on the treachery of other Frenchmen. Thus the death of Roland was ascribed to the treachery of Ganelon, the defeat of Francis I at Pavia to the betrayal of the Constable of Bourbon, and the loss of the Franco-Prussian War to the treason of Bazaine. No doubt the blame for the present disaster would be laid at the door of the whole republican system. Alba said that Pétain undoubtedly intended to restore the monarchy, and he thought this would conduce to the improvement of Franco-Spanish relations and might well be acceptable to the French peasantry.

Mr Duff Cooper is in trouble with the press, whom he has criticised, and has himself been criticised on all sides for trying to send people into the homes of the citizens of this country to investigate their owners' morale. The campaign against "Cooper's Snoopers" has thrown Duff Cooper himself into discredit. Certainly he has not produced many results as Minister of Information, and I think there are signs that Chamberlain was justified in refusing to give him a job.

Monday, August 5th
At 1.30 a military agreement was signed in the Cabinet Room by the P.M., Halifax and representatives of the Polish Government, including General Sikorski. A photographer, for the first time in history, took a photograph of the signatories in the Cabinet Room. Afterwards we went out into the garden and drank champagne. Winston prowling round and proposing toasts to the common cause, etc.

In a minute on the production of the U.P. weapon (which gave satisfactory results the other day at Dover), the P.E. fuse, etc., the P.M. urges that the greatest facilities be given by the Ministry of Supply to the scientist in charge, Dr Crowe. He says: "The whole character of the war both by sea and land in 1941 may be affected by the development of these weapons."

Interest centres on Operation scipio, by which it is hoped that General de Gaulle may be enabled to land in French West Africa and seize power. The forces employed are to be French troops, but the main difficulty is the decision about the escorting British men-of-war. Are they to engage ships of the Vichy Government if the latter attempt to intercept General de Gaulle's forces? H.M.G. are anxious to avoid this. This afternoon the P.M. signed a letter to the General agreeing to recognise a French "Council of Defence" in the French Colonies to which all anti-Vichy elements can rally. De Gaulle's agents will leave by air tomorrow for Nigeria with copies of this document.

Operation RAZZLE, for burning the German crops, is also under discussion, but only a fraction of these are within range of our aircraft.

Tuesday, August 6th
The day was an uneventful one except for the news that the Italians are advancing into British Somaliland and have proceeded a considerable distance towards Berbera. Materially the loss of this territory would be slight, but psychologically, in Italy and the Near East, the effects would be lamentable. We are moving the Black Watch from Aden to Berbera.

Winston was in a nervous and irritable frame of mind in the evening, occupied with the question of obtaining from the U.S. the fifty destroyers we so badly need. He refuses to contemplate a promise to give Canada, and thus the U.S., a lien on our warships if these islands are conquered and brands any such proposal as defeatism. We could only give such an undertaking in return for an Anglo-U.S. Alliance. Thus Winston declares that the only *quid pro quo* we could give the U.S. would be the lease of air and naval bases in the West Indies. This would be justifiable because it is in our interest to encourage a strong Anglo-American defence line in the Western Atlantic.

W. protested strongly at the noise being made in the Private Secretaries' room and finally threatened to sack the next offender. This next offender was the Chief of the Air Staff, but the real culprit is Desmond Morton whose voice would penetrate the ramparts of a mediaeval castle.

Wednesday, August 7th

Winston has gone off to East Anglia to inspect defences, taking with him Randolph and Major Jack Churchill.[1] I am afraid his naturally affectionate nature disposes him towards nepotism. He has given Duncan Sandys an important job at the Cabinet Offices, under Ismay, and a staff job is being arranged for Randolph.[2]

I had a very busy day, alone most of the afternoon and immersed in a jungle of unimportant but harassing detail. The piles of desperately boring letters awaiting my signature became increasingly unmanageable.

Desmond Morton tells me the Secret Service have absconded with £13,000,000 in francs which they discovered in the court-yard of a French bank in occupied France. This money will be used to finance de Gaulle. So the Secret Service are not entirely useless.

The King of Sweden [Gustav V] has telegraphed to the King and to Hitler offering his services as a mediator. It is apparently the King's personal initiative. The F.O. draft declining King Gustav's offer, which will be considered by the Cabinet tomorrow, is a masterpiece of dignified language.

Dined with Lady Wolverton, Marion Hyde and Esmé Glyn.[3] Marion tells me that though the King and Queen appreciate Winston's qualities, and see that he is the man for the occasion, they are a little ruffled by the off-hand way in which he treats them. They much preferred Chamberlain's habit of going to the Palace regularly once a week and explaining the situation in a careful unhurried way. Winston says he will come at 6.00, puts it off by telephone till 6.30 and is inclined to turn up for ten hectic minutes at 7.00. Unfortunately the King, doubtless on

[1] Winston Churchill's younger brother, to whom he was devoted. He lived at No. 10 and was a member of the staff mess. He married the lovely Lady Gwendeline Bertie by whom Winston had also been captivated in his youth. Their children were John, Peregrine and Clarissa.

[2] This is a libel. He was given a job in the Commandos but had a staff job later, before being parachuted into Yugoslavia.

[3] The elder of Lady Wolverton's two daughters was a lady-in-waiting to Queen Elizabeth. The younger, Esmé, worked hard in the Women's Voluntary Service as adjutant to Lady Reading. She later married Nigel Birch, M.P., who held high political office and was created Lord Rhyl.

the advice of Alec Hardinge, has chosen to oppose Winston on a number of questions, about which it would have been more tactful to remain silent, namely the appointment of Beaverbrook as Minister of Aircraft Production, the gift of a Privy Councillorship to Brendan, and the offer of a peerage to Ironside. But Winston, however cavalierly he may treat his sovereign, is at heart a most vehement Royalist.

Relations between the King and the Prime Minister soon became excellent and even Queen Mary developed an immense admiration for Winston. The Prime Minister was, in fact, always scrupulous in consulting as well as informing the King on all matters of major importance and never missed his weekly audience if he could possibly avoid it. Suspicions which the King and Queen may have had about Winston's support of the Duke of Windsor rapidly evaporated when the Duke made difficulties in connection with his appointment as Governor of the Bahamas and the Prime Minister himself sought the King's permission to reply to the Duke's complaints with considerable severity. As the war proceeded the King and Queen became as devoted to Winston Churchill as he consistently was to them.

Having dropped Esmé in a taxi at Tothill Street (headquarters of the Women's Voluntary Service), where she is spending the night on duty, I went back to No. 10 and found Winston rending the Chiefs of Staff who are being unenthusiastic about the projected Operation SCIPIO in West Africa. De Gaulle came to sign an agreement; Newall, Dill and the Vice Chief of the Naval Staff (Admiral Philipps, minute but brilliant) talked with Ismay about the situation in Somaliland and the possibilities of invasion here; Desmond Morton and General Spears waited dutifully in my room for three hours in case they should be needed.

The First Lord told me on the telephone about 1.00 a.m. that a troopship had been torpedoed off Ireland. This depressed Winston greatly; however he recovered when he heard that nearly all the men had been saved and that there were no valuable stores on board, merely remarking that the navy were not being as successful against U-boats as in the past. (We have lost much shipping lately.)

Thursday, August 8th
Another busy day. After an early lunch I heard from the Air Ministry that violent fighting had taken place over a convoy off St Catherine's Point.[1] We appear to have destroyed a large number of German aircraft, but several ships in the convoy were sunk, two by E-boats. I told the P.M. this while he was lunching with Mrs Churchill and Dr Beneš[2] and he said: "And the British navy let them (the E-boats) sink those poor little ships in broad daylight!"

According to the Joint Intelligence Committee's weekly summary, which is a document well worth perusing, the result of Germany's delay in attacking this country is that "a small cloud of doubt as to Germany's invincibility has arisen on the European horizon". There are reports that Italy is pressing Germany to take the offensive in the North Sea and that Germany is urging an Italian offensive in the Mediterranean. Personally I think that the German attack on this country, whether by air or by invasion, will not be delayed much longer: Germany is probably gathering herself for a formidable blow. But it is comforting that an eminent German recently confided to a neutral that Germany's position was "splendid but hopeless".

As regards Russia, where Molotov recently made a speech attacking this country and the U.S., and reaffirming Russia's friendship with Germany, the F.O. comment:

> M. Molotov's speech need not be taken altogether at its face value. The Soviet Government have no friends in the world and no spiritual affinities with other Governments. They merely enter into temporary diplomatic associations with countries for purely opportunist purposes. They distrust and are distrusted by those with whom they associate, but take

[1] Southern point of the Isle of Wight.
[2] Prime Minister of Czechoslovakia, forced into exile when the Nazis occupied his country.

care not to let their distrust be exploited by others (i.e. by us). Hence the anxiety they display to re-emphasise on every suitable occasion the friendly character of their relations with Germany.

Friday, August 9th

The bag in yesterday's attack on a convoy off the Isle of Wight seems to have been about sixty German aircraft for the loss of sixteen. Five ships in the convoy were sunk and a number damaged.

Went to Chequers, motoring down with Mrs Churchill and Mary. Mr Eden, Sir John Dill, Sir Archibald Wavell* (C. in C., Middle East) and Ismay came to dine and sleep. About two minutes before dinner it transpired that the P.M. had invited the First Sea Lord but had omitted to tell anybody! This occasioned some hectic rearranging of the dinner table. I sat between Ismay and the First Sea Lord (Pound). Towards the end of dinner we had a triangular discussion, Eden, Ismay and I, about the fall of France. Both Eden and Ismay seemed to think that her shame had been so great that she could never rise again. W. disagrees.

After the ladies had gone, a variety of subjects were discussed, beginning with the attack on the convoy yesterday. Winston seemed to think we must go on using these coastal vessels as bait, although he admitted that "the surviving bait are getting a bit fed up". In drawing the German attack thus we stood to lose little (Pound pointed out that we even had a surplus of coasting vessels) while in the ensuing aerial battles we definitely proved to ourselves and to the world that we were superior to the Germans. Winston said the enemy must be "less all-powerful" in the air than we had supposed. If their strength were as great as we had believed, they would have come again today; they would have been bombing our ports incessantly. Eden could not understand why the Germans expended so great an effort against comparatively unimportant objects. It was suggested that they still thought they could starve us out and did not realise the unimportance of these coastal convoys. In that case it hardly looks as if the Germans are conserving everything for an invasion and mass-attack.

Pound suggested that the Germans had made a great mistake in going on, after they had proved the weakness of the French army, to strike a knock-out blow: they should have stopped after crossing the Somme and turned on us. Eden pointed out that the Germans probably thought, as did we, that the French would rally. The P.M. said that this mistake, if it was one, merely made the Germans slightly less admirable, but one could not detract from the brilliance of their strategy and of their unhesitating advance through Abbeville and Boulogne to Calais – and nearly to Dunkirk. The men of Calais were the bit of grit that saved us by stopping them as Sidney Smith stopped Napoleon at Acre.

The conversation turned to home defence, and Winston and Eden both said that the only real worry was the acute shortage of small-arms ammunition. But think where we should have been if the fighting had begun in March and had still been going on in France! Dill said that might be true, but in actual fact people never ran out of small arms ammunition. Their real requirements always fell below what they estimated. Eden said the new "Molotov Cocktail" was a vast improvement on the old and the anti-tank mine on the beaches had been shown to be most devastating. In fact the latter had already accounted for too many of our own people: Winston instanced the golfer who recently drove his ball on to the beach; he took his niblick down to the beach, played the ball, and all that remained visible afterwards was the ball which returned safely to the green.

The P.M. said: "Fancy, next year we shall have ten armoured divisions!" Eden and Dill dissented, saying that we should not have the equipment. "Well," said Winston, "if you'll produce the men (cries of "oh, we can do that") I'll see you get the weapons." Then we should be able to undertake formidable raids on the continent. This autumn we should land small forces of 5,000 men (and all the Generals seemed enthusiastic about this idea of taking the offensive), thus giving valuable experience and training to individual brigades or battalions which would form a core for future operations. We had much open to us: a landing in Holland followed by a destructive raid into the Ruhr; the seizure of the Cherbourg peninsula; and invasion of Italy. Wavell suggested Norway: "We shall need skis for that," said Winston, "and we don't want to go and get Namsosed again. We've had enough of that." Eden said that Sicily would be the soft spot in Italy's armour, because the Sicilians had always been anti-fascists.

The P.M., turning to Wavell, said that he promised he would not ask him to effect a landing in enemy territory until we could clear the air over the place of disembarkation. There was every hope that with the P.E. (photo-electric) rocket, the "Spaniel" (a rocket which pursues aircraft and is not dependent on accurate aiming), and a similar radio-rocket for use at night, we should be able to make it difficult for enemy aircraft to operate – and then the possibilities of offensive action would be great indeed.

After dinner Winston, the Generals and Pound retired to the Hawtrey room for a conference, and I arranged papers in the box and read various memoranda until nearly 3.00 a.m. At one moment a German raider came over the house and we all stumbled out into the garden to look. The First Sea Lord fell down first one flight of steps and then, having picked himself up disconsolately, he tumbled down another, ending in a heap on the ground where a sentry threatened him with a bayonet. He came back saying, "This is not the place for a First Sea Lord." Winston's comment was, "Try and remember you are an Admiral of the Fleet and not a Midshipman!"

Saturday, August 10th
In a telegram to the Prime Ministers of Australia and New Zealand, promising that we will abandon the Mediterranean and send our fleet eastwards in the event of Japan attacking Australia or N.Z., Winston has written: "If Hitler fails to invade and conquer Britain before the weather breaks, he has received his first and probably fatal check."

Sir Stafford Cripps has sent an interesting letter from Moscow to Lord Halifax about the future of the British Empire. He speaks of the new international groupings, of which there will be four:

(a) An Asiatic, probably under Japanese but possibly under Sino-Japanese hegemony.

(b) A Euro-Asiatic, including the Baltic states and part of the Balkans, under Russia.

(c) A European, including Scandinavia, part of the Balkans and the Middle East, under one European power.

(d) An American under the U.S.A.

Into these groups the British Empire does not naturally fall as a unit. Cripps' solution is for us to be associated closely in an Anglo-Saxon group with the U.S., G.B. being the European outpost of this group. Such an idea would, in addition, make it easier for the British Government to move to Canada in case of necessity. Winston wrote on this paper a note for circulation, which he afterwards tore up. It ran as follows:

> It seems to me that the ideas set forth by Sir S. Cripps upon the post-war position of the British Empire are far too airy and speculative to be useful at the present moment, when we have to win the war in order to survive. In these circumstances, unless any of my colleagues desire it, it seems hardly necessary to bring this excursion of our Ambassador to the U.S.S.R. formally before the Cabinet.

Later on, at lunch, Winston gave me his own views about war aims and the future. He said there was only one aim, to destroy Hitler. Let those who say they do not know what they are fighting for stop fighting and they will see. France is now discovering what she was fighting for. After the last war people had done much constructive thinking and the League of Nations had been a magnificent idea. Something of the kind would have to be built up again: there would be a United States of Europe, and this Island would be the link connecting this Federation with the new world and able to hold the balance between the two. "A new conception of the balance of power?" I said. "No," he replied, "the balance of virtue."

I lunched *en famille* with the P.M., Mrs C. and Mary, and it could not have been more enjoyable. Winston was in the best of humours. He talked brilliantly on every topic from Ruskin to

Lord Baldwin, from the future of Europe to the strength of the Tory Party. When he spoke of our lamentable lack of equipment, of that "boob" Inskip, etc., he said: "We shall win, but we don't deserve it; at least, we do deserve it because of our virtues, but not because of our intelligence." He said that the Tory Party was the strength of the country: few things need to be changed quickly and drastically; what conservatism, as envisaged by Disraeli, stood for was the gradual increase of amenities for an ever larger number of people, who should enjoy the benefits previously reserved for a very few (i.e. a levelling upwards, not a levelling downwards). The future depended not on the political system, but, once every man had sufficient, on the inner heart and soul of the individual. He was in a very friendly and garrulous mood and extremely pleased by some of the examples of bad verse (such as that by Edmund Gosse's housemaid) which I quoted to him:

> *Oh, Moon, lovely Moon, with thy beautiful face*
> *Careering throughout the boundaries of space*
> *Whenever I see thee, I think in my mind,*
> *Shall I ever, oh ever, behold thy behind.*[1]

Lord Beaverbrook rang up to say that the Germans had bombed an important factory at Rochester heavily but had contrived to miss with all their bombs. The Almighty is not always against us, he said, "In fact God is the Minister of Aircraft Production and I am his deputy."

After lunch I went for a long walk with Mrs Churchill and Mary to the summit of a neighbouring hill. Inadvisedly I raced Mary to the top, and though I won I reached my objective feeling iller than I have ever felt and was quite unable to see or think. Having recovered sufficiently, I walked home with Mrs C. discussing what could be done to make Lord Bessborough acceptable to Peggy, and others, as Chairman of the French Welfare Committees, etc., to which office Winston has appointed him.

---

[1] Had she lived a hundred years later she would have.

Arrived back in time to receive de Gaulle and Spears who came to discuss the former's proposed action at Dakar and in West Africa. I spent a very busy evening with papers and innumerable telephone conversations with Lord Lloyd about a propaganda matter.

Sir R. Gordon Finlayson, C. in C. Western Command, and Sir H. Pownall,[1] who commands the Home Guard, came to dine and sleep. Colonel Jacob and Prof. Lindemann also arrived. At dinner I sat between Mary and Jacob and, when not discussing bloodsports with the former, listened to Winston. He mentioned the numerous projects, inventions, etc., which he had in view and compared himself to a farmer driving pigs along a road, who always had to be prodding them on and preventing them from straying. He praised the splendid *sang-froid* and morale of the people, and said he could not quite see why he appeared to be so popular. After all since he came into power, everything had gone wrong and he had had nothing but disasters to announce. His platform was only "blood, sweat and tears".

He sent Prof. and me for some of his cherished graphs and diagrams and began to expound the supply position. Beaverbrook, he said, had genius and, what was more, brutal ruthlessness. He had never in his life, at the Ministry of Munitions or anywhere else, seen such startling results as Beaverbrook had produced; and Pownall, looking at the Aircraft Production charts, agreed that there had never been such an achievement. W. regretted that the Ministry of Supply had shown themselves incapable of producing similar results for the army.

He proceeded to examine the statistics, calling on Prof. for frequent explanations, and declaring that we were already overhauling the Germans in numbers (our production already exceeds theirs by one third). It was generally agreed that Hitler's aircraft position *must* be less good than we had supposed; otherwise why the delay, why the sparsity of attack?

After dinner (i.e. about 11.15!) we walked up and down beneath the stars, a habit which Winston has formed. When he

---

[1] Chief of Staff to Lord Gort in the British Expeditionary Force, 1939–40.

came in I showed him a letter from Nelson to Lord Spencer
(First Lord of the Admiralty), written a week after the Battle
of the Nile, which I had found in one of the rooms. It began:
"My Lord, was I to die at this moment want of frigates would
be found stamped on my heart. No words of mine can express
what I have and am suffering for want of them . . ." I suggested
to W. that he might so begin a "Former Naval Person" telegram
to Roosevelt, substituting "destroyers" for "frigates". He
answered that we were certainly going to get the destroyers
from America. But it is curious how history repeats itself even
in small details.

The Generals retired to the Hawtrey room to discuss the
Home Guard until 2.00 a.m. when we went to bed.

Sunday, August 11th
Walked in the garden with Jacob. He says that Beaverbrook is
a pirate; he steals the things which his colleagues, such as the
Minister of Supply, want and there is a real danger that he will
cause trouble with his Labour colleagues, especially as the P.M.
supports all his demands and backs him against Sinclair and
Morrison.[1] I think that Beaverbrook should be made Minister
of Munitions, with a Tory as Minister of Supply under him, and
Morrison should be sent to the Ministry of Information. Jacob
comments that Beaverbrook as Minister of Aircraft Production
is still Beaverbrook the Press King: he attaches supreme importance to the numbers of aircraft he can produce, as he formerly did
to the numbers of the *Daily Express* he could sell. "Circulation" is
his paramount interest.

Jacob thinks the P.M. should invite people from the War
Office and Admiralty, as well as the Generals, down here so
that they might realise how forceful and competent a person he
is. At present the departments are driven to exasperation by
the flow of enquiries, demands and comments which reach them
every morning from No. 10 and from Ismay's staff (now to be
known as the Office of the Minister of Defence).

Speaking of Chamberlain Jacob described him aptly as "a

[1] Herbert Morrison.

perfect Chairman of the Board of Directors, but not a good Managing Director".

Air Marshal Bowhill (C. in C., Coastal Command) came to lunch, also the Randolph Churchills. The chief excitement was another big aerial engagement and I kept on having to ring up Fighter Command to discover "the latest score". W. was very excited and kept on saying that "the swine had needed three days in which to lick their wounds" before they came again and that their air superiority was clearly less than we had feared.

The P.M. spoke on the telephone to Beaverbrook, who is coming tonight. B. (whose comment scrawled on a bit of paper to explain why this week's totals of aircraft deliveries are smaller than last week's, is: "Bevin's holiday and more holidays to come – and the Germans too perhaps") talked of his troubles with Herbert Morrison. He said that Morrison is never in his office and has no idea how to run a business: he tries to work it on the same lines as the L.C.C. They discussed the possibility of Morrison being replaced and agreed that tonight, when Ernest Bevin is coming, would be a good opportunity to approach the subject. The best way of influencing Morrison is through Bevin.[1]

After lunch I was soundly beaten by Mrs C. at croquet and then walked to the top of Beacon Hill with Mary. We sat on the top in the sunshine and prattled gaily, looking at the magnificent view of the plain below. Even though she takes herself a little seriously – as she confesses – she is a charming girl and very pleasant to look upon.

After tea I accompanied the P.M. to a rifle range nearby, where he fired with his Mannlicher rifle at targets 100, 200 and 300 yards away. He also fired his revolver, still smoking a cigar, with commendable accuracy. Despite his age, size and lack of practice, he acquitted himself well. The whole time he talked of the best method of killing Huns. Soft-nose bullets were the thing to use and he must get some. But, said Randolph, they are illegal in war; to which the P.M. replied that the Germans would

[1] As events showed, it was the worst. Ernest Bevin* detested Morrison. In any case, though Churchill always listened to Beaverbrook, he had no intention of taking part in his political intrigues (without which life had no zest for Beaverbrook).

make very short work of him if they caught him, and so he didn't see why he should have any mercy on them. He always seems to visualise the possibility of having to defend himself against German troops!

Beaverbrook and Bevin* arrived, and I dined alone with them and Winston. Grouse has been specially ordered, it having become legal to shoot them on August 5th this year. Winston politely hinted before dinner that it was a good thing to leave politicians to talk alone (they want to work on Bevin about the Morrison question) and so I retired discreetly as soon as I had procured myself a cigar. During dinner it was amusing to hear Beaverbrook flatter Bevin, calling him a natural House of Commons man and saying that he was the only orator in the Labour Party. Bevin said the war would be won in the Middle East and it was essential, for the sake of morale in this country, to deal the Italians a resounding blow. One was enough; after that they would collapse. Beaverbrook said he thought the morale in this country was all right, and when we received set-backs we braced ourselves the more. Bevin was doubtful and considered that success was sorely needed. I wondered who knew best, the newspaper magnate or the Labour leader. I am inclined to think the latter.

There were a number of sly allusions to capitalism and socialism and, I thought, a certain atmosphere of *gêne*, but this wore off by degrees. Agriculture was discussed, both Beaverbrook and Bevin considering themselves experts on the subject, and the former tried to persuade the P.M. that it was advisable to plough up 2,000,000 acres. "1,500,000," said Winston, "you are looking at what you think will be useful after the war. We have got to use all the labour we have to win the war and after that we'll make this country a fit place to live in." Talking on the same subject he said he did not think much of "that young man", by whom I understood him to mean Rob Hudson, the Minister of Agriculture.

Bevin asked for two things: (i) a Ministry of Buildings, to be responsible for all government construction and to co-ordinate this with the needs of the building trade; (ii) to be allowed to be in charge of amusements, from philharmonic concerts to horse-racing, in order that the public's entertainment might not be neglected in war-time. We have not got to be gloomy in order to be worthy of winning the war. The P.M. assented heartily. "There's nothing like singing to keep your spirits up," said Bevin finally. "As you know I have organised more strikes than anybody in the country, and when we ran out of money I always got the men to sing."

After dinner there were the usual starlight walks, Beaverbrook coming in after a few minutes and protesting it was a loathsome habit of the P.M. Then politics were discussed and, from what I heard, a ministerial reshuffle. Beaverbrook wants Greenwood to go; the other night he even announced to his guests at dinner that there were three ministers who were rotten – Greenwood, Sinclair and Duff Cooper (a nice thing for a Minister of the Crown to say publicly). I gather that it was being suggested Bevin should go to some other post and that he was asserting he must stay at the Ministry of Labour.

The P.M. asked me to come and talk to him while he was undressing and was most genial. He said Bevin was a good old thing and had "the right stuff in him" – no defeatist tendencies. He expatiated on the debt we owed to our airmen and claimed that the life of the country depended on their intrepid spirit. What a slender thread, he exclaimed, his voice tremulous with emotion, the greatest of things can hang by! He has cause to be elated: today our fighters accounted for about seventy German planes over the Channel.

Monday, August 12th

At the P.M.'s request I had breakfast with Bevin at 8.15. He was a little on his guard in these unaccustomed surroundings, but soon became more at ease and even ate honey off his knife. We talked about the press. He said that he thought the great fault of the newspapers had been, and was, to pander to such a low level of intelligence. The Berrys[1] had done a great disservice by trying to monopolise the provincial press: it was worse to have the newspapers controlled by one private interest than

[1] Lords Camrose and Kemsley and their estimable partner, Lord Iliffe.

by the State, though both alternatives were undesirable. The present lack of competition had killed the profession of journalism and there was no longer a school of experience which could produce men like Spender and Garvin for the future.

Left for London at 11.15, speeding to London most dangerously in order to be back for the Cabinet at 12.30. I drove in the police-car with Sawyers,[1] the butler, who said that he had been with Lord Wigram and remembered me as a page, coming in a carriage to pick up Neville and insisting on keeping my feathered hat on (I remember thinking it a cruel waste to carry such a beautiful thing under one's arm).

Lunched with Grandfather and Peggy. The party included the Cranbornes,[2] Mrs Ronnie Greville,[3] Mrs Simon Elwes[4] and some others. I sat between Lady Cranborne and Mrs Elwes, and found the former particularly agreeable.

Tuesday, August 13th

Telegram from Sweden to the effect that the Germans are embarking on the Norwegian coast for the purpose of invasion.

The P.M. is very much on edge, concerned with the quickest method of sending reinforcements to the Near East before the expected attack on Egypt. The War Office and the Admiralty want to send these via the Cape; Winston is intent on a dash through the Mediterranean (Operation HATS).

The other problem is the provision of R.A.F. pilots, W. being convinced that the shortage is partly due to the Air Ministry's policy of keeping too many pilots for training and ground jobs. Beaverbrook and Archie Sinclair are, as ever, at it hammer and tongs.

---

[1] Sawyers went everywhere with Churchill, of whom he took the utmost care. He was a considerable character and would have made a fortune on the stage. His memory of me dated from the 1920s, when Neville Wigram and I were pages of honour to George V.

[2] Robert Cecil, later 5th Marquess of Salisbury.* His wife Betty was the daughter of Lord Richard and Lady Moyra Cavendish.

[3] Affluent owner of Polesden Lacey near Reigate, where she entertained lavishly. King George VI and Queen Elizabeth spent their honeymoon there.

[4] Daughter of Lord Rennell, former Ambassador in Rome.

Had tea with Mary and Clarissa Churchill in Mary's sitting-room. It is difficult to make conversation to two entirely different types of person. Whatever I might say to interest one would, whether it succeeded or not, be certain to bore the other.

At No. 10 I heard the astonishing result of today's air battle: seventy-eight German planes destroyed for certain and we only lost three pilots. This is indeed a victory and will do much for the public morale. The Germans can hardly sustain their present losses with equanimity and it looks as if the tide may be turning. Prof., unlike most prophets, hopes for a crack in the German front this winter.

The long discussions on how to reinforce the Middle East continued after dinner, Winston (who did not have his sleep this afternoon) being in the worst of tempers. He has written today to Eden:

> I am favourably impressed with General Wavell in many ways, but I do not feel in him that sense of mental vigour and resolve to overcome obstacles, which is indispensable to successful war. I find, instead, tame acceptance of a variety of local circumstances in different theatres, which is leading to a lamentable lack of concentration upon the decisive point . . . Pray do not forget that the loss of Alexandria means the end of British sea power in the Eastern Mediterranean, with all its consequences.

In his reply Eden said that the main trouble in the Near East was the absence of sufficient equipment for those troops who were already there. Referring to the C. in C., he wrote: "Dill and I were much perturbed at your judgment of Wavell. Neither of us knows of any General Officer in the army better qualified to fill this very difficult post at this critical time."

The question everyone is asking today is, what is the motive of these gigantic daylight raids, which cost so much and effect so little? Are they reconnaissance in force, or a diversion, or just the cavalry attack before the main offensive? Presumably the next few days will show.

Wednesday, August 14th

In the afternoon I accompanied the P.M. to a meeting at the Admiralty Upper War Room. I walked back with him across the Horse Guards Parade and he confided to me that it was very difficult to make "those fellows" (the First Lord and the First Sea Lord) be sensible about sending troops through the Mediterranean. They were so confoundedly cautious.

Dined at the Mirabelle with Zara Mainwaring, whose charm and good looks were emphasised by the fact that she was beautifully dressed. We went on to see an amusing, gripping but impossible spy story called *Night Train to Munich*.

Thursday, August 15th

The President has sent a message to the effect that he can persuade Congress to let us have our fifty destroyers if we give him an assurance, not necessarily for publication, that we will not allow the British Fleet to be scuttled or surrendered, and if we sell or lease to the U.S. naval and air bases in all British possessions from Newfoundland southwards (this rather smacks of Russia's demands on Finland). In his reply Winston says he is cheered by this information and continues: "You will, I am sure, send us everything you can, for you know well that the worth of every destroyer you can spare to us is measured in rubies."

In Somaliland we have met with disaster, our strong fortified position at Tug Argan having been overwhelmed by vastly superior Italian forces. The blow against Egypt can hardly be long delayed, but there we shall be in a position to make a stiffer resistance.

When the P.M. makes his own arrangements he is inclined to forget to tell any of us and then to forget himself. Thus today at 4.00 the room was full of military dignitaries, Eden, Dill, Wavell and Ismay, and the P.M. was quietly enjoying a whisky and soda in the smoking-room at the House. While we waited I reminded Wavell about Mary Roxburghe (who was stranded in Palestine) and he said that he would attend to the matter personally when he got back to Cairo.

Today there took place the greatest and most successful air

battle of all. The figures of enemy planes destroyed kept on mounting and mounting until finally Winston, consumed with excitement, got into his car and drove off to Fighter Command at Stanmore. When he came back he told me the total was well over a hundred and asked me to ring up the Lord President, who is in the country recovering from an operation. I did so and found Mr Chamberlain somewhat cold at being disturbed in the middle of dinner. However he was overcome with joy when he heard the news and very touched at Winston thinking of him. It is typical of W. to do a small thing like this which could give such great pleasure. "The Lord President was very grateful to you," I said to Winston. "So he ought to be," replied W., "this is one of the greatest days in history."

Everybody is very elated and Somaliland falls into the background: the German confirmed losses have risen to 161, with a good many "probables" in addition and we have lost but thirty-four machines and eighteen pilots.

After dinner the P.M. sat down and dictated straight off a "directive" about operations in the Middle East. I thought it a masterly document, long but clear and to the point. First of all he considered how we could best assemble the maximum number of troops in the Delta area, then what our tactics should be. This is the first time I have seen his long experience as a strategist and student of war put into effect with such rapidity and confidence. He will discuss the matter tomorrow with Eden and Dill; but, of course, time presses and the Italians may not give us an opportunity to make all the dispositions we could wish. Somaliland is to be evacuated, and although this sounds like "sour grapes", the necessity is in itself a virtue since we need the Somaliland troops elsewhere.

To bed just before 2 a.m.

Friday, August 16th
12.30 p.m. Another air-raid warning has sounded and the Central War Room tell me Chatham is being heavily bombed, as well as Kenley where the P.M.'s squadron is stationed.[1] The P.M. has

---

[1] No. 615 Squadron of which he was Honorary Air Commodore.

decided to hold the Cabinet as usual, but there has been difficulty in extricating some of its members who have gone to ground. Beaverbrook looks a little blue because he says the Germans are concentrating on his aircraft factories (yesterday they destroyed Short's, an important bomber factory at Rochester).

Lunched with Grandfather and Peggy. Lady Ward, the Reggie Felloweses, Lady Victor Paget and an American called Bertram Cruger were there. I sat between the notorious Daisy Fellowes, friend of the Duke of Windsor and leader of the most decadent cosmopolitan set in Paris, and Lady Victor Paget. I talked to Cruger afterwards and said I hoped we won this war without American help (he having said he felt sure America would come in). He said he sympathised with that feeling, but that our complacency, if we won single-handed, would be unbearable. He has been urging Duff Cooper, who is a friend of his, to send documentary newsreels to America, on the grounds that they are the most effective propaganda; but he has met with scant success.

At about 5.00 p.m., while I was with the P.M. in his bedroom, the sirens sounded once again, for the third time in twenty-four hours. I ran downstairs to find out from the Central War Room what we were to expect and, tripping up at the bottom, arrived with such a noise that the C.I.G.S. thought a bomb had fallen. I spent the "warning" having tea on the lawn with Mrs Churchill, Mary and Seal, and left for Stansted just before the all-clear sounded. A bomb had fallen in the middle of the Kingston by-pass and necessitated a traffic diversion.

Lord Bessborough's train being two hours late – owing to a bomb on the railway line – I dined alone with Lady Bessborough and Moyra and afterwards went for a moonlight walk with Moyra.

Saturday, August 17th
A hot and sunny day devoid of aerial activity. In the morning Moyra and I, having visited the garden for the sake of the peaches, walked to look at the wreck of a JU.88 which had crashed nearby.

Sunday, August 18th

I said, half seriously, that my motive for coming to stay was to see one of these great air battles. I got my wish: after several warnings in the morning, we eventually had a grandstand view of a fight from the terrace of the house. It was after lunch and we were sitting on the terrace looking towards Thorney Island with the Portsmouth balloons just visible over the trees to our right. Suddenly we heard the sound of A.A. fire and saw puffs of white smoke as the shells burst over Portsmouth. Then to our left, from the direction of Chichester and Tangmere, came the roar of engines and the noise of machine-gun fire. "There they are," exclaimed Moyra, and shading our eyes to escape the glare of this August day we saw not far in front of us about twenty machines engaged in a fight. Soon a German bomber came hurtling down with smoke pouring from its tail and we lost sight of it behind the trees. A parachute opened and sank gracefully down through the whirling fighters and bombers. Out of the mêlée came a dive-bomber, hovered like a bird of prey and then sped steeply down on Thorney Island. There were vast explosions as another and then another followed, and my attention was diverted from the fight as clouds of smoke rose from the burning hangars of Thorney aerodrome. In all, the battle only lasted about two minutes and then moved away seawards, with at least two German aircraft left smouldering on the ground.

There seemed to be more machines about because the A.A. guns kept on firing, and presently, standing on the terrace balustrade, I saw four of the barrage balloons at Portsmouth collapse in flames. A number of bombs fell and one seemed to be of the "screaming" variety.

When peace was restored Moyra, Jean Meade (who had come over to lunch and was in ecstasies about the *"pain perdu"*) and I sat on the terrace in high spirits, elated by what we had seen.

After tea Moyra and I again played tennis until she was summoned away to deal with casualties at Chichester Hospital.

Today's bag was 141 certainly destroyed for ten pilots lost.

Monday, August 19th

Drove up to London without adventure, though the Kingston by-pass was still impassable. Found Miss Watson in a deplorable state of nerves, German aircraft having passed close to her window during the week-end.

The P.M. seems to have made an exception of Horace Wilson in the general forgiveness he has bestowed on the Men of Munich. Today H.J.[1] sent a note attached to a letter: "Mr Seal. The P.M. may be interested to see." Winston put a red circle round the word "interested" and wrote at the bottom "Why?".

I dined with Grandfather and Mother at Argyll House.

Back at No. 10 I read the first edition of the speech which the P.M. is to make in the House tomorrow and on which he has spent many hours this afternoon. It is curious to see how, as it were, he fertilises a phrase or a line of poetry for weeks and then gives birth to it in a speech. On many occasions recently I have heard him speak of our bombing attacks on Germany and say that even if Hitler is at the Caspian these attacks will bring him back to defend his home. Now I see that the Caspian is featuring in the speech! The sentence I like most is that referring to the German air claims (which included a statement that we lost 150 machines yesterday); if these claims continue Hitler's "reputation for veracity will be seriously impugned".

The P.M. went to bed shortly after midnight expressing delight that the Germans had refrained from raiding on a big scale today and saying they were making a big mistake in giving us a respite.

Tuesday, August 20th

At 9.00 I was commanded to stop the hammering on the Horse Guards Parade. This is an almost daily complaint and must cause considerable delay in the measures being taken to defend Whitehall.

Lunched with Mother and Miss Bondfield,[2] the first (and

---

[1] Sir Horace John Wilson was often referred to as H.J.
[2] Member of Ramsay MacDonald's administration. The first female Privy Councillor.

only) woman ever to be a Cabinet Minister. Her experience as a Trade Unionist and in other fields is very wide and her conversation proportionately interesting. Speaking of the future she said that peace must depend on the success of economic federation. Each nation should be left to develop its own culture and genius within its traditional frontiers, but the economic basis must be far wider. She would like to hear this emphasised every week by some responsible statesman. She told of the reactions to Munich of the United States, where she was at the time, and traced back the mistakes of recent years to the raising of American tariffs in the first place, then to Ottawa (which arose from America's action),[1] to the rejection of the Lytton report on Manchuria and so to the failure of collective security over Abyssinia.

Although the gallery was crowded I made my way down to the House to hear the P.M. speak.[2] It was less oratory than usual and the point of chief interest to the House was the account of the bargain with America about the lease of air-bases in the West Indies (he did not divulge what we hoped to get as a *quid pro quo*). On the whole, except for bright patches – like that about "the Führer's reputation for veracity", which had a great success – the speech seemed to drag and the House, which is not used to sitting in August, was languid. The P.M. ended by comparing Anglo-American co-operation (will it one day be unity?) to the Missouri river and saying, "Let it roll on!" I drove back with him in the car and he sang "Ole Man River" (out of tune) the whole way back to Downing Street.

Dined with Audrey Paget at the Mirabelle (where Lord Kemsley, quite out of the blue, presented me with an enormous cigar), took her to see a satisfactory thriller called *Cottage to Let* and went on to an empty, dull and sordid nightclub called "Slippin". We flirted more brazenly than ever and at one moment

---

[1] The Ottawa Agreement of 1931 initiated the policy of Imperial Preference for trade between Britain and the Dominions.

[2] This speech contained the sentence "Never in the field of human conflict has so much been owed by so many to so few", but it did not strike me very forcibly at the time. I saved the first draft from the waste-paper basket. It is now on loan to Chequers.

it looked like becoming more than a flirtation; but I feel a little conscience-stricken about committing the crime for which Socrates was condemned.[1]

Wednesday, August 21st

A busy morning composing gushing letters for the P.M.'s signature.

There is a hitch about Operation MENACE (ex-SCIPIO) since it seems unlikely that de Gaulle could effect an unopposed landing at Dakar.

The Americans are trying to make the provision of destroyers into the other half of a bargain involving the lease of bases in Bermuda, etc. This is obnoxious to the Cabinet who wish the two questions kept entirely separate and both based on the goodwill the two countries feel towards each other. As Winston proposes to say, in a telegram to the Canadian P.M., "it would be better to do without the destroyers, sorely as we need them, than to get drawn into a haggling match between the experts as to what we ought to give in return for the munitions. Immediately people would say, 'How much are they worth in money?' and 'Is not advantage being taken of our being hard pressed?' Any discussion of this kind would be injurious to the great movement of events. Each should give all he can without any invidious comparison."

The P.M. also makes this clear to Roosevelt, but ends his telegram from "A Former Naval Person" by saying: "Although the air attack has slackened in the last few days and our strength is growing in many ways, I do not think that bad man has yet struck his full blow. We are having considerable losses in merchant ships in the North-Western Approaches, now our only channel of regular communication with the Oceans, and your fifty destroyers, if they came along at once, would be a precious help."

After dinner, while the P.M. sat upstairs with Eden discussing the Middle East and Operation MENACE, I read an interesting paper about the future by Duff Cooper which will be before

[1] Corrupting the youth.

the Cabinet tomorrow. He proposes the establishment of a committee, representing all parties and including Chamberlain, Attlee and Sinclair, to present to the Government and to the public some idea of the post-war world. He maintains that for Europe a federal plan should be drawn up as a democratic answer to Hitler's "New European Order". For this country proposals should be put forward to deal with unemployment, to give equal educational opportunities to all, to sweep away privilege and to bring men nearer to equality. No country would be better qualified to lead the way than Great Britain since no country has done more in the last fifty years in the way of social reform. It is noteworthy that this paper has been written by a Conservative and that the proposed committee will be largely Conservative in composition: as in Disraeli's time perhaps the Tory party may prove to be the initiators of social revolution. Lord Halifax has produced slightly improved terms of reference for the committee.

Graeco-Italian relations are at breaking point, but Greece declares that rather than submit she "will set the Balkans on fire". It is thought that Mussolini will not actually attack for the time being – and while he delays Turkey increases daily in strength. The Germans, having temporarily abandoned their mass raids, today machine-gunned the residents of Bournemouth and the Scilly Isles.

Thursday, August 22nd
The P.M. is not unnaturally indignant because the gun – his gun – so laboriously installed at Dover was not ready to fire in reply to some shore batteries from the other side which bombarded first a convoy and then Dover today.

The Cabinet discussed the financial situation. Our reserves of gold and foreign securities are desperately low and we can only carry on a few months longer. Nevertheless the Cabinet decided to go on placing orders for armaments in the U.S., in the belief that after the Presidential election the American Government might show itself more generous and helpful. The Lord President in a letter to Winston says that we must gamble on the chance of obtaining American support; and Winston, in the Cabinet, said it would be better to give the Americans a lien on British industry rather than run short of supplies. In the last resort we may requisition wedding rings, gold ornaments, etc., in order to shame the U.S.; but the amount so raised would be only about £20 million.

I was just peacefully asleep when the sirens went. I refused to be disturbed, but was of course subsequently aroused by the all-clear. There is a double sting about air-raids at night. I gather that at No. 10 the P.M. strode about the house, having been aroused by gunfire in North London, wearing his flowery dressing-gown and a tin hat.

Monday, August 26th

At No. 10 I found the P.M. not yet returned from Chequers. The news is not too good: our shipping losses by submarine are becoming serious. London has been bombed – by a single aircraft on Saturday night – and in retaliation we sent eighty-nine bombers over Berlin last night. We may therefore expect a big raid on London tonight, I fear. However perhaps Goering will exhaust his air force: an R.A.F. officer (Group Captain Cochrane), whom I met at Hinchingbrooke on Saturday, told me that in the last war Goering drove the Richthofen Squadron to death when he took over the command.

The first air-raid warning – which came to nothing – sounded just after lunch. The P.M., who thought it would be serious owing to last night's adventures, ordered everybody to the shelter and then telephoned to the C.A.S. to express disgust that tonight we were going to bomb Leipzig rather than Berlin. "Now that they have begun to molest the capital," he said, "I want you to hit them hard – and Berlin is the place to hit them."

I dined with Sidney Cuthbert, who is on the King's Guard at St James's Palace. We fed out of the way well and afterwards a piper of the Scots Guards marched round the table playing to us. He had just started a second performance, and was well launched into "Speed Bonny Boat", when we were told that the sirens were sounding. So, relinquishing our cigars, we made for the Palace shelter, the officers changing from their immaculate blue mess-kit into battledress and steel helmets.

It is now 12.30 and the all-clear has not yet sounded. This distraction is merely due to a few single aircraft, and because of them production has stopped and even the newspapers have given up printing. The searchlights, concentrated through the warm haze on first one spot then another, have been magnificent to see and from time to time (as at this moment) we have heard the drone of enemy aircraft overhead and heard the noise of anti-aircraft fire. The P.M. has driven everybody to the shelter except myself, John Peck, Herbert Morrison (who has been hiccuping loudly over a whisky and soda), Archie Sinclair and Air Marshal Courtenay.

I stood in the garden, heard midnight strike on Big Ben, watched the searchlight display and wondered at the unaccustomed stillness of London. Not a sound, and scarcely a breath of air. Then suddenly the noise of an engine and the flash of a distant gun.

The P.M., undressed at midnight, came down in his particularly magnificent golden dragon dressing-gown and, tin hat in hand, retired to sleep in the shelter. I sat a long time gossiping with Brendan and Prof. and supposing that this is the first of many such disturbed nights.

After pacing the lawn for some time the P.M. finally retired to bed in the air-raid shelter where, unaroused by the all-clear at 3.45 a.m., he spent the night. I sat up till after 2.00 and then, convinced that my vigil was useless, went to bed – but was not allowed to sleep peacefully or long.

Tuesday, August 27th
One of the most immediate questions is the extension of training for R.A.F. pilots and its transfer abroad where it may take place unhampered. Beaverbrook says he does not see the point in this transfer, and W.'s reaction to that is: "I attach the greatest importance to your opinion, but you must either face the facts and answer them effectively and with a positive plan or allow the opinion of those who are responsible to prevail."

The P.M.'s system of working includes the enlistment of outside authorities to vet and supplement the labours of the officially responsible department. Thus today he sends over to

P. J. Grigg at the War Office a batch of telegrams from India with the following mandate: "I will from time to time send you other Indian telegrams in order that you may warn me if amid all their wordage there is anything being done counter to the policy now agreed."

When I returned to No. 10 after an early dinner, there was a good deal to do and I was deeply involved in arranging papers when, at about 9.30, the sirens began. I went up to tell the P.M. that it was all due to one aeroplane and stayed to drink some coffee and smoke a cigar. Winston, to his obvious regret, refused brandy and demanded iced soda-water, saying that he was ashamed of the easy life he led and had never before lived in such luxury. Desmond Morton said that the P.M.'s staff had different views on this question of an easy life! W. went on to declare that his object was to preserve "the maximum initiative-energy". "Every night," he said, "I try myself by court martial to see if I have done anything effective during the day. I don't mean just pawing the ground; anyone can go through the motions; but something really effective."

Got away shortly after midnight, in between two air-raid warnings, having heard from Desmond Morton that the Cameroons had just announced their secession to de Gaulle.

Wednesday, August 28th
The P.M. set forth on a journey to inspect the South-East defences and so we had a quiet day. I was even able to go to sleep in the afternoon, having been infected by Winstonian habits.

I dined with Seal at the R.A.C. The inevitable air-raid came at 9.00 while our bombers were setting off to bomb Berlin. The P.M. came back at about 11.00, having seen numerous air battles and been much affected by the plight of those whose houses have been destroyed or badly damaged by raids. He was, he said, determined that they should receive full compensation up to £1,000 and made a note to the effect that he would browbeat the Chancellor of the Exchequer on the subject next day.

The air-raid lasted till 4.00 a.m.; the searchlight displays were magnificent but ineffective; and we heard bombs falling not far away, in Chelsea and on the south side of the river.

Morton tells me that the French Congo has now declared for de Gaulle.

Thursday, August 29th
Kingsley Wood came about compensation and proved himself the perfect yes-man. Afterwards I enjoyed listening to him pandering to Beaverbrook and Brendan, both of whom flattered him and treated him as an inferior being.[1]

Lunched with Seal at Wyndham's and had a most interesting discussion about Munich and wisdom-after-the-event. He pointed out that it was only the events after Munich which united the country and made it ready for war. In September 1938 there would have been a strong anti-war party.

Friday, August 30th
Motored to Chequers with Mrs Churchill and Pamela. I found at the last moment that the P.M. was going to stop at Fighter Command, but though disappointed at missing this I thought it would be rude to tell Mrs C. I did not want to go with her.

General Ismay came and also the Joint Planners, representing the three services, whose duty it is to plan our military operations. They are Air Commodore Slessor who seems to be the most forceful of the three, Brigadier Playfair and Captain Daniel, R.N. I showed them the house and garden before the P.M. arrived and when telling Captain Daniel of Nelson's letter about "want of frigates" was surprised to find he knew it almost by heart and the approximate date on which it was written.

At dinner, fortified by 1911 champagne, the P.M. talked brilliantly, though less epigramatically than usual. He said there were only three things that worried him: when, as yesterday,

---

[1] He suggested on one occasion that as we were providing the Dutch Government with vast financial support the present unequal division of Shell and Royal Dutch, with forty per cent owned by Shell and sixty per cent by Royal Dutch, should be remedied. We should demand a fifty-fifty re-organisation. Churchill, who objected to taking advantage of another country's misfortunes, said that he never again wished to hear such a suggestion.

the proportion of our air losses was too high; the startling shipping losses in the North-Western Approaches, where lay the seeds of something that "might be mortal" if allowed to get out of hand; and the gun batteries at Gris Nez which would make the passage of our convoys through the Straits almost impossible and would mean that Dover might be "laid in ashes". He proposed to destroy those batteries – from the sea. (Captain Daniel wants to do it by landing troops.)

The reason why he had brought the Joint Planners down was to give them his general idea, which they could elaborate, of the campaign of 1941. He would not look as far as 1942, which must "be the child of 1941", but would like to discuss the offensive action we should be able to take next year in order to turn the tables on the Germans and make them wonder, for a change, where they were going to be struck next. The essential prerequisite was the command of the air over the beaches where we should disembark our troops and armoured divisions. We had a large number of weapons, well on the road to development, which could help us in this: the A.I., which would for the first time be used in a Beaufighter plane tomorrow night and would soon be available in sufficiently large numbers to discomfort the enemy "night prowlers", unescorted as they were by fighters; the "Yagi" (now called "Elsie") or wireless-controlled searchlights; and above all the P.E. fuse which was cheap, and easy to produce, and would shortly be given its trial in the clear atmosphere of Malta. Once these weapons were available, and the likelihood of being "Namsosed" again had passed away, we could land on the continent.

He then outlined a number of possibilities which he wished the Joint Planners to study in the months to come: the capture of Oslo and the consequent undoing of Hitler's first great achievement; the invasion of Italy by sea; the cutting off of the Cherbourg peninsula (this might be used as a feint, because he did not wish to fight in France); and, most attractive of all, a landing in the Low Countries followed by the seizure of the Ruhr, or at any rate North German territory, so that the enemy might be made to experience war in his own land. Forces of 100–120,000 men could be used, and if these operations were successful, who could tell to what they might lead?

Brigadier Playfair suggested it might be dangerous to use the P.E. fuse at Malta, in case its existence should become known and steps taken to parry it. But the P.M. said that there was no reason why it should be distinguished from accurate A.A. fire, and, moreover, if it were successful at Malta not only should we be able to plan our other operations with confidence, but also the fleet would once again have a secure base which would be fatal to Italy's communications with Libya and would alter the whole situation in the Mediterranean.

After dinner I did a certain amount of work, interrupted by periodic excursions into the garden to watch the searchlights fruitlessly attempt to pick up German aircraft as they passed overhead. To bed by 2.00.

Saturday, August 31st

I had to break to the P.M. at 8.30 that three more big ships had been torpedoed off the Bloody Foreland (one of them 15,000 tons, carrying children to New York). This distressed him particularly, because the North-Western Approaches are a very sore spot which shows no immediate sign of healing. On the other hand the news of our raids on Berlin last night is excellent: we seem to have found our objectives and damaged them severely.

Beaverbrook rang up and, speaking of the heavy attacks which are developing this morning (in good weather conditions for our fighters, I think), said that he felt sure the enemy was now trying to reach a conclusion over here. He is satisfied with our fighter production figures.

There are more signs of German shipping concentrations at Emden (which we bombed last night) and off the Norwegian coast. Possibly a raid is contemplated, but I think serious invasion must depend on the ability of the German air force to obtain the mastery – and that seems more than doubtful.

Sir Roger Keyes came to lunch and the Joint Planners stayed. The P.M. talked a lot. Pouring out another glass of brandy, and eyeing us all benevolently, he said that these Planners, on whose deliberation so much depended, could not afford to have more than one glass of brandy; but it was different for him who had only to take the responsibility. It was curious but in this war he had had no success but had received nothing but praise, whereas in the last war he had done several things which he thought were good and had got nothing but abuse for them.

Speaking of the Americans, who favoured many of the measures, such as violating Swiss neutrality in the air, which we are now taking, he said that their morale was very good – in applauding the valiant deeds done by others!

Sir R. Keyes then became the centre of conversation, the P.M. beginning by saying: "I make myself detestable to everybody (i.e. by his refusal to let sleeping dogs lie or acquiesce in inactivity) except Roger whose dupe I am." This is true because he has given Keyes a job out of loyalty and affection and in so doing has much angered the younger men in the navy. He told Keyes how he hoped that he would be able to undertake a raid on the Channel Islands soon, and Sir R. said that would be easy. The provision of air protection would however be difficult, insisted Slessor.

Keyes said he hoped we should seize Casablanca when we took Dakar, but the P.M. replied that de Gaulle, who would have to be consulted, was now on the high seas. Apparently de Gaulle's movements will be disguised by the fact that he will speak twice weekly on the wireless from London – from records already made. Similarly a bogus notice appeared in the press the other day to the effect that Larminat,[1] now in Equatorial Africa, had lunched with the P.M. On the whole I formed the impression that one of Sir R. Keyes' major characteristics was a well-developed tendency to self-glorification.

The P.M. went to see the fighter pilots at Uxbridge, and watched a great battle in progress, while I went for a series of walks, alone, with Mrs Churchill and with Pamela. Unfortunately while I was on one of these, enjoying the magnificent evening,

---

[1] General de Larminat. Rallied to de Gaulle in 1940. Captured Brazzaville for the Free French. Committed suicide in 1961 when appointed by de Gaulle to try the French generals who had rebelled in Algiers.

the P.M. returned, decided to work, demanded his box, found it in complete disorder and was most displeased. I felt a worm that had neglected its duties.

Sir H. Dowding, C. in C. Fighter Command, and Sir C. Portal,[1] C. in C. Bomber Command, came to dinner. Dowding is splendid: he stands up to the P.M., refuses to be particularly unpleasant about the Germans, and is the very antithesis of the complacency with which so many Englishmen are afflicted. He told me that he could not understand why the Germans kept on coming in waves instead of concentrating on one mass raid a day which could not be effectively parried. Ismay suggested that they might be short of planes and have to use bombers twice daily. There was a great discussion about the ethics of shooting down enemy pilots landing by parachute: Dowding maintaining it should be done and the P.M. saying that an escaping pilot was like a drowning sailor. Otherwise he was in a very ruthless frame of mind.

Portal told me it was not true that the captured German airmen were, as is commonly reported, exceptionally young. On the contrary their average age was twenty-five or twenty-six.

A pressing question is how often air-raid sirens should be sounded in order to attain the maximum security and the minimum disturbance. Lord Beaverbrook is for none; the Air Marshals are for lots. The Cabinet must decide.

After dinner the First Lord rang up from Brighton to say that enemy ships were steering westwards from Terschelling. The invasion may be pending (though I'll lay 10–1 against!) and all H.M. Forces are taking up their positions. If these German ships came on they would reach the coast of Norfolk tomorrow morning.

The P.M. and the Air Marshals, with Lindemann, looked at diagrams showing the working of the German Headache beam which, directed from Germany, guides the bombers to their objectives whatever the weather conditions or the visibility. We, having learnt of this, are in process of discovering how to jam

[1] Later Lord Portal of Hungerford.*

and how to divert it. Diversion is more fun: it sends the enemy to wrong destinations.

The final figures for today's fighting are eighty-five certain, thirty-four probable, thirty-three damaged. We lost thirty-seven aircraft, twelve pilots being killed and fourteen wounded. Our increased losses are due to the fact that the Germans have now thought of armouring their planes behind – a precaution we took long ago – and the fighting is therefore much harder. The P.M. was deeply moved by what he saw this afternoon at Uxbridge: he said that what he saw there brought the war home to him.

NINE

LONDON BOMBARDED
SEPTEMBER 1940

Sunday, September 1st
The supposed invasion proved to be nothing, but three of
our destroyers, which were investigating matters, ran into a
minefield and one was sunk.

I walked with Ismay round the camp of the soldiers (Coldstream now) who guard Chequers. He quoted to me by heart
passages from the P.M.'s *World Crisis* (particularly the tribute
to the British army after the Somme) which he considers some
of the finest prose in English literature. His admiration for the
P.M., as a man who has himself experienced the warfare which
he now directs, knows no bounds.

At lunch the P.M., talking of *Why England Slept*,[1] turned to
me and said, "You slept too, didn't you!" – a good-natured jibe
at my professed "Munichois" views!

In the afternoon I went with the P.M., Lindemann and Ismay
to Uxbridge, headquarters of No. 11 Group which controls all
the Fighter Squadrons in the South-East. We talked to Air
Marshal Park[2] who confirmed the P.M.'s view that the Germans
must already have developed their maximum attack and could
not stand the strain much longer as far as an air offensive was

---

[1] A book written by John F. Kennedy, later President of the United States.
[2] Air Chief Marshal Sir Keith Park. Commanded 11 Group, the main fighter
force in the Battle of Britain, was later A.O.C. in C., Egypt for a year and
then in command of the R.A.F. during the siege of Malta when Lord Gort
was Governor.

concerned. The P.M. expressed delight at the success of our pilots, but said, "It is terrible – terrible – that the British Empire should have been gambled on this." He had already remarked at lunch, talking of Poland and the failure of France to maintain its position in Eastern Europe, "This is one of the most unnecessary wars, and it will probably be one of the most terrible." The Poles, he pointed out, had fought much better than the French and had shown infinitely greater spirit.

After talking to the Air Marshal, we went to the operations room, with its maps, its men and W.A.A.F.s in shirt-sleeves acting as croupiers, its coloured lights and intricate apparatus. There were no raids of importance in progress – the enemy having been smitten harder than he liked both yesterday and this morning – but it was interesting to see how the reports of the R.D.F. (Radar), and observation corps were shown on the map. This room is in the bowels of the earth, fifty feet or more underground.

When we returned to Chequers I heard that a brand-new cruiser, the *Fiji*, escorting de Gaulle and his party to their objective, had been torpedoed. "The Admiralty," said Winston, "is now the weak spot; the air is all right."

Air Marshal Park and his wife came to dinner as did two Coldstream officers from the soldiers guarding Chequers. Their names were John Sparrow (a barrister – Fellow of All Souls)[1] and Rickards, an Eton Master. It amused me mildly that Mrs C., who does nothing but profess democratic and radical sentiments, should put off inviting any of the officers to dine until the guard consisted of the Coldstream. The Oxford and Bucks Light Infantry were never invited inside. At dinner the P.M., thinking of our new weapons, said that we could not hope to pile up sufficient men and munitions to outmatch the Germans. This was a war of science, a war that would be won with new weapons.

Monday, September 2nd
Drove up from Chequers with Lindemann who described to me the new weapons and their prospects of success.

[1] Later Warden of All Souls.

Sir Stafford Cripps telegraphs from Moscow that the Russo-German alliance is very close, closer indeed than before since Russia is afraid of Germany and friendship is a means of defence. We must not rely on any breach between them or look for divergence of policy. This is the opinion I have held all along and it is interesting that such an ardent supporter of the extreme Left as Cripps should support it.

Movements of German bomber squadrons to advanced bases in France are thought to indicate an intensification of air attack towards the end of this week. It is already on a sufficiently large scale!

Postal censorship reports show that the morale of the country is extremely high. There is much hatred of Hitler but little of Germany. France is spoken of with supreme contempt and little sympathy. It is widely realised that the support we are getting from America is paid for in hard cash.

I dined rapidly with Zara and Betts at Pruniers, where we sat on high stools against the counter and fed most expensively. I then went back to No. 10 in time for an air-raid. Winston returned with Beaverbrook, having dined well at the American Embassy, and was most importunate, demanding papers, information, etc. He dictated to me a telegram for Lothian, apparently oblivious of the fact that I can't write shorthand. I managed somehow to scrawl down what he said and to get it off to America: it was an instruction about the exchange of aide-memoires on the destroyer question which were due for signature in Washington within an hour.

Tuesday, September 3rd

Went to a service at Westminster Abbey to commemorate the first anniversary of the war. The King and Queen were to have gone, but an air-raid warning sounded just before the service began. However the P.M. and a good many Ministers attended. I rescued Eden and Dill from a garden where they had been isolated by an over-zealous verger and where they would otherwise have been left and forgotten.

Bishop Hensley Henson, the new Canon, preached an eloquent fighting sermon, containing much alliteration, many fiery denunciations, a good deal of politics and no Christianity – which was what Winston had come to hear.

Wednesday, September 4th

Attended the funeral of Sir J. J. Thomson[1] in Westminster Abbey, as representative of the P.M. It was moving in itself: the procession of clergy in their black vestments, the sunlight blazing diagonally on the coffin and altar, the almost garish effect of the many candles. It was also moving because it seemed to me that in him the Trinity which I knew so well had passed away: though only a figurehead in the college, he was representative of a period in its history.

Returning to No. 10 I busied myself with the question of appointing a new Master, my last job before handing over patronage questions to Tony Bevir. The College want to leave the Mastership in abeyance till after the war, but Brendan thinks this would be a mistake, as the office is one of more than academic importance, and I agree with him. So it has been decided to try and persuade George Trevelyan[2] to accept.

September 5th–15th

Stayed at Helperby and greatly profited from the rest and quiet. We walked partridges most days, played tennis and gambled. Mother and Philip left on the 11th. Aunt Celia[3] was very cheerful and exceedingly hospitable, and Uncle Clive did his best to provide us with partridges to shoot and was lavish with his remarkable '63 and '70 port.

While I was away, the great raids on London started and much damage was done, Buckingham Palace being singled out for attack.

---

[1] Master of Trinity College, Cambridge. Nobel Prize winning physicist who, with Lord Rutherford, first split the atom and was thus one of the originators of nuclear fission.

[2] Eminent historian and successor to J. J. Thomson as Master of Trinity.

[3] My mother's greatly loved twin sister, Lady Celia Coates, married to Sir Clive Coates of Helperby Hall, Yorkshire. She celebrated her hundredth birthday in 1984, being the last surviving person to have known Mr Gladstone.

Sunday, September 15th

Motored back to London after lunch, stopping at Hinchingbrooke for tea. I have caught Betty Harris's[1] cold and as she has come out with chicken-pox this morning I am in quarantine for that miserable disease.

I reached London in time for the air-raids, and the noise of guns and bombs was deafening all night. The house shook and the reports were so loud that it seemed as if the guns were firing from the garden outside. But we brought down 186 German planes today, for the loss of thirteen pilots, and it looks as if Hitler cannot keep up this pressure for long.

Monday, September 16th

Mother, who leaves for Badminton today, thank God, said at breakfast that if one looked on all this as ordinary civilian life it was indeed hellish, but if one thought of it as a siege then it was certainly one of the most comfortable in history.

At No. 10 there is a certain chaos caused by the fact that the building is thought to be unsafe. The basement is being fitted up for the P.M. to live and to work in, and meanwhile much of the time, both by day and by night, is being spent in the disagreeable atmosphere of the Central War Room. We may move altogether: possibly to the newly-constructed Church House, Westminster. Brendan suggests Bridgewater House as a solid stone building.

I am disappointed to hear from Desmond Morton that Operation MENACE (ex SCIPIO) has been abandoned because the Admiralty allowed French ships to get to Dakar first. I wonder if Vichy got wind of the proposed coup?[2]

Tuesday, September 17th

After another night of loud explosions, apparent earthquakes and general discomfort, I went early to No. 10, where I found

[1] Lady Celia Coates' younger daughter. My first cousin and close friend, she married William Harris, Q.C., who was serving in the Coldstream Guards.

[2] It was said that Free French officers dining at l'Ecu de France shortly before they sailed, rose to their feet in the restaurant and drank "à Dakar". This may have got back to Vichy through a member of a foreign embassy who was also dining in the restaurant.

the P.M. up and about early, having spent the night in the
C.W.R. Brendan and Prof. and Tony had slept with the staff in
bunks in the air-raid shelter (at No. 10).

We lunched off beer and bottled tongue and then I went down
to the House to hear the P.M. make a statement on the air-raids,
etc. Just as he was about to speak, the spotters on the roof
(who now supplement air-raid warnings by blowing whistles
when the enemy are really near) became active and the House
of Commons repaired to its dug-outs. I remained in my room
having so far preserved a healthy contempt for these alarums
and excursions – except after dark when the shell splinters fly.
The P.M. subsequently spoke very eloquently.

Some telegrams from de Gaulle arrived, expressing his disappointment at the abandonment of MENACE and declaring his intention to proceed against Dakar by land.

I walked back to No. 10 and just as I was about to enter there
was a vast explosion. I met the P.M. who swore he had seen,
from his bedroom window, a bomb hit Buckingham Palace.
Everybody was packed off to the shelter, but it transpired that
the noise was due to a time-bomb in the Palace garden which
had been purposely exploded.

8.00 p.m. is about zero-hour for the night raid and the
accompanying gun fire. The Private Secretaries now have a car
at their disposal, with a soldier as driver, and so I went home
in that about 8.30 with my tin helmet firmly pressed down over
my ears and my eyes fixed on the gun flashes. The early advent
of the equinoctial gales has made raiding less easy today, the
westerly wind reaching great strength.

Wednesday, September 18th
Lunched with Father at the Travellers after going down to the
House, where the Cabinet met, and returning during an air-raid
while the exhaust of our fighters streaked the blue sky with
white lines and circles.

After lunch I showed No. 10 to a Japanese journalist, who is
to write an article on the P.M. for the paper *Asaki*, and extolled
Winston's merits to him in the most lavish terms. With typical
Japanese contempt for the truth he explained to me how he

proposed to say that he had shaken hands with the P.M., noted the eagle look in his eye, etc., etc. I said I must draw the line at his producing a fictitious conversation.

Miss Violet Markham[1] came to see me to talk about the effect of air-raids on the people. It is, she pointed out, a question of *"pourvu que les civiles tiennent"*. At the moment nothing was being done to ensure their safe transport home – the buses stopped running in raids – and no steps were being taken to feed them when they came out of shelters after long, cold and weary vigils. I rang up Sir John Reith (Minister of Transport) and arranged that she should go and see him and promised to see that further steps were taken from here if satisfactory results were not achieved. It is clearly most important that everything possible should be done to lighten the cross which the people of London have got to bear – particularly as their lot will become increasingly unpleasant as the winter draws on.

Back to No. 10 to sleep. The P.M. went over to the C.W.R. for the night with Seal. Brendan, Prof. and Jack Churchill slept in the shelter at No. 10, in quarters resembling third-class accommodation on a Channel steamer. The typists and servants sleep on mattresses in the bigger room in the shelter. Enemy aircraft boomed overhead and once or twice I looked out into the garden to watch the shells and the bombs, until the falling shell splinters – one of which came unpleasantly near – drove me in. One splinter is embedded firmly in the inside wall of our room as a result of last night's activities.

After Brendan, Jack Churchill and I had gossiped for a little I went over to the C.W.R. and had a whisky-and-soda with Seal, Ismay, Hollis and the rest. Pug Ismay was giving his usual description of the French collapse and the helplessness of the statesmen and Generals. So I hurried away to No. 10, a bomb falling close as I entered the Foreign Office arch. Then Brendan and I did some sightseeing, watching the A.A. barrage at work on planes directly over our heads. There was an orange glow

[1] Mrs James Carruthers, who retained her maiden name. She was one of the best-known and respected social workers in the country and was an associate of my mother, at whose suggestion she came to see me at Downing Street.

as a balloon above us collapsed in flames and then, in the direction of the river, we saw a parachute descending through the moon-beams. "A parachutist," said one policeman. "A pilot escaping; that orange glow was an enemy plane down," said another (the big fat one who guards the door); but a third said, "No, it is coming down too fast, it's something worse than that." A few seconds later he was proved to be right: a landmine exploded on the County Hall and even the windows in Downing Street and the F.O. were shattered. Slept uncomfortably in the shelter.

Thursday, September 19th

The P.M. is sufficiently undismayed by the air-raids to take note of trivialities. Yesterday he sent the following note: "First Lord. Surely you can run to a new Admiralty flag. It grieves me to see the present dingy object every morning. W.S.C."

MENACE is on again, de Gaulle and our commanders with him having made the strongest representations.

The Bomber Command have been instructed to make the heaviest possible bombing attack on Berlin as soon as the weather is suitable. This morning Winston said that as the Germans were dropping these parachute mines indiscriminately, we must say that we would drop two for every one of theirs.

The Germans are making more tentative peace-feelers through Stockholm. Needless to say these are not even considered. Despite their successes, and our present discomfiture, the Germans cannot be too happy:

  i. They have another cold and hungry winter before them.

 ii. The destroyer agreement with America has made a deep impression in Rome and Berlin.

iii. There appears to be some estrangement with Russia over the settlement of the Roumanian question.

iv. It is obvious that France is becoming increasingly Anglophile and that the R.A.F. victories have had a tonic effect on Europe.

America is sitting on the fence as usual and Mr Hull[1] declares that the likelihood of the U.S. giving us assistance in the event

[1] American Secretary of State.

of trouble with Japan – if we reopen the Burma Road next month – must depend on the progress of the Battle of Britain in the next few weeks. The Americans still do not realise that their own fate, as well as that of Civilisation, hangs on the result of that battle and it is no use just oozing goodwill and saying, as one of their journalists did the other day, that the attacks on London made Americans quite "ill with anger".

I had a talk with Sir Walford Selby, Ambassador in Lisbon, who came to see the P.M. He said that the Anglo-Portuguese Alliance had greatly helped to keep Spain out of the war and Salazar's influence had been very useful to us at Madrid. Salazar was the hardest of bargainers and suspicious, but entirely honest. Selby said he considered the Germans had been laying the foundations of their present military power in 1926 and 1927. By giving way to Brüning and Stresemann[1] we had weakened them and strengthened German militarism.

Friday, September 20th

General Catroux,[2] who may be used to head a revolt against Vichy in Syria, came to see the P.M. He looks forceful and is, I am told, much the greatest "name" that de Gaulle has to dispose of.

I motored down to Chequers with Randolph Churchill, who was pleasant but as usual talked a lot of vituperative nonsense about Horace Wilson, etc. We followed the P.M. and Mrs Churchill to Dollis Hill where the Cabinet's emergency headquarters are. We inspected the flats where we should live and the deep underground rooms, safe from the biggest bomb, where the Cabinet and its satellites (e.g. me) would work and, if necessary, sleep. They are impressive but rather forbidding; I suppose if the present intensive bombing continues we must get used to being troglodytes ("trogs" as the P.M. puts it). I

---

[1] German Chancellor in 1923 and a prime mover in the negotiations for the Locarno Treaty of 1925, an attempt to make a future war between France and Germany impossible.

[2] The only senior French General to rally to de Gaulle (who was inclined to be jealous and therefore to denigrate him).

begin to understand what the early Christians must have felt about living in the Catacombs.

At Chequers were the P.M. and Mrs C., Randolph and Pamela (whose baby is expected hourly), Mary and General Ismay. We dined well and not too seriously. I repeated to Mrs C. what Violet Markham had told me and she wants to start a mobile canteen to feed the dreary and depressed citizens as they emerge from public shelters in the early hours. Violet Markham, having failed to move the Ministry of Food, is starting one herself. I also told the P.M. what Violet M. had told me about transport difficulties and he asked me to prepare a note on which he could take action.

We talked about the possibility of the Germans using poison gas, but the P.M. and Ismay are confident that nothing new, or more devilish than mustard gas, is available. He is doubtful whether invasion will be tried in the near future, but says that there is no doubt every preparation has been made. He is becoming less and less benevolent towards the Germans (having been much moved by the examples of their frightfulness in Wandsworth which he has been to see: a landmine caused very great devastation there) and talks about castrating the lot. He says there will be no nonsense about a "just peace". I feel sure this is the wrong attitude – not only immoral but unwise. We should aim at crushing them and then being firm but magnanimous victors.

Towards bedtime the P.M., very animated, reminisced about the South African War (the last enjoyable war, he called it) and the beauties of the Veld. His thirst for talking military strategy is unquenchable.

Saturday, September 21st
Summer has returned and the weather is glorious, but that did not console me for being summoned to the presence before 8.00 a.m. It is quite difficult to sleep in this perfect quiet after five nights of incessant bombardment.

I was kept pretty busy all day. Part of the morning was spent planning an adequate air-raid shelter with office-of-works architects and the P.M., who was clad in his air-force blue, zip-fastened cloth overall which he straps tightly round his stomach and in which he looks like an Eskimo.

The Sandyses came to lunch and afterwards, while the P.M. slept, we played croquet on the lawn. I subsequently snatched three-quarters of an hour to go for a walk up Beacon Hill with the charming, if somewhat tense, Mary.

Lord Gort and Sir Hugh Dowding came to dinner. Conversation turned at first to the German use of landmines in their air-raids. As these cannot be aimed, and mean indiscriminate slaughter, the P.M., though averse to such action on principle, is bent on retaliation. He proposes that one should be dropped on an open German town for each dropped in this country. "It is the only language they understand," said Lord Gort.

Sir H. Dowding said the Poles in our Fighter Squadrons were very dashing but totally undisciplined. It was generally agreed they were magnificent fighters. "When we have abolished Germany," said the P.M., "we will certainly establish Poland – and make them a permanent thing in Europe." He suggested that one Pole was worth three Frenchmen; Gort and Dowding said nearer ten!

It becomes daily more apparent how well prepared the enemy is for invasion. The P.M. thinks that from the North Foreland to Dungeness is the real danger point and that the most dangerous condition will be fog. Ismay is sceptical about the Germans being able to keep contact in thick fog. Gort says he would guarantee to land on that coast in a fog and he points out that once landed the Germans will push straight ahead. He is afraid of the mentality of the British army which, based on Lady Butler's picture of "The Thin Red Line", is always to fall back in order to keep the line intact. This was what ruined the French: against rapid penetration by small forces the only thing to do is to stand firm and let isolated detachments get through. The P.M., Dowding and Gort think that the first wave of invaders would be storm troops – all picked men – lightly armed and conveyed in fast motor boats. The second would be tanks, landed from craft with specially constructed bows. The third would be heavy artillery and the mass of the infantry. The first two should be able to effect a landing before darkness or the fog lifted. But, of course, meanwhile our bombers would be throwing their full weight against the ports of embarkation. The P.M. seems rather more apprehensive than I had realised about the possibility of invasion in the immediate future and he keeps on ringing up the Admiralty and asking about the weather in the Channel.

Dowding produced a paper ("masterly" the P.M. described it to Beaverbrook) about the prospects of night-interception in the near future: a skilful blending of the A.I. (which was tried for the first time last night in a Beaufighter, albeit without results) and the G.L. (wireless-controlled A.A. and searchlight).

I gather that it is presumed the Germans would use this "beam", by which they guide their aircraft, to guide an invading force also; and this would give them great advantage in a fog.

It is interesting that on the German side no new weapons have so far been produced. Their "beam" has long been used in America for guiding aircraft at night; the magnetic mine is only an improvement on an old weapon; there is nothing new, in the scientific sense, in the parachute mines they let fall on London. This is all in striking contrast to their military strategy which, in France, was daringly and successfully new. Scientifically we have high hopes of being the side to produce the new weapons.

Sunday, September 22nd

Barker[1] awoke me on the telephone to dictate a telegram from Roosevelt who has heard from a "most reliable source" in Berlin that the invasion will be put in train at 3.00 a.m. today.

The P.M., though slightly sceptical (as who would not be after so many false alarms throughout the summer), kept himself busy telephoning to people about it all morning. I aroused Lord Gort (whose flat was bombed last night for the second time in succession) and he said that frankly he did not think invasion very likely. I then went and told Mrs C. and Mary who were sitting side by side in the same bed, with trays on their laps, and who treated the whole matter as a most entertaining joke.

---

[1] Charles Barker, Chief Clerk at No. 10. Efficient and entertaining, he was popular with the Private Secretaries. An expert on old silver. He had two intelligent men, Pat Kinna and Donald MacKay, working under him and jointly they kept the office in apple-pie order.

What is not entertaining is the fact that we lost another large number of ships off the Bloody Foreland last night, as well as the night before. These losses are assuming serious proportions and the P.M. is very displeased with the Admiralty.

The P.M. gave vent to a most horrific display of abusive epithets when he saw a telegram about Sir S. Syme, Governor General of the Sudan, who is said to be "bored with the war". So strongly did he feel that he had to call me back and say, "Don't put it to Cadogan in quite those terms." (The report had come from Lampson[1] at Cairo.)

12.50 p.m.: The prospects do not look good for invasion. Pouring rain and a gale blowing up. It is significant, particularly in view of what the P.M. said last night, that the Germans are reported to be practising disembarkation under cover of a yellow vapour intended to represent fog.

Sir F. Pile, C. in C. Anti-Aircraft, and General Lock of the War Office came to lunch, when there was a good deal of talk about the P.E. fuse, etc. We talked of France, the P.M. expressing surprise at the speed with which we had been able to re-orientate ourselves to the collapse of an ally upon whose support so much seemed to be staked. He said that a fortnight before the débacle, when the possibility first began to dawn on him, he had thought to himself that the position would be little worse than if Germany had right at the beginning masked France and thrown the full weight of her air force against us. Mary, who seldom speaks when her father is present, thought of a *bon mot*, confided it to me and then interposed nervously, "Never before has so much been betrayed for so many by so few."[2]

After lunch the troop of Generals, the P.M. and Prof. (who says, *sotto voce*, that Dowding's "masterly" paper is his first admission of a number of facts which have been impressed on him for ages) retired to the Hawtrey room to discuss the Egyptian battle which now seems to be opening. The P.M. is

---

[1] Sir Miles Lampson, British Ambassador to Egypt, created Lord Killearn. Large and imposing, he was wont to treat the wayward King Farouk as an incorrigibly naughty schoolboy.

[2] At that time variations on this theme had not become as fashionable as they did subsequently.

full of confidence and says that we have enough good troops out there to do what is necessary "unless, of course, our men fight like skunks and the Italians like heroes". But he feels the opposite is more likely to be the case.

I have made a note about London transport difficulties and have shown it to the P.M. who has sent it to Sir J. Reith with the following minute: "Action this Day. Minister of Transport. This matter certainly requires your attention and I shall be glad to receive your report on the subject."

Motored up from Chequers after tea. The P.M. drove with Gort whom he seems to like. I shall not be surprised to find him back in high military office before long. On the way up we stopped at Lord Gort's twice bombed flat, which is a mess of charred wood and water. The P.M. was most compassionate, but Lord G. seemed unmoved by the havoc.

As we drove to No. 10 I noticed how many houses, in Berkeley Square and Bruton Street, are crumbled to dust. It almost makes me think I had better give up sleeping on the third floor at Eccleston Square.

The report about invasion today came from Kirke, the American Chargé d'Affaires in Berlin, who was right about the invasion of Holland and Belgium – though a change in the weather made him twenty-four hours too soon on that occasion.

I went home to dine with Father. Before we sat down there were loud explosions and the sky became red with the glow of a large fire south of the river. We climbed to the top of the house to look at it and as we watched we heard the whistle of a falling bomb close at hand. It struck a building about a quarter of a mile away, in the direction of the Abbey, and in the flash of the explosion I saw the house topple over sideways. It was nightmarish, and with our tails between our legs we crept downstairs to the dining-room.

Before going to my uneasy couch I went into Philip's room and knelt by the window. The night was cloudless and starry, with the moon rising over Westminster. Nothing could have been more beautiful and the searchlights interlaced at certain points on the horizon, the star-like flashes in the sky where shells were bursting, the light of distant fires, all added to the scene. It was magnificent and terrible: the spasmodic drone of enemy aircraft overhead, the thunder of gunfire, sometimes close sometimes in the distance, the illumination, like that of electric trains in peace-time, as the guns fired, and the myriad stars, real and artificial, in the firmament. Never was there such a contrast of natural splendour and human vileness. Later thick palls of smoke rose from the Embankment where bombs had fallen on Dolphin Square – and it went on all night long.

Monday, September 23rd
Today at dawn MENACE takes place. During the morning the Admiralty telephoned the messages from Dakar as they came in. So far (12.30 p.m.) all seems to be going according to plan.

Lunched with Betty Montagu in Hyde Park. A few shells burst over our heads, but otherwise it was warm and peaceful.

When I got back I found that MENACE was proceeding less favourably. The French had opened fire and all prospects of a peaceful landing had had to be abandoned. I told the P.M. who said, cheerfully, "Let 'em have it. Remember this: never maltreat your enemy by halves. Once the battle is joined, let 'em have it."

Dined with Philip at Wellington barracks and sat between the Commanding Officer and Peter Carrington.[1] Afterwards, despite the fact that all the lights went out owing to enemy action, Philip, Lionel Berry,[2] Captain Lindsay and I played bridge.

Tonight we bomb Berlin with 120 heavy bombers.

Tuesday, September 24th
Father, I am glad to say, goes off to Badminton today to stay with Queen Mary. He is badly in need of sleep and quiet, but has borne up wonderfully under all the strain of the bombardment.

David is now in the French ship *Chevreuil*, the officers and crew of which are apparently quite unskilled in nautical matters

---

[1] Many years later, Minister of Defence and Foreign Secretary. By a remarkable feat of in-breeding he is at once my first cousin once removed and my second cousin.

[2] Eldest son of Lord Kemsley.

– a fact which alarms him considerably. Today I learn from secret sources that she is to be used to capture the French Island of St Pierre and to bring the fishing fleet home. Poor David will be most alarmed when he knows he is to put to sea with the French.

MENACE is not proceeding according to plan. The Vichy French are resisting fiercely and the P.M. tells me he is afraid this may have a bad effect. A rapid and bloodless *fait accompli*, for which we all hoped, would have been accepted in France; this hard fighting may have different results. We are unlucky in having bad visibility in which to operate.

Mr Chamberlain has offered to resign, since his operation is giving him trouble and he is not well enough to stay in London and stand the noise. The P.M. has asked him to remain and to return when he is well, saying: "Let us go on together through the storm. These are great days."

Dined with Betts and Janet Margesson at the former's flat. I had a cantankerous political argument with Jan, which was silly because she obviously does not understand what she is talking about and has swallowed a large number of catchwords which she has ill-digested. But at this moment, when our lives and liberties are at stake, it is annoying to hear such travesties of the facts as that this country financed Nazi Germany and made Hitler's rise to power possible by subsidies.

I travelled home in an armoured car but was hardly in bed when I was aroused by the fall nearby of incendiary bombs. These started a number of glaring fires, uncomfortably close, and the thick pall of smoke in the night, together with a catch in the throat due to smoking too many cigarettes, gave me the unpleasant feeling that the Germans were using gas (a not unlikely eventuality).

Wednesday, September 25th

MENACE has proved a miserable fiasco, with what results it is only too easy to prophesy. I sat most of the morning in the Central War Room, where Winston holds most of his meetings now, and after the position had been fully examined, first by the Chiefs of Staff and service Ministers and then by the Cabinet, Winston came out and dictated to Mrs Hill a telegram calling off the expedition and ordering the fleet back to Gibraltar (which Rock the French bombed yesterday in retaliation for MENACE). This may be the end of de Gaulle; it will at any rate give his cause a serious set-back.

Sir John Reith has answered Miss Markham's criticisms very unsatisfactorily. He rang me up to ask if I agreed with his reply and I told him I did not think it met her main point, which is to provide transport to get people off the streets, even if they then have to wait in traffic jams. He promised to look into this and I attached a note to that effect to his reply for the P.M. to see.

The P.M. has today signed a letter which I drafted to George Trevelyan expressing the hope that he will accept the Mastership of Trinity. After consulting Jim Butler,[1] who works at the C.W.R. now, I wrote to Winstanley and asked him to drop the hint to Trevelyan that if he refused, the Mastership would *not* be left in abeyance but would be offered to some other person, probably less acceptable to the Fellows.[2]

Dined at home and then went to call on Zara and Betts. Zara told me she was engaged to Ronald Strutt,[3] after knowing him for only ten days. Betts said all people in love were intolerable, but Zara had a dreamy, blissful unwarconscious look on her face which it did me good to see. Betts talked much nonsense about religion and the ineffectiveness of our propaganda in America, her remarks on the latter being based entirely on hearsay. It is a waste of time, and exasperating, to talk to most women on serious subjects. Sex, the Arts and the Abstract seem to me the only topics to discuss with women.

Thursday, September 26th
Everybody is perturbed about Dakar and people seem to think that once started we should have gone through with it. In fact

[1] Professor Sir James Butler, notable classicist and historian, had been one of my Directors of Studies at Trinity. Subsequently Chief Editor of the Official War Histories. A shy but lovable scholar of profound erudition.

[2] I deliberately let it be thought that the choice might fall on Lindemann when I paid a visit to Trinity, a stratagem of which Lindemann himself knew nothing.

[3] An officer in the Coldstream Guards, afterwards Lord Belper.

we were not strong enough to do so after the *Resolution* was torpedoed.

In an interview with General Sikorski Lord Halifax said that he sometimes wondered whether the threat of invasion to this country was not designed to prevent us from reinforcing Egypt. It is more than possible that the whole Axis effort will be thrown in that direction: we have enough to meet the Italians there, but if the Germans join in we shall be hard pressed. Sikorski thinks Rome should be bombed. Halifax said it had a very special position in the world. Sikorski replied that London had also.

That part of Africa which has already declared for de Gaulle seems to be holding firm in spite of Dakar. The Cameroons sent an encouraging telegram to Winston and I sent an immediate reply in which, trying to copy the Churchillian style, I said that H.M.G. knew that the French in the Cameroons would "continue to struggle side by side with the peoples of the British Empire until France is freed and restored and the shadow of German tyranny has been driven from the face of the earth for ever". By a Gargantuan effort I got this approved and through to the Ministry of Information in time for tonight's broadcasts and tomorrow's papers.

Friday, September 27th
During breakfast the bombers came and were most disturbingly close. Apparently eighteen, out of a big raid of 250, had managed to break through our fighter defences. They were over again later in the morning and I stood on the terrace at No. 10 with the Chief Whip trying to see them.

The papers in New York and this country are now stigmatising Dakar as a major blunder. It will be difficult for Winston to escape criticism.

At 12.15 p.m., while I was over at the C.W.R. where the Cabinet was meeting, Sammy Hood rang me up to say that Germany, Italy and Japan were to sign a Three-Power pact. I took this information into the Cabinet and gave it to Winston who looked pensive. Of course we have known for some time that Germany and Japan were negotiating something and presumably the recent Ciano–Ribbentrop conversations at Rome were on the same subject. This brings into the open anything that still remained obscure and the U. S. must surely now define her position. Unfortunately this accursed presidential election does not take place till November and until that issue is decided America is paralysed. Later, on going in to the Cabinet Room, I heard the P.M. proclaim that one of the clauses of the Agreement was "aimed plum at the United States".

Overheard in the Cabinet: the P.M. – "Personally I should like to wage war on a great scale in the Middle East. By next spring I hope we shall have sufficient forces there." He has been taking tremendous pains lately about the despatch of reinforcements to Egypt and the position of the Australian and New Zealand contingents in that part of the world.

Herschel Johnson lunched with me at the Travellers. He tells me that he thinks Roosevelt will get in and that America will almost certainly give us credits when it is made clear to the Government and people that there is no alternative if we are to be saved from bankruptcy.

Monday, September 30th
At No. 10 I found Cabinet changes in the air. Chamberlain is now clearly too ill to continue and I gather that Halifax has advised Winston to accept his resignation, already proffered but at first refused. Probably Halifax will become Lord President, Eden S. of S. for Foreign Affairs, Oliver Lyttelton[1] (hitherto politically unknown) S. of S. for War, Morrison Home Secretary and Beaverbrook Minister for all branches of supply. John Anderson may go to the Dominions Office and then become Viceroy (this will break Sam Hoare's heart).[2] Such a reshuffle would solve the supply problem, to the solution of which Herbert Morrison was an obstacle, but I expect Beaverbrook will favour aircraft at the expense of tanks and other army equipment.

There was an air-raid in the lunch-hour. Admiral Tovey,[3] who

[1] Later Viscount Chandos.*
[2] Hoare believed he had been promised the reversion of the Viceroyalty of India when Lord Linlithgow retired. Churchill knew nothing of any such undertaking and felt no obligation to consider it.
[3] Commanded the Home Fleet, 1940–43, and was thereafter C. in C., The Nore.

was lunching with the P.M., was in the shelter. I gather the P.M. has him in mind for a high naval appointment, possibly C. in C., Home Fleet.

George Trevelyan has accepted the Mastership of Trinity. In his letter to the P.M. he says: "I am touched by your kindness and fortified by your good opinion. In your great way, and in my small way, we have been called to unexpected destinies, since the time when as your junior at Harrow I admired from a distance the driving force of your character, which is now our nation's great support."

David Margesson tells me he is opposed to Eden going to the F.O. or being Lord President. He wants Anderson, our best administrator, to be in the War Cabinet (the P.M. wants Eden) and he thinks that if Oliver Lyttelton is to come into the Government he should go to the Ministry of Supply (the idea occurred to him while we talked). He is a business man and he works for the Ministry now. Beaverbrook is being tiresome. He doesn't want to be responsible for all supply questions and has refused to dine with the P.M. tonight to discuss the problem with Winston and David, on the grounds of a temperature – a very last minute and political temperature!

TEN

BRITAIN BESIEGED
OCTOBER 1940

Tuesday, October 1st
Beaverbrook has written to the P.M. as follows:

> My Dear Winston. I gathered from our conversation tonight that you expect me to undertake more responsibilities. But my asthma drives me to the unhappy conclusion that the cold weather and sharp winds bring my labours to nothing. I have tried many devices but nights pass in procession without any sleep for me. If I live through the war I shall give you thanks for winning it, even though you may die now. For the example you gave the nation in the last four months and the leadership of the dark days of the flight from France decided the battle in our favour. Your devoted Max. Sept. 30. 1940.

In another letter he says he is going to resign. Of course, he is a crafty man and what he says is not necessarily the truth, but Brendan tells me that he really is suffering a great deal.

Halifax has been given the choice of becoming Lord President, and Number Two in the Government, or remaining where he is. He has chosen to remain and has written to propose that John Anderson should be Lord President and a member of the War Cabinet. He writes that he is "doubtful whether Anthony" (whom Winston wishes to make Lord President if Halifax prefers the F.O.), "would in fact do your tying-up jobs in the Cabinet as well as J.A. J.A. has got that sort of orderly mind which

Neville had – and which I don't think Anthony has . . . I have reached these conclusions independently of David Margesson."

Eden, for his part, says he will do anything asked of him. His personal predilection is to remain at the War Office.

David Margesson told me last night that the P.M. would not make up his mind. He is always taking decisions and then repenting of them. David says life would be much easier if people would take a clear line. I have sometimes felt that about his own daughter.

Sir Stafford Cripps' comments on Soviet reactions to the Germano-Japanese-Italian pact are that while the pact will make Russia less well-disposed to the Axis, it will make her more afraid and therefore more subservient. Thus our only policy is to aim at convincing Russia that her hope of self-preservation lies in a victory for this country. I think that there are signs of the thieves falling out among themselves: M. Kiosseivanoff, former Bulgarian Prime Minister, says that Germany and Italy have quarrelled over Italy's wish to invade Greece; and the U.S.S.R. must know that Italy hates her and that Germany uses but despises her.

Lunched with Pat Hancock most exquisitely at the Jardin des Gourmets. He is P.S. to Dalton whom he thinks brilliant but unlovable.

Went home to bed and found Mother, just returned from Badminton, with the news from Lord Claud Hamilton[1] that Chamberlain has cancer.

Wednesday, October 2nd
Busy Cabinet making. Herbert Morrison was recalcitrant about accepting the Home Office, probably because he thinks the offer a reflection on his success at the Ministry of Supply – which it is. He is an unpleasant-looking man and not much good as a Minister. John Anderson is to be Lord President, Andrew Duncan Minister of Supply, Oliver Lyttelton President of the Board of Trade, Lord Cranborne Secretary of State for the Dominions, Caldecote Lord Chief Justice, Reith Office of Works,

---

[1] Brother of the Duke of Abercorn and Comptroller to Queen Mary.

Moore-Brabazon[1] Minister of Transport. Bevin is to come in to the War Cabinet and Kingsley Wood also. Brendan says the latter has "oiled his way in" by flattery; he and Eden, whom Brendan calls "the film star at the War Office", lay it on very thick – and most successfully. I think all these appointments will be well received in the country, except for Kingsley Wood's entry into the War Cabinet.

The matter which chiefly interests the Cabinet at the moment is our attitude to the Vichy Government. Halifax comes perilously near advocating appeasement, saying that all we require is an assurance that the French Colonies are "healthily anti-German and anti-Italian". If they are, it does not matter whether they are nominally under Vichy or de Gaulle. We must be careful not to let de Gaulle down, I feel very strongly; but perhaps there is no harm in our flirting with M. Baudouin, through the Embassy at Madrid, about questions of interest to both countries.

The French, of course, want us to let food into France through the blockade; but it will be difficult to devise a means of guaranteeing it from falling into German hands. Should the Germans decide to take over the whole of France, it looks as if the Vichy Government – presumably minus Laval – might fly to North Africa; and then of course the whole of the French Empire would rejoin us in active resistance to the enemy. Meanwhile the Monarchists, under the Comte de Paris, are active and have the support of Weygand and his friends.

At the same time as the Government is being reconstituted, the Chiefs of Staff, who are sound, but old and slow, are being purged. Newall goes to New Zealand as Governor General and will be succeeded as Chief of the Air Staff by Portal. Pound will, I suppose, cease to be First Sea Lord and in any case there is to be a drastic change in the higher naval command. This is

---

[1] Holder of Pilot's Licence No. I. M.P. since 1918 and Churchill's Parliamentary Private Secretary at the Air Ministry in 1919. Succeeded Beaverbrook as Minister of Aircraft Production in 1941. Quoted at a nominally private gathering as saying he hoped Germany and the Soviet Union would destroy each other. This effectively ended his political career, but Churchill made him a peer in 1942.

certainly called for: the continued loss of merchant shipping is serious and the navy has not shown up well of late.

David Margesson went down to see Mr Chamberlain because the latter's letter of resignation was not considered suitable and he had to be persuaded to write another. This he did, accompanying it with a private one from which the following is an extract: "It is kind of you to think of putting me forward for so great an honour as the Garter, but you will, I think, not misunderstand me when I say that I prefer to die plain 'Mr Chamberlain' like my father before me, unadorned by any title. This applies to the Garter just as much as to a peerage which you once before suggested to me."

David tells me he is wonderfully brave. He fought hard for peace and his hardest for victory. He has been greatly maligned; but I believe historians, if they try to throw themselves back into the conditions in which decisions were taken, and refrain from judging solely by what happened afterwards, will mix their censure with much praise for his honest efforts.

Thursday, October 3rd
The P.M., Cabinet, Chiefs of Staff, etc., all went off for a trial day at Dollis Hill and John Martin and I remained alone at No. 10 dealing placidly with our business, unhampered by bells, visitors and the general atmosphere of rush which surrounds the P.M.

It is terrible how our new weapons are being talked about. Philip tells me that he has several times heard descriptions in general terms of what is obviously the A.I.

Sumner Welles has told Lothian that the new Japanese pact with the Axis has knocked Isolationism on the head once and for all in the U.S.

Friday, October 4th
Went with Mrs Churchill to Chingford to see the damage in the P.M.'s constituency. We toured the place with the Mayor and some of the councillors and inspected the havoc wrought by bombs and parachute mines. The saddest sight was the homeless refugees in a school. One woman, wheeling a baby in a pram,

told me she had twice been bombed out of her house and kept on saying disconsolately: "A load of trouble, a load of trouble." One woman said: "It is all very well for them," (looking at us!) "who have all they want; but we have lost everything." We lunched with the Mayor and civic dignitaries in a pub called "The Cock" at Epping. Civic dignitaries are strangely boring people.

Monday, October 7th
Dined at home where I found that Father and Mother have accepted an invitation from Grandfather and Peggy to go to Madeley, which is being opened up. This will mean the removal of furniture from Eccleston Square and I shall live as a troglodyte at No. 10. Mother is much disgruntled at leaving London – she is afraid of nothing – but Father is desperately anxious to go. He will also be able to effect great economies by living at Madeley and that becomes increasingly necessary. The move is a big and weary undertaking which must be put in hand quickly – as the sight of so many gutted and crumbled houses, increasing in number every day, makes clear.

Madeley Manor in Staffordshire was a regency house at the southern end of my grandfather's once extensive property in Cheshire and Staffordshire. He had sold Crewe Hall and most of the Cheshire estates in the 1930s. When the raids on London became heavy he opened Madeley, in which the family had not lived for a century, and invited his eldest daughter, Lady Annabel Dodds (formerly O'Neill), and my mother, neither of whom had houses in the country, to move there with their husbands. His two other daughters, Lady Celia Coates and the Duchess of Roxburghe, had their own houses in the country, the one at Helperby in the North Riding of Yorkshire, the other at Floors Castle, Kelso, where they were both most hospitable to me when I was able to escape from duty.

Today German and Italian troops entered Roumania. Eden says this is obviously part of a pincer movement aimed at the Middle East – but the Germans will have no easy task in advancing through Anatolia in the face of Turkish opposition. The threat to the Bosphorus and the Aegean is now immediate and Eden wants to fly out to Egypt this week-end.

Tuesday, October 8th
When I reached No. 10 I found everybody crouching in the shelter because bombs had fallen in the Horse Guards Parade and on the War Office.

The P.M. made a long speech in the House to which I listened. He discussed the bombing of London, our attitude to Japan and the position of Spain (a fine passage which the F.O. did their best to make him omit). I heard the P.M. tell Halifax on the telephone that he set great store on speaking of Spain as "a leading and famous member of the family of Europe and of Christendom".

He was skilful in dealing with Dakar and insisted that "this series of accidents and some errors" should be regarded in its true perspective. His peroration with its reminder that "long dark months of trial and tribulation lie before us", with misfortunes, shortcomings, mistakes and disappointments, was eloquently spoken and enthusiastically received. "Death and sorrow," he said, "will be the companions of our journey, hardship our garment; constancy and valour are our only shield. We must be united; we must be undaunted; we must be inflexible. Our qualities and our deeds must burn and glow through the gloom of Europe till they become the veritable beacon of its salvation." I followed the speech from a flimsy of the P.M.'s notes, which are typed in a way which Halifax says is like the printing of the psalms. Afterwards John Peck and I corrected the official report and altered the text in many places to improve the style and the grammar; for the P.M.'s speeches are essentially oratorical masterpieces and in speaking he inserts much that sounds well and reads badly.

Before the speech Randolph, recently elected M.P. for Preston was introduced, amidst applause, by Winston and David Margesson (a fact which, said R., made him shiver). The applause, needless to say, was for Winston whose popularity in the House, as in the country, remains untarnished.

The P.M., dressed in his blue "siren-suit", dined with Eden

in his new dining-room at No. 10 – formerly the typists' room in the basement and now redecorated and reinforced. He was in great form – as always after a speech has been successfully achieved – and amused Eden and me very much by his conversation with Nelson, the black cat, whom he chided for being afraid of the guns and unworthy of the name he bore. "Try and remember," he said to Nelson reprovingly, "what those boys in the R.A.F. are doing."

Prof., whom I talked to after dinner, is rather gloomy about the initial lack of success won by the A.I., G.L., etc., and he also says he thinks the Germans, who started the war behind us in this respect, have produced new aircraft types while we have been left standing. He alternates between startling optimism and querulous pessimism.

The air in the shelter went wrong in the middle of the night and I almost stifled. That coupled with the fact that John Martin tossed about ceaselessly in his bed above mine made the night most uncomfortable.

Wednesday, October 9th
A scandal is brewing owing to the dishonesty of Bob Boothby, Parliamentary Under Secretary to the Ministry of Food, in pushing the case of a Czech called Weininger – whom in addition M.I.5 suspect of being a spy – in return for ten per cent of the proceeds. This is rare in English politics, but extremely serious in the case of a member of the Government.[1]

The P.M. went to a meeting of the Conservative Party to accept the Leadership. I read the typescript of his speech and saw that in giving the reasons for his acceptance he intended to say: "I have always faithfully served two supreme public causes – the maintenance of the enduring greatness of Britain and her Empire and the historic certainty of our Island life. Alone among the peoples we have reconciled democracy and tradition . . .

---

[1] Boothby forcefully asserted his innocence. That this was generally accepted is shown by the fact that Churchill made him a K.B.E. in 1953 and in 1958, presumably after full consideration by the Political Honours Scrutiny Committee, Macmillan recommended him for a peerage.

The Conservative Party will not allow any party to excel it in the sacrifice of party interests and party feelings." This is his apologia for Conservatism.

The F.O. Weekly Summary gives an unpleasant picture of life in Poland. The Russians are taking whole families and dividing them up, sending the men to Siberia, the women to South Russia, the children elsewhere. So, many Poles are trying to escape to the German-occupied area where last week twenty men were shot in one place, and the remaining male members of the town subjected to a mass flogging, because one Polish bandit shot one German gendarme. There is much to be said for the theory that civilisation stops at the Rhine and the Danube, the frontiers of the Roman Empire.

Sir S. Cripps advocates our reaching a rapid compromise with the U.S.S.R. on the present vexed issue of the assets of the Baltic States – recently occupied by Russia – which we have frozen. Cripps feels that now is the moment to "cash in" on the malaise caused in Russia by the recent Japanese pact with the Axis.

Betty Montagu and Mrs Crosthwaite[1] came to dinner and Mother and I went with them to inspect one of the Rest Centres – in Kentish Town – provided for those whose homes have been destroyed. These were in a lamentable state a few days ago, owing to the lack of co-ordination between the various central and local authorities responsible for them; but there has been a great improvement and the one we saw was much better than I had expected. The inmates, who stay for anything from two to ten days, sleep on rough mattresses on the floor and have army blankets. The sanitary arrangements consist of unscreened buckets; the only lighting is from hurricane lamps, though electricity is to be installed shortly; the atmosphere is hot and stuffy; the building, an L.C.C. elementary school, is solid but not underground or safe from a direct hit; there is not really enough space and many of the mattresses are laid in the passage. On the other hand the food is good and well-prepared, there was a

[1] Indefatigable social worker and mother of my Foreign Office friend, Moore Crosthwaite.

piano playing and the people were dancing, the atmosphere is one of willingness to be helpful and of sympathy, there are few complaints and the cheerfulness of the homeless, as of the staff, is remarkable. I suggested they should procure electric fans which would make a great difference to the air in the building.

We motored back through the clear night, leaving Mrs Crosthwaite at the shelter, and saw parachute flares at which tracer bullets, which seemed to be red, were being fired. A number of bombs fell on and near Victoria Station and shook the house most unpleasantly.

Thursday, October 10th
In the early hours a bomb hit St Paul's Cathedral. Today I have been one year at No. 10 and I have seen many changes in the interval.

Lunched with Philip at Wellington barracks and played billiards. The Commanding Officer showed me a subversive pamphlet handed to Grenadier Guardsmen outside a cinema and I subsequently gave this to the P.M. for whatever action he might think appropriate.

I talked to the P.M. while he was changing into his siren-suit for dinner and described what we had seen at the rest centre at Kentish Town. He told me to procure for him a full report on the subject of both rest centres and shelters, showing who was responsible for what. I asked Bridges to supply this. The P.M. went off after dinner to see A.A. and Searchlights at Richmond and Kenley.

Friday, October 11th
There are two unexploded bombs on the Horse Guards Parade. "Will they do us any damage when they explode?" asked the P.M. lying in bed. "I shouldn't think so, Sir," I said. "Is that just your opinion," he replied, "because if so it's worth nothing. You have never seen an unexploded bomb go off. Go and ask for an official report." Such is the result of hazarding opinions to the P.M. if one has nothing with which to back them. But I was vindicated by the experts.

To Chequers for the week-end. I drove down with a slightly

affected, opinionated and supercilious youth called Alastair Forbes,[1] a friend of Mary. He was in the Dakar expedition. Venetia Montagu was at Chequers; and the C. in C., Home Forces, Sir Alan Brooke, the C. in C., Anti-Aircraft Defences, Sir F. Pile, and Ismay came to dine and sleep.

At dinner I sat between Mary and Diana. The P.M was cheerful, despite the facts that our air results today and yesterday have been bad. He proclaimed that "the man's effort is flagging". He talked with Brooke about the French campaign, called Gamelin a "barber's block" who knew about nothing but artillery, repeated the oft-told story about *supériorité de nombres, supériorité d'armes, supériorité de méthodes* – and a shrug.[2]

He said that Georges, the only French General with intellect and ability, had been worn out by a two-year struggle for his rights with Gamelin. He wanted to send him a message: "*en penser souvent, en parler jamais*" – that was all. The French "Maginot Line complex" was discussed. Winston said that a fortified line was useless without a field army to manoeuvre within it. Brooke and Ismay declared that the French had refused us the information we required about the disposition of their troops because they despised our army and thought of themselves as the invincible, experienced soldiers. Brooke described how the winter had been wasted and no progress had been made with the extension of the Maginot Line north of Luxembourg. All agreed in praising the tank and lamenting the fact that we neglected the evolution of our own discovery. Randolph said that the Germans had taken twenty years to learn what it had taken us twenty years to forget about tanks. They had obtained the information they wanted from the "Purple Primer" sold to them by Lieutenant Baillie Stewart;[3] but in England that Primer had remained unread and unappreciated.

[1] Enlisted as a marine and was attached to the Free French, on whose sometimes vicious activities at their Duke Street headquarters he reported indignantly. Became a favourite of Ann O'Neill and after she married Lord Rothermere he wrote regularly for the *Daily Mail*.

[2] General Gamelin's reply to Churchill, when in May 1940 he asked what accounted for the German breakthrough. When Churchill asked him what he proposed to do about it, he merely shrugged his shoulders.

[3] Imprisoned in the Tower of London before the war for treason.

The conversation turned to General Hobart, an erratic genius on tanks whose services are not being used. Brooke said he was too wild, but Winston reminded him of Wolfe standing on a chair in front of Chatham and brandishing his sword. "You cannot expect," he said, "to have the genius type with a conventional copy-book style."

Some apprehension was expressed about the vulnerability of Chequers, which would make an easy target for bombs. "Probably," said Winston, "they don't think I am so foolish as to come here; but I stand to lose a lot, three generations at a swoop." (Randolph's and Pamela's son was born two days ago.) Certainly there is a danger: in Norway, Poland and Holland the Germans showed it was their policy to go all out for the Government, and Winston is worth more to them than the whole Cabinets of those three countries rolled into one. To bed at 2.15 a.m.

Saturday, October 12th

A glorious day, the beginning of St Luke's Summer I hope. I was kept busy all day, with brief interludes. At lunch we talked chiefly of the air-raids and their effects. The P.M., sitting in his siren-suit and smoking an immense cigar, said he thought this was the sort of war which would suit the English people once they were used to it. They would prefer all to be in the front line, taking part in the Battle of London, than to look on helplessly at mass slaughters like Passchendaele.

After lunch we all walked to look at the craters caused by some bombs which fell all too near the house a few nights ago. I think it was chance that they fell so close, but the P.M. and Ismay incline to the view that it was a trial shot and may well have been done on purpose.

Two of the Coldstream officers came to tea. The P.M., talking of the official policy of restricting consumption and expenditure, said, "Personally I prefer to make my number by increased effort rather than by self-denial." We also spoke of Fifth Column dangers and the P.M. said he much disliked locking people up and the suspension of Habeas Corpus. In any case he thought "those filthy Communists" were really more dangerous than the fascists.

I have persuaded the P.M. to take up the question of heating, etc., in private shelters during the winter and he says he will try and put a stop to the proposal to impose the purchase-tax on oil stoves, thermoses, etc.

Cripps and several of our Balkan Ministers now telegraph that Russia is likely to become more amenable, presumably because of the German domination of Roumania. The Soviet are making up their differences with Iran and with Turkey, and though bashful as far as we are concerned they may be open to discreet blandishments. The press is complicating matters, to the fury of Cripps, by publishing reports of Anglo-Soviet-Turkish-Greek-Yugoslav collaboration in the face of Axis threats to South-Eastern Europe. This has already had the effect of making the Russians draw in their horns.

That most charming of men, Sir John Dill, arrived to dine and sleep, as did the Lord Privy Seal and Mrs Attlee. I sat next to Diana and Venetia Montagu (whom Ruby Linsday[1] unjustly accuses of halitosis) and had a vehement conversation about ambition with Diana.

The P.M. is obviously worried about the possibility of an attack on Chequers and says that he does not object to chance "but feels it a mistake to be the victim of design". With the evolution of the German "beam" methods, he fears that accurate blind bombing may become a reality.

After dinner, politics and the House of Commons were discussed. Attlee said that David Margesson, in all his dealings with the Labour Party since 1931, had always been absolutely straight. Even Randolph agreed about his remarkable ability as Chief Whip. The P.M. considered that Ramsay MacDonald had made a great and unnecessary mistake in 1931: the National Government had been a sham and its effect had been to destroy party politics and thus to remove the opportunity for back-benchers to attain ability through experience. This was the reason for the dearth of talent in the back benches on both sides

[1] Rosemary Hinchingbrooke's mother.

of the House. Ramsay MacDonald had in 1931 lost the place which, by his raising of the Labour Party to a power in the land, he had formerly won for himself in history. Attlee and the P.M. then fell to swapping stories of their electioneering experiences and the P.M. said that he had learned one great lesson from his father: never to be afraid of British democracy.

Randolph thought that Baldwin had destroyed the fire in politics by adopting the technique of humble frankness which was intended to, and did, count on the generosity of his opponents and remove the sting from their attack. Attlee answered that this was a true estimate.

I heard that the War Office had this evening received two direct hits, that the National Gallery had been hit and that a bomb had fallen near King Charles' statue and had gone through to the underground, where in spite of the Government's disapproval thousands congregate every night, causing a hundred casualties. This report later proved to be exaggerated. The accurate bombing much disturbed the P.M., Attlee and Dill who all feel that Whitehall – and particularly No. 10 – is extremely dangerous. The P.M. is thinking on authoritarian lines about shelters and talks of forcibly preventing people from going into the underground and allotting to each a place of safety so that the optimum dispersal may be achieved.

Sunday, October 13th
In a note to Lord Halifax the P.M. writes: "Bombing of military objectives seems at present our main road home."

The Attlees stayed to lunch and Lady Digby[1] and Major General Hobart came. Winston's only noteworthy remark during lunch was, "A Hun alive is a war in prospect." Afterwards the Home Guard was discussed at length.

Master Winston Churchill, Randolph's four-day-old son, lay crying in his pram before the front door, open to inspection.

I walked up Beacon Hill and admired the autumn colouring of the beech trees. It is a glorious and exhilarating place. Then Diana Sandys and I walked to the Happy Valley where we sat

[1] Pamela Churchill's mother.

and talked politics. I defended David Margesson and Halifax; we both expressed our loathing of Hore-Belisha.

Lady Digby tells me her nephew Ronald Strutt, who has deserted his post as Captain of the Guard to spend the week-end with Zara Mainwaring, is a bore, heavy in hand and only interested in horses, though certainly possessed of a nice character. I think Zara deserves to marry somebody more sparkling, but if she will insist on getting engaged after ten days' acquaintanceship she may have to pay the penalty.

Sir H. Dowding, Sir Dudley Pound and the new C.A.S., Sir Charles Portal, dined and, with the exception of Dowding, slept. After dinner there was air conversation: the bombing of London, the smallness of the bombs we have been using, the difficulties in the way of using the A.I. and our other inventions, which are still in their teething stage. There was much speculation why the Germans have not yet made a mass night raid on London (I fear it is to come) concentrating on one small area with first incendiaries and then high explosive. Portal says we intend to do this on Germany when we have the necessary strength. Dowding says that the German attack has been almost exclusively lacking in purpose: they show no signs of concentrating on detailed objectives or concentrating their striking force for one purpose. Presumably the advantages of so doing will one day dawn upon them as has, at last, the idiocy of letting their valuable bombers be destroyed in scores by daylight, when they can be much more alarming by night and when their fighters can maintain a nuisance value by day. For the last week the German day raids have taken place with impunity: large forces of fighters have come at great height, dropping their bombs at random and departing before they can be intercepted. We have accounted for few.

After dinner I conversed with Randolph whose fantastic arguments make one shudder. He talks of world domination as the greatest ideal and says he admires the Germans for desiring it. He wants it to be our aim and decries our ineptitude in the last century for not including South America and the Dutch East Indies in the British Empire. My thesis that Hitler's mistake was not to realise just how far he could go, and not to consolidate the gains he had made without war, he denounced as wishy-washy and, becoming at once arrogant and insolent, said it was people like me and Ramsay MacDonald and Baldwin that deprived this country of its greatness. Randolph is a most unattractive combination of the bombastic, the cantankerous and the unwise; and yet at times he makes shrewd and penetrating comments and at times he can be pleasant. He has none of Winston's reasonableness.

Today, in the Children's Hour, Princess Elizabeth spoke for the first time on the wireless. Diana Sandys and I, who listened, were embarrassed by the sloppy sentiment she was made to express, but her voice was most impressive and, if the monarchy survives, Queen Elizabeth II should be a most successful radio Queen.

The P.M. has today written, for the consideration of the Chiefs of Staff, a masterly paper on our strategy in the Mediterranean and elsewhere. The salient point is the re-occupation of Malta by the Mediterranean Fleet which can only be accomplished when the island has been reinforced with men, guns and U.P. weapon, etc. The strength of the Mediterranean Fleet is to be increased, more divisions are to be sent to the Middle East, with bombers and fighters too, so that by January we shall have a large army there and unquestionable naval control of the Eastern Mediterranean. These plans are to be pursued without pandering to the Vichy Government: we should continue to put pressure on the French in the belief that this will not fundamentally change the increasingly Anglophile sentiments of most Frenchmen. The P.M. believes it is becoming more and more difficult for the Vichy Government to drive the country into war against us however stringently we may impose the blockade, however strongly we support de Gaulle, however many unfortunate naval incidents occur. We must also maintain our strength at home and must prepare mobile divisions for amphibious operations on the continent. For the Bomber Command the great German battleships *Bismark* and *Tirpitz* must be primary objectives so that the *King George V* may be released for the Mediterranean.

I told the P.M. how much I admired this review, and he

replied that it was by no means in a finished state: he had just written down what he had in his head. It shows great breadth of vision.

As the P.M. said goodnight to the Air Marshals, he told them he was sure we were going to win the war, but he confessed he did not see clearly how it was to be achieved. Prof. and I, discussing the matter afterwards, thought that if the U.S.A. came in, Russia "turned ugly" – as she has every reason to do – and Italy received a setback in North Africa, the end might well be sooner than was expected. Such a sequence of events would break their hearts, said Prof.

Prof. now attaches great hopes to the aerial mine-barrage which is being developed. (The U.P. weapon.) It works on the same principle as the naval wire barrage and should be very effective against night raiders. To bed at 2.00 a.m.

Monday, October 14th
Motored up to London with Prof. Almost every street is now scarred by bombs and the piles of debris and shattered houses are tragic to see.

Wednesday, October 16th
I returned from Cambridge to London, which has been very heavily raided and has suffered severely during the last two nights. Leicester Square is a desert, Pall Mall is badly damaged (the Carlton has collapsed and the Travellers was hit) and a bomb just missed No. 10, doing great damage to the Treasury and wrecking some of the rooms in No. 10 itself. Coming into Liverpool Street by train I saw such devastation by the railway line as is impossible to describe. Poor London.

Thursday, October 17th
A very busy day for me, but I had time to go with Brendan and others to inspect the basement and refuges at No. 11, where we may have to live in future after the raiding hours have begun.

The Spanish Minister of Foreign Affairs tells Sam Hoare that Hitler is going to meet Franco on the Pyrenees. He may try to bully F. into letting German troops attack Gibraltar through Spain.

I received an alarming letter from Miss Markham about the fall in morale among the citizens of London and the still unsolved transport problem. I showed this to the P.M. who dealt with it at a "shelter meeting" he held during the afternoon. A committee has been set up to enquire into the question of heating private shelters and providing oil-stoves, etc., which I brought to the P.M.'s notice last week-end.

Dined at the C.W.R. with Seal, Bridges, Wilkinson and Ismay. The food comes out of tins but the company is sufficiently entertaining to compensate for that.

Slept at No. 10 after talking to Jack Churchill in the P.M.'s dining-room till bed time. I had not fallen asleep before the crash of a falling bomb dragged us all from our beds. The air was thick with smoke and the choking smell of sulphur and gunpowder. Once outside the house I walked in my dressing-gown towards the Treasury which was hidden in a dense cloud of smoke. In Whitehall a bomb had made a huge crater just outside the Home Office, but when the smoke had cleared I could see the real havoc, the complete destruction of a large part of the Treasury. Our shelter at No. 10 – on the site of the old seventeenth-century Cockpit – is only about forty yards away from where the bomb fell. Four members of the Home Guard were trapped – and I fear killed – beneath the debris. I followed the demolition squad and A.R.P. men along an underground passage beneath the ruins, but we could get no reply to knocks and calls from the room in which the men had been caught.

This is the second hit within four days in almost the same place. Brendan and I said we thought it could only be a question of days before No. 10 fell a victim. Jack Churchill and Prof. were shivering with alarm.

Friday, October 18th

The great advantage of being young is that one can sleep after such events without opening an eyelid. But it is disconcerting to be woken up with the news that there is a mine in St James's Park which may blow to pieces everything within four hundred yards. The P.M. refused to leave No. 10 when I reported this unwelcome prospect and was chiefly worried about the fate of "those poor little birds" in St James's Park lake. By the time I returned from breakfast the mine had been rendered innocuous by the gallant Unexploded Bomb squad and the danger was over.

Miss Nettlefold[1] and Mrs Crosthwaite confirm Violet Markham's statement that the morale of Londoners has deteriorated. There is less of "We can take it" and an inclination to say "This must stop at all costs". It appears that transport muddles have much to do with it. The shelter situation is improving and will improve.

Travelling by underground is revolting now. Trains are sparse and travellers are legion.

The P.M. went off to Chequers. Tony and I remain in London. The whole establishment at No. 10 is to be moved over to the more solid Office of Works and C.W.R. during the week-end.[2] Owing to a mistake about the cars I had to walk a mile through the "blitz" to dine with Sidney Cuthbert on Guard at St James's Palace. It is alarming to walk that distance when the guns are firing and enemy planes are overhead; moreover Whitehall and Trafalgar Square are full of craters and pitfalls. Dinner, which the King provides on a lavish scale, was excellent and I liked Sidney's two brother officers, Anthony Balfour and Eddie Hope. The latter, who seems to be a sensible Tory – my favourite brand of Conservative Radical – is nursing a constituency in Islington. We had an involved argument about whether Duff Cooper was justified in throwing Caporetto[3] in the teeth of the Italians during a broadcast: Sidney and Hope thought he was: Balfour and I said it was (a) cheap, (b) impolitic (when so many Italians are opposed to the war).

[1] A social worker whose family had been well-known iron and steel masters.
[2] The Churchills had a flat over the C.W.R., above ground level, where the offices of the staff were also installed. It was thenceforward known as No. 10 Annexe. On the floor above that, Professor Lindemann and Desmond Morton had their offices, and there was also a "Mess" in which the No. 10 staff dined, established with an admirable Swedish cook supplied by Brendan Bracken.
[3] Caporetto was the humiliating defeat by the Austrians which the Italians suffered in the First World War.

A night at No. 10 which, owing to a downpour of rain, would have been quiet had it not been for an unimportant telegram, marked Most Immediate, that arrived at 3.00 a.m. Eden, who is now in Egypt, in order to gratify his self-esteem has arranged for a private cypher which does not go through the War Office. We are supposed to decypher these telegrams ourselves but, not having the time, we suborn a military cypherer. However, it was no easy task to get hold of him at 3.00 a.m. Eden is worried about the weakness of our air force in the Middle East – a fact which has worried our people out there, and the F.O. in London, for many weeks.

Saturday, October 19th
The Minister without Portfolio, Arthur Greenwood, has shocked the Treasury by suggesting that his economic experts should consider a number of problems of the present and future and the methods of dealing with them. Measures which he thinks should be visualised are, amongst others: (i) lower limit for income-tax exemption, (ii) extension of the scope of the purchase tax, (iii) forced saving. He also discusses an upper limit of spendable income and the possibility of a capital levy now or after the war. Sir Kingsley Wood objects to Greenwood trying to steal the Treasury's thunder and points out that he has got some of the ablest economists in the country, such as Keynes and Denis Robertson,[1] to advise him. Nevertheless I think the title of Greenwood's paper, "The Urgent Need for an Enquiry into the Economic and Financial Outlook", is one that contains much truth in itself.

I have been reading a telegram from Smuts, dated October 12th, in which he as usual makes some shrewd observations.

The neutral report that the Brenner meeting decided on a big offensive upon Egypt via Constantinople and Syria confirms the fears I have repeatedly expressed in previous messages. Such a move would be the greatest danger facing the British

---

[1] Fellow of Trinity College, Cambridge, and University Professor of Political Economy.

Empire now that the blitzkrieg against Great Britain has been partially checked . . . The reported plan is likely because it is grandiose enough to appeal to a mind like Hitler's. It promises vast results if successful, as it would open the way to Baghdad and Persia and the oil, and it would cut vital Empire communications and give Mussolini hope . . . The great counter-attack on land which the P.M. has foreshadowed may take place not in Western Europe, where conditions favour Germany, but in the Middle East where they are against her.

Smuts emphatically underlines the necessity of building up a strong force in Egypt and of co-operating with potential allies *before* they are overrun: "We should be there in time to co-operate fully with Greece and Turkey . . . I am myself suspicious of Russia. Is she not going to betray us again and has Germany not already bribed her with promises of Constantinople?"

After dining at home I was driven back to Downing Street in one of the army cars which are now at our disposal. Seeing an immense glow ahead I told the driver to go along the Embankment and we saw a big warehouse east of the County Hall entirely enveloped in flames. The fire obviously made the surrounding district an easy target and so we made for Downing Street with all speed. As we entered Whitehall a high explosive bomb seemed to hit the Admiralty on the Horse Guards Parade. I jumped out of the car at the entrance to the Treasury passage. I had not walked five yards before a parcel of incendiaries fell all round me. I threw myself flat on the ground in the mud and none fell nearer than ten yards from me. One set the F.O. roof on fire; two more fell among the ruins of the Treasury; several fell in the open. Somewhat shaken, I clambered into No. 10, through the shelter emergency exit, and spent the evening in the P.M.'s strengthened basement dining-room.

The night was peaceful except for periodic telephone calls which said "Purple" or "White" or something equally useless to people in a shelter and for the sound of the electric fan which resembles an enemy aeroplane.

Sunday, October 20th

Today began the move from No. 10 to the Office of Works. Only the Cabinet Room and that next door are to remain furnished. It is sad to leave the old building, especially as I fear it will not survive the Battle of London.

As I was sitting at the C.W.R., drinking lager with Tony Bevir, I said what a remarkable man Smuts was and how shrewd in the comments he sends from thousands of miles away. Tony suggested he might be Prime Minister if anything happened to Winston (which God forbid). This seemed to me a great Imperial idea: to have a Dominion politician as Prime Minister of England would be a living proof of the solidarity of the Commonwealth; and Smuts, a member of the Imperial War Cabinet in the last war, the man whose tact broke the Welsh coal strike at a critical moment, has the experience, the wisdom, the drive and the reputation to prove himself a worthy successor to Winston. There would, of course, be difficulties: the jealousy of the other Dominions, the strength of opposition and division of opinion in South Africa; but the idea seems to me so grandiose that I wrote to Mother and proposed that she should put it to Queen Mary with the idea of its filtering through to the King. The King chooses the Prime Minister and can send for whomsoever he wishes. It is thus wise to let the thought reach H.M. and I shall also suggest it to David Margesson and others.

General Smuts' reputation stood high, not only with Churchill, but with all parties in the Cabinet, with the leaders of the armed forces and with informed opinion throughout the Commonwealth and Empire. The South African policy of apartheid, to which Smuts would have subscribed (though with less emphasis and conviction than the Nationalist Party) did not at this period occupy anybody's thoughts. It was as a wise elder statesman, with military knowledge and governmental experience in the First World War, that Smuts was respected and admired. Careful attention was always given to his suggestions, and not only in the wide field of strategy. Thus when Sir Stafford Cripps was appointed Minister of Aircraft Production in 1942, it was done at the suggestion of Smuts.

The P.M. has taken up the transport problem with vigour and has sent drastic proposals to Moore-Brabazon for the use of private cars, lorries, etc., to get the people off the streets.

Monday, October 21st

Rode on Wimbledon Common in fine rain; my first exercise for weeks. Eccleston Square is in chaos, most of the furniture departing for Madeley; No. 10 is in chaos, most of the furniture going over to the Office of Works. I spent much of the day looking through one of Pitt's speeches, of the 3rd of February 1800, to find certain passages applicable to the present day for the P.M. to see. The sentence which struck me as most appropriate was: "It is only from the alliance of the most horrid principles with the most horrid means, that such miseries could have been brought upon Europe." I was also interested by his conservative declaration that "whatever may be the defects of any particular constitution, those who live under it will prefer its continuance to the experiment of changes which may plunge them in the unfathomable abyss of revolution, or extricate them from it only to expose them to the terrors of military despotism."

Philip rang me up and said that two bombs had burst on the Officers' Mess at Wanstead, where he was, the night before. Fortunately he was not even scratched, though the room in which he was had been destroyed.

In the last few days two convoys have suffered badly, one losing seventeen ships and the other fourteen (it is due to the Germans using R.D.F. [radar] captured in France). This naturally preys on the P.M.'s mind greatly; but the position should be better when the American destroyers are in commission and when our new anti-U Boat craft are ready.

The P.M. made a gaffe. He is speaking on the wireless in French tonight, and just before dinner he came into the room, where the French B.B.C. expert and translator, M. Duchesne,[1] was standing, and exclaimed: "Where is my frog speech?" M. Duchesne looked pained.

---

[1] His real name was Michel Saint-Denis. He was an eminent French theatre director, also joint founder of the Old Vic Theatre School and an influential figure in the English theatre as a teacher of acting.

Saturday, March 8ᵗʰ

CHEQUERS
BUTLER'S CROSS · AYLESBURY
BUCKS

At dinner this evening there were present, besides the Prime Minister, General de Gaulle, General Spears, Mr Menzies (Prime Minister of Australia), Duncan and Diana Sandys, Tommy Thompson and myself.

We talked of Germany and the Germans.

De Gaulle said that the important thing for people living in an occupied territory was to remain aloof and superior. The Germans knew that they were inferior beings and were susceptible on the point. Moreover, this being so, it was important to show that the war was a world war. The Germans could see themselves as lords of Europe, but the idea of the world gave them vertigo. As for Hitler he said: "Vous le le prendrez bas et cette fois il n'y aura pas un Doorn".

Duncan Sandys was very bloodthirsty. He wanted to destroy Germany by laying the country waste and burning towns and factories so that for years the German people might be occupied in reconstruction. He wanted to destroy their books and libraries so that an illiterate generation might grow up. Louis Spears replied that this would make the Germans more sturdy and virile, while their western conquerors would be growing effete on the fruits of victory. In his view Richelieu was the greatest of modern European statesmen. He had

Individual page from Sir John's diary, Saturday March 8th 1941.

Sunday. 11/May/1941

10, Downing Street,
Whitehall,

I walked out into Downing Street at 8.0 am on my way to the early service at Westminster Abbey. It was really a summer day with blue skies, but the smoke from many fires lay thick over London and obscured the sun. Burnt paper, from some demolished paper mill, was falling like leaves on a windy autumn day.

Whitehall was thronged with people, mostly sightseers but some of them civil defence workers with blackened faces and haggard looks. One of them, a boy of 18 or 19, pointed towards the Houses of Parliament and said: "Is that the sun?" But the great orange glow at which we were looking was the light of many fires south of the river. At Westminster Abbey there were fire-engines and the policeman at the door said to me: "There will not be any services in the Abbey to-day, Sir", exactly as if it were closed for spring cleaning. I turned towards Westminster Hall on the roof of which I could see flames still leaping. Smoke rose from some invisible point in the file of Parliament buildings beyond. I talked to a fireman. He shewed me Big Ben, the face of which was pocked and scarred, and told me a bomb had gone right through the Tower. The

Individual page from Sir John's diary, Sunday May 11th 1941.

The Prime Minister with his Private Office taken on the author's departure to join the R.A.F., September 29, 1941. *Front row:* the author, the Prime Minister, John Martin, Anthony Bevir. *Behind (L to r):* Leslie Rowan, John Peck, Miss Watson, Commander Thompson, Charles Barker.

Laying the Prime Minister's wreath at the Cenotaph,
November 11th, 1940.
Below: Mrs Churchill and the author. Chequers, 1941.

Some influential advisers.
Above left: Lord Beaverbrook.
Above right: Brendan Bracken.
Left: Professor Lindemann (later
Lord Cherwell).
Below: Lord Halifax and
Lord Cranborne (subsequently
Marquess of Salisbury).

Neville Chamberlain.
Winston Churchill.

Meeting of the Governments exiled in London, held at St. James's Palace on June 12, 1941. On the right of King George VI, Mr Gerbrandy (Dutch Prime Minister), on his left General Sikorski (Poland). At extreme right, Edward Bridges, Brendan Bracken, Desmond Morton. At extreme left: R.A. Butler, the author, Sir Archibald Sinclair.

Private Secretary at War: the author as a fighter pilot.

Dined with Father and slept at Eccleston Square for the last time for many a long day. Most of the furniture has now gone.

Tuesday, October 22nd
Rode on a splendid chestnut of Louis Greig's in Richmond Park, where a thick mist made riding hazardous owing to the large number of bomb-craters and unexploded bombs.

During a Cabinet Meeting at the House I talked to Colonel Moore-Brabazon, the new Minister of Transport, who has seen Violet Markham and told me she was most helpful. He sounds as if he is at last going to get things moving, unlike Reith (whom M.-B. described as "sticky").

Mrs Churchill was abusive. She seemed to expect me to make the arrangements for a visit to Glasgow she is making on Thursday and as I was extremely busy owing to the move, and also object to acting as Mrs C.'s private secretary, I gave most of the instructions to Miss Hamblin,[1] Mrs C.'s secretary. She was furious and said I gave myself airs, etc., etc., much to the amusement of Brendan who was sitting in the car with her while all this transpired. Mrs C. considers it one of her missions in life to put people in their place and prides herself on being outspoken.

Left by train for Scotland to accompany the P.M. on one of his tours. The party included Mrs Churchill (calmed and assuaged by this time), the C.I. G.S., Ismay, Commander Thompson and Victor Cazalet[2] who was told three times that he was not wanted but appeared on the platform and brazenly asked Winston to take him.

I dined at the same table as Ismay and Victor Cazalet. Ismay said that at the time of Munich there was no thought in the Government of waiting until we were better prepared. To avert war, not to postpone it, was the sole object.

---

[1] Grace Hamblin. Churchill's secretary before the war, his wife's during and after it. A tower of strength to the Churchill family, all of whom were fond of her. Wise and competent, she became the National Trust's curator of Chartwell after Churchill's death.

[2] Owner of Fairlawne near Tonbridge. Conservative M.P., outstanding racquets and tennis player and supporter of Churchill in the pre-war struggle for re-armament.

Later in the evening the P.M. said a lot of people talked a lot of nonsense when they said wars never settled anything; nothing in history was ever settled except by wars. He said that what we are now going through is of importance only on the stage of history, by which I suppose he meant that we are achieving nothing constructive but are definitely influencing the future course of events and are laying up a stock of experience from which other generations may learn.

There was much talk about the British army and its lack of good officers. The P.M. said that every prospective officer should follow General Gordon's recommendation and read Plutarch's *Lives*; Dill said a study of Stonewall Jackson was the best possible course. The present trouble was that officers were admirably versed in weapon training but had little stimulus to use their imagination and look at military problems with a broad view.

Wednesday, October 23rd

We had breakfast in a siding and steamed in to Coupar Angus at 9.00 a.m. General Sikorski and his entourage boarded the train, the P.M. put on his strange hat, expressed indignation at the failure to produce his iced soda-water, and finally sallied forth in pouring rain to inspect a Polish battalion. We drove to a place called Tentsmuir where more Poles were drawn up and then stood by the roadside while first a mobile column and then the infantry, performing a kind of goose-step (which knocked all their steel helmets awry), marched past. Later we looked at a camp and at some beach defences north of the Forth. At St Andrews we walked in a procession along the coast for the same purpose, Mrs Churchill being draped in the overcoat of a Polish General. The Poles seemed hardy and fit and gave the impression of being anxious to tear every living German in shreds.

Sikorski and his suite came to lunch on the train, after we had waited for some time on St Andrews platform while the P.M. signed autograph books and formed an object of great excitement to the crowd. I sat with two distinguished and gallant Poles, General Paskiewicz who commanded a division and won the equivalent of three V.C.s and Colonel Klimecki. The former looked grim, expressed his contempt for the French and disgust with the Russians, but spoke little. The latter, with steely blue eyes and a courteous manner, talked of methods for extracting from Poland intelligence about Germany.

After lunch the Poles, accompanied by a charming M.P., bearleader, Colonel Mitchell,[1] departed and Lord Rosebery[2] joined us. We made an extensive tour of Rosyth dockyard and spent much time on the great new battleship, *King George V*, completing in dry dock before doing her trials. We saw the luxurious ward-room and sick-bay, officers' compartment, kitchens and turrets. In descending through the tiny hole into one of the 14–inch turrets both the P.M. and Lord Rosebery all but got stuck. The P.M. had a long talk with the C. in C., Home Fleet, Sir Charles Forbes,[3] and then, dressed in his yachting cap and navy-blue brass-buttoned suit, addressed the ship's company about their ship and the necessity of having her in good trim before the *Bismarck* was out and at sea.

Mrs Churchill left with Lord Lamington, and the rest of the party saw many parts of the dockyard and a huge coastal command aerodrome. Then we left by train for Dalmeny and found the Duchess of Kent[4] and Mary Herbert[5] at the station. We crossed the Forth Bridge, the P.M. obviously delighted by the stirring reception given him by all the people, civilians and others, who had seen him that day.

Ismay and I drove to Edinburgh and dined in the train while the P.M., C.I.G.S., and Thompson dined with Lord R. at

---

[1] Sir Harold Mitchell, M.P. In 1953 he lent Churchill his Jamaican house at Ocho Rios for a holiday after a busy visit to Washington.

[2] Harry, 6th Earl of Rosebery, son of the Liberal Prime Minister and brother of Peggy Crewe. Regional commissioner for Scotland till 1945 and then Secretary of State. Leading racehorse owner, keen cricketer (at one time, as Lord Dalmeny, Captain of Surrey) and Master of Foxhounds.

[3] C. in C., Home Fleet, 1938–40, and then C. in C., Plymouth.

[4] Princess Marina of Greece, married to Prince George, Duke of Kent, King George V's youngest son.

[5] Lady Mary Hope, sister of the Marquess of Linlithgow, Viceroy of India, and married to Sidney Herbert, afterwards Earl of Pembroke. She was a great friend of both my parents.

Dalmeny. I played backgammon most successfully with Ismay while the P.M. talked to Dill and worked until 2.00 a.m. I heard the tail-end of a discussion in which Dill was being lectured on the desirability of employing General Hobart (who is disliked by the army – and by Dill): "Remember," said the P.M. with a meaning look at Dill, "it isn't only the good boys who help to win wars; it is the sneaks and the stinkers as well."

Thursday, October 24th

The train was very late and we had breakfast in comfort before reaching King's Cross. The P.M. passed the time in abusing the Foreign Office with Dill, who complained that the middle ranks in the Diplomatic Service were so poor. The P.M. said a large number should be pensioned off: "What is wanted in that department is a substantial application of the boot."

I drove back with him to No. 10. He said as the passers-by cheered, "I represent to them something which they whole-heartedly support: the determination to win. For a year or two they will cheer me." He pointed out that we were not yet a nation in arms: it took four years for a nation to reach its peak in war production; Germany had reached that maximum state, while we were only at the end of the second year of our effort. I asked him what he thought of the *King George V*. He replied that she was "a monument to Chatfield's folly". A four-gun turret had been taken out of her to allow for aeroplane hangars and she had been armed with 14–inch guns instead of the 16–inch he would have liked to see. Chatfield had been able to overrule some weak and ignorant First Lord, because, the P.M. said, "You see, Neville never seemed to think it mattered who he appointed to the Admiralty."

I found our new apartment at the Office of Works in a state of chaos. As Brendan said, to call it a mad-house would be an insult to lunatics. So I spent most of the day at No. 10 ministering to the wants of the P.M. who elected to work in the Cabinet Room.

John Martin and I dined at the C.W.R. and then repaired to Downing Street when, after drafting a message from the P.M. to the Polish nation, I sat in the underground dining-room with

Jack Churchill and Brendan and listened to the latter's most amusing account of electioneering with the P.M. and in particular the Westminster Election of 1923.

Friday, October 25th
At 4.00 a.m. a box was brought to me containing two Most Immediate telegrams from Hoare in Madrid. The French Ambassador had told him that the Vichy Government would, at a meeting today at noon, decide whether to hand over Toulon, their ports and their fleet to Germany. Pétain and Weygand were against it; Darlan and Laval in favour. It was suggested that a telegram from the King or the P.M. to Pétain might turn the scales. I got back into bed determined to leave the telegram till the P.M., who was sleeping the night in the tube at Down Street,[1] should awake at 7.00. But when I thought of the short interval allowed us I got up, seized the telephone, rang up Alec Cadogan, arranged that the American Embassy should send a message through their Chargé d'Affaires at Vichy, spoke to Lord Halifax and was generally cold and hectic until about 7.30.

The P.M. came back and got into bed at No. 10 to draft a message from the King. He told me that he "had an instinct" this was going to happen and that was why he had sent a telegram to Sam Hoare for communication to the French Ambassador last week. Brendan confirmed that the P.M. had been very uneasy about the whole question for the last few days – and particularly last night. An air-raid alarm drove us all into the shelter and an influx of many people from the half-ruined Treasury caused such a disturbance that the P.M. could hardly concentrate on his drafting. Moreover I was dressing in the inner shelter and he had to sit in the outer. The alarm passed and he went back to bed in his room, but a few minutes later the "Jim Crow"[2] sounded once more and we all went scurrying for safety. Such were the conditions in which this vitally important document, in a race against time, had to be composed. Meanwhile, on the

---

[1] Until the early 1930s there had been a station at Down Street, off Piccadilly. The London Transport Executive converted it into a comfortable, indeed luxurious, air-raid shelter.

[2] Early warning signal of an air-raid.

P.M.'s instructions, I had arranged for the telegrams to be cabled to Washington for transmission to the President who, it is hoped, may encourage Pétain and Weygand to resist. But the wretched old Marshal has had to have an interview with Hitler – who has also been seeing Franco – and it is doubtful whether there is much he can do, especially as Darlan and the navy are fanatically Anglophobe.

In three days' time we were to have backed de Gaulle in an assault on Libreville. This will now have to be postponed or cancelled.

Sunday, October 27th

Lord Bessborough tells me that the de Gaulle headquarters in London are appalling and he thinks that unless something is done about them Winston, whose personal prestige is involved, may suffer. He also thinks that the influence of Spears is pernicious and says that Winston has always had bad judgment. Certainly it is true that Spears' emphatic telegrams persuaded the Cabinet to revert to the Dakar scheme after it had, on the advice of the Chiefs of Staff, been abandoned.

Monday, October 28th

Arrived back at Downing Street Annexe (as we call the Office of Works flat) to find everybody completely befogged about what has been happening in France. The F.O. have no information but are trying to obtain some through the Americans.

I found the P.M. in his bedroom at the C.W.R. with Beaverbrook and told him that Athens had been bombed this morning. "Then we must bomb Rome," he said without hesitation and asked me to summon the Chiefs of Staff at once.

Wednesday, October 30th

Having breakfasted scrappily I went to No. 10 and spent most of the morning there dictating. I had an interesting talk with one of the P.M.'s visitors, an American newspaper magnate called Ingersoll, who is amazed by the spirit of the people of London but, quite justifiably, not impressed by the welfare arrangements. He wanted to know all about the P.M.'s habits, whether he drank tea or coffee for breakfast and a score of other journalese Americanisms.

Violet Markham came to see me. Yesterday afternoon Mrs C. and I went to look at her canteen in Southwark, where her initiative has been well repaid, and also saw the miles of underground shelter, in a converted tube, where thousands spend the night. Mrs C., who was ridiculously overdressed in a leopard-skin coat, was loudly acclaimed and both she and I were impressed by the universal cheerfulness in squalid conditions.

Violet Markham gave me the advice I wanted about Mrs Crosthwaite's plea that the services of the trained professional social workers are not being used. She also shed an interesting light on the inefficiency and lack of sympathy shown by the L.C.C. in dealing with the shelter and other kindred problems. This has given rise to a feeling among the poor that "they" – the authorities – are being callous. She confirmed what I had heard, that the trouble at rest centres and elsewhere was very largely due to local jealousies and the obtuseness of Borough Councils; but she says that in particular during the last few weeks all her illusions about the L.C.C. have vanished. The transport problem is much improved and Colonel Moore-Brabazon has shown great vigour and determination.

The P.M. lunched with Herbert Morrison and I was bidden to drink brandy with them. The P.M. began by saying that he had never doubted the ability of London to stand up to bombardment, though Herbert Morrison said he had not been sure how they would take it. The P.M. cited the wonderful courage of the Cockney regiments in the last war and pointed out that a large portion of the navy was recruited from London[1] (it appears that nearly the whole navy is drawn from Chatham, Portsmouth and Plymouth). He told us that Beaverbrook had produced figures to prove that only about thirty per cent of the R.A.F. pilots came from Public Schools, the remainder being products of the Elementary Schools and professional classes. It was striking that none of the aristocracy chose the R.A.F. – they left it to the lower middle class. The P.M. then waxed

[1] In which Churchill included Chatham.

eloquent on the disappearance of the aristocracy from the stage and their replacement by these excellent sons of the lower middle classes. He paid a tribute to what they had done for England. Morrison, to my surprise, said it would be a pity if they vanished altogether. The P.M. commented on the difference between this country and France: there the aristocracy had been separated from the people by a gulf of blood; here they were sinking noiselessly and unresisting into the background. I had a feeling that the P.M. was flattering Morrison by his praise of the lower orders, and Morrison the P.M. by his admiration for many of the qualities of the upper classes. It made me feel rather uncomfortable.

The P.M. then proceeded to slang Baldwin, Ramsay MacDonald and the unnatural National Government. He stigmatised Baldwin as "the greatest of non-statesmen", said that this was the most unnecessary war in history and proclaimed that it was a war far harder to win than to avoid.

After dinner at the C.W.R. Ismay and I went to Down Street tube station where the P.M. was dining with Bevin. With General Crossman, commanding the London A.A. defences, we penetrated into the bowels of the earth and extricated the diners. Bevin, who had been well plied with brandy, was extremely loquacious. He and I got into a lift together and had great difficulty in getting out owing to his insistence on trying to open the gates before the lift had stopped. Then a policeman tried to arrest the P.M. for having too bright side-lights and was finally dismissed with a loud "Go to Hell, man".

Finally we reached Raynes Park and stumped across a wet field to see a battery of A.A. guns and the G.L. set which controls their fire. It was raining, no enemy aircraft entered our sector, and the guns remained silent; so after looking at the G.L., a clumsy contrivance like a caravan, and walking round the guns, we repaired to the Officers' Mess and the P.M., dressed in his R.A.F. overcoat, sat in a chair looking strangely like Napoleon while Bevin chattered and the officers gave us whisky. The P.M. said that when the G.L. and the other apparatus were perfected the war would take a different aspect: the air would cease to be formidable and the land and sea would come back to their own. It was a long way off, but it would come. Bevin said this was the dawn of a new era – whether he meant in war or in the application of these wireless miracles to other spheres I do not know. The officers seemed very pleased with the G.L. and confident of its ultimate success when the present teething troubles had been overcome.

Thursday, October 31st
Rose at 7.00, dressed in the P.M.'s empty bedroom and went off to Richmond to ride Louis Greig's horse. After a refreshing gallop I had breakfast with the Greig family and Victor Cazalet. On the way up to London Louis Greig and Cazalet told me of Weizmann's[1] new discovery of 120 per cent octane oil which may revolutionise flying. It is apparently being strongly opposed by the oil interests and has met with great obstruction in high circles. It is deplorable that vested interests in this country should be able to act in such a way.

Lunched with Jasper Rootham[2] at White's. Determined to join the army and forbidden to do so by Civil Service rules, he has resigned from the Treasury and will join up next month. Presumably he will be taken back after the war, but he is still badly off, his pay stops and generally speaking I think he is most gallant. He complains that the Government makes provision for conscientious objectors, but none for those who are forbidden to fight and conscientiously object to not doing so.

We talked about Neville Chamberlain and Horace Wilson and he had formed a more definite opinion than I had of the former's dependence on the latter. We agreed that Horace, though a good and genuinely public-spirited man, was fatally addicted to the policy of cautious advance and excessive circumspection in every task he undertook.

The P.M. felt ill, was sick and went off to Down Street where

---

[1] Chaim Weizmann, first President of Israel, whom Churchill admired and respected.
[2] My predecessor as junior Private Secretary to Neville Chamberlain. The Treasury, quite disgracefully, declined to reinstate him after the war, in which he served as a liaison officer with the Yugoslav guerillas. He joined the Bank of England and on retirement wrote elegant verses.

he had no dinner ("which I much resented – but it was very good for me"). I dined with John Martin and John Peck at the C.W.R. The latter, who has a gift for the ridiculous, amused himself by typing the following minute:

Action this Day

Pray let six new offices be fitted for my use, in Selfridge's, Lambeth Palace, Stanmore, Tooting Bec, the Palladium and Mile End Road. I will inform you at 6 each evening at which office I shall dine, work and sleep. Accommodation will be required for Mrs Churchill, two shorthand typists, three secretaries and Nelson.[1] There should be shelter for all and a place for me to watch air-raids from the roof. This should be completed by Monday. There is to be no hammering during office hours, that is between 7a.m. and 3 a.m.

W.S.C.

31.10.40.

The above, very realistically produced, entirely convinced Morton, Jacob, Seal, Ismay and others of its authenticity – which only goes to show the state of attrition to which all these moves and constantly changing plans have reduced the P.M.'s entourage.

At the end of a year at war during which he had been at the forefront in the Norwegian disaster, the Dunkirk episode, the invasion threat and the battle of Britain – not to mention the battle of the Atlantic which was now threatening survival – it would have been surprising if Churchill had not been tense with emotion and turbulent in mood.

He did not shout, as actors in films and television productions imagine; nor did I ever see him drunk, as the media and the less well-informed writers sometimes suggest that he frequently was. But never notably considerate, except to those in pain or in trouble, he was more than normally inconsiderate and demanding during the last months of 1940. He complained of

[1] The black cat.

delays when there were none; he changed carefully prepared plans at the last minute; he cancelled meetings and appointments without caring for anybody's convenience but his own; and he was continually insisting on personal amenities which gave much trouble to overworked people and were, in a small way, diversions from the war effort. The sound of hammering, often on account of building activities he himself had set in train, caused outbursts of fury, and his staff spent much time searching Whitehall for the source of the irritant in the hope of appeasing their sometimes unreasonable master.

Mrs Churchill, at one stage in the summer of 1940, wrote him a letter on the subject. Long experience had convinced her that when she really wanted him to pay attention written representations were more effective than oral. He may have accepted the rebuke, but it was some months before he reformed. If, however, he had been unjustly angry, he seldom failed to make amends, not indeed by saying he was sorry but by praising the injured party generously for some entirely dissociated virtue.

So if John Peck's spoof minute was an imaginative parody, it was not altogether wide of the mark.

Churchill's ill-tempered phase was a passing one, nor was it constant. What was constant was the respect, admiration and affection that almost all those with whom he was in touch felt for him despite his engaging but sometimes infuriating idiosyncrasies.

ELEVEN

MEDITERRANEAN DILEMMA
NOVEMBER 1940

Friday, November 1st
After the P.M. had had his afternoon sleep we left for Chequers.
I travelled with him in his car and after a sticky beginning found
him most affable. He was dressed in his R.A.F. uniform and we
stopped at Northolt to inspect the Hurricane Squadron, No. 615,
of which he is Honorary Air Commodore. They had been up four
times today and told us of their experiences in the Mess while we
drank whisky and soda. When we continued our journey the P.M.
talked about the Italians, whose impertinence in sending bombers
to attack this country has much annoyed him. He said he intended
to attack Rome before long, as soon as we had enough Wellingtons
at Malta. Last night our bombers successfully attacked Naples
from there and today the press, ignorant of the truth, is chortling
about the magnificent 3,000 mile flight from England to Naples
and back. I said to the P.M. that I hoped if we bombed Rome we
should be careful to spare the Coliseum. The P.M. answered that
it wouldn't hurt the Coliseum to have a few more bricks knocked
off it and then, becoming pensive, quoted:

> *While stands the Coliseum Rome shall stand*
> *When falls the Coliseum Rome shall fall . . .*[1]

We talked about the Public Schools and he said he wished he
had learned Greek. He said he would go down to Harrow to

[1] From Byron's *Childe Harold's Pilgrimage*.

hear School Songs if I would arrange it, and then he reverted to his lament about the almost entire failure of Eton, Harrow and Winchester to contribute pilots to the R.A.F. I repeated Lord Bessborough's condemnation of the de Gaulle headquarters and the P.M. said that de Gaulle was definitely an embarrassment to us now in our dealings with Vichy and the French people. I also told him what Louis Greig had said about Weizmann's discovery of 120 per cent octane oil and he said that if I could show him that the oil interests really were opposing this for their own ends he would soon put a stop to their machinations.

He gave it as his view, emphatically, that Roosevelt would win the election by a far greater majority than was supposed and he said he thought America would come into the war. He praised the instinctive intelligence of the British press in showing no sign of the eagerness with which we desired a Roosevelt victory. He said he quite understood the exasperation which so many English people feel with the American attitude of criticism combined with ineffective assistance; but we must be patient and we must conceal our irritation. (All this was punctuated with bursts of "Under the spreading Chestnut Tree").

"I should now like," said the P.M. as we neared Chequers, "to have dinner – at Monte Carlo – and then to go and gamble!" He proceeded to expound the pleasures of chemin de fer and the exultation he found in gambling on the Riviera.

Despite his excellent humour, the P.M. was still suffering slightly from the effects of yesterday's sickness and he went straight to bed. I dined with Mrs Churchill, Mary, Judy Montagu and Ismay. I spent most of the evening bickering with Mary who was feeling cantankerous and is in any case a shade too prim. Ismay and I then talked about the megalomania of Sir Roger Keyes who has had the effrontery to suggest that the P.M. should appoint him his deputy to preside over the Chiefs of Staff.

Saturday, November 2nd
I spent the whole day indoors at my writing table, coping with a stream of incoming pouches and outgoing orders.

The First Lord, the First Sea Lord and the C.I.G.S. came to lunch. Speaking of Vichy, and their recent negotiations with the Germans, the P.M. said, "Owing to our unexpected resistance they have been able to market their treachery at a slightly higher rate than would otherwise have been possible." He referred to them with loathing and said that while he could understand people being wicked he could not understand their being so contemptible. He now thinks the invasion is off, but that can only be because of our constant vigilance. If we relaxed that, invasion would be an imminent danger. But of course this meant our keeping great forces immobilised at home, and similarly the North African threat meant our concentrating all the rest we possessed in Egypt. Thus the Axis powers could keep our forces concentrated in one or two spots while they amused themselves elsewhere.

Nevertheless the P.M. is determined that all possible, by land, sea and air, shall be done for Greece and when, after a long post-prandial discussion, Dill drove away at tea-time the P.M.'s last words were, "Don't forget – the maximum possible for Greece." Similarly in a minute this morning to the C.A.S. about sending air support to the Greeks, the P.M. wrote: "Perhaps you will say that all I propose is impossible. If so, I shall be very sorry, because a great opportunity will have been missed, and we shall have to pay heavily hereafter for it. Please try your best."

It was one of those days when almost everything went wrong: the electric light spasmodically failed; the Green Line telephone was out of order; a telegram to Eden in Cairo, bidding him stay there, was unduly delayed in despatch; I incurred the P.M.'s displeasure by sending up to London the flimsies of some minutes he had dictated and wanted again. I was rushed off my feet by an overwhelming volume of papers; Peggy Crewe rang up about some trifling Air Raid Precaution troubles in Chelsea which she wanted me to put right; I spent ages with Mrs Churchill poring over some notes of Violet Markham's about lack of compensation for Civil Defence Workers and the unsympathetic attitude of the L.C.C. as regards welfare work.

The new C. in C., Bomber Command, Sir Richard Peirse,[1] two pilots from No. 615 Squadron, and the Coldstream Company Commander, Sir George Forestier-Walker, came to dinner, when the conversation was mostly on fighter tactics and bombing prospects. The German fighters can outfly ours, but their pilots are very timid. We have some new bombers on the way, Halifaxes, Manchesters and Stirlings which will be most destructive, and by the end of next year the P.M. hopes to be bombing "every Hun corner" every night. Peirse tells me that the much-vaunted American "Flying Fortresses" are obsolete and we have refused to take them. As regards bombing Rome, the P.M. said to Peirse, as he said to me yesterday, "We must be careful not to bomb the Pope; he has a lot of influential friends!" After dinner the P.M. with great pride showed the young air-force officers some of his albums of aircraft production; he is never happier than when displaying the spectacular strides that have been made since Beaverbrook and the new government came into power.

The P.M., closeted with Peirse and Ismay, produced another telegram to Eden which Ismay is to submit to the Chiefs of Staff tomorrow.

However unjust it may be, the collapse of Greece without any effort by us will have deadly effect on Turkey and on future of war . . . Quite understand how everyone with you fixed on idea of set-piece battle at Mersa Matruh. For that very reason unlikely it will occur . . . No one will thank us for sitting tight in Egypt with ever growing forces while Greek situation and all that hangs on it is cast away . . . New emergencies must be met in war as they come and local views must not subjugate main issue . . . Trust you will grasp situation firmly (abandoning negative and passive policies)[2] and seizing opportunity which has come into our hands. Safety

[1] C. in C., Bomber Command, until replaced by Sir Arthur Harris in 1942, when he went to India as A.O.C. in C. Caused a scandal by running off with General Auchinleck's wife.
[2] The sentence in brackets was subsequently omitted.

First is the road to ruin in war even if you had the safety which you have not.

All this was interspersed in a longer and much more detailed telegram.

Sunday, November 3rd

The P.M. was upset by a broadcast made by the First Lord (A. V. Alexander) giving an extravagant picture of what we were doing, and would do, for Greece. "Such a nice fellow – but, really . . ." he said. Of course the press have blazoned his remarks across their front pages and false hopes will be raised.

Then a telegram came from Eden saying he must return in order to discuss the position with the P.M. I took it up to his bedroom, written in pencil, and waited while he drafted a reply telling Eden to wait till he had seen the P.M.'s latest telegram – which the Chiefs of Staff are sending off this morning. He lay there in his four-post bed with its flowery chintz hangings, his bed-table by his side. Mrs Hill sat patiently opposite while he chewed his cigar, drank frequent sips of iced soda-water, fidgeted his toes beneath the bedclothes and muttered stertorously under his breath what he contemplated saying. To watch him compose some telegram or minute for dictation is to make one feel that one is present at the birth of a child, so tense is his expression, so restless his turnings from side to side, so curious the noises he emits under his breath. Then comes out some masterly sentence and finally with a "Gimme" he takes the sheet of typewritten paper and initials it or alters it with his fountain-pen, which he holds most awkwardly halfway up the holder.

A note arrived from Lord Beaverbrook, announcing his resignation because of asthma (actually he is cross with the Air Ministry and piqued because the P.M. has thrown some cold water on his grandiose scheme for making Faraday House the seat and centre of Government – thus upsetting all the Post Office arrangements). The P.M. smiled wryly when I gave him the note, knowing that Lord Beaverbrook resigns every few days; and then he rang him up and said if he did so there would be a public outcry, it would be called desertion, and anyhow why couldn't he just take a fortnight's or a month's holiday.

Lunch was a quiet meal: the family, myself and a Coldstream officer called Waddilove. We listened to a Winstonian dissertation on Sadowa[1] and Austria and Bismarck. Waddilove said that Bismarck was the last German who knew where to stop; the P.M. said he would show these present Germans where they were to stop – in the grave.

After lunch I played backgammon with Mrs Churchill while the P.M. thought out the speech he is to make in the House on Tuesday to the accompaniment of Strauss waltzes on Mary's gramophone. Having received sufficient inspiration he went into the Hawtrey room to dictate the speech to Mrs Hill, and I walked in the pouring rain with Mary and Judy.

After tea the three Chiefs of Staff and Lady Portal (wife of the C.A.S.) arrived to dine and sleep, as did Prof. The purpose is to discuss the plan, which they have been working on all day, for assistance to Greece. Ismay says there is nothing we can do on a sufficiently large scale to save the Greeks and the C.O.S. seem rather unenthusiastic about the P.M.'s determination to throw considerable forces into the fray even at the expense of weakening Egypt. Ismay thinks that concentrated air-attack, with little opposition, will break Greece as it broke Poland and France.

The P.M. is highly delighted by the Italian admission of their casualties in Africa which are more than ten times as great as ours. He says that "the Italians are easier to kill than to catch".

After dinner, before leaving the dining-room, projects for capturing Pantellaria ("by 300 determined men, with blackened faces, knives between their teeth and revolvers under their tails", as the P.M. envisaged the operation) and Rhodes were discussed. The Pantellaria scheme could be left to Sir R. Keyes and his commandos; he has been pressing to be allowed to do it. Rhodes would be a harder job, but the P.M. thinks it would be agreeable to seize it and give it to Turkey: the Turks would

[1] The decisive victory of the Prussians in the Austro-Prussian War of 1866.

not be able to resist the offer and then they would be embroiled with Italy.

For long hours I sat up while assistance for Greece was discussed, the numbers of aircraft we could send was ascertained, telegrams were received from Eden saying that if troops were sent from Egypt Wavell would be prevented from carrying out a prospective hard blow at the Italians and Eden was told not to be faint-hearted, parochially minded, over-cautious, etc., etc. During an interlude I took Dill to look at some despatch riders, who had just arrived, in order to prove to him that the military mackintosh was not waterproof.

Prof. thinks it fantastic that no plan should have been ready for instant use in the event of an Italian attack on Greece. Ismay's reply is that no ready-made plan is applicable to the special circumstances existing when the attack is made and that as far as Greece was concerned our previously worked out plans depended on French co-operation. We had intended to occupy Crete in such an event and we had already done so. My impression is that we are now going beyond what is intended because the P.M. realises the moral and strategic value of preventing a Greek collapse. He thinks the Greeks will fight well (and cites the wars of 1911 and 1921 to show they are not despicable). They may well prove a match for the aggressors on land – and it is up to us to provide air support.

From 9.00 p.m. till 2.00 a.m. telegrams to Eden were drafted and redrafted and finally in a state of complete exhaustion we all went to bed after 2.00. London had its first night free of air-raids for many a long day.

Monday, November 4th
The P.M. has ordered enquiries to be made into Violet Markham's two points about compensation for Civil Defence workers in case of death and about the unsympathetic attitude of the L.C.C. as regards welfare work. I am to take these points up with the departments concerned.

The P.M. is much impressed by the slackening of air attacks and says it is not all due to the weather. The Germans have to continue them in order to try and hide their defeat, but evidently they do not like the reception they get or the retaliation on Berlin.

Depressing news from the sea: two big armed merchant cruisers, the *Laurentic* and the *Patroclus*, have been torpedoed together with a merchant ship off Ireland.

When I got up to find out the news the P.M. was already down, in his siren-suit, bidding farewell to the departing Chiefs of Staff. Shortly afterwards we ourselves left for London.

I lunched with Father at White's and then, after spending enough time in the office to put some semblance of order into my overflowing trays, I motored down to Ardley in the pouring rain and arrived there as darkness fell. Mother was there staying with Joan and Ann. She told me that my suggestion about General Smuts as a successor, if need should ever arise, to the P.M. much affected Queen Mary, who said that it was an idea which had greatly appealed to King George V. She therefore passed it on to the King who reacted favourably.

Tuesday, November 5th
Polling day in the U.S. A close contest is generally expected.

Wednesday, November 6th
After an idle morning, during which it poured for the fifth day in succession, I drove Mother up to London and went to No. 10. The Greeks are holding out well; the presidential election has gone the right way; and the Admiralty are much exercised by the apparent presence of another pocket battleship in the Atlantic.

After dinner at the Central War Room (endless tinned soup and sausages) John Peck and I went over to No. 10 and, sitting in the P.M.'s dining-room, drank brandy and gossiped with Brendan (who tells me he wants to buy the *Observer*) and Jack Churchill.

Thursday, November 7th
I was on duty from 8.00 a.m. till 9.30 and then had breakfast at Wyndham's. (The Travellers is bombed and in disuse.)

The House of Commons met for the first time at Church

House, which is thought to be safer than the Palace of Westminster. The Cabinet was also held there and as I was in attendance on the P.M. part of the time I had time to steal into the Assembly Room where the House meets and watch that sparse gathering of M.P.s in their small and unwonted surroundings. The official gallery is on a kind of rostrum behind the Speaker's Chair. I noticed that Rab Butler, on the Front Bench, so far followed the traditions of the House as to put his feet up on the Table.

The amount of papers in the P.M.'s box is becoming unwieldy. In order to keep a full and comprehensive diary of events I ought to give a summary of the matters dealt with; but it would be a whole-time job to summarise this farrago of operational, civil, political and scientific matter.

The P.M. was much displeased by a minute in a War Office file which referred to one of "his scribbles" as being unintelligible. He sent a furious minute to P. J. Grigg demanding an apology and deploring that the officer in question (General McCready, A.C.I.G.S.) should have made more use of his critical faculties than of his intelligence.

Seven bombs in succession shook our equanimity at the C.W.R.

Friday, November 8th

At night I dined at the C.W.R. and then, leaving Seal and Bevir to cope with the P.M. at the C.W.R. (where he fed not wisely and all too well with Eden, who today returned from Cairo), I went over to No. 10 and read *Madame Bovary* before going to bed.

We bombed Munich in force.

Saturday, November 9th

Rode early at Richmond on Louis Greig's horse and had breakfast with him and his family afterwards. He is the soul of hospitality and affability.

I am amused to see the following minute by the P.M., attached to an earlier one he had written about assistance for Greece: "Although I bowed before the difficulties so industriously assembled by the Joint Planners in their report of August 31st, and the general attitude of negation, I should be very much obliged to the C.O.S. Committee if they would kindly read my minute and see if there was not something in it after all."

The P.M. spent most of the morning dictating a speech he is to make at a Mansion House lunch today and with the composition of which he was so behindhand that he asked to be allowed to be half an hour late for lunch.

Tony Bevir gave Desmond Morton, John Peck and me an excellent lunch at the United Universities Club. We talked of the incapacity of Archie Sinclair and the fact that "the Prof." shows signs of breaking up under the strain. Desmond also retailed two of the P.M.'s latest remarks, one to General Sikorski who wanted foreign exchange: *"Mon Général, devant la vieille dame de Threadneedle Street je suis impotent"*; the other a 2.00 a.m. Parthian shot at the Chiefs of Staff: "I am obliged to wage modern warfare with ancient weapons."

Horace Wilson rang me up to say that Mr Chamberlain died this evening. He had cancer but his death was painless. I rang up Seal who has gone with the P.M. to Ditchley, fearing an attack on Chequers by the light of the waxing moon.

One can be quite comfortable these days in spite of the bombs. I had a bath in the P.M.'s bath at No. 10, and then sat in his downstairs room in my dressing-gown, reading *Madame Bovary* and drinking some delicious brown ale provided by Barker.

Sunday, November 10th
Went to the early service in Westminster Abbey. The altar is now set up in the nave before the gates of the choir. The Dean asked our prayers for Mr Neville Chamberlain as if he were still alive – the news will not be published till this afternoon.

I breakfasted at No. 10 and then went over to the Annexe for the morning, after wrestling with the Duke of Westminster's[1] secretary about His Grace's lady-friend who has been seized by M.I.5 on her arrival in this country. The Duke wants Winston

---

[1] Bendor, 2nd Duke of Westminster. Old friend of Churchill with whom he made several military expeditions by armoured car in the First World War. Churchill hunted wild boars on his Normandy estate and painted many pictures when staying at his other French property near Bordeaux.

to intervene – a monstrous suggestion which I trust the P.M. will resist.

The Free French forces seem to be making a successful attack on Libreville in Gabon, but their activities are now rather an embarrassment in our relations with Vichy. De Gaulle has been asked to come back to London, and Spears too; but the P.M. doubts whether they are on sufficiently good terms to come back on the same ship.

There are rumours from the Balkans that Russia might join in an Axis advance south-eastwards so as to ensure her control of the Black Sea ports and the Straits. She is pursuing a policy of the most abject "appeasement" towards Germany.

Our Balkan Missions are pouring in telegrams which stress the psychological necessity of supporting Greece; but the problem is best summed up in the F.O. weekly political summary:

> We are still paying for our failure to re-arm in good time. Our military resources in the Eastern Mediterranean do not permit us to disperse our strength and the air help which Greece so sorely needs can be given only at the expense of other interests. The problem of aid for Greece is a military one which has been gravely complicated by the collapse of France. But, from the political point of view, the advantages of swift and effective help are pre-eminent.

The raids, which began early, were very intense and drove me and *Madame Bovary* out of the P.M.'s sitting-room into the shelter after a very short attempt at concentration. The sky and the balloons were reddened by two fierce fires, but the nights are becoming cold for street-prowling in dressing-gowns and bedroom slippers, however remarkable the sights.

Monday, November 11th
Rose at 7.00 and while it was yet dark (summer time is to continue throughout the winter) set out to ride at Wimbledon. The ground was white with the first frost of the winter, but the sky was blue, streaked with pink clouds, and the leaves, though

now a dull brown, were still on the oak trees. The bomb craters are filling with pools of water.

At 10.15 I laid a wreath on the Cenotaph, as representative of the Prime Minister. There was no ceremony: the traffic was just stopped, I placed the wreath and a large number of press photographers clicked their cameras.

The P.M. came back from Ditchley at lunch-time. Afterwards he went to sleep but had to be disturbed owing to the shriek of bombs nearby. He soon got tired of the shelter and returned to his bedroom, where he gave me a lecture on the excellence of his teeth-cleaning apparatus, an electrical appliance which spurts water at a high velocity into his mouth and removes the taste of cigars. He said that if young men like me were sensible enough to use them they would never have bad teeth.

He is very cross with Archie Sinclair who (after the attack in the Beer Cellar at Munich) gave an interview to the *Daily Express* saying that dictators were military objectives. The P.M. thinks this may cause unpleasant reactions on himself and says such a statement almost amounts to incitement to assassination. But, if you are allowed to bomb Heads of States, surely you may shoot them?

Today we have shot down more raiders than usual and, for the first time over England, at least eight Italian planes amongst them. The P.M. gave a whoop of joy when I told him.

After dinner I sat in the dining-room and talked at length to Brendan. He thought it a tragedy that Philip Sassoon didn't leave Trent to the P.M. (Brendan cannot bear Chequers.) He also spoke of the beauties of a certain Stene Chapel, near Banbury, built by Nathaniel Crewe, Bishop of Durham and Oxford. We also discussed the shipping situation which is very serious.

Tuesday, November 12th

Lord Lothian has drafted a telegram for the P.M. to send to Roosevelt. It stresses very frankly our need for American support in obtaining the Irish naval bases, in guarding Singapore, in getting more ships and above all in buying munitions and aircraft on credit. It is intended to make R. feel that if we go down, the responsibility will be America's. Brendan tells me the

P.M. thinks it so admirably written that he could not improve a word of it; but it will go before the Cabinet for consideration.

At 12.00 noon the P.M. rose in the unfamiliar surroundings of Church House and paid before the House of Commons his moving and eloquent tribute to Mr Chamberlain. The noise of Seal and Miss Watson coming on to the dais (which takes the place of the official gallery), the coughs and creaks from members, were very disturbing in the small chamber used for debate, and I did not think the P.M.'s delivery was equal to the magnificence of his language and the balance of his phrases. I was struck by his words when, in speaking of the verdict of the future, he said:

> History with its flickering lamp stumbles along the trail of the past, trying to reconstruct its scenes, to revive its echoes, and kindle with pale gleams the passion of former days. What is the worth of all this? The only guide to a man is his conscience. The only shield to his memory is the rectitude and sincerity of his actions. It is very imprudent to walk through life without this shield, because we are so often mocked by the failure of our hopes and the upsetting of our calculations; but with this shield, however the fates may play, we march always in the ranks of honour.

Tommy Lascelles,[1] with whom I talked after lunch at Wyndham's, said that only the P.M., of living orators, could make one realise what it must have been like to hear Burke or Chatham.

Our depression at the huge shipping losses in the North Western Approaches, which if continued at their present rate would bring us to our knees, has been relieved by the success of the Fleet Air Arm in destroying the Italian fleet in Taranto harbour and setting fire to Durazzo and Valona, the only supply ports for the Italian army in Greece.

[1] Sir Alan Lascelles (only Churchill called him Alan rather than Tommy) was Hardinge's successor as the King's Private Secretary. He was a wise counsellor, well-read, a good historian and a lover of Wagner. He wrote the best of letters and when, one day, his diaries are published they will doubtless be a document of unusual importance. Married the younger daughter of a Viceroy, Lord Chelmsford.

Wednesday, November 13th

The First Lord is a queer fish. I congratulated him on the Taranto affair and he said the praise was due to Cunningham,[1] C. in C., Mediterranean. "But," he continued, "in fairness to Pound I must say that I suggested it to him the other day and he telegraphed it out to Cunningham." This unself-conscious egotism is probably due to Mr A.'s disappointment that the P.M. is going to steal the Admiralty's laurels by himself announcing the victory in the House.

The P.M. frantically composed his speech and I drove down to Church House with him while he discoursed upon the difference this event makes to the whole of our naval disposition and the panic which the Italians, in their inner harbour, must have felt at the unexpected attack. His description of "this glorious episode" to the House was greeted with enthusiastic cheers from an assembly hungry for something cheerful.

A vile, hot and hectic afternoon, starting with a tour of the new building operations[2] – where the P.M. leapt deftly over girders and crawled through holes – and ending with great pressure of work.

The Molotov visit to Berlin may presage any of three things:

i.   A Peace offensive (no one but me subscribes to this view!).

ii.   Pressure on Turkey for the control of the Straits. Russia would be anxious to be sure of the Black Sea ports. This is the most likely interpretation of the meeting.

iii.   A division of power in the Far East and Asia, Russia taking, in some form or another, Iran and Afghanistan.

This rumour comes from Craigie[3] in Tokyo.

At dinner in the C.W.R. I had a talk with Sir Reginald Dorman

---

[1] Sir Andrew Cunningham, known as A.B.C., First Sea Lord after Sir Dudley Pound's death in 1943.

[2] These excursions, of which I always seemed to be the victim, were made because Churchill, as a keen amateur builder, was fascinated by the work in progress to make the Central War Room more bomb-proof. He examined the plans and suggested alterations, including the construction of brick traverses.

[3] Sir Robert Craigie, British Ambassador.

Smith (Minister of Agriculture in Chamberlain's government), who says that the P.M.'s recent letter to the farmers (saying "stick it and don't grumble") has had a deplorable effect. It was written by Beaverbrook, who in many respects is a mischievous person. Dorman Smith spoke enthusiastically of Chamberlain and agreed wholeheartedly with a letter I received this morning from Arthur Rucker saying: "Neville's last months were a bitter tragedy, but I believe that he will some day be regarded as the greatest Englishman of his times."

Thursday, November 14th
Rode in Richmond Park on Jean Greig's large brown horse and gratefully drank in the cold clear morning air after nights of air-conditioning. At breakfast I listened to a discourse by Louis Greig on the iniquitous behaviour of Beaverbrook, who is, of course, at daggers drawn with Louis' chief, Archie Sinclair, and is stealing all the materials required by the Ministry of Supply.

Neville Chamberlain's funeral took place in Westminster Abbey at noon. Tony and I were among the ushers. A huge congregation assembled, and froze as they sat beneath the shattered windows. All the Ministers were there in the choir stalls; the P.M., David, and most of the War Cabinet were pall-bearers. The Duke of Gloucester represented the King, and the Chiefs of Staff represented the three services. The time and place had been a well-kept secret, announced to both Houses in secret session; for a judiciously placed bomb would have had spectacular results.

I noticed the look of blank indifference, almost of disdain, on Duff Cooper's face, the boredom of Bevin. Only Anderson and Hankey sang the hymns. Lady Oxford marched out at the end of the service, side by side with Lord Horder,[1] and among the family mourners. Publicity is her God.

In the afternoon the P.M. set out for Ditchley; but having heard, just before he started, that a German operation entitled MOONLIGHT SONATA was likely to take place tonight, he changed his

---

[1] Prominent and fashionable general practitioner. Neville Chamberlain's doctor.

mind before he had gone far and returned to London. This operation is known from the contents of these mysterious buff boxes, which the P.M. alone opens, sent every day by Brigadier Menzies.[1] It is obviously some major air operation – possibly stimulated by our success at Taranto – but its exact destination the Air Ministry find it difficult to determine. In any case we all decided to take the necessary precautions and to sleep in the safest place.

One of the two best kept secrets of the war (the other was nuclear research) was our possession of the Enigma machine, provided with immense courage by the Poles, that enabled us to decipher at Bletchley first the signals of the German Luftwaffe and later those of the German navy and army as well. These deciphered signals were known in central Government circles by the code-word Boniface *and their circulation was so closely restricted that not even the Prime Minister's secretaries were supposed to see them, although we soon became aware of their origin. Brigadier Menzies used to deliver them personally to No. 10, in ancient buff-coloured boxes marked V.R.I. and the Prime Minister himself kept the only key. Sometimes he would forget and show one of us a particularly interesting intercept; but that was later in the war.*

Immense credit is due to the French cryptologists who worked on Enigma alongside the British until the collapse of France and never spoke a word to the Vichy Government. The Free French, who were notoriously liable to leak, were not told the secret; nor, until shortly before they came into the war, were the Americans who were thought to be only marginally better at keeping secrets. The Russians were provided with information but not informed of its source.

Although the first successful "decrypts" were produced early in 1940, it was not until the end of May – the time of Dunkirk – that it became possible to decipher the Luftwaffe signals within a short period of their interception. The German naval signals were mastered in the early summer of 1941 and those of the army in 1942.

[1] Brigadier Stewart Menzies, head of M.I.6 and referred to as "C".

A typical incident happened just before lunch today. The P.M. had invited Cross, the Minister of Shipping, to lunch and was showing him great affability. Suddenly he charged back into the room at No. 10, where I was telephoning, and whispered hoarsely in my ear, "What is the name of the Minister of Shipping?" "Cross," I whispered back furtively, because the Minister was standing in the doorway. "Oh," said the P.M. "Well, what's his Christian name?" Cross must have heard the whole conversation.

John Peck and I dined at Down Street Station ("the burrow", Winston calls it) where we fed excellently, and slept there in great comfort. The P.M. spent the night at the C.W.R. to await the MOONLIGHT SONATA, and became so impatient that he spent much of the time on the Air Ministry roof.

Friday, November 15th
London had a quiet night but Coventry was subjected to violent bombardment – possibly the First Movement of the Sonata, which may continue throughout the moon period.

The P.M. has sent a real snorter to Lampson, in Egypt, who in a private telegram to Eden stigmatised one of the decisions of the Cabinet as "crazy".

P. J. Grigg, whom I saw this morning, was loud in his condemnation of his master, Eden. "Complete junk," he called him.

Moyra Ponsonby lunched with me at Pruniers, and after eating oysters on high stools against the counter, we went together to Zara Mainwaring's wedding at the small and exceedingly attractive Chelsea Old Church.[1] There were few people in the church, as the service was at 1.45, but the bride looked radiantly lovely compared with her somewhat morose-looking bridegroom. With astonishing inappropriateness the last hymn chosen was "Through the Night of Doubt and Sorrow" – which before the wedding night seemed a strange choice.

Flushed with champagne I motored down to Camfield to stay the week-end with Audrey Paget.

---

[1] Entirely destroyed by a land-mine the following April.

Saturday, November 16th

Audrey and I rode for an hour and then I took her, lovely in her new M.T.C. uniform,[1] to Cambridge where I lunched in Hall at Trinity with the Master and Fellows on the occasion of the installation of George Trevelyan as Master. I sat between the Dean, Hollond, and the distinguished and charming Dr Adrian, a Nobel Prize winner and probably future Master of Trinity. The Vice Master, Winstanley, made a beautifully turned speech welcoming Trevelyan and the latter replied with a review of the history of the College and a sombre lament on the war and the future.

Monday, November 18th

When I got back to No. 10 Annexe the P.M. was downstairs looking at Intelligence Reports, putting red ink circles round the names of Greek towns and chortling as he thought of the discomfiture of the Italians. Then, after expressing to me his disgust with Admiral Somerville[2] who let twelve Hurricanes bound for Malta take off from an aircraft carrier too soon, so that eight came down in the sea and were lost, he went to bed and slept until the Cabinet was due.

Towards dinner-time, while I was desperately coping with mountainous papers on my desk, the P.M. appeared and, bidding me bring a torch, led me away to look at girders in the basement, intended to support the building. With astonishing agility he climbed over girders, balanced himself on their upturned edges, some five feet above ground, and leapt from one to another without any sign of undue effort. Extraordinary in a man of almost sixty-six who never takes exercise of any sort.

Tuesday, November 19th

A morning of extreme gravity at Church House where the P.M.'s "Cuspidor" had vanished! The real gravity of the situation

---

[1] She was driving for the Polish officers as a member of the Military Transport Corps. "What is it like?" I asked her one day. "Well," she replied, "I have to say Yes, Sir, all day and No, Sir, all night."

[2] Admiral of the Fleet Sir James Somerville, commanding Force H in the Mediterranean. Later C. in C. of the British Fleet in the Far East.

at present lies (i) in the submarine menace, which without the use of bases in Eire is a pressing problem; (ii) the continued failure to deal with the night raiders, which reduced Coventry to ashes despite its quantity of A.A. guns and the 100 Hurricanes which were sent up to defend it. It is vitally important to make the A.I. and the Beaufighters function efficiently or the Germans may be sensible enough to concentrate their attack on town after town and Sheffield, Birmingham, Bristol, Southampton may share Coventry's fate. The P.M. and the Air Ministry are cudgelling their brains.

The Greeks continue their astonishing successes and are now well established on Albanian soil. They are demanding fighter support and in a minor degree we are confronted with the same problem as during the Battle of France. However it looks as if the Greeks of today may avenge the submission of their ancestors to the military supremacy of Rome, and Byron did not die in vain.

I went with the P.M. to Down Street for the night and dined excellently, far beneath the level of the street, with Sir Ralph Wedgwood (brother of the egregious Colonel Jos.[1] and Chairman of the Railway Executive), Cole Deacon (the Secretary) and his wife. The L.P.T.B. do themselves well: caviar (almost unobtainable in these days of restricted imports), Perrier Jouet 1928, 1865 brandy and excellent cigars.

After dinner the Defence Committee, consisting of the Chiefs of Staff, the service Ministers and Pug Ismay, met to discuss the unending topic of air-reinforcements for the Middle East and the difficulty of supplying Greece without dangerously weakening Egypt. That megalomaniac Sir R. Keyes was sent for in the armoured car to attend part of the meeting, presumably connected with "special combined operations".

After midnight I took in a long list of places bombed in London tonight and news of a heavy attack on Birmingham with streams of bombers passing over the country on their way there. "Complete failure of all our methods," commented the P.M. grimly. "Four days have passed since Coventry and no remedy has been found."

[1] Colonel Josiah Wedgwood, outspoken Labour M.P. and friend of Churchill.

Wednesday, November 20th
I breakfasted very well at Down Street and then went to No.
10 where the P.M. worked in the Cabinet Room, demanding
many things which were difficult to find and showing great
reluctance to be photographed by Cecil Beaton who was waiting
patiently outside.

The P.M. feels that as we can hardly give any other sort
of help to Greece we should do all we can financially. In a
minute to the Chancellor of the Exchequer: "I do hope that
this will not be an occasion for the Treasury to do one
of their regular departmental grimaces, which no doubt
are very necessary in ordinary circumstances, but would be
very much out of place now." Another acrobatic tour of the
girders.

Thursday, November 21st
At about 6.00 p.m., Winston having left for Chequers with Seal,
I went over to No. 10 to make up a little lost sleep. But David
Margesson walked in to gossip and disturbed my slumbers. In
common with most Tories – and with Brendan – he is cross with
Bevin who made a speech yesterday condemning the private
profit motive. Whether Bevin is right or wrong, he should not
in a time of supposed national unity raise party issues. There
would be terrible trouble if Conservative Ministers went about
denouncing socialism and proclaimed their panaceas for the
future. David is also annoyed by the continued attacks on him
and points out that the critics of his rigid control of the party in
the House forget that the British Constitution is run on a
two-party system and eschews a multiplicity of political cliques.
In actual fact since 1931 there had been many occasions when
backbenchers had opposed the Government's policy – e.g. the
India Bill and the National Defence Contribution – and David had
often had to warn the Government to modify its intentions
because of feeling in the House. David also said that people who
blamed him for his appointments, always forgot the successful
ones such as Andrew Duncan. The P.M. has taken up the
cudgels on his behalf (as has Attlee!) and wrote a strong letter

to Vyvian Adams[1] recently when the latter attacked David on the adjournment.

Friday, November 22nd
The Greek successes make us all feel better. Rosy prospects of Italy being driven out of Albania and suing for peace begin to unfold, although still based on a good deal of wishful thinking. But the continued shipping losses (more today) are a canker which urgently needs the surgeon's knife. The night raiders are ravaging Birmingham tonight, but the threat they present is as nothing to that of the submarines.

Saturday, November 23rd
The economic position in Spain is so bad, largely owing to the incompetence and corruption of the Government and their mishandling of an American offer to supply a limited amount of food under guarantees, that Sam Hoare foresees a total collapse entailing the fall of Spain into Axis clutches. Being a born appeaser, Sam H. recommends large credits to Spain and the turning of a blind eye to some supplies from the U.S. percolating through to Germany and Italy.

The censorship reports on letters from France bear witness to the growing volume of support for this country, the rapacity of the Germans, and the striking contrast between the two zones. In unoccupied France there is dazed and listless acquiescence combined with veneration for Pétain. In occupied France there is a spirit of revolt and defiance, longing for an English victory, and a refusal to be either appeased or abashed by the Germans.

After dinner – as usual at the C.W.R., where I am becoming tired of tinned soup and sausages – I took over to the F.O. a Former Naval Person telegram urging Roosevelt to allow controlled amounts of food into Spain in order to avert a collapse. So Sam Hoare *has* been listened to! I drank a glass of rum

---

[1] Conservative M.P. for Leeds and Director of Home Intelligence at the Ministry of Information.

with Bill Bentinck,[1] Fitzroy Maclean* and Edward Warner and listened to Bill B.'s comments on the P.M.'s "rococo style".

Sunday, November 24th

Yugoslavia seems to be on the brink of the abyss and Sir Ronald Campbell[2] has sent a request for permission to assure the Prince Regent that if he resists Axis pressure we will "supply him with all the help in our power". This of course is small, but we can at least guarantee to restore the country when victory has been won. Ronnie Campbell's proposed communication to the Yugoslavs was typical of the F.O. at its worst: long-winded, reserved and unilluminating.

The P.M. and Halifax both think that the prospects held out by the Greek triumph are great, but the P.M. in a minute to Halifax says: "I greatly fear a German attack through Bulgaria. Every effort should be made to firm up Turkey and Yugoslavia against this. The impending fortnight is momentous."

Lunched at White's where I met and conversed with Lord Lloyd, whose life as Colonial Secretary is much burdened by Jews and Arabs. He is a strong man and yet a curiously uncertain one – and a little bit inclined to whine. He expressed great hopes that the P.M. would be careful in his dealings with de Gaulle and Spears, who returned from Africa this week-end, and would at all costs not re-employ Spears.

Went to the American Embassy to get a telegram which had just arrived from the President (about the French fleet) and found Herschel Johnson, now Head of the U.S. Mission to the Court of St James, sitting alone sadly typing the telegram with one finger. Such is the effect of Sunday afternoon even in war-time. Pétain has promised to let the President know before the *Richelieu* or the *Jean Bart* are moved from Dakar and Casablanca into the Mediterranean.

A quiet night. London has been very little bombed for the last

[1] Victor Frederick William, last Duke of Portland. During the war he was Chairman of the Joint Intelligence Committee to the great satisfaction of the three service departments and of the Intelligence Services.

[2] Sir Ronald Ian Campbell. easily confused with Sir Ronald Hugh Campbell, Ambassador in Paris and in Lisbon.

week in spite of clear weather. The Germans have apparently learned that they cannot break our spirits by fear and they are wisely concentrating their night efforts on industry. Bristol suffered tonight; Southampton last night.

Monday, November 25th
Rode in a fog at Richmond on an excellent old hunter of Louis Greig's.

The P.M. returned at lunch-time and busied himself with picking holes in a F.O. telegram giving the pros and cons of pushing Turkey into war. He demanded a report on the subject while he was having lunch – an unreasonable request which caused much perturbation to me and the F.O. Having settled the matter to everybody's satisfaction but the P.M.'s, Jim Bowker and I went off to lunch harmoniously at the Wyndham Club. Jim points out that the reasons for keeping Turkey out of the war are stronger than those for driving her in; but the whole question depends on whether we shall be able to bring her in at the psychological moment.

Spent much time running between No. 10 and the Annexe (the Marines, who act as messengers at the Annexe, move so slowly and with such dignity) in order to procure papers which the P.M. demanded.

Thursday, November 28th
I got back to No. 10 by 9.30 and was disgusted to find that in my absence (on forty-eight hours' leave) the *Daily Express* had published an article by Mr Ingersoll of the American paper *P.M.* who described his interview with Winston and added a large and inaccurate account of what I had told him. He described me as a "dark, slim man in the middle thirties"! and proceeded to put into my mouth the cheapest account of a largely fictitious conversation. Winston was, I believe, furious and I feel both ashamed and angry.

Lady Londonderry[1] has written a deplorable letter asking the

---

[1] Edith, Marchioness of Londonderry, wife of Churchill's cousin who had been Secretary of State for Air in Ramsay MacDonald's National Government. Travel to Northern Ireland was strictly limited to those on military or civilian business.

P.M. to relax the restrictions in force in order to let relations and guests go over to Northern Ireland for the wedding of Derek Keppel[1] and Mairi Stewart. I wanted to send a damping reply to this outrageous request, but Mrs C., who can never resist an opportunity of taking the opposite view, insists on being polite and would get Winston to intervene with the Home Secretary if she could.[2]

Dined at the C.W.R., worked a little and then John Martin and I sat gossiping with Brendan at No. 10 until after midnight. Brendan was feeling in an iconoclastic mood and spent most of the time attacking Chamberlain for his failure to rearm the country. It seems to me that the blame must be sought in the theory of Government upheld by the Baldwin régime: namely that it is the function of democratic government to act in accordance with public opinion rather than to form public opinion. From 1931–38 the people of this country were against rearmament and pacifist in sentiment. The Government did not attempt to oppose the people's wishes; perhaps their fault lay in pandering to those wishes by statements tending to over-estimate our strength and readiness. We were lulled by Baldwinian assurances into a sleep from which it took more than the mere outbreak of war to disturb us.

Today John Peck, who lunched with me at the Wyndham, aptly described Randolph Churchill as "carrying on a perpetual preventive war".

Friday, November 29th
The P.M. having gone to Chequers yesterday to celebrate his sixty-sixth birthday and the christening of his grandson, life in London was quiet and there was time to dispose of much accumulated correspondence.

I had breakfast at No. 10, went for a walk in the cold sunlight, visited Coutts and broke my resolution to give up smoking Chesterfields.

Jim Bowker took me down to dine and spend the night in a charming Regency house he has taken on the Green at Kew

---

[1] Elder brother of my friend Cynthia Keppel.
[2] This would undoubtedly have led to a hostile Parliamentary Question.

(No. 71). Its rooms are beautifully proportioned, its view on both sides is of grass and trees, its external appearance is as pleasant as the interior. After dinner we settled down comfortably, Jim to finish some work, I to browse in a coarse but attractive book of Defoe's called *Moll Flanders*. But it was a noisy night, the worst since MOONLIGHT SONATA, and the sky was red with fires and flares. Periodically we slipped off our chairs and lay prone on the floor as a bomb came whistling down in the vicinity. Just as I had got into bed three fell together and shook the house to its foundations.

Saturday, November 30th
We got up in the dark, breakfasted and returned to London. The F.O. now begin work at 9.00 a.m. – two hours earlier than normal.

It is the P.M.'s birthday and the atmosphere is thick with messages and telegrams of congratulation.

The P.M. has at last completed his long letter to Roosevelt, on the lines suggested to him by Lothian. I was put to great exertions having the letter printed for the Cabinet, having it telegraphed to Washington and besieging the Treasury, Foreign Office and Admiralty with demands for comments.

The main focus of the letter is the serious shipping position. "The decision for 1941 lies upon the seas", is the predominant note.

The danger of Great Britain being destroyed by a swift overwhelming blow, has for the time being very greatly receded. In its place there is a long gradually maturing danger, less sudden and less spectacular, but equally deadly . . . It is in shipping, and the power to transport across the oceans, particularly the Atlantic Ocean, that in 1941 the crunch of the whole war will be found. If, on the other hand, we are able to move the necessary tonnage to and fro across salt water indefinitely, it may well be that the application of superior air power to the German homeland and the rising anger of the German and other Nazi-gripped populations, will bring the agony of civilisation to a merciful and glorious end. But let us not underrate the task . . .

He ends by a reference to the financial question which both sides know must soon be broached (Lothian has already said so indiscreetly to pressmen on his return to the U.S.). One extract, which the Chancellor of the Exchequer has now recommended should be altered, runs as follows:

While we will do our utmost, and shrink from no proper sacrifice to make payments across the Exchange, I should not myself be willing, even in the height of this struggle, to divest Great Britain of every conceivable saleable asset, so that after the victory was won with our blood and sweat, and civilisation saved and the time gained for the United States to be fully armed against all eventualities, we should stand stripped to the bone. Such a course would not be in the moral or economic interests of either of our countries.

He gives details of the assistance we need: merchant shipping, destroyers, American help in obtaining the Eire bases, use of American men-of-war to convoy American merchant vessels; and he ends a fifteen-page letter by saying: "If, as I take it, you are satisfied, Mr President, that the defeat of the Nazi and Fascist tyranny is a matter of high consequence to the people of the United States and to the Western Hemisphere, you will regard this letter not as an appeal for aid, but as a statement of the minimum action necessary to achieve our common purpose."

Lunched at the Wyndham with Charles Peake and Sammy Hood, who tell me Duff Cooper is very lazy. They are anxious that we should be rid of George Steward from No. 10 as being indolent and ineffective. I stood up for him then and afterwards with Brendan.

I dined at White's with Pat Hancock. We drank excellent burgundy, smoked huge cigars and became very mellow. Pat describes Dalton as capable but unlovable.

Note on an Intelligence Summary in which Leros was called by its Greek name: General Ismay. Leros only is to be used in these reports. Also Constantinople instead of Istanbul."

TWELVE

MARKING TIME
DECEMBER 1940

Monday, December 2nd
I have never spent a more exacting day. Although the P.M. did
not return from Chequers till after lunch (and was greeted with
yet another letter of resignation from Lord Beaverbrook), I was
confronted with the necessity of dealing with birthday greetings,
the ordinary post, Parliamentary Questions (Miss Watson being
ill) and the usual medley of current operational matters.

The P.M., Mrs C. and Eden dined at the Annexe, which is
now coming into full use, and I acted as watchdog.

Am re-reading *Pride and Prejudice* at the behest of Pat
Hancock who says my character has many of Mr Darcy's traits.
Curiously enough Gay always used to say he was her ideal
character in fiction, but I don't think Pat meant it in an altogether
complimentary sense.

Tuesday, December 3rd
The P.M. began by saying he would work at the Annexe,
where he had breakfast, and then, maddened by hammering,
transferred the seat of Government to No. 10. As always when
these last-minute changes of mind take place, there was much
confusion and a good deal of ill-temper.

At 12.00 noon the Chiefs of Staff arrived to discuss operation
WORKSHOP, by Sir Roger Keyes and his Commandos, in the
Mediterranean. [The proposed seizure of the Italian island of
Pantellaria.] While this was happening I read a curious document

by Liddell-Hart who advocates peace with Germany since he believes we can only overthrow the Nazis by propaganda and cannot, in the military field, expect more than a stalemate, with exhaustion, disease and devastation on both sides, if indeed we are not defeated. This document, which has been privately circulated, is thought by the Admiralty to show traces of enemy propaganda and to be not spontaneous. The First Lord has written on it: "Probably no technical correspondent has more responsibility than Liddell-Hart for the accepted military theories propagated before the war and which were so disproved in the Battle of France. I should have thought he would have preferred to hide his head rather than produce still yet another theory as pregnant with defeat as his former theories, which are now proved heresies."

Personally, although preferring anything to the triumph of Nazi principles, which I believe a compromise peace would imply, I cannot help shuddering at the picture which Liddell-Hart presents to the imagination and which may not be far from the truth: Western Europe racked by warfare and economic hardship; the legacy of centuries, in art and culture, swept away; the health of the nation dangerously impaired by malnutrition, nervous strain and epidemics; Russia and possibly the U.S. profiting from our exhaustion; and at the end of it all compromise or a Pyrrhic victory. A terrible glimpse of the future; and yet I know we should be wrong to hesitate, because so great a moral question is at issue. In one thing I believe Liddell-Hart may be right: he says that the fear of sharing Napoleon's fate must embolden Hitler himself, and the belief, based on much that we say over here, in a worse-than-Versailles if they are defeated must encourage the Germans to resist desperately. I am convinced, despite all that Winston says, that a firm but just declaration of peace aims would have a powerful psychological effect in our favour.

Before lunch I listened to a little monologue by the P.M., addressed to the Chiefs of Staff, on the means of helping Greece, by preparing advanced air bases, and on the desirability of putting severe economic pressure on Ireland in order to make her lend us the bases we so badly need. As regards Greece, Sir

John Dill said: "What is Germany doing?" "They are preparing something terrible, said the P.M. He pointed out how carefully the attack on Poland had been planned, how Mussolini had been drawn into war by the sight of the overwhelming strength deployed against France, and how doubtful Pétain now is, having presumably been told something of Germany's might, about our ability to withstand the attack that is to come.

Back at No. 10 I worked the epidiascope in the Cabinet Room and showed the P.M. and Sir R. Keyes large-scale photographs of the objective of OPERATION WORKSHOP.

The P.M.'s comment on the First Lord's note about Liddell-Hart is: "It is out of date and he seems more a candidate for a mental home than for more serious action."

The P.M. changed his mind at least eight times as to whether he would sleep and dine at No. 10 or at the Annexe and three times as to what time he would see Dr Dalton (whom he dislikes).

At dinner he conspired with Cranborne, Rob Hudson, Kingsley Wood and Oliver Lyttelton about the means of bringing pressure to bear on Ireland. Refusal to buy her food, to lend her our shipping or to pay her our present subsidies seem calculated to bring De Valera to his knees in a very short time. On the other hand the Irish are an explosive race and economic coercion might mean trouble. But the issues at stake justify risks.

Wednesday, December 4th
In speaking to the C.A.S. the P.M. demanded that in view of the Germans' systematic attack on each of our towns in turn, we should reconsider a real mass-scale attack on one German town followed by the publication of a list of German towns which we shall duly devastate if the Germans continue their present policy against us.

My time has been much occupied with the vexed question whether the church bells should be rung on Christmas Day.[1]

[1] In the preceding summer it had been decreed that church bells were only to be rung as a signal of invasion.

The P.M. was disposed to say yes in reply to a Parliamentary Question, but after much discussion the C. in C., Home Forces, has produced such overwhelming arguments against it that the P.M. has agreed to refuse. I was in a position to get the Question answered affirmatively before the contrary arguments could be marshalled, and I all but did so; but then the thought of the responsibility that would be mine if any disaster occurred on Christmas Day made me pause.

After lunch David Margesson asked me whether Beaverbrook had withdrawn his resignation. We both agreed it was time he went; he has done his job. "Who would you suggest putting in his place? Moore-Brabazon?" I asked. "Stafford Cripps", was the astonishing reply from the Tory Chief Whip. David pointed out that Stafford Cripps' outstanding ability was being wasted in Moscow, where little can be done as is now lamentably clear, whereas at home Cripps would not only be a great asset as a Minister but also a counter-weight to Bevin in the Labour Party. Bevin is inclined to throw his weight about too much.

I remarked to David on the excellence of Winston's latest long letter to the President. David answered that he wished W. were as great an administrator as he is leader, orator and writer. The criticism is a fair one.

"This place," said the Prime Minister, as he entered the Annexe after the evening Cabinet, "is too hot. Tell them to turn off the central heating." And the same man complained, on the hottest of June nights at Admiralty House, because his fire had not been lit!

Thursday, December 5th
At 8.30, as soon as it was light, I mounted one of Louis Greig's horses and galloped round Richmond Park, relieving my lungs of nights of air-conditioning and glorying in the cold sunrise.

Cripps, whose telegrams are always to the point and never long-winded like some Ambassadors, says in speaking of Anglo-Soviet relations: "While I do not advocate impatience or irritation I disagree that we should at present appear helpful or forthcoming. Having received no encouragement whatever as regards either our political or our commercial proposals, we

365

should at all costs avoid the appearance of running after the Soviet Government (which would only be interpreted as weakness) and should await advances from them." Seldom do left-wing ideologists take so realistic a view. Cripps, I feel sure, will go far, whether Right or Left are in control. He is much the ablest man in the Labour Party.

After dinner John Peck and I sat down to the three-hour task of sticking Lord Lothian's comments on the P.M.'s letter to Roosevelt on pieces of paper next to the P. M.'s original text. It was a complicated and laborious job but we thought we did it rather skilfully.

Friday, December 6th
The P.M. was not at all gracious about our handiwork and complained that we had had parts of the text retyped instead of sticking in every unamended word of the print. However his irritability was due to the fact that he did not care for many of Lothian's alterations and he described the whole thing as a "bloody business".

Lunched with Arthur Rucker. We talked of old times at No. 10 and the great differences that have taken place. Arthur said he chiefly remembered the unimportant incidents such as when he stole my umbrella; I said that keeping a diary helped one to remember the more important events. "A very dangerous document," commented Arthur. And I suppose this one is.

As we walked back we met P. J. Grigg, who after running down his Secretary of State as usual, said that the only time he had any real power was when he was Private Secretary (to Winston as Chancellor of the Exchequer).

Monday, December 9th
Motored from Hinchingbrooke back to London, where the great excitement is the beginning of our offensive against the Italian army in Egypt. The P.M., who returned from Chequers after lunch with a cold in the head, said to the C.I.G.S. on the telephone: "So we shan't have to make use of General Papagos[1]

[1] Commander in Chief of the Greek army in its outstanding success against the Italian aggressors.

after all!" implying that at last our generals are living up to the Greek example of boldness and initiative.

Tuesday, December 10th
The news from North Africa is increasingly good. Though the operation is a small one, it shows the inability of the Italians to stand up to attack – if indeed any proof were required.

Wednesday, December 11th
The P.M. had been going down to Harrow today, with all the Old Harrovian members of the Government, to hear School Songs. However his cold is heavier and the trip had to be postponed.

In the Censorship Report (which incidentally shows a certain lower-class opinion, apparently worked on by propaganda, that the war is being engineered for financial and upper-class interests), I marked a number of passages which I thought particularly interesting and I noticed that the P.M. marked in red ink one phrase quoted from a letter: "It's difficult to think politically, or socially, in classes any more . . . *there's a kind of warmth pervading England.*" An extract that amused me was from a letter written by an East End Jew:

> It is terrible here at night – every night. Lord God, what have we done to deserve it? Death rains from the Clouds . . . Now, there is abundance of food which, though dear, we could well pay for; (never was the shop so profitable; people pay what you ask without question) but the raids, the machine-gunning, it is murder. The English are not so highly strung as we. They do not seem to mind until they actually see some of their own family killed in front of their noses. Then, instead of being frightened or praying, they say: "Damn those bloody bastards".

Just before dinner the P.M. rang up the King to tell him the glad news that Sidi Barrani had fallen. "My humble congratulations to you, Sir, on a great British victory – a great Imperial victory."

It is the first time since war began that we have really been able to make use of the word victory.

One of the P.M.'s first reactions – a curious one – was to ask to see and peruse the two books General Wavell has written.

Thursday, December 12th
At Church House the P.M. made a subdued but very welcome statement on the North African operations.

Drove myself down to Chequers in my own car and arrived there an hour before the P.M. I had tea in the White Parlour with Mary, who has an adorable sheepdog puppy and who was full of charm and gossip. She was also very anxious to read my diary but was with difficulty restrained.

Lord Lothian died suddenly in Washington; a tragic blow to our relations with the United States where his ability was so marked and his drive so fruitful.

Mrs Churchill having a migraine, Mary and I dined alone with the P.M. He began by saying he was going to read his book (Boswell's *Tour to the Hebrides*) – "you children can talk" – but the tastelessness of the soup so excited his frenzy that he rushed out of the room to harangue the cook and returned to give a disquisition on the inadequacy of the food at Chequers and the fact that ability to make good soup is the test of a cook. Having mastered his indignation he began to lament the death of Lothian and to demand who he should put in his place. He would like to try L.G. if he could trust him. I suggested Cranborne or Vansittart. He had thought of both and considered Cranborne particularly suitable. But as the evening wore on he "sweetened to the idea of L.G.", as he put it, saying that his knowledge of munitions problems and his fiery personality marked him out. He thought L.G. would be willing to serve and in order to sweeten the pill of serving under Halifax (which I suggested would be an obstacle from L.G.'s point of view) he would make him a member of the War Cabinet. He believed L.G. would be loyal to him; if not he could always sack him. The suitability of Cranborne, on which he had waxed eloquent, slowly receded into the background, and when I suggested that Cripps was being wasted in Russia, he replied that he was a lunatic in a country of lunatics and it would be a pity to move him.

Mary left us and I had a long tête-à-tête with Winston over the brandy. He grew very expansive, elated by the thought of our successes, continually growing in size, in North Africa. He spoke of the dignity of the Italians, who possessed every requisite for Empire except courage, and of the terrible miscalculation they had made about us. We had had a wonderful escape in these last months and it was now difficult to remember what we had been through.

Talking of the future he sketched the European Confederations that would have to be formed ("with their Diets of Worms") and shuddered as he thought of the intricate currency problems, etc. He did not understand such things and he would be out of it. He did not wish to lead a party struggle or a class struggle against the Labour leaders who were now serving him so well. He would retire to Chartwell and write a book on the war, which he already had mapped out in his mind chapter by chapter. This was the moment for him; he was determined not to prolong his career into the period of reconstruction. I said I thought he would be demanded by the people; there was no other leader. (This was not just Boswellian; there is not at present any man of the right calibre, nor any sign of one on the horizon.)

After a few slashes at Baldwin for not making better use of the sanctions period against Italy, he moved from the dining-room, with his multi-coloured dressing-gown over his siren-suit, rang up Gwylym Lloyd George to sound him about his father, and then stood beaming in front of the fire in the Great Hall. He asked if I had heard L.G. during the debate in which the Chamberlain Government fell. I said I had, and deplored Chamberlain's mistake in saying "I have my friends" to the hostile minority in the House. The P.M. said it had been a wonderful opportunity for him: the stars in their courses had fought on his side. He had been able to defend his chief to the utmost and only to win esteem and support in so doing. No one could say he had been disloyal or had intrigued against Chamberlain – "and I never have done that sort of thing".

Remarking that tomorrow was Friday, 13th, I said that last year, on Friday, November 13th, the B.B.C. had gloated over the date as having been a bad one for German submarines. Four hours later the *Royal Oak* was sunk. "I wrote that communiqué," replied Winston laconically. I subsided.

After some observations on the utility of his system of personal minutes to Ministers, and some praise by me of the effectiveness of "Action this Day", the P.M. retired into the Hawtrey room and dictated telegrams to the Dominions and the U.S. To bed at 1.20 a.m.

Friday, December 13th

When the P.M. spoke to Halifax about the Washington appointment, H. suggested Eden (who would not take it) and then Lord Dudley, but seemed quite to approve of L.G.

The Chief of the Air Staff spoke about ABIGAIL, an operation whereby we shall single out a German town, as they singled out Coventry, and destroy it, at the same time allowing a list of German towns destined for a similar fate to become known. The moral scruples of the Cabinet on this subject have been overcome.

There was a question, much discussed on the telephone, whether the Duke of Devonshire[1] was to be given the Garter. The P.M. kept on repeating that he was not bad as Dukes go and that anyway there was "no damned merit about it".

General de Gaulle and Major Morton came to lunch. The P.M. held forth in his execrable but expressive French. There was a good deal of purring over Sidi Barrani, which de G. said would make an excellent name for the battle. "No," said the P.M., "it should be called the Battle of Libya." There was an interlude while we talked about eating octopuses, as the Italians do, and as I have done in Sicily; then we got on to the serious topic of war. What were the Germans going to do? De Gaulle said, as Winston said last night, that Spain seemed the obvious

---

[1] Edward, 10th Duke of Devonshire, successively Under Secretary for the Dominions, India and the Colonies under Chamberlain and Churchill. At this time the Garter and the Thistle were still bestowed on the recommendation of the Prime Minister, a practice Mr Attlee renounced in 1945.

objective, and through Spain Africa. But the Spanish people, *"fier et misérable"*, might well resist.

De Gaulle said he thought we should make more of the fact that we stood alone, *"le champion du monde"* against Hitler, and if we were accepted as such all our actions would be excused; Oran would seem natural, merely because the world was at stake. Winston said he was inclined to lay stress on the fact that we were fighting the Nazis rather than Germany, even though many an Englishman now had murderous thoughts towards the whole German race. "But," objected de Gaulle, "we fought the last war against the Hohenzollerns and German militarism; we crushed them both; and then came Hitler – *et toujours le militarisme allemand*. So there was something to be said for those who blamed the Germans as a whole."

De Gaulle said that Laval hated this country, but would try and keep out of war. Darlan, on the other hand, might well take an opportunity to bring in the French fleet against us: *"La France ne marchera pas, mais la flotte – peut-être."*

The conversation then turned to the relationship of de Gaulle and Spears, which is correct though not cordial (de G. finds S. intelligent but egotistic and hampering because of his unpopularity in the War Office, etc.). After lunch Ismay arrived and a future operation of the Free French forces was discussed. I went for a long solitary walk through the woods and up the hills, almost killing myself by going too fast up a steep hill (it is shattering to be in such a bad state of training – and I have visions of joining one of the Commandos!).

I had tea with Mary and some Coldstream officers and then the P.M. worked till dinner-time. We wanted news from the War Office ("that House of Shame", Pug calls it): the C.I.G.S. had gone off for ten days' leave and the V.C.I.G.S., in charge of the W.O., was found to know less up-to-date news than anyone else in the building. People condemn the Civil Servants; but what of the serving officers!

The V.C.N.S. (Tom Phillips) and Prof. came to dinner. We began with talk of the Sidi Barrani operation, COMPASS as it was called, the best-kept secret of the war. The P.M. said he had been living on hopes of it for five weeks and had been terrified some sandstorm would give the men on the spot a chance to back out. It had been well planned and brilliantly executed, unlike Narvik which of all the fiascos for which he had had any responsibility had been the worst – except for Dakar.

What a monstrous thing, exclaimed the P.M., that Lothian should not have allowed a doctor to be called ("I had at last come to like Philip, after years of prejudice"). "Is anyone here a Christian Scientist?" "Well," said Prof., "I am if you divide the two words – a Christian and a Scientist." "I am willing to admit you may have some claim to be the latter." "Which is the only one of the two on which you have any qualifications to judge."

The P.M. reverted, in some detail, to his ideas for the future. We had got to admit that Germany was going to remain in the European family. "Germany existed before the Gestapo." When we had won he visualised five great European nations: England, France, Italy, Spain and Prussia. In addition there would be four confederations: the Northern, with its capital at The Hague; the Mitteleuropa, with its capital at Warsaw or Prague; the Danubian, consisting of Bavaria, Württemberg, Austria, Hungary, etc., with its capital at Vienna; and the Balkan with Turkey at its head and Constantinople as its capital. These nine powers would meet in a Council of Europe, which would have a supreme judiciary and a Supreme Economic Council to settle currency questions, etc. Each power would contribute an air cohort – Prussia included – and boys of sixteen would be selected for it. Once enrolled they would be under no national jurisdiction, but they would never be obliged to co-operate in an attack on their own country. All air forces, military and civil, would be internationalised. As regards armies, every power would be allowed its own militia, because Democracy must be based on a people's army and not left to oligarchs or Secret Police. Prussia alone would, for a hundred years, be denied all armaments beyond her air contingent. The Council would be unrestricted in its methods of dealing with a Power condemned by the remainder in Council.

The English speaking world would be apart from this, but closely connected with it, and it alone would control the seas, as the reward of victory. It would be bound by covenant to respect the trading and colonial rights of all peoples, and England and America would have exactly equal navies. Russia would fit into an Eastern re-organisation, and the whole problem of Asia would have to be faced. But as far as Europe was concerned, only by such a system of Confederations could the small powers continue to exist and we must at all costs avoid the old mistake of "Balkanising" Europe.

There would be no war debts, no reparations and no demands on Prussia. Certain territories might have to be ceded and certain exchanges of population, on the lines of that so success-fully effected by Greece and Turkey, would have to take place. But there should be no pariahs and Prussia, though unarmed, would be secured by the guarantee of the Council of Europe. Only the Nazis, the murderers of June 30th, 1934,[1] and the Gestapo would be made to suffer for their misdeeds.

But all this was a thing of the still distant future: we might have to give it one hundred years to work. At present he could utter no such ideals when every cottage in Europe was calling for German blood and when the English themselves were demanding that all Germans should be massacred or castrated.

We all liked this "Grand Design", powerfully expounded as it was and I very much hope that Winston may live to lay its foundations. My only comments, unvoiced, were, "Supposing the members of the European Council divided themselves into axes or armed camps? War would still be possible, even with national militias, and the international air contingents could easily fly their machines home – even though they had become *dépaysé* at sixteen. Moreover, would the mere disarmament of Prussia render impotent the traditions of force and ruthlessness in which generations have been reared or eradicate the evil teaching impregnated by Nazism in the minds of young Germans?" What-ever Winston would have replied, his scheme is a noble and lofty one, worthy of his fine imagination and his sensitiveness to the lessons history has taught. His reverence for tradition (which

[1] The Night of the Long Knives when Hitler had the S.A. (brown-shirt) leaders and his predecessor as Chancellor, General Schleicher, murdered by black-uniformed S.S.

he would never allow to warp his judgment of what is expedient) is shown in his statement that Spain should remain a separate unit because of the individuality with which her past, as well as her geographical position, invests her.

We ended dinner by discussing a projected German operation, which seems aimed either at Ireland or Spain. The P.M. thinks Spain; he would go that way if he were Hitler. We discussed our strategy either in the event of Spain resisting or allowing German troops to pass.

The P.M. was much incensed by a request of Seal's that all the staff at No. 10 should be allowed a week's Christmas leave. He said that we should all go on working as usual with the exception of one and a half hours off for divine service! Continuity of work never harmed anyone.

A late despatch rider brought telegrams from Tangier announcing the intention of the Spanish Government to take over the International Zone. This together with their allowing two damaged Italian submarines to escape from Tangier has infuriated H.M.G. and the F.O. have drafted a – for them – severe telegram threatening not to allow the Spaniards the cargoes of wheat they want and without which Spain, *"fier et misérable"*, will starve.

The P.M. thinks this a sign of big things to come and believes the projected German operation (called FELIX), about which we know, will be in Spain. This may entail a drastic re-organisation of four or five of our own operations (BRISK, SHRAPNEL, EXCESS, CHALLENGE, etc.) which are pending, as he considers it would be undesirable to have our forces and our transports "sprawled" about the world at such a moment.

The F.O. had foolishly kept no copy of their telegram and I had laboriously to dictate it back to the Resident Clerk (who failed to produce a shorthand typist) a task which took me until nearly 3.00 a.m.

Saturday, December 14th
At about 6.00 a.m. Nelson woke me by climbing on to my bed and preparing to go to sleep on my feet. I am a little suspicious of black cats: they always seem to frequent me on the eve of

great events. The Treasury Cat (or "Munich Mouser" as the Churchills call him) very seldom paid me any attention, but on two or three occasions I found him curled up on my blotting pad at No. 10: once at the time of the Norwegian crisis and once at the worst moment of the Battle of France. But perhaps Nelson, on the eve of a Spanish crisis, may portend another Trafalgar.

The P.M. was amusing last night about the North African campaign. He said we had taken the right course: we had risked sending troops and material to Egypt when still under the threat of invasion at home, and we had sent substantial air assistance to Greece in spite of the fact that we were preparing for a "Spring of the Lion" in North Africa. But if events had taken a different course, as they might have, what would history have said? He quoted dramatically from a mythical history book of the future, denouncing the criminal gambler who sent overseas the divisions which might have turned the scale against the German invasion at home, or the vacillators who sent to Greece the aeroplanes which could have turned the North African fiasco into a success. It was a good commentary on my favourite, and boring, thesis about the ease of being wise after the event.

Pound, Portal and Haining (the V.C.I.G.S.) arrived at 11.00 and went into conference with the P.M., Ismay and Phillips until lunch-time. Sir Roger Keyes arrived late and Lord Halifax, who thought we were at Ditchley and went there by mistake (the fault being the P.M.'s) only reached Chequers at the end of lunch. There was the usual chortling over our North African exploits and the effect they would have on our prestige in the world. "We have now reached the stage," said Phillips, "where we shall suddenly find we have got many more friends than we thought." The P.M. enjoys mocking the Italians, whose civilisation and achievements he greatly admires but of whom he finds it easy and irresistible to make fun.

I found Haining very agreeable and informative on the methods of obtaining information from enemy prisoners and occupied territories. Apparently as far as the latter is concerned we worked on a system with the French, and their defection left a gap in our organisation.

After lunch the conference about Tangier and Spain continued in the Hawtrey room. I drove off through the blizzard to Ditchley, taking with me one of the telephone girls, a nice creature whose attitude to life was largely summed up in the fact that the thing she chiefly admired in Chester was the new café. Her husband was in the balloon barrage and she said military discipline had taken something away from his character which could never be replaced.

Ditchley is a lovely house and still kept up in pre-war style. On arrival, about an hour before the P.M., I found Ronnie Tree* and his very attractive wife, Mrs Churchill, Lady Cranborne and Brendan. General Alexander,[1] the new C. in C., Southern Command, an unusually delightful person, arrived to dine and sleep. The P.M. spent most of the time before dinner showing him the Prof.'s albums, while I sat in my Louis Quinze office and drank an Old Fashioned cocktail.

The Trees, who are very hospitable, put the house entirely at the P.M.'s disposal. They are of course delighted to have him, but it must be something of a trial when he arrives with such a vast following.

There was a large dinner party, at which I sat between the Duchess of Marlborough and Ronnie Tree, with both of whom I had very pleasant conversations. After dinner there was a film: Charlie Chaplin's *The Great Dictator* which has not yet been released in this country and which everyone has been eagerly awaiting. Mary Rose Fitzroy[2] and Dinah Brand,[3] who are living here but have been turned out for the week-end, came over for the film and stayed to talk and eat afterwards. That affected marine, Alastair Forbes, and a young Australian called Booth, handsome but rough, to whom I gathered Dinah Brand is engaged, were also of the party.

The film, at which we all laughed a great deal – Mary Rose moaning pitifully with excessive mirth – being over, Winston dictated to me a short telegram to Roosevelt, asking whether

[1] Later Field Marshal Earl Alexander of Tunis.
[2] Sister of John, Duke of Grafton, my contemporary at Harrow and Cambridge. She married Francis Williams.
[3] Delightful daughter of the Hon. Robert Brand, the Treasury adviser. Afterwards Mrs Christopher Bridge.

L.G. would be acceptable as Ambassador, and went to bed early. He twice complimented me on my "beautiful handwriting", which he esteems far beyond its real merits. Roger Keyes, who has been scheming to come to Ditchley for the last two days, rang up and asked point blank. Winston, who is at long last becoming bored with his importunity, refused to speak to him and sent a snubbing answer through me.

Sunday, December 15th
I arose in a leisurely way in my luxurious bedroom, had breakfast and settled down to work with the December sun streaming in through the windows.

General Wavell's comments on past and future operations in North Africa are now beginning to arrive. He says: "Rome will not be unbuilt in a day, but hope recent and future events will shake foundations." Meanwhile we heard last night that Laval has been dismissed and Flandin, who is a little better, put in his place. Also communications with Switzerland have been cut; the last message to reach New York was: "Something big is coming." The P.M. inclines to think this means, not an invasion of Switzerland (which would be pointless) but the preliminaries of an operation against Spain.

Comes a telegram from South Africa saying that Smuts, impressed by the German military potential, thinks our propaganda in the U.S. must be more aggressive and that we must make a supreme effort to bring in America as a belligerent. The military and air power of the British Commonwealth, together with the economic blockade, will be insufficient to bring about Germany's fall even in 1942.

The interminable wrangle between the M.A.P. and the Air Ministry goes on, like The Brook, for ever. But Winston, in a minute this morning to Beaverbrook, says: "I am definitely of the opinion that it is more in the public interest that there should be sharp criticism and counter-criticism between the two departments than that they should be handing each other out ceremonious bouquets."

Beaverbrook is also in trouble from some quarters about the activities of his newspapers which have attacked certain

Ministers. He replies: I do not agree with Low.[1] I have rarely done so. I do not interfere with Low. I have never done so." He goes on to say that he would be much more useful outside the Government and earnestly wishes to resign, and at the end: "The aircraft industry is in good shape. The best work I have done so far is dispersal. That is a policy I adopted in the face of opposition and amidst turmoil and abuse. The little bit of credit I will get on your day of victory will be due to the same policy of dispersal." Result: the usual soothing and appreciative reply from the P.M. who says: "Anyhow, let us keep plodding on together and see how things look in another year. I think they will look much better. Yours ever, W."

At lunch I sat between Richard Law,[2] who is staying here, and the officer commanding the guard. Towards the end Winston and Lord Cranborne, who arrived this morning, had a discussion about the sanctions period and agreed in denouncing Baldwin's thesis that we could exert pressure no further than it might be done with safety.

It was suggested that the Duke of Aosta,[3] now Viceroy of Abyssinia, might be used to head a movement against Mussolini. "Yes," said Winston, "he would desert his tired and about-to-be-emasculated army, enter a sumptuous aeroplane and return to restore the soul of Italy to Democracy!" Mr Justice Singleton,[4] who was lunching, thought that Mussolini might save his position by changing his régime. Winston said that he gave the blighter the credit for being a brave man who would go down with his ship, and, as far as changing his policy was concerned, "I believe it is not in his character; I am sure it is not in his reach."

After lunch the P.M. went off to Blenheim with Lady Cran-

---

[1] The *Evening Standard* cartoonist.
[2] Parliamentary Under Secretary, and later Minister of State, in the Foreign Office. A son of the former Prime Minister, Bonar Law. He was briefly Minister of Education in 1945.
[3] Cousin of the King of Italy and Commander of the Italian army in Abyssinia.
[4] Judge of the High Court and previously an M.P. Commissioned by Churchill to examine all the evidence available about the strength of the German air forces.

borne, and I went for a walk with Ronnie Tree, his wife and Richard Law. I changed my mind about Ronnie Tree, whom I had always looked upon as the epitome of an idle rich Tory M.P. I found him interesting and sensible in his views of the Conservative future: there must be a new Tory Democracy, prepared to sacrifice wealth and vested interest, radical but sensible. In Ronnie Tree's view, the indispensable pre-requisites were to reform the central office, pay candidates' expenses – and get rid of the Chief Whip. I agreed in all but the last. He thought Lloyd George too old for Washington, and I agree. We have the examples of Petain and Hindenburg to warn us. Cranborne, he considered, would be ideal: a man who was already looking ahead to the 1950s, he would be able to make the speeches which American opinion would appreciate.

We reached the front door just as the P.M. and Lady Cranborne returned from Blenheim. The P.M. went straight to bed, to sleep and to work, while I had tea and talked with the charming and modest Lady Cranborne.

Sir R. Keyes, in spite of all injunctions, arrived! He was greeted by an indignant P.M. who, however, agreed to talk to him. His whole aim is to undo the decisions reached at yesterday's conferences, namely that operations WORKSHOP and EXCESS, in which he was to have taken part, should be postponed in view of the threat of developments in Spain or elsewhere. We were all thunderstruck by his audacity: he carries the Zeebrugge spirit too far into private life.

Eden arrived for the night and made himself extremely affable. Ronnie Tree thinks him a future P.M., but I feel that many as are his qualities, they are not very solid.

At dinner Richard Law said to me that the secret of Hitler's power was his demand for sacrifice. The P.M. understood this and his own speeches were brilliant in this respect, but Bevin thought that he could buoy people up by promising them higher wages and better times. He was wrong.

We saw *Gone with the Wind* which lasted till 2.00 a.m. I thought the photography superb. Scarlett reminded me a little bit of Audrey. The P.M. said he was "pulverised by the strength of their feelings and emotions".

After some conversation between the P.M. and Eden about N. Africa I got to bed at 3.00 a.m.; but the P.M., throwing himself on a chair in his bedroom, collapsed between the chair and the stool, ending in a most absurd position on the floor with his feet in the air. Having no false dignity, he treated it as a complete joke and repeated several times, "A real Charlie Chaplin!"

Monday, December 16th
When the P.M.'s party had left Ditchley for London, I said goodbye to Mrs Tree and drove to Ardley. David was just home, after an agonising ordeal on the *Chevreuil* off the coast of Scotland where it seemed at one time as if they were done for. He feels very bitter about the French.

Tuesday, December 17th
In the morning the sun shone brilliantly and while Ann, who is lazy, stayed behind, David, Joan and I walked over to Middleton, visited Lady Jersey and went on to have a drink with Diane Maxwell.[1]

In the afternoon we motored over to Stene to see the Chapel built by Nathaniel, Lord Crewe, Bishop of Oxford and of Durham. The chapel contains the only marble altar in the Church of England, but its real glory are the tombs of the Crewe family, exquisitely sculptured in marble and retaining their original colouring. The inscriptions are most pleasing. Thus of Temperance Crewe, wife of the Speaker, Sir Thomas, it is written:

> *Coniunx Casta, Parens felix, Matrona pudica;*
> *Sara viro, mundo Martha, Maria Deo.*

And in the English inscription she is described as a woman

> *who with her lott was well contented,*
> *who lived desyred and dyed lamented.*

---

[1] Only daughter of Sir Austen Chamberlain, married to Colonel Terence Maxwell, soldier, banker and industrialist.

Little of the episcopal palace remains, but what does forms a very charming country house which David much covets.

Wednesday, December 18th
Motored to London in ice and fog.

After lunch the visit to Harrow, which I had done much to make possible, came off. The P.M. drove down with Mrs Churchill; I with David Margesson; and Amery, Moore Brabazon, Geoffrey Lloyd[1] and Jack Churchill also came. If Sir Donald Somervell, the Attorney General, had not been prevented from coming, all the Old Harrovian members of the administration would have been present.

The school sang well in spite of its depleted numbers, and Winston thoroughly enjoyed himself. An extra verse had been inserted into "Stet Fortuna Domus" in his honour and he asked for two extra songs, "Giants" and "Boy". He sang lustily, as did we all, and seemed to remember most of the words without referring to the book. Before "Forty Years On" he made a brilliant impromptu speech to the school, saying how much Harrow Songs had meant to him, what an inspiration they had been at certain stages of his life, and pointing out that although Hitler claimed the Adolf Hitler Schools had shown their superiority to Eton, he had forgotten Harrow! He then said that after the war the advantages of the Public Schools must be extended to the whole country, on a broader and better basis. He was wildly applauded.

When we got back to No. 10 the P.M. saw Halifax and offered him the Ambassadorship to Washington, L.G. having refused on grounds of age. David Margesson told me in the car on the way to Harrow that Eden would go to the Foreign Office and perhaps Amery to the War Office. David thinks Rab Butler should be given his chance and sent to the India Office.

Friday, December 20th
Over to the Annexe at 8.30. The P.M. gave me a manuscript letter he wished sent to Halifax. It appears that Halifax left the

---

[1] Later Lord Geoffrey-Lloyd.*

decision about Washington in the P.M.'s hands and the P.M. has decided he shall go. Probably Sir Gerald Campbell will be made Minister and thus H. will be able to return frequently to this country where he will still be a member of the War Cabinet.

Before lunch the P.M. discoursed to me on the difficulty of his interview with Halifax, who told him yesterday that both his judgment and his inclination were against going to Washington. But, said the P.M., he would never live down the reputation for appeasement which he and the F.O. had won themselves here. He had no future in this country. On the other hand he had a glorious opportunity in America; because unless the U.S. came into the war we could not win, or at least we could not win a really satisfactory peace. If Halifax succeeded in his mission over there, he would come home on the crest of the wave. The P.M.'s judgment has, I think, been considerably influenced by the monthly Censorship Reports which show Halifax to be unpopular over here and to have inherited the criticism that was Chamberlain's.

The P.M. lunched with Beaverbrook and L.G. and upset everybody very much by appearing to listen to the former's wild remarks about the proposed Cabinet reshuffle (consequent on Halifax's appointment) and to a suggestion that L.G. should enter the Government in some agricultural capacity, in which he would certainly quarrel with Rob Hudson.

Everyone waited for the departure to Chequers, but when all was ready the P.M. suddenly went off to his bedroom and slept – keeping us all hanging about for hours. I talked to David Margesson who told me that if he had "carried bigger guns" he would so much have liked to go to Washington. He had been pressed to go to the War Office, but had refused because he did not think himself suitable for the job. The P.M.'s present intention was that he should go to the Dominions Office, where his lack of departmental experience – he had been in the Whip's office since 1924 – would not matter so much. Actually I think his great organising capacity, about which Gay and Jan wax eloquent to the disparagement of all his other qualities, might be very advantageous in the proverbially incompetent War Office.

Saturday, December 21st
Quiet reigned.

Among the papers returning from Chequers was a letter offering a peerage to Lord Hugh Cecil[1] "to repel the onset of the Adolf Hitler Schools, to sustain the aristocratic morale, and to chide the bishops when they err; and now that I read in the newspapers that the Eton flogging block is destroyed by enemy action, you may have more leisure and strength. Anyhow I should like to see a brother Hughligan in the legislature . . ."

In a note to Lord Halifax: "We have not had anything from the U.S. that we have not paid for and what we have had has not played an essential part in our resistance."

David Margesson rang up Chequers and afterwards told me on the telephone that he had been pressed into accepting the War Office. I congratulated him warmly and sincerely. He said he was pleased in that it was a great honour, but he was very diffident about his capacity to undertake it. I said I should have to treat him with greater respect in future. "No you won't, old boy," he replied.

He will have to speak in the House which will give his former subjects a chance of getting their own back. He thought they would enjoy that, and I have little doubt they will make the best of their opportunities.

Sunday, December 22nd
Went to the early service in St Faith's chapel, lit with candles and crowded.

Lunched with Sammy Hood, and then after an afternoon's work drove down to Farnham to stay with the Kemsleys. The

---

[1] Son of the 3rd Marquess of Salisbury, Prime Minister at the turn of the century. Best man at Churchill's wedding and leader of the rebel "Hughligans" in the Commons, a group which had included Churchill. Devout Churchman and prominent member of the Church Assembly. Became Provost of Eton in 1936 though he had hated his own schooldays there and disliked schoolboys.

The "Hughligans" were a group of four young Tory M.P.s who frequently attacked their own Government, of which A. J. Balfour was Prime Minister, shortly after the turn of the century.

last thing I did before leaving was to release the information about the Cabinet changes; the first thing I heard on arrival was Lord Kemsley receiving the news from his office. He gave instructions that Halifax's and Eden's appointments were to be applauded but David Margesson was not to be greeted with open arms.

During dinner, at which Lord and Lady K., Pam and Lionel Berry, and an atrociously affected young man called Sir John Phillips were present, we had a hot discussion about the War Office appointment. I upheld David's appointment very strongly and emphasised his organising ability. Lord Kemsley said a good businessman would have been better. I pointed out that the Government of the country is based on the House of Commons: we already have four outsiders in the administration, Duncan, Woolton, Reith and Oliver Lyttelton; to appoint another would be to make a mockery of Parliamentary institutions – and anyhow David ought to be given a chance, by the public and the press.

Tuesday, December 24th

Came up from Farnham early and found a great accumulation of work. After lunch the P.M. signed a number of books, which he is giving us all as Christmas presents, and sent off presents to the King and Queen: a siren-suit for the King and Fowler's *English Usage* for the Queen! As he left the room he said, remembering our plea for a Christmas holiday, "A busy Christmas and a frantic New Year."

Dined at the C.W.R. gaily festooned with Christmas decorations. We are not going to bomb Germany tonight, but should they attack us we shall return in great force tomorrow. However with the aid of bad weather, it looks as if the Luftwaffe will get the credit for respecting this *Stille Nacht, heilige Nacht*.

In a letter to the P.M., General Catroux, discussing the prospects of winning over Syria and French North Africa, holds out little hope of securing Weygand (which is an expectation generally entertained). He says: *"Weygand, sous ses apparences de modéstie est un orgueilleux qui hésitera à avouer qu 'il s'est trompé en signant un déplorable armistice."* ["Weygand, with his apparent modesty, is a conceited man who will hesitate to admit that he erred in signing a deplorable Armistice."]

Wednesday, December 25th
The first Christmas Day that I can remember spending in London. I went to the Abbey for the early service, where hundreds of people came, through the gloom and the blackout, and knelt in the candle-lit nave.

I had breakfast at the Wyndham and read a little of a book called *The Importance of Living*, by a Chinese philosopher called Lin Yutang, given me by Gay for Christmas. It is amusingly written, but not very profound.

I cat-burgled 66 Eccleston Square in an attempt to get a bottle of champagne for the typists; but after hazardous descents down drainpipes I found the inner doors barred against me.

Nicholas Lawford[1] dined with me at White's and as Lord Gort was the only other person present he joined us. We had a very long conversation during and after dinner, ranging from the megalomania of Sir Roger Keyes to the weakness of the French, but centring on the Battle of France and Dunkirk. Lord G. was critical of the information he had received from home and confirmed that he had received no warning of the Belgian collapse; but the subject on which he chiefly dwelt was the order sent to him, after the Amiens gap had been made, to march south and join the French. He said that the reports of the French having crossed the Somme, and being in a position to march northwards and close the gap had no truth in them. But the Cabinet and Chiefs of Staff seemed to think that he could march his nine infantry divisions southwards, against eight armoured German divisions in the gap and a reserve of motorised divisions behind. The order which he received took no account of the reality of the situation, scouted the tactical impossibility of facing an army about while it was engaged with the enemy on the other side, and did not consider the position of the Belgian army on Gort's left flank. History would have much to say on this order.

[1] V. G. Lawford, amusing and erudite second private secretary at the Foreign Office.

Had he tried to obey it, he would have lost the whole B.E.F. and the war.

He said that it was only by good fortune, and by some sort of premonition, that he had made arrangements for the protection of his left flank. If he had not done so, the position would have been desperate when the Belgians collapsed.

He talked very modestly throughout, never vaunting himself or complaining of his treatment; but he obviously has a certain grievance against those in authority and feels the injustice of holding up the publication of his despatches. He spoke with the utmost contempt of Hore-Belisha.

The unofficial Christmas truce has been kept by both sides. We have not bombed Germany, nor they us.

Saturday, December 28th [At Helperby, in the North Riding of Yorkshire]

Hunted with the York and Ainsty (North), which met at Helperby. We drew all the small coverts, which I know so well from shooting, and spent much of the morning cantering indecisively about Brafferton Springs. In the warmth and the sunshine even the poorness of the scent could not spoil our pleasure. Finally a fox from Thibet[1] broke well away and we had an exhilarating run, through Pilmoor and across country, jumping a dozen good fences. My hireling was the best of jumpers, but during a second run in the afternoon it landed in a ditch and fell. We were both unhurt and continued an enjoyable hunt until dusk.

Sunday, December 29th

The Germans added to their growing list of atrocities by showering thousands of incendiaries on the City and destroying the Guildhall and eight Wren churches (thank Heavens that Mother and I took the trouble to make a tour of them and admire their beauties one summer's evening two years ago).

---

[1] One of the coverts on the Helperby estate amicably shared by pheasants and foxes.

Tuesday, December 31st

Having reached Downing Street at 7.45 a.m., set to work to cope with arrears and spent much of the day in attendance on the P.M., who was in mellow mood especially when inspecting two of Herbert Morrison's new domestic shelters (intended, I suspect, as rivals to Anderson's successful creation) upon the stresses and strains of which he could demonstrate his technical knowledge as a builder.

Eric Seal is going to try to wangle me into the army, by support of the P. M., over the head of the recalcitrant Foreign Office, but says I must wait till the spring.

Dined at the C.W.R., where General Ismay plied Tommy Thompson and me with brandy and regaled us with stories of the field of battle, and then proceeded upstairs to drink to the New Year in champagne.

THIRTEEN

RECONNAISSANCE BY THE U.S.A.
JANUARY 1941

Wednesday, January 1st

The P.M. has circulated a minute about preserving the secrecy of documents which suddenly makes me feel rather conscience-stricken about this diary. I haven't the heart to destroy it and shall compromise by keeping it locked up here, even more strictly than hitherto.

This evening the P.M. met his Waterloo when inspecting the girders and constructions above the C.W.R. He would not wait for me to return with an effective light and, using only the torch in the handle of his walking-stick, sank up to his ankles in thick liquid cement.[1]

Desmond told us of M.I.5's discovery that Muselier[2] and several of his staff were traitors, agents of the Vichy Government who had betrayed our intentions at Dakar (we have documents to prove it). When he told the P.M., the latter gave orders that they should be arrested tonight and de Gaulle informed by special messenger.

I stayed on duty late, until the P.M. in the early hours ascended to the roof to look at the stars and the new moon. Eden and Kingsley Wood spent much of the evening here discussing the question of financial assistance from America. I

---

[1] When I said he had met his Waterloo, he replied, "How dare you! Anyhow, Blenheim, not Waterloo."

[2] The sole French naval officer of flag rank to rally to de Gaulle. He therefore commanded the French navy. De Gaulle disliked him.

sat in the room while the P.M. drafted a forceful telegram to Roosevelt, not hiding from him the dangerous drain on our resources. Sombre though the telegram was, with its warning that only by American financial help could Hitlerism be "extirpated from Europe, Africa and Asia", the P.M. seemed to enjoy drafting it and his *obiter dicta* to Kingsley Wood who sat perched on the edge of his armchair, were not particularly depressing. But he obviously fears that the Americans' love of doing good business may lead them to denude us of all our realisable resources before they show any inclination to be the Good Samaritan.

M.I.5 went off to arrest Muselier, another Frenchman and two French ladies. One of the ladies was found in bed with a doctor attached to the Free French forces. In the house of the other was found the Second Secretary of the Brazilian Embassy, stark naked. It was through the Brazilian Embassy that information was passed to Vichy. The Admiral himself was found to be in possession of dangerous drugs.

Thursday, January 2nd

The P.M. told Brendan, whose help I had solicited, that I could not join up. So that is that until the spring, when I shall try again.

Friday, January 3rd

Nothing worth recording in the war, except that the defences of Bardia[1] have at last been pierced.

The Germans remain ominously quiet. Many people think the invasion is really being prepared. In any case it seems clear that we have got to expect havoc from air-raids on an increasing scale. Big fire-raids are the order of the day. The devastation of the City was followed by a concentrated attack on Bremen.

Saturday, January 4th

Ordinary routine duties and not very onerous. Biting wind and intense cold made it unpleasant to venture out. Sir Walter Layton has sent the P.M. an interesting poem by an American woman, called "The White Cliffs". Very good propaganda for us.

[1] Italian held town in Libya.

Dorothy Sayers[1] has sent a poem which represents what a great many people in this country are feeling:

THE BURDEN OF IRELAND

O never trouble Ireland; her lamps are shining bright,
While the wicked cities of England are plunged in fear and night,
For Ireland may go lightly and draw her easy breath,
With the hard heart of England set between her and death.

O never trouble Ireland, for she may sleep sound
While the reek of blood and burning goes up from English ground.
She lies down lightly with a smile upon her lips,
Her bulwarks built of English bones and the wreck of the English ships.

O never trouble Ireland; her fields are green with mirth,
While the sharp share of battle ploughs the cursed English earth;
She may wrap her from the winter in a warm English cloak,
For the naked breast of England is wrapped in fire and smoke.

O never trouble Ireland, for Ireland is free –
It is only the men of other lands that groan for liberty.
It is only cruel England thinks such men worth a stir;
But do not trouble Ireland – it does not trouble her.

Say only of Catholic Ireland that she remained at home
When the Pagan and the apostate set heel on the neck of Rome,
When the Cross lay under the fylfot, bowed down to the axe and rod,
And the dirty English Protestant went out to die for God.

[1] Writer of excellent detective stories and creator of the amateur sleuth, Lord Peter Wimsey. A dedicated Anglican.

And say of gallant Ireland, she does not stand alone;
She sits in the shield of England's arm and bites her to the
bone.
She has shortened the sword of England without shewing
fight –
God rest you merry, Irish men, let nothing you affright.

And say of conquered Ireland that she has won her war;
She has taken the bounty of England to settle the English
score,
She has spilt the blood of England without drawing blade –
And England may go lightly now, for all her debts are paid.

But do not trouble England with a tale of Irish wrongs,
Or wring the heart of England with the old heroic songs,
Or bend the Irish blarney to woo the English ear –
For the laughter of England will not be good to hear.

And trouble not for Ireland; though St Patrick lies asleep,
St Andrew and St David and St George are on the deep,
St Michael of the Angels shall guard our Western wall,
Our Lady of Victories pray for us all.[1]

Sunday, January 5th
Bardia has fallen and the P.M., in a peculiarly charming letter
to the King, refers to today as "Bardia Day". In a great tribute
to the King, he says, "Your Majesties are more beloved by all
classes and conditions than any of the princes of the past."

Monday, January 6th
Lunched at the Wyndham where I sat with Horace Wilson and
Peter Loxley.[2] The former talked of the method of governing
by committees. He says the P.M. does not understand the use

---

[1] Dorothy Sayers did not take account of the large number of Southern
Irishmen who came to England to volunteer for service in the British armed
forces despite their Government's craven neutrality.

[2] Highly regarded member of the Diplomatic Service, killed in an air crash on
the way to the Yalta Conference in February 1945.

of them, but both he and Peter considered they served a purpose in providing for decisions without the passage of long and innumerable letters. Beaverbrook – who has just sent another letter of resignation – looks at the same question from another angle. He refused the chairmanship of the new Production Executive because, like a businessman, he believes that committees complicate and slow up decisions which ought to be taken by one man. Beaverbrook and Horace illustrate very clearly the difference between the civil servant's and the businessman's approach. The new plan, which is being published today, for eliminating many committees and establishing two new ones, the Production Executive and the Imports Executive, looks as if it may simplify a machinery which was becoming too intricate.

Vansittart has written a violent paper about Germany, denouncing any attempt to distinguish Germans from Nazis or to hold out hopes of gentle treatment when we have won, and saying that if we look for a revolution from that placid and disciplined people we shall, in the words of Nietzsche, "starve upon expectations". The P.M. disagrees with this outburst and writes in reply: "I contemplate a reunited European family in which Germany will have a great place. We must not let our vision be darkened by hatred or obscured by sentiment. A much more fruitful line is to try to separate the Prussians from the South Germans . . . The expressions to which I attach importance and intend to give emphasis are 'Nazi tyranny' and 'Prussian militarism'." What a contrast between the erratic, feverish genius and the wisdom of a statesman!

We are now making overtures to Vichy because we have hopes that the French may continue the war in North Africa and we realise that Pétain is so widely venerated in France that to attack him is both useless and impolitic.

I was at No. 10 from 2.00 p.m. till 8.15 and had an exhausting time what with the issue of press communiqués about the new Production Executive, etc., and wrangles with Lord Beaverbrook. The P.M. had his sleep and while he was dressing treated me to a discourse on the siege of Ladysmith and why he always remembered January 6th. On the way over to the Annexe for dinner, he said, "I think Anthony is putting his hand on the Foreign Office. I see a different touch in the telegrams."

I was on duty after dinner when an encouraging telegram came which makes it look as if Tobruk may fall close after Bardia. Then we shall have to make a decision: whether to press on to Benghazi or whether to stop and divert our striking force elsewhere. The threat of a German advance into the Balkans, and the slowing up of the Greek offensive in Albania in the face of more determined resistance, give cause to think. It would be disastrous to let the Greek triumph end in defeat, as did the victories of the Finnish army last winter.

The P.M. worked intensively till 2.00 a.m. and sent yet another eloquent note to Lord Beaverbrook, ending "Danton, no weakness". Then he went to bed and, as he snuggled beneath the bed clothes, smiling at the thought of Bardia and, he hopes soon, Tobruk, he had the grace for once to apologise for keeping me up so late.

Tuesday, January 7th
Brendan tells me that he argued ceaselessly last night with Lord B. about his resignation, but all to no avail. He is determined to go. No bad thing in itself, but it will upset the P.M. terribly.

Thursday, January 9th
I was at No. 10 from 4.00 p.m. till dinner-time, the main preoccupation being with General de Gaulle, since it has now been discovered that the documents incriminating Admiral Muselier were false and had been forged by two disgruntled officers of the Free French forces. The P.M. was greatly pleased because de Gaulle "behaved like a Gentleman", was not at all cantankerous about the episode, and said that his only interest was to see that honour and justice were satisfied.

James Stuart[1] came to No. 10 and was offered, and accepted, the post of Chief Whip. He had been deputy to David Margesson, now promoted to the War Office.

---

[1] Afterwards Viscount Stuart of Findhorn.

Friday, January 10th

The President's envoy, Mr Hopkins,* was lunching with the P.M. and they were so impressed with each other that their tête-à-tête did not break up till nearly 4.00. Then we left for Ditchley, I travelling down with Brendan. Brendan said that Hopkins, the confidant of Roosevelt, was the most important American visitor to this country we had ever had. He had come to tell the President what we needed and to form an opinion of the country's morale. He could influence the President more than any living man. At Lisbon Ronnie Campbell had made a bad impression by saying that "the morale of the lower classes was wonderful" – a remark which offended the liberal and democratic Hopkins. But apparently Hopkins had been much impressed by Halifax, whose religious views and variety of interests would, he said, appeal to Roosevelt. While we were thus discoursing, an icy mist descended and we collided with a fish-and-chips wagon which burst into flames. Nobody was hurt and we arrived safely at Ditchley.

Besides the Trees, Venetia Montagu was there, Dinah Brand (with her Australian beau) and the Captain of the Guard, a former schoolmaster, who seemed very intelligent. Before dinner we drank and thawed while Winston pointed out, in reply to Mrs Tree, that Wavell had done very well but that the Italians were the sort of enemy against whom any General should be only too happy to be matched.

Dinner was an exquisite meal at which I sat next to Mrs Tree. Afterwards Winston smoked the biggest cigar in history and became very mellow. There was an interlude in which I talked to the exceptionally pleasant Dinah, after which Winston retired to bed with a very full box and in an excellent temper while I whiled away the time arranging the box in my beautiful working room below.

After the drafting of a long and intricate telegram to Wavell, for consideration by the Chiefs of Staff, we went to bed at about 1.30. The point of the telegram was that in view of the imminence of a German attack in the Balkans we must relax our effort in Libya, once Tobruk has fallen, and divert a part of our forces to the aid of Greece. The army authorities in the Middle East are in despair at this; they believe the Balkan threat is only a bluff.

Tobruk is proving a tougher nut to crack than we had supposed. It may take a week, the P.M. says.

Saturday, January 11th
Very annoyed at being disturbed early by the P.M.

He is delighted by the new American bill which allows British warships the use of American ports and contains wide powers for the President in every sphere of assistance to us. He says this is tantamount to a declaration of war by the United States. At any rate it is an open challenge to Germany to declare war if she dares. In view of this bill it will be more difficult for us to resist the American tendency – which Kingsley Wood lamented to me yesterday – to strip us of everything we possess in payment for what we are about to receive.

Ronnie Tree went off to his constituency and his wife, at 4.00 a.m. this morning, had to rush off with her squadron of mobile canteens to Portsmouth which received the full force of the blitz last night. So at lunch we had no host or hostess, although the son of the house[1] – a trooper in the Life Guards – came in towards the end. But Mr Hopkins arrived and his quiet charm and dignity held the table. He said that the new Presidential bill would arouse loud controversy, but he felt sure it would succeed. He told us of the Duke of Windsor's recent visit to the President on his yacht when the former spoke very charmingly of the King (a fact which touched Winston), and he said that the Duke's entourage was very bad. Moreover H.R.H.'s recent yachting trip with a violently pro-Nazi Swede did not create a good impression. It was the astounding success of the King and Queen's visit to the U.S. which had made America give up its partisanship of the Windsors.

Winston expressed the opinion, forcibly, that socialism was bad, that jingoism was worse, and that the two combined, in a kind of debased Italian fascism, was the worst creed ever designed by man.

[1]   Michael Tree, married Lady Anne Cavendish.

The Marquesa de Casa Maury[1] (formerly Mrs Dudley Ward) came at tea-time and also Oliver Lyttelton and the Prof. Brendan, who had taken Hopkins over to Blenheim, said that Hopkins had told him his mission was to see what we needed so that we might get it – even if it meant transferring to us armaments belonging to the U.S. forces. The President was resolved that we should have the means of survival and of victory.

Dinner at Ditchley takes place in a magnificent setting. The dining-room is lit only by candles, in a large chandelier and on the walls. The table is not over-decorated: four gilt candle sticks with tall yellow tapers and a single gilt cup in the centre. The food is in keeping with the surroundings, though I notice some attempt to be less lavish since Lord Woolton's recent strictures on over-feeding.

The P.M. has been troubled by *The Times'* attack on his new Production Executive, etc., and indeed the criticisms voiced there reflect a widely-felt complaint. So he has taken the trouble to write a full explanation to Geoffrey Dawson,[2] and at dinner he expounded his views, emphasising that he had no use for committees in a purely advisory capacity but that there was no one man today who could be an economic dictator or maintain a position similar to his, on the military side, as Minister of Defence. His exercise of this office was only made possible by the power which he possessed as Prime Minister.

When the ladies had gone, Mr Hopkins paid a graceful tribute to the P.M.'s speeches which had, he said, produced the most stirring and revolutionary effect on all classes and districts in America. At an American Cabinet meeting the President had had a wireless-set brought in so that all might listen to the Prime Minister. The P.M. was touched and gratified. He said that he hardly knew what he said in his speeches last summer; he had just been imbued with the feeling that "it would be better for us to be destroyed than to see the triumph of such an impostor".

---

[1] A woman of exceptional charm, for many years friend, confidante and mistress of the Prince of Wales (Edward VIII).

[2] Editor of *The Times*. Strong supporter of Munich and of appeasement. Friend of Lady Astor and Lord Lothian and member of the so-called "Cliveden Set". About to hand over his editorship to Robin Barrington-Ward.

When, at the time of Dunkirk, he had addressed a meeting of Ministers "below the line" he had realised that there was only one thing they wanted to hear him say: that whatever happened to our army we should still go on. He had said it.

After the war he could never lead a party Government against the Opposition leaders who had co-operated so loyally. He hoped a national Government would continue for two or three years after the war so that the country might be undivided in its efforts to put into effect certain principles – or rather measures – of reconstruction. He then proceeded to give – after saying that the text of the American bill that morning had made him feel that a new world had come into being – a graphic description of the future, as he visualised it, from an international point of view. He began by saying that there must be a United States of Europe and he believed it should be built by the English; if the Russians built it, there would be communism and squalor; if the Germans built it, there would be tyranny and brute force. He then outlined his ideas, which I have related before, in the quick unhesitating manner which means he has really warmed to his subject.

He asked Hopkins what he thought, and the reply, slow, deliberate, halting was a remarkable contrast to the ceaseless flow of eloquence to which we had listened. Hopkins said that there were two kinds of men: those who talked and those who acted. The President, like the Prime Minister, was one of the latter. Although Hopkins had heard him sketch out an idea very similar to the P.M.'s, Roosevelt refused to listen to those who talked so much of war aims and was intent only upon one end: the destruction of Hitler. Winston hastily explained that he had been speaking very freely and was just anxious to let Hopkins realise that we were not all devoid of thoughts of the future: he would be the first to agree that the destruction of "those foul swine" was the primary and over-riding objective.

At this point Mrs Tree evicted us forcibly from the dining-room to see a film of the Mormons called *Brigham Young*. I sat next to Mrs Dudley Ward and thought I understood why the Prince of Wales felt the way he did. The film, though it had its *longueurs*, was a moving one and stimulating to one's thought.

It showed the great quality of simple faith (which, as Tennyson pointed out, is more than Norman blood) and the nobility of refusing to compromise with the principles one has deliberately adopted as right. After this film was over we saw some German news films which included a scene at the Brenner meeting, which with its salutes and its absurdity was funnier than anything Charlie Chaplin produced in *The Great Dictator*. To bed by 2.00 a.m.

Sunday, January 12th
The P.M.'s respect for General Smuts' wise and comprehensive telegrams is shown in the final sentence of a telegram he has just sent to the General: "Most grateful for all your help and above all for your sure-footed judgment which marches with our laboriously reached conclusions."

Lunch lasted a long time, but eventually, while the P.M. conferred with Prof. and Mr Justice Singleton about the strength of the German air force, I managed to go out for a walk with my host and hostess, whom I like more and more. They live ostentatiously but are the opposite themselves.

The discussion after dinner was largely about America, and in particular the American principle of coping with unemployment by providing work instead of a dole – a plan which costs four times as much or would, at any rate, in England. The P.M. asked what the Americans would do when they had accumulated all the gold in the world and the other countries then decided that gold was of no value except for filling teeth. "Well," said Mr Hopkins, "we shall be able to make use of our unemployed in guarding it!"

We saw several films including *Night Train to Munich*, which I had seen before. In the middle the telephone rang and I was told that H.M.S. *Southampton* had been destroyed by dive-bombers in the Mediterranean. When I took the P.M. aside afterwards and broke the news to him, he was less upset than I expected, though he bitterly regretted that he had been dissuaded from allowing Operation WORKSHOP[1] to go through. "I

---

[1] The seizure of Pantellaria.

flinched," he said, "and now I have cause to regret it." I asked Prof. why the U.P. weapon had not come into play and he replied that the service experts had decided dive-bombing was no longer a danger and that the U.P. should be adapted for use against high-altitude flying.

From midnight till 2.00 a.m. the P.M., smoking a phenomenally large cigar, paced about in front of the fire at the far end of the library and gave, for Hopkins' benefit, an appreciation of the war up to date. Ronnie Tree, Oliver Lyttelton, Prof., Tommy Thompson and I sat and goggled, while Hopkins occasionally made some short comment. He began by discussing the future. The question of populations was important. Germany had sixty millions on whom she could count; the remainder were at least a drag and potentially a danger. The British Empire had more white inhabitants than that, and if the U.S. were with us – as he seemed in this discourse to assume they actively would be – there would be another 120 millions. So we were not outmatched in numbers any more than we were in courage and resolution. He did not believe that Japan would come in against the threat of Anglo-American armed resistance and he thought it more than probable that the Germans would be obliged to occupy the whole of France, thus driving the French to take up arms again in North Africa. (He later said he believed that if he had gone to Bordeaux in those last fateful days he would have been able to tip the balance in favour of further resistance overseas.)

Turning to the past, he sketched the whole history of the war, Norway, the trap when we marched our men right up into Belgium, his visits to France, the air battles, Libya, and, above all, the threat of invasion. He believed that Oran had been the turning-point in our fortunes: it made the world realise that we were in earnest in our intentions to carry on. He sketched the possibilities of invasion, of "lodgements", of the use of gas, but he said he now felt quite confident, even though it was wrong to say that we should actually welcome invasion as so many people were now feeling. I think Hopkins must have been impressed.

With Oliver Lyttelton*, who radiates charm, I had what he

called "a little whisky-and-soda treason before going to bed". We discussed the Government and he told me he had no opinion of Bevin's capacity, though he thought Morrison was doing his job well.

Monday, January 13th
Having breakfasted with Mrs Churchill, Venetia Montagu and Mrs Dudley Ward, I cleared up the remnants of a week-end's input and output from boxes, and the P.M. was ready to leave for London by 10.45.

I travelled with the Prof. There was an unreasonable outburst of anger from the P.M. en route because a box (with a few quite unimportant papers) had not reached us when we left for Ditchley and we could not induce the car containing it to stop when we met. The P.M. stopped his car by the side of the road, just outside Oxford, and threatened to wait an hour till the box was retrieved. Fortunately we only waited three minutes.

I invited Jan Margesson and Betty Montagu to lunch at the Mirabelle and we sat talking, most pleasurably, till past 3.00. Jan had been attending, as a delegate, a meeting of a Communist-organised "People's Convention" which the P.M. recently instructed the Home Secretary to watch carefully. The present Communist policy is apparently to support the war (which they denounced a very short time ago) but in so doing to sow every possible dissension and disrupt the national effort. They don't look as if they are making much headway, but the Cabinet is today considering the possibility of suspending the *Daily Worker*, a difficult decision owing to deep-rooted feelings about the freedom of the press. I led Jan to believe that the Government's policy was to ignore all such movements and organisations because of their insignificance.

That Janet Margesson, daughter of the ultra-Tory Chief Whip, should be a member of the Communist Party seemed less surprising then that it would now. After all Mrs Churchill was a dedicated Liberal, much disliking the Conservative Party except in her husband's constituency; and Mrs Attlee told me that she had voted Conservative until 1945. Stanley Baldwin's elder son was a Labour M.P. and neither Asquith's nor Lloyd George's sons were ostentatiously Liberal in their political sympathies.

In my own family my father was a Conservative, but my mother, a staunch Liberal, would vote Labour rather than Conservative if no Liberal were standing. In 1945 she voted Conservative, saying shame-facedly to me, "I have never done such a thing before, but as you are with Winston I just felt I had to support him."

In the mid 1980s the public would be surprised if Mr Thatcher was a socialist or if Mrs Kinnock or Mrs Wedgwood Benn were Tories. In the 1930s and 1940s such a state of affairs would not have seemed remarkable, and it may well be that family divergencies in politics were wholesome.

Tuesday, January 14th

The P.M. went north to Scapa Flow to see Lord Halifax off to the United States and to visit the Fleet.

Prince Paul of Yugoslavia[1] is terrified at the prospect of our sending great assistance to Greece. He feels sure it will bring the Germans down. The P.M.'s reaction to his panicky telegrams from Belgrade is that the Germans will not be either hurried or deflected from their carefully laid plans by any minor troop movements on our part. Prince Paul is like a man in a cage with a tiger, "hoping not to provoke him while steadily dinner-time approaches".

Wednesday, January 15th

The terrible problem of the strength of the German air force, into which Singleton has been enquiring, has produced many complications which kept me busy for much of the day. The conclusion reached seems to be that the Germans are very little superior to us except in long-range bombers. Their main advantage lies in the short distance they have to come.

---

[1] Cousin of the murdered King Alexander and regent for the young King Peter. Married to the dazzlingly beautiful Princess Olga, sister of the Duchess of Kent.

Having dined frugally at the C.W.R. I joined a party at the Ecu de France consisting of the Hinchingbrookes, Martin Charteris,* Mrs Simon Whitbread, Colonel Clark, Faith and Betty Montagu. Everybody was in a delightful frame of mind and we went on to the Four Hundred where we enjoyed our-selves greatly until after 2.00 a.m.

Thursday, January 16th
Sir Stafford Cripps reports that Russia looks like standing aside and letting Germany have her way in the Balkans. He considers a German offensive through Bulgaria is assured within the next few months and thinks it will be synchronised with other offensives elsewhere. He says: "If events go badly for Turkey then she (Russia) may attack that country and Iran or make very large demands on them. It is likely that she will make demands on Iran as soon as Turkey is thoroughly engaged with Germany." So one leader of the extreme Left has no illusions left about Russian intentions.

It seems clear that Germany must make a determined effort to reach a decision, at whatever cost, before American help becomes effective. The spring is going to be critical, and it makes one shudder to see the reports from many and different sources of the manufacture and storage of German gas bombs.

Friday, January 17th
Helen Dashwood gave a dance at West Wycombe, in aid of the Red Cross, and I went there for the weekend. It seemed to be a children's party, at which Fitzroy Maclean and I were the only adults, but later in the evening, as more people arrived, things livened up considerably. In any case it was lovely to hear a band and to see people dancing.

Monday, January 20th
Thick snow gave way to thicker slush and I goaded my car through miles of it from West Wycombe to London, accompanied by two sodden journalists to whom I gave a lift.

The P.M. did not return to London till after lunch, so John Martin and I fed unhurriedly and well at Boodles and I listened to his description of the Scottish trip which seems to have been almost farcical at times, especially when the U.P. weapon was fired in the P.M.'s honour and all but ended in exploding on top of the whole party.

The Cabinet was at 5.00 at the C.W.R., as always on Mondays, and afterwards the P.M. was feeling very polite. He even went so far as to say (after I had fetched him his red ink pen and much else besides): "Will you add yet another to all the kindnesses you have been heaping on my head by turning out the electric fire?" which is not the way he usually asks for things.

Heavy air attacks have taken place on Malta, and it is thought possible that the next German move will be either an attack on Malta or an invasion, by German and Italian forces, of Tunis with the idea of destroying any chance of renewed French activity and of reinforcing the sorely beleaguered Graziani[1] in Libya. But we are not letting the grass grow under our feet.

After dinner I was on duty while the P.M. held a Defence Committee Meeting. Having finished my work, I read M. Dupuy's (the Canadian Minister) enlightening report on his visit to Vichy, where he found Pétain much more alert than we had supposed and anxious for a British victory. The one fear that many Frenchmen had was that a British victory would mean the return of the old politicians who had brought about France's downfall. It had been impressed upon Dupuy that the appearance of Anglo-French tension must be preserved in order to hoodwink the Germans and Laval; but secret discussions could take place behind this veil. The French have two great levers against Germany: their fleet and their Colonies. We have one great bargaining counter with them: the relaxation, under guarantees, of the blockade in certain articles. Dupuy ends his report with the words: "The problem of Franco-British relations depends on two things – goodwill and psychology. The goodwill already exists on both sides – there remains the question of psychology."

The Foreign Office weekly summary describes how in Poland the Germans, having failed to terrorise the Poles, are now trying

[1] Marshal Graziani, commander of the Italian armies in North Africa. Soundly defeated by General Wavell.

to demoralise them by the encouragement of gambling, erotic literature and improper displays and the banning of more serious forms of entertainment. An interesting foretaste of Hitler's New Order.

The P.M. went to bed, very benevolently, about 2.00 a.m. and spent a rotten night.

Tuesday, January 21st

The House of Commons met, in the old House. David Margesson made his first appearance as a Minister and had forty Questions to answer, a heavy task which he achieved with great credit. Then, after Questions, the House debated Manpower, Production and Supply. The P.M. sat on the Front Bench, and I in the box, while Bevin read out a long oration. Everybody yawned, and the incorrigible Mr Austin Hopkinson[1] even suggested rudely that to save Mr Bevin trouble the Clerk of the Table should read the speech for him; but the House sat up with a start and gaped when Industrial Registration, to make possible conscription in industries of national importance, was announced. After Bevin had spoken for over an hour, Lord Winterton[2] rose and made an eloquent attack on the Government. He said, with some truth, that there was danger of our forming a kind of "Maginot Line Complex" about American help. We must not rely on any but our own efforts.

Gave Barker a late but extensive lunch at Boodles and was surprised to find what bloodthirsty and merciless sentiments he nurtured towards Germany. I find less and less support for my belief that when we have won, mercy should season justice.

Wednesday, January 22nd

The debate in the House continued and I spent most of the day there until the Police shouted "Who goes home?" at 4.00 p.m.

---

[1] Independent M.P. for the Mossley division of Lancashire who asked endless irritating Parliamentary Questions.

[2] 6th Earl Winterton. Irish peer who was M.P. for Horsham and sat in the House of Commons for forty-five years, rising from being Baby of the House in 1904 to Father of the House. Amiable but eccentric, and very outspoken, he held Cabinet office briefly in 1938–39 and then, as a backbench Privy Councillor, became a gadfly stinging all administrations impartially.

At the end of questions Morrison made a statement on the suppression of the *Daily Worker*, and although the House was clearly in favour of this Aneurin Bevan[1] pressed the P.M. for a debate and carried his point.

I lunched with Eric Seal at the House, and then we both went into the box to hear the P.M. wind up the debate. He did so extremely well, explaining his reasons for the new committee machinery (which has been much criticised) with the utmost clearness and cogency. The House was entertained by his quips and his mastery of the art of anti-climax. He expounded the little understood facts about the slowness of changing from peace to war production and the increased need of manpower, in industry rather than the forces, as that transfer takes place. He answered the demand for a dictator on the Home Front, to correspond with the Minister of Defence on the military side, by disparaging dictators in general and by pointing out that he could only maintain his ascendancy as Minister of Defence because he was also Prime Minister. In general he welcomed criticism even when, for the sake of emphasis, it parted company with reality.

Tobruk fell.

I am continually impressed by the P.M.'s genuine love of democracy; viz. a recent minute to the Foreign Secretary about Egypt:

I trust the time will come when the interests of the Fellaheen will be cherished by H.M.G., even if some of the rich pashas and landowners and other pretended nationalists have to pay the same kind of taxes as are paid by wealthy people in Britain. A little of the radical democratic sledge-hammer is needed in the Delta, where so many fat, insolent class and party interests have grown up under our tolerant protection.

---

[1] Labour M.P. for Ebbw Vale. Made himself leader of an unofficial opposition and was thought by Churchill, rightly or wrongly, to subordinate national interest to political advantage. Churchill usually outwitted him, brilliant debater though he was. A thorn in Attlee's flesh in the post-war Labour Government, but a major contributor to the establishment of the Welfare State.

Friday, January 24th

The P.M. took Mr Hopkins off to see the batteries at Dover. I could have gone, but preferred to drive myself down to Chequers independently and to clear up the considerable amount of work which confronted me.

In the late afternoon I drove Jack Churchill to Chequers. Mrs Churchill, Lady Gwendeline Churchill, Judy Montagu and Mary were there, and the P.M. and Harry Hopkins arrived about 7.00.

At dinner Hopkins said how impressed he had been to see when dining with Bevin, Morrison and Sir Andrew Duncan, on what friendly and familiar terms a great industrialist could be with Labour leaders. Such a thing could not happen in America.

Hopkins told the P.M. that during the afternoon at Dover he had heard one workman say to another, as Winston passed, "There goes the bloody British Empire." Winston's face wreathed itself in smiles and, turning to me, he lisped, *"Very nice."* I don't think anything has given him such pleasure for a long time.

The P.M. said he did not now see how invasion could be successful and he now woke up in the mornings, as he nearly always had, feeling as if he had a bottle of champagne inside him and glad that another day had come. In May and June, however, he had been sorry when the nights were over and he had often thought about death, not, he said, "that I much believe in personal survival after death, at least not of the memory". He was not, he said, much worried by the chance of being bombed – in this connection he is fond of quoting M. Poincaré's[1] statement, "I take refuge beneath the impenetrable arch of probability".

Jack Churchill asked when we were going to recapture British Somaliland. The P.M. replied that we must concentrate on the major operation. As Napoleon said, *"Frappez la masse et le reste vien par surcrôit."*

[1] President of the French Republic in the First World War and subsequently for two years Prime Minister. In the Third Republic Prime Ministers normally lasted only a few months and sometimes only weeks.

Hopkins thought that a statement to the effect that any move by Japan against American interests in the East would be considered an unfriendly act by Great Britain, would have a most important effect in the U.S. The P.M. was delighted and promised to say this as soon as the President let him know the time was ripe.

After dinner I read to the C.I.G.S.[1] on the "Scrambler" (our new telephonic secrecy device) a long telegram from the P.M. to Wavell protesting against the latter's enormous demand for rearward services. Wavell had well over 300,000 men in North Africa but could only put 45,000 into the field. The C.I.G.S. didn't like this telegram and subsequently I had to ring him up again so that he and the P.M. might wrangle about it. Eventually the P.M. agreed to tone down the wording, but said that plain-speaking was necessary in war and he didn't see why Wavell should want still more Y.M.C.A.s etc. behind the lines.

At midnight the P.M. and Harry Hopkins came into my office and talked. The P.M. was much impressed by the fact that there are 200,000 white civilians in Abyssinia and he is a little worried about their fate when "those savage warriors, who have been burned with poison gas" get among them. If the Duke of Aosta will surrender in time, the P.M. thinks we might be able to hold the Abyssinians back.

"Never give in," said the P.M., "and you will never regret it." A negotiated peace would be a German victory and would leave open the way for another and final "spring of the tiger" in a few years' time. Hopkins agreed and said that Lindbergh,[2] and others in America who favoured a negotiated peace, really desired a German victory. The P.M. wound up by saying that after the last war he had been asked to provide an inscription for a French war memorial. His suggestion, which was rejected, had been: "In war fury, in defeat defiance, in victory magnanimity, in peace goodwill."

The P.M. summoned me into his bedroom and, as he

---

[1] Sir John Dill.
[2] Famous American aviator who became a standard-bearer for the Isolationists.

undressed, said very nicely that he didn't think there was much point in his letting me join up in the Guards, though there was every point in my wanting to do so. This was not like the last war when every man was needed, and there were too many able men who had gone into the army and were doing jobs which did not make full use of their capacities. If things really started to move, he promised to let me go and to see that I was well placed. He would take care of my interests and he would not forget. He thought a commission in the Marines, which he could procure for me, was the thing. I should not need much preliminary training. I said, "What about a Commando?" "You mightn't get a commission in that," he replied. I said I wouldn't mind going in the ranks, but he said that was silly (which I don't think it is).

I put in a plea, rather feebly, for permission to go soon on the grounds that members of the Diplomatic Service were too inclined to see life from the drawing-room sofa angle and that it would be an excellent thing to have a wider experience. But I was told that this war was not being waged in order that I might complete my education.

Saturday, January 25th
The Duke and Duchess of Marlborough came to lunch and conversation was much more general than usual. Harry Hopkins talked about Lisbon and the undesirable Americans there.

The P.M., alarmed by the number of papers in his box, worked all the afternoon in bed. I arranged for Mrs C. and Mr Hopkins to go and see West Wycombe, but Mr Hopkins fell asleep and Mrs C. decided not to go – which distressed Helen Dashwood very much. From her voice on the telephone she sounded like one who has returned from a Safari and seen no trace of the lions she has been promised.

A considerable amount of work was done, including a letter to the editor of the *Daily Mirror*, protesting against that newspaper's Fifth Column attitude, and an enormous memorandum to David Margesson about manpower, the army's excessive dependence on rearward services and the distribution of the thirty-seven divisions we now have available.

Sir John Dill came after tea and contributed his unaffected charm and urbanity.

I sat between Judy Montagu and Mary at dinner, the former very agreeable and forthcoming (and apparently smitten by the graces of Bruce Grimston[1]), the latter, although in reality intelligent and sensible, inclined this evening to be captious and tiresome.

Over the brandy Hopkins showed the P.M. and Dill the details of the American rearmament programme, which I had already perused. It is clear that gigantic efforts are being made, but the P.M. warned Hopkins that the results could not be expected for about eighteen months. Our own war factories were only just beginning their full production (e.g. last week our ammunition output doubled).

Then the C.I.G.S. produced the papers about Operation VICTOR, a military exercise which has been taking place during the last few days as practice against invasion. The papers include an able appreciation of the advantages and tactics of invasion written, as if by the German Staff, by General Weeks[2] of the War Office. It is very comprehensive and sensible, much impressed the P.M., and would certainly do great credit to the Germans if genuine. I was asked to read this out aloud, and afterwards an account of the first stages of the exercise. This account contained, as an appendix, a broadcast by the P.M. on the beginning of invasion. I read this out aloud and its language caused much amusement, though the P.M. promised he would produce a far better one in the event and said that the sham one was a good example of the mistake of using conventional adjectives, attached to conventional nouns, merely for the sake of effect. If he did have to make such a speech he would end it: "The hour has come; kill the Hun."

There was some discussion about Eire, Dill putting forward the theory that the Germans would invade Ireland as a diversion, like they did Norway, before the main attack materialised.

---

[1] Younger son of the Earl of Verulam. Good-looking, amusing and a gallant R.A.F. pilot. Killed in action in Bomber Command as was his brother Brian.

[2] Sir Ronald Weeks, subsequently Chairman of Vickers Ltd and of the English Steel Corporation.

The rest of the evening was spent in the Great Hall, where the gramophone played and the P.M., in the intervals of discoursing to Hopkins or Dill, tripped a little measure. Hopkins seems doubtful whether we shall have any warning of invasion, but the P.M. and Dill are confident that complete surprise is impossible.

I drank five different sorts of alcohol, in an effort to stifle a cold, but remained quite sober.

Sunday, January 26th

I arranged for Mr Hopkins to go to West Wycombe and then on to see the Fred Crippses (Mrs C. and Lady Gwendeline Churchill both suspect he is attracted by Mrs Cripps[1]). The lady proved so attractive that he stayed to lunch. Mrs C. made a great fuss about Mr Hopkins going to West Wycombe as she felt she ought to have gone too. But I managed to pacify her. In fact Mr H. did not want her to go with him.

In thanking the P.M. for his tribute to him in the House the other day, Beaverbrook writes: "You have given me a certificate of character which will carry me through my days. And that is good for me. Because there is a difference between us. You will be talked of even more widely after you are dead than during your lifetime. But I am talked of while I live, and save for my association with you, I will be forgotten thereafter." Lord B. knows how to lay it on – and also how to forward his own cause in his unceasing struggles with the Air Ministry, of which the P.M. said to me on Friday that he was heartily sick.

Hamish St Clair Erskine (of the Guard) came to lunch and was entertaining. Dill had gone and Hopkins was not back, so we had a rest from war and politics and talked about food and people.

Sir Charles and Lady Portal arrived at tea-time and, as Mrs C. was still out, the P.M. escorted them up to the Long Gallery for tea, together with Hopkins and Prof., who came today. We started talking about the Classics, Portal being a Wykehamist

---

[1] Violet, previously one of the Duke of Westminster's four wives. Married to Fred Cripps, brother of Sir Stafford but far from sharing his political and dietary views.

and thus presumably learned, and the P.M. said that the use of the new pronunciation in Latin was one of the few things he felt passionate about. Latin spoken in the old way was beautiful to hear; the new way was not only ugly but by hiding the resemblance between English and Latin words removed one of the first utilitarian arguments in favour of the Classics.

We got on to the House of Lords and the P.M. said that in England our architecture produced our manner of living and not vice versa. Thus the two-party system owed its supremacy here partly to the shape of the Houses of Parliament. You had to be on one side or the other and it was difficult to cross the floor. He had done it and he knew. Indeed he had re-done it, which everybody said was impossible. They had said you could rat but you couldn't re-rat.

During dinner the P.M. was very hilarious and in the same amiable frame of mind as he has been the whole week-end. He mentioned Generis Mainwaring[1] (pronouncing the G as a J) and I told him she had been bitten by a rat and nearly died. He asked if she had grown a tail and couldn't keep off the subject for at least five minutes. Afterwards he reminisced about the Cuban campaign and South African War.

When the women had gone to bed, I listened in the Great Hall to as interesting a discussion as I ever hope to hear. We sat in a circle, Portal, Hopkins, Jack Churchill, myself and Prof., while the P.M. stood with his back against the mantelpiece, a cigar between his teeth, his hands in the armpits of his waistcoat. Every few seconds he would start forward, trip over the marble grate, walk four or five paces, turn abruptly and resume his position against the mantelpiece. All the while a torrent of eloquence flowed from his lips, and he would fix one or another of us with his eye as he drove home some point. He talked of the past, the present and the future, and the subject matter of his talk was roughly as follows:

In recent history two men had been the most harmful influence in English politics, Joseph Chamberlain and Baldwin. The first

[1] Daughter of Sir Richard and Lady Magdalen Williams-Bulkeley and mother of Zara Mainwaring.

had pushed us into the Boer War and, by setting Europe against us, had stimulated the Germans to build a fleet. The second had dominated the scene for fifteen years. He had pushed out of public life the men with the greatest experience, L.G., Birkenhead, etc.; and he had made possible the resurgence of Germany and the decay of our own strength. He was just sufficiently good to be suffering now acutely for what he had done. This led to a digression about the "Carthaginian peace" of Versailles: we had exacted 1,000 millions in reparations; we and the U.S. had contributed 2,000 millions in loans to set Germany on her feet again and rebuild her power. It was possible that in some twenty months we and the U.S. would again have to make a peace settlement and there would once more be those who wished to help Germany on to her feet. "Only one thing in history is certain: that mankind is unteachable."

There was some discussion of currency problems, the P.M. coming out strongly in favour of "the commodity dollar", the rate of which would be fixed by the prices of a number of selected commodities. He compared the currency problem to that of daylight saving; by a little tampering with the clock great benefits could be reaped; but by overdoing it in either direction all advantage must be lost. Hopkins agreed that the present financial system was unsatisfactory, and said that the President was in favour of some such scheme as the P.M. had outlined; but the opposition of Wall Street had been intense. However in favour of the financiers, the P.M. pointed out that today everybody wanted credit but nobody had any patience with creditors.

The P.M. said that when the war was over there would be a short lull during which we had the opportunity to establish a few basic principles, of justice, of respect for the rights and property of other nations, and indeed of respect for private property so long as its owner was honest and its scope moderate. We could find nothing better than Christian ethics on which to build and the more closely we followed the Sermon on the Mount, the more likely we were to succeed in our endeavours. But all this talk about war aims was absurd at the present time: the Cabinet Committee to examine the question had produced a vague paper, four-fifths of which was from the Sermon on the Mount and the remainder an election address.

Japan and the U.S. was the next topic, and Hopkins expressed the belief that if America came into the war the incident would be with Japan. The P.M. said that the advantage of America as an ally to the disadvantage of Japan as an enemy was as 10 to 1. Why, look at their respective power of steel production – and "modern war is waged with steel". Besides Japan must have been greatly affected by the fate of the Italian navy, which on paper had been so strong. "Fate holds terrible forfeits for those who gamble on certainties."

The P.M. sat down heavily on the sofa, said he had talked too much, and asked Hopkins for his views. Speaking slowly but emphatically, Hopkins stated that the President was not much concerned with the future. His preoccupation was with the next few months. As far as war aims were concerned, there were only very few people in America, liberal intellectuals, who cared about the matter; and they were nearly all on our side. He believed the same to be true of people in this country. All he would say of the future was that he believed the Anglo-Saxon peoples would have to do the rearrangement: the other nations would not be ripe for co-operation for a long time. He thought the problems of reconstruction would be very great, greater than the P.M. had implied, and we should have to send men to the conference table who were tough and not sentimental.

As far as the present was concerned, there were four divisions of public opinion in America: a small group of Nazis and Communists, sheltering behind Lindbergh, who declared for a negotiated peace and wanted a German victory; a group, represented by Joe Kennedy, which said "Help Britain, but make damn sure you don't get into any danger of war"; a majority group which supported the President's determination to send the maximum assistance at whatever risk; and about ten per cent or fifteen per cent of the country, including Knox,[1] Stimson[2] and most of the armed forces, who were in favour of immediate war.

---

[1] Frank Knox, U.S. Secretary of the Navy.
[2] Henry L. Stimson, U.S. Secretary of the Army.

The important element in the situation was the boldness of the President, who would lead opinion and not follow it, who was convinced that if England lost, America, too, would be encircled and beaten. He would use his powers if necessary; he would not scruple to interpret existing laws for the furtherance of his aim; he would make people gape with surprise, as the British Foreign Office must have gaped when it saw the terms of the Lease and Lend Bill. The boldness of the President was a striking factor in the situation. He did not want war, indeed he looked upon America as an arsenal which should provide the weapons for the conflict and not count the cost; but he would not shrink from war.

I talked to the P.M. as he went to bed and found him most communicative and benign. Nobody is more lovable than he when he is in this frame of mind. He recounted to me the difficulties in the way of an invader whose lines of communications would be cut and who could not dominate the air during the daytime. But, I said, the Germans must know this as well as we do and surely the implication is that they will not invade. "To tell you the truth," he said, "that is what I think, and so does Portal. But the others don't think so." He said he would not feel so confident, remembering as he did Neville Chamberlain's conviction a year ago that Germany would not invade Holland and Belgium, were it not for the fact that we had air superiority in the day and that we were not pinning our faith in the Maginot Line, "a great China Wall", but in our troops *behind* the beaches who would attack any lodgment and make each separate one into a Sidi Barrani, a Bardia or a Tobruk.

He snuggled down beneath the bedclothes, I gave him his Boswell's *Tour of the Hebrides*, and smiling sweetly he wished me goodnight.

Monday, January 27th
Hopkins, who has smoked most of my Chesterfields, departed with the Prof. who is giving him an album of statistics showing our possessions and our requirements. The P.M. worked in bed till eleven and then went up to London, while I got into my car and drove to Ardley. It has been a particularly agreeable

week-end, interesting and not too hectic, and the P.M. has throughout been at his most entertaining and shown the sunniest side of his disposition. He said last night at dinner that he hated nobody and didn't feel he had any enemies – except the Huns, and that was professional! Few men are as good-natured, and it is an interesting spotlight on No. 10 last winter that he should have been regarded with such dislike and mistrust.

Thursday, January 30th

As a result of last night's meeting, the P.M. drafted at No. 10 a telegram to the Turkish President asking that in view of the certainty of a German move through Bulgaria we should be allowed to base a number of squadrons on Turkey. From every source news comes that Germany's intentions in the Balkans are serious, and from whatever angle the Chiefs of Staff regard the matter it remains evident that Turkey is the key to the situation. Hence the P.M.'s telegram.

I went to see David Margesson at the War Office about the pay of army nurses, a matter which Queen Mary wished me to raise with the P.M. David was quite prepared to be helpful, and very friendly, although his first suggestion, true to form, was that the nurses should increase their earnings by trading their charms to the troops! I thought the War Office a horrid crowded place, but the Secretary of State's room is by contrast rather distinguished and its occupant gains in dignity by the fact that one has to walk the whole length of the room before one reaches his desk (a technique, as I pointed out to him, much utilised by foreign dictators).

Friday, January 31st

Spent most of the morning coping with the affairs of our new Mess at No. 10 Annexe, which is to open on Monday, Tommy Thompson, whose job it is, having shirked part of the responsibility.

Today and yesterday, for the first time in weeks, there have been numerous daylight raids and bombs have been dropped. This period of quiet has been partly due to the weather, but is doubtless also on account of the great German preparations which are taking place. There can now be little hesitation in predicting a German move through Bulgaria, which has finally succumbed to German influence and infiltration and where heavy German concentrations are taking place. The point at issue is whether Turkey will resist and will concert measures with Yugoslavia in time.

Meanwhile Derna has fallen and the C.I.G.S. is disappointed because, contrary to expectation, Wavell says he cannot hope to take Benghazi before the end of February. The P.M. has decided that our main effort must now be diverted to the Balkans where Germans, and not Italians, will have to be faced.

FOURTEEN

BRIGHTER NEWS
FEBRUARY–MARCH 1941

Sunday, February 2nd
The Roumanians, in the course of their civil upheaval, are committing sadistic atrocities unsurpassed in horror. For instance they have been taking hundreds of Jews to cattle slaughter-houses and killing them according to the Jews' own ritual practices in slaughtering animals. The P.M. has sent a minute to the Foreign Secretary: "Would it not be well to tell General Antonescu that we will hold him and his immediate circle personally responsible in life and limb if such a vile act is committed. (Some specific atrocity forecast in an F.O. telegram.) Perhaps you may think of something more diplomatic than this." It seems that we are back in the time of Mr Gladstone and the Bashi-Bazouks.

Monday, February 3rd
Everything is marking time in the military sphere, except in Italian East Africa where the prospects become brighter daily. Meanwhile the P.M. is busy with appointments of new Under Secretaries and High Commissioners. He wants to get rid of Malcolm MacDonald by sending him as High Commissioner to Canada and Winterton is to be offered the High Commissionership in South Africa.

Lunched at the Wyndham Club, where I sat with Clifford Norton who was interesting about Vansittart, whose P.S. he was. Our meeting Horace Wilson in the passage started us on the old, old topic of responsibility for the war. Norton said that Van had been uttering warnings about Germany since 1932, and that he and Eden had really seen eye to eye on the matter; but Eden could not stand it being thought that any opinion he uttered in the Cabinet was really the voice of Van.

After spending some of the afternoon at No. 10, I went to have a drink with the S. of S. for Air and Lady Sinclair in their flat above the Air Ministry. Catherine and Elizabeth Sinclair were there, as well as Hugh Seely,[1] a number of airmen – and Frances Day.[2] Conversation was general and entertaining and Archie Sinclair laid himself out to be pleasant. I like Lady Sinclair despite her austerity.

On late duty, but the P.M. obligingly thought of going to bed at 11.30.

Tuesday, February 4th

Represented the P.M. at General Metaxas's[3] memorial service in the Greek Church, Moscow Road. The Kents were there, and I sat in the row behind them with the Secretaries of State for Air, War, and Foreign Affairs. Lady Oxford slithered into a stall at the side and afterwards managed to pose with all the celebrities in turn as they left the church in front of a battery of photographers. I agree with Winston in thinking the Duchess of Kent the most beautiful woman I have ever seen. She is excellently dressed, her hair is as well done as it can be, and her natural beauty is only increased by the taste with which she paints and clothes herself.

The service was quite short. Some Orthodox priests emerged from behind the painted screen, accompanied by a man with an

---

[1] Sir Hugh Seely, 3rd Bt., was a Liberal M.P. appointed to be Sir Archibald Sinclair's Joint Parliamentary Under Secretary. Created Lord Sherwood at Sinclair's request, he expressed republican sentiments in the Smoking Room of the House of Commons and Churchill thereupon ordered the submission for the peerage to be retrieved. It was too late; the King had signed it.

[2] Well-known, good-looking and popular actress, born in the U.S.A. but anglicised.

[3] Greek Prime Minister who had restored King George II to the throne, put an end to the anarchic Greek Parliamentary situation, and thereafter ruled firmly but well.

Imperial and a deep bass voice, and chanted, unintelligibly to most of the congregation, for half an hour in front of the draped catafalque, on which candles burnt and a chalice of incense stood. It was much less impressive than Mount Athos,[1] but there was the same air of languid indifference strangely combined with devotional attention on the part of the Greeks present. Sheik Hafiz Wahba[2] and General de Gaulle lent an incongruous touch to the scene.

Today I talked to Malcolm MacDonald, who is reluctant to accept Canada. The P.M. admits that he has not done badly at the Ministry of Health, but obviously does not much care for him and repeated both to James Stuart and to me that he would have great opportunities in Canada. He adopted the same attitude when Halifax was reluctant to go to America.

I also saw Tom Johnston,[3] whom the P.M. thinks one of the best of the Labour Party. He is to be offered the Scottish Office.

Strange negotiations are going on between Germany and France. Pétain seems to be obstinately refusing to take back Laval or to modify the terms of the Armistice and he has, as his great bargaining counters, the threat to continue the war with the fleet and in the Colonies. The Germans are clearly furious with Vichy and even Darlan seems to have incurred their wrath.

The Mess had its opening night and looks like being a success. The cook is evidently first-rate and the company is stimulating. Desmond and Brendan expressed a good many anti-Chamberlain and anti-Baldwin sentiments and it was unanimously agreed that Kingsley Wood ("Little Joe" as Brendan and Beaverbrook call him) was the arch time-server. There was no dissent from Eric Seal's judgment that appeasement backed by strength may be good policy; appeasement through weakness is fatal. We had a

---

[1] In 1934 I had spent ten days in the monastic republic of Mount Athos.

[2] Saudi Arabian Minister.

[3] Scottish journalist M.P., originally with extreme left-wing views. Among the first to warn of the Nazi danger, he was appointed Regional Commissioner for Scotland by Chamberlain in 1939, with Lords Rosebery and Airlie as his deputies. On accepting the Scottish Office he made the unusual proviso that he should be assisted by a council containing all the previous Secretaries of State for Scotland.

long discussion on the reform of the Civil Service, begun by my begging Brendan to get the P.M. to make use of the present opportunity to initiate retirement in the Civil Service from forty-five onwards with a proportionate pension. Eric and Desmond put forward the view that each new entrant to the Civil Service should do a year's training to discover his bent and that some time after the age of thirty he should, if suitable, go to something equivalent to the Staff College before receiving higher promotion.

Wednesday, February 5th

Being on duty at 8.30 a.m. I read Keynes's interesting counter-blast to Hitler's new order, which states our war aims – and the hollowness of Germany's – in the economic sphere, promises drastic measures to deal with unemployment and proclaims a currency based on the exchange of goods. The Treasury have hacked it about a little and Sir Orme Sargent[1] has redrafted it entirely; but I prefer Keynes's original, which is pungent and comprehensible to the inexpert.

The Censorship Report on Home Opinion, which I am summarising for the P.M., makes it clear that there is a general expectation that this war must bring the end of class distinction and the abolition of great inequalities of wealth. There is no anti-democratic feeling. Obviously – and rightly – the fact that rationing and shortages affect the rich very little, since they can pay the extra price and feed in well-stocked restaurants, is causing some bitterness. A demand for war aims comes only from the intelligentsia and the main feeling seems to be hatred of the Germans and a demand for their annihilation – this particularly from the working classes. Employers and Labour both claim that the other is profiting from the war.

Edward Bridges and Prof. both dined in the Mess which promises to be a great success.

---

[1] Witty and cynical Under Secretary at the Foreign Office who was loved and respected by all his colleagues and universally known as Moley, though far from being a mole. Succeeded Sir Alexander Cadogan as Permanent Under Secretary after the war. Churchill set great store by his judgment.

Thursday, February 6th

At the House the P.M. paid a tribute to Lord Lloyd, who died on Sunday. He spoke of him simply and well and said that, though an imperialist and in some ways an authoritarian, he had been among the first to see the danger of Nazism and had worked in complete harmony with his Labour colleagues. His knowledge of the Moslems was great and since the King-Emperor had under his rule more Moslems than any other Prince, Lloyd's loss was especially heavy.

In the evening the P.M. got busy with the appointment of large numbers of Under Secretaries and Ministers. Lord Moyne* succeeds Lloyd, Ernest Brown[1] becomes Minister of Health instead of Malcolm MacDonald, and Tom Johnston S. of S. for Scotland. The P.M. told me he was delighted with the "lay-out" which includes the Editor of *Forward* (Tom Johnston) and the Premier Duke[2] (Under-Secretary for Agriculture) and thus shows the breadth of the administration.

Tommy Dugdale, who has just come back from Palestine, is to be Deputy Chief Whip.

Friday, February 7th

The P.M. went off on a tour to Colchester. At about 10.30 I was able to ring up and give the good news that Benghazi had surrendered. Wavell had doubted his ability to take it before the end of the month.

I met Philip at Euston and travelled with him to Crewe, dining on the train and proceeding from Crewe to Madeley in a taxi. The first impression of Madeley is pleasing, in spite of the overcrowding with furniture and pictures from Crewe, Crewe House, Horsley and Eccleston Square. The rooms are well proportioned and spacious and large fires burn in every grate.

---

[1] Eloquent Baptist Liberal-National, renowned for his loud voice. A man of high quality, he was successively Minister of Labour, Secretary of State for Scotland (though as English as could be), Chancellor of the Duchy of Lancaster and briefly, in 1945, Minister of Aircraft Production. He lost his seat at Leith in the 1945 election.

[2] Bernard, 16th Duke of Norfolk and Earl Marshal. Brilliant organiser of state functions, including two coronations and Churchill's State Funeral.

Saturday, February 8th

Mother, Philip and I walked far in the morning, through the park and round by the village. The surrounding country is undulating and pretty, quite unspoilt by the sight of an occasional colliery and the nearness of the Potteries and the Five Towns. The house outside is much less attractive than within, in fact distinctly disappointing as it was built in a good period (c. 1800).

Peggy arrived at lunch-time and made herself very agreeable. She particularly wanted to hear "all the low-down" about Muselier's mistaken arrest, of which she had already heard. Secrets do not last long.

After tea I went to see Grandfather in his room upstairs. He has had a touch of pleurisy, which at eighty-three is serious. However he looks astonishingly well and youthful; his cheeks have sunk a little but his appearance is still distinguished; he is growing deaf, and he sometimes stutters a little, but his eye and brain are clear and he expresses himself well if sometimes haltingly. His memory is remarkable, both for what he has seen and what he has read. We talked of politics. He said the Prime Minister had greatly mellowed of recent years and had, he thought, lost the sudden fits of unreasonable temper to which he had once been subject. He agreed that Baldwin would receive the roughest treatment at the hands of posterity, rougher than Chamberlain, but he did not believe this would be entirely justified although Baldwin's understanding of foreign affairs had been very slight. In other circumstances he might well have been a great Prime Minister. He had the capacity as his handling of the Abdication had shown.

Sunday, February 9th

Constant rain. We went to Mattins in the old red sandstone church which was almost filled by a large congregation.

After dinner we listened to Winston's first-rate broadcast, triumphant and yet not over-optimistic, addressed very largely to American ears. He mentioned the gallantry of the police which I had suggested that he should do.

At this stage of the proceedings I decided to leave the three fat volumes of my diary locked up at Madeley because its indis-cretions were considerable. I also felt it would be a pity if it were burnt in some conflagration during the blitz. On leaving Madeley on February 10th I wrote as follows:

I am confident that we have won. We shall see much serious damage and undergo many trials and dangers; but with the certainty of American material help and the determination of the people, the ultimate issue cannot be in doubt. The aftermath is unforeseeable, but there is reason to hope that we have learnt enough from the experiences of the recent past to see the folly of allowing the ideal to part company from the practical.

As soon as I got back to London I could not resist keeping a small pocket diary and the entries grew fuller as the days went by. I soon added to this much longer notes written after occasions which seemed to me particularly interesting, especially travels with the Prime Minister and week-ends at Chequers. In the entries that follow I have inserted these in their proper place. They account, however, for occasional repetitions in the narrative.

Tuesday, February 11th
Went to the Sinclairs' flat on top of the Air Ministry to have a drink with Lady S. and Catherine. Air Marshal Sir Philip Joubert de la Ferté was there, and I thought him most entertaining, if a shade specious.

Douglas, one of the nicest people in the Treasury, dined in the Mess. Brendan says we must not have so many Civil Servants to dine: they are dreary.

Wednesday, February 12th
Frantic arguments at dinner between Desmond and Brendan about theology and in particular the Church of Rome. Very late with the P.M.: read Pepys.

Beaverbrook told the P.M. on the telephone that in three things he had shown great vision: in his treatment of Hopkins;

in his treatment of Wendell Willkie;[1] in the timing of his broadcast last Sunday, which had just caught the American public on the right reaction.

Desmond Morton told me that there was great opposition to the P.M.'s decision not to press on to Tripoli but to divert our effort to Greece and Turkey. In continuing our African campaign we had the practical certainty of winning all North Africa and holding an impregnable position. In forming a bridgehead in Greece we ran the risk of another Dunkirk. The C.I.G.S. felt so strongly about it that he was almost thinking of resigning, and the military were making a determined effort to get Wavell to intervene. There was no constitutional means of forcing Wavell to obey; c.f. the old controversy between Haig and Lloyd George. Desmond pointed out that this was the vital decision of the first stage of the war.

To Sir John Anderson, who has shown himself unsympathetic to a complaint of Burgin[2] about the Government's indifference to certain cases of suffering, the P.M. has minuted: "When one is in office one has no idea how damnable things can feel to the ordinary rank and file of the public."

Saturday, February 15th
Nose to the grindstone all day in the absence of everybody but Seal, Barker and myself (the first taking no part in routine work). The noise of workmen strengthening our block of buildings is enough to induce lunacy.

Monday, February 17th
Philip and I both went on leave. Drove P. up to Helperby, stopping to lunch with the Sandwiches at Hinchingbrooke.

---

[1] Wendell Willkie, wholly dedicated to the cause of the Allies, was Republican candidate in the 1940 presidential election. He brought to England a message from Roosevelt and the verse, in the President's handwriting, "Sail on, O Ship of State" by Longfellow. Churchill received Willkie with courtesy and took much trouble to inform him about the current state of affairs.

[2] Leslie Burgin, M.P., had been Minister of Supply in Chamberlain's administration, but was dropped from the Government in May 1940.

Mother, Aunt Celia and Colin[1] at Helperby. Am reading Baudelaire's *Fleurs du Mal*.

Wednesday, February 19th

We had been going to hunt, but snow made it impossible to our great disappointment. So I read Dostoevsky's *The Idiot* (which is a wonderful book), slept and, in the afternoon, walked with Philip through the driving snowflakes. During the afternoon an enemy raider surprisingly descended from the clouds and dropped eight bombs nearby – one hitting a train full of chocolate. Aunt Celia upset a silver kettle of scalding water over Lady Graham, but this was not cause and effect. Father arrived from Madeley.

Thursday, February 20th

Snow still falling and no signs of its force diminishing. Emerged once or twice from the house, but for health not pleasure. Passed the day with bridge, sleep and Dostoevsky.

Friday, February 21st

Brilliant sunshine and warmth, but the snow is deep and takes a lot of melting. Philip, Mother and I walked to Myton in the morning to look at an exceedingly beautiful Charles II farmhouse.

Saturday, February 22nd

Lady Chesterfield[2] came over to lunch from Beningbrough. The same party as yesterday, with the addition of Uncle Clive, waited in the kale field, this time ineffectively, but had a very good pigeon shoot in the evening. In Carr's plantation I got twelve, shooting with accuracy.

---

[1] Colin Dodds (later Crewe), elder son of Lady Annabel Dodds by her second husband.

[2] Enid, last Countess of Chesterfield, owned Beningbrough Hall in the North Riding and bred racehorses. "Who was the architect?" I once asked her when shooting woodcock in the bracken near the house. "Gainsborough," she replied. "*Gainsborough?*" I asked incredulously. "Oh, well, perhaps it was Vanburgh. I have a yearling by one and a house by the other. It is so confusing."

Wednesday, February 26th

Lunched late at the Wyndham and then went to Hatchards to buy myself some books as a birthday present from David. There I met and conversed with Nancy Tree, Sir Godfrey Thomas, Catherine Sinclair and Juliet Henley. Hatchards is a twentieth-century coffee-house.

Chips Channon (just back from Yugoslavia) and Norman Brook dined. I was on late duty, the P.M. spending the evening composing his speech for the debate in the House tomorrow on the Disqualification of Members (or Malcolm MacDonald) Bill. This afternoon I heard the Chief Whip and Brendan pitch into Attlee because the Labour Party have decided not to put on the Whips for tomorrow's debate. To bed at 3.15 a.m.

After dinner the P.M. dictated his speech, which was full of historical allusions and legal intricacies, on the Disqualification of Members Bill, which has been occasioned by the appointment of Malcolm MacDonald as High Commissioner for Canada. The P.M. will get away with it of course, but I think he is unwise to use his personal influence with the House in an instance which is of little immediate importance. By so doing he may weaken his power on an occasion when it is really necessary. He is a great House of Commons man and loves to make use of his Parliamentary art; but I believe his prestige in the House would be even greater if he only appeared there on rare and solemn occasions.

In the early hours news came from the Admiralty of another serious disaster to a convoy. Brendan and I commented gloomily on the great threat to our lifeline which is developing and will continue to develop. He suggested I should not tell the P.M. tonight as it would prevent him sleeping. But at 3.00 a.m. he asked me point-blank if there was any news from the Admiralty and I had to tell him. He became very pensive. "It is very distressing," I said weakly. "Distressing!" he replied. "It is terrifying. If it goes on it will be the end of us."

Thursday, February 27th

The P.M. spent all day at the House where he delivered his speech in the afternoon. I was at the F.O. most of the morning checking certain historical allusions with the help of Gaselee.[1]

Heard the P.M.'s speech which was amusing and well-received in spite of its length. The issue at stake – the holding of "offices of profit" under the Crown by M.P.s – seemed of greater academic than immediate interest; but it was a good lesson in the intricacies and obscurities of British Constitutional practice. I took a long time checking the speech with the Official Reporter.

Friday, February 28th
The P.M. spent the morning at No. 10, presiding over a meeting of the Import Executive about the means of relieving our shipping difficulties. I was in attendance most of the time, working in the congenial atmosphere of No. 10 which is so preferable to the gaunt and dusty Annexe.

Heard that Sandy Vereker[2] had committed suicide. A tragic waste of charm, good looks and talent.

Monday, March 3rd
Rode at Richmond and saw a perfect sunrise. A soft blue sky and a watery sun and the birds singing as if spring were already here. Drove Louis Greig to London and said on a sudden impulse that I should like to be in a bomber crew. He promised to arrange a medical interview for me and I think that if I can tell Winston the R.A.F. have a place for me he may let me go (however obstructive he is about the army or navy).

Spent much time trying to get somebody to write an obituary for Sandy Vereker.

Lunched and laughed with Betty [Montagu] at the Civil Service Canteen in the National Gallery. The P.M. has a cold and is staying at Chequers.

[1] Sir Stephen Gaselee was the immensely erudite Foreign Office Librarian, always dressed as if King Edward VII were still on the throne.
[2] Only son of Lord Gort. A contemporary of mine at Harrow and Cambridge. A gifted painter, a keen Wagnerian (his room at Harrow was adorned by his own excellent paintings of scenes from *The Ring*) and the best-looking young man of my generation. He hated military life, as a reaction from his father, but acquitted himself well on the Dunkirk beaches. He shot himself when seriously concussed after a crash on a motor-cycle.

I may here pay a tribute to Louis Greig. He rose from nothing to considerable wealth and quite a lot of influence, partly by marrying a rich woman but more particularly by a genuine and constantly pursued ambition to pull strings on behalf of other people. He seldom if ever pulled them for himself but he thoroughly enjoyed helping others.

During the war he lent me a horse to ride in Richmond Park and I often used to stay the night at Thatched House Lodge, the Greigs' house in the Park. He died after the war, loved by a great many people to whom he had given pleasure without ever seeking any return. His two singularly pleasant daughters (one of whom, Jean, was happily married to Joe Cooper, the pianist) died, far too young, not long after their father.

Tuesday, March 4th

The P.M. returned from Chequers at noon and saw Colonel Donovan,[1] just back from the Balkans, where the stage is set and the curtain about to rise.

The P.M. had Herschel Johnson and Winant* to dine and discussed with them the American bases problem. I had to rush away from the dinner-table three times in order to procure various telegrams. It is very difficult to find what the P.M. wants because his descriptions are so elliptical. To bed 12.30 a.m.

Wednesday, March 5th

Busy and interesting day, during which vital and far-reaching issues were under discussion.

I only managed to snatch a quarter of an hour for lunch and went to the National Gallery where I found Miss Campbell, formerly Mr Chamberlain's personal private secretary. We talked of former days at No. 10 when the atmosphere was quieter – and much less gay. Winston's régime is certainly entertaining.

---

[1] "Big Bill" Donovan. Won the Congressional Medal of Honour in France in 1918. He was a successful lawyer of humble Irish immigrant origin. With much help from the British, he created from nothing the American Intelligence system in the Second World War, founded the Office of Strategic Services (O.S.S.) and was thus indirectly an originator of the C.I.A.

Today has been one of great activity and varied interest. At 11.30 the P.M. met Lord Moyne and Cranborne, Herschel Johnson and Winant, the new U.S. Ambassador, in the Cabinet Room at No. 10, to discuss the vexed problem of the American bases in the West Indies, which we have given on lease for ninety-nine years in return for fifty obsolete destroyers. The West Indian Colonies themselves, the oldest of the Crown, are resentful and their feelings are shared by many people here in view of the conditions which the Americans have demanded and which amount to capitulations. Both sides are haggling and ill-feeling has arisen. Bridges thinks that if the Government accepted all the American desiderata they would be defeated in the House of Commons. The Colonial Office are frightened that in the heat of conflict we shall cede much that will afterwards be most regrettable. Lord Cranborne sees in the American attitude a dangerous emphasis on hemisphere defence: an inclination to make special concessions to Canada because she is an American nation; a tendency which might well lead to Western hemisphere isolationism after the war.

But the P.M. is ill-satisfied with the point of view expressed by his colleagues. He believes that the safety of the state is at stake, that America in providing us with credits will enable us to win the war which we could not otherwise do, and that we cannot afford to risk the major issue in order to maintain our pride and to preserve the dignity of a few small islands.

I think his view is statesmanlike, but America, if she persists, is going to arouse a lot of bitterness in England and set back the cause of Anglo-American unity.

While the P.M. was trying to reach a *modus vivendi* on this question, an alarming telegram arrived from Eden. It showed the Greek situation in a sombre light. Eden, Dill and Wavell have found General Papagos discouraged and obviously weakened by the loss of Metaxas. They have accepted a strategic position which will mean that our troops will find themselves in a dangerous plight. Yugoslavia is weak and vacillating; Turkey is in no position to do anything but remain on the defensive. Eden says: "This is as tough a proposition as ever I have known."

Last night David Margesson told me how much he disliked

the whole venture upon which we are about to embark. Many others feel the same. It was thrust upon us partly because, in the first place, the P.M. felt that our prestige in France, in Spain and in the U.S., could not stand our desertion of Greece; partly because Eden, Dill, Wavell and Cunningham (who has now telegraphed to point out the extreme length to which his resources are stretched) recommended it so strongly.[1] But the danger of another Norway, Dunkirk and Dakar rolled into one, looms threateningly before us.

More telegrams came. The P.M. went very late to lunch with Oliver Lyttelton, and I snatched a quarter of an hour for a quick mouthful. After his afternoon sleep, the P.M., emerging from beneath the bedclothes and yawning, said, voicing his waking thought: "The poor Chiefs of the Staff will get very much out of breath in their desire to run away." I showed him a telegram from Eden urging that a high decoration for General Papagos would help matters. "Too cheap," he commented with a disgusted gesture.

The Cabinet met at 5.00 and afterwards the P.M. drafted a telegram to Eden urging that we should not be justified in preventing the Greeks from accepting German terms if they felt themselves unable to resist. If they wished to fight, well and good; we should have to do our utmost.

This telegram was discussed at a 10.00 p.m. Defence Meeting.

Thursday, March 6th

Rush continued. Very short handed. The P.M. harangued the Chiefs of Staff at No. 10 continuously from 11.30 to 1.30.

Lunched with Father at the Turf, which was full. I am glad to see the sideboard is less groaning with cold meat than when last I was there; but certainly the rich can still feed sumptuously.

Rab Butler dined with me in the Mess, where Brendan's flow of eloquence was ceaseless and very funny. The P.M. was cross because he could not find any of us during dinner, but was laughed out of his ill-temper by Brendan who compared him to

[1] Wavell, having been opposed to the whole scheme of intervention on behalf of Greece, veered round and became its warm exponent.

Mr Sparrow[1] (from Nathaniel Gubbins in the *Sunday Express*).
Slept upstairs, out of the shelter, for the first time.

Friday, March 7th
Very anxious decisions have been in the air, making the P.M.
impatient, the atmosphere electric and the pace tremendous.

In the morning I went over to see Vansittart in the F.O. to
let him know what the P.M. is thinking about the American bases
question. He was emphatic about the importance of reaching
agreement before the American press becomes vociferous.

Travelled down late to Chequers. Pug and Edward Bridges
came, also Oliver Stanley. There was a good deal of reminiscing
about the early stages of the war and, later, a number of
important telegrams telephoned down from London.

The P.M. was much happier. His mind is relieved now that a
great decision has been irrevocably taken. He was witty and
entertaining.

Saturday, March 8th
Sir Arthur Salter and Sir William Beveridge[2] came to lunch and
talked of shipping and manpower. The P.M. pulled their legs a
good deal and kept on winking at Tommy Thompson and me,
the others present. He said that socialism was folly, that the
profit motive was essential to efficiency, and many other things
that must have shocked Salter. Beveridge said he thought there
would be a Conservative reaction after the war.

A short but much needed walk, followed by tea with Pamela
Churchill in the Great Hall. Mr Menzies,[3] the Australian Prime

---

[1] Mr Sparrow was the curmudgeonly husband in the Sparrows' nest which
was a feature of Nat Gubbins' column.

[2] Author of the Beveridge Plan and thus of the Welfare State. A Liberal who
was a gifted economist and social scientist. Originally a civil servant, he
became Vice Chancellor of London University and Master of University
College, Oxford. Created a peer in 1946.

[3] Sir Robert Menzies, Prime Minister of Australia until the Labour Party won
a General Election in 1941. He spent several months in England and was
invited to attend the War Cabinet meetings. A staunch imperialist, he
returned to power in 1949 and won a reputation for wisdom and statesman-
ship. On his retirement the Queen appointed him Lord Warden of the Cinque
Ports. She had already made him a Knight of the Thistle.

Minister, came to stay; so did General de Gaulle, General Spears, and Duncan and Diana Sandys. An interesting evening, punctuated with rumours of an impending naval battle and news of a blitz on London, the first for weeks. The Café de Paris was hit and a hundred people trapped. Mr Hopkins rang me up from New York at 3.00 a.m. to say the Lease and Lend Bill had passed.

At dinner this evening there were present, besides the Prime Minister, General de Gaulle, General Spears, Mr Menzies, Duncan and Diana Sandys, Tommy Thompson and myself.

We talked of Germany and the Germans.

De Gaulle said that the important thing for people living in an occupied territory was to remain aloof and superior. The Germans knew that they were inferior beings and were susceptible on the point. Moreover, this being so, it was important to stress that the war was a world war. The Germans could see themselves as lords of Europe, but the idea of the world gave them vertigo. As for Hitler, he said: *"Vous ne le prendrez pas, et cette fois il n'y aura pas un Doorn."*[1]

Duncan Sandys was bloodthirsty. He wanted to destroy Germany by laying the country waste and burning towns and factories, so that for years the German people might be occupied in reconstruction. He wanted to destroy their books and libraries so that an illiterate generation might grow up.

Louis Spears replied that this would make the Germans more hardy and virile, while their Western conquerors would be growing effete on the fruits of victory. In his view Richelieu was the greatest of modern European statesmen. He had understood the Germans and at the Diet of Ratisbon he had so divided them that they took centuries to unite. The P.M. replied that this was not applicable to modern conditions, though Prussia must be separated from South Germany.

The P.M. said he was in no way moved by Duncan's words. He did not believe in pariah nations, and he saw no alternative

[1] "You will not capture him, and this time there will not be a Doorn." Doorn was the country house in Holland where Kaiser Wilhelm II found asylum when the British and French Governments wanted to put him on trial after 1918.

to the acceptance of Germany as part of the family of Europe. In the event of invasion he would not even approve of the civil population murdering the Germans quartered on them. Still less would he condone atrocities against the German civil population if we were in a position to commit them. He cited an incident in Ancient Greece when the Athenians spared a city which had massacred some of their citizens, not because its inhabitants were men, but "because of the nature of man". This impressed Mr Menzies.

Mr Menzies contributed to the discussion by a slightly irrelevant, though amusing, account of the way in which an insect called the Cactoblastus, imported from California, destroyed the dense growth of Prickly Pear jungle in Australia. Duncan hoped for a similar *deus ex machina* to deal with the Germans.

The conversation turned to Rome and Carthage. The P.M. drew a comparison between this country and Carthage, but pointed out that the Carthaginians were vanquished because they lost command of the sea. Mr Menzies said that moreover they had not had a Winston Churchill (forgetting Hannibal!). Anyhow, said the P. M., the Almighty had given Carthage a raw deal last time and might alter the outcome on this occasion.

Sunday, March 9th
Saw de Gaulle off and talked with Colonel Donovan who came to see the P.M. and told me about his Balkan and Peninsular tour.

Sir Alan Brooke, C. in C., Home Forces, came to dine and sleep. Prof. L. and Alastair Forbes dined also and there was a lot of flippant conversation about metaphysics, solipsists and higher mathematics. Afterwards the gramophone played marches and old-fashioned songs of a martial kind (such as the P.M. loves) while W.S.C. gave us a display of arms drill with his big game rifle. To bed at the record hour of 11.30 p.m.

Monday, March 10th
The P.M. has been suffering from bronchitis and is not going back to London. His capacity for work is totally unimpaired and his temper is scarcely ruffled. He came down to lunch with

Mary, Tommy Thompson and me. Afterwards he told us about Robert Graves's book on the American War of Independence (*Sergeant Lamb*), which he is reading with particular enjoyment, and lamented the difficulties caused by the bases agreement.

Lord Moyne (S. of S. for the Colonies) and Sir Richard Peirse (C. in C., Bomber Command) came for the night. Big bombs (the new 4,000–pounders) alternated with West Indian bases as the main topic and I sat up late arranging the P.M.'s complex papers about the latter.

Tuesday, March 11th
Early bedside conference with Lord Moyne. The P.M. decided to tackle the bases problem with the American Ambassador this afternoon.

His bronchitis is still bad, but in spite of everybody's wishes he insisted on returning to London in time for the usual Tuesday lunch with the King. I dined with Eileen[1] and Tommy Davies at the Dorchester. The others in the party included Fitzroy Maclean (who has resigned from the F.O. to become a private in the Camerons).

Wednesday, March 12th
Went to the House with the P.M. and heard him sing a paean of praise to the U.S. for having passed the Lease and Lend Bill. He described it as a second Magna Carta (using words suggested by Professor Whitehead of the F.O.).[2]

He then saw the Bermudan delegates and spoke to them so charmingly about their losses over the bases question that they told me they thought he felt it as keenly as they themselves. I quoted *The Tempest* to them: "the still-vexed Bermoothes".

Brendan invited his financier-collector friend, Chester Beatty,[3] to dine and Cole Deacon of the Railway Executive also

---

[1] A childhood friend married to Colonel Thomas Davies, Grenadier Guards.

[2] This was the only occasion I remember during the war when Winston Churchill used somebody else's draft, or at any rate a portion of it, in making a speech to the House of Commons. In all other cases the text was entirely his own.

[3] A successful mining engineer, born an American but naturalised a British subject. Chairman of Selection Trust and other large mining enterprises.

came. I made an allusion to Roumania being the Botany Bay of the Roman Empire, which incensed Brendan – though I believe he is Irish and not Australian at all.

Tuesday, March 18th
The P.M. made a speech at the Pilgrim's luncheon. Lunch was at 1.15: he was still dictating his speech at 1.30!

Left at 6.30 to stay the night with Lilly[1] and Tom Motion at Serge Hill for a day's hunting. Cousin Nelly[2] was there – a very delightful personality, aristocratic in the true sense, intelligent, dignified and of great simplicity. We talked of the three Sheridan sisters[3] and particularly Caroline Norton.

Wednesday, March 19th
Hunted with the Hertfordshire, accompanied by my host and hostess. We met at Putteridge and a thick mist gave way to radiant heat and sunshine. We did not find till late, but there could have been no better day for riding about the countryside which is exquisite in this part of the country. We finally found in a ploughed field to which we were led by two Miss Harrisons (of the famous eight sisters)[4] and had a short but fast run before the fox went to ground. He got up from a furrow twenty-five yards in front of hounds and the chase was spectacular.

Back to London after tea. The P.M. had the Americans Biddle[5] (Ambassador to all our fugitive allies over here) and

---

[1] Best looking of the six daughters of the 3rd Earl of Verulam. My mother's first cousin. My father fell briefly in love with her before he met my mother and when, at my mother's suggestion, she became a lady-in-waiting, King George V found her so attractive that Queen Mary thought it prudent to dispense with her services.

[2] Lady Helen Graham.*

[3] Sheridan's three beautiful and talented grand-daughters were Lady Dufferin, Mrs Norton and the Duchess of Somerset. Caroline Norton wrote verses and novels, was a pioneer of the Married Women's Property Act and had an intimate, though probably platonic, relationship with Lord Melbourne. She was a well-known figure in Victorian intellectual circles and George Meredith portrayed her as "Diana of the Crossways".

[4] The eight daughters of Major J. F. Harrison of King's Waldenbury, Hitchin, were ardent riders to hounds.

[5] U.S. Ambassador to all the exiled foreign Governments in London.

Harriman* (President R.'s personal representative on shipping and supply questions) to dinner and as there was a heavy raid he took his guests and his whole private office up to the roof of the Air Ministry to watch the fun. He quoted to us Tennyson's prescient lines about aerial warfare.

Thursday, March 20th
At the House for Questions and the Cabinet. There was a scene over Boothby who is committing breaches of privilege. On the way home in the car the P.M., speaking of this, said he would have no part in the matter; if there was one thing in the world he found odious, it was a man-hunt.

Our master having gone to dine at the Other Club,[1] we took the opportunity of playing noisy and childish games in the Mess, and were much excited by the news that the *Scharnhorst* and *Gneisenau* had been located in the Atlantic and might well be intercepted.

Saturday, March 22nd
Very busy. Tony Bevir has many qualities but he is apt to vanish for hours at a stretch and leave a solitary colleague to bear the heat and burden of the day.

Jack Churchill was quite entertaining in the Mess (he is often very boring) and gave vivid descriptions of F.E. (Lord Birkenhead).

The diplomatic battle for the soul of Yugoslavia is reaching its height and sways either way with vertiginous speed.

Sunday, March 23rd
During the course of the morning I strolled out for a few minutes and walked into the Abbey where, even in this sceptical age, hundreds of people were attending a service in the nave in observance of the National Day of Prayer.

Edward Bridges and Bill Cavendish Bentinck dined. The latter is witty and talks well; also has good judgment, I think. He is

---

[1] Dining Club founded by Churchill and F. E. Smith (Lord Birkenhead) in 1911 when they were both blackballed from The Club.

au courant with what is going on and full of ideas on the subject.

Tuesday, March 25th
The message which I drafted for the P.M. to send to the Greeks on their Independence Day was published in this evening's paper:

> Mr Churchill, the Prime Minister, has sent the following message to the Greek people, who yesterday celebrated Greek Independence Day:
> "On this day of proud memories, I would add one brief tribute to those which the whole civilised world is paying to the valour of the Greek nation.
> One hundred and twenty years ago, all that was noblest in England strove in the cause of Greek independence and rejoiced in its achievement. Today that epic struggle is being repeated against greater odds, but with equal courage and with no less certainty of success. We in England know that the cause for which Byron died is a sacred cause: we are resolved to sustain it."

While the Prime Minister always wrote his own speeches I became, at this period and again when I returned to No. 10 at the end of 1943, the principal drafter of messages, prefaces, etc. Although Mr Churchill at his best was beyond plagiarism, it was possible to imitate his style fairly closely on matters which were not of supreme importance and I reached the stage where I could draft most of his shorter compositions without his correcting them. Having thus acquired a certain ability to imitate his style I did, after 1951, write quite a number of his speeches although very few of those, and then only on ceremonial occasions, which he delivered to Parliament.

Thursday, March 27th
Walked round St James's Park lake with Rab Butler who has, somewhat reluctantly, come to admire the P.M. though he still clearly does not think much of his own Secretary of State [Anthony Eden].

A great day. Revolution in Belgrade, which puts an entirely different complexion on events in the Balkans and turns darkness into dawn. The P.M. is overjoyed and I should be too, if I had not got a liver attack. He announced the glad tidings in two speeches, at a Conservative Association meeting and at a T.U.C. meeting. The whole country is in ecstasies.[1]

News of Keren's[2] fall was the final cause of rejoicing. P.M. thrilled, but says we must now expect bad news.

Friday, March 28th
To Chequers, arriving just in time for dinner. Party consisted of P.M., Sir John Anderson, Pug, Tommy, Mary and Pamela. Chief excitement was report of naval engagement with Italians off Crete – this time a true one. Talk ranged from foreign policy to the home front. P.M. said people were very much happier in the war than might have been expected. Anderson went further and thought the war might prove to have been a real blessing to the country. He is a pompous ass, but clever.

The P.M., in praising Chamberlain's courage during his illness, said that he knew not the first thing about war, Europe or foreign politics. Discourse on the Admiralty: Pound the best brain in the navy, though the most cautious. Alexander would have had to face much hostile criticism if he had not been a Labour man.

Saturday, March 29th
A family luncheon party after which the P.M. gave me a short lecture on the various invaders of Russia, especially Charles

---

[1] The Regent of Yugoslavia, Prince Paul, was summoned by Hitler in March 1941 and reluctantly obliged to sign a pact with the Axis. This caused a revolution in Belgrade. On March 26th General Simovic deposed the Regent, declared King Peter ruler of the country and formed an anti-German government. The Germans thereupon diverted troops southwards, bombed Belgrade and occupied the country. The King had to escape to London and the former Regent was placed in custody by the British. The Yugoslav diversion, preceded in March by the British landing in Greece, may have caused Hitler to postpone his invasion of Russia, originally planned for May 1st.

[2] Keren, in Eritrea, had been tenaciously defended by the Duke of Aosta's Italian army.

XII. Later Sarah took Mrs C., Tommy and me over to see her new and luxurious (but very filmstar) house at Waddesdon.

Mr Winant, Averell Harriman, Mr Menzies and the Cranbornes came for the week-end. I sat next to Menzies at dinner and had a lively conversation with him about Ireland, the English and the Diplomatic Service.

Sunday, March 30th
The Duke and Duchess of Kent came to lunch. I sat between Lord Cranborne, who is exceptionally agreeable, and Averell Harriman. Afterwards the Duke inspected the Guard while I struggled with his chauffeur-less car and the Duchess. Mr Menzies photographed the proceedings assiduously.

The news of the great naval victory off Cape Matapan, for which we have been waiting, came through just after the Kents had left and was greeted with yells of delight. "How lucky the Italians came in," said the P.M.

Sarah came to tea and there was more photography by Mr Menzies. Prof. arrived.

"The tearing up of the paper fleet of Italy," was Winston's comment on today's news.

Monday, March 31st
This has been a wonderful week-end, the culmination of a week of victories. Our visitors are Winant, Harriman, Menzies, the Cranbornes.

The P.M. has been elated by the naval victory following so close on the Yugoslav revolution, the fall of Keren and the capture of Harar.[1] He emphasises the effect it will have on Japan and he has written a letter to Matsuoka,[2] now on his way to Vichy, in a similar vein, though somewhat more threatening, to

[1] Town in Ethiopia defended by the Italians.
[2] Japanese Foreign Minister and moving spirit behind Japan's decision to join the Berlin – Rome Axis. He also wanted to make friends with the Soviet Union and isolate the U.S.A. In April 1941 he went to Moscow, via Rome and Berlin, but Hitler told him nothing of his plan to invade Russia. Thus he looked foolish when, on reaching Moscow, he signed a treaty with the Soviet Union just before it was attacked by his Axis allies. He had to resign.

that he sent last June to Mussolini. He begins by asking: "Will Germany, without the command of the sea or the command of the British daylight air, be able to invade and conquer Great Britain in the spring, summer or autumn of 1941? Will Germany try to do so? Would it not be in the interests of Japan to wait until these questions have answered themselves?" He asks seven other equally pertinent questions and concludes: "From the answers to these questions may spring the avoidance by Japan of a serious catastrophe, and a marked improvement in the relations between Japan and the two great sea powers of the West."

The P.M. told me he was now sure Germany would attack Yugoslavia before Greece or Turkey and he is very hopeful on that front.

The naval news has stirred him to compose several brilliant telegrams, to Roosevelt, etc., and he has spent much of the week-end pacing – or rather tripping – up and down the Great Hall to the sound of the gramophone (playing martial airs, waltzes and the most vulgar kind of brass-band songs) deep in thought all the while.

In the evening Diana Quilter took me, with Middy Gascoigne, Brigadier Gibbs and a guardsman called Arnold Vivian, to see the Stepney Shelters. We drank sherry and ate smoked-salmon sandwiches at Diana's First Aid Post and were then escorted to the crypt of Christchurch, Spitalfields; the Kent and Essex Hay-yard (which was deserted); the Tilbury shelter; the Arches, Watney Street; and Gooche's. They have greatly improved; some are even cheerful, though it is terrible to see human beings living in such cramped conditions. But many were well dressed and few looked miserable. Two personalities impressed me: Father Groser who has organised a social centre at the Arches, with a canteen and lectures or debates every night; and the nurse, young but downright and completely self-possessed, at Gooche's.

FIFTEEN

AFRICAN REVERSE: GREEK FIASCO
APRIL 1941

Wednesday, April 2nd
Glamorous pay-party at Claridges, organised by Ann O'Neill.[1]
There has been nothing like it since the war. Our party was
Middy, Terence, Rosemary Hinchingbrooke, Betty Montagu,
Martin Charteris, Diana Quilter and others. It was wonderful to
see a display of real evening dresses again and to meet people
I had not seen since 1939. All London was there and the gaiety
was great.

In the early hours I went on to the Four Hundred with Martin,
Rosemary, Betty and Peter and Diana Tiarks. War is a great
cure for blasé-ness as far as these sort of entertainments go. It
would all have seemed commonplace and dull two years ago.

Thursday, April 3rd
We have been compelled to evacuate Benghazi in face of the
German advance from Tripoli. The P.M. is greatly worried, but
Pug refuses to take it too tragically. However the proposed visit
to Liverpool and Manchester this evening is cancelled.

[1] Born Ann Charteris, she married my cousin Shane, Lord O'Neill, who was
killed in action in 1944. She then married Esmond, Viscount Rothermere,
and finally Ian Fleming, the creator of James Bond. Vivacious and quick-
witted, she sought the company of men of power. Lord Beaverbrook
unkindly dubbed her "Idiots' Delight", but she delighted many men and some
women who were by no means idiots.

Sunday, April 6th
We heard on the wireless that Germany had invaded both Greece and Yugoslavia.

Monday, April 7th
There is no news from the Balkan front but that from Libya is bad. The German attack has taken us by surprise and an armoured brigade has been cut up.

Budget: income tax ten shillings in the pound. Nobody seems to mind. Brendan says the House and the Country take a masochistic pleasure in it, like flagellating friars.

After dinner (to which Brendan invited Sir Walter Layton) there was a short Chiefs of Staff meeting. The P.M. confided to me that he thought Wavell, etc., had been very silly in North Africa and should have been prepared to meet an attack there.

There was a film display in the Air Council room at the Air Ministry. I went with the P.M. We saw a new propaganda film, and the latest *March of Time*.

Tuesday, April 8th
The P.M. spent all the afternoon composing his speech for tomorrow. After dinner I took part of it round to the American Embassy to show Winant. He made four pertinent observations in respect of the effect on U.S. opinion and I was deeply impressed by his unassertive shrewdness and wisdom. I afterwards explained these points to the P.M. who accepted them.

While I was with the Ambassador a blitz started. He did not even raise his head. Massawa has fallen into our hands; but the news from Yugoslavia is disturbing and the Germans have already entered Salonica.

Wednesday, April 9th
I listened to the P.M.'s speech on the war situation in the House of Commons. It was well received. He painted a picture dark and yet encouraging, and he stressed that the Battle of the Atlantic was the real issue of the war. He did not attempt to minimise the hazards with which we are faced in Greece and North Africa. He explained how unity in the Balkans had been

a possibility. If Yugoslavia, Greece and Turkey had stood firm together, they could have presented to Germany a strong front defended by seventy divisions.

Thursday, April 10th
The P.M. was terribly upset by a serious motor smash involving Duncan Sandys.

Left for a tour of the South-West with the P.M., Winant, Harriman, Mrs Churchill, Mary, Ismay, Tommy and a batch of officers connected with the new technical inventions. We all slept on the train.

Friday, April 11th
Good Friday. Reached Swansea at 8.00 a.m. and spent the morning among the City's battered ruins and inspecting detachments of Civil Defence Workers. The centre of the town has not a house standing. I was amazed by the eagerness and cheerfulness of the population. W. had a great reception.

We went on by train to Cardigan and motored from there to Aberporth on Cardigan Bay, where we saw a noisy but interesting display of rockets, U.P. projectors, etc., such as would have delighted the Prof.'s heart if he had not been laid up with a chill at Marlow. The firing of the rockets was bad and at the first display a childishly easy target was repeatedly missed; but the multiple projectors seemed promising; so did the aerial mines descending with parachutes.

During the morning at Swansea I walked much of the time with Mr David Grenfell, local M.P. and also Minister of Mines, who began life as a miner. He talked in Welsh to most of his constituents.

We slept on the train at a wayside station called Whitland.

Saturday, April 12th
Arrived early at Bristol. Bathed and breakfasted with the P.M. and Harriman at the Grand Hotel. The rest of the party joined us from the train and led by the Lord Mayor we walked and motored through devastation such as I had never thought possible. Swansea is mild in comparison. There had been a bad raid

during the night and many of the ruins were still smoking. The people looked bewildered but, as at Swansea, were brave and were thrilled by the sight of Winston who drove about sitting on the hood of an open car and waving his hat.

At the university the P.M., as Chancellor, conferred honorary degrees on Winant and Menzies and made an excellent impromptu speech in which he likened the fortitude of Bristol to that which we are accustomed "to associate with Ancient Rome and modern Greece". The gowns and pageantry were a strange contrast to the smoking ruins just outside.[1]

Reached Chequers for dinner. Mr and Mrs Eden and Sir J. Dill came. A hectic night starting in gloom and ending in glad momentous news from the U.S.A. – Winant received a telegram for the P.M. from Roosevelt announcing America's intention to extend her patrol area as far west as the 25th meridian.

Sunday, April 13th

Easter Day. The C.I.G.S. took Mary and me to the early service in his car. The Chiefs of Staff, Eden, Amery, Horace Seymour[2] and Pug met all the morning to discuss Iraq, where a pro-axis coup d'état has taken place under Rashid Ali, and Yugoslavia, where resistance to the Germans by the semi-mobilised army seems to be stiffening a little. In Libya we heard that the Germans had taken Bardia and attacked Tobruk.

I asked Harriman if he did not think last night's news from the U.S. might mean war with Germany. "That's what I hope," he said.

At lunch I sat between Brendan (who shuns Chequers except on rare occasions) and Seymour. Afterwards the conclave continued till tea-time, Amery, who had been summoned about Iraq, pushing himself into the Yugoslav discussions. When the

---

[1] Menzies, who spoke poorly on this occasion, told me afterwards that he never spoke with notes. He always found it was politically more impressive, and seldom risky, to speak impromptu. In this discovery he was luckier than most politicians.

[2] A diplomat since before the First World War. Minister at Teheran in the 1930s, an Under Secretary in the Foreign Office for the first half of the war and then Ambassador to China.

P.M. went to sleep Mary and I went for an invigorating walk in the fresh wind, she overbrimming with life and gaiety.

Menzies arrived for dinner, at which only the P.M., Mary, Harriman and Tommy were present in addition. Afterwards we talked, pulled Mary's leg and played the gramophone. The P.M. worked till 2.15 a.m.

Wednesday, April 16th
Organised resistance in Yugoslavia has ceased. In Greece the Germans are entering Volo and there is much talk of a stand in the pass of Thermopylae. We are holding our own at Tobruk.

Gladwyn Jebb came to dinner. A raid started in the middle and grew, in the course of the night, to be the worst London has yet had. During it I went to the American Embassy in the armoured car to discuss a telegram with Winant and also met his wife. Later, as 450 planes droned over London, bombs came down like hailstones and on my way to No. 10, at 1.45 a.m., I had quite a disagreeable walk.

During this period of the war Jack Churchill and I slept on the top floor of 10 Downing Street itself, in the Prime Minister's and Mrs Churchill's former bedrooms, which were still furnished. This was comfortable, but also noisy and vulnerable. In the autumn of 1944, when I returned to Downing Street during the "V" weapon bombardment, I slept for a time in the underground quarters beneath the Central War Room where all the rest of the Secretaries slept, as well as the Chiefs of Staff and members of the Cabinet Offices. This was certainly safe, but it looked and smelt like a battleship and one emerged in the morning gasping for fresh air.

Thursday, April 17th
London looks bleary-eyed and disfigured. There is a great gash in the Admiralty. St Peter's, Eaton Square, has been hit (and Mr Austin Thompson[1] killed), Chelsea Old Church is demolished, Jermyn Street is wrecked. Mayfair has suffered badly.

[1] Much loved vicar of St Peter's, Eaton Square. He went out on to the steps of the church to call people into the comparative safety of the solidly-built edifice and was struck by a bomb.

After breakfast Eric Seal and I walked in the sun on the Horse Guards Parade and found Pamela Churchill and Averell Harriman also examining the devastation. The streets were soon full of people intent on sightseeing. The roads everywhere were covered with glass.

In the evening Brendan regaled us with his electioneering experiences, which are remarkably funny, and Pug told for the twelfth time the story of Gamelin and the defeat of France.

Our planes set out to bomb Berlin and thus showed we are not afraid of reprisal threats.

Friday, April 18th
Got up and rode early on the Thatched House Lodge chestnut, afterwards breakfasting with Louis.

Lunched with Esmé Glyn at the Carlton Grill. She took me to see her mother's house in St James's Place gutted by fire and by a landmine yesterday morning. Only the shell remains and there was still a fire burning inside. The butler was stalwartly saving what he could from the ruins. Except for No. 23, Jimmy Rothschild's house, the whole street of charming houses is laid waste. Rain added to the desolation of the scene.

The P.M. saw the press editors to prepare their minds for grave possibilities in Greece. At 6.00 he left for Ditchley.

A statement was issued to the press that we would bomb Rome if Athens or Cairo were bombed and that we should continue to raid Berlin, not as reprisals but as policy, whenever convenient.

Saturday, April 19th
After dinner another raid started and rapidly increased in intensity. As I write a bomb has exploded close by and there seem to be many aircraft overhead.

Tony says that London is now beginning to look a little like what he expected it to be thirty-six hours after the outbreak of war. Certainly as I walk through the streets I look at London's landmarks more carefully now, with a feeling that it may be the last time I shall see them.

Sunday, April 20th
Early service at Westminster Abbey and then walked down the
Embankment in the sun. London from Westminster Bridge on
a spring morning is very different from the day when Wordsworth
saw it, but it now has a modern splendour. Boadicea's[1] statue
is a monument to successful imperialism (*aet.* 1902):

> *Realms that Caesar never knew*
> *Thy posterity shall sway.*

Monday, April 21st
The P.M. returned from Ditchley at 11.30 and immediately had
a Defence Committee. Today is a critical day in the history of
the war as far as Greece is concerned. Final decision to evacuate
was taken.

Lunched with Father at the Turf, one of the few surviving
clubs. Sammy Hood dined in the Mess. I was on late duty and
very late it was, the P.M. almost finishing his box.

A momentous decision was taken today, not only in Greece.
Operation TIGER[2] was adopted.

Tuesday, April 22nd
To the new House (the old has been damaged) for Questions
and a short statement as to why there should be no statement!
Tripoli has been bombarded by the fleet, though it is not yet
clear with how much success. The P.M. had Hore-Belisha to
lunch and it was a strange coincidence that for the first time a
press photographer was seen to be waiting outside the Annexe.
I asked David Margesson, who was also lunching, whether he
thought the P.M. had anything in mind for Belisha. He said he
thought the P.M. had, at the back of his mind, because he saw
incipient opposition in that quarter and Winston is inclined to

---

[1] Now called Boudicca, with the same pedantry that turns Jehovah into
Yahweh, thus demonstrating an academic ambition to be thought clever by
dethroning names that have been in general use for centuries. Adam and
Eve have miraculously escaped so far.
[2] The despatch at great risk through the Mediterranean of tanks required to
enable Wavell to take the offensive.

defeat opposition by means of favour rather than by fear. David
has the lowest opinion of Belisha; so has Duff Cooper with whom
I also talked of him this afternoon.

Wednesday, April 23rd

The surrender of the Western Greek armies and departure of
the Government were made public.

The Home Censorship Report (on letters sent abroad from
this country) is for the first time a little bit alarming. It shows a
certain amount of discontent. People seem to think that "the
ruling classes" are doing well out of the war – which they
certainly are not. There is a good deal of criticism of the
Government and a lot of the B.B.C. In particular people seem
to be getting sick of the hearty propaganda of the "Are we
downhearted?" kind, sponsored by the Government. Brendan
points out that there is bound to be criticism of the Government:
its "honeymoon period" is over and "the grim realities of
marriage" have to be faced.

Tommy Dugdale dined with me. We had a long talk, largely
about the tendency to discontent visible in the House and in the
country.

Thursday, April 24th

With the P.M. in the Upper War Room, Admiralty, most of the
afternoon. We walked back down Whitehall and he expatiated
on the beauty of the Banqueting Hall, saying he could not think
why it had not been copied for Government offices. He told me
that today New Zealand troops were fully engaged at Thermopylae – an historic event which he had been certain would
happen. I remember how blood red the pass looked when I went
by it at sunrise, seven years ago, on the way to Athens from
Salonika.

The P.M. left for a tour of Liverpool and Manchester.

Dined with Clarissa Churchill at the Coq d'Or. She is singularly
beautiful and talks well, but is cold and, I think, callous. However
I found her sympathetic this evening and we had quite interesting
conversations, punctuated with awkward silences, at the Four
Hundred to which we repaired after dinner.

Friday, April 25th
A medical interview for the R.A.F. Passed A.1. in everything but eyesight in which I was border-line. Was told I might be able to fly – as a pilot – if I had contact lenses. If I chose to get them at my own expense I could be reconsidered, but without any guarantee that I should be taken. The various medical tests lasted over two hours and were very thorough.

Sunday, April 27th [at Hinchingbrooke]
Faith and I did some firing practice after tea with a heavy revolver of hers.

Winston spoke on the wireless, less vividly than usual, but painting a sombre picture of the position in the east and bidding us to turn our eyes westwards.

Monday, April 28th
Back at No. 10 there is a tense feeling as the evacuation of our troops from Greece is now taking place.

The P.M.'s speech has been well received though there is inevitably some disillusionment after the brilliant successes of the last few months. Many people think too much emphasis has been laid on the part played by Anzacs and New Zealanders. From the papers one would hardly suppose British troops had been fighting in Greece or Africa at all. It was, of course, the same at Gallipoli in the last war.

There is some consolation in the fact that our successes in Abyssinia and East Africa proceed undiminished.

On late duty. Most of the time the P.M. spent at a Defence Committee considering urgent problems arising out of the Mediterranean situation and in particular Operations TIGER and JAGUAR. To these Defence Meetings come the Lord Privy Seal (Attlee), the Foreign Secretary, the three service Ministers, the Chiefs of Staff, and Ismay, Hollis and Jacob.

Tuesday, April 29th
To the House for Questions. The P.M. had three tiresome ones (about War Aims, small War Cabinet, etc.) and gave the same answer to all three in succession: "No, Sir."

An afternoon of busy operational discussions: we must save Egypt and Suez at all costs. The evacuation of Greece seems to have been fairly successful and we have got over 40,000 away out of 55,000 all told. The Germans are crowing, but are furious about Winston's speech yesterday.

Wednesday, April 30th
To the House with the P.M. who made a brief statement on the result of the evacuation from Greece. Lunched at the Trafalgar Square canteen with Christopher Eastwood,[1] who says Moyne is a surprisingly effective Colonial Secretary though he tends to trust the Colonial Office too much.

Dined with Mrs Churchill at 7.30 and took her to Stepney where Father Groser showed us the Arches shelter, his social centres and various other shelters. Mrs C., who looked beautiful, was followed by an admiring crowd of women and made quite a good speech standing on a chair in the shelter. The doctor who went round with us (Cronin by name) said the people were very brave in spite of the havoc and devastation around them, but that they were annoyed (a) by the constant claims that we could defeat the night bomber (b) by the insincere attitude of the press towards our defeats in Africa.

[1] Pleasant Colonial Office official who was a friend of John Martin.

SIXTEEN

HESS, CRETE AND THE BISMARCK
MAY 1941

Thursday, May 1st
The day was spent breathlessly arranging Government changes, whereby Lord Spitfire (i.e. Beaverbrook) becomes Minister of State, Moore-Brabazon goes to the Ministry of Aircraft Production, Mr Leathers, Minister of Shipping and Transport.

Lunched with Mother at the Spanish restaurant in Swallow Street. She is a really remarkable woman, disinterested without being priggish, good and yet not smug, intelligent but always humble and, finally, never afraid to say and do what she believes. I could not have chosen a more desirable parent, had I been given the choice.

Left for a tour of Plymouth after dinner with the P.M., Mrs Churchill, First Sea Lord, his Secretary (Brockman),[1] Averell Harriman, Pug and Tommy. Plymouth has been cruelly laid waste in the last fortnight.

On the way to Paddington in the car, the P.M. told me that Leathers was entirely his own choice and that he hoped great things of his experience and tried ability.

Friday, May 2nd
We awoke in the train which was stationary on the line somewhere in Devonshire between banks of primroses and violets.

---

[1] Ronald Brockman, Naval Secretary to two First Sea Lords and then, for sixteen years, Mountbatten's devoted and efficient Secretary in all his various offices, including the Viceroyalty of India. Rose to be Vice Admiral. Knighted 1965.

At 9.30 we drew into Plymouth where we were greeted by the two M.P.s Lady Astor (also Lady Mayoress) and Mrs Rathbone,[1] who squabbled like two she-cats until the P.M., who was still shaving when we arrived, emerged on to the platform.

The whole party went to Admiralty House, Devonport, to meet the new C. in C., Sir Charles Forbes. Then began the morning's tour of the dockyard. Brockman and I did not go to Mount Batten, but waited to get the news and then proceeded to the North Yard where we looked at the melancholy ruins of a terrace of lovely houses in which Brockman's had been. The P.M. arrived in a launch and we then walked for miles, along quays, through workshops, over ships. We saw *Centurion*, now a decoy ship made to look like one of the *K.G.V.* class. Just before lunch we reached the R.N. barracks, where bombs had killed a number of sailors. There was a gruesome sight in the gymnasium: beds in which some forty slightly injured men lay, separated only by a low curtain from some coffins which were being nailed down. The hammering must have been horrible to the injured men, but such has been the damage that there was nowhere else it could be done.

The men lunched in the barracks, in a room decorated with a frieze of wooden ships representing the Armada, designed by Wylie.[2] We had a revolting lunch (tepid Brown Windsor soup, etc.) and then returned to Admiralty House so that the P.M. might sleep.

At 3.30 we drove round Plymouth. It has suffered five heavy raids in nine nights and scarcely a house seems to be habitable. It is far worse than Bristol: the whole city is wrecked except, characteristically, the important parts of the naval establishment. Mount Edgecumbe, where we used to land from the sea, is burnt out as well. In Plymouth itself I saw a bus which had been carried bodily, by the force of an explosion, on to the roof of a

[1] Intelligent and vivacious American constrained by her husband's constituents to take on his Plymouth seat after his death in an air crash. Thus the second American woman (after Lady Astor) to be a British M.P. Later married Sir Paul Wright and was Ambassadress in the Congo and the Lebanon.

[2] Well-known painter of naval scenes and actions.

building some 150 yards from where it had been standing.

We had tea at Lady Astor's house. At 6.30 we left the scene of horror and desolation on the return journey to Chequers, where we arrived at midnight.

There was news to make the P.M. gravely depressed. A long telegram from Roosevelt explaining that the U.S. could not cooperate with us in preventing Germany from seizing the Azores and Cape Verde Islands; news that one of the ships containing many tanks for the reinforcement of Wavell (Operation TIGER) had developed serious engine trouble; a signal that H.M.S. *Jersey*, one of Lord Louis Mountbatten's destroyers, had sunk at Malta blocking the Grand Harbour; and finally the fact that the Iraqis, who opened fire on our troops this morning (two hours before we had intended firing on them!) were fighting well and were not proving to be the rabble we expected.

So the P.M., in worse gloom than I have ever seen him, dictated a telegram to the President drawing a sombre picture of what a collapse in the Middle East would entail. Then he sketched to Harriman, Pug and me a world in which Hitler dominated all Europe, Asia and Africa and left the U.S. and ourselves no option but an unwilling peace.

It is clear that Spain, Vichy and Turkey are waiting on the result of the issue in North Africa, where Tobruk still resists valiantly. If Suez were to fall the Middle East would be lost, and Hitler's robot new order would receive the inspiration which might give it real life.

In a less dark mood the P.M. said that this moment is decisive: it is being established not whether we shall win or lose, but whether the duration of the war will be long or short. With Hitler in control of Iraq oil and Ukrainian wheat, not all the staunchness of "our Plymouth brethren" will shorten the ordeal.

I think it is largely Plymouth that has caused him such melancholy – he keeps on repeating: "I've never seen the like."

Mrs C. said to me suddenly in the train this morning: "Jock, do you think we are going to win?" I said truthfully and unhesitatingly: "Yes."

Saturday, May 3rd

Too little sleep made the P.M. irritable all the morning and morose at lunch when he discovered that Mrs C. had used some of his favourite honey, sent from Queensland, to sweeten the rhubarb.

A lovely spring day. Everything is very late, but the trees are at last beginning to come out.

Eric Duncannon and Moyra Ponsonby came to stay. Eric is making up to Mary and Mrs C. thinks he is going to propose, which worries her. Eric was really only invited for lunch tomorrow, but pretended he was invited for the week-end. Mary is disconcerted by Mrs C.'s cold view of the idea and by Sarah's frank ridicule.

The P.M. broadcast to the Poles and did it superbly, though there was a terrible rush to have it ready in time. We dined at 9.30. The P.M., some of whose worries have been relieved and who is inspired by the fact that a real fight is taking place at Tobruk, was very mellow and stayed up till 3.30 laughing, chaffing and alternating business with conversation. Eden, who came to dine, was made to stay the night in spite of his lacking even a toothbrush; but the C. in C., Fighter Command got away at 3.00.

The P.M. said to Eric Duncannon and me that Tobruk was playing the same part as Acre did against Napoleon. It was a speck of sand in the desert which might ruin all Hitler's calculations.

Sunday, May 4th

The clocks put forward an hour, making double summer-time. It was obvious that Eric was expected to make advances to Mary and that the prospect was viewed with nervous pleasure by Mary, with approbation by Moyra, with dislike by Mrs C. and with amusement by Clarissa – who arrived for lunch, looking quite beautiful, with Captain Hillgarth, Naval Attaché at Madrid and a fervent disciple of Sam Hoare.

At lunch I sat next to Clarissa while Eric was on her other side. We had a three-cornered conversation on a rather tiresome intellectual plane.

We all went into the rose-garden to bask in the sun and while I lingered behind to show the P.M. some service telegrams about Iraq, Eric and Clarissa went off for a long walk, leaving Mary. His motives were either Clarissa's attraction, which she did not attempt to keep in the background, or else the belief that it was good policy to arouse Mary's jealousy. Having returned from his walk, and Clarissa having gone, Eric proceeded to go to sleep until such time as he could make a dramatic entry into the Long Gallery at tea-time when we were all assembled together with Sarah Oliver and the Dashwoods, who had come over from West Wycombe. I think all this is a flutter, which pleases Eric's theatrical feelings and stirs Mary's youthful emotions, but will have no serious consequence.

Meanwhile the P.M., tempted by the warmth, sat in the garden working and glancing at me with suspicion from time to time in the belief that I was trying to read the contents of his special buff boxes.

The C. in C., Bomber Command (Peirse) came to dine and sleep. Lady Goonie[1] and I had a talk about calling people by their Christian names[2] ("Dear Bracken called me Goonie the first time I ever saw him").

The P.M. worked till after 2.00 a.m. in bed, almost emptying a very full box while the Prof. sat in his bedroom acting as a wastepaper basket and I stood at the foot of the bed collecting those papers with which he had dealt.

Monday, May 5th
Reached London in a state of exhaustion. Lunched at the Travellers which reopened today. The Library is being used as a dining-room and I sat there with Sammy Hood, Peter Loxley and Roger Makins.

Rode at Richmond for an hour, then slept at No. 10, and finally took my car to pick up Betty Montagu and go to Chobham

[1] Lady Gwendeline Churchill, wife of Major Jack Churchill.
[2] This familiarity has now become almost universal, but it used to be reserved for relations, contemporaries and close friends. Churchill asked me to call him Winston shortly after the war, but intimately as both my wife and I knew Lady Churchill, we never called her Clemmie to her dying day.

to spend a night with Rosemary and Hinch. Dropped Betty at Jacqueline Dyer's[1] house and had a drink there with Jacqueline, Zara and Ronnie Strutt.

We had a party in the evening at a very nice country club nearby. Zara and Ronnie came, Peter Cazalet,[2] Diana Tiarks and Martin Charteris. Dinner was excellent but the evening was less successful afterwards. We danced to the gramophone, but Ronnie Strutt stood glumly in front of the fire and for some reason the party just did not go.

Wednesday, May 7th

Lunched at the Travellers, sitting next to the C.A.S. with whom I broached the subject of entering the R.A.F. After discussing the matter with Mother last night I am prepared to resign from the F.O. if necessary.

The P.M. wound up a debate on the war in the House, scoring a great Parliamentary success and utterly confounding Lloyd George and Hore-Belisha.

He went early to bed elated by his forensic success. I pointed out to him that it was just a year since the debate in which Chamberlain fell.

Tonight we shot down more night raiders than ever before: at least twenty-three fell to guns and fighters.

Thursday, May 8th

The Cabinet met at the House and I had a conversation with the dynamic and excellent Tom Johnston, S. of S. for Scotland, who told me of the incredible tactlessness shown by many employers in Lanarkshire. He said the morale of the workers on Clydeside was much better since they had been bombed and he could not help wishing Lanarkshire would be bombed too.

Eric Seal is going on a special mission to the U.S. and we are to have a new Principal Private Secretary. Meanwhile Brendan,

---

[1] Later Mrs Vincent Paravicini.
[2] Celebrated trainer of steeplechasers. Succeeded to Fairlawne after his brother, Victor, was killed with General Sikorski. After the death of his first wife he married Zara (née Mainwaring), at the time of this diary entry Mrs Ronnie Strutt.

to whom I entrusted the task, has failed to persuade the P.M. to release me for the R.A.F. and before taking further steps I shall have now to wait till Seal's successor is installed.

Our biggest raid on Germany: 380 aircraft.

Friday, May 9th

The Bessboroughs and Eric lunched at the Annexe and afterwards Mary came to tell me she was engaged to Eric. I was relieved to be able simply to wish her happiness: I had feared she might be going to ask my opinion.

The P.M. went off to Ditchley very excited about Operation TIGER. The convoy has passed through the narrows between Sicily and N. Africa and only one ship out of five, carrying a huge consignment of tanks for Wavell, has gone down. The P.M. thinks this will have far-reaching consequences on the war. He said to me: "The poor Tiger has already lost one claw and another is damaged; but still I would close on what is left."

Saturday, May 10th

Things are going better again – in Iraq, in Spain (where the Falange[1] and Suñer[2] have been worsted), and there are bright prospects in N. Africa now that TIGER is through.

The full moon. Just as I was going to bed one of London's worst raids started and I descended to the shelter where my bed was periodically shaken by the explosion of bombs on the Horse Guards Parade. It was strange that on every occasion I awoke about five seconds before the bomb actually exploded.

Sunday, May 11th

Awoke thinking unaccountably of Peter Fleming's book *Flying Visit*[3] and day-dreaming of what would happen if we captured Goering during one of his alleged flights over London.

[1] Spanish fascist party founded by Miguel Primo de Rivera.
[2] Spanish Foreign Minister. Brother-in-law of General Franco and considered strongly pro-German.
[3] An amusing fantasy, published in the early months of the war, about the embarrassment caused by Hitler's unheralded arrival in England by parachute.

I walked out into Downing Street at 8.00 a.m. on my way to the early service at Westminster Abbey. It was really a sunny day with blue skies, but the smoke from many fires lay thick over London and obscured the sun. Burnt paper, from some demolished paper mill, was falling like leaves on a windy autumn day.

Whitehall was thronged with people, mostly sightseers but some of them Civil Defence workers with blackened faces and haggard looks. One of them, a boy of eighteen or nineteen, pointed towards the Houses of Parliament and said, "Is that the sun?" But the great orange glow at which we were looking was the light of many fires south of the river. At Westminster Abbey there were fire-engines and the policeman at the door said to me, "There will not be any services in the Abbey today, Sir", exactly as if it were closed for spring cleaning. I turned towards Westminster Hall, on the roof of which I could see flames still leaping. Smoke rose from some invisible point in the pile of Parliament buildings beyond. I talked to a fireman. He showed me Big Ben, the face of which was pocked and scarred, and told me a bomb had gone right through the Tower. The one thing that had given him great pleasure during the night was that Big Ben had struck two o'clock a few minutes after being hit. It was still giving the proper time.

I stood on Westminster Bridge and thought ironically of Wordsworth and 1802. St Thomas's Hospital was ablaze, the livid colour of the sky extended from Lambeth to St Paul's, flames were visible all along the Embankment, there was smoke rising thickly as far as the eye could see. After no previous raid has London looked so wounded next day.

After breakfast I rang up the P.M. at Ditchley and described what I had seen. He was very grieved that William Rufus's roof at Westminster Hall should have gone. He told me we had shot down forty-five which, out of 380 operating, is a good result.[1] Great excitement over an E. Phillips Oppenheim story concern-

---

[1] An exaggerated estimate given by Fighter Command. Thirty-three was the true number.

ing the Duke of Hamilton[1] and a crashed Nazi plane. The Duke flew to London and I had been going to Northolt to meet him; but he was switched straight through to Ditchley.

I had walked over to the Foreign Office during the morning in order to gossip with Nicolas Lawford, a clever and amusing diplomat, who was Anthony Eden's Second Private Secretary and was on duty over the week-end. As I entered the room he was on the telephone. He turned round and said to the person to whom he was speaking, "Hold on a minute. I think this is your man." Lawford, holding his hand over the receiver, explained that it was the Duke of Hamilton who had got some fantastic story, which he refused to reveal in detail, and that he wanted the Prime Minister's Secretary to meet him at Northolt aerodrome, to which he intended to fly. He also wanted Sir Alexander Cadogan to go. Lawford handed me the telephone. It might, of course, be a lunatic pretending to be a Duke. The caller declined to be more specific but said he could only compare what had happened to an E. Phillips Oppenheim novel and that it had to do with a crashed Nazi plane. At that moment I vividly remembered my early waking thoughts on Peter Fleming's book and I felt sure that either Hitler or Goering had arrived. In the event I was only one wrong in the Nazi hierarchy. I telephoned to Ditchley and the Prime Minister instructed me to have the Duke driven directly there, but I was to ensure it really was the Duke and not a lunatic.

Monday, May 12th
The P.M. returned from Ditchley bringing the Duke of Hamilton with him. I managed to have a few words with the Duke, while the P.M. was excitedly talking to Eden, and to elicit that the occupant of the crashed Nazi plane was Rudolph Hess. There has never been such a fantastic occurrence.

[1] Douglas, 14th Duke of Hamilton and Brandon. Skilful pilot and pugnacious amateur boxer. The first man to look down on Mount Everest, having organised an expedition to fly over it. A Conservative M.P. for ten years before succeeding his father. When Hess, whom he had only seen once, at the Berlin Olympic Games, arrived in Scotland, Hamilton was serving as Group Captain in the R.A.F.

Lunched with John Martin whom the P.M. has definitely appointed Principal Private Secretary, at the Travellers.

Dined with Philip in the Mess of the 4th Battalion, Grenadiers, at Wanstead. We had a delicious dinner, with champagne, etc., and afterwards played bridge. The 9.00 news was turned on and I heard an announcement of a German communiqué about Hess's disappearance. Nobody paid any attention or seemed to grasp what it meant. I said nothing. Back at No. 10 in time to hear of a statement on the subject which the P.M. has drafted for publication.

During the afternoon Mary told me that her engagement to Eric was off – and that she felt at the bottom of her heart it would never be on again.

Tuesday, May 13th

The Hess story has, of course, made everyone gape. This morning, after returning from the House with the P.M., I saw an account of Hess's interview with Kirkpatrick, which is only being shown to Eden, Attlee and Beaverbrook. It is clear that Hess is no traitor but genuinely believes he can persuade us that we cannot win and that a compromise peace is obtainable. His essential prerequisite is the fall of the Churchill Government. The poor Duke of Hamilton feels acutely the slur of being taken for a potential Quisling – which he certainly is not.

In the Travellers at lunch-time there was no other topic. The rumours and theories are diverse and amusing.

Wednesday, May 14th

During the later afternoon "C", Alec Cadogan, Duff Cooper and Brendan assembled in my room at No. 10 and I listened to many intelligent theories and suggestions about Hess. Cadogan says that if only the parachute had failed to open, he would be a happier and more efficient man. The handling of the whole business is difficult but very important psychologically.

Thursday, May 15th

The day started badly. I summoned the D.N.I.[1] for the P.M. instead of the D.M.I.[1] The P.M. answered Questions (inadver-

[1] Directors of Naval and of Military Intelligence.

tently letting fall in answer to a supplementary that the Ministry of Economic Warfare was connected with propaganda) and then proposed a resolution thanking the House of Peers for their message of condolence on the loss of the Chamber of the House of Commons.

Gladwyn Jebb dined and made a great fuss about this morning's Question, maintaining that the P.M. had jeopardised the secrecy of Dr Dalton's organisation. Desmond and I thought him very silly about it all and concluded that his motive was to be able to go back to Dalton and say that he had given us a piece of his mind. Incidentally the P.M. had refused to see Dalton about it as he cannot bear the sight of him.

Monday, May 19th
Reached London at lunch-time and burst in on a farewell luncheon party which Brendan was giving for Seal in the Annexe. It ended with short, embarrassed speeches punctuated by witticisms from Brendan.

Brendan had Commander Fletcher (A. V. Alexander's P.P.S.) to dine. While the P.M. and the Defence Committee were deciding how to react to Vichy's latest treason in Syria (where German planes have been allowed to use aerodromes), I gossiped with Antony Head and the C.I.G.S.'s two A.D.C.s (Nutting and MacDonald Buchanan) in the C.W.R.

Before going to bed the P.M. told me he expected the German attack on Crete to begin tomorrow.

Tuesday, May 20th
The Germans are attacking Crete. At the House the P.M. made an impromptu statement covering Aosta's surrender, our recapture of Sollum and the Cretan adventure. On the way back in the car I showed him two urgent telegrams about Syria. He said, "We must go in" and immediately summoned a Defence Committee.

Lunched with Tommy Lascelles and discussed whether very great men usually had a touch of charlatanism in them.

At 5.00 the P.M. sped down to the House again and interrupted their business to give them the latest "hot news" from Crete, clasping a tattered postcard on which I had scrawled the last signal.

Wednesday, May 21st
Another brief statement in the House of Commons on Crete where the fight is hard but so far successful. There is a general demand for the execution of German parachutists who are alleged to have landed in New Zealand uniforms.

Thursday, May 22nd
The navy are having a heavy task off Crete and have lost a lot of ships, including *Gloucester* and *Fiji*. I expressed grief to the P.M. who replied, "What do you think we build the ships for?" He deprecates the navy's way of treating ships as if they were too precious ever to risk.

Tom Troubridge dined in the Mess. An interesting discussion on Germany, especially propaganda. Troubridge said the Germans loved jazz which is prohibited by the Nazis: instead of broadcasting that, the B.B.C. produce programmes of German music! He said the obtuseness of the Ministry of Information was largely due to the warring cliques within it.

The *Bismarck* and another German ship are out, probably on a substantial raid in the Atlantic. Now is the time to test the efficacy of American naval help.

Friday, May 23rd
Lunched with Herschel Johnson at Claridges to meet members of the American Embassy.

Drove my own car to Chequers. P.M. arrived later from a tank inspection, bringing with him David Margesson, Pownall (the new Vice Chief of the Imperial General Staff), Macready (Assistant C.I.G.S.), Averell Harriman, Jack Churchill and Ismay.

An entirely male party. The P.M. laments very strongly that the tanks which he asked Wavell to send to Crete were not sent. They might have made the whole difference to the battle.

The *Bismarck* is near Iceland, hotly pursued by the *Prince of*

Wales and the *Hood*. There is an excellent chance of catching her at dawn in the Denmark Straits.

Saturday, May 24th
Awoken at 6.00 a.m. by the Duty Captain, Admiralty, who said *Prince of Wales* and *Hood* were engaging *Bismarck*. At 9.00 when I emerged from my bedroom Mrs Hill told me the *Hood* was lost.

In the morning there was a conference on conscription in Northern Ireland, an issue which is impassioning Eire and causing unfavourable repercussions in the U.S. and Canada. The P.M. is very insistent on conscription. The Prime Minister of Northern Ireland (Andrews)[1] arrived, accompanied by two of his Ministers, and others present were Herbert Morrison, Bevin, Cranborne, John Anderson, Bridges and Pownall (who has just given up the post of G.O.C. Northern Ireland). At lunch I sat next to Pownall. He is optimistic about Crete and thinks the odds slightly in favour of our victory: yesterday he would have laid 6–4 on; today he thought it about evens. He pointed out that we had had three great victories in this war which counted for much more than our various military catastrophes. These victories were the success of the R.A.F. in defeating the daylight bomber, of the navy in keeping the seas open, and, above all, of the civilian population in holding firm against air bombardment.

Crete is now serious, as became clear during the afternoon and evening. The Germans are fighting with blind courage and have complete control of the air. The crux of the matter is how long the navy can carry out its dangerous task of preventing seaborne landings.

First night of the Chequers cinema, which the P.M. has had installed. The guests of the day had all gone. Andrew Cavendish,[2] who is one of the officers at the camp, dined and afterwards we saw a film in the Great Parlour: Marlene Dietrich in *Seven Sinners* – very alluring.

[1] Rt. Hon. J. M. Andrews, Prime Minister of Northern Ireland, 1940–43.
[2] Subsequently 11th Duke of Devonshire. Minister of State for Commonwealth Relations in Harold Macmillan's Government.

All ships are converging on the *Bismarck* and the C. in C. proposes to attack at 9.00 a.m. tomorrow.

Sunday, May 25th
Bismarck has been lost during the hours of darkness. A day of fearful gloom ensued. The P.M. cannot understand why the *Prince of Wales* did not press home her attack yesterday and keeps on saying it is the worst thing since Troubridge turned away from the *Goeben* in 1914. He rated the First Lord and the First Sea Lord continuously, both on this account and because in the Mediterranean the navy shows, he thinks, a tendency to shirk its task of preventing a seaborne landing in Crete since Cunningham fears severe losses from bombing. The P.M.'s line is that Cunningham must be made to take every risk: the loss of half the Mediterranean fleet would be worthwhile in order to save Crete.

The Fred Crippses came to lunch, and Beaverbrook afterwards in a new (and very vulgar) suit to celebrate his birthday. The P.M. treated us to a discourse on the heroism of China and Chiang Kai-shek, for whom he longed to be able to do something.

Winant came at tea-time and stayed till after 8.00, putting very forcibly Roosevelt's objections to conscription in Northern Ireland.

The P.M. cheered up at dinner, which was a family affair (by which I mean Ismay, Tommy, Jack Churchill, self and the Prof., who is soon to be a peer). He criticised Wavell very heavily about tanks for Crete and expressed amazement that W. should have thought he could get reinforcements ashore after the fight had begun. He considered the Middle East had been very badly managed. If he could be put in command there he would gladly lay down his present office – yes, and even renounce cigars and alcohol!

After dinner we had a film: *Western Union* (with Red Indians and all the Wild West trappings) and the P. M.'s favourite *March of Time*.

With a final comment that these three days had been the worst yet, he went to bed at 2.15 a.m. There is, however, still a chance that the *Ark Royal* and the *Rodney* may catch the

Bismarck before she reaches the French port for which she seems to be making.

Monday, May 26th

Left Chequers at 12.30, following the P.M.'s cortège in my car at breakneck speed. The Cretan situation seems slightly better and at the P.M.'s instigation the Chiefs of Staff have sent a signal to the C. in C. that no risk can be considered too heavy to win the battle.

Rowan,* our new Private Secretary from the Treasury, arrived.

Brendan and Desmond both think President R.'s speech tomorrow might be very important to the outcome of the war. It looks as if Vichy, Japan, Spain are all lined up waiting to fall on the British Empire if it shows any further signs of disintegration.

Tuesday, May 27th

To the House, where the P.M. made a statement on Crete and the *Bismarck* and announced the Government's decision not to introduce conscription into Northern Ireland. This culminated in a dramatic scene when we rushed to the P.M., just after he had sat down, a slip of paper saying the *Bismarck* had been sunk.

The Crete situation is deplorable. It seems that we are finished there owing to lack of air support.

Went to have first fitting for contact lenses as I am now resolved to get into the R.A.F. as a fighter pilot if humanly possible, even at the cost of resignation from the Diplomatic Service.

Wednesday, May 28th

My head is full of plans for a new life in the R.A.F. and, of course, of improbable day-dreams on the subject.

Decision to withdraw from Crete was taken.

Thursday, May 29th

Rode at Richmond. Melville[1] rode the horse I usually ride and it ran away, throwing him into a sandpit.

P.M. much upset by telegram from Wavell who shows some sign of defeatism. "He sounds a tired and disheartened man," said the P.M.

Attended conference in Desmond's room with Prof. and Victor Rothschild[2] about security as regards cigars, etc., sent to the P.M.

---

[1] Ronnie Melville, Principal Private Secretary to the Secretary of State for Air. A first-class classicist with a fine sense of humour. Afterwards held a number of senior posts in Whitehall, including two Permanent Under Secretaryships. He does not list riding among his hobbies in *Who's Who*.

[2] Victor, 3rd Lord Rothschild. A notable scientist, whose research tended to concentrate on intimate biological matters, he was a Fellow of Trinity College, Cambridge, Chairman of Shell Research, Chairman of the Royal Commission on gambling, first head of the Central Policy Review Staff (the "Think Tank") and a winner of the George Medal for unravelling fiendish enemy booby-traps. His incisive comments brought terror to some, but admiration to all.

SEVENTEEN

THIEVES FALL OUT
JUNE 1941

Monday, June 2nd

Late in the afternoon I accompanied the P.M. and Mrs Churchill to Chartwell where they plan to have a few days' rest. I am sleeping in the cottage which the P.M. built with his own hands and have his very comfortable bedroom.

We dined in the cottage; the P.M., Mrs C., Tommy, Miss Whyte[1] and I. Mrs C. and I played backgammon; the P.M. professed extreme tiredness and at one moment even lay prostrate on the dining-room floor while Mrs C. and I continued to rattle the dice and Tommy sipped his brandy pensively.

After dinner the P.M. went up to the big house and worked till 1.30, dictating to Miss Layton[2] while I sat in his study, looked at his books, and plied him with papers when supplies ran short.

He is much perturbed by the fact that the rearguard, consisting of Royal Marines, was left behind in Crete. He blamed the navy and went so far as to describe it as a shameful episode.

---

[1] A cousin of Clementine Churchill who was Mary's guide, philosopher and friend, known as Moppet and much loved by the whole family.

[2] One of Churchill's personal secretaries, pleasant to look at and good-natured. At a stop on a return flight from Moscow, the Russians erroneously judged her to be Churchill's mistress and toasted her effusively. She married, went to live in South Africa and, as Elizabeth Nel, wrote a book, *Mr Churchill's Secretary*, of which Lady Churchill highly approved.

Tuesday, June 3rd

It was cold and raining, so that the P.M., lying dismally in bed, decided to go back to London after lunch and curtail his holiday.

He said to David Margesson on the telephone that he had no doubts of the wisdom of what we had done in Crete though sometimes he had doubts about the Greek campaign. However we had at least done what was honourable.

I started reading *My Early Life*,[1] of which I found an annotated copy in the office, with the object of using some of the facts in it when I come to make my bid for release.

I had lunch alone with the P.M. and the Yellow Cat, which sat in a chair on his right-hand side and attracted most of his attention. He was meditating deeply on the Middle East, where he is intent on reorganising the rearward services, and on Lord Beaverbrook who is proving particularly troublesome. The P.M. said that Lord B. just did not begin to understand how to get on with the military. While he brooded on these matters, he kept up a running conversation with the cat, cleaning its eyes with his napkin, offering it mutton and expressing regret that it could not have cream in war-time. Finally he said some very harsh things about Wavell, whose excessive caution and inclination to pessimism he finds very antipathetic.

After dinner in the Mess I went to see first Desmond and then Archie Sinclair about Louis Greig who has, as I heard by chance, become involved with a company of financial crooks. In view of his great and continuous hospitality to me I should like to give him a hint, but thought it better to do so through Archie Sinclair.

Wednesday, June 4th

Lunched at the Travellers between Moley Sargent and Horace Wilson. The former thinks Sir M. Robertson's[2] plans to reform

---

[1] Winston Churchill's account of his childhood and youth.

[2] Joined the Foreign Office in Queen Victoria's reign and was at various times Ambassador in Buenos Aires, Chairman of Spillers Ltd, Chairman of the British Council and a Member of Parliament. He regularly interviewed aspirants for the Diplomatic Service (including me) and asked searching questions.

the Diplomatic Service (which have now been adopted by the Cabinet) good though he doubts the wisdom of amalgamating the Diplomatic and Consular Service as the duds are bound to be pushed into the consular posts and our Consular Service will suffer. We talked of Horace after he had left and Sargent thought he had suffered greatly from Chamberlain pushing him into something for which he had no qualifications and by which his reputation and his future were bound to be compromised. Both Sargent and Horace said No. 10 was partly to blame for the inadequacy of our news and propaganda to the U.S.: the spokesmen of the service departments were terrified of saying anything that might incur the Prime Minister's displeasure and so took refuge in silence.

The Kaiser died, in obscurity and contempt. *The Times* said: "History will some day have to assess the respective responsibilities of the crowned and uncrowned demagogue in bringing ruin upon the head of the German people and calamity on the peaceful civilisation of Europe."

Thursday, June 5th
Rode in Richmond Park, jumping several hurdles and having two long breakneck gallops.

New appointments are under consideration, connected with the establishment of a ministry of light, fuel, heat, etc. Beaverbrook has refused an offer of Agriculture *and* Food. Brendan says that he takes up more of the P.M.'s time than Hitler.

Criticism of the Crete episode is rife; the press are being cantankerous; and the Government will have to face an important debate in the House next week. Our propaganda is very much at fault, at home and abroad.

Friday, June 6th
Lunched with Jim Bowker at the Travellers. He spoke of the determination of the Turks not to commit themselves. He was critical of our fighting in Crete, believing that we had still failed to understand the lessons that complete domination of the air is

a decisive factor and that when the Germans attack they do so ruthlessly and without reserve.

The P.M. returned, instead of going straight on to Ditchley, on account of telegrams from Washington which show that Pétain and Weygand have both agreed to military co-operation with Germany, and of difficulties connected with the Free French, General Spears, Syria and innumerable complications related to matters of prestige and *amour propre*.

On late duty. The P.M. dictated his speech for next Tuesday, rather cantankerous in tone and likely, unless substantially toned down, to cause a good deal of unfavourable comment. Pug says he thinks it is impossible to run a war efficiently if so much time has to be devoted to justifying one's actions in the House of Commons. At the risk of seeming smug he maintains that no error or misconception was made in the direction of the campaign from this end. General Freyberg[1] specifically said he was not afraid of the air.

Went to bed exhausted at 2.30 a.m.

Saturday, June 7th
The Prime Minister saw the editors of the newspapers this morning with a view to damping down their criticism and explaining the position.

De Gaulle is showing himself highly-strung and quarrelsome. Desmond Morton actually thinks he might go over to Vichy. Much will depend on events in the very near future.

The P.M. went off to Ditchley at tea-time and I spent a peaceful evening reading *My Early Life* (with a view to proving to the P.M. that he would have left no stone unturned to take an active part in the war if he had been me) and listening to a fiery denunciation of Horace Wilson's pettiness by Anthony Bevir.

---

[1] Soldier of heroic fame who won a V.C. and three D.S.O.s, was wounded countless times, almost swum the Channel, was G.O.C. of the New Zealand forces from 1939 to 1945, was Governor General of New Zealand after the war and ended as Governor of Windsor Castle. His wife, Barbara Jekyll, was a childhood friend of my mother at the Viceregal Lodge in Dublin.

Sunday, June 8th

Went to church early at Westminster Abbey. Anthony and Brendan are occupying their minds in a search for a successor to Cosmo Cantuar in case anything should befall that prelate. I have put forward the suggestion of Robert Moberley, Bishop of Stepney.

Today our forces, together with those of de Gaulle, advance into Syria for the implementation of Operation EXPORTER. It may mean war with Vichy; but the P.M. is convinced that this would not imply war with France.

Meanwhile negotiations between Germany and Russia are proceeding and look like ending, in the very near future, with a complete alignment of the two countries or an invasion of Russia if she proves recalcitrant. Having so wholeheartedly taken over the mantle of appeasement, I think Russia is more likely to collaborate than to fight.

Barclay, an interpreter attached to the Ministry of Defence, dined in the Mess. He says that he has been following the deliberations of Mr Arthur Greenwood's committee on reconstruction after the war and that they give him no confidence. Lord Reith's contribution on material reconstruction, e.g. town-planning, is the only one that is at all practical and businesslike. The rest talk airily of freedom, equality, justice – and all the other things which J. S. Mill wrote about much more competently and which, I think, seem a mockery to the subdued nations of Europe.

Tuesday, June 10th

Rode in a torrential downpour. Spent most of the day at Church House listening to the debate on Crete. Hore-Belisha spoke well, if acrimoniously, but he has not got the sympathy of the House. Lord Winterton, who is both fluent and amusing, attacked his own party and Labour, employers and workmen, with equal versatility and expressed the hope that the P.M. would not take refuge from criticism in rhetoric. He also objected strongly to the P.M. comparing Lloyd George to Marshal Pétain.

The Prime Minister wound up the debate with a forceful speech lasting one and a half hours, in which he denied the

House's right to have information on tactical matters and objected to being called to account for every phase of the war. Did Hitler call the Reichstag to explain the loss of the *Bismarck* or Mussolini feel constrained to give an apologia for Italian disasters in Africa? He also said some harsh things to Hore-Belisha, though not as harsh as he had originally intended.

I corrected the speech for Hansard, which took a long time, and then went to have a drink with the Sinclairs. There was a young man there called Michael Young,[1] a friend of Rosemary Hinchingbrooke, who extolled to me the virtues of Communism and asked me if the Communists at Cambridge in my time had not been "the élite of the students". I offended him deeply by referring to their personal uncleanliness.

For the first time since war broke out I feel discontented and unsettled, bored by most people I meet and destitute of ideas. I certainly need a change and think an active, practical life in the R.A.F. is the real solution. I am not anxious to immolate myself on the altar of Mars, but have reached the stage of thinking that nothing matters.

Lunched today with Colly Barclay[2] at the St James's Club. He is rather dismal, but like me he feels the intolerable position of living a life of pampered ease and comparative safety in the midst of all this suffering and danger.

Wednesday, June 11th

Lord Simon, the Lord Chancellor, has seen Hess and it becomes increasingly clear that the latter came here of his own volition, that he utterly misconceived politics and opinion in this country, that there is very little valuable information to be got out of him. Although Hitler's personal friend and right-hand man, I doubt if he knew as much of plans and production even as Brendan; certainly no more.

Shigemitsu, the lame Japanese Ambassador, came to say

[1] After a diverse and distinguished academic career, he was created Lord Young of Dartington, the *avant-garde* and occasionally notorious progressive school which was the object of his and Rosemary Hinchingbrooke's adulation.
[2] Step-son of Sir Robert Vansittart. Entered the Foreign Office in the same year as I did.

goodbye to the P.M. at No. 10. I suppose he is being recalled on account of his known Anglophile views.

Dined with Clarissa Churchill in a good Soho restaurant. I enjoyed my evening greatly and see how right Gay is in her praises of Clarissa: she is extremely agreeable and one of the most intelligent of women, more balanced than most. She tells me that after a few weeks in the Communications Department of the F.O. she is being paid £6 a week free of tax – almost as much as I get – with short hours and no skill attached to the job. After dinner we walked in Regent's Park till 11.00 p.m. when it began to be dark, and then adjourned to the Four Hundred till 1.15 a.m.

Thursday, June 12th
The Honours List. Prof. L. gets a barony which will cause anger in many quarters and especially at Oxford, but not as much as when it is learned that he proposes to call himself Lord Cherwell of Oxford.

The President of the Royal Society, Sir Henry Dale, accompanied by Professors A. V. Hill and A. C. Egerton and by Sir Henry Tizard, came to No. 10 to admit the P.M. a Fellow. He kept them waiting forty minutes, during which time I conversed with them pleasantly, and then signed his name in their historic book which starts with "Charles R. Founder" and contains every great name since, people so diverse as Sir Winston Churchill (father of the first Duke of Marlborough), Sir Isaac Newton, Queen Victoria and Freud!

At 12.00 began the Meeting of Allied Representatives in the picture gallery at St James's Palace. I attended and sat at a table with Edward Bridges, Nicholas Lawford and Roger Makins. The P.M. made a powerful speech of invective against the enemy, which he enjoys and at which he excels. The representatives of ten nations sat round the long table and listened appreciatively, but the dignity of the scene was marred by such modern appliances as microphones, cinema apparatus and innumerable photographers. This did not disturb the P.M. who shook his finger at the microphone as if it had been the Führer himself that he was addressing. When he came to a passage in which he spoke of the stain on the German name which nothing would eradicate for hundreds of years, Van (who today becomes Lord Van) became wreathed in appreciative smiles. Hatred and harsh words are the methods which he prescribes.

The meeting adjourned for lunch and Brendan took me to White's to have a gin and lime. Later in the day one of the Free French representatives made this mystifying statement to Desmond Morton: "Ah, that is Bracken. I have heard of him. He has the vocabulary of Mr Churchill but of the left."

In the afternoon representatives of our nine Allies spoke: Sikorski, Pierlot (the Belgian P.M. who is most eloquent), Gerbrandy (the Dutchman), the speakers on behalf of Free France, Czechoslovakia, Norway, Greece, Yugoslavia and Luxembourg. Only Ethiopia was left out: there is no Ethiopian, of sufficient standing, in England. At 4.00 came the King, in naval uniform, and walked round the room talking to all in turn. Evidently the meeting was a success and Eden, in his winding-up speech, expressed the hope that it would be the first of those which, on a basis of international collaboration, should settle the peace and reorganise Europe.

Chief interest now centres on: (1) the prospect of a Soviet – German clash which, according to many and diverse sources, seems imminent. I can't see the sense of it from Hitler's point of view unless, as Bridges suggests, the intention is to dissuade the U.S. from war; (2) the now declared intention of the U.S. Government to take over the occupation of Iceland from us very shortly; (3) Syria, where progress is slow but where General Spears and the War Office believe all opposition will crumble after an initial display of resistance.

The P.M. was much impressed by a photograph of today's conference, brought by a young man from the *Daily Sketch*, and said it was the most artistic grouping he had ever seen, better than any of the groups painted by Sargent, etc., on similar occasions and yet quite haphazard.[1]

[1] See photograph of Exiled Governments.

Friday, June 13th
Attlee tells me he had to converse with the Czech representative, Sramek, in Latin yesterday.

Sunday, June 15th
Today our offensive in North Africa began. Great hopes are placed on this Operation BATTLEAXE (formerly TIGERCUBS and afterwards BRUISER). For the first time British armoured forces meet the Germans on equal terms and without marked air inferiority.

Monday, June 16th
Summer, hot and sunny, at last.

Lunched with George Rendel[1] at the Travellers. He has been given the job of working out the reform of the Foreign Office. He says that amalgamating the Diplomatic and Consular services is like amalgamating the House of Commons and the L.C.C. Their functions are different; their scope is different.

In the afternoon the P.M. broadcast to Rochester University from which he receives an honorary degree. A very-well-phrased speech, the burden of which was "United we stand; divided we fall".

After dinner I went for a walk round Westminster with Brendan. His knowledge of houses and architects is remarkable and he told me much that was interesting about the precincts of Westminster Abbey and School and the neighbouring streets.

The fighting round Sollum[2] is very fierce. At dinner in the Mess we all, except Brendan and Tommy, thought that Russia would give way to Germany without a fight. That Germany is prepared to fight there can be no question. Sir Stafford Cripps, just back from Moscow, whom I saw today, says that the issue of war rests entirely with Hitler: Stalin will have no choice one way or the other.

---

[1] A man of great goodness and a devout Roman Catholic who was head of the Foreign Office Eastern Department when I joined it in 1937. He was, however, incorrigibly long-winded in the minutes and memoranda he wrote, to the grave dissatisfaction of the Under Secretaries and the Secretary of State.

[2] On the Egypt – Cyrenaica frontier.

Tuesday, June 17th

The P.M. went to Chartwell for the afternoon after hearing that Vichy troops had captured Kynteira in Syria, forcing a British battalion to surrender. This looks bad and I fear the prospect in the Western Desert is none too bright either. Later the prospect seemed still gloomier.

Wednesday, June 18th

Operation BATTLEAXE has obviously failed and we have to face the bitter fact of being beaten by the Germans on equal terms. Indeed we should have had superiority were not Wavell so lavish with his rearward services and so cautious about using his full strength. The P.M. is gravely disappointed as he had placed great hopes on this operation for which Operation TIGER had been staged. Fortunately it will not appear as a major defeat as we merely return to our positions after a sharp and costly battle; but neither the general public nor the Germans know what hopes were set by the Cabinet (though not by Wavell or Dill) on a successful offensive.

In the afternoon, as the P.M. had gone off to see a rocket demonstration, I went riding and dallied pleasantly in a large wood at Richmond where bank after bank of rhododendrons in full flower surrounded me on every side. I have never seen such profusion. At Exbury the quality may be greater, but not the quantity. The heat was tropical and the air heavy with the scent of flowers. I rode in this wood for half an hour, forcing my way along the overgrown footpaths, and then galloped full tilt down the avenue to White Lodge, jumping a series of hurdles and a stream on the way.

Brendan had Walter Elliot[1] to dinner and also an American, Glancey by name, who is head of General Motors and is working with Harriman. He gave us impressive forecasts of what American industry can produce. He was enthusiastic about the pros-

---

[1] Erudite Scottish M.P., highly acclaimed as Minister of Agriculture and of Health, and as Secretary of State for Scotland. At one time regarded as a future Prime Minister. His wife, daughter of Sir Charles Tennant and half-sister of Lady Oxford and Asquith, was made a peeress in her own right and worked assiduously in the House of Lords.

pects next spring if we can hang on till then. For example America will be producing small arms ammunition at the rate of 1,000,000 rounds an hour. Walter Elliot said that to win this war soldiers should give up studying any military history since the Plantagenets and Angevins: we had returned to the feudal military conception of knights and peasants, only now the knights rode in tanks and the peasants were infantry. Armour has come back to its own.

While waiting for the P.M. to return I played backgammon with Mrs C. and enlisted her support for my R.A.F. project. She advises me to put my application to the P.M. in writing. Mrs C. spoke in no unmeasured terms of her relief that Mary had broken off her engagement with Eric.

When the P.M. came back he was in good spirits, less perturbed than I had expected by the fiasco of BATTLEAXE, and told me that he was now busy considering where next we could take the offensive.

Thursday, June 19th
French advances for an armistice in Syria reached us through Washington.

At the House of Commons Tommy Dugdale lamented to me the first signs of a new class feeling between the two sides of the House. The Tories, conscious of the great sacrifices they are making financially and of the exceedingly high wages being paid to war workers, are cantankerous about the many reports of slackness, absenteeism, etc., in the factories. The Labour Party resent this criticism and blame the managers and employers for any shortcomings. A Conservative M.P., Henderson Stewart, discussed the matter with me in very strong terms: he wants the P.M. to have stringent investigations made in all factories.

Lunched with Peggy Crewe at the Ritz. She says that criticism of the Government is increasing, though not of Winston personally. I certainly have the impression that discontent is growing, and it is inevitable with so many setbacks.

John Peck and I agreed that the P.M. does not help the Government machine to run smoothly and his inconsiderate treatment of the service departments would cause trouble were it not for the great personal loyalty of the service Ministers to himself. He supplies drive and initiative, but he often meddles where he would better leave things alone and the operational side of the war might profit if he gave it a respite and turned to grapple with labour and production.

Audrey Stanley,[1] Diana Quilter, John Martin and I went to see *Patience* well produced at the Savoy Theatre. After dining at absurd expense in the Savoy Grill we proceeded to the Four Hundred to drink gin and discourse. Audrey Stanley said that the P.M. would go down in history not as a great Prime Minister but as a great poet.

Friday, June 20th
Departed at 9.15 for Dover with the P.M. and a large party including Archie Sinclair, Mr Glancey, Sir R. Keyes and Dill, besides several generals and Desmond Morton. We saw an 18–inch gun on a railway mounting, a formidable object with a brass plate "H.M.G. Boche-Buster". I could not bear the prospect of seeing more guns and so went to Dover Castle with the Vice Admiral, Dover's Flag Lieutenant (a charming youth called Gibb), and after telephoning to Ismay about the P.M.'s latest project – the replacement of Wavell by Auchinleck – awaited the arrival of the party. The haze and heat made it impossible to see the coast of France, so the P.M. consoled himself by ordering the firing of rounds by the U.P. batteries.

At lunch on the train I sat with General Loch, head of the A.A. Section in the War Office. He is an erudite man but much of his learning was lost owing to the softness of his voice and the frequency of the tunnels. We talked of Hore-Belisha, and Loch, though disagreeing with him as a politician and administrator, defended him as a man.

Left the train with the P.M. at a small station and spent the afternoon at Chartwell. The garden was glorious. After a long

[1] Lady Audrey Talbot, first wife of the ebullient, clever and frequently offensive Edward, Lord Stanley of Alderley, who was a bosom friend of Randolph Churchill and Evelyn Waugh.

sleep the P.M. in a purple dressing-gown and grey felt hat took me to see his goldfish. He was ruminating deeply about the fate of Tobruk since the failure of BATTLEAXE and contemplating means of resuming the offensive. He continued this train of thought in the cottage, conversing the while with the Yellow Cat and with Desmond about his garden.

Back in London an emissary from Marshal Pétain came to see the P.M., sponsored by "C".

The P.M. received a letter from H. G. Wells suggesting measures to relieve German pressure on Russia. "Russia is his only religion," the P.M. said to me with contempt.

Saturday, June 21st

The *Daily Mail* is full of schemes for reorganising the War Cabinet. The P.M. is nettled and fretful about the attitude of the press (just as I remember his predecessor being) and said to Beaverbrook that he must have more control of the whole war machine or else go. These murmured threats of resignation to Lord B. are indeed a turn of the tables.

The *Daily Mirror* has a front-page headline about "War Minister's daughter going to Washington as delegate to Red conference". Jan, of course. In an interview she said it was Munich that turned her socialist. I well remember that at Hinchingbrooke in October 1938 she was the only person who supported me in defence of Munich!

Returning from lunch, limp with the heat, I found Lord Louis Mountbatten* who recently played a heroic part in the naval action off Crete. He described how he sank several "Caiques" and foolishly, being old-fashioned, didn't shoot the men in the water; subsequently when his own ship was sunk the Germans machine-gunned him and his crew as they swam. He said that Crete emphasised the lesson which ought to have been learned long ago: that no naval or military operation should be undertaken without strong air cover. The navy felt a little aggrieved at their inclusion in the Cretan defeat: they had performed the task allotted to them, namely the prevention of a German seaborne landing.

During the morning I went to Waterloo to greet, on the P.M.'s behalf, Mr Fraser,[1] P.M. of New Zealand.

After lunch I took to the War Office telegrams from the P.M. appointing Auchinleck C. in C., Middle East, and transferring Wavell (in whom the P.M. has never really had much confidence) to India. David Margesson greeted me with: "Well, what do you think of that little bitch Jan?" and then went on to say that he approved of the Wavell change. The C.I.G.S., whom I also saw, obviously disapproves but thinks that it is no use keeping Wavell as he has not got the P.M.'s confidence. Wavell, he says, has got twice Auchinleck's brain. In any case he thinks it a mistake to send Wavell to India where he will arrive with the reputation of "failed B.A.".

To Chequers in time for dinner. Party consisted of P.M. and Mrs C., Mary, Judy Montagu, Tommy, Mr and Mrs Winant, Mr and Mrs Eden, Edward Bridges.

During dinner the talk turned to the demand for an Imperial War Cabinet. "Well," said the P.M., "you can easily turn the War Cabinet into a museum of Imperial celebrities, but then you have to have another body to manage the war."

The P.M. says a German attack on Russia is certain and Russia will assuredly be defeated. He thinks that Hitler is counting on enlisting capitalist and right-wing sympathies in this country and the U.S. The P.M. says he is wrong: he will go all out to help Russia. Winant asserts that the same will be true in the U.S. After dinner, when I was walking on the lawn with the P.M., he elaborated this and I said that for him, the arch anti-Communist, this was bowing down in the House of Rimmon. He replied that he had only one single purpose – the destruction of Hitler – and his life was much simplified thereby. If Hitler invaded Hell he would at least make a favourable reference to the Devil!

During dinner there was much talk on the U.S. coming into the war and also on Pétain's emissary, who has made it clear

---

[1] Emigrated from Glasgow to New Zealand in his youth. Once his shyness was penetrated, gold shone and he was seen to be a sincere, unassuming and deep-thinking statesman.

that what was holding Frenchmen back from us was their uncertainty about our victory and about the U.S. coming in. Eden said this was a contemptible attitude and compared very unfavourably with that of the Yugoslavs. "I hate *all* Frenchmen," he said to me, half-laughing, half-serious, when after dinner I showed him a telegram about de Gaulle's hurt feelings over something connected with peace negotiations in Syria.

When I was alone in the garden with the P.M. he said to me, "You will live through many wars, but you will never have such an interesting time as you are having now – and you may get some fighting later on." He then spoke of Wavell and Auchinleck and said it had been very difficult. I wondered if Wavell might not sulk and refuse India, but the P.M. said he had been afraid of just putting him on the shelf as that would excite much comment and attention. I suggested (as the C.I.G.S. had) that Wavell would use his pen after the war; the P.M. replied that he could use his too and would bet he sold more copies.

There were various nocturnal prowls before we went to bed. During one of them Eden, while holding forth on some topic, took a step backwards and disappeared head over heels into the deep ha-ha and barbed-wire fence at the edge of the lawn.

Sunday, June 22nd
Awoken by the telephone with the news that Germany had attacked Russia. I went a round of the bedrooms breaking the news and produced a smile of satisfaction on the faces of the P.M., Eden and Winant. Winant, however, suspects it may all be a put-up job between Hitler and Stalin (later the P.M. and Cripps laughed this to scorn).

Eden rushed off to the F.O. for the day; the P.M. decided to broadcast and actually came down to the Hawtrey room at 11.0 a.m. to prepare it; Sir Stafford and Lady Cripps motored over to discuss the situation and ended by staying to lunch and dine. Mr Fraser, the dull Labour Prime Minister of New Zealand, came to lunch and to stay the night, as did Cranborne and Beaverbrook.

At lunch the P.M. trailed his coat for Cripps, castigating Communism and saying that Russians were barbarians. Finally he declared that not even the slenderest thread connected Communists to the very basest type of humanity. Cripps took it all in good part and was amused.

During the afternoon I braved the heat and walked with Lady Cripps up to Beacon Hill. She is intelligent and sensitive and obviously very observant.

The P.M.'s broadcast was not ready till twenty minutes before he was due to deliver it and it gave me great anxiety, but even more so to Eden who wanted to vet the text and couldn't. But when it was made it impressed us all: it was dramatic and it gave a clear decision of policy-support for Russia.

After the ladies had left the dining-room there ensued a vivacious and witty debate between the P.M., supported in spirit but not much in words by Sir S. Cripps, on the one hand and Cranborne and Eden on the other. Fraser tried to make a few commonplace observations but could scarcely get a word in. Edward Bridges and I sat, fascinated and yet convulsed with laughter. The question at issue was: "Should there be a debate in the House on Tuesday about Russia?" Eden and Cranborne took the Tory standpoint that if there was it should be confined to the purely military aspect, as politically Russia was as bad as Germany and half the country would object to being associated with her too closely. The P.M.'s view was that Russia was now at war; innocent peasants were being slaughtered; and we should forget about Soviet systems or the Comintern and extend our hand to fellow human beings in distress. The argument was extremely vehement. I have never spent a more enjoyable evening.

Later, the night being very warm, we all walked in the garden and I gossiped with Edward Bridges while the P.M. continued an onslaught, begun at dinner, on the people who had let us in for this most unnecessary of all wars. He was harsh about Chamberlain whom he called "the narrowest, most ignorant, most ungenerous of men". At dinner it had been Chatfield whom he belaboured and the people at the Admiralty and elsewhere whose desire for "absurd self-abasement had brought us to the verge of annihilation".

On going to bed the P.M. kept on repeating how wonderful

it was that Russia had come in against Germany when she might so easily have been with her. He is also very pleased with our daylight sorties by fighters which, today and yesterday, accounted for fifty-eight enemy planes over France for the loss of three pilots. We seem to command the daylight air over enemy territory as well as our own.

Monday, June 23rd
The P.M. is now toying with the idea of an armed raid on the French coast while the Germans are busy in Russia. Now, he says, is the time "to make hell while the sun shines".

Went down to Ardley for the night to see David who is on leave. He is violently opposed to my joining the R.A.F. His reasons were many of them offensive (such as my practical incapacity in which he and Philip firmly, but wrongly, believe) but I did not mind as I knew they were in reality based on nothing but affection and the fear that I should be killed. Joan supports my intention.

Tuesday, June 24th
There is something to be said for "influence" – at least so I thought this morning when stopped in Birdcage Walk for speeding and then let off because the policeman recognised me as Private Secretary to the P.M.

The House of Commons met for the first time in the Chamber of the House of Lords, their Lordships having removed to the Royal Gallery. It is an inconveniently long way from the new Chamber to the P.M.'s room and as I had to run from one to the other three times in this tropical heat I all but succumbed.

Brendan invited Vincent Sheean[1] and Duncan Sandys to dinner and there ensued a violent religious argument, Sheean being an atheist and Brendan and Duncan, rather surprisingly, both being stalwart partisans of Christianity, as of course were Desmond, John Martin, Anthony and myself. Brendan is very sensitive to any anti-religious opinion and has, I think, a religious

---

[1] A somewhat brash Irish-American author and playwright of not very high quality.

temperament beneath his blasphemous exterior. The level of argument was not very high, but there was a compensating intensity of feeling.

Wednesday, June 25th

The troubles of the Ministry of Information have reached a climax and it is now essential to define what powers Mr Duff Cooper has and what his relations with the service departments are to be. Sammy Hood, with whom I lunched at the Travellers, says it is impossible to carry on as at present.

In Secret Session the P.M. told the House of Commons the facts about the shipping position and the Battle of the Atlantic, which show real signs of improvement. Last week-end Winant told me America hoped next year to build 2,000,000 tons of shipping more than was scheduled.

Finished *My Early Life* while the P.M. discussed his new proposal for sending a Cabinet Minister to take up permanent residence in the Middle East. This has been stimulated by a telegram from Randolph. Oliver Lyttelton has been selected.

Thursday, June 26th

Lunched with the George Rendels, one of their daughters and Sir W. Malkin (Legal Adviser to the F.O.) at the Ladies' Carlton. George told me some more about the F.O. reform which he is working out and said he hoped to increase efficiency by making people's positions less secure. He also talked of the Balkans, and of the chances we missed in Bulgaria. But Balkan solidarity proved illusory owing to the general antagonism to Bulgaria, the fact that none of the Balkan States had air forces, and the determination of H.M.G. to believe everything Prince Paul said and suspect everything King Boris said.

Saturday, June 28th (at Madeley)

Grandfather told me some interesting things about Lord Randolph Churchill, whom he had known well, and who, he said, could be more offensive than any man though he could also be more charming. He had an encyclopaedic memory only surpassed by Mr Gladstone.

Sunday, June 29th

In the afternoon I lay on a chaise longue in the sun reading Shelley's *Alastor*, Keats' *Endymion* and excerpts from Lord Chesterfield's *Letters to his Son*.

Mother had gone up to London to broadcast and during dinner we listened to her admirably conceived and delivered appeal on behalf of the various girls' societies. She is a most accomplished speaker. The postscript to the news was by an American journalist, Quentin Reynolds, who addressed himself to Dr Goebbels personally. I agreed with Grandfather in thinking it one of the most effective broadcasts I had ever heard. England and America had, he said, only one point of difference: the English drove on the left of the road and the Americans on the right; we were both going to drive down the same road, each keeping our own side, until together we reached its end – Berlin.

Monday, June 30th

The Russians, who are being driven back by the Germans, are showing unbelievable reticence to our military mission in Moscow. Molotov will tell us nothing beyond what is in the official communiqués. Now, in their hour of need, the Soviet Government – or at any rate Molotov – is as suspicious and unco-operative as when we were negotiating a treaty in the summer of 1939. I suppose our own left wing will say it is all the fault of H.M.G.

The announcement was made today of Beaverbrook's appointment as Minister of Supply (where, with more specific duties, he may become less importunate). Andrew Duncan goes to the Board of Trade and Oliver Lyttelton becomes Minister of State with special duties in the Middle East.

Finding the Annexe stuffy on these hot summer evenings the P.M. now proposes to dine and work at No. 10. I was on duty there until 1.30 while the terms of the communiqués about the new Middle East appointments, and the methods of announcing them, were thrashed out. Eden, whom Brendan now calls Robert Taylor,[1] came over and complained vociferously about

[1] A good looking, if "flashy" American film actor, whose most recent films had been *Escape* and *Flight Command*.

Stafford Cripps who, he says, changes his opinion every few minutes and wants to teach him (Eden) how to manage Foreign Affairs.

EIGHTEEN

LULL IN THE STORMS
JULY 1941

Tuesday, July 1st

The P.M. gave different instructions to me, Rowan and Ismay about the Middle East announcements. He is petrified of a leakage through some foreign Embassy which would enable Lord Haw Haw[1] to be first with the news.

Lunched at the Reform with Charles Fletcher Cooke,[2] whom I used to know at Cambridge as a socialist President of the Union. I found that his views of the desirability of state control had been shaken by working as a civil servant in the Admiralty. It was not the Administrative Grades which he criticised but "the people who walk about all day with tea-pots". He was beginning to think there was something to be said for private enterprise. His suggestion about recruiting civil servants is that they should serve a five-year apprenticeship and then be given a lump sum down and sent out into the world for ten years to make their way. Those that did so would afterwards be taken back and given key jobs.

---

[1] William Joyce. His affected voice earned him his nickname and his daily broadcasts from Berlin caused more amusement than alarm. Tried at the Old Bailey after the war and hanged for treason.

[2] A Cambridge contemporary and ardent socialist debater in the Union. Later became a barrister of merit, a Conservative M.P. and Parliamentary Under Secretary at the Home Office.

Wednesday, July 2nd
The changes in the Middle Eastern Command and the appointment of Oliver Lyttelton have a good press, though the removal of Wavell has caused surprise.

The Bishop of Birmingham, the notorious Dr Barnes,[1] came to see me, in Anthony Bevir's absence, about a crown living in his diocese. He described how the church of St Jude was next door to a pork butcher and all the pigs had been driven into the church during a bad raid. "Quite right too, I thought," added this Prince of the Church.

Thursday, July 3rd
The Russians are being driven back on all fronts but seem to be fighting hard and not disheartened.

Brendan had an M.P., Archie James, and the London Editor of the *New York Times* to dinner. We talked about the Ministry of Information and the general consensus of opinion seems to be that the Government's new compromise scheme for improving it is worthless. It should either be expanded and given great powers or contracted and the control of publicity vested in the individual departments concerned.

Friday, July 4th
I foresee an outcry: the I.L.P. maintain that Beaverbrook, before the formation of the present Government, offered to finance Peace candidates. The P.M. denied this in the House the other day. McGovern[2] now produces a circumstantial account for which Maxton will vouch – and most people will believe Maxton before Beaverbrook.

Saturday, July 5th
Alone with Barker at No. 10, the P.M. having gone to Chartwell in search of peace. So I was kept more pleasantly busy than is usually the case now with this large staff.

[1] Right Revd E. W. Barnes, a Cambridge don of high intellect, but outspokenly iconoclastic and much criticised by most Anglicans.
[2] Independent Labour Party M.P. for the Shettleston division of Glasgow.

Gave Jasper Rootham lunch at the Travellers. He rejoices in exchanging the Civil Service for a tank. He told me that the one member of Chamberlain's Government who opposed the return of the Irish bases to De Valera in 1938 was Lord Hailsham[1]

In the late afternoon I sat beneath the tree in the garden at No. 10 and read and re-read T. S. Eliot's poem *Burnt Norton*. His sense of rhythm and his use of words are beyond praise. His meaning is less easy to assess.

Sunday, July 6th

Went to church early at Westminster Abbey. A quiet day of blazing heat and sunshine. Part of it I spent trying on my contact lenses, which are not comfortable, and part in reading A. J. A. Symons' astonishing, highly readable book, *The Quest for Corvo*.

Dined at Claridges with Herschel Johnson and talked most agreeably till 11.00. I elaborated my thesis that Hitler has been so impressed by the skill of his own staff-work, and by the speed and regularity with which his objects have been achieved, that he has ceased to believe anything impossible. Whereas our authorities are apt to take a gloomy view of an operation, and in any case to prepare a very slow timetable, German operations have invariably succeeded – at any rate on land – and German squadrons and divisions are moved from east to west or north to south in as many days as our forces require weeks. Thus I believe that Hitler did not contemplate the possibility of a check in Russia: everything would work out with the same clockwork precision as before. Perhaps it will; many of our experts think so; but I do not.

Herschel said that an American resents the indifference of an Englishman; he would not mind mere rudeness. An American is often offensive, but he does not understand silent contempt.

As I left Herschel told me that Monty Sherman had once said to him, "I never feel able to criticise anyone's motives." Monty,

[1] Quintin Hogg, 1st Viscount Hailsham, Lord Chancellor twice and also Secretary of State for War. Had the distinction of producing a son who was also Lord Chancellor twice, for even longer than himself, and First Lord of the Admiralty.

though very tolerant, was a man who often condemned people's actions.

Tuesday, July 8th

After lunching with Father at the Turf, I got back to No. 10 and went down to talk to the P.M. while he was preparing to go to sleep. "I hear you are plotting to abandon me," he said. "You know I can stop you. I can't make you stay with me against your will but I can put you somewhere else." I said yes, but I hoped he wouldn't; and after I had taken out one of my unfinished contact lenses to show him, he said I might go and agreed that the short, sharp battle of the fighter pilot was far better than the long wait of a bomber crew before they reached their objective. He made a few remarks about how wrong I was to go when I knew the routine of the office (though he clearly thought I was right) and said he would not have let me if the bombing in London had been heavy, but as there was a lull he couldn't say no.

The tropical heatwave, which started more than three weeks ago, continues – at well over 90° in the shade.

Wednesday, July 9th

Philip, to whom I told the P.M.'s decision on the telephone, was not at all elated. He takes the same view as David of my practical incapacity – and I think for the same affectionate reasons.

The P.M. and most of his family went down to Chequers for the night, for Lady Goonie's funeral tomorrow. Being in attendance I drove Diana Sandys there in my car. The sentries refused to let us in, but we forced an entrance by the back door. The Sinclairs also came.

At dinner I sat between Lady Sinclair and Mrs Churchill. The P.M. talked afterwards of the political future, the conversation arising from his congratulations to Archie Sinclair on his K.T. [Order of the Thistle] and Archie saying that a K.G. for Anthony Eden would ruin his chances of being P.M. Winston said that Eden now had a serious competitor: Oliver Lyttelton, who was *persona grata* to the Conservative Party and who had an opportunity of establishing his reputation in Egypt. Anthony

Eden was not supported in the House or in the party though personally he, Winston, admired his great moral and physical courage. "He would equally well charge a battery or go to the stake for his principles – even though the principles might be wrongly conceived and he might charge the battery from the wrong angle." Oliver Lyttelton was "tough and stuffy" – and ready to take responsibility.

After dinner the P.M. and Archie talked till 2.00 a.m. while I played the gramophone for them. The P.M. showed Archie with great glee the parody of "To be or not to be" written at the time of Napoleon's invasion threat and now hung in the passage at Chequers. They talked of what should be done with the enemy leaders after the war. The P.M. thought that when the war was over there should be an end to all bloodshed, though he would like to see Mussolini, the bogus mimic of Ancient Rome, strangled like Vercingetorix in old Roman fashion. Hitler and the Nazis he would segregate on some island, though he would not so desecrate St Helena. But we still had a long way to go.

The P.M. inveighed against defeatism and said it would be better to make this island a sea of blood than to surrender if invasion came. He had been impressed by a letter from Reynaud to Pétain, sent some weeks ago, in which the former recalled how the Generals had said to him that after the Franco-German Armistice England would have "her neck wrung like a chicken" in three weeks. Reynaud had sent copies of this letter through the American Ambassador at Vichy to the P.M. and to the President. It is impressive reading.

Finally the P.M. and the S. of S. agreed that the French had acted shamefully in demanding more fighter squadrons from us after they knew the battle was lost.

The P.M. seems reconciled to my joining the R.A.F. and, as he went to bed, said that a fighter pilot had greater excitement than a polo-player, big game shot and hunting-man rolled into one. I owe my release largely to Mrs C.'s spirited intervention on my behalf.

Thursday, July 10th

The whole party went off to Lady Goonie's funeral in the morning and returned to lunch bringing with them Clarissa and Peregrine.[1]

After lunch I drove Clarissa up to London. She had been shy and silent at lunch (realising no doubt that she is not at present held in high esteem by her relations) but was more cheerful in the car.

Friday, July 11th

Rode and bathed at Richmond. Each succeeding day is if possible hotter than the last.

Went to Cowes to stay with Father at the Squadron, almost succumbing to the unbearable heat in the train to Portsmouth. Cowes itself was cool and fresh, and I delighted in its narrow streets and familiar smells after an absence of almost two years.

Colonel Charteris,[2] deafer than ever but still gay and debonair, was staying at the club; also Major Saville, a charming old man who told me of his life as a cowboy in Colorado in the year 1880.

I broke to Father my intention of joining the air force. He said: "I'm sorry", but was less obviously disturbed than I had feared and seemed to forget all about it.

Monday, July 14th

Returned from Cowes with Father. At Winchester Clarissa got into the train, with all her mother's effects in a number of trunks, and I travelled with her to Waterloo where she unloaded her trunks on me for deposit at No. 10.

There are to be changes in the Administration, with a view to disposing of Duff Cooper and Lord Hankey. It is proposed that Brendan – very much against his will, he says – should be

---

[1] Younger son of Major Jack and Lady Gwendeline Churchill.
[2] Owner of Cahir, Co. Tipperary. A friendly, generous man, well known in both racing and yachting circles and loved by Irishmen of all persuasions. During "the troubles" his castle was occupied forcibly by De Valera and the Sinn Fein leaders and on regaining his property he was surprised to find they had all signed their names in the Visitors' Book. He married a lady from the music-hall stage known as "The Copper Queen".

Minister of Information, a job in which every holder of the office has failed but for which he has great qualifications. Rab will be President of the Board of Education. The P.M. wants to make Duncan Sandys Financial Secretary to the War Office (Dick Law succeeding Rab at the F.O.). This will cause accusations of nepotism.

Very hot and trying searches for a telegram which Eden, Desmond and I thought did not exist and which the P.M. swore did. It did; and the P.M. suggested I should perform hari-kiri.

Feel strongly that I am achieving nothing here but living very comfortably on false pretences and growing lazy through the lack of incentive to effort.

Tuesday, July 15th
Went to the House with the P.M. who made a statement on Production (criticisms in the recent debate have galled him), Syria and the Russian alliance.

Desmond says there are signs that Vichy is playing a double game and that the emissary from Pétain and Huntziger,[1] who came the other day, was not all that he appeared to be. The aim may be to cause a breach between ourselves and de Gaulle.

Brendan tells me that the letters and requests he gets from people wanting honours and jobs defy belief.

Wednesday, July 16th
The Russians, though still retiring, are evidently taking severe toll of the Germans who, for the first time, are short of fighter support. Thus our daily raids on Northern France are serving their purpose, even though they are not a sufficiently formidable diversion and we ought to do something more. But as usual the attitude of the Chiefs of Staff is as negative as it can be.

I talked to Dr Wellington Koo, the new Chinese Ambassador, who told me how effective the "scorched earth" tactics, now being used by the Russians against the German invader, can be.

[1] Commanded the French 2nd Army in May 1940. Subsequently rallied to Pétain, though he had been more in favour of continued resistance than most of the French Generals and de Gaulle thought well of him.

They were widely adopted in China against the Japanese. H.E. was full of optimism; he did not see how the immense anti-Axis front could fail. Like the P.M. he is impressed by the numbers now opposed to Germany: 1,200 million, or three-quarters of the world's population.

Lunched with Milo Talbot at the Junior Carlton and discussed the situation which would arise if the Nazis were overthrown and the German Generals offered peace, with their armed strength unbroken. I believe that then will be the moment to declare peace aims – and specifically at that. German resistance would be sustained by the fear of a Carthaginian peace. A generous offer, demanding in return the disarmament of Germany under strict guarantees, might well tempt a war-weary people to coerce even the army leaders. We also discussed Russia. I now think that Russia's action in 1939 and subsequently was due to fear and a wish to appease rather than the Machiavellian hope of seeing Europe so devastated that the seeds of Communism could be planted successfully in the shell holes. So they paid Danegeld.

The P.M. apparently wanted to make Duncan Sandys Under Secretary for Foreign Affairs – the most important and responsible of the Under Secretaryships. Eden has tactfully expressed a preference for Richard Law on grounds of experience. So Duncan will go to the War Office. Stirred by this example of nepotism John Peck offers me £5 to suggest that the best choice for Minister of Information would be Vic Oliver.

Thursday, July 17th
A report of Brendan's appointment as Minister of Information has appeared in the newspapers – leaked from Heaven knows where – and at lunch-time in the Travellers I was bombarded with questions.

At 5.30 Harry Hopkins appeared, having suddenly arrived from America in a bomber, laden with ham, cheese, cigars, etc., for the P.M. and American cigarettes which, to my envy, he gave to Tommy.

Friday, July 18th
Went to Chequers, where there is a large party: Harry Hopkins, Averell Harriman and his daughter Kathleen,[1] Pamela Churchill, Pug, Brendan. The latter is filled with gloom at his new appointment and says he hates the very idea of it.

Harry Hopkins is full of optimism about American production, especially with regard to tanks for the Middle East and an American maintenance staff there.

I sat next to Kathleen Harriman at dinner. She is pretty but convinced of the superiority of the United States in all things.

Saturday, July 19th
General Alexander, C. in C., Southern Command, came to lunch.

At tea-time the Soviet Ambassador[2] arrived, bringing a telegram for the P.M. from Stalin who asks for diversions in various places by English forces. It is hard for the Russians to understand how unprepared we still are to take the offensive. I was present while the P.M. explained the whole situation very clearly to poor, uninformed Maisky.

Sir Alan Brooke (C. in C., Home Forces), Colonel Bob Laycock[3] (who commanded the S.A.S. battalion in Crete) and Peregrine Churchill came to dine and sleep. Sir Dudley Pound also.

Sunday, July 20th
Better weather, though since St Swithin's day there has been no whole day without rain.

---

[1] Competent hostess and constant companion of her father when he was Ambassador in Moscow, 1943–46.
[2] Ivan Maisky, Soviet Ambassador in London for eleven years. Churchill had known and liked him since the 1930s. He was evidently more popular in London than in Moscow; Stalin incarcerated him for four years.
[3] Formerly an officer in the Blues and intimate friend of Antony Head. He led the Commandos in Crete and in 1943 succeeded Lord Louis Mountbatten as Chief of Combined Operations and a member of the Chiefs of Staff Committee. After the war he was Governor of Malta. He combined charm with driving energy. He married a daughter of the Marquesa de Casa Maury (Mrs Dudley Ward).

Raymond Gram Swing, the American wireless commentator, came to lunch. So did Professor Lord Cherwell.

Sat on the lawn a great part of the afternoon, dozing, conversing spasmodically and playing backgammon with Mrs C.

The P.M. dictated a clever reply to Stalin which made me very late for dinner and caused me considerable inconvenience afterwards (long conversations with Eden, Pound, Sargent, etc., on the channel by which it should be sent – a matter which the P.M. had already decided).

The Attlees came to dine and sleep and Sir Richard and Lady Peirse to dine. We listened to Raymond Gram Swing's masterly commentary after the news. It almost seemed to be addressed to those in the room: the remarks about the P.M. and Harry Hopkins were surely made in the light of the lunch-time conversation and in the knowledge they were listening.

After dinner we had a deplorable American film, *Citizen Kane*,[1] based on the personality of William Randolph Hearst. The P.M. was so bored that he walked out before the end. Kathleen Harriman thought it wonderful and said that all Americans did. The fact that we did not, revealed to her much about English people. I replied that the fact Americans did, revealed to me nothing about Americans.

After the film we sat up till 3.00 while the P.M. talked about food supplies and imports. Hopkins said that the export of finished steel goods such as knives and aluminium fishing rods to the U.S., while of no economic importance, was playing into the hands of the Isolationists, who declared that America was sending us products she could ill afford in order that we might support our exports. Nonsense, of course; but the political issue was quite considerable when vast Lease-Lend appropriations were before Congress. Hopkins also said that the U.S. could and should send us more food.

Finally Attlee and Harriman were yawning so much that Hopkins insisted that the P.M., in irrepressible spirits, should go to bed. When Winston started on what he was going to do

[1] Not thought deplorable by most people. It brought fame and celebrity to Orson Welles.

to the Nazi leaders after the war – and the Nazi cities during it – Hopkins said that he, Winston, only read the bits of the Bible that suited him and that they were drawn from the Old Testament. "I'm not surprised they all leave you, the way you go on: there's Tommy lost at least two stone, there's Jock going into the Air Corps (beware of the coloured gals in Alabama if you go to be trained there), there's Seal gone to the United States, and you have to give that girl (Mrs Hill) of yours a medal to have her stay." At that moment everybody started looking at their watches and the P.M. was forcibly taken to bed.

Monday, July 21st
On the way back to London we all, in a great cortège of cars, stopped at Northolt to see the new big bombers. A Stirling, a Halifax, a Lancaster, a B.17 (Flying Fortress) and a B.24 (Liberator) were all drawn up for inspection. With the Attlees, Pamela, and Kathleen Harriman, I climbed inside most of them and was astounded by the intricacy of the mechanism as well as thrilled by the expanse of the wings and the sense of power. Then the five planes took off and flew past, very low, while we stood in a vast group which included Archie Sinclair, the C.A.S., Peirse, Moore-Brabazon and numbers of American officers and experts. The Lancaster was the most impressive of all, though the Flying Fortress, designed for civilian use, is the most beautiful.

Lady Malcolm[1] (daughter of Lillie Langtry, "The Jersey Lily") took me to the first night of the Vic-Wells Ballet at the New Theatre. I had expected to be bored but was entranced. We saw *Giselle* and *The Prospect Before Us*. Robert Helpmann may not be Massine nor Margot Fonteyn Danilova, but their performance was as good as any I have seen in the Ballet Russe before the war. The other members of the party were Americans, Mrs Johnny Dodge, and Drexel Biddle's right-hand man, Rudolph Schön, whom I found very conversible at dinner at La Coquille. He refuses to agree that the war may now be a

[1] Her father was not Mr Langtry but Prince Louis of Battenberg. She was thus a half-sister of Lord Louis Mountbatten.

short one, though he admits the potential effect of heavy bombing on German towns. But he thinks we have got to beat them militarily.

Tuesday, July 22nd
The more I see of the Chiefs of Staff's conclusions, the more depressed I am by the negative attitude they adopt. They seem convinced that their function is to find reasons against every offensive proposal put forward and to suggest some anodyne, ineffective alternative. Their excuse may be shortage of equipment, shipping and manpower; but they show no disposition to improvise or to take risks.

The P.M. held a meeting on American aircraft, since Harry Hopkins and Averell Harriman think we are not making full use of the B.17s and B.24s we have received.

Brendan, very scathing after his first day at the Ministry of Information ("Bloomersbury" he calls it), invited Lord Moore[1] to dine and our new P.P.S., Colonel Harvie-Watt[2] was also there. We talked of price stabilisation and wages. Brendan says that no Chancellor of the Exchequer has had the courage to say that if you are to have any chance of successfully stabilising prices, you must prevent an all-round rise in wages.

Wednesday, July 23rd
Another meeting with the Americans, this time about tanks.

My contact lenses are at last finished and today, for the first time, I wore them with the lenses fitted.

Bob Coates,[3] just back from Iceland, dined with me in the Mess and afterwards I took him, by invitation of Brendan, to

---

[1] Garrett, afterwards 11th Earl of Drogheda, Managing Director and Chairman of the *Financial Times* and an outstanding Chairman of Covent Garden. A man of wide knowledge and great sensitivity. married to a pianist of high quality.

[2] M.P. for Richmond, Surrey. He wrote for Churchill excellent weekly summaries of proceedings in the House of Commons. Chairman of Consolidated Goldfields after the war.

[3] Elder son of Sir Clive and Lady Celia Coates. Commanded a battalion of the Coldstream Guards, won a D.S.O. and was the best of good company.

see a number of films at the Ministry of Information. There were newsreels of the Russian war, arrived via Sweden this morning, and an admirable English propaganda film, called *Target for Tonight*, about an R.A.F. bomber squadron.

Thursday, July 24th

Lunched with the P.M. and Mrs Churchill at the Annexe. The other guests were Sir William[1] and Lady Jowitt, Lady Ridley, Lady Wimborne (Alice), Sir Henry Strakosch, Venetia Montagu and Mr Chuter Ede.[2] I sat between Lady Jowitt, gushing and talkative, and Lady Wimborne, who looks very young and has lots to say.

The P.M. said that one of the most striking things about this age was "the lamentable lack of Charlotte Cordays".

Sir Henry Strakosch is optimistic about German oil. He thinks they only have five million tons' reserve and that if the Russians hold out another two months Germany will be exhausted for lack of it. Sir W. Jowitt, an intellectual and distinguished-looking man, was eloquent in his denunciation of Vichy – the most contemptible thing in history.

If Brendan is to be believed, he has already tackled the Admiralty and persuaded them to be more generous with their supply of straw for the Ministry of Information bricks.

De Gaulle is behaving abominably in Cairo: quarrelsome and neurotic. Oliver Lyttelton seems to be treating him tactfully in order to avoid a breach.

On late duty at No. 10 where future strategy in the Middle East was being discussed. First Harry Hopkins and then the P.M. spoke to President Roosevelt on the telephone, and the P.M., forgetting he was not on the "scrambler", said some things about a certain rendez-vous which he afterwards bitterly regretted.

---

[1] A Liberal M.P., of strikingly handsome appearance, converted to Labour. Minister of National Insurance in Churchill's Government and Lord Chancellor when Attlee took office in 1945.

[2] Prominent Labour M.P. Home Secretary in Attlee's post-war government.

Friday, July 25th

Rode and bathed at Richmond. Louis Greig says he can make arrangements to prevent my call-up being delayed so that, if I pass the medical, I can start my training soon. Accounts reaching the P.M. show that the training schools in the U.S. are hard and spartan and the standard very high. Meanwhile one of my contact lenses is being troublesome – letting in bubbles.

Spent the night at Horsley with Grandfather and Peggy, who are most agreeable hosts.

Saturday, July 26th

Returned to London, giving a lift to a vivacious Frenchwoman, whose conversation was so enjoyable that I exceeded the speed limit and was apprehended.

Went to Badminton with Philip. It is a large, beautiful grey house. Mother and Jack Coke[1] were there when we arrived and also Lord and Lady Coke, who had come over to tea. Queen Mary who had invited us because of her great affection for Mother, although she never has guests to stay, came in to tea and later I walked with her in the garden, telling her many things which, in view of her great discretion, I thought I might safely say. She was grateful and said how sadly she missed the information which in the last war the King had always confided to her.

The Duchess of Beaufort,[2] who had been working in a canteen, was back in time for dinner and I thought her downright, frank manner very attractive. She loathes Jack Coke with a deep and unalterable conviction.

Sunday, July 27th

The Duke of Beaufort arrived from Windsor for a late breakfast. At 11.00 we went to church in the church attached to the house, a fine building with good marble tombstones of various Dukes

---

[1] Uncle of Lord Leicester and equerry to Queen Mary from 1937. Friendly, entertaining, but alarmingly indiscreet.
[2] Mary, daughter of Queen Mary's eldest brother, Prince Adolphus of Teck, who was created Marquess of Cambridge in 1917, and of Lady Margaret Grosvenor.

of Beaufort, executed by Italian sculptors. We sat in a large gallery at the back of the church, in huge armchairs and confronted with immense prayer books dating from the eighteenth century, looking down on the congregation below.

Before lunch Mother and I walked with the tedious Louise, Dowager Duchess of Beaufort, to look at her house in the village and resplendent garden. The village of Badminton is unspoilt and beautiful.

In the afternoon Queen Mary motored Mother and me into Bath, and we gave a lift in the car to a hot and embarrassed private soldier from the Badminton guard. I had not been to Bath for some five years. Under the auspices of Lady Noble we went over several houses in Lansdowne Crescent – including Moley Sargent's flat – and in the famous Royal Crescent. Their interiors were exquisite and redolent of Jane Austen and Fanny Burney. We had tea with Lady Noble, whose dining-room in Park Crescent is embellished with large paintings by Sert. We also saw the mayor's house, in itself fine but tastelessly decorated.

Back at Badminton I had another long conversation with Queen Mary in her private sitting-room, which, in the best royal tradition, is crammed with family photographs. H.M. was very pleasant and talkative. I can see why Mother has formed so great an affection for her. She has dignity which is natural and knowledge which is unaccompanied by arrogance or affectation.

Philip had returned to Sandhurst, where he is taking a tank course, by the time we returned from Bath. We dined, as last night, in the small oak-panelled dining-room, with the family device of a portcullis engraved on the panels. The Queen wore a mass of jewels, diamond collar and bracelets, brooches and necklaces, which she carries without any appearance of ostentation or overdressing. In obedience to Lord Woolton we only had two courses but four pages and footmen to serve them. Altogether the Queen's household is a strange mixture of simplicity and royal state.

When we had listened to Harry Hopkins broadcasting (rather poorly, I thought), and the Queen had gone upstairs, Jack Coke and I had a somewhat acrimonious argument about the war.

Monday, July 28th

Back in London, where there had been a small raid last night in retaliation for some bombs we dropped on Berlin. After lunch I sat with the P.M. and Mrs Churchill in the garden while they told me about a book of Cecil Beaton's – *My Royal Past* – with which they are both delighted. The P.M. also talked about the long speech on production which he is to make tomorrow and which is eagerly awaited by his growing body of critics. Apparently he has been working on it all the week-end – until 10 to 5 one morning. It is very important from the point of view of informed opinion in the country.

Today I kept my contact lenses in for two hours without the appearance of a bubble.

Tuesday, July 29th

The Production debate, in which the P.M. made a very long speech that failed wholly to satisfy the critics and the newspapers, who demand the appointment of a Minister of Production.

Leslie and I spent the whole afternoon correcting the Hansard proof, so shocking are the acoustics of the House of Lords.

Drank sherry with Lady Sinclair and Sylvia Henley. We discussed leakages. Lady S. said that the surest way of making people repeat things was to say "Don't quote me". This prefix always convinced people that the statement was important and true. Sir Archibald Sinclair never told her anything: he was what Lady Violet Bonham-Carter called "in a Trappist mood".

Wednesday, July 30th

Was present at the signing of the Russo-Polish treaty in the Secretary of State's room at the F.O. It was signed against a background of spotlights and a foreground of cameramen by the P.M., Eden, Sikorski and Maisky, while a bust of the Younger Pitt looked down, rather disapprovingly I thought. Although this treaty abrogates the Soviet-German treaty of 1939, and leaves the frontier question unsettled, it has caused a lot of Polish heart-burning, including, I believe, the resignation of the President. To a Pole, a Russian has no advantages over a German – and history makes this very understandable.

Auchinleck, the new C. in C., Middle East, dined with the P.M. and I had a conversation with him beforehand. He thought the situation in the Western Desert had been mishandled – "not by the High Command, but tactically I mean". He entirely discounted the possibility of the Germans moving an armoured division from Libya to the Russian front. He thinks de Gaulle is mad and consumed with personal ambition, which makes him care little for our fortunes in the war. But, says A., Oliver Lyttelton has handled him very well. Auchinleck is an impressive man, but – as one sometimes finds on a racecourse – looks do not always bear great relation to form.

Thursday, July 31st
The P.M. walked back from the House after the Cabinet, a thing he has never done before, and though he was talking to me at the top of his voice about war memorials (a train of thought engendered by the Cenotaph) hardly anybody in the street recognised him.

On late duty at No. 10. The P.M. returned from the Other Club, somewhat cantankerous, and dictated voluminous notes about the war until 2.15 a.m.

Meanwhile Desmond has made the horrifying discovery that the press, or at any rate Lord Camrose and his staff, have found out about the most closely guarded secret of the war: namely the contents of those buff boxes which "C" sends to the P.M.[1] Leakages increase in number and seriousness.

---

[1] If Desmond Morton's information was correct, Lord Camrose and his staff showed commendable discretion; for no word of what was subsequently called the Ultra Secret was printed till several decades after the war.

NINETEEN

SPECIAL RELATIONSHIP CONFIRMED
AUGUST 1941

Friday, August 1st
I went to the Air Ministry for my "medical", with my contact lenses in place, and – oh rapture! – was passed entirely fit. On my return I visited Horace Wilson, who was sympathetic and prepared to be helpful, and then bearded Harvey and Mallet at the F.O., who were the very opposite but were reluctantly persuaded to acquiesce.

The P.M. disappeared to Chequers and I shall not see him for a fortnight as he is very shortly off on a historic journey (Operation RIVIERA). He is as excited as a schoolboy on the last day of the term. Brendan has persuaded him, against his will, to take two newspaper reporters.

Dined with Hugh Dodds;[1] among much that was boring he gave me some interesting news about France and said that southern France could only be restored to its honour and life by a German occupation. He thinks we should work for this. Desmond Morton thinks so too.

---

[1] Second husband of my Aunt Nancy (Annabel). He had been Consul in Addis Ababa and Tripoli, and ended his career as Consul General in Nice. He got into trouble, unfairly, with the Foreign Office for transporting the Duke and Duchess of Windsor over the Pyrenees in June 1940 while leaving his subordinates to deal with the flood of other refugees and escaped prisoners of war who swarmed into Nice.

Saturday, August 2nd

The Russians seem to be holding their position and the situation at Smolensk is satisfactory. If they can but hold another three months the war is as good as won and Napoleon's precedent will have been followed with almost uncanny exactitude.

In the evening I went to see Clarissa who is in hospital with lumbago and looks radiantly attractive in bed.

St Swithin who, since July 15th, has been very jealous of his reputation, showed signs of relenting today and the sun shone with the brilliance of a month ago.

Sunday, August 3rd

We raided Berlin heavily last night.

The P.M. left for the north with a retinue which Cardinal Wolsey might have envied.

Monday, August 4th

Received a moving letter from Mother: "Well, Darling, I am glad (I think), absolutely thrilled anyhow, and *very* proud to hear of my new Air Force son. I hope the *ardua* won't be too tedious or exacting and that the *astra* will fulfil all your hopes concerning them . . . Father has said very little, and is reluctantly resigned."

Sat next to John Addis[1] at lunch. He tells me he is the twelfth child of a twelfth child!

The P.M.'s absence makes an astonishing difference: there is practically nothing to do, though Attlee – who is deputising in the P.M.'s absence – keeps on ringing up to know whether there are any papers for him to sign, like a child with a new toy it is longing to use.

Went to see Diana Quilter, who is working in the prisoners-of-war depot at Trent. Apparently all the prisoners think Hitler made a big mistake in going into Russia; and apparently they all have a real loathing of us. Diana says she is convinced our fate would be worse than that of the Poles if the Germans ever got here.

---

[1] Entered the Foreign Office in 1938 and succeeded me at No. 10 in 1945. Eventually Ambassador in Peking.

From Diana's house I went to comfort Clarissa in her nursing home, but finding Colly Barclay there, and knowing him to be an ardent suitor, I did not stay long.

Tuesday, August 5th
The P.M. being away, an unnatural calm reigns. I represented him at the memorial service for Sir Emsley Carr (proprietor of the *News of the World*) at St Dunstan's in the West, Fleet Street and, giving Sammy Hood a lift back in my staff car, learned that the German Trans-ocean Wireless had already broadcast that the P.M. and Roosevelt were to meet.

Motored to Stratford on Avon after lunch to stay with the Sandwiches in a very ancient house once inhabited by Shakespeare's daughter and, for a time, by Shakespeare himself.

We went to see an extremely enjoyable performance of *The Merchant of Venice*, and the two principal actors, Baliol Holloway (Shylock) and Margaretta Scott (Portia), came back to dine afterwards and to talk about the stage.

Monday, August 11th
Back in London I found everything quiet and even "the military" admitting that the Russian army was technically better equipped and trained than had been expected. Apparently part of Russia's successful stand has been due to her using her whole bomber force for army co-operation. Stalin is confident he can hold out till winter without losing Moscow, Kiev, or Leningrad.

There seemed to be little doing and so I went to bed early, thus missing the arrival of a telegram from the P.M. about the joint declaration – in effect a statement of war aims – which President R. wishes published. The Cabinet met at 1.00 a.m. and substantially accepted the P.M.'s view on the subject.

Tuesday, August 12th
The Cabinet met at 10.00 to resume last night's discussions. The P.M. appears to have cajoled the President into accepting the terms of the joint declaration which he desires. Moreover the President and the P.M. have concerted measures against Japan.

Wednesday, August 13th

The P.M. sent another batch of telegrams which were very entertaining and showed great satisfaction with his conversations. In parts they were flippant: e.g. "See also Roosevelt – Churchill message to dear, old Joe" – who is being promised a great deal of material help.

The "Home Opinion" Censorship Report displays a great upward surge of public morale as a result of Russia's continued resistance. Indeed a great many people seem to hope for victory by Christmas. There is little reservation in the enthusiasm shown for Russia and practically no defeatism, but some bitterness against vested interests, Mr Bevin, and in particular ablebodied men and women who live in comfort at such places as Harrogate, disregarding the war as far as they can and concentrating on food and amusement.

A Pole, Count Zamoyski,[1] and Ronnie Melville dined with me. Zamoyski, who strikes me as sensible and realistic, is nevertheless very resolute in his hatred of Germany and wants as much destruction as possible done now, since he does not believe that we could destroy Germany's strength in cold blood after the war. A nice Christian frame of mind we are all reaching! Z. also confirmed what I have been told previously, that the Russian occupation of Poland was on the whole more terrible than the German.

Thursday, August 14th

At 3.00 p.m. Attlee announced on the wireless the meeting of the P.M. and Roosevelt and read the Declaration of War Aims which they had agreed. It sounded tame, though the significance of America agreeing to collaborate in keeping the aggressor states disarmed is considerable.

Friday, August 15th

Went to Euston House at 8.45 a.m. for the formalities connected with joining the air force and left at 12.00 with 2/6d pay, an Aircraftsman 2nd Class in the R.A.F.V.R.

---

[1] A.D.C. to General Sikorski. Married a rich lady and settled in England, spending much of his time playing bridge (rather badly) at White's Club.

I was given three written tests in Mathematics, Intelligence and General Knowledge. They were very searching, to my surprise. To be confronted with even elementary algebra and geometry is disconcerting after eleven years – and I felt rather foolish when I remembered recording, on another form, that I had won "credits" in the School Certificate in Elementary and Advanced Mathematics. Fortunately I remembered about Pythagoras. The Air Vice Marshal on the Selection Board seemed to think some technical knowledge of engineering desirable; which was a blow. He discounted my theory that ability to ride a horse was useful for a pilot but said that sailing a boat was. By dint of heavy wire-pulling it looks as if I shall be able to be called up when I wish: namely about September 30th. In company with six other men clasping Bibles I swore allegiance in very solemn terms to the King, his Heirs and Successors.

Went down to West Horsley for the night with Mother. We had a delightful evening. I trotted out my thesis that our contribution to the Peace Settlement must be the acceptance of Washington instead of London as the centre of gravity of the Anglo-Saxon World, the British Isles becoming the English Speaking outpost in Europe. Why, said Mother, should we make this sacrifice in order to establish a lower basis of political and commercial morality – which would in effect be the result? There is force in this.

Saturday, August 16th
Peacefully denuded the loganberry bushes in the garden for half an hour (what occupation can be more agreeable?) and then drove M. to London.

The reactions to the Churchill – Roosevelt meeting are now crystallising, and the significance of the declaration is more appreciated as the initial disappointment that something more startling did not emerge wears off.

At the Ministry of Information Brendan provided a display of the films of the Prime Minister's voyage which have just been flown back to London. They were not yet cut or edited and some of the effects produced – in particular the singing of "Onward Christian Soldiers" at the service on H.M.S. *Prince of*

Wales – were almost unbearably funny. Lord Cherwell and Inspector Thompson[1] in yachting caps were also mirth giving, not to mention the gestures and twitchings of Tommy Thompson who always contrives to be in the forefront of the photographic battle. Nevertheless the films, which lasted over an hour, when suitably bowdlerised should provide a good record of an historic occasion.

Monday, August 18th
I lunched with Mrs Churchill and Mary at No. 10. Mary is shortly going away to join the A.T.S.

Afterwards, the cat being away, it seemed reasonable that the mice should play tennis, and Leslie Rowan and I played two energetic sets in Eccleston Square.

Brendan asked us all to the Ministry of Information to see the finished version of the Churchill – Roosevelt film. I could never have believed so good a result could be achieved from so uninspiring and amorphous a farrago of material. It was typical of Brendan to think of asking all the P.M.'s servants and to meet them himself at the entrance to the Ministry, not allowing the films to begin without them. The comment of Moley Sargent, whom I took in my car, was that the P.M. looked more like Mr Pickwick every day.

Had a conversation with Sir Frederick Leith Ross[2] who was Mr Asquith's private secretary in 1910. He considered that Cabinet business was much more easily and efficiently conducted when no papers were circulated and Ministers conveyed decisions to their departments by word of mouth. There had never in his experience been any subsequent argument about the nature or scope of a decision.

Jack Churchill, Desmond and I discussed the rising annoyance in the House of Commons at the P.M.'s personal resentment of criticism – which is meant to be helpful – and the offence which has been given to many people, including Ministers, by his

[1] Churchill's senior detective who had been with him, in good times and bad, for a great many years.
[2] One of the most revered civil servants of his generation. Chief economic adviser to the Government from 1938 to 1946.

treatment of them. Desmond goes so far as to say that the P.M. is losing many people's friendship. The P.M. himself does not expect to retain his popularity if he wins the war for us: he has before him the examples of Wellington and Disraeli amongst others. But that he should lose his personal friends owing to the impatience of his manner is unfortunate – and unfair to one so innately lovable and generous.

Tuesday, August 19th
The P.M. arrived back in London. The Cabinet met him at King's Cross; Leslie Rowan, John Peck and I greeted him on the steps of the Annexe as he emerged from his car, smiling broadly, still dressed in his nautical clothes. Ralph Assheton[1] had brought his wife and child to see the return; nobody else was there.

John Martin told me he had heard Roosevelt say that he did not intend to declare war: he intended to wage it.

Wednesday, August 20th
Just before going down to dress for dinner the P.M., nodding his head gloomily, said that the situation was very grim. I suppose he was referring to the German progress in the Ukraine and towards Leningrad; or perhaps to certain failures and disappointments in our production. It is an attitude very dissimilar from that of the general public, whose optimism is almost too buoyant at present.

After dinner the P.M. asked me about the tests I had undergone at Euston House. I described the questions in the Intelligence test (which would appeal to a crossword puzzle enthusiast who was also fond of tricky mathematical problems, e.g. Philip) and the P.M. said that if that was the standard, Nelson and Napoleon would have been considered unsuitable. What, he wanted to know, was the use of catering for a lot of "chessplayers who would die young of epilepsy"?

He was incensed by a letter from the cranky, pacifist Duke

---

[1] Financial Secretary to the Treasury in 1942 and Chairman of the Conservative Party from 1944 to 1946. Created Lord Clitheroe.

of Bedford and ended his scathing remarks on the subject by saying he was so glad that when this war was over he would be old enough "to leave it all: the scorn that I have for them." By them I think he meant politics. Whatever may in fact happen, he certainly now has the intention of washing his hands of politics after the war and retiring to Chartwell to write a book. But he thinks it will be a long war yet; and can he retain his position until the end of it? There are no signs of his popularity diminishing or authority weakening, and this American journey, coupled with his speech on Russia,[1] has regained any prestige he had lost. But public opinion is fickle.

Thursday, August 21st

Mr Fraser, Prime Minister of New Zealand, who improves very much on acquaintance, came to say goodbye to the P.M. I showed him Dorothy Sayers' bitter poem about Ireland, which greatly took his fancy and so, although it is unpublished, I sent him a copy.

Hardly had he left when another Dominion Prime Minister, Mackenzie King[2] of Canada, arrived, and after being greeted by the P.M., went straight into a meeting of the Cabinet.

Dined at the Ritz with Zamoyski and Lipski, who was Polish Ambassador in Berlin when war broke out and subsequently joined up as a private in the Polish army in France. They were both very scathing about the French. Lipski told me that opposite the Saar, where he had been posted, there was a complete gap in the Maginot Line: the French, uncertain which way the Saar plebiscite would go, had thought it proper to economise when the Line was originally built. Lipski also described to me the German schools for Leaders, which he had visited. These were vast establishments, with every possible sporting amenity and great forests for shooting, where the chosen *Jugend* were subjected to much physical culture (though decadent games like

---

[1] His speech broadcast on the day Russia was invaded.

[2] Liberal Prime Minister of Canada for long periods. A son of the Manse, an astute politician, but disliked and distrusted by many who worked for him. The King gave him the Order of Merit, though his achievements were not those for which the Order was created by Edward VII.

golf and tennis were excluded) and a good deal of Nazi political theory.

Lipski's description of his escape from France was fascinating. He is going to write a book about it. He told me he had learned more during one year as an army private than in twenty as a diplomat.

Zamoyski devoted half an hour to asking that the P.M. should include encouraging words about Poland in his broadcast next Sunday. The Polish Government is facing great difficulties with its own people who hate the idea of an alliance with Russia. Only the P.M.'s prestige can persuade them to accept the situation. Mr Eden is not sufficient – but it is difficult to insinuate this fact tactfully.

Friday, August 22nd
Negotiated with the F.O. on the Polish question and reached agreement with Eden and Strang[1] on a note which I am to submit to the P.M.

Went to Madeley for the week-end. Grandfather and Peggy, Father and Mother were there.

Saturday, August 23rd
Pouring rain all day; but today is the last of St Swithin's forty.

Grandfather produced some of his magnificent 1902 Hock and 1858 brandy.

Sunday, August 24th
After dinner we heard Winston's splendid speech on the wireless, describing his American journey, and containing a spirited message to each of the enslaved countries.

Monday, August 25th
Travelled to London with Peggy, whose company made the train journey seem short. She told me two things I had never

---

[1] A man of ability and tireless energy chosen in the summer of 1939 as head of the mission to Russia, which vainly sought to reach an understanding with the Soviet Government. An outstanding bureaucrat, he was Sir Orme Sargent's successor as Permanent Under Secretary at the Foreign Office and was given a peerage.

suspected: that Grandfather was highly-strung; that Mother, had she wished, could have married Lord Halifax. She had, said Peggy, more admirers than Aunt Celia or Aunt Nancy – which I can believe, as her intrinsic worth is great and her unworldliness so endearing.

Today our long-planned invasion of Persia began. I am afraid it is an aggressive and not really warranted act, which is difficult to justify except on the, in this case dubious, principle of *Salus populi surprema lex.*

Tuesday, August 26th

The Persian adventure has started successfully, though we do not seem to have a very large force employed.

Saw a Czech Jew, Dr Rabinovicz, who wants to publish a book of extracts from the P.M.'s speeches and writings on the Jewish problem. Discouraged him.

Miss Rees, of the Gt Marlborough St Labour Exchange, brought to see me a Miss Hewitt, nominally though not effectively in charge of woman labour at the Royal Ordnance Factories. She painted a lamentable picture of disorganisation, lack of training facilities and petty departmental jealousies. I am taking the matter up with Lord Cherwell with a view to approaching the P.M., because production is seriously hampered. It is difficult because Lord Beaverbrook, as Minister of Supply, is jealous of outside interference. Miss Hewitt told me that her experience had thrown her, a professed socialist, into the arms of private enterprise. She had seen what state control and a salaried administration could produce.

The P.M. is angry to find that Haining, lately V.C.I.G.S., and now Intendant General in the Middle East, is no good. So Oliver Lyttelton says. The P.M. suspects, very possibly with justice, that the War Office, and in particular Dill, strongly recommended him to send out Haining because they wanted to get rid of him.

Churchill himself was inclined to offer posts abroad to those of whom he found it convenient to be rid. There was quite a bit of "my language fails, go out and govern New South Wales" in the despatch of Hoare to Madrid, Cross to Canberra, Malcolm

MacDonald to Canada, Dorman-Smith to Burma and even Lord Halifax to Washington. He failed to persuade Lord Winterton to be High Commissioner in South Africa, but prevailed on Lord Harlech, who had been Secretary of State for the Colonies, to go instead.

Wednesday, August 27th

In the morning the P.M. had a conference with Halifax, who is just back from Washington, Beaverbrook, Sinclair and Eden about supplies from America and to Russia. Meanwhile Maisky complains that we are in effect doing nothing for Russia: we say we cannot form a "second front" and we only supply inadequate armaments. Thus the U.S., in spite of all the fanfares, has only delivered five bombers to the U.S.S.R. It is difficult to see what we can do: geography, and shortage of trained, equipped men, make a military diversion out of the question. We are sending a lot of fighters and are helping economically. It is no use recriminating, but after all when we were fighting alone and for our lives the Russians were actually supplying Germany with the material means of attacking us.

The military situation is not good today. The Germans are driving south-eastwards, behind Kiev, and threaten to cut off the southern armies of the U.S.S.R. and turn all their positions on the Dnieper.

Spent an hour at the dentist owing to an air force decision that two of my teeth, which my dentist said need not be filled, should be filled.

I was on late duty and most of the time was occupied with de Gaulle, whose attitude is deplorable and whose pronouncements, private and public, are intolerable. The P.M. is sick to death of him.

Laval was shot to the dissatisfaction of nobody here. At last a Charlotte Corday! [He was only wounded.]

Thursday, August 28th

At lunch-time we heard the news that the Persians had ceased to resist.

Friday, August 29th

The P.M. has telegraphed to Stalin offering further help in aeroplanes. He has also telegraphed to Hopkins about the disquiet which the Cabinet are feeling at the slowing-down of the tempo in America and the apparent check to the growing open assistance we were receiving.

To Chequers, driving down with Tommy and Mary. Brigadier Shearer, who was formerly managing director of Fortnum and Mason and is now on the Staff of the C. in C., Middle East, was the only guest. Points from the conversation at dinner were:

Jubilation over our success in Persia, which had been very well received all over the world. The P.M. said that last Sunday morning he had had qualms. We had been doing something for which we had justification but no right. The man in the street, on the other hand, seemed elated that we had at last taken a leaf from Hitler's notebook. In support of this Shearer quoted the liftman at his hotel, a figure who played in his conversation the same recurring role as the schoolboy in Macaulay's essays.

Referring to a certain operation, the P.M. said he mistrusted set pieces which were rehearsed, like a play, so fully that nothing could go wrong – and then just before the performance the theatre caught fire or the Lord Chamberlain withdrew his licence.

Mr Churchill showed considerable optimism. He compared the situation in the Middle East a year ago, when we had but 80,000 ill-equipped troops, with that today, when apart from a tremendous army, we are in possession of Syria, Iraq, Abyssinia, Eritrea, both Somalilands and Persia, and are confident in the Western Desert.

The Yugoslav revolution when Prince Paul fled, might well have played a vital part in the war: it caused Hitler to bring back his Panzer divisions from the north and postponed for six weeks the attack on Russia.

Shearer thought Hitler had made two bad miscalculations: (i) in attacking Russia (about which his Intelligence was bad); (ii) in failing to go into Syria when he could still have done so and could have made our hold on Suez precarious.

Saturday, August 30th

The P.M. stayed in bed for lunch, working at his box. He had spent most of the morning composing a long letter to Auchinleck about the future and I all but died of heart failure trying to get hold of it in time to catch Brigadier Shearer at Paddington on his return to the Middle East.

The Halifaxes arrived at tea-time. Lord Halifax, whose reputation in this country and the U.S. makes him out a reactionary and an obscurantist, seemed very Liberal in his conversation with the P.M. over the tea-table in the Long Gallery. He was emphatic that we must "cough up supplies for Russia", and he said, in discussing the future of the Conservative Party, that Secondary Schoolboys were on the whole better educated than Public Schoolboys. To this Winston said, "They have saved this country; they have the right to rule it." He was referring to the R.A.F. pilots, the majority of whom had come from the Secondary Schools.

The P.M. considered that the only hope for the Tory Party at the next election was to choose young candidates who had won their spurs in the war. To succeed in politics a man should enter the H. of C. if possible in the twenties.

They discussed the fourth point of the Atlantic Charter, which declares for freedom of trade and access to raw materials. The P.M. thought that this would in fact be achieved and foresaw a great increase in wealth as a result. Halifax said the Tories would not object, except perhaps Amery.

When he went to bed, after tea, the P.M. who is always talking about my joining up – with approval – said, as he unlocked one of his "buff boxes": "You will have to forget a great many things. Be wise rather than well-informed. Give your opinion but not the reasons for it. Then you will have a valuable contribution to make."

The Edens arrived and also the American Ambassador. At dinner I sat next to Mrs Eden,[1] whom I found easy to get on

---

[1] Beatrice, first wife of Anthony Eden, was the daughter of Sir Gervase Beckett. The Edens were divorced in 1950 and in 1952 he married Clarissa Churchill.

with. Over the brandy, the P.M., periodically supported by Halifax and Eden, made an impassioned appeal to Winant to realise the importance of the issues hanging on America entering the war. (Winant, of course, like Roosevelt, is no sufferer from illusions about this.) The P.M. said that after the joint declaration, America could not honourably stay out. She could not fight with mercenaries. Better she should come in now and give us no supplies for six months than stay out and double her supplies. If she came in, the conviction of an Allied victory would be founded in a dozen countries. This was "a war of science and psychology". America could not produce men, or the ships to transport them, for years: we did not ask for that, but we must have an American declaration of war, or else, though we cannot now be defeated, the war might drag on for another four or five years, and civilisation and culture would be wiped out. If America came in, she could stop this. She alone could bring the war to an end – her belligerency might mean victory in 1943. (Eden thought 1942.)

Winant said that on the day he was killed, Purvis[1] had told him he thought the U.S. might be in the war next March. This prospect seemed to give Winston little satisfaction. He thought the delay too long. He asked whether he should not commit a calculated indiscretion on the subject. Winant said it was better to leave that to his Government.

Eden said that we had now won the war for existence; we had not yet started the war for victory.

As a less serious epilogue, the P.M. discoursed on egalitarianism and the White Ant. He recommended Lord Halifax to read Maeterlinck. Socialism would make our society comparable to that of the White Ant. He also gave an interesting account of the love life of the duck-billed platypus.

After dinner we saw films of the Russian campaign. Coward, the wounded R.A.F. officer in charge of the roof-spotters, murmured to me as an alleged German plane was coming down

[1] Dynamic head of the British Purchasing Commission in the U.S.A. where he had great influence. Killed in a flying accident.

in flames: "That's a Spitfire!" But Russian propaganda is effective even if it parts company with strict veracity.

Sunday, August 31st
As it was hot and sunny, the P.M. got up before lunch and sat in the garden with Halifax, Winant and, when they arrived, Prof. and Lord Melchett.[1]

The P.M. went off to see a "bombard" display, the Halifaxes left, and Mrs Churchill and I played croquet at which she, being an expert, beat me hopelessly.

Lord Gort and Admiral Somerville (Commanding Force "H") dined. As the conversation, about the defence of Gibraltar, seemed likely to be tedious, I slipped away at the end of dinner and, with Mary, saw a sentimental film about a circus.

The P.M. would not stop talking and we did not go to bed until 3.00 a.m. Lord G. seems to be enjoying himself as Governor and C. in C. of Gibraltar.

---

[1] Henry, 2nd Lord Melchett, son of Sir Alfred Mond, creator of I.C.I. and of Mond Nickel.

TWENTY

FIRST GOOD-BYE TO DOWNING STREET
SEPTEMBER 1941

Monday, September 1st
While waiting for the P.M. to start for London, I read the Home
Censorship Report. The increasing support for, and admiration
of, Russia is striking. So is the high proportion of facile optimists
who think the war will be over by Christmas. There is a certain
dread of the approaching winter and a renewal of raids.

We are forgetting about sirens. None sounded in London
during August and only one in July. There has been no proper
air-raid since May.

Wednesday, September 3rd
Moore-Brabazon has raised a storm by saying in a recent
extempore speech that he hoped the Russians and Germans
would exterminate each other (a sentiment widely felt). Tanner,
of the A.E.U., maliciously announced this at a meeting of the
T.U.C. The P.M. spoke to Moore-Brabazon on the telephone
and was quite particularly nice about it, although the matter may
well cause him trouble when the House meets. He told M.-B.
not to worry about anything but producing more aeroplanes, the
production of which is giving great anxiety.

On late duty. The P.M., after holding a C.O.S. meeting,
expressed himself forcibly about the pusillanimity and negative
attitude shown by our military advisers. "And you are one of
the worst," he said to the indignant Pug Ismay.

Thursday, September 4th

Acute indigestion. Barker says I eat too fast.

The following typical example of Lord Beaverbrook's style is the beginning of a paper he has circulated to the Cabinet: "The Royal Air Force bombs asked for by the Air Ministry under its expansion programme cannot be made, cannot be filled and cannot be thrown . . ."

As Mary and Judy Montagu are tomorrow joining the A.T.S., Mrs Churchill and Venetia Montagu gave a large farewell dinner party at the Dorchester. When the P.M. arrived he was clapped right through the hotel. I sat between Diana Sandys, who talked interminably about her children and evacuation, and an attractive girl with large deep-set blue eyes, a fringe and great intelligence. Her name is Fiona Forbes – a sister of Mary's friend Alastair, who improves on acquaintance – and I thought her fascinating. Having lived in France and passed her Baccalaureat, she is really well educated and sensitive too.

The older members of the party – Brendan, Barbara Rothschild, Pug, the Trees, Rupert Belville, etc. – melted away and the younger ones went a round of the night clubs. Mary, Judy, Fiona Forbes, Rosemary Scott Ellis, Bruce Grimston, Anthony Coates, Tommy Buckhurst, Alastair Forbes, Juliet Henley and I went first to the Four Hundred, then to the Nut House to see the Cabaret, and finally to the Coconut Grove to eat bacon and eggs.[1] Home by 4.30 a.m.

The P.M. had retired at 10.00 to see Eden and Maisky who brought him telegrams of grave significance from Stalin.

Friday, September 5th

In view of these telegrams the Prime Minister cancelled his projected trip to Dover. The Russians are hard pressed, both in the fighting and in supply questions, and Stalin, going directly to the point, raises a number of fundamental issues. We look like being faced with a decision of the same kind as that in the closing stages of the Battle of France: throw in everything to

---

[1] All the young men, apart from Alastair Forbes and myself, were later killed in action.

save our Allies or reserve our strength in case the worst happens. Fortunately in this case our cupboard is not so bare.

The P.M. and Mrs Churchill have given me a lovely silver cigarette case from Cartier with the inscription: To Jock from Winston and Clementine Churchill. May 10th, 1940–October 1st, 1941." It is particularly generous of them and I am both touched and gratified.

Saturday, September 6th (At Stansted)
Spent the day shooting. It was dull and misty and admirable for duck. I stood in a cluster of bullrushes, behind a large bush, and shot twenty-three (twenty-one mallard and two teal) at the first stand. Later I accounted for three more.

Having shot brilliantly I subsequently failed entirely to cope with the partridges, only destroying four, although there were several probables and, I regret, a number damaged. Colonel Eben Pike[1] was with us for the duck and Robin Baring[2] arrived at lunch-time to pursue the partridges.

Eric, who was at his simplest and most charming, told me he can still think of nothing but Mary Churchill.

Monday, September 8th
The P.M. arrived back from Ditchley, his attention divided between his speech in the House tomorrow and supplies for Russia.

Tuesday, September 9th
The House has reassembled for one week and I went down to hear the P.M. make a statement on the situation. His speech, which dealt with the U.S., Persia and Russia, was quite well received although, for the first time, a number of members left while he was still speaking. He himself thought it a very good speech, "well-designed" as he said to me on the way back in the car.

[1] A First World War Grenadier married to Olive Snell, the portrait painter, and father of two beautiful daughters.
[2] Lord Bessborough's nephew. Afterwards senior partner of Panmure, Gordon, Stockbrokers.

The Chiefs of Staff only kept their tempers with the utmost difficulty when they attended a meeting at No. 10 to hear the views and complaints of Sir Roger Keyes on combined operations.

Tommy Dugdale dined with me in the Mess. We talked about the formation of a "second front" in Europe and he said, with great truth, that the general public have no conception of the meaning in war of time and space. They cannot visualise the practical difficulties in the way of landing an army on the continent and of bringing armed assistance to Russia. Tommy told me that the Labour Party is now terrified of the Communists and is devoting all its energy and power to combating them.

Personally I think that the trend is towards the employment of our maximum effort in the Middle East, where our forces would form a southward extension of the Russian line, using Basra and Suez for purposes of supply. At present it looks as if Western Europe will be out of the picture for some time, though Desmond and Tommy Dugdale both think the German air attacks on England will start again when winter stabilises the Russian front.

Thursday, September 11th
Desmond Morton tells me that we know from secret sources that the Third International has given orders to its followers in this country to keep alive discontent with the alleged inadequacy of support for Russia in order to use this to overthrow the Churchill Government when the time is ripe. Further he says that Stalin is lukewarm in his determination to go on fighting and Molotov is definitely opposed to so doing; but there are others, representing Russian youth organisations, who are resolute.

There is much speculation on the interview which the P.M. is to have with de Gaulle tomorrow. Sparks will fly, but de Gaulle apparently thinks he can appease the P.M. by playing the "Soldier of France", etc. Meanwhile he continues to use very anti-British language in his conversations with others.

The P.M. was dining with Beaverbrook at No. 12. I took them in a large file of papers on gas warfare, about which the P.M. has sent many instructions and minutes in the last year. I sat with them while they talked about it and reviewed our present much improved position in this respect. Beaverbrook is convinced the Germans will use gas. He says he is certain of it. Winston thinks Hitler's followers may prevent him *if* they consider they are fighting a losing battle.

The P.M. worked till 2.00. I sat beside him most of the time and tried to answer his questions. The King has offered him the Lord Wardenship of the Cinque Ports (in succession to Lord Willingdon). The idea was Anthony Bevir's, who suggested it *sub rosa* to Alec Hardinge. The P.M. is much attracted by the historic splendour of the appointment, which was held by Pitt, Wellington and Palmerston, but daunted by the rates, taxes and cost of upkeep of Walmer Castle.

Monday, September 22nd
I find the P.M. has been busy with the missions to Russia and that it has been decided to give large numbers of fighters and supplies of munitions to the Soviet Government at great expense to ourselves. But, as the P.M. says, it is worthwhile in order to keep Russia in the war.

The Minister of State (Oliver Lyttelton) returned from Cairo and dined with the P.M., who has much to discuss with him.

Tuesday, September 23rd
Rode at Richmond. Louis Greig, just back from Canada where he has been accompanying the Duke of Kent, tells me the Air Training Schools are excellent and advises me to go there.

Francis Brown,[1] my successor at No. 10, arrived. It seems odd to recall a Brigade Intelligence Officer of the Coldstream Guards to become an untrained Private Secretary and to let me go off to become an untrained aircraftsman. Being responsible I feel rather guilty, but nevertheless not repentant.

After drinking a few gins and lime with Herschel Johnson at White's I went to dine with Sylvia Henley and Juliet. Back to

[1] Passed first into the Foreign Office in 1938. Being under twenty-five when the war broke out (as, indeed, was I) he joined the Coldstream Guards, re-joined them when I returned from the R.A.F. in December 1943, was wounded in Normandy and died at an early age after the war.

No. 10 on late duty. The P.M. spent the time till 2.00 a.m. in discussing the dissensions in the Free French movement. A breach between de Gaulle and Muselier threatens to cause a public rift in the movement. De Gaulle is autocratic and right wing; Muselier is a Liberal (and a very loose-living one) who wants de Gaulle's powers to be delegated to a Council. The P.M., who is heartily sick of the Free French, ended by handing the whole matter over to the reluctant Eden.

Thursday, September 25th
The new Lord Warden left Victoria at 12.45 to visit his Cinque Ports, travelling in the new railway coach which has been prepared for him and taking with him Mrs C., Jack Churchill, Tommy, John Martin (for today only) and me. Walmer Castle disappointed its new owner and Mrs C. in particular thought it gloomy and unwieldy. Having a liking for feudal relics I admired the deep moat and the bastions, and was also interested to see the chairs in which Mr Pitt read and the Duke of Wellington died.

We proceeded by car to Manston, saw and had tea with the P.M.'s Fighter Squadron (No. 615) and looked at the Hurricanes. I had a long talk with the Squadron Leader who showed me the cases of maps, food, matches, money, etc., carried by all fighter pilots in case they should come down in France. We also saw a short film of the Squadron's latest attack on an enemy convoy. I met Air Vice Marshal Leigh-Mallory who succeeded Park in command of No. 11 Group.

We spent the night in a quiet siding, half a mile from a stone marking the centre of England and a few miles short of Coventry.

The P.M. dictated half of his speech for the House of Commons next Tuesday. It promises to be one of his best.

Friday, September 26th
We arrived at Coventry platform and the P.M. was not dressed. He always assumes he can get up, shave and have a bath in fifteen minutes whereas in reality it takes him twenty minutes. Consequently he is late for everything. Mrs C. seethed with anger.

Lord Dudley (the Regional Commissioner) and the mayor met us. We went to the centre of the town, where the P.M. inspected a parade of the Civil Defence Services, and then to the Cathedral. The German bombers assuredly did their worst at Coventry.

The P.M. *will* give the V sign with two fingers in spite of the representations repeatedly made to him that this gesture has quite another significance.

We toured very thoroughly the Armstrong Siddeley factory, where aircraft parts and torpedos are made, and the P.M. had a rousing reception. As we entered each workshop all the men clanged their hammers in a deafening welcome.

I drove with Jack Churchill whom some of the crowd took for Maisky.

The Whitley bomber factory is a hotbed of Communism and there was some doubt of the reception the P.M. would get. But his appearance with cigar and semi-top-hat quite captivated the workers who gave him vociferous applause. We saw the lines of finished bombers and amongst them a rickety biplane built in the same factory during the last war. A new Whitley took off and flew past, a Hurricane pilot did stunts, and No. 605 squadron of Hurricanes flew over in astonishingly tight formation. When we drove away the men and women of the factory quite forgot their Communism and rushed forward in serried ranks to say goodbye. But I was disgusted to hear that their production-tempo had not really grown until Russia came into the war.

We lunched on the train, after visiting the cemetery where Coventry's air-raid dead are buried in one common grave. Lord Dudley lunched with us.

At 2.30 we reached Birmingham and there visited a tank factory, where the enthusiasm was even greater than at Coventry, and the Spitfire works at Castle Bromwich. Last of all we saw a display of aerobatics by two test pilots, one in a Hurricane and the other in a Spitfire. Their performance was so daring as to be positively frightening and we all shuddered as Henshaw, the Spitfire pilot, flew over us upside down, some forty feet from the ground.

The drive back to the station was a triumphant procession. The crowds stood on the pavements, as thick as for the opening of Parliament in London, for miles and miles along the route. They waved, they cheered, they shouted: every face seemed happy and excited. I have seen the P.M. have many enthusiastic receptions, but never one to equal this. It is clear that his name and fame are as great today as they have ever been. He was deeply moved.

We spent the night in a siding. There was a storm cloud owing to the non-arrival of a pouch but after much lightning and many claps of thunder (some of which were telephoned to John Peck at No. 10), the sky cleared with the advent of dinner and lots of champagne.

The P.M. finished his speech and I tried laboriously to teach myself mathematics. To bed at 2.00.

Saturday, September 27th
We reached Liverpool. The P.M., in his curious semi-naval garb, toured the new aircraft-carrier *Indomitable*. After we had climbed up and down endless companions and seen the aircraft on deck, he made a speech to the assembled ship's company. I am always impressed by his skill in suiting his words to his audience. On this occasion he spoke of the man-of-war and his wife, or sweetheart, the aircraft carrier who goes out to find his dinner for him and sometimes cooks it or has it done to a turn so that the man-of-war may eat it. It was thus with the *Bismarck*, it might well be the same with the *Tirpitz*.

The docks at Liverpool are a scene of great devastation. Many acres have been entirely cleared of buildings by the bombs.

The P.M. visited C. in C., Western Approaches, at his headquarters, where Lord Derby,[1] also awaited him, and then the party returned to the train for lunch.

In the afternoon we slept and I played some backgammon with Mrs Churchill. It was a stiflingly hot day for so late in the year. We reached Chequers before 6.00. Clarissa was there and

---

[1] Edward, 17th Earl of Derby. Secretary of State for War in the First World War and then Ambassador in Paris. Both his sons, Edward and Oliver, held ministerial office. He had great influence in Lancashire of which he was Lord Lieutenant.

Venetia Montagu. We all sat in the garden and the P.M. Played with Mary's dog, Suki, which is a very engaging poodle.

Oliver Lyttelton (the Minister of State) came for the week-end with his son Anthony, a precocious youth who is a private in the Marines.

The P.M. was in a happy frame of mind at dinner. Having described Mr Granville, M.P., as "the son of a bitch", he remarked that there must have been a great many bitches in the last generation.

After dinner we saw a bad English film, *Cottage to Let*, produced by Anthony Asquith. Later a pouch arrived containing the following telegram: *"Général Catroux à Ld. Warden des Cinque Ports. Reçevez je vous prie mes chaleureuses félicitations pour votre élévation a la pairie qui réjouit tous mes camarades Français Libres. Général Catroux."* The P.M. was highly entertained and sent the following reply: *"Mille remerciements mais ce n'est pas si grave que ça. Vive La France Libre.* (signed) Mister Churchill."

Sunday, September 28th

Mr Winant came to lunch, bringing with him Mr Myron Taylor, U.S. representative at the Vatican. Mr Hanson, leader of the Opposition in the Canadian Parliament, also came and brought with him four of his colleagues with whom he is touring England.

So we were fourteen men to lunch and Clarissa. The latter, who is recovering from her illness, was obviously bored with poor Anthony Lyttelton and showed it. She has very bad manners.

I had a talk with Winant about the Vatican. He said that he was sure the late Pope would have taken a much more forcible line against the Axis, but the present Pope was a very skilful diplomat and was, Winant believed, playing his hand with the utmost intelligence. I think, and said, that there are times when it may be more right, and more paying in the long run, to kick over the traces.

The P.M. talked to me while he was dressing for dinner. He said that so far the Government had only made one error of judgment: Greece. He had instinctively had doubts. We could and should have defended Crete and advised the Greek Government to make the best terms it could. But the campaign, and the Yugoslav volte-face which it entailed, had delayed Germany and might after all prove to have been an advantage. (I was surprised at the P.M.'s assertion that he had doubted the wisdom of going to Greece. I seem to remember his influencing the decision in favour of an expedition and Dill being against it. Incidentally he has now got his knife right into Dill and frequently disparages him. He says he has an alternative C.I.G.S. in mind: Sir Alan Brooke, C. in C., Home Forces.) He went on to say that we cannot afford military failures. As regards all this talk of a diversion on the Western Front, a landing on the continent could only have one outcome. The War Office would not do the job properly; indeed it was unfair to ask them to pit themselves against German organisation, experience and resources. They had neither the means nor the intelligence. But critics would ask how we were going to win the war and that was difficult to answer. On one or two occasions lately I have heard him say he thinks it will last for several years more in all probability.

Finally he said that he ought really to have procured me a commission in the R.A.F. straight away. There was no advantage in going through the ranks. I disagree and said so, but was squashed.

While the P.M. was in his bath I was able to persuade him to delete a passage in his speech referring to Persia in which he spoke of the Foreign Office "in all its long and chequered career".

At dinner there was much good-natured but scathing comment on Hore-Belisha, Winterton, Jack Seely[1] and Oliver Stanley

---

[1] Major General J. E. B. Seely, later Lord Mottistone. At Harrow with Churchill who was always fond of him. Secretary of State for War (at Churchill's suggestion) in Mr Asquith's Government. He was not highly regarded at the War Office and his tenure of office unfortunately coincided with the Curragh mutiny, when British officers at the Curragh feared they would be ordered to march against Ulster. He was a man of great good nature and unflinching courage but, unlike most brave men, he was boastful. It was alleged that there was a delay in publishing his book, *Fear and Be Slain*, because the printer ran out of capital "I"s. People laughed at him, but they loved him.

(who, said the P.M., was really suited to be Dean of a Cathedral, walking round the monastic fish-ponds and contemplating some academic "mot" which he could bring out next time he was invited to dine with the Fellows of his old College). The P.M. admitted that he had been responsible for the appointment of Jack Seely as S. of S. for War: he had suggested it to Asquith during a cruise on the *Enchantress* on the only occasion on which Asquith had mentioned politics, and at the time it had seemed to him to have distinct possibilities. Oliver Lyttelton recalled how just after Munich Crinks Johnstone[1] had told Duff Cooper he had been the worst S. of S. for War of the century and Duff Cooper had replied: "How dare you say such a thing in the presence of Jack Seely."

The P.M. launched an attack on Shinwell who had refused office in May 1940, because he thought the post offered him was inadequate to his deserts, and now took refuge in talking of the Government as a lot of "pinchbeck Napoleons". Then he reminisced about Harrow, where he said he had spent the unhappiest days of his life, and told how he and F. E. Smith had been booed when they went there in 1912. However he was going down again to hear the songs (he repeated several word-perfect by heart) and would recall me from wherever I then might be so that I could accompany him.

After dinner we saw an American film called *John Doe*, which I enjoyed, and the P.M. then closeted himself with Oliver Lyttelton in the Hawtrey room and talked so long, as well as dictating telegrams, that I did not get into bed till 3.35. The P.M. said he supposed I was looking forward to the R.A.F. and lights out at 10.00 p.m.

Between the hours of 2.00 a.m. and 3.00 a.m. the Prof., who arrived at lunch-time today, gave me a brief and very clear exposition of certain navigational questions. He was a little pained to find reposing on top of his charts, papers and boxes a work entitled *Teach Yourself Mathematics*.

---

[1] Liberal Whip, *bon viveur* and friend of Sir Archibald Sinclair (who was not a *bon viveur*).

Monday, September 29th

I am rather sad to say goodbye to Chequers. Though gloomy, it is comfortable and the surrounding country is glorious. I have had much fun there and it has been the scene of very many interesting conversations to which I have listened.

Reached London at 1.00 p.m. Leslie Rowan gave John Martin and me lunch at the Union Club. I shall miss them.

At 3.00 p.m. the Private Secretaries, Barker and Tommy assembled at No. 10 and were photographed with the P.M. in the garden. "Well," said the P.M., "let me have three copies and put them down to Mr Colville; they are being done in his honour. And, by the way, we had better have a photograph of the Cabinet. They are an ugly lot, but still."

John Martin gave a sherry party to say goodbye to me. Brendan's cook, Mrs Norgren, did her very best, with notable results, and she made me a cake with a little aeroplane on it. The whole of Whitehall seemed to be there, from the P.M. and Mrs Churchill downwards. The P.M. told me he would not for the world miss an opportunity of seeing me off the premises! Mother also came and obviously enjoyed herself. So did I, immensely, but I found it a little tedious to be asked by a hundred people when I was off and where I was going.

I dined in the Mess for the last time as a member of the P.M.'s staff.

Tuesday, September 30th

I galloped round Richmond Park, where autumn tints are just beginning to appear and where the sun shone on a million cobwebs wet with dew among the long grass. Louis and Lady Greig, with their usual kindness, begged me to come and stay whenever it was convenient.

I packed frantically all the morning. At lunch-time, when the P.M. had returned from the House of Commons after making a highly successful speech, I went into the Cabinet Room to say goodbye to him. He said it must only be "au revoir" as he hoped I should often come back and see him. He ought not to be letting me go, and Eden had been "very sour" about it and about recalling a trained officer from the army to take my place; but I had so much wanted to go and he thought I was doing a very gallant thing. He said, "I have the greatest affection for you; we all have, Clemmy and I especially. Goodbye and God bless you." I went out of the room with a lump in my throat such as I have not had for many years.

BIOGRAPHICAL NOTES

BIOGRAPHICAL NOTES

(Indicated by * in the text)

Alanbrooke, Field Marshal, 1st Viscount, K.G., G.C.B., O.M., G.C.V.O., D.S.O. (1883–1963)
Uncle of Sir Basil Brooke, Prime Minister of Northern Ireland, he was educated mainly in France and distinguished himself as a gunner in World War I. He went from being G.O.C., Southern Command, in 1939 to lead the 2nd Corps in Lord Gort's British Expeditionary Force, and he fought a successful holding action against the advancing Germans on the eastern flank in May 1940. He was briefly in command of the troops sent to northern France after Dunkirk, but returned home to be once again in charge of Southern Command and, thereafter, of Home Forces. From the end of 1941 he was C.I.G.S. for five years, at once spellbound and exasperated by Churchill and gravely disappointed not to be given command of Operation OVERLORD. He was an admirer and faithful supporter of Montgomery. After the war he was appointed Lord Lieutenant of London, the Master Gunner of St James's Park, Chancellor of Queen's University, Belfast and Constable of the Tower. He was a keen naturalist with a passion for bird-watching.

Alexander of Hillsborough, Albert Victor Alexander, 1st Earl, K.G., C.H. (1885–1965)
Fought in World War I, first in the ranks and then as an officer, and was elected Labour M.P. for Sheffield (Hillsborough division) in 1922. In Ramsay MacDonald's 1929 Government he was First Lord of the Admiralty, the office to which he returned in May 1940. Good-natured, friendly but distastefully egotistic, he was regarded with affection rather than admiration by the Admirals

and also by Churchill who always referred to him as Albert Victor. He was a Baptist lay preacher and a dedicated Non-Conformist. From 1946 to 1950 he was Minister of Defence and after 1955 Leader of the Opposition in the House of Lords. A Viscount in 1950, an Earl (on Conservative recommendation) in 1963, he was made a Knight of the Garter just before his death.

Amery, the Right Hon. Leopold C.H. (1873–1955)

Harrow, Balliol and All Souls between them produced this prodigy of energy, mental and physical, minute in height but vast in intellect. He professed to speak seventeen languages, but was never put to the test. He worked for ten years at *The Times*, and became a Birmingham M.P. in 1911. For part of World War I he was assistant secretary to the War Cabinet and made such an impression on the leading politicians that he was soon, in succession, First Lord of the Admiralty, Secretary of State for the Colonies, for the Dominions and finally, from 1940 to 1945, for India. There were those who thought he was *too* clever and there were others who objected to his casting his net a little far outside his own waters. He was, however, certainly one of the best-known political figures in the first half of the twentieth century.

His elder son Jack, who was at school with me and had considerable charm, unfortunately became a fascist, broadcast enemy propaganda from Italy during the war and was hanged for treason after it. So excessive a retribution would surely not have been his fate had his father not been eminent. His other son, Julian, who strove valiantly to save his brother, went into politics early, married Harold Macmillan's daughter and held several ministerial offices.

Auchinleck, Field Marshal Sir Claude, G.C.B., G.C.I.E., C.S.I., D.S.O. (1884–1981)

A man who gave immediate confidence. From Wellington and Sandhurst he went into the Indian Army and fought in Egypt and Mesopotamia in World War I. After a spell in England in 1940 as G.O.C., Southern Command (when he greatly impressed Churchill), he was appointed C. in C. in India. Then for two depressing years he commanded in North Africa, while Rommel swept all before him and Auchinleck, excellent soldier though he was, was let down by his army commanders. An unsuccessful general has to be replaced whether or not personally at fault, and "the Auk", as he was called, took his failure with dignity and without reproach. He returned to India as C. in C. for four years and was appointed, in 1947, Supreme Commander in India and Pakistan. The Indians loved him as did all who served under him, and though he retired to live in Marrakech he came back to England in 1974 when the Army Council gave a huge luncheon party in the Royal Hospital at Chelsea, to celebrate his ninetieth birthday. He outlived all his contemporary Generals.

Avon, Anthony Eden, 1st Earl of, K.G., M.C. (1897–1977)

From Eton and Christ Church, Oxford (where he won a First in Oriental Languages), and after three years' active service with the King's Royal Rifle Corps, he went into Parliament at the age of twenty-six as Conservative Member for Warwick and Leamington. He became Parliamentary Private Secretary to Sir Austen Chamberlain at the Foreign Office and then, cherished by Stanley Baldwin, he rose quickly in the ministerial hierarchy. He was Lord Privy Seal with responsibility for League of Nations affairs and, in 1935, Foreign Secretary. Objecting to Neville Chamberlain's interference, and to the general belief that Sir Robert Vansittart was *de facto* Foreign Secretary, he shunted the latter sideways and resigned from the former's administration in January 1938. When war broke out he returned to office as Secretary of State for the Dominions, was given the War Office by Churchill in May 1940, and was back at the Foreign Office the following December. Despite frequent efforts to provide him with experience in home departments, he remained firmly attached to the Foreign Office until he became Prime Minister in 1955. He and Winston Churchill sometimes squabbled, but until Churchill's last year in office they were good friends and faithful colleagues. Indeed Eden, who was a man of the highest integrity, was never anything but faithful. By his first wife, Beatrice Beckett, he had two sons, one of whom was killed in Burma, flying in the R.A.F. His second wife was Clarissa Churchill.

Beaverbrook, Maxwell Aitken, 1st Lord (1879–1964)

Many people thought he was evil. He was, in fact, impish and he was capable of great kindness. Born a son of the Manse (all influential Canadians seem to have been sons of the Manse), he made a fortune at an early age by deals which, whether or not actually dishonest, were certainly "borderline". He came to England in 1910, basking in the friendship of the Conservative leader Bonar Law, himself a Canadian, and within six months was Conservative M.P. for Ashton-under-Lyne of which he had never heard a few months before. He bought the derelict *Daily Express* in order to provide an organ for the Conservative Party and he bought and sold, at a profit, the Rolls Royce Company. Between the wars he became a highly successful press lord, circulation being his prime objective. He had a genuine enthusiasm for the British Empire, but he was an arch-appeaser of the dictators. Yet when he was made Minister of Aircraft Production in May 1940, he performed miracles of production and made a major contribution to winning the Battle of Britain. Later in the war he was markedly unhelpful, upsetting any apple-cart in sight, becoming infatuated by Stalin and urging a Second Front in totally unsuitable conditions. He opposed the planning of a Welfare State, and as the end of the war drew near he was more excited by the prospect of a return to party strife than by possible methods of winning the peace. After 1945 his influence on politics was muted, and his relationship with Churchill became distant though always amiable. In 1953, when Churchill had his stroke, nobody rallied more wholeheartedly to his help.

Bevin, Rt. Hon. Ernest (1881–1951)

This unwieldy, unlettered Trade Unionist, formerly General Secretary of the Transport and General Workers' Union, Chairman of the General Council of the Trade Union Congress and a leader of the 1926 General Strike, was a splendid Minister of Labour during the war, an undaunted tower of strength both to Churchill and to Attlee. In 1945 he became Foreign Secretary, in preference to Hugh Dalton whom Attlee had originally intended for the post, and it fell to him to confront Molotov and the intransigent Soviet delegations, when they threw heavy spanners into the works at every conference assembled to negotiate peace treaties. The Foreign Service, whose members all came from backgrounds totally different from his, were devoted to him. Indeed, it may be doubted if there was ever a more loved and respected Foreign Secretary.

Bevir, Sir Anthony, K.C.V.O., C.B.E. (1895–1977)

Scholar of Eton and Hertford College, Oxford, he was badly gassed when serving with the King's Liverpool Regiment in World War I. He worked in the Colonial Office between the wars, was transferred to the War Cabinet Office in 1939 and thence, in 1940, to succeed Cecil Syers (q.v.) at No. 10. He was not ideally suited to cope with Churchill's unusual régime, and so all patronage matters, apart from the Honours' List and the appointment of Lord Lieutenants, were placed in his hands. He worked in a room of his own (previously Sir Horace Wilson's) and there was not a bishop or dean in England whom he did not know. He held this post for twenty-five years, took large quantities of snuff, occasionally lost the office keys and was always at hand to give wise and practical advice to anybody who applied to him. He was among the kindest of men.

Boothby, Lord, K.B.E. (1900–1986)

In his early parliamentary days many people thought him a future Prime Minister. Elected for Aberdeenshire as a Conservative in 1924, he started well as Parliamentary Private Secretary to Winston Churchill when Chancellor of the Exchequer. He was much influenced by Lloyd George, but not by that elder statesman's strange addiction to Hitler and Mussolini, and he became an energetic member of the pre-war anti-appeasement group in the Commons. His appointment by Churchill in 1940 as Parliamentary Secretary to the Minister of Food was brought to a dramatic end in 1942 when he was accused, doubtless falsely, of improper dealings over some Czechoslovak gold. After the war he was one of the leading exponents of a united Europe and became a well-known figure on television.

Bracken, Brendan, 1st and last Viscount (1901–1958)

His rise in the world was astonishing. An unruly, truant boyhood in Ireland, adolescent years spent with an uncle in Australia, education sought and obtained from an imaginative headmaster of Sedbergh when he pretended to be three years younger than he was: all this was the prelude to being Member of Parliament for Paddington at the age of twenty-nine, having in the meantime forced himself on Winston Churchill as a disciple, founded *The Banker*, bought *The Economist* and become Chairman of *The Financial News*. Underneath a mop of wiry, uncontrolled red hair, behind thick glasses and a pretended ruthlessness, lay a heart of gold; and he had a memory so remarkable, for people, events and the architecture of houses, that when Brendan was available no books of reference were required. In the years immediately before the war, and during the war itself, he was a bright comet sweeping across the skies, afraid of nobody, jolting Churchill out of melancholy or intemperate moods, and proving a strikingly successful Minister of Information, in contrast to his three predecessors in the post. Yet he was a lonely man, disguising the fact with incessant and, latterly, repetitive conversation, but genuinely loved by all who dug beneath the physically unattractive façade.

Bridges, Edward, 1st Lord, G.C.B., G.C.V.O., M.C., F.R.S., (1892–1969)

Son of the Poet Laureate, Robert Bridges, he was educated at Eton and Magdalen College, Oxford. He won the M.C. in World War I and then served in the Treasury until in 1938 he was appointed Secretary to the Cabinet in succession to Sir Maurice Hankey, the first holder of the office. Throughout the war he and General Ismay, on the military side, were the twin pillars on which the Prime Minister rested for they were first rate administrators. From 1945 till his retirement in 1956 he was Permanent Secretary of the Treasury and a great power in the land. Friendly, apt to give one a playful punch in the tummy on meeting, he was a forceful and outspoken man with a high sense of public service and propriety.

Butler of Saffron Walden, Lord, K.G., C.H. (1902–1982)

Son of a distinguished Indian civil servant who became Master of Pembroke College, Cambridge, R. A. Butler, always known as "Rab", was President of the Cambridge Union in 1924 and went on to be one of the most eminent British statesmen of the mid-twentieth century. A staunch supporter of Munich, appeasement and Neville Chamberlain, he became in due course a loyal colleague and admirer of Churchill, though to some extent a rival of both Anthony Eden and Harold Macmillan, with neither of whom he was on anything more than polite terms. He was the leading influence in reviving the fortunes of the Conservative Party after its defeat in 1945 and the policies he advocated, not far different from those of the Labour leader Hugh Gaitskell, were known as "Butskellism". He held every senior ministerial post, including the Home Office, Foreign Office and Exchequer, and as Minister of Education in 1944 he gave his name to an Education Act of lasting importance; but twice, in 1957 and 1963, he failed to be chosen Prime Minister. He ended his career, happily, as Master of Trinity College, Cambridge.

Cadogan, Right Hon. Sir Alexander, O.M., G.C.M.G., K.C.B. (1884–1968)

A younger son of the 5th Earl Cadogan, he was at Eton and Balliol and passed top into the Diplomatic Service in 1908. He was Ambassador to China, 1933–36, and when Anthony Eden managed to dispose of Sir Robert Vansittart in 1936, he was appointed Permanent Under Secretary. Calm, sage in counsel and the very reverse of "flashy", his diaries, published after his death, caused astonishment by their outspoken and sometimes vituperative comments. From 1946 to 1950 he represented Britain at the Security Council of the United Nations and in 1952 Churchill appointed him Chairman of the B.B.C., an office he fulfilled admirably in spite of knowing nothing about radio or television. His wife, Lady Theodosia, daughter of the 4th Earl of Gosford, had rather too forceful a character and an idiosyncratic personality.

Chandos, Oliver Lyttelton, 1st Viscount, D.S.O., M.C. (1893–1972)

An engaging buccaneer, son of a Cabinet Minister and educated at Eton and Trinity, Cambridge, he had an excellent record as a Grenadier in World War I and then made large profits in tin. Brought into the Government in 1940 as President of the Board of Trade, partly by the influence of Brendan Bracken, he was prominent in governmental deliberations but a surprisingly poor performer in the House of Commons. He was Minister of State in Cairo in 1941, with a seat in the War Cabinet, and dealt patiently with the explosive tantrums of General de Gaulle. Minister of Production, 1942–45, he was Secretary of State for the Colonies in the 1951 Government, but retired in 1954 to be Chairman of Associated Electrical Industries. Married to

Lady Moyra Osborne, a daughter of the Duke of Leeds, he had two sons and a daughter. He was a rumbustiously agreeable companion, primed with entertaining political and commercial gossip, and he wrote two books in faultless English prose.

Channon, Sir Henry (1897–1958)

An American who went to Christ Church, Oxford, married Lord Iveagh's daughter, Honor, and became Conservative M. P. for Southend in 1935. He was Parliamentary Private Secretary to R. A. Butler when Under Secretary at the Foreign Office (1938–41) and he entertained splendidly and amusingly at his house in Belgrave Square, where both R. A. Butler and, later, Lord Wavell used to stay. He was a leading light in London café society, a great friend of Lady Cunard, of Prince Paul of Yugoslavia and of his neighbours, the Duke and Duchess of Kent; but his main claim to fame is that he wrote with great elegance. *The Ludwigs of Bavaria* is an entertaining book of quality and his diaries are an enthralling peepshow of certain elements of London society between the wars. His only child, Paul, became a Minister in Mrs Thatcher's Government of the 1980s.

Charteris of Amisfield, Lord,
G.C.B., G.C.V.O., Q.S.O.
(New Zealand) (b. 1913)
The younger son of Lord Elcho
(killed in 1916) and Lady Violet
Benson, daughter of the 8th Duke
of Rutland, he went to Eton and
Sandhurst and fought in the war
with the 60th Rifles. Attractive,
energetic and the best of good
company, he married in 1944
Gay, younger daughter of David,
Viscount Margesson. In 1949 he
became Private Secretary to Princess Elizabeth, in succession to
the author of these diaries, and in
due course (1972–77) was a much
liked Private Secretary to the
Queen. On retirement he was
chosen as Provost of Eton, the
statutes having to be amended by
the Privy Council since, having
been to Sandhurst, he had no
university degree. He was also
appointed Chairman of the
National Heritage Memorial
Fund, an assignment he performed with diligence and good
taste. Under the tuition of Mr
Oscar Nemon he developed great
aptitude as a sculptor.

Cherwell, Frederick Lindemann,
1st and last Viscount, C.H.
(1886–1957)
To those he liked the Prof., as he
was called, was generous, helpful
and entertaining. Against those
who had displeased him he waged
a vendetta. He inherited a fortune
arising from waterworks in Ger-

many, studied physics in Berlin
under the great Professor Nernst
and became a friend of Einstein.
He was a keen tennis-player (tennis champion of Sweden), he was
always immaculately dressed and
had a liking for high society. Two
of his claims to enduring fame are
that he revived the moribund
Clarendon Laboratory at Oxford,
which under his direction became
the foremost centre of low-
temperature research in physics;
and that throughout the war he
was Churchill's interpreter in all
technical matters, whether scientific or economic. He had the
capacity to explain the most
difficult problems in clear, simple,
well-expressed English. He
detested Germans (despite his
successful years of study in
Berlin) and ruthlessly, though
unavailingly, plotted the destruction of their trade and industry.
He looked with contempt on Jews
and coloured people: he was arrogant and impervious to argument
when his mind was made up. Yet
he was good company when in
the mood, never boastful of his
achievements, and a loyal friend
to Churchill and to many others.
He was an acquired taste, but a
pleasing one, despite his obvious
faults, to those whom he found
acceptable.

Churchill, Hon. Randolph
(1911–1968)
Born with numerous golden

spoons in his mouth: outstandingly handsome in his youth, a natural orator, an original wit, showing a mastery of language and the son of an already famous father. Most of these gifts he dissipated, disappointed in his political ambitions, making friends easily but losing them more easily still. His father, determined that his only son should be more cherished than he had been, eagerly introduced him, when he was still a boy, to the stimulating company of such men as Lloyd George and Lord Birkenhead. As a result he was unnaturally precocious and found most of his contemporaries dull. He was imaginative and original in his ideas, but he became self-indulgent, excessively addicted to drink and, when he felt like it, inexcusably abusive. Yet when he exerted his charm, those who had vowed never to let him over their threshold again almost invariably relented. He was a talented journalist, and some of the books he wrote won acclaim; but his early promise came to little, both his wives were tried too hard, and the efforts of his mother to counteract her husband's excessive indulgence of their son won Randolph's seldom relenting hostility. Latterly, too, he squabbled with his father, devoted though he was to him. He grew up in the shade of a giant of the forest, and that may have inhibited his own development.

Perhaps Winston Churchill himself would have been a less bright meteor in the sky if his own father, Lord Randolph Churchill, had not died young.

Colville, Lady Cynthia,
D.C.V.O., D.B.E., F.R.C.M.
(1884–1968)
Twin daughter, with Lady Celia Coates, of the Marquess of Crewe, by his first marriage to Sibyl Graham of Netherby, and granddaughter of Richard Monckton-Milnes. Married in January 1908, the Hon. George Colville. From her early married days she became deeply involved in the affairs of the desperately poor borough of Shoreditch, where she started a school for mothers, a home for babies and other welfare schemes. She was a staunch Liberal, with a large number of socialist friends, Chairman of a Juvenile Court and President or Chairman of numerous charitable organisations. She was a dedicated Anglo-Catholic, a long-serving member of the Church Assembly, an outstandingly good public speaker and a woman who took endless pains for others without ever thinking of herself. From 1923 till 1953 she was a lady-in-waiting to Queen Mary on whom she had great influence. Despite her sometimes radical views George V was fond of her and used to ask her to race on his famous cutter *Britannia*.

Colville, David (1909–1986)

Eldest son of the Hon. George and Lady Cynthia Colville. Educated at Harrow and Trinity College, Cambridge; joined Lloyds Bank in 1931 and was Treasurer of the Bank when war was declared. Married, 1933, Lady Joan Child-Villiers, daughter of the 8th Earl of Jersey, with magnificent Titian-red hair. After five years' service in the R.N.V.R. he was invited by Mr Anthony de Rothschild to join the Rothschild bank, of which he became the first non-member of the family, and the first Christian, to be a partner. He had a high reputation in the City.

Colville, Hon. George (1867–1943)

Youngest son of the 1st Viscount, 11th baron, Colville of Culross K.T. (who was Chief Whip in the House of Lords in the Derby and Disraeli administrations, Chairman of the Great Northern Railway and Lord Chamberlain to Queen Alexandra) by the Hon. Cecile Carington. A mathematician of some ability, his Wykehamist education convinced him that ambition was, if not a sin, at least an error. So he was content to be, after a few years at the Bar, Secretary of the Institute of Chartered Accountants, a post he held till his retirement. He was a carpenter of exceptional ability making,

amongst much else, a fine copy of a Jacobean chair from an oak tree he had himself planted at the age of three. He was a skilful helmsman in small boat racing, a pillar of the Royal Yacht Squadron and Commodore of the Island Sailing Club, Treasurer of King's College Hospital and Chairman of the Professional Classes Aid Council. He had an attractive simplicity of character and a total integrity which made him many friends.

Colville, Philip (b. 1910)

Second son of the Hon. George and Lady Cynthia Colville. Educated at Harrow and Trinity College, Cambridge. Joined Cazenove and Akroyd, stockbrokers, but accepted a partnership in R. Nivison and Co. shortly before the war. He enlisted in the Grenadiers, fought in France in May/June 1940, became adjutant of the 4th battalion and served with the 6th Guards' Tank Brigade from the summer of 1944 to the final defeat of Germany. A keen yachtsman, owning a *Dragon* class boat for over thirty years, he was at one time rear-Commodore of the Royal Yacht Squadron. Also a first-class bridge player and an unconscionably lucky card-holder. He is Treasurer and financial adviser to King's College Hospital and a member of the Council of the Royal National Lifeboat Institution.

Crathorne, Thomas Dugdale, 1st Lord (1897–1977)

A wise and much loved habitué of No. 10, who had formerly been Parliamentary Private Secretary to Lord Swinton and to Stanley Baldwin. Conservative M.P. for Richmond (Yorks.), he was an almost daily caller when I first went to Downing Street. He went with the Yorkshire Hussars to fight in the Middle East, and came back in 1942 to be Chairman of the Conservative Party. In 1951 he was Minister of Agriculture, but in 1954 he felt obliged to resign because of the mishandling by his department of the Crichel Down affair. Ennobled in 1959.

Crewe, Robert Crewe-Milnes, 1st and last Marquess of Crewe, K.G. (1858–1945)

Son of the celebrated man of letters, Richard Monckton-Milnes, Lord Houghton, and Annabel, sister and heiress of the last Lord Crewe, whose great estates in Cheshire and Staffordshire he inherited as well as his father's house and land at Fryston, near Ferrybridge, with a famous library.

After Harrow, while still at Trinity College, Cambridge, he became engaged to Sibyl Graham, daughter of Sir Frederick and Lady Hermione Graham of Netherby. She died suddenly after seven years of marriage, a sorrow he described poignantly in verse (for he wrote good poetry), leaving him disconsolate with four children under six. A Liberal follower of Mr Gladstone, in 1892 he was appointed Viceroy of Ireland at the early age of thirty-four. In 1895 he inherited the Crewe estates, was created Earl of Crewe and three years later married Lady Margaret Primrose, aged eighteen, younger daughter of the former Prime Minister, Lord Rosebery. He was tall, handsome and a well-informed, attractive talker: she fell in love with him across the dining-room table at Mentmore.

When the Liberal Government of 1905 was formed, he was given high Cabinet office, being Secretary of State for the Colonies, and later for India, Lord President, and Leader of the House of Lords, with the unenviable task of taking the Parliament Bill, limiting the Lords' powers, to the Upper Chamber. Mr Asquith is on record as saying that there was no member of his Cabinet on whom he relied so much. His speeches read well, but were poorly and hesitantly delivered, reflecting the caution with which he chose his words. In 1911 he was given the Garter and created a Marquess.

He was briefly President of the Board of Education and, surprisingly enough, Chairman of the L.C.C.; but although he was for six years Ambassador in Paris (1922–28), Lord Lieutenant of

London, leader of the Liberals in the Lords and Secretary of State for War in the 1931 National Government, his political career effectively ended when Lloyd George succeeded Asquith as Prime Minister in 1916.

His tastes were catholic, though his religion was Anglican. Of scholarly inclination, well-read in all branches of literature, a good historian and a competent classicist, he was at the same time devoted to the Turf, a breeder of racehorses, and a lavish host, perhaps the last of the Whig grandees. There was no better company when he was in expansive mood, but he nevertheless seemed detached from human beings, except for his wife, and was dutiful rather than affectionate to his daughters. He lost both his sons, one by each marriage, when they were still young and this heart-breaking experience probably accounted for his apparent lack of interest in other people, masked though it was by unwavering courtesy.

Cripps, Hon. Sir Stafford, C. H., F.R.S., K.C. (1889–1952)
Product of Winchester College and University College, London, he was a son of the 1st Lord Parmoor. His wife, Dame Isabel, was an intelligent Eno's Fruitsalts heiress. He did well at the Bar, became steadily more radical in politics and was elected Labour M.P. for Bristol East in 1931, standing on the far left of the party. He was a devout Christian, a vegetarian and a foe to alcohol. He moderated his political views considerably after being Ambassador in Moscow, 1940–42, and returned to London to a seat in the War Cabinet and the leadership of a House of Commons which had a vast Conservative majority. From 1942 to the end of the war he was Minister of Aircraft Production.

In the post-war Labour Government he was, first, President of the Board of Trade and from 1947 Chancellor of the Exchequer, the very emblem of austerity. Austere he may have been, but he was honest through and through and nobody had a more kindly smile. He was clever, but not always sensible.

Daladier, Edouard, G.C.M.G. (1884–1970)
One of the leaders, with Léon Blum, of the French Front Populaire in the early 1930s, he moved steadily to the right. He was French Prime Minister at the time of Munich and an ardent appeaser of Germany. He reluctantly led France into war in September 1939; but two months before the German offensive of May, 1940, resigned in favour of Paul Reynaud and became Minister of Defence in an unstable Cabinet. After the collapse of France, he

might have been willing to carry on the war from North Africa, but he was incarcerated in a ship by the supporters of Pétain and all efforts to communicate with him were frustrated. After the Munich Conference in September 1938, which gave Hitler his way with Czechoslovakia, Neville Chamberlain asked the King to confer on Daladier the Grand Cross of the Order of St Michael and St George.

Dalton, Dr Hugh (1887–1962)

Labour M.P. for Bishop Auckland, educated at Eton and King's College, Cambridge, he was a leading light in the Labour Party, Minister of Economic Warfare in the war and Chancellor of the Exchequer (he had hoped for the Foreign Office) in Attlee's 1945 Government. However, in 1947 he had to resign on account of a Budget leak for which he was not responsible; for though sharp, he was honest. He had a first-class brain, but never quite lived down Queen Victoria's reference to him as "Canon Dalton's horrid little boy".

Darlan, Admiral J. F. (1881–1942)

As Commander-in-Chief of the French Navy before the war he made it an efficient fighting force. Although jealous of the Royal Navy and at heart anti-British, he co-operated loyally until the fall of France. He then became a leading appeaser of the victorious Germans and his Anglophobe sentiments were strengthened by the sinking of the French fleet at Oran in July 1940. By then he was Minister of Marine and in 1941 he rose still higher to become Pétain's Vice President and Foreign Minister. He put Syrian airfields at the disposal of the Germans when, in May 1941, they planned to bring military aid to Rashid Ali's anti-British insurrection in Baghdad. Yet in November 1942, happening by accident or design to be in North Africa when the Anglo-American Operation TORCH took place, he made an agreement with the American General Mark Clark and gave orders, in Marshal Pétain's name, for the French military commanders to stop resisting the Allied landings. Without these orders the operation would have been far more costly. This sudden turn of coat led Vichy and the Germans to denounce him, but it also aroused indignation in England and the United States where a deal with this friend of Germany was regarded with horror. The problem was resolved when a young royalist Frenchman assassinated him on Christmas Eve 1942.

De La Warr, Herbrand Sackville, 9th Earl, G.B.E. (1900–1976)

Always known as Buck, he was a

man of great good looks, irresistible to women. He declared himself a conscientious objector on reaching military age, but since he was no coward he served before the mast in a minesweeper. Joining the Labour Party, he held office in Ramsay MacDonald's Governments of 1924 and 1929–31 and then, having followed MacDonald and Snowden into a National Labour Party, he was Parliamentary Secretary in several departments before becoming Lord Privy Seal in 1937, President of the Board of Education and First Commissioner of Works. In 1951, by which time he had become a Conservative, he was appointed Postmaster General and he had the task of piloting through Parliament the bill establishing Independent Television of which he personally (like Churchill and Eden) strongly disapproved. Apart from being Chairman of the Royal Commonwealth Society and other multifarious activities, he was, with Brendan Bracken, co-secretary of the Other Club. One of his sisters, the glamorous Lady Idina, had five husbands, including the Lord Erroll who was murdered in Kenya in 1941.

Dill, Field Marshal Sir John, G.C.B., C.M.G., D.S.O., D.S.M. (U.S.) (1881–1944)
There were few more likeable human beings. Hailing from Co. Armagh, he went to Cheltenham College and Sandhurst, and fought with the Leinster Regiment in the South African War. He was a staff officer in France for most of World War I, but took part in several engagements, was wounded and won the D.S.O. He acquired such a reputation in the army that he was disappointed not to be made C.I.G.S. by Hore-Belisha in 1937, and again not to be C. in C. of the B.E.F. in 1939. In both cases Lord Gort, his junior in rank, was preferred and he had to be content to command I Corps under Gort from September 1939 to April 1940. He was then recalled to the War Office to be Vice Chief of the Imperial General Staff. On May 27th, at the climax of the Dunkirk evacuation, he succeeded General Ironside as C.I.G.S.

Neither the Secretary of State, Anthony Eden, nor Eden's successor, David Margesson, had anything but praise for him. However, he was a tired man and Churchill found him unsufficiently vigorous. So after the Atlantic Charter meeting with Roosevelt in August 1941, he was left behind to be the British representative with the Combined Chiefs of Staff in Washington. It was here that he came into his own, performing an invaluable service for his country, winning golden opinions from the Americans, forming a strong personal friendship with General Marshall, and finally, when he died in Washington, being given the high American distinction of burial in Arlington Cemetery.

Dodds, Lady Annabel
(1881–1948)
Eldest daughter of the Marquess of Crewe and Sibyl Graham of Netherby. In 1902 she married the Hon. Arthur O'Neill, M.P. for Mid-Antrim, who was the elder son and heir of Lord O'Neill. He died at Ypres, while serving with the 2nd Life Guards, the first M.P. to be killed in World War I. She had five O'Neill children. In 1922 she married Major Hugh Dodds and had two more sons. She had the capacity of making her companions feel more intelligent and amusing than they really were, and she was a "great lady" without being at all arrogant or ostentatious. When her father died in 1945 she changed her name to Dodds-Crewe.

Dowding, Air Chief Marshal
Hugh, 1st Lord, G.C.B.,
G.C.V.O., C.M.G.
(1882–1970)
Educated at Winchester and the Royal Military Academy, Woolwich, he was a Lieutenant Colonel in the Royal Artillery in World War I before joining the Royal Flying Corps. A member of the Air Council, 1930–35, and then appointed C. in C., Fighter Command. A principal architect of victory in the Battle of Britain, and a decisive influence in the decision not to send additional fighter squadrons to France in June 1940, which would have dangerously denuded the home defences, he was retired by the Air Ministry with much tactlessness in the following November. This was done on the doubtless true grounds that he was exhausted. He was justifiably hurt at not being promoted to Marshal of the R.A.F. but Churchill made him a peer.

Duncan-Sandys, Lord, C.H.
(b. 1908)
Son of a Conservative M.P. with a New Zealand wife, he was educated at Eton and Magdalen, Oxford, before passing into the Diplomatic Service in 1930. He served at the Embassy in Berlin in the last days of the Weimar Republic and was elected Conservative M.P. for Norwood in 1935, the year in which he married Winston Churchill's eldest daughter, Diana. In 1936, having learned from a brother territorial officer details of the shortage of anti-aircraft guns, he raised the matter in the House of Commons. Hore-Belisha, Secretary of State for War, sought to court-martial him, but parliamentary privilege as well as family loyalty were at stake and his father-in-law came powerfully to his rescue in debate. "The Sandys Case" was headline news.

From 1941 onwards his political career blossomed. He held at different times the portfolios of Works, Supply, Housing and Local Government, Defence, Aviation, the Colonies and Commonwealth Relations. Hard-working, imaginative, humorous and, as far as I was concerned, pleasant company, he was almost always at odds with the civil servants in his various departments, disliking some and distrusting most.

He was, in the years after the war, a leading proponent of European Unity and instigated Winston Churchill to make the United Europe movement a crusade.

He was made a peer in 1974, and became president of the Civic Trust, which he had founded, and Chairman of Lonrho Ltd.

Gamelin, General Maurice Gustave (1872–1958)

He hoodwinked both his own countrymen and the British into believing him a great General. The man who did not think so was his second in command, General Georges, who would have had his place had he not been gravely wounded in the bomb attack which killed King Alexander of Yugoslavia at Marseilles in 1934. His claim to fame arose from his having been on Marshal Joffre's staff in 1914 and written the directives at the battle of the Marne. He had also defeated a Druse rebellion in Syria and been Inspec-

tor General of the Army. He was interned by the Vichy Government and incarcerated by the Germans at Buchenwald Concentration Camp in 1943.

Gaulle, General Charles de (1890–1970)

Few men in history have risen to the pinnacle of power so fortuitously. An unknown brigadier who had made a profound study of tank warfare and been taken up, right at the end of the day, by Paul Reynaud, he came to London without expecting to lead a Free French movement. Nor would he have done so if any leading French politician had been available. However, Winston Churchill saw in him the very reverse of the defeatism which he had found in France and, once he had made his choice, he did not go back on it, though he was often tempted to do so by de Gaulle's arrogance, suspicions and ingratitude. De Gaulle was a patriot; but he was also a nationalist, and to him the erasure of the 1940 shame and the recovery of French greatness were all that mattered. Churchill protected him from the dislike and distrust of the Americans, but he was exasperated when de Gaulle took steps, often not in the general Allied interest, without consultation; nor could he stomach the General's absurd conviction that the British wished to seize the French colonies, notably Syria and the Lebanon (which the British would have paid any price *not* to possess). All the same, even when de Gaulle, as President of the Republic, was giving rein to his Anglophobe instincts by blocking British entry to the Common Market, he did on several occasions make it clear that he recognised the debt he owed Churchill.

Geoffrey-Lloyd, Lord
(1902–1984)

After Harrow and Trinity, Cambridge, he was private secretary to both Sir Samuel Hoare and Stanley Baldwin before being elected in 1931 Conservative M.P. for the Ladywood division of Birmingham. He then became Parliamentary Private Secretary to Baldwin as Prime Minister. On Baldwin's retirement he was promoted to be Under Secretary at the Home Office and in 1939 was Secretary for Mines and later for Petroleum. In this capacity, and as Chairman of the Oil Control Board, he was responsible for PLUTO, the pipeline under the Channel required for Operation OVERLORD. In 1951 Churchill made him Minister of Fuel and Power and under Harold Macmillan he was Minister of Education. A gentle, unassertive man of ability, he was made a peer in 1974 and devoted his retirement to the brilliant organisation of the Leeds Castle Foundation, bequeathed by his great friend and constant hostess Olive, Lady Baillie, daughter of Lord Queenborough and owner of the castle.

Goering, Field Marshal
Hermann (1893–1946)

He had a way of persuading foreigners, including Lord Halifax, that he was "a good chap", whereas he was in fact ruthless, egotistic and "kinky" to boot. He won fame as an airman by taking command of "the Richthofen Circus" after Richthofen was killed in World War I. One of Hitler's earliest followers, he was wounded in the abortive Nazi "putsch" at Munich in 1923, after which he was air adviser to the Danes and Swedes. In 1932 he became President of the Reichstag, which he probably arranged to have burned down, and Prime Minister of Prussia. Because of his record he was appointed Commander in Chief of the Luftwaffe in 1933 and presided over the air-raids on Britain in 1940–41. Sentenced to death at Nuremberg in 1946, he cheated the hangman by taking an anally secreted cyanide pill.

Gort, Field Marshal John
Standish Vereker, 6th Viscount,
V.C., G.C.B., D.S.O. (and 2
bars), M.C. (1886–1946)

When the American General Patton visited him in Malta in 1943, he said he had come to see the bravest man in the British army. Gort was indeed brave, with a V.C., three D.S.O.s and a M.C. to his credit in the 1st World War. He served in India and in Shanghai, and was Commandant of the Staff College. Hore-Belisha picked him in 1937, junior though he was to many other generals, to be C.I.G.S. He was not the ideal choice, hard though he worked, and he was soon at daggers drawn with Hore-Belisha who nevertheless recommended him for command of the B.E.F. He had two generals senior to himself, Dill and Alan Brooke, as his Corps Commanders. When the crunch came in May 1940, with the B.E.F. cut off and almost surrounded, it was Gort who took the decision to withdraw to Dunkirk for embarkation. Had he not done so, almost every trained officer and N.C.O. in the British army would have been lost and it is doubtful whether Britain could have fought on. So it may well be that he changed the course of history. To his disappointment he was never again given an active command, but after a year as Governor of Gibraltar, where he extended the small airfield with most beneficial consequences for the 1943 campaigns, he was Governor and Commander in Chief of Malta, during much of the Island's terrible siege. His organisation of the defence was masterly. His last appointment was High Commissioner in Palestine in 1944 and there, by sheer force of personality, he preserved the peace between Jews and Arabs. But cancer struck, and he returned home to die in 1946, his services inadequately recognised.

Graham, Lady Helen, D.C.V.O. (1879–1945)
Eldest daughter of my mother's aunt the Duchess of Montrose, who was born Violet Graham of Netherby. Lady Helen was President of the Y.W.C.A. and was the first lady-in-waiting to the Duchess of York (Queen Elizabeth, the Queen Mother) of whom, and of whose children, she became an intimate friend. Well-read, a water-colourist of distinction, a frequent contributor of short stories to *Blackwood's Magazine*, a dedicated Scot though never a nationalist, she was withal humble and unself-assertive. There was no better advertisement for the schoolroom, governess-controlled upbringing of Victorian young ladies at its best.

Greig, Group Captain Sir Louis, K.B.E., C.V.O. (1880–1953)
As a young man played Rugby Football for Scotland, became a doctor, and was appointed medical officer at Osborne, the junior college for naval cadets. Among them was the then delicate Prince Albert, afterwards Duke of York and King George VI. In the war

Greig fought with the Royal Marines, was taken prisoner by the Germans and then joined the R.A.F., becoming a Wing Commander in record time. He became Comptroller and Equerry to the Duke of York whom he partnered at tennis at Wimbledon (without notable success). He married Miss Phyllis Scrymgeour, was appointed deputy-ranger of Richmond Park and resided there, at Thatched House Lodge. In World War II he was personal assistant to Sir Archibald Sinclair, Secretary of State for Air.

Grigg, Sir Percy James, K.C.B., K.C.S.I. (1890–1964)
Educated at Bournemouth School and St John's, Cambridge, he was Private Secretary to Churchill at the Exchequer (1924–29). He was always known as P. J. After being Chairman of the Board of Inland Revenue, he went to India as financial member of the Viceroy's Executive Council. Thence, in 1939, he arrived in Whitehall, like an explosive rocket, as Permanent Under Secretary at the War Office. He had no opinion of Hore-Belisha, his Secretary of State, or of most other people's Secretaries of State. He said exactly what he thought and did not care a fig for those superior to him except, on occasions, the Prime Minister. Clever and hardworking, though holding truthfulness to be a cardinal virtue, he thought tact a social affectation.

To everybody's surprise, including his own, Churchill found him a parliamentary seat at Cardiff and in 1942 made him Secretary of State for War to replace David Margesson who was sacrificed as a scapegoat after the fall of Singapore.

He left politics when the war ended, became Deputy Chairman of the National Provincial Bank, a director of I.C.I. and other leading companies and Chairman of Bass.

Halifax, Edward Wood, 1st Earl of, K.G., O.M., G.C.S.I., G.C.I.E. (1881–1959)
A Fellow of All Souls who was also a M.F.H., a devout practising Anglican, Viceroy of India, Foreign Secretary, British Ambassador in Washington at a crucial period in Anglo-American relations, and the holder of eighteen honorary degrees is a subject worthy either of Dryden or of W. S. Gilbert. Calm and unhurried, he shared Neville Chamberlain's dedication to peace at almost any cost, and although capable of cunning in his diplomacy he was taken in by Goering. He went so far as to suggest that *we* might satisfy the Germans by letting them have the *Portuguese* colonies. He was, all the same, a good and fascinating man, who was a great success in Washington with Roosevelt, Cordell Hull and Harry Hopkins. He was much helped in Delhi as

well as in Washington by his admirable wife, born Lady Dorothy Onslow. Of their three sons one was killed in action, but another, though severely maimed, held many political offices and was himself made a peer.

Hankey, Sir Maurice, 1st Lord, G.C.B., G.C.M.G., G.C.V.O. (1877–1963)
This long-standingly eminent Civil Servant went from Rugby and the Royal Naval College at Greenwich to be a Captain in the Royal Marine Artillery; but several years before World War I he became Secretary of the Committee of Imperial Defence and in 1916 Lloyd George, with whom he worked closely, made him the first Secretary of the Cabinet. He combined these two key functions between the two world wars, but still found time to be Secretary at the Versailles Peace Conference, Clerk of the Privy Council and Secretary to five Imperial Conferences. In 1938 he thought it time to retire, but Neville Chamberlain made him a peer and inveigled him into the War Cabinet as Minister Without Portfolio. At Chamberlain's request Churchill, who had been the object of Hankey's deep suspicion, retained him in office, first as Chancellor of the Duchy of Lancaster and then as Paymaster General and Chairman of the Scientific Advisory and Engineer-

ing Advisory Committees. He continued busily to take the chair of numerous other governmental and semi-governmental committees after the war.

Harriman, Hon. W. Averell (b. 1891)
Son of the fabulously rich American railway king, E. F. Harriman, Averell struck out on his own at an early age, founding the successful banking enterprise Brown Brothers Harriman, and excelling at everything, from polo to croquet, to which he set his hand. In 1941 he came to Britain, as President Roosevelt's special envoy, to organise the supply of equipment. He became a friend of the Churchills and a frequent visitor to Chequers until, in 1943, he was sent as Ambassador to Moscow and formed an amiable personal relationship with Stalin. After the war he was Governor of New York and adviser to successive Democrat Presidents. When Mrs Harriman died, he married Randolph Churchill's first wife, Pamela, who became in her own right a significant feature in the Democrat Party in Washington. As late as 1983, when he was over ninety, the Harrimans visited the Kremlin and had an interview with Brezhnev in the hope of improving Soviet-American relations. By 1985 Averell Harriman and Molotov were the last survivors of the men of power in World War II.

Home of the Hirsel, Alexander Douglas Home, Lord, K.T.
(b. 1903)

Eldest son of the 13th Earl of Home and Lady Lilian Lambton, daughter of the 4th Earl of Durham. Educated at Eton and Christ Church, Oxford, he was elected, as Lord Dunglass, M.P. for South Lanark in 1931 and became Parliamentary Private Secretary to Neville Chamberlain in 1937, accompanying him to the Munich meeting with Hitler in 1938. He married Elizabeth, daughter of the Headmaster of Eton and Dean of Durham, the Very Revd C. A. Alington. He was incapacitated during the war by spinal tuberculosis, but in 1951 he became Minister of State at the Scottish Office and succeeded his father as Earl of Home. He was soon promoted to be Secretary of State for Commonwealth Relations, Leader of the House of Lords, Lord President and, from 1960–63, Foreign Secretary. In 1963, on Harold Macmillan's retirement, he renounced his peerage and became Prime Minister. He lost the 1964 General Election by four seats and the Conservative Party, in their folly, replaced him as leader by Edward Heath whom he nevertheless served faithfully as Foreign Secretary, 1970–74. A man universally loved and admired, by political opponents as well as supporters, he was devoid of vanity and did not know the meaning of rancour or jealousy. A lover of the countryside, he was happiest watching birds, catching salmon at his home on the Tweed or shooting grouse at his other home, Douglas in Lanarkshire.

Hopkins, Harry L. (1890–1946)

He came from a humble home, the son of a harness-maker in Sioux City, and his sympathies were always for the poor and downtrodden. Thin, with wispy hair, always untidy and obviously frail, he nevertheless had piercing, intelligent eyes, a winning smile and a slow, impressive way of speaking. He worked for welfare organisations in the New York slums until he became a friend of Averell Harriman and, through him, of President Roosevelt. The President appointed him Secretary of Commerce in 1938 and he was soon established in the White House as Roosevelt's intimate friend and adviser. The British had represented everything he disliked, especially their far-flung Empire; but he was captivated by Queen Elizabeth when she and King George VI went to Washington in the spring of 1939, and in January 1940, he fell beneath the spell of Winston Churchill, whom he had expected to dislike. After France fell in 1940, he had recognised the British to be the sole active champions of a free world. He used his influence with the President to accelerate the provision of supplies for Britain. He worked closely with Lord Halifax. Later on he became an equally strong partisan of Russia, was foolish enough to advocate a Second Front in 1942 and at the end of the war trusted the word and goodwill of Stalin to an imprudent extent, as did Roosevelt and the State Department. He was much hampered by recurring ill-health, but he was always an honourable man and a sincere idealist.

Hore-Belisha, Leslie, Lord (1893–1957)
Educated at Clifton, St John's, Oxford, Paris and Heidelberg, and President of the Oxford Union after a respectable war record, he aspired to be a second Disraeli. So he fought and won the Devonport division of Plymouth for the Liberals in 1923, spoke fluently in the House, was Parliamentary Secretary to the Board of Trade in 1931, Financial Secretary to the Treasury a year later and then (1934–37) Minister of Transport. There he became a national figure by introducing pedestrian crossings lit by Belisha beacons. The publicity he received did him no good, for he pursued it too diligently when, in 1937, Chamberlain gave him the War Office.

He did much for the welfare and comfort of the troops. However, on matters of army organisation and future strategy he fell foul of the military establishment, tending to consult his unofficial adviser, Liddell-Hart, rather than the Army Council. His fall came when on visiting the British Expeditionary Force in France in November 1939, he crossed swords with the Commander in Chief, Lord Gort, over a matter of pill-boxes. At home Sir Horace Wilson, Sir Edward Bridges, Sir Alexander Hardinge (the King's Private Secretary) and his own new Permanent Under Secretary, P. J. Grigg, all turned against him. In January 1940, Chamberlain demanded his resignation and offered him instead the Board of Trade, which Churchill advised him to accept, but which he foolishly declined. His political career was at an end, though he was briefly Minister of National Insurance in Churchill's caretaker government of 1945. In 1954 he was made a peer.

Ironside, Field Marshal 1st Lord, G.C.B., C.M.G., D.S.O. (1880–1959)
Having fought in the South African War (where his adventures supplied John Buchan with the portrait of Richard Hannay in *The Thirty-Nine Steps*), and been a gunnery officer in the 1st World War, Edmund Ironside was given command of the British forces at Archangel in 1919. His career thereafter was a varied one, but it included three years as Com-

mandant of the Staff College, and, in 1936, Eastern Command. Distraught by obsolete equipment and by governmental inactivity, he paid visits to Churchill at Chartwell and declared that the army was unprepared for war. He was informed by Lord Gort in the summer of 1939 that he was the C. in C. designate of the British Expeditionary Force. In the event, on September 3rd the Secretary of State, Hore-Belisha, obtained Cabinet approval for Gort to be C. in C. and for Ironside to replace him as C.I.G.S. He was not a success in the post and was succeeded in July 1940, by Sir John Dill, being compensated by a brief command of Home Forces and the rank of Field Marshal. The next year he was given a peerage.

Ismay, General Lord, K. G., G.C.B., C.H., D.S.O. (1887–1965)
Son of a senior Indian civil servant, he was educated at Charterhouse and Sandhurst, joining the army in 1905 and winning his D.S.O. in a campaign against the Mad Mullah who dominated Somaliland for more than twenty years. He had long service in India, on the North-West Frontier as a young officer and at headquarters later, being Military Secretary to the Viceroy, 1931–33. He transferred to the Committee of Imperial Defence in London in 1936 and became its Secretary, in succession to Sir Maurice Hankey, in 1938. He was thus the natural choice to be Chief of Staff to Churchill, as Minister of Defence, in 1940. He was the main channel of communication between Churchill and the Chiefs of Staff, of whose committee he was a full member, and he was equally trusted by both. Nobody did more to oil the wheels on the sometimes bumpy road between the service chiefs and the politicians and it was due to him more than anyone else that the confrontations between the two in World War I were avoided in World War II. His ability and dedication to hard work was matched by his personal charm. He was universally known as Pug, for he looked like one and when he was pleased one could almost imagine he was wagging his tail.

He had married a well-endowed wife and after the war he looked forward to a peaceful life, caring for his herd of Jersey cows. It was not to be. In 1951 Churchill inveigled him, against his wishes, into becoming Secretary of State for Commonwealth Relations and in 1952 he was elected, for five years, Secretary General of N.A.T.O. Honours and directorships were heaped on him, but he remained what he had always been, a straightforward, hardworking and totally honourable army officer.

Jacob, Lieutenant General Sir Ian, G.B.E., C.B. (b. 1899)
Son of Field Marshal Sir Claud Jacob, educated at Wellington, the Royal Military Academy, Woolwich, and King's College, Cambridge. A man of tireless industry (nicknamed "Iron Pants" by Antony Head), he was far above the average in both intelligence and common sense. As one of General Ismay's two principal lieutenants in the Office of the Minister of Defence, he was liked and respected by Churchill as a true professional and accompanied him on several of his foreign tours and visits. After the war he was Director of Overseas Services at the B.B.C. until summoned by Churchill in 1952 to be Chief Staff Officer to Field Marshal Alexander as Minister of Defence. He was released after a brief interval and was Director General of the B.B.C., 1952–60. Invariably public spirited and obedient to duty, and a sharp observer of people and events.

Kennedy, Joseph P. (1888–1969)
As Kennedy knew all the tricks of the financial trade, and had himself made a fortune by dealing, President Roosevelt chose him to be the first Chairman of the S.E.C. (Securities Exchange Commission) established to control Wall Street under Roosevelt's "New Deal". A Boston Irishman and an uncompromising Roman Catholic, he brought his eight children with him when he came to London as Ambassador in 1937. They were all enthusiastically received, but in the war Kennedy advised his government that Germany would win, and when the bombs began to fall on London, the American Embassy was, to Roosevelt's disgust, the first to flee from the capital. He was withdrawn by the President at the end of 1940, but had the satisfaction, and then the sorrow, of watching the career of two of his brilliant sons, Jack and Bobby. The eldest, Joe, was killed in action in the air force.

Keyes, Admiral of the Fleet Lord, G.C.B., K.C.V.O., C.M.G., D.S.O. (1872–1945)
Nobody would stint praise to Roger Keyes for the dash and gallantry with which he commanded the raid on the U-boat bases at Zeebrugge and Ostend in 1918. Indeed his entire naval career was a distinguished one, recognised by Parliament in 1919 with a vote of thanks and a cheque for £10,000. Of courage and of drive he had plenty: of modesty he had scarcely any.

That was the root of the trouble in 1940. On May 7th he went down to the House of Commons (to which he had been elected in 1934 for North Portsmouth) in uniform and wearing rows of medals, to speak against

Chamberlain. He then rushed off to Belgium to support King Leopold and returned to England bristling with indignation against the Chiefs of Staff, bombarding the Prime Minister with demands for action, combined with his own advancement, and causing the maximum irritation in Whitehall with the minimum of useful results. He asked to preside over the Chiefs of Staff; he even asked to be Deputy Prime Minister; and Churchill, still under the spell of Keyes' record in World War I, did go so far as to appoint him Director of Combined Operations, though he was tactfully removed in 1941 to make place for Lord Louis Mountbatten.

Kirkpatrick, Sir Ivone, G.C.B., G.C.M.G. (1897–1964)

This forthright Roman Catholic from Downside and Balliol fought throughout World War I with the Inniskillings and entered the Diplomatic Service in 1919. As First Secretary at the Embassy in Berlin, 1933–38, he was convinced that the Nazis intended war and he wholeheartedly disliked the policy of his appeasing chief, Sir Nevile Henderson, and of the Munich Settlement. Returning to Whitehall, he was made director of the foreign division of the Ministry of Information, where he was contemptuous of Duff Cooper's activities, and then controller of the European Services of the B.B.C., a function he performed with energy and fruitful results. In 1949 he was permanent Under Secretary of the German Section of the Foreign Office, from 1950 to 1953 British High Commissioner in Germany and finally, from 1953 to 1957, Permanent Under Secretary of State. On retirement he was appointed Chairman of the Independent Television Authority.

Laval, Pierre (1883–1945)

Between the wars he was always to the fore in French politics, sometimes Prime Minister and sometimes Foreign Minister. His views were extremely right wing and he sympathised with the fascists. When France fell in 1940 he was the most outspokenly pro-German member of the Vichy clique, often causing embarrassment to Marshal Pétain, to whom the Germans appointed him Vice President in 1942. After the war he was tried for treason and executed in October 1945.

Liddell-Hart, Sir Basil (1895–1970)

Undoubtedly a great military historian and invariably helpful to students, though his teaching that in any future war defence must have the advantage over attack lost him his prestige in 1940, as did his belief that Britain would lose the war. He had been military correspondent of *The Times* and was Hore-Belisha's unofficial adviser, to the fury of the Generals, when Belisha was Secretary of State for War. He left a library of great importance to students of military history and after the war became a friend and frequent companion of Field Marshal Montgomery.

Lloyd of Dolobran, George, 1st Lord, G.C.S.I., G.C.I.E., D.S.O. (1879–1941)

Educated at Eton and Trinity College, Cambridge, he worked at the British Embassy in Constantinople and in the Middle East before becoming a Conservative M.P. in 1910. He was much concerned with the Arab revolt and with Lawrence of Arabia. In 1918 he was appointed Governor of Bombay, an office he held for five years. He was the creator of the Lloyd barrage across the Indus, which irrigated thousands of square miles. In 1925 he succeeded Field Marshal Lord Allenby as High Commissioner in Egypt and was made a peer. However, he fell into disfavour at home and resigned in 1929.

He was a resolute man, unbending in his views, but dynamic both in speech and action. Unlike Churchill, he was an unwavering supporter of the Arab cause, but they joined forces in opposition to Baldwin's Government of India Bill, in demanding rapid rearmament and in opposing Neville Chamberlain's foreign policy. He was an active and enthusiastic Chairman of the British Council and President of the right-wing Navy League. There was no more dedicated imperialist. Churchill, who respected his energy and intelligence, made him Secretary of State for the Colonies in 1940. Seeing a certain amount of him socially as well as officially, I was deeply impressed by the brilliance of his conversation and the shrewdness of his judgment. In January 1941, he became Leader of the House of Lords, but died a few weeks later. He married a sister of Sir Alan Lascelles and his son, David, held ministerial office under Churchill and Eden from 1952 to 1957.

Maclean, Sir Fitzroy, Bt., C.B.E. (b. 1911)

A man of action who is also a master of the English language. Joining the Diplomatic Service in 1933, he wrote a highly acclaimed account of an adventurous journey through little visited southern provinces of the Soviet Union made when he was on the Embassy staff in Moscow. Transferred back to London in 1939, he decided to take an active part in the war. He escaped from his reserved occupation in 1941 by declaring himself a parliamentary candidate, joined the Cameron

Highlanders as a private (and, in 1942, the S.A.S.) after being elected Conservative M.P. for Lancaster, a seat he held till 1959. In 1943 he was promoted to Brigadier and chosen to lead the British mission to Tito, with whom he worked closely for two years of guerilla warfare, establishing a most friendly personal relationship. He was from 1954 to 1957 Financial Secretary at the War Office and he wrote a series of excellent books of which the best-known is *Eastern Approaches*. He married the delightful and intelligent daughter of the 16th Lord Lovat, widow of Sir Eric Phipps' younger son, Alan, a naval officer killed in the war.

Margesson, David, 1st Viscount, M. C. (1890–1965)

After Harrow and Magdalene College, Cambridge, he joined the 11th Hussars and won the Military Cross in World War I. Entering the House of Commons in 1922, he became a Whip in 1926 and Chief Whip in 1931. He controlled the Government majority in the House with exemplary skill, employing a mixture of charm (with which he was exceptionally endowed), disciplinary threat and organising ability. Loyal to Baldwin and Chamberlain, he was equally so to Churchill when circumstances changed, and no member of the 1940 Coalition Government, Conservative, Lib-

eral or Labour, thought ill of him. Churchill made him Secretary of State for War in December 1940. He gave every satisfaction, being on most amicable terms with the C.I.G.S., Sir John Dill; but in 1942, after the fall of Singapore, he was thrown to the wolves as a scapegoat, albeit an entirely unblemished one. In 1916 he married an American heiress, Frances Leggett, by whom he had three intelligent children; but he and his wife lived separate lives.

Martin, Sir John, K.C.M.G., C.B., C.V.O. (b. 1904)

A first-class classical product of the Edinburgh Academy and Corpus Christi, Oxford, he had a shy and retiring disposition combined with a ready wit, a delectable sense of humour and a conscientious devotion to the public service. Coming to No. 10 from the Colonial Service, with the secretaryship of the Palestine Royal Commission and the admiration of Chaim Weizmann behind him, he quickly won favour, went with the Prime Minister to the Atlantic Charter Meeting, the Casablanca, Tehran, Cairo and Quebec conferences and on several visits to Washington and Moscow; but he was too law-abiding to keep a diary. That is a pity as his writing is as agreeable as his conversation. After the war was deputy Under Secretary State in the Colonial Office a High Commissioner in Malta, 1965–67. His wife, Rosalind, is a daughter of a former Provost of Oriel, Sir David Ross.

Mary, Her Majesty Queen (1867–1953)

Tall and regal, with a magnificent presence. Her mother, Princess Mary of Cambridge, immensely fat and adored by the populace, was a grand-daughter of King George III; her father, the Duke of Teck, was the morganatic child of Duke Alexander of Württemberg and Countess Rhédey. The Tecks were poor, and the Duchess extravagant, so that Princess Mary of Teck seldom had new clothes and lived in strained circumstances at the White Lodge in Richmond Park, placed at the family's disposal by Queen Victoria. She was selected, doubtless with little enthusiasm on her part, to marry the heir to the throne, the Duke of Clarence. He died while they were engaged and her tryst was, with Queen Victoria's approval, transferred to George, Duke of York, whom she much preferred, though when he became King George V she held him in awe and was unsuccessful in mitigating his authoritarian treatment of their children. Queen Alexandra, her not very intelligent but strikingly beautiful mother-in-law, never liked her; but Queen Victoria, conscious of the fact, went out of her way to

provide affectionate compensation. As Queen Mother she was an immensely popular figure. She had a sense of humour, a social conscience and an unswervingly rigid sense of duty. She was a discriminating collector of jade and objets d'art and catalogued, with minute attention to detail, many of the royal possessions.

Meade-Fetherstonhaugh, Admiral the Hon. Sir Herbert, G.C.B., C.B., D.S.O. (1875–1964)

An Admiral of no great brains, but of charm, gallantry and fine seamanship. He commanded the constantly active flotilla of destroyers at Harwich in World War I. He was always known as Jimmy Meade. Although in 1940 he was sixty-five, nothing would induce him not to serve again. So he became second mate in a coastal trader and was at one stage, in the interval of commanding the Houses of Parliament Home Guard, Commodore of a convoy of merchantmen sailing through U-boat infested waters. One of his sisters married my father's second brother, also an Admiral, so that there was a family connection.

Molotov, Vyacheslav M. (b. 1890)

His face was not his fortune, for it portrayed intransigence and the conviction that there was only one side to every case, namely that which represented Soviet policy. He was Chairman of the Council of People's Commissars and effectively Foreign Minister. One of the few high-ranking officials who lasted the course with Stalin into whose disfavour he never seemed to fall and whose moods he reflected faithfully. His name is for ever attached to the infamous Molotov – Ribbentrop Pact of August 1939 which allied Nazi Germany to Soviet Russia and provided for the partition of Poland as well as the seizure by Russia of the democratic Baltic States, Latvia, Lithuania and Estonia. After the war his consistently negative attitude destroyed all hope of a harmonious settlement with the Western Allies and of a generally acceptable German peace treaty. He was still alive in the mid-eighties, a nonagenarian relic of past misdeeds.

Morrison of Lambeth, Herbert, 1st Lord, C.H. (1888–1965)

Riding on the crest of a wave, as a result of his much praised leadership of the London County Council (1934–40), he became a powerful influence in the Labour Party, in and out of Parliament. He had been its Chairman in 1928. Having been Minister of Transport for two years in Ramsay MacDonald's 1929 Government, his next taste of office was in 1940 when the Labour Opposition joined Churchill's Coalition. He began as Minister of Supply, frequently thwarted by Lord Beaverbrook whose piracy for aircraft production purposes made a heavy dent in the goods Morrison could produce. In October 1940, he was moved to the Home Office and the new Ministry of Home Security, and there he remained till 1945, being admitted to the War Cabinet in 1942, but never taking his eye off the preparation of Labour's next election campaign. He was dynamic, he was tireless and with both fascists and Communists he was ruthless; but he and Ernest Bevin formed a bitter rivalry and hostility.

In 1945 he was the leader of those in the Labour Party who opposed the continuation of the Coalition till after the defeat of Japan and demanded a return to party politics. He became Lord President, was for a time responsible for economic planning and led the House of Commons, through which he piloted the various nationalisation measures. In 1950, when his adversary, Bevin, fell ill, he was for a year an incompetent and unpopular Foreign Secretary; but his eye had long been fixed on ousting Attlee and becoming Prime Minister, for he was not short of ambition. In the end it was Hugh Gaitskell, and not Morrison, who succeeded to the leadership of the party.

*Morton, Major Sir Desmond,
K.C.B., C.M.G., M.C.
(1891–1971)*

A devout Roman Catholic, educated at Eton and Woolwich, he was shot through the heart in World War I but miraculously survived, though he always looked pale and ill. He ended that war as A.D.C. to Field Marshal Haig.

He lived at Edenbridge and was thus a neighbour of the Churchills at Chartwell. He had become head of the Industrial Intelligence Centre and, whether with or without authority is uncertain, he supplied Churchill with much information valuable to him in the 1930s when he was trying to warn the government and the country of the danger ahead.

In May 1940 Churchill brought him to 10 Downing Street and sought to use him as his liaison with the Foreign Office, an experiment much resented in that quarter. He was at an early stage involved with de Gaulle and the Free French and later became the Prime Minister's contact with the Allied governments in London and some branches of the Secret Service. However, his usefulness declined and the Prime Minister, though certainly not wishing to be unkind, made less and less use of his services. He resented this the more because he had given the impression in many quarters that he was the Prime Minister's right-hand man. Churchill did procure a K.C.B. for him and in 1946 persuaded Attlee to appoint him U.K. delegate to the Inter-Allied Reparations Agency; but because he had been over-ambitious he died a sad and embittered man.

*Mountbatten of Burma, Admiral
of the Fleet, 1st Earl, K.G.,
G.C.B., O.M., G.C.S.I.,
G.C.I.E., G.C.V.O., D.S.O.
(1900–1979)*

Younger son of Admiral of the Fleet Prince Louis of Battenberg (1st Marquess of Milford Haven) and Princess Victoria of Hesse, a great-grandson of Queen Victoria and godson of both Queen Victoria and the Tsar Nicholas II. He had an illustrious naval career, including the command of H.M.S. *Kelly* in the battle of Crete, and he married Sir Ernest Cassell's energetic heiress, Edwina Ashley. He was Chief of Combined Operations, 1941–43, Supreme Allied Commander in South East Asia, 1943–46, Viceroy and Governor General of India, 1947–48, C. in C., Mediterranean, 1952–54, First Sea Lord, 1955–59 and Chief of the Defence Staff, 1959–65. Churchill admired his courage, but mistrusted his judgment and deplored his outspoken support, while still a serving officer, of the Labour Party. He therefore declined to agree to his being First Sea Lord until a week before his own resignation. His was the unique case in modern times of a member of the Royal Family actively involved in major political and operational affairs. He was murdered by the I.R.A. while on holiday in Ireland.

Moyne, Walter Guinness, 1st Lord, D.S.O. (and bar) (1880–1944)

Third son of the 1st Earl of Iveagh, he was elected to Parliament as Conservative M.P. for Bury St Edmunds in 1907 after fighting in the Boer War and being seriously wounded. In the 1st World War he fought at Gallipoli and later won a D.S.O. and bar on the Western Front. He was Under-Secretary of State for War and subsequently financial secretary at the Treasury when Churchill was Chancellor of the Exchequer. In 1925 he joined the Cabinet as Minister of Agriculture, an office in which (unlike most Ministers of Agriculture) he won considerable acclaim.

Created a peer in 1932, he was chosen by Churchill in 1941 to succeed Lord Lloyd as Secretary of State for the Colonies, and he was then sent out to Cairo to hold the important post of Resident Minister in Cairo. There, in 1944, he was callously assassinated by the Jewish Stern Group. A man of great public spirit and varied interests, he married Lady Evelyn Ersteine, daughter of the

14th Earl of Buchan and had two sons and a daughter.

Norwich, Alfred Duff Cooper, 1st Viscount, G.C.M.G., D.S.O. (1890–1954)

His claim to fame stemmed at least in part from being married to the beautiful Lady Diana Manners. In the Foreign Office before the First World War, a brave Grenadier Officer during it and a Tory M.P. after it, he was a witty speaker, an interesting conversationist and the owner of an excellent prose style; but he was idle as a Minister. As Secretary of State for War, and then First Lord of the Admiralty in the 1930s, he was regarded as a light-weight, but he did have the courage of his anti-Nazi convictions when he resigned at the time of Munich.

He could scarcely have been worse as Minister of Information (though, as successor to Lord Reith, he did wear a temporary halo), and when sent to Singapore at the end of 1941 to report on the defences he suggested no useful palliatives. However, as Ambassador to the Free French, first in Algiers, and then in Paris at the end of the war and for two years after it, he helped to restore Anglo-French relations and his letters and despatches home often brimmed over with useful analysis and intelligent anticipation.

Pétain, Marshal Philippe (1856–1951)

The victor of Verdun and suppressor of the French army mutinies in 1917, he ended the First World War as Commander in Chief, was for ten years Vice President of the Supreme War Council and in 1934 Minister for War. Ambassador in Madrid in 1939, he returned to France when the fighting began and joined Paul Reynaud's government, becoming himself Prime Minister on June 16th, 1940. The French, in defeat, distress and despair, needed a father-figure to whom to turn. They had not had one since Clemenceau in World War I. Pétain filled that rôle during the German occupation, but both he and Weygand believed that France had sinned and must expiate her sin by suffering. So although he was not such an ardent collaborator with the Germans as Laval, Darlan and Baudouin, and considered it his main duty to ensure strict adherence to the terms of the armistice with Germany, he made no effort to help the Western Allies and actually condemned de Gaulle to death. Such was the prestige of the father-figure that French officers and colonial officials obeyed instructions from Vichy without hesitation, whatever their personal predilections. After the war he was sentenced to death, but the sentence was commuted to imprisonment on an island off the coast of France.

Portal of Hungerford, Marshal of the R.A.F., 1st Viscount, K.G., G.C.B., O.M., D.S.O., M.C. (1893–1971)

Educated at Winchester and Christ Church, Oxford, he joined the R.F.C. in 1915 and was a skilful, daring pilot. He rose steadily to the top of the R.A.F., was A.O.C. in C., Bomber Command, for most of 1940 and Chief of the Air Staff for the rest of the war. Quiet, unforthcoming and not easy to converse with, he was shrewd in his judgment and seldom averse to risk and adventure. Churchill told me that of the three Chiefs of Staff it was on Portal that he relied most. After the war he was Controller of Atomic Energy at the Ministry of Supply, 1946–51, and then Chairman of British Aluminium, of the British Match Corporation and of the British Aircraft Corporation. Although he displayed no goods in his shop window, he was universally respected and admired.

Portal of Laverstoke, Wyndham, 1st and last Viscount, G.C.M.G., D.S.O. (1885–1949)

Son of Sir William Portal, whose family, of Huguenot descent, made paper for £5 notes at the Laverstoke mill. Wyndham struck out from the family mould and was Chairman not only of Portals, but of Wiggins Teape and the Great Western Railway. Most agreeable in conversation and an affable host, he was ruthless to those who worked for him. After success as a war-time Regional Commissioner, he developed political ambitions and, with the help of Brendan Bracken and Oliver Lyttelton (Viscount Chandos), he obtained a ministerial post as Minister of Housing. He won incidental Prime Ministerial favour by sending both Churchill and Attlee (to whom he sucked up shamelessly, despite his Conservative affiliations) baskets of plovers' eggs from Laverstoke every spring.

Pound, Admiral of the Fleet, Sir Dudley, O.M., G.C.B., G.C.V.O. (1877–1943)
He wore a lugubrious air and his mere entry into the room made the occupants feel grave. Yet, off duty he was said to be cheerful and sometimes almost garrulous. Originator of the Directorate of Plans at the Admiralty, former Chief of Staff to Sir Roger Keyes in the Mediterranean and finally C. in C., Mediterranean, himself, he was recalled to London to be First Sea Lord only six weeks before the outbreak of war. Slow, but sure, he seemed the very antithesis of the new First Lord, Winston Churchill; but in fact they worked well together and Churchill developed an affection for Pound, criticise him though he often did for his cautious approach to problems. He overworked consistently and died, still in harness, after the first Quebec Conference in 1943.

Reith, John, 1st Lord, G.C.V.O., G.B.E., C.B. (1889–1971)
Founding father and, indeed, Dictator of the B.B.C. after a youthful apprenticeship in engineering and a short, sharp interlude on the Western Front. In 1938 he was made Chairman of Imperial Airways. He gave the impression of ruthless efficiency, but the efficiency seemed to desert him when, ennobled for the purpose, he entered the Government. It is hard to say whether he was worse as Minister of Information or as Minister of Transport, but whatever his failures his achievement at the B.B.C. is a claim to enduring fame. His Scottish dourness appealed to some, who thought it a sign of his honesty and virtue (which it probably was). He loathed Churchill, whom he found insufficiently Puritan; but Churchill, who had other worries, took no notice of the fact.

Reynaud, Paul (1878–1966)
A prominent politician of the French Third Republic who, after holding the usual assorted collection of Cabinet offices, went from the Ministry of Finance to succeed Daladier as Prime Minister

two months before the German offensive of May 1940. He had a majority of only one in the Chamber and a divided Cabinet. On May 9th he offered his resignation, but withdrew it the next day when the battle started. He tried to keep France in the war, fighting if necessary from North Africa, and Charles de Gaulle was his special protégé. However, he was overwhelmed by his defeatist colleagues, Pétain, Weygand, Baudouin and others, and resigned in favour of Pétain on June 16th. After arrest by the Vichy Government and two years' imprisonment in Germany, he was again French Minister of Finance in 1948 and took a leading part in drafting the new constitution of the Fifth Republic.

Ribbentrop, Joachim von (1893–1946)
Subservient satellite of Hitler who was a champagne salesman in Canada before World War I, in which he won the Iron Cross. He reverted to wine salesmanship from 1920 until elected a Nazi member of the Reichstag in 1933. In 1936 his subservience gained him the German Embassy in London, where he hit the headlines by giving a Nazi salute to King George VI at a St James's Palace levée and busied himself, not at all effectively, in trying to implant pro-Nazi sentiment in important

people. Recalled to Berlin in 1938 to be Foreign Minister, he obeyed his master's voice unquestioningly, gave his name to the infamous Molotov–Ribbentrop Pact and after the Nuremberg Trials was hanged (very clumsily by the American hangman) as a war criminal. When he was captured in 1945, he wrote a crawling and obsequious letter to Churchill attempting to exonerate himself from all blame for the war. Churchill was revolted by his cringing words and sent no reply.

Rowan, Sir Leslie, K.C.B., C.V.O. (1903–1972)
He came to No. 10 from the Colonial Office, via the Treasury, and was one of the ablest and most endearing men I have known. He had played hockey for England, had been well grounded in the classics at Tonbridge and had shone at Queen's College, Cambridge. Of the brightest intelligence, he was serious of purpose but possessed a rollicking sense of fun. In due course he was Principal Private Secretary, first to Churchill and then to Attlee, ministering to them both at the Potsdam Conference. He returned to the Treasury to be Second Secretary and worked with Sir Stafford Cripps as Chancellor. Why he was not promoted to be head of the Treasury is one of Whitehall's unsolved mysteries. He left to become Managing

Director, and in due course Chairman, of Vickers Ltd and died too soon.

Rucker, Sir Arthur Nevil, K.C.M.G., C.B., C.B.E. (b. 1895)

Son of a Fellow of the Royal Society, and educated at Marlborough and Trinity College, Cambridge, he entered the Civil Service after three years in the trenches and was Private Secretary to several Ministers of Health. In 1939 he became Neville Chamberlain's Principal Private Secretary and was wholly uncritical of his policies. He remained with Chamberlain, by then Lord President of the Council, throughout the summer of 1940 and subsequently returned to the Ministry of Health as Deputy Secretary. A man of great goodness, with a sparkling sense of humour, but sometimes blinded by his loyalty.

Salisbury, Robert Cecil, 5th Marquess of, K.G. (1893–1972)

Grandson of a Prime Minister, descendant of Queen Elizabeth I's all-powerful minister, Lord Burleigh, and owner of Hatfield House, he was a political figure of major importance for some twenty years. Having fought as a Grenadier in the First World War, he was, as Lord Cranborne, elected Conservative M.P. for South Dorset in 1929. Representing, with Anthony Eden, the younger element in the Tory Party, he was Parliamentary Under Secretary at the Foreign Office, 1935–38, but resigned with Eden in protest against Neville Chamberlain's interference in foreign affairs. Back in office in 1940, he was soon Secretary of State for the Dominions, and at one stage for the Colonies, Lord Privy Seal and Leader of the House of Lords. On two occasions Churchill had his name on the list to be Foreign Secretary. His influence in the Conservative Party, in and out of office, was dominant and he held a series of high offices between 1951 and 1957 when he resigned on the Cyprus issue. He and his wife Betty, daughter of Lord Richard and Lady Moyra Cavendish, were on the closest terms of friendship with both the King and Queen and the Churchills; but "Bobbety" Salisbury was interested in everybody and was as ready to listen to the views of unimportant people as to those of Kings and Cabinet Ministers.

Sherfield, Roger Makins, 1st Lord, G.C.B., G.C.M.G. (b. 1904)

There have not been many diplomats or civil servants to rival Roger Makins in distinction and intelligence. From Winchester he went to Christ Church, Oxford, won a first in history and was elected a Fellow of All Souls. Years later his elder son did the same, so that, perhaps uniquely, father and son were Fellows of All Souls at the same time.

Rising rapidly in the Diplomatic Service, which he entered in 1928, he married Alice, daughter of Dwight D. Davis of Davis Cup fame. Anthony Eden was greatly impressed by his abilities; and so was Harold Macmillan, after he had served as his No. 2 in North Africa. So, too, was Winston Churchill in his dealings with him at the British Embassy in Washington.

He had already served twice on the staff at the Washington Embassy when, in 1953, he was appointed Ambassador. Thence he was wafted by Harold Macmillan in 1956 to be Joint Permanent Secretary of the Treasury, which was not a post for which his experience, wide though it had been, qualified him; but from 1960 to 1964 he was a successful Chairman of the Atomic Energy Commission. In so-called retirement he was amongst much else Chairman of Hill Samuel, of the Industrial and Commercial Finance Company (I.C.F.C.), of A. C. Cossor, of Raytheon International and of Wells Fargo Ltd. He was also Chancellor of Reading University, a superb ballroom dancer and the owner of one of the loudest and most totally sincere laughs in the United Kingdom.

Simon, John, 1st Viscount, G.C.S.I., G.C.V.O., K.C. (1873–1954)

The son of a Congregational minister, he was educated at Fettes and Wadham, Oxford, and was a Fellow of All Souls. A brilliant advocate, he was not popular with his fellow barristers who proclaimed, "There'll be no moaning at the Bar when he puts out to sea." Shattered by the death of his first wife for whom, before he made a fortune at the Bar, he could not afford the medicaments she needed, he went in to Parliament as a Liberal in 1906, was Solicitor General and then Attorney General in Asquith's pre-war Government, was one of the Ministers originally opposed to Britain entering the war, but became Home Secretary, 1915–16. After the war he was Chairman of the Simon Commission sent to India in 1928 to study constitutional reform when Lord Irwin (later Lord Halifax) was Viceroy. In 1931 he led a section of the Liberal Party into Ramsay MacDonald's National Government, was a most unpopular Foreign Secretary (1931–35), a somewhat more esteemed Home Secretary (1935–37), and Chancellor of the Exchequer with great influence (1937–40). In 1940 Churchill made him Lord Chancellor, but did not put him in the War Cabinet. He was capable of taking great trouble to help people in distress, but he never succeeded in overcoming the dislike of those who worked for him.

Spears, Major-General Sir Edward Louis Bt., K.B.E., C.B., M.C. (1886–1974)
Bilingual in English and French, he made his name as British liaison officer with the French armies in World War I. Between the wars he was Conservative M.P. for Carlisle and a strong supporter of Churchill, who always thought well of him. At Bordeaux in 1940 he did his best to rally the French and it was he who brought de Gaulle to England. He later quarrelled with that emotional general over the affairs of Syria and the Lebanon. He also quarrelled with the French authorities in Beirut when he was British Ambassador to Syria and the Lebanon in the last years of the war. After the war he was Chairman of Ashanti Goldfields. His first wife was the gentle American authoress, Mary Borden, author of *Jane Our Stranger*.

Spears wrote beautiful English and explained his subject with clarity. Churchill once told me that to understand the history of World War I, I need do no more than read two of Spears' books, *Liaison 1914* and *Prelude to Victory*.

Stanley, Col. Right Hon. Oliver, M.C. (1896–1950)
Second son of the 17th Earl of Derby. A master of epigram inside and outside the House of Commons and much sought after as a wit. He fought throughout the First World War, married Lord Londonderry's daughter and was elected Conservative M.P. for Westmorland in 1924. He held many portfolios, Transport, Labour, the Board of Trade and, from January to May 1940, the War Office. However, he was more impressive in debate than in administration, and Churchill did not offer him an office he thought acceptable when the 1940 Government was formed. He did, however, return to the Government in 1942 as Secretary of State for the Colonies. In opposition, after the war, his rapier thrusts in debate were of value to the Conservative Party.

Strakosch, Sir Henry, G.B.E. (1871–1943)
By birth an Austrian, he was naturalised in 1907 and in due course was Chairman of Union Corporation and of *The Economist*. Business relationship with Brendan Bracken turned into personal friendship. He was a financier of unusual skill, responsible for the foundation of the Central Banks of both India and South Africa. He reorganised the currency of several European states

and dominated the Financial Committee of the League of Nations. At Bracken's instigation he gave Churchill, often short of money before the war, investment advice and Churchill felt under an obligation to him. He also found his views on international financial matters valuable.

Syers, Sir Cecil, K.C.M.G., C.V.O. (1903–1981)

A Dominions Office official who was Private Secretary briefly to Stanley Baldwin as Prime Minister and then, from 1937 to 1940, to Neville Chamberlain. He went on to be Deputy High Commissioner in South Africa under Lord Harlech and High Commissioner in Ceylon, 1951–57, ending his career as Secretary of the University Grants Committee. Intelligent, efficient, a trifle jaunty, but an admirable colleague with a well-developed sense of the ridiculous.

Templewood, Samuel Hoare, 1st and last Viscount, G.C.S.I., G.B.E., C.M.G. (1880–1959)

It was not without justification that he was called "Slippery Sam". The son of a Norfolk baronet, his intelligence was matched, or even surpassed, by his natural bent for intrigue. Educated at Harrow and New College, Oxford, he married Lady Maud Lygon, daughter of the 6th Earl Beauchamp, and when presenting to his constituents his apologia for the Hoare–Laval Pact of 1935 (which would have given part of Abyssinia to Italy) he caused astonishment and amusement throughout the country by declaring that in his hurry to report to them he had "left Lady Maud and the luggage" in Paris. M.P. for Chelsea, he was Secretary of State for Air in 1922, and subsequently for India and for Foreign Affairs, First Lord of the Admiralty and Home Secretary. It was in this last office, which he combined with Lord Privy Seal, that in 1937–39 he was a powerful, influential and strongly appeasing member of Chamberlain's Cabinet. There was a dire moment in 1939 when, had anything happened to Chamberlain, he might well have been Prime Minister. His own great ambition was to be Viceroy. In 1940 Churchill, who was not one of his admirers, sent him as Ambassador to Madrid where he performed a most useful service in countering the pro-German influence of General Franco's supporters.

Thurso, Archibald Sinclair, 1st Viscount, K.T., C.M.G. (1890–1970)

Head of the Caithness Sinclair clan, he went to Eton and Sandhurst and, although an officer in the Life Guards, became Winston Churchill's second in command of the 6th Royal Scots Fusiliers in

1916. He stayed with Churchill, whom he worshipped, as Personal Secretary at the War Office, 1919–21, and then at the Colonial Office. However, in 1922 he was elected Liberal M.P. for Caithness and Sutherland. When the National Government was formed in 1931, he did not join those Liberals who, under Sir John Simon, remained loyal to Ramsay MacDonald and Stanley Baldwin. After a brief tenure of the Scottish Office, he and his chief, Sir Herbert Samuel, left the National Government on the issue of Free Trade. In 1935 he succeeded Samuel as Leader of the Opposition Liberals, vigorously opposed Chamberlain, Munich and appeasement, declined to bring his party into the Government in September 1939, but became, to his great satisfaction, Churchill's choice as Secretary of State for Air in 1940. He retained that office, in constant controversy with Lord Beaverbrook, till the end of the war. His wife, Marigold, daughter of the notoriously flighty Lady Angela Forbes, had a stronger character than her husband and was a pleasant, if alarmingly determined, woman.

Tree, Ronald (1897–1976)
Affable and public-spirited owner of Ditchley Park, possessed of a substantial Marshall Field fortune from Chicago, he was a British subject, educated at Winchester, and was elected Conservative M.P. for a Leicestershire constituency. His first wife was a stimulating niece of Lady Astor, with exquisite taste, and his second, Marietta, daughter of an Episcopalian bishop, was a U.S. Ambassador to the United Nations and is now a city planner, involved in many civic and cultural activities.

Wavell, Field Marshal, 1st Earl, G.C.B., G.C.S.I., G.C.I.E., C.M.G., M.C. (1883–1950)
This well-read Wykehamist, who loved poetry, was considered by many the finest soldier in the British Army. In 1937 Lord Gort, as Military Secretary, was about to put forward his name to be C.I.G.S. when Hore-Belisha surprisingly chose Gort himself instead. Having commanded in Palestine and Transjordan, he was G.O.C., Southern Command, before being sent in 1939 to take charge of the British Army in Egypt. When Italy came into the war Wavell won two successful campaigns against General Graziani, but in 1941 the arrival of Rommel and the Germans on the scene changed the situation. His handling of the Greek and Crete campaigns that spring was not adept, at least so Churchill thought, and he was badly checked in the Western Desert, despite the arrival of many new tanks and guns by means of

Operation TIGER. So at the end of 1941 he was relieved of his command and sent off to India, first as C. in C. and then, from 1943 to 1947, as Viceroy until Mountbatten came out to replace him and organise Indian independence. He was shy and not good at expressing himself orally so that Churchill never grasped his best qualities. He did, moreover, preside over a grossly over-manned H.Q. in Cairo and he seemed to Churchill more interested in building up a large body of supporting personnel in Egypt than in taking offensive action.

Waverley, Sir John Anderson, 1st Viscount, G.C.B., O.M., G.C.S.I., G.C.I.E., F.R.S. (1882–1958)

His company and his appearance were pontifical. Brendan Bracken, who had a *penchant* for creating nicknames, called him God's Butler, but he was on a par with Lord Hankey as one of Britain's greatest twentieth-century administrators.

Of comparatively humble origin, but with a distinguished academic career at George Watson's College and Edinburgh University, he passed top into the Civil Service in 1905 and quickly rose to be Chairman of the Board of Inland Revenue, Under Secretary in Ireland during the distressing Black and Tans period, and, from 1922, Permanent Under Secretary at the Home Office. There he made necessary preparations to deal with a General Strike and established the basis of air-raid precautions. Ten years later he was appointed Governor of Bengal and narrowly escaped two terrorist attempts on his life. Back in England he became independent M.P. for the Scottish Universities, and in 1938, at the time of Munich, was Regional Commissioner for London and the Home Counties. Neville Chamberlain appointed him Lord Privy Seal, responsible for manpower and civil defence, and in 1939 he was promoted to be Home Secretary. Later in the war he was Lord President of the Council and from 1943 till the fall of Churchill's Government Chancellor of the Exchequer. The Lord President's Committee, of which he was Chairman, was the main instrument for regulating home affairs. The smoothness with which the country's civil administration was conducted, and its economic resources maintained, was in large part due to his calm and steady administrative skill. He was also responsible, with Lord Cherwell, for the British contribution to the atomic bomb programme, deadly secret and known as TUBE ALLOYS. At one stage, when the Prime Minister and Eden were setting off together on a foreign journey,

Churchill suggested to the King that, should they both be killed, Anderson, as a non-party statesman of proved ability, might be the man to send for as Prime Minister.

After the war he was made a Viscount, and in addition to being Chairman of the Advisory Committee on atomic energy, and Chairman of the Port of London Authority, he threw himself energetically and successfully into reviving the fortunes of the Covent Garden opera. He disliked personal publicity and he was an uninspiring speaker in either House of Parliament, but by his quiet efficiency and capacity for hard work he was a major contributor to winning the war.

Weygand, General Maxime (1867–1965)

He was commanding the French Army in the Middle East when summoned urgently in May 1940 to succeed General Gamelin in charge of the Allied armies in France. Active, apparently tireless and impressive in speech, he owed his high reputation mainly to having been Chief of Staff to Marshal Foch, who was reputed to have said: "When France is in danger, send for Weygand." The mystery of his birth added to his fascination for the French public. Some said his father was the Archduke Maximilian, Emperor of Mexico, others that he was a son of the appalling King Leopold II of Belgium, and yet others that he was the illegitimate offspring of a jewish businessman in Bruges who had a gardener called Weygand. Whatever the truth, it was too late for him to prove his worth by the time he was called to command in 1940; but he was infuriated by the failure of the British to accept defeat as inevitable once the French Army had been crushed. In September 1940, after three months as Minister of National Defence in the Vichy Government, he was sent to Algeria as Governor General and there were hopes in London and Washington that he might defect to the Allies. The same thought must have occurred to the Germans, for in 1942 the imprisoned him for three years, and so, after the war, did the French.

Wilson, Sir Horace John, G.C.B., G.C.M.G., C.B.E. (1882–1972)

By nature modest and retiring, educated at Kurnella School, Bournemouth, and the London School of Economics, he was by the late 1930s one of the most powerful men in Britain, an *eminence grise* without whose advice the Prime Minister seldom moved. This was not his fault, or indeed his desire. Having been Permanent Secretary at the Ministry of Labour before he was forty, he was appointed Chief Industrial Adviser to the Government in 1930, imported to No. 10 by Stanley Baldwin in 1935 and retained with ever increasing influence by Neville Chamberlain. He knew little about defence or foreign affairs, but was plunged into the deep end of both by the Prime Minister, and in 1939 he was also made Permanent Secretary to the Treasury and Head of the Civil Service. Churchill, who regarded him with aversion, removed him from No. 10, but left him at the Treasury, where he pursued his duties efficiently. Kind-hearted, conscientious and a good Christian, he had much blame heaped on his head, a good deal of it unjustly.

Winant, Hon. John Gilbert (1889–47)

A gentle, dreamy idealist, whom most men and all women loved, he had been Governor of New Hampshire and looked like Abraham Lincoln. He came to England, with President Roosevelt's full confidence, as a welcome contrast to his defeatist predecessor, Joseph P. Kennedy. He was soon a personal friend of the Churchill family and there was seldom a week-end when he did not go to Chequers. He fell in love with Sarah Churchill, though the relationship was an innocent one. He was an introspective man, unhappily married. In 1947, no longer employed, but renting a house in South Street where he was only happy talking about old times, he suddenly returned to America and committed suicide.

Wood, Sir Kingsley (1881–1943)

Insignificant in appearance, and considered by some to be a time-server, he nevertheless carried weight in the counsels of the Conservative Party. Son of a Wesleyan minister in Hull, he became a solicitor, set up a thriving practice in London while still in his twenties, was elected to the L.C.C. and, in 1918, to Parliament. He was amiable to all and easily accessible; and even though he was a poor speaker he was a good manipulator. He had much to do with establishing a Ministry of Health and was therefore smiled upon by Neville Chamberlain. He was also the most efficient of Postmaster Generals and made the Post Office so popular (temporarily) that in 1933 Stanley Baldwin put him in the Cabinet. In 1938 he became Secretary of State for Air, which was an ill-judged appointment as he knew nothing of the armed services and rearmament was at last beginning in earnest. Churchill, with encouragement from Chamberlain and Margesson, sent him to the Treasury where the poor man had to bear the odium of the first swingeing war-time Budget. He called in Keynes, Brand, Robertson and others to advise him, increased taxation to a scarcely bearable extent and balanced his budgets. He adopted the idea of P.A.Y.E. and died, suddenly, on the morning of the day he was to announce it.

Woolton, Frederick Marquis, 1st Earl of, C.H. (1883–1964)

The successful import of non-politicians into the War Coalition included Sir Andrew Duncan, Lord Leathers, Oliver Lyttelton and P. J. Grigg. As successful as any of them was Lord Woolton, who kept the nation wholesomely fed in spite of the devastation of merchant shipping by U-boats. A man with a strong social conscience, he began his adult life with energetic efforts to lessen the impact of poverty and was warden of a settlement in Liverpool dockland. Unfit for military service, he worked as an economist in the War Office during World War I and was involved in commercial and industrial mat-

ters. Almost by accident he joined the Liverpool, Manchester and Birmingham retail chain called Lewis, becoming Managing Director in 1928 and later Chairman. He was by then an important industrialist.

He made a favourable impression on Sir Horace Wilson who persuaded Chamberlain to withdraw him from the job of providing clothing for the army and to make him, in April 1940, Minister of Food. He worked miracles of organisation and became a national figure. In 1943 he was brought into the War Cabinet as Minister of Reconstruction. When Churchill was defeated in 1945, Woolton, who had once been a Fabian, was so angry with the electorate that he joined the Conservative Party, and in 1946 Churchill asked him to be Party Chairman. He so remained until 1955 and was in addition made Lord President in 1951. Though an endearing man, he was vain and inclined to be pompous, as well as sometimes indiscreet; but few served their country better.

GLOSSARY

GLOSSARY

A.A. = Anti-Aircraft
A.C.I.G.S. = Assistant Chief of Imperial General Staff
A.C.2. = Aircraftsman 2nd Class
A.D.C. = Aide de Camp
A.E. = Anthony Eden
A.E.U. = Amalgamated Engineering Union
A.F.H.Q. = Allied Forces Headquarters
A.I. = Airborne Interception
A.M. = Air Ministry
A.O.C. = Air Officer Commanding
A.O.C. in C. = Air Officer Commanding in Chief
A.R.P. = Air Raid Precautions
A.T.S. = Auxiliary Territorial Service
A.V.M. = Air Vice Marshal

B. 17 = Flying Fortress Aircraft
B. 24 = Liberator Aircraft
B.E.F. = British Expeditionary Force

B.G.S. = Brigadier, General Staff
B.O.A.C. = British Overseas Airways Corporation

"C" = Brigadier Menzies, head of the Secret Service
C.A.S. = Chief of Air Staff
C.I.D. = Criminal Investigation Department
C.I.G.S. = Chief of Imperial General Staff
C. of E. = Church of England
C.O.S. = Chiefs of Staff
C.W.R. = Central War Room

D.M.I. = Director of Military Intelligence
D.N.I. = Director of Naval Intelligence

E-boat = German torpedo boat
E.D.C. = European Defence Community
E.A.M. = Political organisation of Greek Communists
E.L.A.S. = Combatant

organisation of Greek
Communists

F.O. = Foreign Office
F.W. 190 = Focke Wulf 190
German aircraft

G.H.Q. = General
Headquarters
G.L. = Radar-controlled
searchlight
G.O.C. = General Officer
Commanding

H.B. = Hore-Belisha (Leslie)
H.E. = His Excellency
H.E. bomb = High-Explosive
bomb
H.M. = His or Her Majesty
H.M.G. = His Majesty's
Government
H.M.S = His Majesty's Ship
H. of C. = House of Commons

I.C.I. = Imperial Chemical
Industries
I.L.P. = Independent Labour
Party
I.O.U. = I owe you
I.R.A. = Irish Republican Army

JU. 88 = Junkers 88 German
aircraft

K.G. = Knight of the Garter
K.T. = Knight of the Thistle

L.C.C. = London County
Council
L.D.V. = Local Defence
Volunteers (Home Guard)

L.G. = Lloyd George
L.P.T.B. = London Passenger
Transport Board

M. and B. = antibiotic drug
M.A.P. = Ministry of Aircraft
Production
ME. 109 = Messerschmitt 109
German aircraft
M.F.A. = Minister for Foreign
Affairs
M.I.5 = Internal Security
Service
M.I.6 = Overseas Intelligence
Service
M. of I. = Ministry of
Information
M.P. = Member of Parliament
M.T.C. = Military Transport
Corps

N.C. = Neville Chamberlain
N.C.O. = Non-Commissioned
Officer
N.Z. = New Zealand

O.C.T.U. = Officer Cadet
Training Unit
O.S.S. = Office of Strategic
Services

P.A. = Personal Assistant
P.E. = Photo-Electric
P.F. = Proximity Fuse
P.G. = Paying Guest
P.M. = Prime Minister
P. of W. = Prisoner of War
P.P.S. = Parliamentary Private
Secretary
P.Q. = Parliamentary
Questions

P.S. = Private Secretary
P.W.E. = Political Warfare
Executive

R.A.C. = Royal Automobile
Club
R.A.F. = Royal Air Force
R.A.F.V.R. = Royal Air Force
Volunteer Reserve
R.A.S.C. = Royal Army Service
Corps
R.C. = Roman Catholic
R.C.A.F. = Royal Canadian Air
Force
R.D.F. = Radio Direction
Finding (Radar)
R.M. = Royal Marines
R.M.S. = Royal Mail Steamer
R.N. = Royal Navy
R.N.V.R. = Royal Naval
Volunteer Reserve

S.A. = Sturmabteilung
S.A.S. = Special Air Service
S.A.S.O. = Senior Air Staff
Officer
S.H.A.E.F. = Supreme
Headquarters Allied
Expeditionary Force
S.H.A.P.E. = Supreme
Headquarters Allied Powers
Europe
S.O.E. = Special Operations
Executive
S. of S. = Secretary of State
S.S. = Schutzstaffel
s.s. = steam ship
S.W.C. = Supreme War Council

T.A.B. = Typhoid anti-bacillus

Tube Alloys = code name for
atomic research
T.U.C. = Trades Union
Congress
T.R.H. = Their Royal
Highnesses

U-boat = Untersee-boot
(German submarine)
U. J. = Uncle Joe (Stalin)
U.N.O. = United Nations
Organisation
U.N.R.R.A. = United Nations
Relief and Rehabilitation
Administration
U.P. = aerial minefield
U.X.B. = unexploded bomb

V.1 = Vergeltungswaffe
(German flying bomb)
V.2 = German rocket
V.C. = Victoria Cross
V.C.I.G.S. = Vice Chief of
Imperial General Staff
V.C.N.S. = Vice Chief of Naval
Staff
V.E. = Victory in Europe
V.R.I. = Victoria Regina et
Imperatrix

W.A.A.F. = Women's Auxiliary
Air Force
W.O. = War Office
W.V.S. = Women's Voluntary
Service

Y.M.C.A. = Young Men's
Christian Association
Y.W.C.A. = Young Women's
Christian Association

INDEX

(Names marked with an asterisk* are included in the biographical notes. Married names of women mentioned in the text are placed in brackets after the entry, as are titles subsequently conferred when they differ from the original surname. The title Right Honourable for Privy Councillor has been omitted.)

PIERS PAUL READ

THE VILLA GOLITSYN

When Simon Milson is unexpectedly invited to stay with his old friend in the South of France, he is ordered by the Foreign Office to discover whether Willy Ludley committed a monstrous act of treason many years ago. In the faded splendour of the Villa Golitsyn, Simon finds his former hero a changed man, racked by a mysterious sense of guilt and drinking himself to death . . .

'A gripping story of treachery'

Paul Theroux

'Highly professional . . . There's a good deal of deft juggling of ideas about politics and personal passion'

Observer

'Fluent, suspenseful and well-plotted'

Spectator

'As if a story dreamed up by Eugene O'Neill had been dramatised by John le Carré . . . Substantial and vivid'

New York Times

'THE VILLA GOLITSYN keeps exploding . . . Like Graham Greene, Read mixes espionage and religion, dishonesty and faith'

Time

sceptre

MARY RENAULT

THE CHARIOTEER

'Let us say, then, that the soul resembles the joined powers of a pair of horses and a charioteer. Now the horses and drivers of the gods are of equal temper and breed, but with men it is otherwise . . .'

Socrates

With men it is the unequal black horse given to bolting and travelling at will that throws the soul into confusion. This is the story of homosexual love told with rare compassion and beauty. The hero, lyrical always about his love, reads Socrates as a balm to his divided soul. He aspires to the well-matched horses of the gods but is tied to his dual nature. The poignancy of the story is heightened by its bleak and terrible setting in a hospital for the wounded of Dunkirk.

'Miss Renault masters a lyrical style, meticulous and probing, and introduces us into a world of emotion so delicate and private that the reader often feels like an intruder'

New York Times

'One of the best novels of its time'

The Listener

SIMON WINCHESTER

OUTPOSTS

'How is the Empire?,' George V asked in 1936. Fifty years on
Simon Winchester reveals the truth.

'Simon Winchester had the good idea of visiting the assorted
far-flung islands which are all that remain of the Empire. He
travelled 100,000 miles back and forth from Antarctica to the
Caribbean, from the Mediterranean to the Far East to write
OUTPOSTS and has come up with a fascinating and important
book'

The Sunday Times

'A splendid idea, and done very well. It is the little, obscure
unknown places which give us the best parts of the book'

The Guardian

'Simon Winchester puts his finger on the tiny pulse, his ear to
the small patch of ground, and for such a dwindled subject he
packs an unbelievable quantity of information'

Observer

'Original and enjoyable'

Lord Beloff

MARY RENAULT

THE MASK OF APOLLO

Once again Mary Renault has performed a magic trick in bringing to life the places and people of Ancient Greece.

Out of the Fourth century BC strides the figure of Nikeratos, the gifted tragic actor who travels through classical Greece with a company of players. Watched over by Apollo himself, he marches forward to his meetings with many famous men, including Plato, and to his fateful encounter with events that could alter the state of power in the ancient world forever.

'Utterly convincing . . . a superbly controlled performance'
New York Times

'Miss Renault has an unnerving genius for making the remote past live without diminishing its remoteness and alien glitter'
The Sunday Times

'Here is skill, charm and considerable imagination . . . she is writing better than ever'
Life

WILLIAM McILVANNEY

THE BIG MAN

The big man is Dan Scoular, a working-class legend of physical prowess, fighting for his heritage – a decaying community in a small Ayrshire town – fighting to keep it afloat and intact.

'Inspiring and harshly funny. As in Orwell at his fiercest best, McIlvanney's outrage is all the more potent for being tranquil. Grand fiction that reads as truly as fact, (which says), "this is where we've been and this where we really are"'
David Hughes in The Mail On Sunday

'A vivid transcription of a small town and the people who live there . . . Wry, funny, tender, largely unsentimental and very readable'
Henry Stanhope in The Times

'Confirms his reputation as the most incisive observer of working-class Scottish life'
Rob Brown in The Guardian

'A novel of great power and microscopic observations . . . Ambitious material, handled with sharpness and poignancy and full of memorable moments and images'
Isabel Quigley in the Financial Times

'A prose of growing assurance, with vivid and memorable results'
Douglas Dunn, Whitbread Book of the Year Winner, in the Glasgow Herald

MELVYN BRAGG

SPEAK FOR ENGLAND

Melvyn Bragg returned to his home town, Wigton, Cumberland, to interview over sixty locals from all walks of life. The result is a memorable testimony to the first three-quarters of this century. The people speak for themselves, for their inheritance, their culture, and for their country.

'These vivid recollections, scrupulously edited, make a book which lays plausible claim to being representative of England's history as lived and felt by her people in the twentieth century . . . The considerable pleasures and insights to be gained from the book are to be found in real memories, the measure of a life'
Dennis Potter in The Guardian

'What leaps from these pages is the authentic voice of direct experience'
The Listener

'Full of humour, hope, common sense, stoicism, courage, decency . . . The voices speaking for England here are not just a collection of characters – odd, outspoken, eccentric – but give a real insight into England, past and present . . . They are intelligent and individual, all sorts, all classes and conditions'
Los Angeles Times

'Fascinating . . . a rich and varied multiple voice, which does indeed "Speak for England"'
Monica Dickens in the Boston Globe

Current and forthcoming titles from Sceptre

PIERS PAUL READ

THE VILLA GOLITSYN

MARY RENAULT

THE CHARIOTEER

THE MASK OF APOLLO

WILLIAM McILVANNEY

THE BIG MAN

MELVYN BRAGG

SPEAK FOR ENGLAND

SIMON WINCHESTER

OUTPOSTS

BOOKS OF DISTINCTION